AN ANTHOLOGY OF
TRADITIONAL
KOREAN LITERATURE

An ANTHOLOGY *of* TRADITIONAL KOREAN LITERATURE

Compiled and edited by
Peter H. Lee

UNIVERSITY OF HAWAI'I PRESS
Honolulu

This book has been published with the support of the
Literature Translation Institute of Korea (LTI Korea).

Library of Congress Cataloging-in-Publication Data
Names: Lee, Peter H., compiler, editor.
Title: An anthology of traditional Korean literature /
compiled and edited by Peter H. Lee.
Description: Honolulu : University of Hawai'i Press, [2017] |
Includes bibliographical references and index.
Identifiers: LCCN 2016042094 | ISBN 9780824866358
(cloth ; alk. paper) | ISBN 9780824866365 (pbk. ; alk. paper)
Subjects: LCSH: Korean literature—To 1900—Translations
into English.
Classification: LCC PL984.E1 A54 2017 | DDC 895.7/08—dc23
LC record available at https://lccn.loc.gov/2016042094

Designed by York Street Graphics

To students and readers of
Korean and world literature

Contents

PROSE

ORAL LITERATURE

Acknowledgments

Special thanks go to the scholars and translators who have provided translations for this volume: Yoo-sup Chang, John Duncan, Heinz Insu Fenkl, Uchang Kim, Youme Kim, Yung-Hee Kim, Janet Y. Lee, David R. McCann, Wenxia Min, Hyunsuk Park, Mark Peterson, Marshall R. Pihl, Richard Rutt, Timothy Tangherlini, and Frits Vos. Translations that are unattributed are by the editor.

For encouragement, I thank my colleagues Robert Buswell, John Duncan, Chris Hanscom, Seong-Kon Kim, and David Schaberg; for technical help, I am grateful to the technology analysts in my department, Michael Bak and Phuong Truong. For this anthology I have had the great fortune of finding in Stuart Kiang a wholly sympathetic editor, and in Pamela Kelley at the University of Hawai'i Press an efficient editor who has skillfully guided the manuscript to publication.

I would also like to acknowledge with thanks permission to reproduce the following material:

"The Tale of Hong Kil-tong," translated by Marshall R. Pihl, *Korea Journal* 8, no. 7 (July 1968): 4–17. Reprinted with permission of the Korean National Commission for UNESCO, Seoul.

Lives of Eminent Korean Monks: Haedong kosŭng chŏn, translated, with an introduction, by Peter H. Lee. © 1969 by the Harvard-Yenching Institute. Used with permission of Harvard University Press.

Selections from *A Dream of Nine Clouds* (pp. 16, 24, 172–177), from *Virtuous Women: Three Classic Korean Novels,* translated

Conventions and Abbreviations

Romanization of Korean names and terms follows the McCune-Reischauer system and certain suggestions made in *Korean Studies* 4 (1980): 111–125. The apostrophe to mark two separate sounds (e.g., *han'gŭl*) has been omitted, as has a hyphen in the given name of Koreans, historical or fictional.

Chinese names and terms formerly transcribed in Wade-Giles have been converted to Hanyu pinyin, the phonetic alphabet promulgated by the People's Republic of China in 1958.

Chinese institutional titles and military ranks have been translated following Charles O. Hucker, *A Dictionary of Official Titles in Imperial China* (Stanford, CA: Stanford University Press, 1985).

Translations of Korean institutional titles, together with Korean terms for linear, area, and distance measurements, generally follow Ki-baek Lee, *A New History of Korea,* trans. Edward W. Wagner with Edward J. Shultz (Cambridge, MA: Harvard University Press, 1984). Chinese *li* and Korean *ri* are rendered as "tricent" (three hundred paces), a third of a mile, following a suggestion made by Victor H. Mair in *The Columbia Anthology of Traditional Chinese Literature* (New York: Columbia University Press, 1994), xxxii.

For translation of Buddhist terms, I have consulted *The Princeton Dictionary of Buddhism,* edited by Robert E. Buswell Jr. and Donald S. Lopez Jr. (Princeton, NJ: Princeton University Press, 2014).

Chinese dynastic histories are cited from the punctuated Zhonghua edition published in Beijing, 1959–1974. Citations from these and other classical texts are followed by references to an accessible English translation when available.

References to Chosŏn dynasty annals are to the *Chosŏn wangjo sillok,* compiled by the Kuksa p'yŏnch'an wiwŏnhoe, 48 vols., 1955–1958. All Korean-language texts were published in Seoul unless otherwise indicated.

Dates for rulers of China and Korea are reign dates. They are preceded by dates of birth and death if required. The Chinese and Korean names of reign eras are untranslated, as are the names of years in the sexagenary cycle.

Companion volumes for this anthology include the following, edited by Peter H. Lee: *Sourcebook of Korean Civilization,* 2 vols. (New York: Columbia University Press, 1993–1996); *Sources of Korean Tradition,* 2 vols. (New York: Columbia University Press, 1997–2001); and *The Columbia Anthology of Traditional Korean Poetry* (New York: Columbia University Press, 2002).

The following abbreviations have been used in the notes and biographical notes to this volume:

KS	*Koryŏ sa.* Edited by Chŏng Inji et al. 3 vols. Yŏnse taehakkyo Tongbanghak yŏnguso, 1955–1961.
PDB	*The Princeton Dictionary of Buddhism.* Edited by Robert E. Buswell Jr. and Donald S. Lopez Jr., Princeton, NJ: Princeton University Press, 2014.
Sourcebook	*Sourcebook of Korean Civilization.* Edited by Peter H. Lee. 2 vols. New York: Columbia University Press, 1993–1996.
SS	*Samguk sagi,* by Kim Pusik. Edited by Yi Pyŏngdo. 2 vols. Ŭryu, 1977.
SY	*Samguk yusa,* by Iryŏn. Edited by Ch'oe Namsŏn. Minjung sŏgwan, 1954.

Preface

An anthology of traditional Korean literature should cover all genres and forms written in classical (literary) Chinese and the vernacular Korean language (consisting of Late Middle Korean and Modern Korean). An early example of such a collection was published by the University of Hawai'i Press in 1981, and it included verses written in literary Chinese and the vernacular, examples of prose and fiction, and a single work of *p'ansori* (musical story telling). Fiction and oral literature were underrepresented, however, because reliable edited collections were unavailable at that time. Hence this new volume, which attempts to provide a more comprehensive selection of works from four major branches of traditional Korean literature: verse, prose, fiction, and oral literature.

In compiling this volume, I solicited input from more than twenty colleagues who have been teaching traditional Korean literature in translation, and its contents reflect their suggestions for a one-volume anthology that will render Korea's literary past credibly and meaningfully. Among other additions, this revised anthology presents for the first time previously undervalued or suppressed texts in Korean literary history, including Koryŏ love lyrics, shamanist narrative songs, and *p'ansori*—creations composed in the mind, retained in memory, sung to audiences, and heard—not read.

It must be remembered that written and oral literature existed side by side in Korea for more than a thousand years. The literati wrote in literary Chinese, their favored means of expression, and continued to do so after the promulgation of the Korean phonetic alphabet by King Sejong in 1446. In effect, Korea was a bicultural society in which literary Chinese (read and written, but never spoken) and vernacular written Korean interacted with a preexisting oral language over a long period. Most verse genres, myths, folktales, folk songs, *p'ansori,* mask dance plays, and puppet plays were narrated, chanted, or sung—their transmission, in other words, occurred in live performance. Thus, while their texts have reached us in written form, what they primarily attest is the primacy of the spoken word.

Translation, it is said, is a dialogue, a negotiation, or even a confrontation between two languages. More properly, translation is "criticism by total immersion, the closest form of reading; thus it offers the reader some sense of the variety of responses a great text can inspire."[1] It is the art of translation that enables these early works of Korean literature to reach across time and space and speak directly to the reader, proving that they can adapt effectively to the changing needs of different times and places without requiring culture-specific knowledge.

David Damrosch's *What Is World Literature?* proposes a threefold definition: (1) world literature is an elliptical refraction of national literatures; (2) world literature is writing that gains in translation; (3) world literature is not a set canon of texts but a mode of reading; a form of detached engagement with worlds beyond our own place and time.[2] It is my hope that the works in this volume will achieve an effective life as world literature.

1. Galassi, "The Great Montale in English," 67.
2. Damrosch, *What Is World Literature?*, 281.

Old Chosŏn (2333–194 BCE)

Wiman Chosŏn (194–108 BCE)

Puyŏ (?–346 CE)

Pon Kaya (42–532 CE)

Koguryŏ (37 BCE–668 CE)

Paekche (18 BCE–660 CE)

Silla (57 BCE–935 CE)

Parhae (698–926)

Koryŏ (918–1392)

Chosŏn (1392–1910)

T'aejo (1335–1408; r. 1392–1398)

Chŏngjong (1357–1419; r. 1398–1400)

T'aejong (1367–1422; r. 1400–1418)

Sejong (1397–1450; r.1418–1450)

Munjong (1414–1452; r. 1450–1452)

Tanjong (1441–1457; r. 1452–1455)

Sejo (1417–1468; r. 1455–1468)

Yejong (1450–1469; r. 1468–1469)

Sŏngjong (1456–1494; r. 1469–1494)

Yŏngsangun (1476–1506; r. 1494–1506)

Chungjong (1488–1544; r. 1506–1544)

Injong (1515–1545; r. 1544–1545)

Myŏngjong (1534–1567; r. 1545–1567)

Sŏnjo (1552–1608; r. 1567–1608)

Kwanghaegun (1575–1641; r. 1608–1623)

Injo (1595–1649; r. 1623–1649)

Hyojong (1619–1659; r. 1649–1659)

Hyŏnjong (1641–1674; r. 1659–1674)

Sukchong (1661–1720; r. 1674–1720)

Kyŏngjong (1688–1724; r. 1720–1724)

Yŏngjo (1694–1776; r. 1724–1776)

Chŏngjo (1752–1800; r. 1776–1800)

Sunjo (1790–1834; r. 1800–1834)

Hŏnjong (1827–1849; r. 1834–1849)

Ch'ŏlchong (1831–1864; r. 1849–1864)

Kojong (1853–1907; r. 1864–1907)

Sunjong (1874–1926; r. 1907–1910)

Introduction

Society

The ancient Korean kingdoms—Koguryŏ (37 BCE–668), Paekche (18 BCE–660), and Silla (57 BCE–735)—were centralized aristocratic states. In all three kingdoms, aristocratic families dominated a social status system based on heredity. In Silla, young elites joined in groups dedicated to an ethos of mutual loyalty, ethical conduct, and service to the throne. Members of these groups, called *hwarang* or the "flower of youth," were considered the "knights" of their time. In the early sixth century, following patterns in the neighboring Chinese empire, a code of administrative law with seventeen grades of officialdom was promulgated in Silla. At the highest level, the function of the conciliar institution in Silla was to render decisions on the most important matters of state such as succession to the throne, declarations of war, and ratification of the state religion. Civil service examinations to select candidates for entry into government service were introduced as early as the eighth century. The examinations tested candidates' knowledge of the Chinese classics in history and literature and awarded the highest rankings to those who had developed proficient writing skills in Chinese.

Sinographs, owing to geographic proximity and the absence of a native writing system, had been introduced into the Korean kingdoms as early as the second century BCE. Used to transcribe the native languages as well as to promote literacy, the sinographs were adopted for inscriptions, for archival use, for administrative and diplomatic purposes, and ultimately for edification—to teach the Confucian classics in the social sphere and Buddhist scriptures in religion. (Buddhism was introduced to Koguryŏ in 372, to Paekche in 384, and to Silla in 527.) The Confucian texts introduced principles and practices dealing with the proper regulation of the social order—concepts like knowledge and wisdom, ceremonies and learning, love and the golden rule, reverence for ancestors, and the mandate of Heaven entered the discourse of ancient Korea molded in the linguistic forms of literary Chinese. If practiced, it was believed, the gentlemanly ideal (Ch. *junzi*; K. *kunja*) would manifest itself in the world in virtues like sincerity and filial piety and imbue all social relations with the qualities of harmony and humanity (Ch. *ren*; K. *in*).

The kingdom of Koryŏ (918–1392), which united the territories of the later three kingdoms and ruled over most of the Korean peninsula, was also a hereditary aristocratic monarchy. Although almost nothing is known about the kin structure of Koryŏ commoners and slaves, a study of records pertaining to upper-class women shows that consanguineous marriage was practiced, and union with patrilateral and matrilateral cousins was frequent. Moreover, succession in the kingdom was nonlinear and flexible—in other words, primogeniture was absent. Daughters could and did receive an equal allotment of the patrimony, in both land and slaves. The majority of households included legally adult sons as well as married daughters with their husbands. In the latter case, marriage was performed in the house of the bride, and the bridegroom moved in—uxorilocal residence. Since these women shared the right of inheritance with male siblings, their status was protected. Married women consequently enjoyed a strong economic position, having retained their rights in their natal family, and children growing up in their mother's family's house developed close emotional ties to their maternal kin. Women did not suffer from separation or the threat of expulsion. Men and women enjoyed free and easy contact.[1]

---

1. Deuchler, *Confucian Transformation of Korea*, 29–87.

This situation stands in sharp contrast to what happened to the status of women in the Chosŏn dynasty (1392–1910), which succeeded Koryŏ. The teachings of Neo-Confucianism—a philosophical outgrowth of Confucianism that explained human and cosmic origins in metaphysical terms—had been introduced to Korea beginning in the late thirteenth century to promote rigorous Confucian education, which became the focus of the curriculum at academic institutions in the kingdom. Officials in the newly formed dynasty believed that the kingdom's government must be staffed and run by men of virtue and talent. To strengthen the government, they implemented an extensive system of civil, military, and technical examinations—and of these the civil service examinations carried the greatest honor and prestige. The *yangban* (two orders) serving as officials in Chosŏn's civil and military bureaucracies were the ascendant social class, and they sought to create nothing less than a new social order rooted in Confucian moral principles. All beliefs, customs, and traditions that did not comply with Confucian teachings were to be rejected as heterodox. These legislators laid the groundwork from which the highly structured patrilineal descent groups characteristic of Chosŏn society emerged. For example, ancestor rituals were shifted to a domestic shrine requiring regular offerings, and these ritual tasks were entrusted to the eldest male member of the household. Women, the ritual practitioners of the past, were excluded from this male domain.

In effect, the scholar-officials of Chosŏn restructured the social order by institutionalizing ancestor worship, the conduct of mourning and funerary rites, patrilineal succession and inheritance, primogeniture, and virilocal residence. They also introduced a distinction between primary and secondary wives (the wives of Koryŏ men had not been subject to a social ranking order); discriminated against secondary sons and daughters (children born of an alliance with a concubine or female slave); barred secondary sons from state examinations and high officialdom; prohibited the remarriage of widows; and indoctrinated women in Neo-Confucian morality. The result was that only one woman, the primary wife, could qualify to become the mother of her husband's lineal heir. Further, the marriageable age for boys was set between sixteen and thirty; and that of a girl, between fourteen and twenty.

There were four classes in Chosŏn society: scholars (literati), farmers, artisans, and merchants; on the margins were public and private slaves and outcasts—butchers, tanners, wickerworkers, shamans, actors (in traveling troupes), and female entertainers.[2]

Canons

To understand the genesis and reception of traditional literary works in Korea, it is helpful to know the broad framework of understanding in which those works were created, including the hierarchy of primary and secondary genres in the traditional canon, and the relations between works written in literary Chinese and those penned in the vernacular. The major texts the Koreans studied after the formation of their states were the Confucian classics—first five, then eleven, and finally thirteen texts. These texts formed the basic curriculum of education for almost a thousand years. The employment of Confucian scholars at court, the establishment of a royal academy, and the recruitment of officials through standardized civil service examinations established the hegemony of the official Confucian canon and ensured its perpetuation. Accepted as binding texts in politics and ethics, the Confucian classics defined the nature and function of the literati, who, as translators of morality into action, enjoyed authority, power, and prestige. Because they were also the writers of their times, they played a major role in forming the canon of refined literature. The literati wrote almost exclusively in literary Chinese, the father language, which utterly dominated the world of letters. Consequently, they adopted as official the genres of Chinese poetry and prose found in the *Wenxuan*

---

2. Eckert et al., *Korea Old and New*, 121, 132–133.

(Selections of refined literature, compiled by Xiao Tong, early 6th cent.), the most widely read and influential literary anthology. The official canon therefore included most genres of poetry and prose. Of the sixty chapters in the *Wenxuan*, the first thirty-five are assigned to poetry. And while no single writer is on record as having tried all of the prose forms, genres such as memorials, letters, admonitions, epitaphs, treatises, discourses, and prefaces all enjoyed a lasting place in the received paradigm of what constituted refined literature.

For practical purposes, the primary genres were the forms of poetry and prose that might be considered for collection in a writer's official works. In Korea—as in China—the three secondary genres were prose fiction, random jottings, and drama. The terms designating fiction in East Asia (Ch. *xiaoshuo;* K. s*osŏl;* J. s*hōsetsu*) were used derogatorily to describe all prose fiction that presumed to offer alternative views of reality by inventing a world other than that sanctioned by established authority. Random jottings were essays generally considered to belong to the genre of literary miscellany, including reportorial, biographical, and autobiographical narratives, as well as poetry criticism. That a literary miscellany was excluded from a writer's collected works, even in the case of a high state minister, indicates its low status in the hierarchy of prose genres. As for drama, it was obviously beneath consideration as the work of itinerant actors, marginalized among the outcasts of society.

To be sure, some Korean writers wrote both in literary Chinese and in Korean, but they knew that vernacular poetry and prose stood little chance of being included in their collected works. In fact, only a handful of such works ventured to include vernacular poetry in an appendix. As in the traditional canon, poetry was the highest of native literary types, but it was not part of the official curriculum. Some writers, including kings, wrote in the vernacular, and no one was censured for doing so. But the place of prose fiction in literary Chinese and Korean was humble. It was considered a recreational form of writing for women, even though, beginning in the eighteenth century, it was undeniably popular among the literati and women of the upper and middle classes.

Literary Chinese remained the preferred medium of educated writers until 1894. It was the educated in Silla who first devised the *idu* (clerk reading) system to facilitate the reading of Chinese texts by providing particles and inflection so that they conformed to Korean syntax; this system was used mostly in administrative papers and public documents. The system used in the Old Korean poems known as *hyangga* was the *hyangch'al* orthographic system, in which sinographs were used phonetically and semantically to represent the sounds of Old Korean. Some graphs were used for their meaning (mostly nouns), while others transcribed verbs, particles, and inflections. This system was used until the thirteenth century. The texts of Koryŏ love lyrics (12th–14th cent.) are recorded in Late Middle Korean, which was a tonal language. The Korean phonetic alphabet *Hunmin chŏngŭm* (Correct sounds for teaching the people), now known as *hangŭl,* was invented by King Sejong in 1443–1444 and promulgated on October 9, 1446. For the first time, it enabled the Korean people to write down texts for native songs (such as the Koryŏ love songs) and poetic forms using an alphabet that conformed to the spoken language. The alphabet consisting of twenty-eight letters (seventeen consonants and eleven vowels) was accompanied, at the time of its promulgation, by a document titled "Explanations and Examples of the Correct Sounds," compiled by a group of linguists in the Hall of Worthies commissioned by the king. After its creation, *hangŭl* underwent several major ordeals in the course of its diffusion—unsurprising, because of the long, almost monopolistic use of sinographs by the literati. Although King Sejo (1455–1468) used the alphabet to annotate Buddhist scriptures, it wasn't until the reform of 1894 that *hangŭl* came to be used in the country's official documents, mixed with sinographs. Since then, the mixed use of two scripts has been a common practice up to the present time.

In the twentieth century, the use of Korean, including *hangŭl,* was suppressed during the Japanese occupation of Korea (1910–1945), and the Korean people were forced to use Japanese. When Korea was liberated from Japan on August 15, 1945, use of the Korean language and alphabet was restored in both South and North Korea.

Primary Sources

Dynastic histories and court-ordered compilations are often reprinted and are in constant circulation. Other publications of anonymous origin include valuable texts (see below) that escaped fire, flood, and the teeth of time for five hundred years and were discovered in the first half of the twentieth century.

For collections of verse and prose in literary Chinese, see Sŏ Kŏjŏng's *Tong munsŏn* (Selections of refined literature in Korea, 1478; reprint 1966–1967) and a sequel, Sin Yonggae's *Sok Tong munsŏn* (1517; reprint, 1966–1967). A Korean translation of *Tong munsŏn* is in progress. In addition, we have more than three thousand collected works of individual authors, now being collected and published in *Hanguk yŏktae munjip* (Collected works of successive generations of Korea). Poems by women poets such as Hwang Chini and Yi Sugwŏn (Okpong), both secondary daughters, were read by posterity. Hwang Chini, whose status as the most renowned woman poet is perhaps disproportionate to the size of her surviving body of work, left four (some say eight) poems in literary Chinese and six *sijo*. Her best pieces are at once of their moment and timeless. Yi Okpong's works are included in anthologies published in Ming China and in Korea (1704; thirty-five poems). The works of Hŏ Nansŏrhŏn are similarly included in anthologies published in Ming China and in Japan.

Silla songs: The primary source for fourteen Silla songs is Iryŏn's *Samguk yusa* (Memorabilia of the three kingdoms, 1285; reprint, 1512, 1954); that for the eleven devotional songs by Kyunyŏ is *Kyunyŏ chŏn* (Life of Kyunyŏ, 1075), by Hyŏngnyŏn Chŏng (fl. c. 1075–1105)—the texts of the eleven songs in *hyangch'al* orthography are in chap. 7, and Ch'oe Haenggwi's Chinese translations in eight heptasyllabic lines are in chap. 8. The *Life* is also included in the *Korean Tripiṭaka*.

Koryŏ songs: A single copy of the anonymous *Siyong hyangak po* (Notations for Korean music in contemporary use, c. early 16th cent.) in woodblock print was discovered in a private library in the early 1950s (reprinted in photolithographic edition, 1955, 1972); and three copies of the anonymous *Akchang kasa* (Anthology of song texts, early 16th cent.?; reprint, 1973) have been discovered to date. Sŏng Hyŏn's *Akhak kwebŏm* (Guide to the study of music, 1493; reprint, 1610, 1655, 1763, 1812, 1968) and *Koryŏ sa* (History of Koryŏ, 1451; reprint, 1955–1961, 1972), chap. 71, provide useful information on the music of Koryŏ.

Lives of Eminent Korean Monks: I have used the text in *Taishō shinshū daizōkyō* (Taishō Tripiṭaka, 100 vols., Tokyo, 1924–1934), T. 50, no. 2065, and consulted a manuscript copy in the Asami Collection, East Asian Library, University of California, Berkeley.

Songs of Flying Dragons: I have used a copy of the 1612 edition (reprint, 1937–1938).

Sijo: The first anthology of *sijo* was Kim Ch'ŏnt'aek's *Ch'ŏnggu yŏngŏn* (Songs of green hills, 1728; in different manuscript editions, 1815; reprint, 1929, 1961), followed by Ch'oe Namsŏn's *Sijo yuch'wi* (*Sijo* collection by topics, 1928, containing 1,405 *sijo*). Songs (*sijo* and *kasa*) by three major Chosŏn poets—Chŏng Ch'ŏl, Yun Sŏndo, and Pak Illo—are included in their collected works or published separately as anthologies. A useful modern edition is that by Sim Chaewan, *Kyobon yŏktae sijo chŏnsŏ* (Variorum edition of the complete *sijo* canon, 1972).

Kasa: "Song of the Pure Land" by Monk Naong (1320–1376) is the earliest extant example. In addition to calendrical *kasa* (e.g., "The Farmer's Works and Days") and those by exiles and travelers (e.g., "Grand Trip to Japan"), there are women's *kasa* that flourished in the southeastern part of Korea from the eighteenth century on dealing with travel, amusement, boating, games, morals, social protest, and satire (e.g.,"Song of a Foolish Wife"); at least six thousand known works, mostly in rolled scrolls, exist, with modern studies and some annotations. A collection of *kasa* in old moveable type exists in 50 vols. (*Kohwaltchabon yŏktae kasa chŏnjip*, 1987–1998) and with annotations in 21 vols. (*Hanguk kasa munhak chuhae yŏngu*, 2005–), both edited by Im Kijung.

Literary miscellany: There is an anonymous collection in manuscript, *Hangogwan oesa* (Unofficial histories), in 140 chapters; the Harvard-Yenching Library has a copy. Another manuscript collection, *Taedong yasŭng* (lit., Cavalcade of unofficial history in Great Korea), containing works by fifty-nine known authors and nine anonymous works from the early fifteenth to early seventeenth centuries, was published in moveable type in 1909–1911. Other collections include *P'aerim* (Forest of unofficial histories, 19 vols., 1969; twenty works repeat those in the *Taedong yasŭng*) and Yun Paengnam's *Chosŏn yasa chŏnjip* (Collection of unofficial histories of Korea, 5 vols., 1934); *Kugyŏk Taedong yasŭng* (1971), a translation of *Taedong yasŭng* into Korean, is unreliable.

Fiction: I have used the latest annotated editions of individual titles, some in excerpts, such as Yi Sangt'aek's *Kojŏn sosŏl* (1997), as well as individual works edited and published by the Minjok munhwa yŏnguso (Korean Culture Institute) of Korea University. See also Kim Kidong's *P'ilsabon kojŏn sosŏl chŏnjip* (Collection of classic fiction in manuscript, 10 vols., 1980; in moveable type, 12 vols., 1976; in old moveable type, 33 vols., 1983) and another collection, *Kojŏn sosŏl chŏnjip* (30 vols., 1980). For a punctuated and annotated edition of fiction in literary Chinese, see Pak Hŭibyŏng's *Hanguk hanmun sosŏl kyohap kuhae* (2005).

Oral literature: The most reliable annotated anthology is Sŏ Taesŏk's *Kubi munhak* (1997). For a complete collection, see *Hanguk kubi munhak taegye* (Systematic collection of oral literature of Korea), edited by Hanguk chŏngsin munhwa yŏnguwŏn (Academy of Korean studies), 82 vols., 1980–1988.

VERSE

Hyangga

In the literary history of Korea, the term *si* was reserved for poetry written in literary Chinese while *ka* designated poems in the vernacular. This difference may well reflect the ideological bias and cultural elitism of men who espoused the classical Chinese literary canon and through their influence at court formed the ruling class in Korea. Yet their labeling of vernacular poetry as *songs* might also reflect another cultural trait, namely, a shared understanding of poetry's genesis in oral performance.[1]

The names of most native poetic genres in Korea contain the graph *ka* 'song' or its cognates (*yo*, *cho*, and the like). If poetry was termed *ka* for other reasons than simply to distinguish it from poetry and songs written in literary Chinese, we might first look to the performance of songs in the life of the ancient Korean people for clues. Religious and civic ceremonies in the northern and southern regions of Korea are vividly recorded in the *Weizhi* (Records of Wei) in the *Sanguozhi* (Records of the Three Kingdoms, comp. 285–297) and *Hou Hanshu* (History of the Later Han, comp. 398–445). According to these descriptions, people high and low, young and old, "all sing when walking along the road whether it be day or night; all day long the sound of their voices never ceases."[2] In Koguryŏ in the north, "men and women gather in groups at nightfall for communal

---

1. By oral, I mean, with Paul Zumthor, "any poetic communication where transmission and reception at least are carried by voice and hearing," and by performance, "the complex action by which a poetic message is simultaneously transmitted and perceived in the here and now." Zumthor, *Oral Poetry*, 22–23.

2. *Sanguozhi* 30:841ff.; *Hou Hanshu* 85:2811ff.

singing and games,"[3] while in Ye's harvest celebration in the tenth month, they "drink, sing, and dance day and night."[4] In Mahan in the south, "they sing and dance together, and drink wine day and night without ceasing. In their dancing, several tens of men get up together and form a line; looking upward and downward as they thump the ground, they move their hands and feet in time with a rhythm that is similar to our (Chinese) bell-clapper dance."[5] What struck the Chinese observers then and strikes the contemporary reader now is the evident love of singing and dancing shared by the people of Korea.

The first recorded song used as a means of incantation occurred in the third month of the year 42, when nine chiefs and several hundred people climbed Mount Kuji and sang the "Song of Kuji" (*Kuji ka*) to greet the sovereign: "O turtle, O turtle/Show your head! /If you do not/We'll roast and eat you." The turtle, according to one reading, symbolizes life. This song, or spell, probably sung by an unlettered shaman, was not composed in writing but comes to us translated into Chinese.

The first description of songs from the kingdom of Silla (57 BCE–935 CE) appears in the *Historical Records of the Three Kingdoms* (*Samguk sagi,* 1146), and this information is augmented in the *Memorabilia of the Three Kingdoms* (*Samguk yusa,* 1285). Like all subsequent vernacular poetic forms in Korea, Silla songs, known as *hyangga,* were sung.[6] The forms and styles of Korean poetry therefore reflect its melodic origins. The basis of its prosody is a line consisting of metric segments of three or four syllables, the rhythm that is probably most natural to the language. In the ten-line *hyangga,* the ninth line usually begins with an interjection that expresses heightened emotion and a change in tempo and pitch, and also presages the song's conclusion.

3. *Sanguozhi* 30:844; *Hou Hanshu* 85:2812.
4. *Sanguozhi* 30:849.
5. *Sanguozhi* 30:852. *Hou Hanshu* 85:2819.
6. Including the eleven devotional songs by Great Master Kyunyŏ (923–973), which his congregation had memorized and sung.

On the basis of the surviving songs, we recognize three forms: a stanza of four lines; two stanzas of four lines; and two stanzas of four lines plus a stanza of two lines. The first form is the simplest and accounts for four of the twenty-five extant works. Nursery rhymes, children's songs, and folk songs retain this simple form, which is easy to sing and memorize. The second form evinces a middle state in the structural development of *hyangga* and occurs three times. The third is the most polished and popular form, appearing toward the end of the sixth century. It has two stanzas of four lines that introduce and develop the main theme, and a final stanza of two lines, in the form of a wish, command, or exclamation, that summarizes a thought developed in the song. This last stanza constitutes a conclusion, at times in a sophisticated manner, and has an epigrammatic quality that makes it memorable and quotable. Structurally, the ninth line begins with an interjection, variously indicated but reconstructed throughout the *hyangga* as *aya* (Ah!). (*Ayayo* occurs once and conveys the same sense.)

A final word about the difficulty of deciphering *hyangch'al* orthography, the system of transcribing the vernacular language of *hyangga* using Chinese graphs. The small number of extant examples, the absence of parallel texts dating from the same period, and our inadequate knowledge of the phonological system of Old Korean all constitute obstacles. Early efforts relied first on the Rosetta Stone of *hyangch'al* transcription: Kyunyŏ's eleven songs,[7] which exist both in *hyangch'al* and in Chinese translation (from 967, in eight heptasyllabic lines), although the latter do not follow the imagery and meter of the original very closely. Subsequent readings, when successful, have taken into account the fact that a *hyangga* is a song that was performed before an audience in an age when speech was privileged over writing. For listeners who presumably shared the same background and expectations, the performance of *hyangga* became a play of complex interactions among song texts, traditions, and beliefs, and we can imagine their response when suasive, affective, and

---

7. Recorded in chapter 7 of the life of Kyunyŏ.

magical tropes were directed at them to arouse and transform their emotions.

Although a modern reader's experience of an old work inescapably involves a sense of distance and alterity, readers are still capable of assimilating such works in ways that make them relevant to their own needs. It is true that traditional literary works, as intertextual constructs, presuppose a basic competence in reading ability—contextual knowledge allows readers to infer a contemporary horizon of expectations, bridging the hermeneutic gap between the text and themselves. What then enables the reader to understand and appreciate the text's meaning is a fusion of horizons, an imaginative dialogue between past and present. In other words, we grasp the essential concern in a work through a creative act of imagination. And since the work's meaning cannot be circumscribed by the intention of its author, we need subtle and scrupulous close readings to discover its past significance and present meaning. To interpret an ancient *hyangga* is like engaging in a conversation—a form of question and answer.

Master Yungch'ŏn (fl. c. 579–632)

SONG OF THE COMET

During the reign of King Chinp'yŏng (r. 579–632), the *hwarang* or "flower of youth" was an elite group of young men who had dedicated themselves to a life of chivalry. Three members were about to embark on a pilgrimage to the Diamond Mountains when they beheld the sudden appearance of a comet violating one of the twenty-eight lunar mansions, the constellation of Scorpius. Filled with foreboding, the three were ready to abandon their journey when Master Yungch'ŏn composed this poem (dated 594), making the comet disappear and transforming a misfortune into a blessing. The king was pleased and bade the three youths to continue on to the mountains.

❧

There is a castle by the eastern sea
Where once a mirage used to play.

Japanese soldiers came,
Torches were burnt in the forest.[1]

When knights visited this mountain,
The moon marked its westerly course,
And a star was about to sweep a path,
Someone said, "Look, there is a comet!"

Ah, the moon has already departed.
Now, where shall we look for the long-tailed star?

Kwangdŏk (fl. 661–681)

PRAYER TO AMITĀYUS

Kwangdŏk, a celibate ascetic who endeavored to practice virtue, is said to have gone to the western paradise of Amitāyus, as he had prayed.

❖

O Moon,
Go to the west, and
Pray to Amitāyus
And report

That there is one who
Adores the Buddha of infinite life and
Longs for the Pure Land,
Praying before Him with folded hands.

Ah, would he leave me out
When he fulfills the forty-eight vows?[1]

1. Or: on the frontier.
1. Vows by aspirants for rebirth in Amitābha's Pure Land; see *PDB*, 34–35.

Tŭgo (fl. 692–702)

ODE TO KNIGHT CHUKCHI

In a celebrated incident, Tŭgo, a member of Knight Chungman's *hwarang*, was forced by the leader of another group to work in the fields as a common laborer. Learning of this, his comrade Chukchi went in search of Tŭgo at the head of a band of more than a hundred fellow knights and obtained Tŭgo's release. This song was composed by Tŭgo before the incident.

All living beings sorrow and lament
Over the spring that is past;
Your face once fair and bright
Is about to wear deep furrows.

I must glimpse you
Even for one awesome moment.
My fervent mind cannot rest at night
In the mugwort-rank hollow.

Sinch'ung (fl. 737–757)

REGRET

Sinch'ung used to play chess with the future king Hyosŏng (r. 737–742) under a pine tree. The prince vowed then that he would not forget his friend. But after ascending the throne, the king failed to remember Sinch'ung, who composed this song and fixed it to the tree. When the tree died, the king suddenly had cause to regret his lapse of memory, and he conferred on his erstwhile friend a title.

You said you would no more forget me
Than the densely green pine
would wither in the fall.
That familiar face is there still.

The moon in the ancient lake
Complains of the transient tide.
I still glimpse your figure,
But how I despise this world.[1]

Master Wŏlmyŏng (fl. 742–765)

REQUIEM FOR A DEAD SISTER

Master Wŏlmyŏng composed this song for a rite of abstinence conducted in memory of his sister. During the ceremony a gust of wind blew the offerings of paper money to the west. In the final line, the assurance of a reunion after death dispels the uncertainty expressed in the second stanza, where the image of leaves fallen from the same tree echoes Homer, who compared the generation of humans to leaves (*Iliad* 6:146–150), underscoring the brevity of human life.

On the hard road of life and death
That is near our land,
You went, afraid,
Without words.

We know not where we go,
Leaves blown, scattered,
Though fallen from the same tree,
By the first winds of autumn.

Ah, I will tend to the path
Until I meet you in the Pure Land.

1. Or: Now I reproach the world.

Master Ch'ungdam (fl. c. 742–765)

STATESMANSHIP

Iryŏn's introductory note to this poem in the *Memorabilia of the Three Kingdoms* says that on the third day of the third month of 765, King Kyŏngdŏk asked that a virtuous monk be brought to him. The master in patched clothes appeared from the south at that time. At the king's request for a song about the art of government, the master composed this lyric.

The king is father,
And his ministers are loving mothers.
His subjects are foolish children;
They only receive what love brings.

Schooled in saving the masses,
The king feeds and guides them.
Then no one will desert this land—
This is the way to govern a country.

Peace and prosperity will prevail if each—
King, minister, and subject—lives as he should.

ODE TO KNIGHT KIP'A

This song was known for its noble spirit and intense emotion. King Kyŏngdŏk himself is said to have praised it highly. The first and second stanzas compare the moon in pursuit of white clouds to the speaker who seeks, among pebbles, the depths of his friend's mind. The knight once stood by the water, the river of time, flowing irreversibly into extinction. The speaker does not deny the river's flow; rather, he accepts it on its own terms. Hence the concluding stanza, in establishing a correspondence between knight and pine, acknowledges that the knight is dead while asserting that his moral beauty endures. His integrity scorns mutability and imposes a sense of order on the landscape. His nobility is that of the mind. The knight represents the principle of growth and order; he is the emblem of an enduring culture.

The moon that pushes her way
Through the thickets of clouds,
Is she not pursuing
The white clouds?

Knight Kip'a once stood by the water,
His face reflecting in the Iro.
Henceforth I shall seek, and gather
Among the pebbles, the depth of his mind.

Knight, you are the towering pine
That scorns frost, ignores snow.

Hŭimyŏng (fl. 742–765)

HYMN TO THE THOUSAND-EYED SOUND OBSERVER

On behalf of her son who had lost his eyesight, Hŭimyŏng composed this song
and had him recite it in front of the Thousand-Armed and Thousand-Eyed Sound
Observer[1] painted on the north wall of Punhwang monastery.

Falling on my knees,
Pressing my hands together,
Thousand-Eyed Sound Observer,
I implore thee.

Yield me,
Who lacks,
One among your thousand eyes;
By your mystery restore me whole.

1. Kwanŭm (Ch. Guanyin), the bodhisattva who "observes the sounds of the world";
PDB, 82–83.

If you grant me one of your many eyes,
O the bounty, then, of your charity.

Monk Yŏngjae (fl. 785–798)

MEETING BANDITS

Intending to spend his last days on South Peak in retirement, the monk Yŏngjae
was crossing the Taehyŏn Ridge when he met sixty thieves. Although the bandits
drew their swords and threatened him, they had heard of his reputation as a poet
and asked him to compose an impromptu song.

In those days I did not know
My true mind—
Now I am awakened from ignorance
And make my way through the forest.[1]

Transgressors hiding in the bushes,
You can turn your light onto others.
If I am stabbed to death,
A good day will dawn.[2]

Ah, such a meager good deed
Cannot build a lofty edifice.

Ch'ŏyong (fl. 875–886)

SONG OF CH'ŎYONG

Ch'ŏyong, one of the seven sons of the dragon king of the eastern sea, married a
beautiful woman. Once, seeing that she was extremely desirable, an evil spirit
assumed human form and forced himself upon her while Ch'ŏyong was away.

---

1. Lines 3–4 can also be read: And am on my way hidden/To cultivate the path.
2. Lines 5–8 can also be read: How can I revert to the state/Where I fear the fallen
transgressors? /If I endure these spears and swords,/A good day will dawn.

Witnessing the scene when he returned, Ch'ŏyong calmly sang the following song. The evil spirit was so moved that it fled. Later, the Ch'ŏyong mask was used to exorcise evil spirits, usually on New Year's Eve.

❀

Having caroused far into the night
In the moonlit capital,
I return home and in my bed,
Behold, four legs.

Two were mine,
Whose are the other two?
Formerly two were mine;
What shall be done now they are taken?

Great Master Kyunyŏ (923–973)

Eleven Poems on the Ten Vows of the Universally Worthy Bodhisattva

Great Master Kyunyŏ was a learned monk who single-handedly revived the Garland school of Buddhism in the tenth century. A prolific commentator and popularizer, he composed songs in the vernacular, taught them orally, and encouraged the congregation to memorize and chant them. A Chinese translation of his songs was made by Ch'oe Heanggwi in 967. The text of his *Eleven Poems* is preserved in chapter 7 of the *Life of Kyunyŏ* (*Kyunyŏ chŏn*, 1075). Poem 6, excerpted here, is an entreaty for the turning of the wheel of dharma.

❀

6
To the majestic assembly of buddhas
In the dharma realm,
I go forth and pray
For the sweet rain of truth.

Wash away the blight of affliction
Rooted deep in the soil of ignorance,

And bathe the sentient fields of the mind
Where good grasses struggle to grow.

Ah, how happy the moonlit autumn field,
Ripe with the fruit of knowledge.

Koryŏ Songs

We do not know when the music and texts of Koryŏ love songs were composed, and the social settings of these feminine-voiced songs have all but disappeared. The texts themselves could have been written down only after the invention of the Korean alphabet in the mid-fifteenth century, when Chosŏn officials wrote new texts as *con-trafactum*[1] for well-known Koryŏ songs. Moreover, we have no textual history to speak of until the *Guide to the Study of Music* (*Akhak kwebŏm*, 1493)[2] and two later compilations. In other words, Koryŏ songs owe their survival to the adoption of their music for court use in the Chosŏn period. It is unclear, however, how the texts, dubbed "vulgar and obscene" and expunged by Chosŏn censors as late as 1490, managed to survive. Perhaps these songs were so popular that no one needed to write them down to remember them, repetition and recurrent refrains making them easy for the unlearned to remember.

In the native poetic tradition, oral delivery was the principal mode of transmission. Although we can identify the speaker's voice as feminine—the locus of unrequited love—the texts themselves do not encode information about the speaker's economic class or social status. We do know that in the Koryŏ period it was not considered

---

1. New text for a popular melody; Sadie, *New Grove Dictionary*, 6:367b–370d.
2. Yi Hyegu, *Sinyŏk Akhak kwebŏm*.

indecorous for women to compose and perform love songs and to take part in public entertainment.

When presented to the public, the songs were accompanied by an orchestra and probably performed before a mixed group. Vocal programs, especially when performed at court, were often supplemented by instrumental dances. The "Monograph on Music" in the *History of Koryŏ* lists thirteen musical instruments in the orchestra,[3] including a six-stringed black zither, a two-stringed fiddle, two kinds of lutes, two kinds of double-reed oboes, two kinds of transverse flutes, two six-leaved clappers (one of wood, the other of ivory), and an hourglass and large barrel drums. The same monograph lists thirty-two Koryŏ songs without musical notation and song texts,[4] three of which are dance music. From contextual clues, eleven appear to be folk songs, eleven are praise songs, five concern women's fidelity, and one treats filial piety.

Late Middle Korean love lyrics are texts that reveal some characteristic features of oral transmission but have reached us only in written form. Although extratextual information on their history and tradition is lacking, a close look at the structure of these songs tells us their provenance. A typical line consists of two or three, rarely four or five, metric segments. The songs are stanzaic, but generally the metrical structure of the first stanza is not repeated identically in subsequent ones—the structure is heterometric rather than isometric. The songs are primarily aural, not visual. They do not explore the possibility of homophony, or wordplay, but their density—the accumulation and intensification of consonantal sounds and key words—reinforces the theme. Repetition, sound patterns running in parallel with syntactic units, the constant presence of meter—these elements distinguish the texts as songs from an oral tradition.

The refrain—the repeated unit of one or more phrases or lines in successive stanzas—is usually a nonsense phrase that allows the

3. *KS* 71:30b–31a.
4. Some with translations into literary Chinese by Yi Chehyŏn.

song to carry a tune.[5] It can evoke the sounds of specific musical instruments (*kusŏng*) and be sung to accompany a particular dance pattern, as in "Ode to the Seasons," where the refrain *aŭ tongdong tari* imitates the sounds of the drum. In "The Turkish Bakery," the succession of sounds in line 5—*tŏrŏ tungsyŏng tarirŏdirŏ tarirŏdirŏ tarorŏgŏdirŏ tarorŏ*—is said to evoke an ensemble of large transverse flute, drum, and large gong in the first half of the line, giving way to a two-stringed fiddle in the rest of the line.

These poets were anonymous: we do not know whether they wrote both the texts and the melodies or even if they performed their own songs. It's understood that they drew their material from a common source of reference—a rhetorical tradition developed over the centuries—but performance was always related to a specific occasion. Whether performed by trained singers or ordinary people, the songs were intended to be heard rather than read, and their rhetorical devices are different from those found in a poem designed for reading.[6] A listener's reaction to singing is immediate, ephemeral, and unique.

Usually we can identify the gender of the speaker (singer) from distinctive verbal features and tropes. A feminine speaker often employs nonsense phrases and repetition, placing her voice close to the roots of lyric,[7] and her subject subsumes the recurrent features of love, especially separation. Most of the songs are by abandoned women—explorations of the torments of love, meditations on the contours of absence. The gender of the song's target audience is male, but the actual audience may have been mixed. Koryŏ audiences would have known the text by heart and could be expected to join the soloist in singing the refrain. Inseparable from performance, these songs were transferable—meant to be sung by others, they functioned as a call for fellowship. Because there has been nothing resembling them in Korean literary history before or since, only repeated readings can bring us closer to the experience of the medieval audience.

5. Chŏng Pyŏnguk, "Akki ŭi kuŭm ŭrobon pyŏlgok ŭi yŏŭmgu," 1–26.
6. Renoir, *Key to Old Poems*, 160.
7. Earnshaw, *Female Voice in Medieval Romance*, 135.

Anonymous

ODE TO THE SEASONS

Virtue in a rear cup,
Happiness in a front cup,
Come to offer
Virtue and happiness![1]
Aŭ tongdong tari

The river in January *aŭ*
Now freezes, now melts.
Born into this world,
I live alone.
Aŭ tongdong tari

You are like a lofty lantern *aŭ*
High up in the air.
In mid-February,
Your figure shines upon the world.
Aŭ tongdong tari

In March *aŭ*
Plums[2] bloom in late spring.
Others envy
Your magnificent figure!
Aŭ tongdong tari

---

1. Stanza 1 also reads: With virtue in one hand, / And happiness in the other, / Come, come, you gods / With virtue and happiness. / *Aŭ tongdong tari.*

Or: We offer virtue to gods / And happiness to ancestors. / We have come to offer / Virtue and happiness.

2. Or: azaleas.

In April without forgetting *aŭ*
Orioles, you've come.
But you, my clerk,
Forget bygone days.
Aŭ tongdong tari

On the feast of irises *aŭ*
I brew healing herbs
And offer you this drink—
May you live a thousand years.
Aŭ tongdong tari

On a mid-June day *aŭ*
I'm like a comb cast from a cliff!
If even for a moment I follow you
Who will look after me.
Aŭ tongdong tari

In mid-July *aŭ*
On the feast of the dead,
I prepare the dainties of land and sea
And pray that we may be together.[3]
Aŭ tongdong tari

This is the full moon, *aŭ*
Of the mid-autumn festival.
This will be the festive day
If only I am with you.
Aŭ tongdong tari

---

3. Also reads: In mid-July *aŭ*/I plant many kinds of seeds/And pray/That I may go with you.

On the double ninth *aŭ*
We eat yellow flowers.
O fragrance of chrysanthemums,
The season's change is late.[4]
Aŭ tongdong tari

In October *aŭ*
I'm like a sliced berry.
Once the branch is broken,
Who will cherish it?
Aŭ tongdong tari

On a November night *aŭ*
I lie on a dirt floor
With only a sheet to cover me.
O lonely life, night without you.
Aŭ dongdong tari

In December I am like *aŭ*
Chopsticks carved from pepperwood
Placed neatly before you:
An unknown guest holds them.
Aŭ tongdong tari

O Cham (fl. 1274–1308)

THE TURKISH BAKERY

I go to the Turkish shop, buy a bun,
An old Turk[1] grasps me by the hand.

---

4. Or: The thatched village is quiet.
1. In the original, *hoehoe*, an Inner and Central Asian Muslim.

If this story is spread abroad,
tarorŏ kŏdirŏ you alone are to blame, little actor!
tŏrŏ tungsyŏng tarirŏdirŏ tarirŏdirŏ tarorŏgŏdirŏ tarorŏ
I too will go to his bed:
wi wi tarorŏ kŏdirŏ tarorŏ
A narrow place, sultry and dark.

I go to Samjang Temple to light the lantern,
A chief priest grasps me by the hand.
If this story is spread abroad,
tarorŏ kŏdirŏ you alone are to blame, little altar boy!
tŏrŏ tungsyŏng tarirŏdirŏ tarirŏdirŏ tarorŏgŏdirŏ tarorŏ
I too will go to his bed:
wi wi tarorŏ kŏdirŏ tarorŏ
A narrow place, sultry and dark.

I go to the well to draw water,
A dragon within grasps me by the hand.
If this story is spread abroad,
tarorŏ kŏdirŏ you alone are to blame, dipper!
tŏrŏ tungsyŏng tarirŏdirŏ tarirŏdirŏ tarorŏgŏdirŏ tarorŏ
I too will go to his bed:
wi wi tarorŏ kŏdirŏ tarorŏ
A narrow place, sultry and dark.

I go to the tavern to buy the wine,
An innkeeper grasps me by the hand.
If this story is spread abroad,
tarorŏ kŏdirŏ you alone are to blame, wine jug!
tŏrŏ tungsyŏng tarirŏdirŏ tarirŏdirŏ tarorŏgŏdirŏ tarorŏ
I too will go to his bed:
wi wi tarorŏ kŏdirŏ tarorŏ
A narrow place, sultry and dark.

Anonymous

SONG OF P'YŎNGYANG

P'yŏngyang *ajŭlkka*
Although P'yŏngyang is my capital
wi tuŏrŏngsyŏng tuŏrŏngsyŏng taringdiri

I love *ajŭlkka*
Although I love the repaired city,
wi tuŏrŏngsyŏng tuŏrŏngsyŏng taringdiri

Instead of parting *ajŭlkka*
Instead of parting I'd rather stop spinning
wi tuŏrŏngsyŏng tuŏrŏngsyŏng taringdiri

If you love me *ajŭlkka*
If you love me I'll follow you with tears
wi tuŏrŏngsyŏng tuŏrŏngsyŏng taringdiri

Pearls *ajŭlkka*
Were the pearls to fall on the rock
wi tuŏrŏngsyŏng tuŏrŏngsyŏng taringdiri

Would the thread *ajŭlkka*
Would the thread be broken?
wi tuŏrŏngsyŏng tuŏrŏngsyŏng taringdiri

A thousand years *ajŭlkka*
If I parted from you a thousand years
wi tuŏrŏngsyŏng tuŏrŏngsyŏng taringdiri

Would my heart *ajŭlkka*
Would my heart be changed?
wi tuŏrŏngsyŏng tuŏrŏngsyŏng taringdiri

Taedong River *ajŭlkka*
Not knowing how wide the river is
wi tuŏrŏngsyŏng tuŏrŏngsyŏng taringdiri

You pushed the boat off *ajŭlkka*
You pushed the boat off, boatman!
wi tuŏrŏngsyŏng tuŏrŏngsyŏng taringdiri

Your own wife *ajŭlkka*
Not knowing how loose your wife is
wi tuŏrŏngsyŏng tuŏrngsyŏng taringdiri

You board the ferry *ajŭlkka*
You had my love board the ferry, boatman!
wi tuŏrŏngsyŏng tuŏrŏngsyŏng taringdiri

Taedong River *ajŭlkka*
The flower beyond the Taedong River
wi tuŏrŏngsyŏng tuŏrŏngsyŏng taringdiri

When he has crossed the shore *ajŭlkka*
When he has crossed he will pluck another flower!
wi tuŏrŏngsyŏng tuŏrŏngsyŏng taringdiri

SONG OF P'YŎNGYANG (WITHOUT REFRAIN)

Although P'yŏngyang is my capital,
Although I love the repaired city,

Instead of parting I'd rather stop spinning
If you love me I'll follow you with tears.

Were the pearls to fall on the rock,
Would the thread be broken?
If I parted from you a thousand years,
Would my heart be changed?

Not knowing how wide the river is,
You pushed the boat off, boatman!
Not knowing how loose your wife is,
You had my love board the ferry, boatman!

The flower beyond the Taedong River,
When he has crossed he will pluck another flower!

Anonymous

SONG OF GREEN MOUNTAIN

Let's live, let's live,
Let's live in the green mountain!
With wild grapes and thyme,
Let's live in the green mountain!
Yalli yalli yallasyŏng yallari yalla

Cry, cry, birds,
Cry after you wake.
I've more sorrow than you
And cry after I wake.
Yalli yalli yallasyŏng yallari yalla

I see the bird passing, bird passing,
I see the passing bird beyond the waters.
With a mossy plow
I see the passing bird beyond the waters.
Yalli yalli yallasyŏng yallari yalla

I've spent the day
This way and that.
But where no man comes or goes,
How am I to pass the night?
Yalli yalli yallasyŏng yallari yalla

Where is this stone thrown?
At whom is this stone thrown?
Here, no one to hate or love,
I am hit and I cry.
Yalli yalli yallasyŏng yallari yalla

Let's live, let's live,
Let's live by the sea!
With seaweed, oysters, and clams,
Let's live by the sea!
Yalli yalli yallasyŏng yallari yalla

I've listened as I went, went,
Turning an isolated kitchen I've listened.
I've listened to the stag fiddling
Perched on a bamboo pole.
Yalli yalli yallasyŏng yallari yalla

I have brewed strong wine
In a round-bellied jar.

A gourdlike leaven seizes me.
What shall I do now?
Yalli yalli yallasyŏng yallari yalla

Anonymous

SONG OF THE GONG AND CHIMES

Ring the gong, strike the chimes!
Ring the gong, strike the chimes!
Let's enjoy this age of peace.[1]

On a brittle sandy cliff,
On a brittle sandy cliff,
Let's plant roasted chestnuts, five pints.

When the chestnuts shoot and sprout,
When the chestnuts shoot and sprout,
Then we'll part from the virtuous lord.

Let's carve a lotus out of jade,
Let's carve a lotus out of jade,
And graft the lotus in the stone.

When it blossoms in the winter,
When it blossoms in the winter,
Then we'll part from the virtuous lord.

Let's make an iron suit of armor,
Let's make an iron suit of armor,
Stitch the pleats with iron thread.

1. Or: Let's perform our duty in this age of peace.

When it has been worn and torn,
When it has been worn and torn,
Then we'll part from the virtuous lord.

Let's make an iron ox and put him,
Let's make an iron ox and put him,
To graze among the iron trees.

When he grazes the iron grass,
When he grazes the iron grass,
Then we'll part from the virtuous lord.

Were the pearls to fall on the rock,
Were the pearls to fall on the rock,
Would the thread be broken?

If I parted from you for a thousand years,
If I parted from you for a thousand years,
Would my heart be changed?

Anonymous

TREADING FROST

After a rain, ah, comes a thick snow.
Do you come, who made me
Tarong tiusyŏ madŭksari madunŏjŭse nŏuji
Lie awake half the night,
Through a pass in the tangled wood,
Through an awful path to sleep?[1]

1. Or: On a path in the tangled wood (or thick with frost),/I think of my love/Who
kept me awake all night./Who'd come by this awful path to sleep?

At times thunderbolts, ah,
My body will fall into the Avici hell[2]
And perish at once—
At times thunderbolts, ah,
My body will fall into the Avici hell
And perish at once—
Would I walk on a different mountain path?[3]

Let's do this or that,
Is your pledge this or that?
Ah, love, living with you is my vow.

Anonymous

WILL YOU GO?

Will you go away?
Will you forsake me and go?
wi chŭngjŭlka O age of great peace and plenty!

How can you tell me to live on
And forsake me and go away?
wi chŭngjŭlka O age of great peace and plenty!

I could stop you but fear
You would be annoyed and never return.
wi chŭngjŭlka O age of great peace and plenty!

I'll let you go, wretched love,
But return as soon as you leave.
wi chŭngjŭlka O age of great peace and plenty!

2. The deepest, largest, and most torturous of the eight great hells; *PDB, 86.*
3. Or: Would I seek another lover's bosom?

Anonymous

Spring Overflows the Pavilion

Were I to build a bamboo hut on the ice
And die of cold with him on the ice,
Were I to build a bamboo hut on the ice
And die of cold with him on the ice,
O night of our love, run slow, run slow.

When I lie alone, restless,
How can I fall asleep?
Only peach blossoms wave over the west window.
Ungrieved, you scorn the spring breeze,
Scorn the spring breeze.

I have cherished those who vowed,
"May my soul be with yours."
I have cherished those who vowed,
"May my soul be with yours."
Who, who persuaded me this was true?

"O duck, O duck,
O gentle duck,
Why do you come
To the swamp, instead of the shoal?"
"If the swamp freezes, the shoal will do, the shoal will do."

A bed on Mount South,
With Mount Jade as pillow,
Mount Brocade as quilt,

A bed on Mount South,
With Mount jade as pillow
Mount Brocade as quilt,

And beside me a girl sweeter than musk,[1]
Let's press our magic hearts, press our magic hearts!

O love, let us be forever together!

Songs of Flying Dragons

The *Songs of Flying Dragons* (*Yongbi ŏch'ŏn ka*, 1445–1447), a eulogy cycle in 125 cantos, was compiled by a royal committee to praise the founding of the Chosŏn dynasty by General Yi Sŏnggye (1335–1408). Preparation for this work, begun in the year 1437, forty-five years after the dynasty's founding, included the inspection of birthplaces and places of residence of four royal ancestors and the collection of oral narratives about the founder's deeds. Composed by the foremost philologists and literary men of their day, the *Songs* were the first experimental use in verse of the Korean alphabet invented in 1443–1444. They are also a manifesto of the policies of the new state, a mirror for future monarchs, and a repository of heroic tales and foundation myths of China and Korea.

The organization of the cycle may be summarized as follows:

a) 1–2   proem
b) 3–109   celebration of military and cultural accomplishments of the six dragons, especially the founder

---

1. Or: a girl with a pouch of musk.

c) 110–124   admonitions to future monarchs

d) 125   conclusion

The Iliadic cantos of the *Songs* present Yi Sŏnggye as possessing unusual gifts of body and character. Set apart from ordinary men in childhood, he has a splendid appearance (cantos 28–29) and superhuman strength (87). Carrying a huge bow (27), he is a supreme archer (32, 40, 43, 45–47, 63, 86–89), a master horseman (31, 34, 65, 70, 86–87), and a superlative tactician (35–36, 51, 60). With these qualities, he pacifies the Red Turbans (33), the Jurchens (38), and the Mongols (35–37, 39, 40–41, 54), and subjugates the Japanese pirates (47–52, 58–62). As a military leader, he is kind to his men (66, 78–79), magnanimous (54, 67, 77), humble (4, 81), and consistent (79). Commending his selfless deeds, heaven sends auspicious omens and portents (13, 39, 42, 50, 67–68, 83–84), underscoring the inevitability of the divine plan, and comes to his aid (30, 34, 37). With heaven as his ally, he is compared to a number of Chinese paragons but surpasses them in moral excellence.

As a creature of flesh and blood, Yi is bitterly aware of the cost of human achievement, inseparable from suffering and loss. Contemplating the horror of war—the corpses that cover the hills and plains—he comprehends the limitations of human activity (50). This is the scene in which the hero recognizes his own mortality, giving his heroic career deeper meaning. As a suffering hero, he is viewed as the incarnation of his people, an embodiment of their struggles. Certainly this was the view sanctioned by Confucian orthodoxy. "When heaven is about to place a great burden on a man," Mencius said, "it always tests his resolution, exhausts his frame and makes him suffer starvation and hardship, frustrates his efforts so as to shake him from mental lassitude, toughens his nature, and makes good his deficiencies."[1] This was how heaven prepares people for great tasks, and the scope of Yi's trials is the measure of his greatness. Thus, building upon the Confucian conception of a man who, by great endurance and action, raises himself to heroic status, the

1. 6B:15; Lau, *Mencius*, 181.

compilers of the *Songs* confer on Yi's deeds a universalizing moral and political significance. The virtuous leader is the upholder of justice and humanity, one who scorns violence and unreason by subordinating his passions and desires to a higher purpose. He is endowed with strength and purpose by his sense of duty, his trust in his mission as a carrier of civilization, and his ability to restore harmony and order on every plane. He looks to the future: to the unified nation, the willing people, and the dynasty that will stand as a symbol of peace and stability.

The cantos that celebrate the statesmanship of Yi Sŏnggye explore the nature and function of kingship, the relations of power and justice, the role of mercy and remonstrance, and the importance of learning and orthodoxy, culminating in the admonitory cantos that conclude the cycle. Here the compilers directly address King Sejong in a series of gracious exhortations that change the focus from the distant and normative to the immediate and real. With poignantly personal utterance, the compilers address the evils that arise from ease and luxury, the role of peace in breeding courage and resolve, the value of modesty and the harm of pride, and the transforming power of virtue as the guardian of order. The final canto ends not only with a prophecy of national greatness but with an allusive rhetorical question.

Here the compilers assert once again that the security of the throne depends entirely upon the ruler's worship of heaven and his dedication to the people. Then they evoke the figure of Tai Kang of Xia, who went on a long hunting trip south of the Luo River and was ambushed on his way back to the capital, losing his throne. The symbolism of this passage lies in the image of the hunt, a political metaphor for the unbound energy of the tyrant whose rapacity disrupts the ideal moral order. Its admonitory appearance in the final canto warns against royal indulgence in tyranny, insisting on the cause-and-effect relationship between the moral energy of the ruler and the welfare of his state. Such was the figure of the ideal Confucian prince, whose lasting virtues were vital to the future of the dynasty.

SONGS OF FLYING DRAGONS

1   Korea's six dragons flew in the sky.[1]
      Their every deed was blessed by heaven.
      Their deeds tallied with those of the sage-kings.

2   The tree, whose roots are deep,
      Is firm amidst the winds,
      Its flowers are good,
      Its fruits abundant.

      The stream, whose source is deep,
      Gushes forth even in a drought.
      It forms a river
      And gains the sea.

27   His arrow was huge beyond compare—
      His father saw it and abandoned it.
      On the same day he rejoiced
      In him whose genius astounded the day.[2]

32   Heaven sent a genius
      In order to save the people.
      Hence he shot with twenty arrows
      Twenty sables in the bush.

---

1. The six dragons are the four royal ancestors Mokcho (d. 1274), Ikcho (d.u.), Tojo (d. 1342), and Hwanjo (1315–1360), followed by Yi Sŏnggye (1392–1398) and Yi Pangwŏn (1400–1418).

2. Except for the first and last cantos (1–2, 125) in the cycle, each canto consists of two verses, the first usually relating to the deeds of Chinese sovereigns and the second to those of Korean kings. From this canto until 110, only the second verse is given. "His" refers to Yi Sŏnggye; "his father" refers to Hwanjo.

43 On Mount Chorae he struck two roebucks
    With a single arrow.
    Must one paint
    This natural genius?

44 It was a polo match played by royal order—
    He hit the ball with a "sideways block."
    People on nine state roads
    All admired his skill.

53 He opened the four borders,
    Island dwellers had no more fear of pirates.
    Southern barbarians beyond our waters,
    How could they not come to him?[3]

70 Heaven gave him courage and wisdom
    Who was to bring order to his country.
    Hence eight steeds
    Appeared at the proper time.

73 Because robbers poisoned the people,
    He initiated land reform.
    First he drove away the usurper,
    He then labored to restore the state.[4]

---

3. Yi Sŏnggye finally subjugated the Jurchen in the north and the Japanese outlaws in the south, letting the inhabitants of even the remotest island in the south enjoy peace. After Yi's enthronement, the king of Liuqiu sent an envoy to pay his respects (1392), and Siam sent an envoy with tribute (1393).

4. Yi Sŏnggye dethroned Sin Ch'ang and set the Koryŏ dynasty in order. He also confiscated the estates monopolized by powerful families, burned the public and private land register in the ninth month of 1390, and enforced new rules for land distribution in 1391.

76   Kind and selfless to his brothers,
     He covered their past misdeeds.
     Thus today we enjoy
     Humane manners and customs.[5]

79   He was consistent from beginning to end.
     Meritorious subjects were truly loyal to him.
     He secured the throne for myriad years.
     Would his royal works ever cease?

80   Though he was busy with war,
     He loved the way of the scholar.
     His work of achieving peace
     Shone brilliantly.[6]

81   He did not boast of his natural gifts,
     His learning was equally deep.
     The vast scope of royal works
     Was indeed great.[7]

82   Upon receiving an old scholar
     He knelt down with due politeness.
     What do you say about
     His respect for scholarship?[8]

---

5. When his stepbrother, who had plotted a revolt in 1371, was involved in a murder case four years later, Yi did everything to help him but could not save his life.

6. Yi loved learning, reading far into and night and discussing the classics with scholars between battles.

7. Yi never boasted of his brilliant exploits. Regretting that his family had not yet produced a scholar, he urged his son, Yi Pangwŏn, to study the classics. The latter passed the higher civil service examination in 1383.

8. When Yi Saek (1328–1396) returned from exile in the eleventh month of 1391, Yi Sŏnggye kneeled to receive him, offering him a cup.

86   He shot six roebucks,
     He shot six crows,
     He flew across
     The slanting tree.[9]

88   He hit the backs of forty tailed deer.
     He pierced the mouths and eyes of the rebels.
     He shot down three mice from the eaves,
     Were there any like him in the past?[10]

89   Seven pinecones,
     The trunk of a dead tree,
     Three arrows piercing the helmet—
     None like him in the past.[11]

110 Your four ancestors never enjoyed peace—
     How often did they move around?
     How did they live,
     In how large an abode?

     When you live in a deep sumptuous palace,
     When you enjoy golden days of peace,
     Remember, my Lord,
     Their hardship and sorrow.

---

9. While still young, Yi Sŏnggye pierced six roebucks and six crows with a single arrow. When a deer ran beneath a slanting tree during a hunt, Yi vaulted over the tree while his horse ran under it, landed in the saddle on the other side, and shot the fleeing animal.

10. Yi Sŏnggye shot forty deer on a hunting trip in Haeju in 1385. During his campaign against the Mongol Naghacu in 1362, Yi shot the rebels in the mouth.

11. To forecast the outcome of a battle against Japanese outlaws in Hamju in 1385, Yi used seven arrows to shoot down seven pinecones from seventy paces away. In 1377, before charging the Japanese outlaws, Yi placed a helmet one hundred fifty paces away and divined the outcome of the campaign by hitting the target three times. On another occasion, his arrows hit the trunk of a dead tree three times.

111   Because the wolves wrought havoc,
       Because not even a grass roof remained,
       They bore hardships
       In a clay hut.

       When you are in a great carpeted room,
       When you sit on a richly woven throne,
       Remember, my Lord,
       Their hardships and sorrow.[12]

112   Anxious only to fulfill the royal cause
       He led his men from camp to camp.
       How many days did he run
       Without doffing his armor?

       When you are wrapped in a dragon robe,
       When you wear the belt of precious gems,
       Remember, my Lord,
       His fortitude and tenacity.[13]

113   Zealous to deliver the suffering people,
       He fought on mountains and plains.
       O how many times did he go
       Without food and drink?

       When you sup on northern viands and southern dainties,
       When you have superb wine and precious grain,
       Remember, my Lord,
       His fortitude and fervor.[14]

12. Jurchen chiefs ("wolves" in line 1) conspired against the life of Yi's great-grandfather. In cantos 110–124, both verses deal with the Yi kings.

13. When Yi was subjugating the north and the south, he never had time to remove his armor.

14. During his campaign against the Jurchen and Japanese outlaws, Yi went without food for days.

114 Wishing to entrust him with a great task,
Heaven flexed his bones and sinews,
And let his body suffer
Wounds and scars.

While the stately guards stand row after row,
While you reign in peace and give audience,
Remember, my Lord,
His piety and constancy.[15]

115 Because he loved men and sought their welfare,
He overawed
The fierce rebels
And caught them alive.

When you have men at your beck and call,
When you punish men and sentence men,
Remember, my Lord,
His mercy and temperance.[16]

116 Seeing the bodies lying in heaps,
He abandoned food and sleep.
Moved by love for his people,
He labored assiduously.

If you are unaware of people's sorrow,
Heaven will abandon you.

---

15. During his campaign against the Red Turbans (1362), Yi suffered a wound below the right ear. In the 1380 campaign against the Japanese outlaws, an enemy arrow hit Yi's left knee.

16. Yi returned the spoils to the people of Liaodong after a battle in 1370; in his campaign against the Mongols in 1362, Yi shot the enemy general with wooden arrows, forcing him to dismount and surrender; and in his campaign against the Japanese outlaws in 1385, Yi urged his soldiers to capture them alive.

Remember, my Lord,
His labor and love.[17]

117   He battled against the king's enemy,
And his fame was unrivaled.
But he never boasted of his deeds.
Such was his virtue of modesty.

If a deceitful minister flatters you,
If you are roused to pride,
Remember, my Lord,
His prowess and modesty.[18]

118   He had many to help him;
Even the Jurchen served him with constancy.
How can we tell in words
How our people gave their hearts to him?[19]

If a king loses his inward power,
Even his kin will rebel.
Remember, my Lord,
His fame and virtue.

119   The brothers rebelled against one another:
But in their heart they were friendly.
Despite their crimes
Their ties remained firm.[20]

---

17. During his 1390 campaign against the Japanese outlaws, Yi saw dead bodies piled up on the plains and hills. Overwhelmed, he could neither eat nor sleep.

18. The first stanza refers to the victories won by Yi Sŏnggye over the Japanese outlaws in 1377, 1378, 1380, and 1385.

19. Yi enjoyed the esteem of Jurchen chiefs in the northeast, and they served under his command.

20. The first verse refers to the rebellion of Yi Sŏnggye's stepbrother in 1371 and Yi Pangwŏn's elder brother in 1400.

If brothers are split,
A villain will enter and sow discord.
Remember, my Lord,
His sagacity and love.

120   Because the government burdened the people,
The people who are heaven to a ruler,
He defied a multitude of opinions
And reformed the system of private lands.

If a ruler taxes his people without measure,
The basis of the state will crumble.
Remember, my Lord,
His justice and humanity.

121   Even though they were rebellious,
They were loyal to their lord.
Hence he forgave them
And employed them again.

If your advisers wrangle before you,
Only to assist and secure the Throne,
Remember, my Lord,
His goodness and justice.

122   His nature being one with heaven,
He knew learning surpassed mere thinking.
Hence he made friends
With learned men.[21]

If a small man wishes to curry favor
And preaches "No leisure for culture,"

21. See Canto 80 above.

Remember, my Lord,
His effort and erudition.

123   Many slandered him;
An innocent man was about to perish.
He narrowly saved
The man of merit from death.

When slanderers craftily make mischief,
When they grossly exaggerate small mistakes,
Remember, my Lord,
His wisdom and justice.[22]

124   Because his bright nature
Was versed in the teachings of the sage,
He proscribed
· Heresy.[23]

If perverse theories of the western barbarians
Threaten you with sin and allure with bliss,
Remember, my Lord,
His judgment and orthodoxy.

125   A millennium ago,
Heaven chose the north of the Han.
There they accumulated goodness and founded the state.
Oracles foretold a myriad years;

May your sons and grandsons reign unbroken.
But you can secure the dynasty only

22. The first verse refers to Yi Sŏnggye's saving of Cho Chun, who had been imprisoned on a false charge in 1400.

23. Upholding Confucian orthodoxy, Yi Pangwŏn closed Buddhist monasteries in
1402 and secularized the clergy.

When you worship heaven and benefit the people.
Ah, you who will wear the crown, beware.

Can you depend upon your ancestor
When you go hunting by the waters of the Luo?[24]

Sijo

The short lyric poem or song called *sijo,* dating from the late
fourteenth to early fifteenth century, was the most popular, elastic,
and mnemonic poetic form of Korea. The *sijo* is typically a three-
line poem sung in the vernacular, each line consisting of four metric
segments or rhythmic groups, with a minor pause at the end of the
second segment and a major one at the end of the fourth:

$$3/4 \quad 4 \quad 3/4 \quad 4$$
$$3/4 \quad 4 \quad 3/4 \quad 4$$
$$3 \quad 5 \quad 4 \quad 3/4$$

An emphatic syntactic division is usually introduced in the third line,
often in the form of an exclamation representing a leap in logic or
development. This introduction of a deliberate twist in phrasing or
meaning—somewhat like the Italian *volta* (twist)[1]—was considered
a test of a poet's originality.

The diction of *sijo,* despite some loanwords from Chinese, is native in the frequency of use of given words. In addition, certain re-
curring epithets and phrases, used for poetic amplification, establish

24. Tai Kang of Xia was excessively fond of hunting. On a trip south of the Luo River,
he dallied for a hundred days, allowing a usurper to prevent his return to the capital and
seize the throne.

1. Between the octave and sestet of the Italian sonnet.

a community of mind and of imagination between poet and audience. While some epithets are dictated by seasonal, topical, and
structural requirements, others are necessitated by the brevity of the
form itself. Indeed, the frequency of verbal parallels and formulaic
expressions, long and short, points to a particular method of creation. The poet's task was to preserve and transmit a living tradition
through a new arrangement of old material, thereby imparting added
significance to the tradition. As a particular sequence of ideas and
topics germinated in the poet's memory, he composed by deploying
phrases, motifs, and themes, each serving as a mnemonic device for
himself and his audience. The countless variations on a theme became a source of pleasure to the auditors in the audience, who were
quick to recognize allusions to earlier versions, to see the worth of
old material in new contexts, and to savor their own aesthetic responses to the poet's creation. By recalling the past, Korean singers
were oral poets drawing on their society's memory bank in order to
renew it through the art of their performance.

The *Songs of Green Hills* (*Ch'ŏnggu yŏngŏn*, 1728), by Kim
Ch'ŏnt'aek, a professional singer and poet (whose background was
that of a commoner), was the first collection of *sijo*. Among the authors represented were kings and princes, female entertainers, and a
large number of anonymous writers. Favored topics include the
brevity of spring and autumn; the phases of love; the sorrow of unrequited love and of parting; the reunion of friends; the onslaught
of old age; *carpe diem* and *carpe florem*; and cherishing the past.
Since the text of most songs varied, possibly with each performance, the great number of song variants collected in the history of
sijo bespeaks its oral nature. The modern variorum edition of the
sijo canon lists 3,335 songs, each with more than thirty or forty
variants.[2]

Korea's lyric-based poetics, in its affective and expressive dimensions, ultimately traces to the major preface to the *Book of Songs:*
"Poetry is where the intent of the heart (or mind) goes. Lying in the
heart, it is 'intent'; when uttered in words, it is 'poetry.' When an

---

2. Sim Chaewan, *Kyobon yŏktae sijo chŏnsŏ*.

emotion stirs inside, one expresses it in words; finding this inadequate, one sighs over it; not content with this, one sings it in poetry; still not satisfied, one unconsciously dances with one's hand and feet."[3]

A large number of *sijo* were composed on the attractions of nature, seen as a realm of intuition where fortune has no power. To scholar-officials serving at court and in the capital, a withdrawal to nature and a life lived in retirement were not simply praiseworthy; they often seemed the wisest course. Let us look at a deceptively simple poem by Sŏng Hon (1525–1598):

> The mountain is silent,
>   the water without form.
> A clear breeze has no price,
>   the bright moon no lover.
> Here, after their fashion,
>   I will grow old in peace.

The four images in the first four lines are all from nature: mountain, water, a breeze, and the moon, and they are qualified by four statements that point to the relationships among them. The first pair of lines contains metaphors with Daoist overtones, for nature, according to Zhuangzi, is not only spontaneous but in constant flux and transformation. The second pair introduces what might be called political metaphors—metaphors of the marketplace that implicitly denounce one way of life and uphold another. Here we are presented with a contrast between attachment to worldly pursuits and freedom therefrom. For this purpose, the speaker has brought in two adjectives: "priceless," here translated as having no price, and "ownerless" or "loverless," translated as having "no lover." The first has two meanings: not worth putting a price on, hence unsold; and having a value beyond all price. A clear breeze is still unsold, for those who cling to worldly power and wealth cannot purchase it. Similarly, the moon has no owner; no one has yet claimed it as his own. Wandering in the vast realm of oneness, transformed and transforming, the

---

3. Liu, *Chinese Theories of Literature*, 69.

poet attains great knowledge, indeed "after their fashion." In the last line, the speaker talks, somewhat ironically, as a man fully awakened, for one who has comprehended the relationship between the phenomenal world and ultimate truth and has taken transformation as his final abode will never grow old. He is impervious to the elements of nature, for nothing can harm him or cause him to suffer. This brief example shows the *sijo* poet in the act of extending the tradition by selecting conventional material and making it new.

U T'ak (1262–1342)

The wind that melted the spring hills
　　came and went without trace.
I wish I could bring it back
　　and blow it over my head.
Would I could melt the white hair
　　grown under my ears.

Sticks in one hand,
　　brambles in the other,
I try to block old age with thorn bushes,
　　and white hair with sticks.
But white hair came by a shortcut,
　　having seen through my devices.

Yi Chonyŏn (1269–1343)

The moon is white on pear blossoms,
　　and the Milky Way tells the third watch.

A cuckoo would not know
   the intent of a branch of spring.[1]
Too much awareness is a sickness,
   it keeps me awake all night.

Yi Saek (1328–1396)

Rough clouds gather around the valley
   where the snow still lies.
Where is the welcoming plum,[1]
   at what place does it bloom?
I have lost my way, alone,
   in the setting sun.

Yi Chono (1341–1371)

That clouds have no intent
   is perhaps false and unreliable.
Floating in midair,
   freely moving,
For what reason do they cover
   the bright light of day?

Kil Chae (1353–1419)

I return on horseback
   to the capital of five hundred years.
Hills and rivers remain the same,

---

1. Alludes to the promise of plum blossoms, as in a poem by Lu Kai of the Song. See Frankel, "The Plum Tree in Chinese Poetry."

1. Refers to the declining royal house of Koryŏ.

but where are the great men of the past?
Alas, the age of grand peace—
   it was only a dream!

Wŏn Ch'ŏnsŏk (fl. c. 1401–1410)

Fortune determines rise and fall,
   Full Moon Terrace is autumn grass.
A shepherd's pipe echoes
   the royal works of five hundred years.
A traveler cannot keep back his tears
   in the setting sun.

Maeng Sasŏng (1360–1438)

FOUR SEASONS BY THE RIVERS AND LAKES

1
Spring comes to rivers and lakes,
   wild rapture seizes me.
I drink thick wine by the river
   with a damask-scaled fish.
I can enjoy a leisurely life
   because of royal favor.
2
Summer comes to rivers and lakes,
   I am idle at the grass hut.
Friendly waves in the river
   only send a cool breeze.
I can keep myself cool
   because of royal favor.

3
Autumn comes to rivers and lakes,
   every fish is sleek.
I cast a net from my boat
   and leave it to the stream's flow.
I can while away my time
   because of royal favor.

4
Winter comes to rivers and lakes,
   snow is a foot deep.
A bamboo hat aslant,
   a straw cape for cloth,
I am not cold
   because of royal favor.

Hwang Hŭi (1363–1452)

Are chestnuts falling
   in the valley of red jujubes?
And crabs crawling in the stubble
   after a harvest of rice?
Wine is ripe, and a sieve seller passes by.
   What can I do but strain and drink?

Yi Kae (1417–1456)

The candle burns in the room,
   for whom has it parted?
Shedding tears outside,
   does it know that its inside burns?
That candle is like me,
   it does not know its heart burns!

Sŏng Sammun (1418–1456)

Were you to ask me what I'd wish to be
    after my death,
I would answer, a pine tree, tall and hardy
    on the highest peak of Mount Pongnae,
And to be green, alone, green,
    when snow fills heaven and earth.

Yu Ŭngbu (d. 1456)

Do you say the wind blew last night
    and frost and snow fell?
Tall drooping pines
    are bent and broken.
What about the flower buds, then,
    what is their fate?

King Sŏngjong (1470–1494)

Stay:
    will you go? Must you go?
Is it in weariness you go? From disgust?
    Who advised you, who persuaded you?
Say why you are leaving,
    you, who are breaking my heart.

Kim Ku (1488–1534)

Until the duck's short legs
    grow as long as the crane's—
Until the crow has become white,

white as the white heron—
Enjoy enduring bliss
    forever.

Sŏ Kyŏngdŏk (1489–1546)

My mind is foolish,
    all that I do seems in vain.
Who would come to the deep mountain
    with its thick clouds, fold upon fold?
I look to see whether you come by chance,
    whenever the fallen leaves rustle in the wind.

Song Sun (1493–1583)

I have spent ten years
    building a grass hut;
Now winds occupy half,
    the moon fills the rest.
I cannot let in hills and waters:
    I will display them all around.

        ❁

I discuss with my heart
    whether to retire from court.
My heart scorns the intent:
    "How could you leave the king?"
"Heart, stay here and serve him,
    my old body must go."

        ❁

Do not grieve, little birds,
    over the falling blossoms:

They're not to blame, it's the wind
   who loosens and scatters the petals.
Spring persists in leaving us,
   don't hold it against her.

Cho Sik (1501–1572)

Wearing hemp clothes in the coldest winter,
   wet with rain and snow in the cave,
I have not had the sun,
   hidden by the clouds.
But, yet, to see the setting sun
   brings tears to my eyes.

Hwang Chini (c. 1506–1544)

I will break the back
   of this long, midwinter night,
folding it double,
   cold beneath my spring quilt,
that I may draw out
   the night, should my love return.

Translated by David R. McCann

Do not boast of your speed,
   O blue-green stream running by the hills:
Once you have reached the wide ocean,
   you can return no more.
Why not stay here and rest
   when Bright Moon fills the empty hills?

❖

Mountains are steadfast,
    but waters are not so.
Since they flow day and night,
    can there be old waters?
Great heroes are like waters,
    once gone, they never return.

❖

Blue mountains speak of my desire,
    green waters reflect my lover's love:
Green waters may flow away,
    but can blue mountains change?
Green waters too cannot forget blue mountains,
    They wander through in tears.

❖

When was I unfaithful to you?
    When did I ever deceive you?
The moon sinks and it's the third watch,
    there is no sign of you.
What can I do about
    the falling leaves in the autumn wind?

Kwŏn Homun (1532–1587)

Nature makes clear the windy air,
    and bright the round moon.
In the bamboo garden, on the
    pine fence, not a speck of dust.
How fresh and clean my life
    with a long lute and piled scrolls!

Sŏng Hon (1535–1598)

The mountain is silent,
   the water without form.
A clear breeze has no price,
   the bright moon no lover.
Here, after their fashion,
   I will grow old in peace.

Chŏng Ch'ŏl (1537–1594)

The juice of bitter herbs has
   more taste than any meat.
My small grass hut is
   a fitting abode for me.
But my longing for my lord
   chokes me with grief.

✦

A dash of rain upon
   the lotus leaves. But the leaves
Remain unmarked, no matter
   how hard the raindrops beat.
Mind, be like the lotus leaves,
   unstained by the world.

✦

Let forty thousand pecks of pearls
   rest on the lotus leaves.
I box and measure them
   to send them off somewhere.
Tumultuous rolling drops—
   how zestful, graceful.

Boys have gone out to gather bracken;
    the bamboo grove is empty.
Who will pick up the dice
    scattered on the checkerboard?
Drunk, I lean on the pine trunk,
    let dawn pass me by.

Milky rain on the green hills,
    can you deceive me?
Sedge cape and horsehair hat,
    can you deceive me?
Yesterday I flung off my silk robe—
    I have nothing left that will stain me.

Im Che (1549–1587)

In a mound where the grass grows long,
    are you sleeping or lying at rest?
Where is your lovely face?
    only bones are buried here.
I have no one to offer a cup,
    and that makes me sad.

Deep among the green valley grasses,
    a stream runs crying.
Where's the terrace of songs,
    where's the hall of dancing?
Do you know, swallow,
    cutting the sunset water?

Cho Chonsŏng (1553–1627)

FOUR SONGS CALLING A BOY

1

Boy, gather your straw basket,
  the sun sets on the western hills.
The fern that grew last night
  may be already withered.
What should I eat in morning and evening
  if there are no fiddleheads?

2

Boy, bring my sedge cape and bamboo hat,
  it rains at the eastern torrent.
With a long fishing rod
  and barbless hook I go.
Fish, don't be startled!
  I came here in high spirits.

3

Boy, bring my morning porridge,
  much work to be done in the southern field.
Who will help me to work
  my clumsy plowing?
Let it be, we can plow in peace
  because of royal favor.

4

Boy, lead a cow to the northern village,
  let's taste new wine.
My face is rosy with drink,
  I'll return on cowback in the moonlight.
Hurrah, I am a Fu Xi[1] tonight,
  ancient glories at my fingertips.

---

1. A Chinese culture hero.

Hongnang (fl. 1576–1600)

I send you, my love,
  select branches of the willow.
Plant them to be admired
  outside your bedroom window.
If a night rain makes them bud,
  think that it is I.

Kyerang (Yi Hyanggŭm, 1513–1550)

Under a shower of pear blossoms
  we parted in tears, clinging to each other.
Now autumn winds scatter leaves,
  are you too thinking of me?
A thousand miles away,
  only my lonely dreams come and go.

Myŏngok (late 16th cent.)

They say dream visits
  are "only a dream."
My longing to see him is destroying me.
  Where else do I see him but in dreams?
Darling, come to me even if it be in dreams.
  Let me see you time and again.

❀

Snow falls on the mountain village
  and buries the stone path.
Do not open the twig gate,
  who will come to visit me here?
My only friend is
  a slice of bright moon.

Ch'ŏn Kŭm (d.u.)

Night draws near in a mountain village,
   a dog barks far away.
I open the twig gate:
   the chilly sky and the moon.
Be still, stop barking at the moon
   asleep over the bare mountain.

Kim Sangyong (1561–1637)

Listlessly I hear the rain
   beat on the wide beech tree leaves.
My grief awakens, and every raindrop
   on the leaves brings sorrow.
Never again shall I plant
   a tree with such broad leaves.

Love is a deceit.
   She does not love me.
She says she comes to me in a dream:
   it is a lie.
Lying awake every night,
   in what dream shall I see her?

Sin Hŭm (1566–1628)

I would draw her face with blood
   that lies stagnant in my heart.
And on the plain wall of a high hall,
   I would hang it up to gaze.

Who has invented the word "Farewell"?
  Who causes me to die?

A rain came overnight;
  pomegranates are in full bloom.
Having rolled up a crystal screen
  by the lotus pond,
Can I unravel this deep sorrow—
  caused by someone I love?

Don't laugh if my roof beams
  are long or short, the pillars
Tilted or crooked, or my grass hut small.
  moonlight that pours on the vines,
The encircling hills,
  are mine, and mine alone.

The person who made a song
  must have had many sorrows.
Unable to say what he wanted,
  he must have sung it.
If song could dispel sorrow,
  I too will start to sing.

Kim Yuk (1580–1658)

Be sure to invite me
  when your wine matures.
I shall invite you
  if flowers bloom in my arbor.
We shall discuss, then, how to live
  a hundred years without worry.

Kim Kwanguk (1580–1656)

Have you seen a person
  who returned from death?
None ever told us he came back,
  no one has seen another return.
Since I know this is so,
  I'll savor life's joys.

❖

Bamboo staff, the sight of you
  fills me with trust and delight.
Ah, boyhood days when you were my horse!
  Stand there now
behind the window, and when we go out,
  let me stand behind you.

❖

Bundle the piles of verbose missives
  and throw them away!
At last I ride home on a swift horse
  whipping the autumn winds.
No bird freed can be happier,
  what freedom, what relief.

Yun Sŏndo (1587–1671)

SONGS OF FIVE FRIENDS

How many friends have I? Count them:
  water and stone, pine and bamboo—
The rising moon on the east mountain,
  welcome, it too is my friend.
What need is there, I say,
  to have more friends than five?

They say the color of clouds is fine,
   but they often darken.
They say the sound of winds is clear,
   but they often cease to blow.
It is only the *water*, then,
   that is perpetual and good.

Why do flowers fade so soon
   once they are in their glory?
Why do grasses yellow so soon
   once they have grown tall?
Perhaps it is the *stone*, then,
   that is constant and good.

Flowers bloom when it is warm;
   leaves fall when the days are cool.
But, O *pine*, how is it
   that you scorn frost, ignore snow?
I know now even your roots are
   straight among the Nine Springs.[1]

You are not a tree,
   nor are you a plant.
Who let you shoot up so straight?
   What makes you empty within?
You are green in all seasons,
   welcome, my friend.

Small but floating high,
   you shed light on all creation.
And what can match your brightness

1. Hades.

in the dark of night?
You see everything but say nothing;
    that's why, O *moon*, you are my friend.

THE ANGLER'S CALENDAR

The image of the fisherman is extraordinarily widespread in the literatures of the world, but nowhere does it play a more important role than in Chinese and Korean poetry. In China, legendary sages and historical recluses were portrayed as fishermen, paragons of an ideal mode of life, seen as pure wise men living detached from troubled times and a confused world, and devoted to self-cultivation.

The origin of fisherman songs in Korea is obscure, but we know they were popular from the Koryŏ dynasty on. There are two versions that preceded Yun Sŏndo's: a *sijo* sequence of twelve songs in the *Akchang kasa* (c. 16th cent.?) and its revision by Yi Hyŏnbo (1467–1555) into a cycle of nine stanzas.[1] The first seems to have been written as Chinese heptasyllabic quatrains with at least one line from Tang poets.[2] Yi Hyŏnbo did away with the repetitions and reorganized the songs, but his adaptations still sounded clumsy, as Yun Sŏndo observed: "Yi's sound pattern is faulty, and his diction and meaning leave much to be desired." For his part, Yun set out to create a cycle of fisherman's songs in the vernacular that would resound with native rhythms. His forty poems/songs depicting the four seasons, titled *The Angler's Calendar* (1651), are not a treatise on the craft of fishing with enumeration of fish and details on bait and each fish's favorite haunts. Instead, the poems are the product of Yun's leisurely life at a favorite retreat, the Lotus Grotto, and they elaborate a dialectical pattern involving two modes of life wherein the happy fisherman's discovery of self and nature is the result of his renunciation of the world, representing the obstacle to his final freedom and illumination.

The songs are written in intricate stanzas that differ from the conventional *sijo* form. The general pattern is as follows (the numerals indicate the number of syllables in each metric segment):

1st line:	3 4 3 4
envoi:	4 4
2nd line:	3 4 3 4
envoi:	3 3 3
3rd line:	3 4 3 4

1. *Nongam chip*, 3:15a–16b.

2. "Because the lines have been borrowed so long . . . because they have been assimilated so thoroughly by latter-day poets, they are now a legacy shared by all poets" (Palumbo-Liu, *The Poetics of Appropriation*, 176). The borrowed lines were from poets such as Zen Can (715–770), Zhang Zihe (742–782), Bo Juyi (771–846), Liu Zongyuan (773–819), Du Mu (803–852), Du Xuanhe (846–914), Dai Fugu (d.u.), and Sikong Shu (837–908).

A pair of four-syllable words is added after line 1 and three-syllable onomatopoetic words after line 2, bringing the total number of syllables to fifty-nine. The
fortieth poem in the sequence has an unusual form, for here the total number of
syllables is seventy-two.

Together with their intricate organization, the poems are marked by flawless
diction and a musical quality that depicts images as well as simulating sounds.
Indeed, in lyrical rhythms Yun succeeded in casting a persuasive depiction of the
fisherman's life. The fourth poem in the spring cycle offers an admirable example
of the poet's technique:

> Is it a cuckoo that cries?
>   Is it the willow that is blue?
> Row away, row away!
>   Several roofs in a far fishing village
>   swim in the mist.
> *Chigukch'ong chigukch'ong ŏsawa.*
> Boy, fetch an old net!
>   The fish are climbing against the stream.

The poem opens with two questions suggesting uncertainty regarding the senses
of sound and sight. In the next two lines we actually do see village roofs, however
insubstantial they may appear, seeming to swim in the twilight. The expression
"*chigukch'ong chigukch'ong ŏsawa*" is an onomatopoetic segment simulating the
movements and sounds of rowing. The last two lines are brisk and forceful and
express a practical and immediate appreciation and delight, with the suggestion
that all these stages follow in sequence. The poem therefore presents nature's mystery, beauty, and bounty in terms of illusory loveliness, actual loveliness, and finally the physical sustenance reaped by those who fish. Thus the poem not only
imparts the felt transcendence of the vision but also reveals an awareness of the
transience of earthly joy and beauty. Yet all this is conveyed with the simplest vocabulary and the utmost economy.

SPRING

1

Fog lifts in the stream before me,
    the sun lances the black hills.
Cast off, cast off!
The night tide neaps, and now
    high water rushes upon the shore.

Chigukch'ong chigukch'ong ŏsawa.
Flowers in river hamlets are fair to see,
　but distant views swell my heart.

2
The day is warm,
　fish float in the blue.
Hoist anchor, hoist anchor!
In twos or threes,
　gulls come and go.
Chigukch'ong chigukch'ong ŏsawa.
Boy, I have a rod;
　have you loaded a flagon of wine?

3
A puff of east wind ruffles
　the stream's surface into ripples.
Raise sail, raise sail!
Let's go to West Lake
　by the East.
Chigukch'ong chigukch'ong ŏsawa.
Hills pass by,
　more hills greet us.

4
Is it a cuckoo that cries?
　Is it the willow that is blue?
Row away, row away!
Several roofs in a far fishing village
　swim in the mist.
Chigukch'ong chigukch'ong ŏsawa.
Boy, fetch an old net!
　The fish are climbing against the stream.[1]

---

1. Another version of lines 7–8 reads: "In the deep and clear stream,/All kinds of fish are leaping." Sim Chaewan, *Kyobon yŏktae sijo chŏnsŏ*, 770–772.

5

The sun's fair rays are shining.
   Water shimmers like oil.
Row away, row away!
Should we cast a net,
   or drop a line on such a day?
Chigukch'ong chigukch'ong ŏsawa.
The Fisherman's Song stirs my fancy;[2]
   I have forgotten all about fishing.

6

Let's return to the shore,
   twilight trails in the west.
Lower sail, lower sail!
How supple and sweet
   willows and flowers on the riverbank!
Chigukch'ong chigukch'ong ŏsawa.
Who would envy three dukes?
   Who would now think of earthly affairs?

7

Let's tread on fragrant grasses
   and pick orchids and angelica.
Stop the boat, stop the boat!
What have I taken aboard
   on my boat small as a leaf?
Chigukch'ong chigukch'ong ŏsawa.
Nothing except mist when I set sail,
   when I row back, the moon.

8

Drunk I lie asleep,
   what if the boat floats downstream?
Moor the boat, moor the boat!

2. Refers to "The Fisherman" in *Chuzi* (Elegies of Chu).

Peach Blossom Spring is near,[3]
 pink petals leap on the stream.
Chigukch'ong chigukch'ong ŏsawa.
I am far removed from red dust—
 the human world.

9
Let's stop angling and see
 the moon through the bamboo awning.
Drop anchor, drop anchor!
Night settles,
 the cuckoo sings a sweet song.
Chigukch'ong chigukch'ong ŏsawa.
The heart shouts its peak of joy,
 I have lost my way in the dark.

10
Tomorrow, tomorrow, we have tomorrow.
 A spring night will soon see the day.
Bring the boat ashore, bring the boat ashore!
With a rod for a cane,
 let's find our twig gate.
Chigukch'ong chigukch'ong ŏsawa.
This angler's life is
 how I shall pass my days.

SUMMER

11
Tedious rain over at last,
 the stream grows limpid.
Cast off, cast off!
Rod on my shoulder,

---

3. The first Chinese *locus amoenus,* created by Tao Qian; see Hightower, *Poetry of T'ao Ch'ien,* 254–258.

I can't still my loud heart.
Chigukch'ong chigukch'ong ŏsawa.
Who has painted these scenes,
  misty rivers and folded peaks?

12

Wrap the steamed rice in lotus leaves,
  you need no other viands.
Hoist anchor, hoist anchor!
I've already got my blue arum hat,
  bring me, boy, my green straw cape.
Chigukch'ong chigukch'ong ŏsawa.
Mindless gulls come and go;
  do they follow me, or I them?

13

A wind rises among the water chestnut,
  cool is the bamboo awning.
Raise sail, raise sail!
Let the boat drift with the current,
  the summer breeze is capricious.
Chigukch'ong chigukch'ong ŏsawa.
Northern coves and southern river,
  does it matter where I go?

14

When the river is muddy,
  no matter if we wash our feet there.
Row away, row away!
I wish to go to Wu River; sad
  are the angry waves of a thousand years.[4]
Chigukch'ong chigukch'ong ŏsawa.

---

4. Lines 4–5 refer to Wu Yuan, a native of Chu, who committed suicide after being denounced by Fu Chai of Wu. Angry, Fu caused his body to be put in a leather sack and thrown into the Wu River; on the bank the people raised a shrine to his memory. *Shiji* (Historical records) 66:2180.

Paddle the boat, then, to the Chu River;
   but don't catch the fish of a loyal soul.[5]

15

How rare is a mossy jetty
   with willow groves, thick and green.
Row away, row away!
Remember when we reach the fishing rock,
   anglers don't fight for the best pool.
Chigukch'ong chigukch'ong ŏsawa.
When you meet a hoary hermit,
   yield him the choicest stream.[6]

16

Whelmed by my exalted mood,
   I had not known day was ending.
Lower sail, lower sail!
Let's beat the stroke
   With a song of roving waves.
Chigukch'ong chigukch'ong ŏsawa.
Who can know how my heart
   always delights in the creak of an oar?

17

The setting sun is splendid.
   Twilight will soon overtake us!
Stop the boat, stop the boat!
Under the pine a path
   winds through the rocks.
Chigukch'ong chigukch'ong ŏsawa.
Do you hear an oriole calling
   here and there in the green grove?

5. Lines 7–8 refer to Qu Yuan (c. 343–278 BCE), who drowned himself in the Miluo
(or Chu) River. *Shiji* 84:2481–2491.
   6. According to tradition, when Emperor Shun went to Mount Li, he was given a field;
and when he went to the Lei stream, he was given a good spot for fishing. *Shiji* 1:33–34.

18

Let's spread our net out on the sand
    and lie under the thatched awning.
Moor the boat, moor the boat!
Fan off the mosquitoes,
    no, flies are worse.
Chigukch'ong chigukch'ong ŏsawa.
Only one worry, even here,
    traitors might eavesdrop.[7]

19

What will the mood of the sky be?
    Winds and storm may rise at night.
Drop anchor, drop anchor!
Who said that a boat swings by itself
    at the ferry landing?[8]
Chigukch'ong chigukch'ong ŏsawa.
Lovely are the hidden plants
    growing along mountain torrents.

20

Look! My snail-shell hut
    with white clouds all around.
Bring the boat ashore, bring the boat ashore!
Let's climb the stone path
    With bulrush fan in hand.
Chigukch'ong chigukch'ong ŏsawa.
O idle life of an old angler,
    this is my work, this is my life.

7. Minister Sang in the original: it is not clear why Sang Hongyang (152–80 BCE) is brought in to serve as a duplicitous courtier here. For Sang see *Shiji* 30:1428–1442.
    8. Allusion to "West Creek at Chuzhou" by Wei Yingwu (b. 736); see Watson, *Columbia Book of Chinese Poetry*, 278.

AUTUMN

21

What is more transcendent
  Than the life of a complete angler?
Cast off, cast off!
Mock not a hoary fisherman,
  he's painted by every great hand.
Chigukch'ong chigukch'ong ŏsawa.
Are the joys of all seasons equal?
  No, autumn has most delights.

22

Autumn comes to a river village,
  the fish are many and sleek.
Hoist anchor, hoist anchor!
Let's be free and happy
  on myriad acres of limpid waves.
Chigukch'ong chigukch'ong ŏsawa.
Behind me the dusty world, but
  joy doubles as I sail farther away.

23

Where white clouds rise,
  branches rustle.
Raise sail, raise sail!
Let's go to West Lake at high tide,
  and at low water to East Lake.
Chigukch'ong chigukch'ong ŏsawa.
White clover ferns and pink knotweeds,
  they adorn every inlet.

24

Beyond where the wild geese fly
  unknown peaks emerge.
Row away, row away!
I'll angle there, of course, but

my zestful spirit is enough.
Chigukch'ong chigukch'ong ŏsawa.
As the setting sun shines,
    a thousand hills are brocade.

25

Silver scales and jade scales,
    did I have a good catch today?
Row away, row away!
Let's build a fire of reed bushes,
    broil the fish one by one.
Chigukch'ong chigukch'ong ŏsawa.
Pour wine from a crock jar
    filling up my gourd cup!

26

Gently, the side wind blowing,
    we return with sail lowered.
Lower sail, lower sail!
Darkness is overcoming the day,
    but clear delight lingers.
Chigukch'ong chigukch'ong ŏsawa.
Who can tire of
    the red trees and crystal waters?

27

A scattering of silver dew;
    the bright moon rises.
Stop the boat, stop the boat!
Far and foggy is the Phoenix Tower,[9]
    to whom should I give this clear light?
Chigukch'ong chigukch'ong ŏsawa.
The jade hare pounds the magic pills;
    would I could feed them to heroes.

9. The palace. In East Asian mythology the hare or rabbit compounds a magical medicine (elixir of life) in the moon.

28
Where is it, where am I?
   Are heaven and earth separate?
Moor the boat, moor the boat!
Since the west wind's dust can't reach us,
   why fan away the empty air?[10]
Chigukch'ong chigukch'ong ŏsawa.
Further, since I have heard no words,
   why should I bother to wash my ears?[11]

29
Frost falls on my clothes:
   I am not cold.
Drop anchor, drop anchor!
Don't complain that the boat is narrow;
   compare it instead to the floating world.
Chigukch'ong chigukch'ong ŏsawa.
We'll live this way
   tomorrow and ever.

30
I want to admire the dawn moon
   from a stone cave in the pine grove.
Bring the boat ashore, bring the boat ashore!
But the path in the empty hills
   is hidden by fallen leaves.
Chigukch'ong chigukch'ong ŏsawa.
Since the white clouds, too, follow me,
   O heavy is the sedge cape!

---

10. In their struggle for power, Wang Dao (276–339) was dismissive of Yu Liang (289–340), who held the position of General Chastizing the West: "A strong wind started to raise the dust, and Wang (Dao), whisking it away with his fan, said, 'Yu Liang's dust is contaminating me!'" Mather, *New Account*, 429.

11. When the sage-king Yao wished to make the recluse Xu You his successor, Xu went to the Ying River to wash his ears.

WINTER

31

The clouds have rolled away,
  the sun's rays are warm.
Cast off, cast off!
Heaven and earth are frozen hard,
  but water as always is clear and cold.
Chigukch'ong chigukch'ong ŏsawa.
The boundless water
  is silk brocade.

32

Mend your fishing line and rod,
  repair the boat with bamboo sheets.
Hoist anchor, hoist anchor!
They say the nets on the Xiao and Xiang
  and the Dongting Lake freeze.[12]
Chigukch'ong chigukch'ong ŏsawa.
At this time no place is
  better than our waters.

33

The fish in the shallows
  have gone to distant swamps.
Raise sail, raise sail!
The sun shines for a moment;
  so let's go out to the fishing place.
Chigukch'ong chigukch'ong ŏsawa.
If the bait is good,
  fat fish will bite, they say.

34

A snow settles over the night—
  What new scenes before my eyes!

12. The Xiao and Xiang rivers and Dongting Lake are in northeastern Hunan.

Row away, row away!
In front lie glassy acres,
   jade hills piled behind.
Chigukch'ong chigukch'ong ŏsawa.
Is it a fairy land, or Buddha's realm?
   It can't be the human world.

35
I've forgotten the net and rod
   and beat the side of the boat.
Row away, row away!
How many times have I wished
   to cross the stream ahead?
Chigukch'ong chigukch'ong ŏsawa.
What if a gale should rise
   and set my boat in motion?

36
The crows hastening to their nests,
   how many have flown overhead?
Lower sail, lower sail!
Darkness envelops our homeward path,
   evening snow lies thick.
Chigukch'ong chigukch'ong ŏsawa.
Who'll attack Eya Lake[13]
   and avenge the shame of soldier trees?[14]

---

13. In 817 the Tang general Li Su took Caizhou in Honan by surprise, capturing Wu Yuanji (783–817). Appearing before the enemy stronghold on a snowy night, he flushed wildfowl from the numerous ponds outside the walls so that their noise might drown out the sound of the approaching army. *Jiu Tangshu* (Old history of the Tang) 33:3680; *Xin Tangshu* (New history of the Tang) 154:4877.

14. Fu Jian (338–385), king of the Former Qin, attacked the Eastern Jin and suffered a crushing defeat in 383. Fearing ambush from every tree and tuft of grass, the retreating army was alarmed by the sound of the wind and whoop of the cranes. *Jinshu* (History of the Jin) 114:2918.

37

Red cliffs and emerald canyons
   enfold us like a painted screen.
Stop the boat, stop the boat!
What does it matter
   if I catch any fish or not?[15]
Chigukch'ong chigukch'ong ŏsawa.
In an empty boat, with straw cape and hat,
   I sit and my heart beats fast.

38

By the river a lone pine,
   how mighty, how towering.
Moor the boat, moor the boat!
Don't scorn the rough clouds—
   they screen the world from us.
Chigukch'ong chigukch'ong ŏsawa.
Don't deplore the roaring waves—
   they drown out the clamor of this world.

39

People have praised my way of life
   in the land of the hermits.
Drop anchor, drop anchor!
Tell me who wore
   the sheepskin cloth at Seven-League Shallows?[16]
Chigukch'ong chigukch'ong ŏsawa.
And for three thousand six hundred days
   let's count the time on our fingers.[17]

15. The original refers to "fish with big mouths and delicate scales," an allusion to Su Shi; see Watson, *Su Tung-p'o*, 91.

16. Yan Guang (37 BCE–43 CE), a contemporary of Emperor Guangwu, retired to Mount Fuchun and spent his time fishing because he wished to decline the latter's offer of a high post. *Hou Hanshu* 113:2763–2764.

17. Refers to Taigong Wang or Lü Shang, a counselor to King Wen of Zhou. *Shiji* 32:1477–1481.

40
Day closes,
   time to feast and rest.
Bring the boat ashore, bring the boat ashore!
Let's tread the path where snow
   is strewn with pink petals.
Chigukch'ong chigukch'ong ŏsawa.
Lean from the pine window and gaze
   as the snow moon crosses the western peak.

Yi Myŏnghan (1595–1645)

If the path of my dreams
   left footprints,
The road outside your window, even of stone,
   would have been worn down.
But no trace remains on dream paths,
   and that makes me sad.

❖

With tears I cling to your sleeves,
   do not shake them and leave.
Over the far-off long dike
   the sun goes down.
You will regret it trimming the lamp
   by the tavern window without sleep.

❖

The morning star has set. A lark
   rises out of the long grass as I take
My hoe and close my twig gate.
   my cloth breeches are wet with dew.
Boy, if these were peaceful times,
   who'd be fretting about his wet clothes?

Prince Pongnim (1619–1659)

What amuses you in the sound
  of rain on the clear stream?
O flowers and trees of the hill,
  you shake and laugh?
Take pleasure, then, while you may;
  only a few more spring days.

Prince Inp'yŏng (1622–1658)

Don't mock a pine
  twisted and bent by the winds.
Flowers in the spring wind,
  can they keep their brilliance?
When winds blow and snow whirls,
  you will call for me.

Yi T'aek (1651–1719)

O roc, don't ridicule the small black birds:
You and the little birds both fly way up in the clouds,
You're a bird,
They're birds.
Really, I can't see much difference between you!

Chu Ŭisik (1675–1720)

A boy stops outside my window,
  tells me it is the New Year.
So I look out my eastern window—
  the usual sun has risen.

Boy, it's the same old sun,
   come tell me in the next world.

❖

What is life, I ponder—
   it is just a dream!
All good things and bad,
   they're dreams within a dream.
If this is so, all right—
   why not enjoy this dreaming?

Kim Sujang (1690–1769)

In my quiet grass hut,
   I sit alone.
The clouds are dozing
   to the low melody of my song.
Who else is there that can know
   the subtle intent of my life?

❖

Standing in your lofty tower,
   don't laugh at this low place.
In the midst of storm and thunder,
   would it surprise you to slip?
We sit on level ground,
   who needs distinctions?

Yi Chŏngbo (1693–1766)

If flowers bloom, I think of the moon,
   if the moon shines, I ask for wine.
When I have all these at once,

still I think of friends.
When can I drink a night away,
   enjoying moon and flowers with a friend?

Cho Myŏngni (1697–1756)

Wild geese have all flown away,
   the first frosts have come.
Long, long is the autumn night,
   many, many are the traveler's worries.
When moonlight floods the garden,
   I feel I am back at home.

Kim Sŏnggi (c. 1725–1776)

Shaking off the red dust,
   a bamboo staff in hand, sandals on foot,
I go into the hills and waters
   with the black zither.
I hear the whoop of a lone crane
   somewhere beyond the clouds.

Kim Ch'ŏnt'aek (c. 1725–1776)

Having given my clothes to a boy
   to have them pawned at the tavern,
Looking up to heaven,
   I question the moon.
Who is Li Bo, that ancient drunkard,[1]
   what is he compared with me?

---

1. A Tang poet known for his poems on wine and the beauty of the moon.

Kim Yŏng (fl. 1776–1800)

Snowflakes flutter—butterflies chase flowers;
   ants float—my wine is thick.
I pluck the black zither,
   a crane dances to my tune.
A dog barks at the wicker gate—
   boy, see if my friend has come.

Pak Hyogwan (fl. c. 1850–1880)

If my lovesick dream
   became the spirit of a cricket,
In the long, long autumn night,
   it would enter my love's room
And wake her from her sleep,
   the sound sleep that has forgotten me.

                ❖

She came to my dream,
   but was gone when I woke.
Where has she gone leaving me,
   the one I long for?
Dreams may be empty,
   but visit me as often as you can.

An Minyŏng (fl. 1870–1880)

Speak, chrysanthemum, why do you shun
   the orient breezes of the third moon?
"I would rather freeze in a cruel rain
   beside the hedge of dried sticks

Than humble myself to join the parade:
　　those flowers of a fickle spring."

Anonymous

At the wind that blew last night,
　　peach blossoms fell, scattered in the garden.
A boy came out with a broom,
　　intending to sweep them away.
No, do not sweep them away, no, no.
　　Are fallen flowers not flowers?

❖

A horse neighs, wants to gallop:
　　my love clings to me, begs me to stay.
The sun has crossed the hill.
　　I have a thousand miles to go.
My love, do not stop me:
　　stop the sun from setting!

❖

The faint moon in a heavy frost;
　　a solitary goose flies crying.
I fancied it brought me news.
　　Was it a letter from my love?
No, I hear only the bird
　　beyond the clouds, incredibly far off.

❖

In the valley where the stream leaps,
　　having built a grass hut by the rock,
I till the field under the moon,
　　among the vast clouds lie down.
Heaven and earth advise me
　　to age with them together.

❀

I have lived anxious and hurt.
    Enough, I would rather die,
Become the spirit of the cuckoo
    when the moon is on the bare hills,
And sing with bitter tears
    to him my forbidden hopes.

❀

What is love, what is it?
    Is it round, is it square?
Is it long, is it short?
    More than an inch, more than a yard?
It seems of no great length,
    but somehow I don't know where it ends.

❀

O love, round as a watermelon,
    do not use words sweet as the melon.
What you have said, this and that,
    was all wrong, and you mocked me.
Enough, your empty talk
    is hollow, like a preserved melon.

Sasŏl Sijo

Sasŏl sijo, a variety of the common *sijo* form, broke with the formal conventions of the *sijo* by adding more than two metric segments in each line (except for the third). Often extended in a chain, these poems are characterized by an abundance of onomatopoeia, a tendency to catalog, striking imagery, and a bold twist at the end. Judging from the extant pieces, mostly by anonymous writers, the form enjoyed great popularity from the eighteenth century on. In addition to structural innovation, the writers introduced new departures in scale, voice, diction, point of view, and rhetorical pattern, drawing frequently on colloquial speech, including taboo words and puns. A marked feature is enumeration—a list of different windows and hinges in the heart, for example, or a catalog of a woman's personal ornaments. The growth of this new form, together with the rise of narrative fiction, drama, genre painting, and popular entertainments such as *p'ansori*, reflected the rise of the middle class and changes in their approach to life.

Sasŏl sijo are also known for their presentation of topics from ordinary low life—especially explicit sex—often with exaggeration, grotesquerie, and caricature. Some poems cast a satiric glance at the corrupt, foolish, and lascivious; others are comic variations on a lovelorn speaker's wish for a metamorphosis to achieve a union. Shorn of classical allusions, these lyrics gain extraordinary freshness by exploring the resources of language that are close to the soil. The sound, color, and feel of the words are robust and original—these are its characteristics. The anonymous poets not only wrote differently but also brought a new dimension to the form. *Sasŏl sijo* gave back poetry—which had long been a monopoly of the lettered class—to the creative sensibility of the common people.

Yi Chŏngbo (1693–1766)

May my love become an alder tree
   of Kŭmsŏng in Hoeyang, and
   I an arrowroot vine in
   the third month or fourth:
Like a spider's web around a butterfly,
   the vine's around the tree,
   tightly this way, tightly that,

wrongly loosened, properly wound,
  bound, then loosened from down below
  all the way to the top,
  tightly winding round and round
  without a single gap, and
  unchanging, day and night,
  it's coiled around, twisting.
Though, in the heart of winter,
  we may bear wind, rain, snow, and frost,
  could we ever be apart?

When the owl hoots,
  atop the distant Wŏrang Rock,
  in the middle of each night:
"Those of old have said,
  the young concubine who,
  hateful and detestable,
  becomes someone's paramour, and
  lures him with her
  cunning wiles, is cursed to
  die a sudden death!"
The concubine replies,
  "O honored wife, do not speak
  such delirious words:
  it's the old wife, who
  mistreats her lord, and is
  so very jealous of the
  concubine, who dies first,
I've heard them say."

Translated by Wen Xiamin

Anonymous

Like a hen pheasant
chased by a hawk
on a treeless, rockless mountain.
Like a ship captain on the high seas,
his cargo a thousand bags of grain,
oars and anchor lost,
rigging broken,
sail torn,
rudder gone,
wind howling, waves billowing,
endless miles to go under a foggy sky,
darkness on all sides,
heaven and earth desolate,
and then to be robbed by pirates.
With what can I liken my sorrow
when you left me two days ago?

❄

Pass where the winds pause before they cross,
pass where the clouds pause before they cross,
the pass of Changsŏng ridge
where wild-born falcons,
tamed falcons,
peregrine falcons,
and yearling falcons pause before they cross—
If they said my love were over the pass,
I would cross it without a pause.

❄

Take apart your cassock and make a coat,
unstring your rosary to make a donkey's crupper.
After ten years of studying

the realm of Śākyamuni,
the Pure Land of bliss,
the bodhisattva Sound Observer,
and "I put my faith in Amitābha,"
now you go away.
At night in a nun's bosom,
you've no time to invoke the Buddha!

❧

Middle- and small-sized needles
dropped in the midst of the sea.
They say with a foot-long pole
a dozen boatmen hooked the eye of every needle and pulled
    them up.
Love, my love,
don't swallow everything you hear
when they tell you a hundred tales.

❧

You, wild hawk,
stop rending my innards.
Shall I give you money?
Shall I give you silver?
A Chinese silk skirt,
a Korean ritual dress,
gauze petticoats,
white satin belt,
a cloudy wig from the north,
a jade hairpin,
a bamboo hairpin,
a silk knife in an inlaid case,
a golden knife in an amber case,
a coral brooch from the far south,
a gold ring set with a blue bell
shaped like a heavenly peach,

sandals with yellow pearl strings,
embroidered hemp sandals?
For a night worth thousands of gold pieces,
give me one chance at your dimples,
lovely and fresh as a flower,
grant me only one night,
priceless as a swift steed!

Translated by Peter H. Lee

Anonymous

Sigh, O thin sigh, through
    what crack have you entered?
With a sliding screen,
    a thin-framed screen, and
    other sliding doors,
    a hinge on the sidepost, and
    on the door, a latch fastened with a
    clang, a lock, fastened firmly, of
    dragon and turtle design,
    a hinged screen folded with a
    clatter, a scroll rolled
    tightly up, through what
    crack could you have entered?
Somehow, on nights when
    you come, I cannot sleep.

Why could you not come? For what reason
    could you not come?
On your way, did they build a fortress of
    cast iron, a wall within the fortress, and
    a house within the wall, then did they put

a chest within the house, a box within
the chest, and bind you in the box,
locking it firmly with a lock, of
dragon and turtle design, on a double bolt?
Why do you not come?
There are thirty days in a month, will there
not be one day you come for me?

❖

Mother-in-law, do not stamp
on the kitchen floor
for hatred of your
daughter-in-law!
Was she payment for a debt,
was she bought for a price?
Father-in-law, severe as a sprig
from the rotting stump of
a chestnut tree,
Mother-in-law, shriveled as
sun-baked cattle dung,
Sister-in-law, sharp as
a new gimlet poking from a straw bag
woven three years ago, and—
like a poor crop on a field
that's made for planting good grain,
having borne a son like
a bright yellow cucumber flower,
who has the bloody flux,
Daughter-in-law, like the bindweed
on a fertile field:
why do they hate her so?

❖

Listen to me, you wench!
When you first saw me you said

you'd stay with me forever:
firmly believing in your words
I sold my house, the land around,
my oven and my kettle,
my horse with a coat of deep ebony,
good rice fields and even my black cow—
didn't I then give it all to you?
For what reason, who has done you wrong,
that you amuse yourself with another?
My love, if you too have deceived me,
would I not deceive you?

When on a cold day with deep snow,
I seek my love, climbing
toward the very heavens:
I take off my shoes to
clutch in my hand,
my socks to hold in my arms, then
helter-skelter,
scurrying, hurrying,
without a moment's rest,
I struggle up panting, and
Yet, though my unshod feet
do not smart with cold,
my heart, under my
tightened collar, chills me.

I loathe them, I loathe them,
I loathe great mansions high above,
Slaves and farms, silken gowns,
silken skirts, violet silk jackets,
knives of amber, braided hair and
precious mineral dyes, are all,

all but the stuff of dreams!
He for whom I wish is a true gallant
   upon a white steed with a golden whip,
   of great height and fair of face,
   a scholar, an orator,
   a singer, a dancer,
   an archer, a chess master, and
   moreover, a gentle lover.

Translated by Wen Xiamin

Kasa

The origin of *kasa* toward the middle of the fifteenth century is traced
to popular songs, didactic folk songs, and the longer *kyŏnggi*-style
songs favored by the literati. What was new in *kasa* was a dramatic
enlargement of scale, allowing lengthier, more sustained treatment of
poetic themes. Unlike the three-line *sijo*, *kasa* tells a story, often adhering to a linear temporal and spatial sequence, although frequently
without a plot in the sense of a causal narrative of events. While the
kasa is said to resemble the Chinese *fu* (rhymeprose, or rhapsody) in
form and technique, it is neither in prose nor rhymed. It is narrative
poetry meant to be sung—or chanted, in the case of *kasa* composed
by literati—and of unlimited length.

    A typical *kasa* line, as in *sijo*, consists of four metric segments,
which is repeated line after line with matched pairings and enumerative
development. A poem generally concludes in a line of 3, 5, 4, and 3/4
syllables in the case of *kasa* composed by literati, and a line of 4,
4, 4, and 4 in the *kasa* by women and commoners. For *kasa* writers,
this simple metric basis invited inventiveness in nearly every other
aspect of poetic development, including narrative technique, sequences

of imagery, and lyric expression. *Kasa* are typically organized according to a pattern. Poems built on a seasonal pattern, for example, unfold a series of nature scenes that evoke each season. If the subject is a single season such as spring, shifting scenes and activities associated with different times of the day provide a structure. Another frequent pattern is based on the rhetoric of argument or complaint—the speaker lists, for example, causes of his present state with an enumeration of the hardships he has encountered, as in poems of exile or unrequited love.

Korean country house poems such as Chŏng Ch'ŏl's "Little Odes on Mount Star" (*Sŏngsan pyŏlgok*, c. 1585–1587) and Pak Il-lo's "Hall of Solitary Bliss" (*Tongnak tang*, 1619) bear similarities to seventeenth-century English country-house poems[1] with descriptions of a paradisal setting—an ideal landscape reflecting the idealized character of the subject, who is associated with traditional paragons of virtue. The "Little Odes on Mount Star," written to praise the elegant life that Kim Sŏngwŏn (1525–1598) had established on Mount Star in South Chŏlla province, catalogues the delights of the four seasons and claims that the expansive landscape reflects Kim's own liberality, freedom, and contemplative retirement. "The Hall of Solitary Bliss" was written on the occasion of Pak's pilgrimage to the hall on Purple Jade Mountain in Kyŏngju where the remains of his teacher Yi Ŏnjŏk (1491–1553) were preserved. Yi had suffered in the 1530 purge but was recalled in 1537 to a high position at court. Caught again in a political purge in 1547, he was sent into exile to the north, where he spent seven years in cold Kanggye transforming the rigors of a political winter into the bliss of a timeless spring. Even in exile Yi had "cultivated virtue, the forthright Way," and history eventually vindicated his name. Subtly underlying the poem is the conviction that the return of moral and political harmony depends upon the return of harmony between humans

---

1. Examples include Ben Jonson's "To Penshurst," Robert Herrick's "Panegyric to Sir Lewis Pemberton," Thomas Carew's "To Saxham," and Andrew Marvell's "Upon Appleton House."

and nature. The ideal landscape, then, provides a setting in which to contemplate the enduring norms of history and culture.

Hŏ Nansŏrhŏn, the elder sister of Hŏ Kyun, the author of the "The Tale of Hong Kiltong," was an accomplished poet in literary Chinese and Korean, and her poem "A Woman's Sorrow" (*Kyuwŏn ka*) is a dramatic narrative on the sorrow of unrequited love.

"Grand Trip to Japan" (*Iltong changyu ka*) was written by Kim Ingyŏm, who, as third secretary, accompanied a Korean diplomatic mission to Japan sent at the request of the Tokugawa shōgun Ieharu (1760–1786). The party, consisting of some five hundred members, left Seoul on September 9, 1763, and reached Edo on March 18, 1764, returning to Seoul in August of that year. Kim's description of the journey is full of entertaining episodes marked by his keen observation, criticism, humor, and wit. The selection presented here shows what was expected of a writer in a foreign country like Japan. The scenes depicted occurred on February 23 and 24, 1764.

Chŏng Kŭgin (1401–1481)

IN PRAISE OF SPRING

What do you think of my life,
    you who are buried in red dust,
Do I match the dead
    in the pursuit of elegant pleasures?
Between heaven and earth
    there are many men like me,
But buried among hills and groves,
    do I not know the utmost joy?
In a small thatched hut
    before an emerald stream,
Among the thickets of pine and bamboo,
    I play host to the winds and moon.

Winter left us the other day, and
    a new spring has returned.
Peach and apricot blossoms are
    in full bloom in the evening sun,
Green willows and fragrant grasses
    are green in a fine drizzle.
As if in the marks of a chisel,
    as if in strokes of a brush,
The deft skill of the Fashioner of Things[1]
    is truly brilliant everywhere.
The birds sing coyly in the wood
    drunk with spring air.
Nature and I are one,
    and the pleasure is the same.
I walk about the brushwood gate
    or sit in the arbor,
Stroll, hum, and chant.
    The day in the hills is quiet,
Few know the true flavor of leisure.
    Come, let's view the hills and waters.
Today walk on the fresh grass,
    tomorrow bathe in the Yi River.[2]
Gather ferns in the morning,
    go fishing in the evening.
Let's strain newly matured wine
    through a turban of kudzu vine,
And drink keeping count of our cups
    with the branches of flowering trees.
Gentle breeze quickly rises

1. Sometimes interpreted as a metaphysical principle responsible for the multiplicity and particularity of the phenomenal world; see Schafer, "The Idea of Created Nature."
2. The abode of Cheng Yi (1033–1108), a Neo-Confucian scholar and philosopher known as the "master of the Yi River."

over the green waters scattering
Clear fragrance on the cups
    and petals on our clothes.
Let me know when the jug is empty—
    I dispatch a boy to a tavern.
A grownup rambles with a stick, and
    a boy carries it on his shoulder,
Humming a verse we walk slowly.
    Sitting alone by the stream,
I wash my cup on the fine sand beach.
    Pouring wine I hold the cup
And look down the clear stream.
    Peach blossoms float down
From Peach Blossom Spring[3] nearby.
    That hill must mark the place.
Between the pines in a narrow lane,
    with an armful of azaleas,
I quickly climb a hilltop
    and sit among the clouds.
A thousand myriad villages
    are scattered everywhere,
With mist and sunglow
    like a brocade spread out in front.
Spring colors are ample
    over the once dark fields.
Fame and name shun me,
    wealth and rank shun me.
Who else is my friend
    but the clear breeze and bright moon?

3. The Chinese *locus amoenus* or ideal place; see Hightower, *Poetry of T'ao Ch'ien*, 254–258.

With a handful of rice and a gourdful of water,[4]
  nothing distracts me.
Well, what do you say
  to a hundred years of a joyful life?

Chŏng Ch'ŏl (1537–1594)

SONG OF LONGING

At the time I was born
  I was born to follow my lord.
Our lives were destined to be joined,
  As even the heavens must have known.

When I was young
  my lord loved me.
There was nothing to compare
  with this heart and love.
All that I longed for in this life
  was to live with him.

Now that I am older,
  for what reason have I been put aside?
A few days ago, serving my lord
  I entered the Moon Palace.[1]
How does it happen since then
  that I have descended to this lower world?
Three years it has been
  since my hair, once combed, became tangled.
I have powders and rouge,

4. *Lunyu* 6:11; Waley, *Analects*, 117–118.
1. Literally, Great Cold Palace (Kwanhan kung).

but for whom would I make myself lovely?
The cares that are knotted in my heart
    pile up, layer upon layer.
It is sighs that build up,
    tears that tumble down.
Life has an end;
    cares are endless.

Indifferent time
    is like the flowing of waters.
The seasons, hot and cold, seem to know
    time and return as they go.
Hearing, seeing,
    there are many things to sense.

Briefly the east wind blows
    and melts away the fallen snow.
Two or three branches have bloomed
    on the plum tree outside the window:
a bold brightness,
    a fragrance deep and mysterious.
At dusk the moon
    shines by the bedside
as if sensing him, rejoicing
    —Is it my lord; could it be?
I wonder, if I broke off that blossom
    and sent it to the place where my lord stays,
what would he think
    as he looked at it?

Blossoms fall, new leaves appear,
    and shade covers.
Silk curtains are lonely;

embroidered curtains are opened.
I close the lotus screen
    and open the peacock screen . . .
How can a day be so tedious,
    so full of cares?
I spread open the mandarin duck quilt,
    take out the five-colored thread,
measure it with a golden ruler
    and make a cloak for my lord
with skill,
    with taste.

Gazing toward the place where my lord stays
    I think of sending to him
these clothes in a jade white chest
    on a pack frame of coral,
but he is so far, so far,
    like a mountain, or a cloud.
Who is there to seek him out
    over the road of ten thousand tricents
When it reached him and was opened,
    would he be pleased?

At night a frost falls;
    the wild goose passes over with a cry.
Alone, I climb the tower
    and open the jade curtain.
Above East Mountain the moon has risen
    and far to the north a star appears.
Is it my lord? Happy,
    tears come unbidden.
Let me extract this brightness
    and send it to the Phoenix Tower:

fix it to the tower
  and illuminate all directions,
that even the deepest mountains and valleys
  may be as bright as day.

Heaven and earth are blockaded
  under a white monochrome.
Men, even birds on the wing
  have disappeared.
With the cold so intense
  here, far to the south,[2]
in the lofty Phoenix Tower
  how much colder it must be!
Would that the sunny spring could be sent
  to warm the place where my lord stays,
or that the sunlight bathing the thatched eaves
  might be sent to the Phoenix Tower.

I tuck my red skirt up,
  roll my blue sleeves halfway,
and as the day declines, by high, thin bamboo
  I lean on a staff, lost in thought.
The brief sun sinks swiftly;
  the long night settles aloft.

I set the inlaid lute
  by the side of the blue lamp
and rest, hoping
  to see my lord, even in a dream.
Cold, cold is the quilt!
  O, when will night become day?

2. In the original, the Xiao and Xiang Rivers that flow into Dongting Lake—rich in mythology and scenic beauty but capable of freezing (in the poet's imagination).

Twelve times each day,
    thirty days each month,
I try, even for a moment, not to think,
    that I may forget these cares,
but they are knotted within my heart,
    they have pierced through my bones.
Even though ten doctors like Pian Que came,[3]
    what could they do with this illness?
Alas, my illness
    is because of my lord.

I would rather die and become
    a swallowtail butterfly.
I would light upon each flowering branch
    one after another, as I went,
till I settled, with perfumed wings
    upon the garments of my lord.
O, my lord, though you forget my existence,
    I shall attend you.

Translated by David R. McCann

Continued Song of Longing

"Lady, who goes there?
    You look so familiar.
Why did you leave
    the White Jade Capital in the heavens,[1]
whom do you seek
    as the sun goes down?"

3. A famous physician during the spring and autumn period; *Shiji* 105: 2785–2820.
1. Where Daoist deities reside.

"Oh, it's you!
   Hear my story now.
My face and ways
   do not merit my lord's favor.
Yet he deigns to recognize me
   when we meet.
I believed in him
   with undivided heart.
I flirted and displayed my charm—
   I might have annoyed him.
His welcoming face
   has changed from the past.
Reclining, I ponder;
   seated, I calculate:
my sins,
   piled high as the mountains;
I don't quarrel with heaven,
   I don't blame men.
I try to untie this sadness—
   it was the Fashioner's doing."

"Fret not, my dear.
   Something eats at my heart, too.
I've served him;
   I know him.
His face once placid as water
   shows little enough of peace these days.
Spring cold and summer heat,
   how did he spend them?
Autumn days and winter skies,
   who served them?
Morning gruel and daily rice,
   did he have enough?

Do you think he slept well
 these long winter nights?"

"I yearn for word of him,
 how I long to hear his news!
But the day is done.
 Will someone come tomorrow?
O tormenting thought!
 Where shall I go?
Led and pushed
 when I climb a high hill,
clouds gather,
 and—why—a mist, too!
When hills and waters are dark,
 how can I see the sun and moon?
What can I see even an inch away?
 A thousand miles is so far . . .
I'll go down to the sea
 and wait for a boat.
Winds and waves
 in turmoil, in shambles.
The boatman is gone;
 only the empty ship.
Standing alone by the river,
 I gaze far into the setting sun.
News from my lord
 is out of the question!
I return when darkness creeps
 under the eaves of my hut.
For whom does that lamp
 in the middle of the wall burn?
Over hill and valley I go,
 back and forth, aimlessly.

Exhausted,
    I sink into sleep.
At last my prayer is answered,
    and I see him in a dream.
But time has stolen
    his face once like jade.
I would tell him all,
    all my heart desires.
But tears flow on and on,
    and I cannot speak.
Unable to tell of my love,
    words stick in my throat.
A frivolous rooster
    wakes me from my slumber.
Ah, everything was a mocking dream.
    Where is my fair one?
Sitting up in my sleep,
    I open the window.
Only the pitiable shadow
    follows me.
I'd sooner die
    and be the setting moon
and shine
    in his window."

"The moon say you, my lady?
    Rather, a driving rain."[2]

---

2. The lady of Mount Shaman, who appeared in a dream to King Xiang (298–265 BCE) and said: "I live on the southern side of Mount Shaman, in the rocky crags of Gaoqiu. At dawn I am the Morning Cloud, and at dusk the Driving Rain." Fusek, "The 'Kao-t'ang Fu,'" 413.

Little Odes on Mount Star

An unknown guest in passing
   stopped on Mount Star and said:
"Listen, master of Mist Settling Hall
   and Resting Shadow Arbor,
despite the many pleasures
   life held,
why did you prefer to them all
   this mountain, this water?
What made you choose
   the solitude of hills and streams?"
Sweeping away the pine needles,
   setting a cushion on a bamboo couch,
I casually climb into the seat
   and view the four quarters.
Floating clouds at the sky's edge come and go
   nestling on Auspicious Stone Terrace;[1]
their flying motion and gentle gestures
   resemble our host.
White waves in the blue stream
   rim the arbor,
as if someone stitched and spread
   the cloud brocade of the Weaver Star,
the water rushes
   in endless patterns.
On other mountains without a calendar
   who would know the year's cycle?
Here every subtle change of the seasons
   unrolls before us.
Whether you hear or see,
   this is truly the land of transcendents.

1. The summit of Mount Mudŭng in Kwangju.

The morning sun at the window with plum trees—
    the fragrance of blossoms wakes me.
Who says there is nothing
    to keep an old hermit busy?
In the sunny spot under the hedges
    I sow melons,
tie the vines, support them;
    when rain nurtures the plants,
I think of the old tale
    of the Blue Gate.[2]
Tying my straw sandals,
    grasping a bamboo staff,
I follow the peach blossom causeway
    over to Fragrant Grass Islet.
As I stroll to the West Brook,
    the stone screen painted by nature
in the bright moonlit mirror
    accompanies me.
Why seek Peach Blossom Spring?
    An earthly paradise is here.
The casual south wind
    scatters green shade;
a faithful cuckoo,
    where did he come from?
I wake from dozing
    on the pillow of ancient worthies[3]
and see the hanging wet balcony

2. The southeast gate of Changan. When the dynasty changed, Shao Ping, marquis of Dongling under the Qin, had to live by raising melons. His melons were called Blue Gate or Dongling melons. See Watson, *Records of the Grand Historian*, 1:130.

3. Refers to a hermit said to have lived before the time of Fu Xi, a Chinese culture hero.

floating on the water.
With my kudzu cap aslant
    and my hemp smock tucked into my belt,
I go nearer
    to watch the frolicking fishes.
After the rain overnight,
    here and there, red and white lotus;
their fragrance rises into the still sky
    filling myriad hills.
As though I had met with Zhou Dunyi[4]
    and questioned him on the Ultimate Secret—
as though an immortal Great Unique[5]
    had shown me the Jade Letters—
I look across Cormorant Rock
    by Purple Forbidden Shallows;
a tall pine tree screens the sun,
    I sit on the stone path.
In the world of man it is the sixth month;
    here it is autumn.
A duck bobbing on the limpid stream
    moves to a white sandbar,
makes friends with the gulls,
    and dozes away.
Free and at leisure,
    it resembles our host.
At the fourth watch the frost moon rises
    over the phoenix trees.

4. Author of *The Diagram of the Supreme Ultimate Explained*, which elucidates the origins of "heavenly principles."

5. Taiyi, the supreme sky god in Chinese mythology, who resides in a palace at the center of heaven marked by the pole star; see Needham, *Science and Civilization in China*, 3:260.

Thousand cliffs, ten thousand ravines,
  could they be brighter by daylight?
Who moved the Crystal Palace
  from Huzhou?[6]
Did I jump over the Milky Way
  and climb into the Moon Palace?
Leaving behind a pair of old pines
  on the fishing terrace,
I let my boat drift downstream
  as it pleases,
passing pink knotweeds
  and a sandbar of white cloverfern.
When did we reach
  the Dragon Pool below Jade Ring Hall?
Moved by a sunset glow,
  cowherds
in green pastures by the crystal river
  blow on their pipes.
They might awaken the dragon
  sunk deep at the pool's bottom.
Emerging from mists and ripples,
  cranes might abandon their nests
and soar into midair.
  Su Shi in his rhymeprose on the Red Cliff
praises the seventh moon;[7]
  but why do people cherish
the mid-autumn moon?
  When thin clouds part,

6. On Mount West Lake in Huzhou.

7. "In the autumn of the year *renxu*, the seventh month, when the moon had just passed its prime, a friend and I went out in a small boat to amuse ourselves at the foot of the Red Cliff" (Watson, *Su Tung-p'o*, 87).

and waves grow still,
   the rising moon
anchors herself in a pine branch.
   How extravagant! Li Bo drowned
trying to scoop up the reflected moon.
   North winds sweep away
the heaped leaves on empty hills,
   marshal the clouds,
drive the snow.
   The Creator loves to fashion—
he makes snowflowers of white jade,
   devises thousands of trees and forests.
The shallows in front freeze over.
   A monk crosses over
the one-log bridge aslant,
   a staff on his shoulder.
What temple are you headed for?
   Don't boast of
the recluse's riches
   lest some find out
this lustrous, hidden world.
   Alone, deep in the mountains,
with the classics, pile on pile,
   I think of the men
of all times:
   many were sages,
many were heroes.
   Heavenly intent goes
into the making of men.
   Yet fortunes
rise and fall;
   chance seems unknowable.

And sadness deep.
　　Why did Xu You on Mount Ji
cleanse his innocent ears?[8]
　　When he threw away his last gourd,
his integrity became even nobler.
　　Man's mind is like his face—
new each time one sees it.
　　Worldly affairs are like clouds—
how perilous they are!
　　The wine made yesterday
must be ready:
　　passing the cup back and forth,
let's pour more wine till we're tired.
　　Then our hearts will open,
the net of sorrow unravel to nothing.
　　String the black zither
and pluck "Wind in the Pines."[9]
　　We have all forgotten
Who is host and who is guest.
　　The crane flying through the vast sky
is the true immortal in this valley—
　　I must have met him
on the Jasper Terrace under the moon.
　　The guest addresses the host with a word:
"You, sir, you alone are immortal."

8. When the sage-king Yao wished to make the recluse Xu You his successor, the latter went into hiding. At Yao's second offer, Xu went to the Ying River to wash his ears.
　　9. The name of a *ci* tune.

Pak Illo (1561–1643)

THE HALL OF SOLITARY BLISS

Long ago I heard of Purple Jade Mountain
And the Hall of Solitary Bliss,
Those cool and quiet places.
But I was a soldier then,
Anxious, with a burning heart.
Danger lurked;[1] our shores were besieged.
Faithful to my duty,
I wielded a glistening spear
And galloped on my armored horse.
But I long for my teacher
Even more now that my hair is gray.
Today I start out at last
With bamboo staff and straw sandals.
Like the Wuyi Mountains,[2]
The peaks look graceful,
And the river winds
Like the Yi.
Such a place
needs a host.
Sages and gentlemen
From Silla of a thousand years
And Koryŏ of five hundred,
How many of you have crossed the lovely pass?
Heaven created it; earth has treasured it
And revealed its secrets to him.

1. *Shijing* (Book of songs) 194:6; Karlgren, *Book of Odes*, 141.
2. In Fujian, 30 tricents south of Chongan county.

Everything has its owner,[3] they say.
How true! Yi Ŏnjŏk is its true owner.

I push aside tangled creepers
And open the elegant, secluded chamber
Of the Hall of Solitary Bliss.
Its beauty is unmatched!
Outside, a thousand stalks of tall bamboo
Surround the emerald stream—
And here, ten thousand books
Line the walls.
The works of Yan Hui and Master Zeng on the left
Those of Zi You and Zi Xia on the right.[4]
He revered the sages of the past[5]
And wrote poems.
In peaceful nature he was so immersed
That he felt at home in all situations.
He called it Solitary Bliss,
A fit name for so elegant a life.
Sima Guang had *his* garden of solitary bliss;[6]
But could it match the beauty of this place?

I enter Truth Nurturing Hermitage
To search for truth.
Winds caress me as I contemplate.
My mind becomes pure and bright:
How marvelous is T'oegye's brush stroke:[7]

---

3. Allusion to Su Shi, "The Red Cliff"; see Watson, *Su Tung-p'o*, 90.
4. Disciples of Confucius.
5. *Mengzi* 5B:8; Lau, *Mencius*, 158. "He" refers to Yi Ŏnjŏk.
6. Sima Guang's (1019–1086) retreat was in Honan, north of Luoyang.
7. T'oegye is the pen name of Yi Hwang (1501–1571), a prominent Neo-Confucian philosopher of Korea.

I see its matchless excellence.
On my walk to the Fish Viewing Terrace,
The rocks show precious traces
Of my teacher's staff and sandals.
The pine he planted retains its ancient air,
How delightful
The unchanging view.
I feel as refreshed as when
I entered his fragrant study.[8]

I think of the past:
High rocks and sheer cliffs
Resemble a mica screen by Longmian.[9]
In the lucid mirror of the pool,
The light of the sky and the shadow of clouds entwine,
A cool breeze and bright moonlight
Dazzle my eyes.
Hawks and fish[10] were
My teacher's friends.
He contemplated, sought truth,
Cultivated learning and virtue.
I cross the stream to a fishing terrace
And ask white gulls near the beach:
Birds, do you know
When Yan Guang[11] returned to the Han house?
The evening smoke settles
On the mossy strand.

8. See *Kongzi jiayu* (School sayings of Confucius), 4:4a.

9. Li Gonglin (1070–1073) of Song lived on Mount Longmian and excelled in verse.

10. *Shijing* 293:3; Karlgren, *Book of Odes*, 191: "The hawk flies and reaches heaven; the fish leaps in the deep."

11. Yan Guang (37 BCE–43 CE), a friend and advisor to Emperor Guangwu (r. 25–58), lived as a fisherman in Zhejiang because he wished to decline the emperor's offer of a high post.

Dressed for spring,
I climb to Yŏnggwi Terrace,
Its beauty unchanging throughout the ages;
My spirits are high.
"Enjoy the breeze and go home singing":[12]
Today I know the pleasures of Zeng Xi.[13]
A light rain
Over the lotus pond beneath the terrace
Scatters pearls
On large jade leaves.
Nature this pure deserves our delight.
How many years have passed
Since Zhou Dunyi[14] left the world?
Only the perennial fragrance of my teacher
Abides!
Through hovering purple mist
A cataract tumbles down
A sheer red cliff—
A long hanging stream.
Where is Incense Burner Peak?
Mount Lu is here.[15]
I look down Lucid Mind Terrace.
My rustic mind cleansed by freshness,
I sit alone
On the terrace,
While the hills are reflected
In the glassy pond with clear breezes.
Birds sing sadly

12. *Lunyu* 11:40; Waley, *Analects*, 160.

13. A disciple of Confucius who uttered the most beautiful passages in the *Analects*. *Lunyu* 11:25; Waley, *Analects*, 160.

14. Zhou Dunyi (1017–1073), a pioneer of Neo-Confucianism in the Song.

15. Also called Nanzhang shan, in Jiangxi; celebrated in the poems of Li Bo and Su Shi.

From green shadows.
I linger and recall
Retracing the master's steps.
As always, spring water is crystal clear
At Cap-String-Washing Terrace;
But in the age of decadence
Men still struggle in the red dust
When they might be better off
Cleansing their cap strings.

I climb Lion Rock
To view Mount Virtue.
Like a jade in its brightness,[16]
My master's brilliance shone here.
Now the phoenix has left, and the hills are bare.[17]
Only a solitary cuckoo sighs at dusk.
The spring from Peach Blossom Cave
Carries fallen petals day and night.
Is this Mount Tiantai?[18] Is it Peach Blossom Spring?
Where is it?
The footsteps of immortals are remote.
I don't know where I am.
I'm not a gentleman
And am far from wise;
But I enjoy the mountain and forget to return home.
Leaning against a rock,
I scan hills and waters
Far and near.

16. "Let (meaning), then, be contained like jade in rocks, that a mountain loom in radiance,/Or cast it like a pearl in water that a whole river gleam with splendor" ("Rhymeprose on Literature" by Lu Ji, in Birch, *Anthology of Chinese Literature*, 210).

17. Li Bo, "Climbing Phoenix Terrace at Jinling"; Liu and Lo, *Sunflower Splendor*, 113.

18. In Zhejiang.

Ten thousand flowers
Weave a brocade,
And their fragrance
Drifts on valley winds.
A distant temple gong
Echoes, riding the clouds.
Even the pen of Fan Xiwen[19]
Couldn't capture this landscape,
So fetching are the views.
They stir the wanderer's heart.
I ramble everywhere
And arrive home late
As the sun sets behind western hills.

On my climb again to the Hall of Solitary Bliss
I look about for traces of his presence.
And here he is;
He welcomes me.
"I see him in the soup and on the walls."[20]
Gazing at the sky and ground
I sigh
And recall his deeds.
This is the desk by the window where he sat,
Oblivious of worldly cares,
Where he read the sages' books
And reaped the fruits of his study.
Thus he continued the tradition, opened a new path,
And brightened the Way for us,
Truly a happy gentleman of the east,

---

19. Fan Zhongyan (989–1052), author of the *Yoyanglou ji* (Record of Yoyang Tower).
20. According to tradition, Shun longed for Yao so intensely after his death that he saw his image on the walls wherever he sat and in the soup whenever he ate.

The only one worthy of the name.
Further, filial piety and brotherly love as roots,
Through loyalty and sincerity,
He became Houji and Jie[21]
At the court of the wise king
And hoped to secure
The peace of Yao and Shun.
But the times were adverse,
The loyal and wise were banished.
In high mountains and deep valleys,
Those who heard and witnessed lamented.
For seven years
He never saw the sun;
He shut the door to search his mind
And cultivate virtue—the forthright Way.
Right prevailed over evil in the end;
The people acclaimed him of their own accord,
And mindful of
His enduring work,
They erected a shrine in Kanggye,
The place of exile,
Remote and poor,
And learned men
Hastened to revere him.

They built an academy on Purple Jade Mountain
Above the springs and rocks.
Numerous students
Pluck the lute and send him poetry

21. Houji or Lord Millet, inventor of agriculture and ancestor of the Zhou people. Jie was a wise minister under Shun.

As though Zhou Dunyi and Luoyang scholars[22]
Were gathered here once again.
I walk around Goodness Embodying Shrine,
Where sacrifices to him never cease.
It's not by chance that he is so honored.

Because we can't
Honor him enough,
He's enshrined in the Confucian shrine—
A lovely custom, a grand affair!
Our civilization matches
That of Han, Tang, and Song.
Ah, we are in Ziyang,
In Cloud Valley.[23]
The waters on Sesim Terrace
Glows with his virtue and favor.
His spirit lingers
Where the dragon reigns,
Wonderful are the workings
Of the Heavenly Artificer!

Overjoyed,
yet unable to fathom
the infinite landscape.
I linger for a month.
I open my rustic mind
To deepen my sincere respect for him
And turn every page of his works.
His thousand words and myriad sayings

---

22. Men such as Shao Yung (1011–1977), Sima Guang (1019–1086), Cheng Yi (1033–1107), and Zhang Zai (1020–1077).

23. Ziyang shan is the place where Zhu Song (1097–1143), Zhu Xi's father, lived.

Are all wisdom, each revealing
A long tradition and ways of thought
As bright as the sun and moon—
Light
Illuminating the dark.

If his thoughts fill our hearts,
If sincere intent directs our minds,[24]
If we order our life to pursue the Way,
If our words are loyal and our deeds faithful,[25]
Then goodness will naturally follow.
Ah, let's ponder his teaching,
Students,
And look
For myriad years to this wise man,
great as Mount Tai,[26] remote as the pole star.
Heaven so high and earth so rich,
They too will dissolve into dust.
None is eternal but the cool wind that blows
Through the Hall of Solitary Bliss.

Hŏ Nansŏrhŏn (1563–1589)

A WOMAN'S SORROW

Yesterday I fancied I was young;
    today, alas, I am aging.
What use is there in recalling
    the joyful days of my youth?

---

24. *Daxue* (Great learning) 1; see Chan, *Sourcebook in Chinese Philosophy*, 86.
25. *Lunyu* 15:6; Waley, *Analects*, 194.
26. Eastern sacred mountain in China.

Now I am old, memory is vain.
   Sorrow chokes me; words fail me.
When Father begot me, Mother reared me,
   when they took pains to bring me up,
they dreamed, not of a duchess or marchioness,
   but at least a bride fit for a gentleman.[1]
The turning of destiny of three lives
   and the ties chanced by a matchmaker
Brought me a romantic knight-errant,
   and careful, as in a dream, I trod on ice.
O was it a dream, those innocent days?
   When I reached fifteen, counted sixteen,
the inborn beauty in me blossomed,
   and with this face and this body
I vowed a union of a hundred years.
   The flow of time was sudden;
gods were jealous of my beauty.
   Spring breezes and autumn moon,
they flew like a shuttle.
   And my face, once beautiful,
where did it go? Who disgraced it so?
   Turn away from the mirror.
Who will love me now?
   Blush not, and reproach no one.

Don't say, "A tavern has found a customer."
   When flowers smiled in the setting sun,
he rode away on a white horse
   With no aim, no fixed place.
Where does he stop to enjoy himself?
   How far he went, I don't know.

---

1. *Shijing* 1:4.

I'll hear no word from him.
    Yet I hope he will remember me,
though changed from what he has been.
    Hush, anxious heart, that longs
for him who abandoned you—
    long is a day, cruel is a month.
The plum trees by my window,
    how many times have they blossomed?
The winter night is bitter cold,
    and thin snow falls.
Long, long is a summer's day;
    and a dreary rain makes my heart ache.
Spring with flowers and willows
    has no feeling for me.
When the autumn moon enters my room
    and crickets chirp on the couch,
a long sigh and salty tears
    in vain make me recall the past.
It's hard to bring this life to an end.
    When I examine myself,
I shouldn't despair so.
    I must unravel my sorrow calmly.

Lighting the blue lamp, I play
    "A Song of Lotus,"
holding the green zither aslant
    as my sorrow commands me.
As though the night rain on the Xiao and Xiang
    beat over the bamboo leaves,
as though the crane returned whooping[2]

2. Ding Lingwei of Liaodong, who studied the Dao during the Han, transformed himself into a crane and flew away.

after a span of myriad years.
Fingers may pluck the familiar tune,
   but who will listen in the room
except for lotus brocade curtains?
   My entrails are torn into pieces.
I would rather fall asleep
   to see him at least in a dream,
But from what enmity
   do the leaves falling in the wind
and the insects piping among the grasses
   wake me from my wretched sleep?
The Herd Boy and Weaver Maid
   meet once on the Double Seven,[3]
however hard it is to cross the Milky Way—
   and never miss this yearly reunion.
But since he left me alone,
   what Weak Water[4] separates us,
making him silent across the water?
   Leaning on the rail, I gaze at the path he took—
dewdrops glitter on the grass,
   evening clouds pass by.
Birds sing sadly in the bamboo grove.
   Many suffer some great sorrow,
but none can be wretched as I.
   Love, you caused me this grief;
I don't know whether I shall live or die.

3. Seventh day of the seventh lunar month.
4. The name of a transcendent stream on which not even a feather can float; see Needham, *Science and Civilization in China*, 3:608–611.

Kim Ingyŏm (b. 1707)

GRAND TRIP TO JAPAN

On the twenty-third I fell ill,
    lying in the official hostel.
Our hosts bring me their poems,
    they are heaped like a hill.
Sickness aside, I answer them;
    how taxing this chore is!
Regulated verse, broken-off lines,
    old style verse, regulated couplets—
some one hundred thirty pieces.
    Because I dashed them off on draft paper,
upon revision I've discarded a half.
    If I have to work like this every day,
it will be too much to bear . . .
    The rich and noble in the city
bring presents, many in kind and amount.
    But I return them all as before.
One scholar, his hand on his brow,
    begs me a hundred times to accept,
rubbing hands together sincerely.
    Touched with pity,
I accept a piece of ink stick.
    When I offer him Korean paper,
brushes and ink sticks,
    he too takes only one ink stick . . .
Before dawn on the twenty-fourth,
    they arrive in streams.
How hard to talk by means of writing,
    how annoying to cap their verses.
Braving my illness,

and mindful of our mission
to awe them and enhance our prestige,
   I exert myself for dear life,
wield my brush like wind and rain,
   and harmonize with them.
When they revise their verses,
   they put their heads together—
their writings bid fair to inundate me.
   I compose for another round;
they respond with another pile.
   I am old and infirm,
and the task saps my vigor.
   I wouldn't mind it if I were young,
but they traveled thousands of miles
   with packed food and waited for months
just to get our opinions.
   If we deny them our writing,
how disappointed they would be!
   We write on and on
for the old and young, the high and low.
   We work as a matter of duty
night and day, without rest.

Poetry in Literary Chinese

A national academy was established in Silla in the seventh century.
In the mid-tenth century, a system of civil service examinations was
instituted in Koryŏ to recruit civilian officials to staff the bureau-
cracy, ensuring that every educated man in Korea would henceforth
be read in the Confucian classics, histories, and literature. The

amount of poetry written in Chinese in all known genres of Chinese origin during the Koryŏ and Chosŏn dynasties is staggering. Great masters of the Tang and Song as well as pre-Tang poets were studied and imitated; Korean writers also profited from the study of others whom they had no intention of imitating.

Perhaps the most renowned scholar, statesman, and poet of Silla, Ch'oe Ch'iwŏn (b. 857), went to China in 868, where he passed the Tang civil service examination and held a number of posts. When he returned home in 885, he found Silla in its decline and withdrew from public service to spend his last years in a monastery. Considered a master of poetry and parallel prose in Chinese, he is included in the "Monograph on Bibliography" in the *New History of Tang*, and his collected works were compiled in 886 and published in both Korea and China.

The Koryŏ civil service examination system, instituted in 958, was open to both hereditary aristocratic families and petty officials in the provinces. Among the three types of examinations, the first tested the candidate's ability in literary composition in *shi* (old-style poetry), *fu* (rhymeprose), *sung* (eulogy), and *ce* (problem essays); the second in the Confucian classics; and the third in miscellaneous subjects. Although knowledge of both classics and literature was recommended, more emphasis was attached to the ability to write poetry and prose in literary Chinese. By 992 the royal academy was established in the capital to teach classics and other subjects such as statutes, mathematics, and calligraphy. The model this academy provided was followed by schools in the provinces. Private academies for the education of the sons of the upper class arose as well, beginning with the academy established by Ch'oe Ch'ung (984–1068) and followed by eleven others. The rise of official and private centers of learning made knowledge of the classics and literature essential for the educated. The prestige attached by the lettered upper class to proficiency in literary composition during the Koryŏ dynasty is reflected in the number of successful candidates for the composition examination (more than 6,000) against that for the classics examination (450). With the examination system in place, old-style poetry and parallel prose gradually gave way to new-style poetry and old-style prose. Thus the prose of the Han and poetry of the Tang and Song began to be studied and imitated.

Four major poets during this period were Yi Illo (1152–1220), Yi Kyubo (1168–1241), Yi Chehyŏn (1287–1367), and Yi Saek (1328–1396). Yi Kyubo published 2,068 poems, and Yi Saek, 6,000. Yi Illo visited Song China and, upon return, formed a literary coterie. He wrote a pentasyllabic quatrain on the wall of a cloister at Ch'ŏnsu monastery while awaiting a friend. A poem left on the door or on the whitewashed wall when a friend was out was cherished by those who could value it. He stressed the importance of diction and the perfection of craft. With Su Shi (1037–1101) and Huang Tingjian (1045–1105) as his models, he wrote poems using the same rhymes or themes as the Chinese poets he admired most. Yi Kyubo held the view that poetry issues from experience in the real world and must respond to the demands of the time. Yi Chehyŏn served seven Koryŏ kings when the dynasty was under Mongol domination and visited China at least six times. He is remembered for preserving nine folk songs current in his day by adapting them into Chinese, an act of cultural legitimation. Yi Saek studied Neo-Confucianism in the Mongol state academy (1348). His poems on the relationship between the examiner and the candidates, the activities of the royal academy, and his own duties as a royal lecturer convey his sense of his role as a Neo-Confucian scholar-statesman. A central concern of poetry, he seems to have thought, is to observe, record, and preserve the native tradition.

In the Chosŏn dynasty the members of the scholar-official class continued to occupy the dominant ruling position they had held during the Koryŏ period. Based on their Confucian knowledge and refinement, these literati enjoyed cultural superiority. As the civil service examinations emphasized literary talent, they led to the development of courtier literature, especially during the reign of King Sŏngjong (1469–1494), and produced excellent poets in literary Chinese. Poems were composed on every conceivable occasion—the courtiers must have thought in verse. Numerous poems were actually inspired by dreams. In such a cultural setting, none could dispute the place of literature in society and culture; even a brutal tyrant like Yŏnsangun (1476–1506) left scores of poems behind.

There are at least three thousand collected works of individual writers from some five hundred years of the Chosŏn dynasty.[1] If each one wrote a hundred poems—and some, like Sŏ Kŏjŏng (1420–1488), wrote as many as six thousand—the total number of poems comes to more than half a million. Neo-Confucian literati in the countryside opposed ornate works and constructed a simple and pure poetic world. The philosopher Yi Hwang (1501–1571), for example, defends poetry as an indispensable element of self-cultivation detached from the mundane world. The three Tang poets from Chŏlla province rejected the contemporary emphasis on complex rhetorical devices and obscure allusions, espoused the simple diction and creativity of Tang poetry, and emphasized genuine emotion through the suggestive portrayal of visual details from nature. The late Chosŏn period was characterized by new literary activities by the practical learning scholars, the "middle people," and commoners. The first group actively absorbed changes in the political and social order and literary trends from the Qing and tried to create an innovative poetic style for the time. During eighteen years of exile, Chŏng Yagyong (1762–1836) experienced the wretched conditions of the common people and urged that Chosŏn-style poetry, with its originality and independence, overcome the constraints of Chinese prototypes. He stopped short, however, of advocating that poets wishing to discover Korean uniqueness should write in the vernacular rather than in literary Chinese. Yi Ok (1760–1812), a member of the lumpen intelligentsia, portrays with a crisp wit the life of city dwellers in the late eighteenth century in his *Women's Songs* (*Iŏn*), comprising sixty-six pentasyllabic quatrains. His poems depict seasonal festivals, marriage scenes, and the pleasure quarters, and delight in conveying the details of women's clothing, hair ornaments, and items

---

1. Kim Sŏnghwan's *Hanguk yŏktae munjip ch'ongsŏ mongnok* lists three thousand works.

of food, trinkets, and cosmetics. They still seem fresh and enjoyable today when seen against the prevailing ideology of the ruling class.

In the nineteenth century, poets trying to find an individual voice addressed topics such as the ephemeral versus the lasting and the virtues of the good life lived in retirement. Some presented vividly concrete images from nature; some tried to adopt colloquial diction; and some concentrated on eulogizing the moral harmony of a righteous mind. By the twentieth century, writing poetry in literary Chinese was seen by intellectuals as mostly an antiquated pastime; Syngman Rhee (Yi Sŭngman, 1875–1965), the first president of the Republic of Korea, was among those who attempted it.

In this section, I have chosen poems that are brief and translatable, relatively free of allusion, and on themes each writer seems better suited to than others.

Ch'oe Ch'iwŏn (b. 857)

ON A RAINY AUTUMN NIGHT

I only chant painfully in the autumn wind,
  For I have few friends in the wide world.
At third watch, it rains outside.
  By the lamp my heart flies myriad miles away.

Chŏng Chisang (d. 1135)

PARTING

After a rain on the long dike, grasses are thick.
  With a sad song I send you off to the South Bank.
When will the Taedong River cease to flow?
  Year after year my tears will swell the waves.

Yi Illo (1152–1220)

CICADA

You drink wind to empty yourself,
 Imbibe dewdrops to cleanse.
Why do you get up at autumn dawn
 and keep crying so mournfully?

NIGHT RAIN ON THE XIAO AND XIANG RIVERS

A stretch of blue water between the shores in autumn:
 The wind sweeps light rain over a boat coming back.
As the boat is moored at night near the bamboo,
 Each leaf rustles coldly, awakening sorrow.

ON THE RIVER ON A SPRING DAY

High high azure peaks—a bundle of brush tips,
 The broad river, far and hazy, spreads beyond the pines.
Files of dark clouds—an array of strange letters,
 A vast blue sky—a scroll of dispatch.

WRITTEN ON THE WALL OF CH'ŎNSU MONASTERY

I wait for a guest who does not come;
 I look for a monk who is also out.
Only a bird[1] beyond the grove
 Welcomes me, urging me to drink.

---

1. The *tihu* (K. *cheho*) bird is supposed to sing *tihu tihu*, meaning "take the pot for wine."

Yi Kyubo (1168–1241)

THE COCK

The cock
   Likes to peck for worms.
I cannot stand to watch it;
   I shout to scatter his flock.
Don't scorn me for what I have done.
   Old and retired, I am idle—
No plans for an audience or an early meal.
   What need have I of a cock to announce the dawn?
I like to sleep to avoid the bright morning.

Yi Chehyŏn (1287–1367)

CONTEMPORARY FOLK SONGS

I carve a small rooster from wood
   And pick it up with chopsticks and put it on the wall.
When this bird crows cock-a-doodle-do,
   Then my mother's face will be like the setting sun.

❖

At a wash place by the stream under a drooping willow,
   Holding the hand of a handsome youth, I whispered.
Not even the March rain falling from the eaves
   Could wash away his lingering scent on my fingertips!

❖

A magpie chatters in a flowering bough by the hedge,
   A spider spins a web above the bed.
Knowing my heart, they announce his return—
   My beloved will be back soon.

Long ago in Silla, Venerable Ch'ŏyong
  Is said to have emerged from the emerald sea.
With white teeth and ruddy lips he sang in the moonlit night,
  And danced in a spring wind with square shoulders and
    purple sleeves.

National Preceptor T'aego (1301–1382)

NOTHINGNESS

Still—all things appear.
  Moving—there is nothing.
What is nothingness?
  Chrysanthemums bursting in the frost.

ON MY DEATHBED

Life is like a bubble—
  Some eighty years, a spring dream.
Now I'll throw away this leather sack,
  A crimson sun sinks on the west peak!

Linked Verse by Five Poets

UPON LISTENING TO THE FLUTE (1442)

Five young scholars at the Hall of Worthies—Sŏng Sammun (1418–1456), Yi
Kae (1417–1456), Sin Sukchu (1417–1475), Pak P'aengnyŏn (1417–1456), and
Yi Sŏkhyŏng (1415–1477)—were granted a leave of absence to study at Chin-
gwan monastery on Mount Samgak, where they composed a number of linked
verses.

Where does it come from, the sound of a flute,
At midnight on a blue-green peak

Sŏng Sammun

Shaking the moonlight, it rings high,
Borne by the wind, it carries afar.

Yi Kae

Clear and smooth like a warbler's song,
The floating melody rolls downhill.

Sin Sukchu

I listen—a sad melody stirs my heart,
I concentrate—it dispels my gloom.

Pak P'aengnyŏn

Always, ever, a lover looks in the mirror,
And amid vibrant silence, night deepens in the hills.

Yi Sŏkhyŏng

Splitting a stone, limpid notes are stout,
"Plucking a Willow Branch" breaks a lover's heart.[1]

Sŏng Sammun

Clear and muddy notes come in order,
The *gong* and *shang* modes unmixed.[2]

Yi Kae

How wonderful, notes drawn out and released,
How pleasant, reaping waves of sound.

Sin Sukchu

Long since I played it seated on my bed.
Where is the zestful player leaning against the tower?

Pak P'aengnyŏn

---

1. A so-called Music Bureau song (written in the style of the folk songs collected by the court of Emperor Wu of the Han in the 2nd cent. BCE) accompanied by a horizontal flute; so is "Plum Blossoms Fall" nine lines later.
2. The first two notes of the pentatonic scale.

Marvelous melodies recall Cai Yan,[3]
Who remembers Ruan Ji's clear whistle?[4]

Yi Sŏkhyŏng

"Plum Blossoms Fall" in the garden,
Fish and dragons fight in the deep sea.

Sŏng Sammun

First, the drawn-out melody startled me,
Now I rejoice in the clear, sweet rhythm.

Yi Kae

How can only a reed whistle in Long
Make the Tartar traders flee homesick?

Sin Sukchu

On Mount Goushi a phoenix calls limpidly,
In the deep pool a dragon hums and dances.

Pak P'aengnyŏn

A wanderer is struck homesick over the pass,
A widow pines in her room.

Yi Sŏkhyŏng

Floating, floating, the music turns sad,
Long, long, my thought is disquieted.

Sŏng Sammun

We were all ears at the first notes,
But can't grasp the dying sounds.

Yi Kae

A startled wind rolls away the border sands,
Cold snow drives through Qin park.

Sin Sukchu

I don't tire of your music,
Should I rise and dance to your tune?

Pak P'aengnyŏn

3. The daughter of Cai Yong (133–193) and a skilled musician.
4. Ruan Ji (210–263), a poet, musician, and lover of wine, was one of the "Seven Worthies of the Bamboo Grove."

Who is that master flautist?
His creative talent is all his own.

Yi Sŏkhyŏng

Prince Qiao is really not dead,[5]
Has Huan Yi returned from the underworld?[6]

Sŏng Sammun

His solo—a whoop of a single crane,
In unison—a thousand ox-drawn carriages.

Yi Kae

Choking, choking, now a tearful complaint,
Murmuring, murmuring, now a tender whisper.

Sin Sukchu

I beg you, flute master,
Hide your art, don't spoil it.

Yi Sŏkhyŏng

Confucius heard Shao and lost his taste for meat;[7]
I too forget to take my meal.

Pak P'aengnyŏn

I cannot help cherishing your heart,
I set forth my deep love for you!

Sŏng Sammun

Hwang Chini (c. 1506–1544)

TAKING LEAVE OF MINISTER SO SEYANG

In the moonlit garden beech tree leaves fall;
  In the frost, wild chrysanthemums wither.

---

5. Wangzi Qiao, or Wangzi Jin, a son of King Ling of Zhou (6th cent. BCE) and a noted player of the *sheng* (mouth organ made from thirteen bamboo pipes), was said to have become a transcendent on Mount Goushi (see above).

6. Huan Yi (d. ca. 392) was a great flautist of the Jin.

7. *Lunyu* 7:13 and 3:25; Waley, *Analects*, 125 and 101. Waley translates *shao*, which Confucius found to be perfect in beauty, as "Succession Dance."

The tower is tall as the sky,
   Drunk, we keep on draining our cups.
Flowing water is cold as the lute;
   Plum fragrance seeps into my flute.
Tomorrow, after we have parted,
   Our love will be green waves unending.

Yi Hyanggŭm (1513–1550)

To a Drunken Guest

The drunken guest clings to my sleeve,
   My gauze sleeve gets torn as I shake him off.
I don't mind the torn blouse,
   I only fear the end of our love.

Great Master Sŏsan (1520–1604)

In Praise of the Portrait of My Former Master

Your white robes are made of white clouds,
   Your blue pupils, strips of water.
Your stomach cradles precious gems,
   Your heavenly light pierces the Big Dipper.

Great Master Chŏnggwan (1533–1609)

At the Moment of My Death

The three-foot-long sword that can split a feather
   I've hidden in the Great Dipper.
In the great void no trace of clouds,
   Now you see its sharp point!

Yi Sunsin (1545–1598)

In the Chinhae Camp

By the sea, the autumn sun sinks;
   Startled by cold, the geese pitch camp.
Anxious, I toss and turn—
   Only a dawn moon on my bow and sword.

Im Che (1559–1587)

A Woman's Sorrow

A beautiful girl, fifteen years old,
   Too shy to speak, sends her lover away.
Back home, she shuts the double gate
   And sobs before the pear blossoms.

Yu Mongin (1559–1623)

A Poor Woman

A poor woman at a shuttle, tears on her cheeks,
   Weaves winter cloth for her husband.
Come morning, she tears a strip for a tax officer;
   No sooner one leaves than another comes.

Hŏ Nansŏrhŏn (1563–1589)

Poor Woman

Till her fingers are stiff with cold,
    She cuts the cloth with scissors
To make a dress for a girl to be married:
    But every year she keeps to her empty room.

Cho Hwi (fl. 1568–1608)

In Peking to a Woman with a Veil

Shy, you veil your face on the street—
    Clear moonlight through faint clouds.
Your slender waist, tightly bound, is a handspan.
    Your new gauze skirt, a pomegranate color.

Yi Tal (fl. 1568–1608)

Mountain Temple

A temple buried in white clouds—
    But monks do not sweep them away.
A guest comes, the gate opens;
    In every valley, yellow pine pollen.

Great Master Chunggwan (fl. 1590)

Upon Reading Zhuangzi

Give me wings, I'll reach a high heaven,
　　With scales, I can dive into a deep pool.
How silly, you dreamer within a dream,
　　Not knowing your body's in a melting furnace.

Kim Ch'anghyŏp (1651–1708)

Mountain Folk

I dismount and ask, "Anybody home?"
　　A housewife emerges from the gate.
She seats me under the eaves
　　And fixes a meal for the guest.
"Where is your husband?" I ask.
　　"Up the hill at dawn with a plow."
It must be hard to furrow the hill;
　　He isn't back even after sunset.
Not a single soul around,
　　Only chickens and dogs on tiered slopes.
"In the woods there are tigers,
　　I can't fill my basket with greens."
"What makes you live alone
　　Among rugged paths in the valley?"
"I know life is easier on the plain,
　　But I am afraid of the king's men."

Nŭngun (d.u.)

WAITING FOR MY LOVE

He said he would come at moonrise;
  The moon is out, but he has not come.
Perhaps he lives among high hills
  Where the moon comes up late.

Pyŏn Wŏngyu (fl. 1881–1884)

TO A FRIEND

Day after day I live, deer for company,
  Bright moon on the water and clouds on the hills.
Nothing except these in the crevice of my heart—
  Shall I send you a painting of autumn sound?

PROSE

Buddhist Hagiography

This section on Buddhist biographical writing begins with selections from two thirteenth-century compilations, the *Lives of Eminent Korean Monks* (*Haedong kosŭng chŏn*, 1215) and *Memorabilia of the Three Kingdoms* (*Samguk yusa*, 1285). The first was compiled by Kakhun (d.u.), abbot of Yŏngt'ong monastery in the capital of Koryŏ, in response to a command from the throne, and it was used by Iryŏn (1206–1289), author of the *Memorabilia,* as one of the primary sources for his compilation. Lost for almost seven centuries, the *Lives* was known only by its title and a few quotations until the discovery in the early part of the twentieth century of a manuscript containing its first two chapters, on propagators of the faith.

The two extant chapters of the *Lives* comprise eighteen major and seven minor biographies and cover a span of five hundred years. The first chapter, which deals with three Koguryŏ monks, two Silla monks, and three monks of foreign origin, throws new and often brilliant light on the development of Korean Buddhism from the time of its introduction to the seventh century. The second chapter deals with Silla monks who went to China or India. In compiling the *Lives*, Kakhun was working within a well-established tradition. He had at least three prototypes, not to mention a large body of historical and literary materials from China and Korea. The Korean sources he cites are documents and records of great antiquity, a few of which are still extant. Among the Chinese sources, he is most indebted for form and style to three Chinese *Gaoseng zhuan* (Lives of eminent monks).[1] He respects the materials at hand and is careful to cite his

---

1. *Gaoseng zhuan*, by Huijiao (497–554); *Xu gaoseng zhuan*, by Daoxuan (596–657); and *Tang gaoseng zhuan*, by Zanning (919–1002).

sources; in cases involving reconstruction owing to the poor condition of the manuscript or kindred materials, he clearly admits his uncertainty.

Because Buddhism enjoyed seven centuries of uninterrupted prestige and protection as the state religion, Kakhun did not have to naturalize monks to promote their status in Korean history. What he wanted to do was prove that his subjects were on a par with their Chinese counterparts in every respect. For this purpose, he brings in Buddhist notables of the past and uses them figuratively, as parallel cases that imply contrast or superiority. As a contrast to Pŏpkong (514–540), for example, Emperor Wu of Liang (502–549) is brought in, only to be dismissed as a less-than-ideal monarch. Pŏpkong, who had renounced the throne to join the religious order, is an ideal ruler, Kakhun argues, for his Buddhist fervor brought about not the downfall but rather the consolidation and prosperity of the kingdom.

The age of Buddhism in Korea began with Pŏpkong, but this would not have been possible unless Silla had been a land chosen and blessed by the former Buddha and unless former kings had accumulated meritorious karma from the beginning of the country's history. Thus arose, from about the beginning of the sixth century, a belief that Korea was the land of the former Buddha,[2] and that the Silla kings, in a manner befitting the rulers of the land, were of the Ksatriya caste.[3] According to Iryŏn, this revelation had been made by Mañjuśrī[4] himself when he appeared in the form of an old man to the Vinaya master Chajang on Mount Wutai and declared: "Your sovereign is of the Ksatriya caste of India, which is far different from other barbarian tribes in the East."[5] When Mañjuśrī appeared a second time, in the form of an old monk, he advised Chajang to return to his country and visit Mount Odae, where ten thousand Mañjuśrīs

2. For example, *SY* 3:132, 137.

3. The second of the four castes of traditional Indian society; *PDB*, 497.

4. "Gentle Glory," one of the most important bodhisattvas in Mahāyana Buddhism; *PDB*, 526–527.

5. *SY* 3:137–138.

always reside.[6] With this episode, Silla became at once not only the land of the former Buddha but also the land of the present and future Buddhas—the permanent abode of the Buddha and bodhisattvas.

The myths and legends engendered by Buddhist piety seem to have determined the very nature of Buddhist biography. The world this kind of writing refers to is presided over by the Buddha with his universal dharma, by miraculous wonders and wondrous miracles, and by the relentless workings of karmic rewards and retributions. Indeed, this referential world, hitherto unknown to the Koreans, existed within a concept of time and space all its own. The subjects of the *Lives* therefore sense the hand of the Buddha working at every moment and in every corner. Prenatal wonders, amazing precocity, feats of endurance, wonder working and miracles—these are the very stuff from which Kakhun worked up his accounts. As the theme in Western hagiography from 400 to 1400 CE was the glory of God through the praise of his saints, so the theme in the *Lives* is the glory of the world of the dharma through the lives of its monks.

Kakhun

LIVES OF EMINENT KOREAN MONKS (1215)

[HAEDONG KOSŬNG CHŎN]

Pŏpkong

Sŏk[1] Pŏpkong was the twenty-third king of Silla, named Pŏphŭng (514–540). His secular name was Wŏnjong, and he was the first son of King Chijŭng (500–514) and Lady Yŏnje. He was seven feet tall. Being generous, he loved the people, and they in turn regarded him as a

---

6. *SY* 3:168 and 170–171.

1. Daoan (314–385), a translator of Buddhist scriptures during the Eastern Jin, was the first to advocate that every monk should take the surname Shi (K. Sŏk; Skt. Śākya), since Śākyamuni was the primary teacher of all monks.

saint or a sage. Millions of people, therefore, placed confidence in him. In his third year (516), a dragon appeared in the Willow Well. In his fourth year (517), the Ministry of War was established, and in his seventh year (520), laws and statutes were promulgated together with official accouterments. After his enthronement, whenever the king attempted to spread Buddhism, his ministers opposed him with much disputation. He felt frustrated, but, remembering Ado's devout vow to bring Buddhism to Silla,[2] he summoned all his officials and said to them: "Our august ancestor, King Mich'u, together with Ado, propagated Buddhism, but he died before great merits were accumulated. That the knowledge of the wonderful transformation of Śākyamuni should be prevented from spreading makes me very sad. We think we ought to erect monasteries and recast images to continue our ancestor's fervor. What do you think?"

Minister Kongal and others remonstrated with the king: "In recent years the crops have been scarce, and the people are restless. Besides, because of frequent border raids from the neighboring state, our soldiers are still engaged in battle. How can we exhort our people to erect useless buildings at such a time?"

The king, depressed at the lack of faith among his subordinates, sighed: "We, lacking moral power, are unworthy of succeeding to the throne. The yin and yang are disharmonious and the people ill at ease; therefore you opposed my idea and did not want to follow. Who can enlighten our errant people to the wonderful dharma?"

For some time no one answered.

In the sixteenth year (529), the grand secretary Pak Yŏmch'ok (Ich'adon or Kŏch'adon), then twenty-five years old, was an upright man. With a heart that was sincere and deep, he resolutely advocated for the righteous cause. To help the king fulfill his noble vow, he secretly memorialized the throne: "If Your Majesty desires to establish

---

2. Ado went to Silla from Koguryŏ in the fifth century. See Peter H. Lee, *Lives of Eminent Korean Monks*, 6n27; for Ado's life, see 50–56.

Buddhism, may I ask Your Majesty to pass a false decree to this officer that the king desires to initiate Buddhist construction? Once the ministers learn of this, they will undoubtedly remonstrate. Your Majesty, declaring that no such decree has been given, will then ask who has forged the royal order. They will ask Your Majesty to punish my crime, and if their request is granted, they will submit to Your Majesty's will."

The king said: "Since they are bigoted and haughty, we fear they will not be satisfied even with your execution."

Yŏmch'ok replied: "Even the deities venerate the religion of the great sage. If an officer as unworthy as myself is killed for its cause, miracles must happen between heaven and earth. If so, who then will dare to remain bigoted and haughty?"

The king answered: "Our basic wish is to further the advantageous and remove the disadvantageous. But now we have to injure a loyal subject. Is this not sorrowful?"

Yŏmch'ok replied: "Sacrificing his life in order to accomplish goodness is the fulfillment of an official's reason for being. Moreover, if it should lead to the perpetual solidarity of the kingdom and the eternal brightness of the Buddha-sun, the day of my death will be the year of my birth."

The king, greatly moved, praised Yŏmch'ok: "Though you are a commoner, your mind conceives thoughts worthy of brocaded and embroidered robes." Thereupon the king and Yŏmch'ok vowed to be true to each other.

Afterward, a royal decree was issued ordering the erection of a monastery in the Forest of the Heavenly Mirror, and the officials in charge began construction. The court officials, as expected, denounced it and expostulated with the king. The king remarked: "We did not issue such an order."

Thereupon Yŏmch'ok spoke out: "Indeed, I did this purposely, for if we practice Buddhism the whole country will become prosperous and peaceful. As long as it is good for the administration of the realm, what wrong can there be in forging a decree?"

Thereupon, the king called a meeting and asked the opinion of the officials. All of them agreed: "These days monks bare their heads and wear strange garments. Their discourses are wrong and in violation of the norm. If we unthinkingly follow their proposals, there may be cause for regret. We dare not obey Your Majesty's order, even if we are threatened with death."

Yŏmch'ok spoke with indignation: "All of you are wrong, for there must be an unusual personage before there can be an unusual undertaking. I have heard that the teaching of Buddhism is profound and arcane. We must practice it. How can a sparrow know the great ambition of a swan?"[3]

The king said: "The will of the majority is firm and unalterable. You are the only one who takes a different view. I cannot follow two conflicting judgments at the same time." He then ordered the execution of Yŏmch'ok.

Yŏmch'ok then made an oath to heaven: "I am about to die for the sake of the dharma. I pray that righteousness will spread, to the benefit of the religion. If the Buddha has a numen,[4] a miracle will occur after my death."

When he was decapitated, his head flew to Mount Diamond,[5] falling on its summit, and white milk gushed forth from the cut, soaring up several hundred feet. The sun darkened, wonderful flowers rained from heaven, and the earth trembled violently. The king, his officials, and the commoners, on the one hand terrified by these strange phenomena, and on the other sorrowful for the death of the grand secretary, who had sacrificed his life for the cause of the dharma, cried aloud and mourned. They buried his body on Mount Diamond with due ceremony. At that time the king and his officials took an oath:

3. *Shiji* 48:1949; Watson, *Records of the Grand Historian*, 1:49.

4. If the Buddha is omnipotent—i.e., if he is truly there.

5. Seven tricents north of Kyŏngju.

"Hereafter we will worship the Buddha and revere the clergy. If we break the oath, may heaven strike us dead."

The gentleman says:[6] "The great sage responds to the blessing of a myriad years. Goodness is born from lucky signs, and righteousness is stirred by favorable auspices. He never fails to respond to heaven and earth, to be coterminous with the sun and moon, and to move the spirits, to say nothing of humans. For once he is confident in the path, he will never fail to obtain assistance from heaven and earth. But a work is valued for its success, and karma for its far-reaching merit. One could take up Mount Tai as if it were lighter than a feather if one could make oneself truly worthy of the confidence of others. How glorious! Yŏmch'ok's death is really the proper way of dying."

In the same year a decree forbade the taking of life. (The above is based on the national history and various documents that the author has rearranged.)

In the twenty-first year (534), trees in the Forest of the Heavenly Mirror were felled in order to build a monastery. When the ground was cleared, pillar bases, stone niches, and steps were discovered, proving the site to be that of an old monastery. Materials for beams and pillars came from the forest. When the monastery was completed, the king abdicated and became a monk. He changed his name to Pŏpkong, mindful of the three garments[7] and the begging bowl. He aspired to lofty conduct and had compassion for all. Accordingly, the monastery was named Taewang Hŭngnyun because it was the king's abode. This was the first monastery erected in Silla.

The queen, too, served the Buddha by becoming a nun and residing at the Yŏnghŭng monastery. Since the king had patronized a great cause, he was given the posthumous epithet of Pŏphŭng, which was by no means idle flattery. Thereafter, at every anniversary of

---

6. Kakhun borrows the lips of a gentleman to express his own views.

7. Three kinds of robes: a patched robe made from nine pieces; a stole, from seven pieces; and an inner garment, from five pieces. The begging bowl stands for a Buddhist monk's way of life.

Yŏmch'ok's death, an assembly was held at the Hŭngnyun monastery to commemorate his martyrdom. In the reign of King T'aejong Muyŏl (654–661), the prime minister Kim Yangdo, whose faith inclined westward, offered his two daughters, Hwabo and Yŏnbo, to serve as maids in the monastery. The relatives of Mo Ch'ŏk, a traitor, were also reduced in rank and made to become servants. Descendants of these two kinds of people serve there even today.

When I was traveling in the eastern capital, I ascended Mount Diamond. Upon seeing a lonely mound and low tombstone, I was unable to stop lamenting. That day, monks assembled there to eat and, when asked, they told me it was the anniversary of the grand secretary's death. Indeed, the more time passed, the more dear he was thought to be. According to the inscription on Ado's tombstone, King Pŏphŭng's Buddhist name was Pŏbun, and his polite name, Pŏpkong. I have distinguished two biographies here, based on the national history and *Sui chŏn* (Stories of marvels). Those who are interested in antiquity will do well to study the matter.

The eulogy says: Usually the sovereign, with the subject's help, can keep established law but cannot innovate. Moreover, there are factors such as the appropriateness of the time and the faith of the people. Thereafter, although King Wŏnjong wished to propagate Buddhism, he could not expect his order to be carried out overnight. But, thanks to the power of his original vow, the prestige of his position, and the counsel of a wise official, he succeeded in making the kingdom prosper by acts of grace and became the equal of Emperor Ming of the Han. How great he is! For who can carp at him? It is, however, wrong to compare him with Emperor Wu (501–549) of Liang, for, while the latter served in the Tongtai monastery as a servant, ignoring his imperial work,[8] the former (Pŏpkong) surrendered his throne first, in order to install his heir, and only afterward became a monk. Of what

---

8. He gave himself up (*sheshen*) as a menial on four occasions, in 517, 529, 546, and 547.

selfishness can one accuse him? As Yŏmch'ok's career attests, king and monk (Skt. *bhiksu*), although physically different, were of the same substance. Indeed. Yŏmch'ok's power was such that he could dispel the clouds of illusion, cause the wisdom-sun of emptiness to radiate everywhere, and fly with the Buddha-sun under his arm.

Pŏbun

Sŏk Pŏbun's secular name was Kongnŭngjong, his posthumous epithet Chinhŭng (540–576). He was the brother of King Pŏphŭng and the son of King Kalmun (500–514). His mother's maiden name was Kim. He ascended the throne at the age of six. Rightly indulgent and rightly benevolent, he attended strictly to business and punctually observed his promises. He rejoiced at hearing the good and strove to uproot the evil.

In the seventh year of his reign (544), the Hŭngnyun monastery was completed, and common people were permitted to enter the clergy. In the eighth year (545), the state of Liang dispatched an envoy, together with the student monk Kaktŏk, who had studied abroad, and some relics. The king sent officials to welcome them in front of the Hŭngnyun monastery. In the fourteenth year (553), he ordered construction of a new palace, east of Wŏlsŏng, and a yellow dragon was seen on the spot. The king, moved by the sight, changed the palace to a monastery and named it the Hwangnyong (Yellow Dragon) monastery. In the twenty-sixth year (566), the Chen (557–589) sent an envoy, Li Si, and the monk Myŏnggwan with more than seven hundred rolls of scriptures and treatises. In the twenty-seventh year (566), the two monasteries Kiwŏn and Silche were completed, as was the Hwangnyong monastery. In the tenth month of the thirty-third year (572), the king held an Eight Restrictions (P'algwanhoe) festival[9] for the repose of officers and soldiers killed in action. The ceremony was

---

9. The first eight (out of ten) prohibitions are not to kill; not to steal; not to commit adultery; not to speak falsely; not to drink wine; not to indulge in cosmetics, dancing or music; not to sleep on fine beds; and not to eat out of regular hours. See *PDB,* 612.

held in the outer monastery and lasted for seven days. In the thirty-fifth year (574), a Buddha image sixteen feet high was cast at the Hwangnyong monastery. Tradition says that it was cast with the gold that King Aśoka shipped to Sap'o (Ulchu). . . . In the thirty-sixth year (576), the *wŏnhwa*[10] were first chosen as the honored youth (*sŏllang*).

At first the king and his officials were perplexed by the problem of how to find and promote the talented among their people. They had the idea that if they could observe young maidens disporting themselves together, the talented among them would emerge and could be elevated to positions of service. In this manner two beautiful girls, Nammu and Chunjŏng, were selected to lead the *hwarang,* a group of about three hundred maidens. But the two who had been chosen were jealous of each other, and Chunjŏng, after plying Nammu with wine until she became intoxicated, pushed her into the river, where she drowned. At this the group became discordant and broke up. Afterward, handsome youths were chosen for the *hwarang* instead. They powdered their faces, wore ornamented dresses, and were respected as the "flower of youth" (*hwarang*), drawing others from various backgrounds into their circle of knighthood. They instructed one another in the path of righteousness, entertained each other with songs and music, and went on pilgrimage to commune with famous mountains and rivers, no matter how far away. From all this, it was believed, a man's moral character could be discerned, and the best among them were recommended to the court.

Kim Taemun, in his *Annals of the Hwarang* (*Hwarang segi*), remarks: "Henceforth, able ministers and loyal subjects were chosen from their circle, and good generals and brave soldiers were born therefrom." Ch'oe Ch'iwŏn (b. 857), in his preface to the *Inscription on the Tomb of Knight Nan* (*Nallang pi*), says: "There is a wonderful and

---

10. "Original flowers," the female leaders of the elite "flower of youth" (*hwarang*).

mysterious way in the country, called *p'ungnyu*,[11] which in fact embraces the Three Teachings and transforms myriad men. It is a tenet of the minister of crime of Lu (Confucius) that one should be filial to one's parents and loyal to one's sovereign; it is the belief of the keeper of the archives of Zhou (Laozi) that one should be at home in the action of inaction and practice the wordless doctrine; and it is the teaching of the Indian prince that one should avoid evil and do many good deeds." Also Linghu Cheng of Tang, in the *Xinluo guoji* (Record of the state of Silla), states that "the *hwarang* were chosen from the handsome sons of the nobles and their faces were made up. They were called *hwarang*, and were respected and served by their countrymen. This was a way to facilitate the king's government." According to the *Annals of the Hwarang*, from *wŏnhwa* to the end of Silla there were more than two hundred knights, of whom the Four Knights were the wisest.

The king ascended the throne as a child and worshiped Buddha ardently. In his later years he shaved his head and became a monk. When he donned a Buddhist robe, he styled himself Pŏbun (Dharma Clouds). He received and retained all the prohibitions and redeemed the three acts—with purity of action, speech, and deed—until his death. Upon his death the people buried him with appropriate ceremony on the peak north of the Aegong monastery. In that year the Dharma master Anham arrived from Sui. . . .

The eulogy says: Great is the power of custom over humans. Therefore, if the king wants to change the fashion of an age, no one can prevent his success, which follows like the downflow of water. After King Chinhŭng first worshiped Buddhism and initiated the way of the *hwarang*, people gladly followed and emulated him. Their excitement in doing so was as great as when visiting a treasure house or going out to the spring terrace. The king's aim was to make the people

---

11. The term in the classical sense means moral influence, the power of customs and manners. During the Three Kingdoms period, the emphasis fell on freedom of spirit, the overturning of convention, and spontaneous emotion.

progress toward goodness and justice and to lead them to the great path. Emperor Ai (7–1 BCE) of the Former Han loved only lust. Ban Gu (32–92 CE) therefore remarked: "The tenderness which seduces man belongs not only to woman, but to man as well." This indeed cannot be compared with our story of the *hwarang*.

Wŏngwang

Sŏk Wŏngwang (542–640) was a resident of the capital of Silla. His secular name was Sŏl or Pak. At the age of twelve he shaved his head and became a monk. His supernal vessel[12] was magnificent and free, and his understanding beyond the ordinary. He was versed in the works of the metaphysical school (*xuanxue*) and Confucianism, and he loved literature. Being lofty in thought, he disdained the world of passion and retired at twenty-nine to a cave on Mount Samgi. His shadow never appeared outside the cave.

One day a mendicant monk came to a place near his cave and built a hermitage there to cultivate the way of religion.

One night while the master was sitting and reciting scriptures, a spirit called to him, "Excellent! There are many religious people, yet none excels you. Now this monk is cultivating black art; but because of your pure thought my way is blocked, and I have not been able to approach him. Whenever I pass by him, however, I cannot help thinking badly of him. I beseech you to persuade him to move away; if he does not follow my advice, there shall be a disaster."

The following morning the master went to the monk and told him, "You had better move away to avoid disaster, or if you stay it will not be to your advantage."

But the monk remarked, "When I have undertaken to do something opposed by Māra himself,[13] why should I worry about what a demon has to say?"

12. *Daodejing* 29; Lau, *Tao Te Ching*, 85–87.
13. The Buddhist devil; *PDB*, 530–531.

That same evening the spirit returned and asked for the monk's reply. The master, fearful of the spirit's anger, said that he had not yet been to see the monk, but that he knew the monk would dare not disobey. The spirit, however, remarked, "I have already ascertained the truth. Be quiet and you shall see." That same night there was a sound as loud as thunder. At dawn the master went out and saw that the hermitage had been crushed under a landslide. Later the spirit returned and said, "I have lived for several thousand years and possess unequaled power to change things. This is nothing to be marveled at." He also advised the master: "Now the master has benefited himself, but lacks the merit of benefiting others. Why not go to China to obtain the Buddha dharma, which will be of great benefit for future generations?"

"It has been my cherished desire to learn the path in China," replied the master, "but owing to the obstacles of sea and land I am afraid I cannot get there." Thereupon the spirit told him in detail of matters relating to a journey to the West.

In the third month, in the spring of the twelfth year of King Chinp'yŏng (589), the master went to Chen. He traveled to various lecture halls and received and noted subtle instructions. After mastering the essence of the *Treatise on the Proof of Reality*,[14] the *Nirvāna Scripture*,[15] and several treatises from the *Tripiṭaka*, he went to Huqiu in Wu harboring an ambition that soared to the sky. Upon the request of a believer, the master expounded the *Tattvasiddhi* and thenceforth requests from his admirers came one after another like the close succession of scales on a fish.

At that time Sui soldiers marched into Yangdu (Nanjing). Here the commander of the army saw a tower in flames. But when he went to the rescue, there was no sign of the fire, and he found only the master tied up in front of the tower. Greatly amazed, the commander set him free. It was during the Kaihuang era (590–600) that the *Summary of*

14. *Tattvasiddhi; PDB*, 900.
15. *Nirvāṇa Sūtra; PDB*, 504.

the Great Vehicle[16] was first promulgated, and the master cherished its style; he won great acclaim in the Sui capital.

Now that he had further cultivated meritorious works, it was incumbent on him to continue the spread of the dharma eastward. Our country therefore appealed to Sui, and a decree allowed him to return to his country in the twenty-second year, *kyŏngsin*, of King Chinp'yŏng (600) together with the *naema* (rank 11) Chebu and the *taesa* (rank 12) Hoengch'ŏn, who at that time served as envoys to China. On the sea, a strange being suddenly appeared out of the water and paid homage to the master: "Would the master please erect a monastery and expound the truth there for my sake so that your disciples can gain outstanding rewards?" The master complied. Because he had returned after an absence of some years, old and young rejoiced alike, and even the king declared his pious respect and dubbed him "Mighty in Goodness."

One day Wŏngwang returned to his old retreat on Mount Samgi. At midnight the same spirit visited the master and asked him about his experiences abroad. The master thanked him and said, "Thanks to your gracious protection, all my wishes have been fulfilled."

"I will not abandon my duty to support you," the spirit replied. "You have an agreement with the sea dragon to erect a monastery, and now the dragon is here with me."

The master asked where the monastery should be built. The spirit replied, "North of the Unmun, where a flock of magpies is pecking at the ground. That is the place." The following morning the master, together with the spirit and the dragon, went there, and after the ground was cleared, they found the remains of a stone pagoda. A monastery was erected, named the Unmun monastery, and there the master stayed.

The spirit continued to protect the master invisibly, until one day when he returned to say: "My end is drawing near, and I wish to re-

16. *Mahāyānasaṃgraha Sūtra*; PDB, 514.

ceive the bodhisattva ordination[17] so that I can be eligible for eternity." The master administered the rites, and they vowed to save each other from endless transmigration. Afterward, the master asked if he might see the spirit's manifestation. The latter answered, "You may look to the east at dawn." The master then saw a large arm reach through the clouds to heaven. The spirit spoke, "Now you have seen my arm. Although I possess supernatural powers, I still am subject to mortality. I shall die on such and such a day in such and such a place, and I hope that you will come there to bid me farewell." The master went to the place as instructed, and there he saw an old black badger whimper and die. It was the spirit.

A female dragon in the western sea used to attend the master's lectures. At that time there was a drought and the master asked her to make rain to alleviate the possibility of a disaster befalling the country. The dragon replied, "The supreme deity will not allow it. If I make rain without his permission, I sin against the deity and have no way of escaping punishment." The master said, "My power can save you from it." Immediately, morning clouds appeared on the southern mountain and rain poured down. But thunder from heaven broke out, indicating imminent punishment, and the dragon was frightened. The master hid her under his couch and continued to expound the scriptures. A heavenly messenger then appeared to say, "I have been ordered here by the supreme deity. You are the host of the fugitive. What shall I do if I am unable to carry out my orders?" The master, pointing to a pear tree in the garden, replied, "She has transformed herself into that tree. You may strike it." The messenger struck it and left. Then the dragon came out and thanked the master. Grateful to the tree that had suffered punishment for her sake, the dragon touched the trunk with her hand and the tree revived.

17. The ordination was administered to the Koryŏ kings by the national or royal preceptor, normally on the fifteenth day of the sixth month. The first king to receive this ordination was Tŏkchong in 1032 (*KS* 5:25a).

In his thirtieth year (608), King Chinp'yŏng was troubled by frequent border raids from Koguryŏ, and he decided to ask for help from Sui to retaliate. He asked the master to draft the petition for a foreign campaign. The master replied, "To destroy others in order to preserve oneself is not the way of a monk. But since I, a poor monk, live in Your Majesty's territory and waste Your Majesty's clothes and food, I dare not disobey." He then relayed the king's request to Sui.

The master was detached and retiring by nature, but affectionate and loving to all. He always smiled when he spoke and never showed signs of anger. His reports, memorials, memoranda, and correspondence were all composed by himself and were greatly admired by the whole country. Power was bestowed on him so that he might govern the provinces, and he used the opportunity to promote Buddhism, setting an example for future generations.

In the thirty-fifth year (613), an assembly of one hundred high seats[18] was held in the Hwangnyong monastery to expound the scriptures and harvest the fruits of blessing. The master headed the entire group. He used to spend days at Kach'wi monastery lecturing on the true way.

Kwisan and Ch'wihang from Saryang district came to the master's door. Lifting up their robes, they said respectfully, "We are ignorant and without knowledge. Please give us a maxim that will serve to instruct us for the rest of our lives."

The master replied, "There are ten commandments in the bodhisattva ordination. But since you are subjects and sons, I fear you cannot practice all of them. So here instead are five commandments for laymen: serve your sovereign with loyalty; tend your parents with filial piety; treat your friends with sincerity; never retreat from a battlefield; and be discriminating about the taking of life. Exercise care in the performance of these commandments."

---

18. The assembly consisted of royal ceremonials to protect the country from various kinds of calamities; see *PDB*, 362–364 and 710. In the second recorded meeting (613), Master Wŏngwang lectured on the Buddhist scriptures.

Kwisan said, "We will follow your wishes with regard to the first four. But what is the meaning of being discriminating about the taking of life?"

The master answered, "Not to kill during the months of spring and summer nor during the six maigre feast days is to choose the time.[19] Nor to kill domestic animals such as cows, horses, chickens, dogs, and tiny creatures whose meat is less than a mouthful is to choose the creatures. Though you may have the need you should not kill often. These are good rules for laymen." Kwisan and his friend subsequently adhered to these rules without ever breaking them.

Later, when the king was ill and no physician could cure him, the master was invited to the palace to expound the dharma and was given separate quarters there. While expounding the texts and lecturing on the truth, he succeeded in gaining the king's faith. At the first watch, the king and his courtiers saw that the master's head was as golden as the disk of the sun. The king's illness was immediately cured.

When the master's monastic years were well advanced, he went to the inner court of the palace by carriage. The king personally took care of the master's clothing and medicine, hoping thus to monopolize the rewards. But except for his monastic robe and begging bowl, the master gave to monasteries all the offerings bestowed upon him in order to lead both the initiated and uninitiated and glorify the true dharma. When he was near the end, the king tended him in person. As the king was to receive the commission to save the people and transmit the dharma after the master's death, the master explained the omens to him in detail. In the ninth year of Queen Sŏndŏk (640), seven days after the onset of his illness, he died sitting upright in his residence after giving his last commandments in a lucid, compassionate voice. In the sky northeast of the Hwangnyong monastery, music filled the air and an unusual fragrance pervaded the hall. The whole nation experienced grief mingled with joy. The burial materials and

---

19. The eighth, fourteenth, fifteenth, twenty-third, twenty-ninth, and thirtieth days constitute the six monthly fast days.

attending rites were the same as those for a king. He was ninety-nine years old. It was the fourteenth year of the Zhenguan era (640). . . . His reliquary on Mount Samgi still stands today. . . .

The eulogy says: Formerly the master Huiyuan (334–416) did not neglect worldly texts. During his lectures he illustrated his points by quotations from Zhuangzi and Laozi in order to make people understand the mysterious purports. Now the commandments for laymen laid down by the master Wŏngwang were really the result of his all-embracing knowledge, and they demonstrate the efficacy of his technique of preaching the dharma according to the receptivity of his listeners. Discrimination in the taking of life is none other than Tang's leaving one side of the net open and Confucius' not shooting at roosting birds.[20] As for his ability to dismiss heavenly messengers and move heavenly deities, he must have possessed unimaginable religious power.

Iryŏn (1206–1289)

MEMORABILIA OF THE THREE KINGDOMS (1285)

[SAMGUK YUSA]

Wŏnhyo

The secular name of the holy monk Master Wŏnhyo (617–686) was Sŏl. He was born under a śāla tree in Chestnut Valley, north of Pulchi village and south of Amnyang county. The master's house was said to be southwest of the valley. One day, as she was passing under the tree, the master's mother felt labor pains and gave birth to him. It was too late to return home, so she hung her husband's clothes on the tree and spent the night under it. This is why the tree is called the śāla, and its unusually shaped fruit, the śāla chestnut.

---

20. *Lunyu* 7:26; Waley, *Analects*, 128.

An old record says that long ago an abbot gave his slave two chestnuts for supper. When the slave complained to an official about his meager rations, the official thought it strange and had the fruit brought to him. Upon inspection, he found that a single chestnut filled a wooden bowl. The official promptly decreed that subsequently only one chestnut should be given. It is from this story that Chestnut Valley got its name.

When the master became a monk, he turned his house into a monastery, calling it Ch'ogae. He built another monastery near the tree and named it Śāla. The master's childhood name was Sŏdang, or Sindang. On the night he was conceived, his mother dreamed that a shooting star entered her bosom. At the moment of the master's birth, five-colored clouds hovered over the earth. This was in the thirty-ninth year of King Chinp'yŏng (617), the thirteenth year of Daye. Wŏnhyo was a clever and versatile child who needed no teacher. The *Lives of Eminent Monks of Tang* and the "Accouts of Conduct" describe his wanderings and religious accomplishments, so I will omit them here and include only some anecdotes from our own sources.

While young the master often had spring fever; once he walked through the streets singing: "Who'll lend me an axe without a handle?[1] I'd like to chisel away at the pillar that supports heaven." The people did not understand his cravings.

King T'aejong Muyŏl (654–661) heard of Wŏnhyo and said, "This monk wants to marry a noble lady and beget a wise son. If a sage is born the country will benefit greatly." At this time a widowed princess lived alone in the Jade Palace. The king dispatched attendants to bring Wŏnhyo to the palace but Wŏnhyo met them halfway, having already come down from Mount South as far as Mosquito Bridge. There he deliberately fell into the stream and doused his clothes. The attendants took him to the palace, where he changed his clothes and spent the night. The princess conceived and gave birth to a son, called Sŏl

---

1. *Shijing* 101 and 158, where the axe stands for a matchmaker.

Ch'ong. Clever and intelligent, Sŏl Ch'ong (c. 660–730) was versed in the classics and histories and became one of the Ten Worthies of Silla. He annotated in the Korean language[2] the customs and names of things of China and Korea, and the six classics and other literary works. These are recommended to any scholar who wishes to elucidate the classics.

After breaking his vow and begetting Sŏl Ch'ong, Wŏnhyo put on worldly clothes and lived in the style of a "little retired gentleman." One day he met an actor who danced with a gourd mask, which struck him as uncanny. He made himself a gourd mask and called it Unhindered[3] after a passage in the *Garland Scripture*,[4] and then composed a song and sang it until many people knew it. He toured the villages singing and dancing so that even usurers and bachelors soon knew the name of the Buddha and called on Amitābha in order to be reborn in his Pure Land. Wŏnhyo's native valley was then renamed Buddha Land, and his monastery was called Ch'ogae, or First Opening. He gave himself the name Wŏnhyo, which means "dawn" in dialect but also indicates that it was Wŏnhyo who made the Buddha-sun shine brightly in Korea.

When he wrote commentaries on the *Garland Scripture* in the Punhwang monastery, he stopped at the fortieth chapter. As he was so busy with public affairs, he was called "The Beginner" in the religious hierarchy. Assisted by a sea dragon, the protector of the faith, he received royal orders while traveling to compile commentaries on the *Adamantine Absorption Scripture*.[5] He placed his inkstone and brush on the two horns of the ox he rode, and soon the people called him Horn Rider. To this day "horn rider" symbolizes a concern with one's own enlightenment and that of others. . . .

---

2. Through the unique system of using sinographs to transcribe Korean words.
3. Without hindrance to achieving enlightenment.
4. *Avataṃsaka Sūtra; PDB*, 84–85.
5. *Vajrasamādhi Sūtra; PDB*, 453.

When Wŏnhyo died, his son, Sŏl Ch'ong, pulverized his remains and cast them into a lifelike image. This he enshrined and worshiped in the Punhwang monastery.

One day, as Sŏl bowed down, the image turned its head to look at him. Its head is still turned to one side. The site of Sŏl's house is said to be near a cave monastery where his father had once lived.

The eulogy says:

Ox horns revealed the mystery of concentration,
the dancing gourd met the wind in myriad streets.
He slept a spring sleep in the moonlit palace and left;
The closed Punhwang monastery casts no shadow.

Ŭisang

The surname of the Dharma master Ŭisang was Kim. In the capital, at the age of twenty-nine, Ŭisang had his head shaved in the Hwangbok monastery and became a monk. Shortly afterward, he thought to travel to China to gauge the extent of the transformations that the Buddha dharma had brought there. As it happened, he went with Wŏnhyo to Liaodong (650) but was captured by a soldier of the Koguryŏ frontier guard and was charged with being a spy. After he had spent dozens of days in confinement he was set free to return home.

In the beginning of the Yonghui era (650–655), Ŭisang sailed on the ship of the returning Tang envoy and so was able to enter China. At first he stopped at Yangzhou. There the governor of the prefecture, Liu Jiren, invited him to stay at the government offices and entertained him in grand style. Afterward, Ŭisang went to the Zhixiang monastery on Mount Zhongnan and had an audience with Zhiyan (602–668). The night before Ŭisang arrived, Zhiyan had a dream: a tall tree with luxuriant leaves shot out from Korea and covered China. In the top of the tree was the nest of a phoenix. Zhiyan climbed to the top of the tree and found a brightly glowing pearl that shone far and wide. After he had awakened, Zhiyan marveled and pondered over the dream. He sprinkled and swept his abode, and waited. Soon Ŭisang arrived. Zhiyan received his guest with special courtesy and addressed him calmly, "Last night in a dream I saw an omen of your coming." He then invited him into his chamber and carefully explained the mysteries of the *Garland Scripture*.

At that time Tang Gaozong was planning to invade Silla, and Silla officials in the Tang capital wanted Ŭisang to return home. He did so in the first year of Xianheng (670). In the first year of Yifeng (676), Ŭisang returned to Mount T'aebaek and built the Pusŏk monastery in accordance with a royal command. There he preached Mahāyāna Buddhism and was rewarded for his prayers.

When Fazang (643–712) sent a copy of his *Notes Plumbing the Profundities (of the Garland Scripture)* (*Tanxuan ji*) together with a personal letter to Ŭisang, Ŭisang gave copies to ten monasteries and ordered them to study it.

Ŭisang wrote the *Diagram of the Dharmadhātu according to the One Vehicle of Hwaŏm* (*Pŏpkye to*)[6] and a commentary (*Yakso*), and everyone, both high and low, made an effort to carry them with him. The *Diagram* was completed in the first year of Xongzhang (668), the year Zhiyan died. Ŭisang was thought to be a reincarnation of the Buddha. He had ten disciples who distinguished themselves as great masters, and the biography of each has been recorded.

Ŭisang is said to have walked on air while circumambulating the pagoda of the Hwangbok monastery with his devotees. Because of this the monks did not set up a ladder. When the devotees also began to circle the pagoda three feet from the ground, Ŭisang looked back at them and remarked, "Ordinary people would think it strange if they saw us. Walking on air cannot be taught to the masses."

The eulogy says:

Parting thorns and braving smoke and clouds, he crossed the ocean.
The gate of the Zhixiang monastery opened, and he received the
    auspicious and precious.

6. *PDB*, 936.

He planted the luxuriant Huayan tree in his home country,
Now spring prevails on the Zhongnan and T'aebaek mountains.

Fazang's Letter to Ŭisang

The monk of the Chongfa monastery in the western capital of Tang, Fazang, sends a letter to the attendant of the Buddha and master of the Great Garland School in Silla.

More than twenty years have passed since we parted, but how could affection for you leave my mind? Between us lie ten thousand miles of smoke and clouds and a thousand folds of land and sea; it is clear we will not see each other again in this life. How can I express, adequately, how I cherish the memory of our friendship? Owing to the same direct and indirect causes in our former existence and the same karma in this life, we were fortunate; we immersed ourselves in the great scripture, and we received its profound meaning by special favor granted us by our late master.

I hear with even greater joy that you have, on your return to your native country, elucidated the *Garland Scripture*, enhanced the Dharma realm, and arisen from causation unhindered. Thus Indra's net is multimeshed and the kingdom of the Buddha is daily renewed; you have widely benefited the world. By this I know that after the death of the Tathāgata,[7] it will be because of you that the wheel of Dharma turns again and the Buddha-sun shines brightly. You have made the Dharma live for us. I, Fazang, have made little progress and interceded even less for others. When I think of you and gaze upon this scripture, I am ashamed that it was to me that our late master transmitted it. But, according to my duty, I cannot abandon what I have received. I only hope to be part of its future causes, direct and indirect, by relying on this karma.

Our teacher's discourses and commentaries, though rich in meaning, are terse in style and difficult for posterity to approach. Hence I

---

7. "One who has thus come/gone," usually "Thus gone one," one of the common epithets of the Buddha; *PDB*, 877.

have recorded his subtle sayings and mysterious purport, with a commentary on their meaning. Master Sŭngjŏn has made an abstract from my writing and will introduce it to your country upon his return to Silla. I beg you to scrutinize its good and bad points; I shall be happy if you would kindly revise it and enlighten me.

If we are reborn in the future, meet again in the Assembly of Vairocana Buddha,[8] receive the boundlessly wonderful Dharma, and practice the immeasurable vows of Samantabhadra,[9] then evil karma will be overthrown in a day.

It is my earnest hope that you will not forget our friendship at various places in our former existence, that you will instruct me in the right path, and that you will inquire after my destiny either through a person or by letter.

First month, twenty-eighth day (of 692)

With respectful salutation,
Fazang

Essays

Works of prose by Korean writers are usually grouped according to the genre classifications in the *Selections of Refined Literature* (*Wenxuan*), by Xiao Tong (501–531), and the *Selections of Refined Literature in Korea* (*Tong munsŏn*), by Sŏ Kŏjŏng (1420–1488). Here we present two pieces, a discourse (*sŏl*) and an essay (*mun*), by Yi Kyubo, and a record (*ki*) each by the monk Sigyŏngam (1270–1350) and Yi Chehyŏn. Yi Kyubo and Yi Chehyŏn have been introduced in the section on poetry in literary Chinese. Sigyŏngam, teacher

8. The "Resplendent" buddha; *PDB*, 949–950.
9. The "Universally Worthy" bodhisattva; *PDB*, 745.

of the national preceptor Pogak (1329–1392) and specialist in the *Scripture on the Descent into Lanka*,[1] left only thirteen prose works. His essay on the virtues of bamboo reflects the point of view of the Meditation school of Korean Buddhism. Yi Chehyŏn's topographical essay describing actual, specifically named places is an exercise in the rejection of worldly temptations for the sake of a principled modesty in landscape, read as a system of signs. Here, as in Thoreau, the criterion of true possession is not ownership but enjoyment.

Next we have three pieces written in the vernacular, an unimportant language for male literati, by three accomplished ladies. The author of "Viewing the Sunrise," Lady Nam of Ŭiryŏng (1727–1823), accompanied her husband, Sin Taeson, to Hamhŭng in the northeast. There she wrote travel records, portraits, and diaries. "Viewing the Sunrise" represents her vivid and lyrical descriptive style at its best. "Lament for a Needle" is a delightful parody of a lamentation (*ae*) or dirge (*cho*), written in graceful language by Lady Yu (n.d.). The author of "The Dispute of a Woman's Seven Companions," also nameless, takes a fling at the members of her own sex. Her little story is told with great simplicity, with art concealing art, to friends gathered around a brazier on a winter night. It is interesting that she praises the perseverance of the thimble, portrayed as having mastered the secrets of life.

Yi Kyubo (1168–1241)

ON DEMOLISHING THE EARTHEN CHAMBER

[KOE T'OSIL SŎL]

On the first day of the tenth month, I came home and saw my sons digging a hole in the earth and building a hut like a grave. I feigned

---

1. *Laṅkāvatāra Sūtra; PDB*, 466–467.

stupidity and asked, "Why are you digging a grave within the premises of the house?"

They replied, "It is not a grave but an earthen chamber."

"Why have you made it?" I asked.

"It will be good for storing flowers and melons during the winter," they replied. "Womenfolk can come here and do their spinning and weaving without their hands getting chilled and chapped; even in winter it will be as warm as spring here."

I grew doubly angry and said, "That it is hot in summer and cold in winter is the regular course of the four seasons. If the opposite comes about, it will be strange and uncanny. The ancient sages taught humans to wear fur garments in winter and hempen ones in summer. This is sufficient for our needs. Building an earthen chamber to turn cold into heat is to resist the ordinances of heaven. In addition, it is inauspicious for men to dwell in holes in winter like snakes or toads. As for spinning and weaving, a proper season is set aside for them. Why should they be done in winter? Also, it is natural for flowers to bloom in the spring and fade in winter. If we reverse the process, we will surely go astray. To grow unseasonable things for untimely pleasures is to usurp the prerogatives of heaven. All this is not what I intend. If you don't destroy the earthen chamber at once, you will not be forgiven and will receive a good flogging from me."

My sons feared my anger and leveled the earthen chamber and made its lumber into firewood. Only then was my mind at peace.

QUESTIONS TO THE CREATOR

[MUN CHOMUL]

> I raise this question because I dislike such species as flies and mosquitoes.

I said to the Creator of the universe: "When Heaven gave birth to humans, it created humans first, and then the five grains so that humans would have things to eat. Then it created mulberry and hemp so that humans would have clothes to wear. This would indicate that Heaven created humans and desires that they live. But it is also true that Heaven created evil things. It created savage animals, such as bears, tigers, wolves, and jackals, and vermin such as mosquitoes, gadflies, fleas, and lice. Inferring from the existence of creatures that do great harm to man, it would seem that Heaven detests humans and wishes them dead. Why is Heaven so inconsistent in its love and hate?"

The Creator replied: "You ask about the birth of humans and other things. But from the remote beginning they came into being of themselves according to the spontaneous workings of nature. Heaven itself does not know why, nor do I. The birth of humans occurred of itself, not because of Heaven. The five grains and the mulberry and hemp came to the world of themselves, not because of Heaven. If so, how could Heaven discriminate among benefits and harms and manage good and evil? He who has the Way accepts good when it comes, without rejoicing, and accepts evil without dread. Because he takes all things as nothing, nothing can harm him."

I asked the Creator: "In the beginning primal material force divided itself into three powers: Heaven above, Earth below, and Humans in between. Since one principle runs through the three, is it possible that there are evil things in Heaven?"

The Creator replied: "Have I not said that nothing can harm a man who has the way? Could Heaven be less than a man with the way and harbor anything harmful?"

"Then, once humans attain the way, can they reach the Jade Palace of the Daoist trinity?"

"Yes."

"Now you have clearly dispelled my doubts. . . . But I am unclear on one point. You say Heaven does not know, nor do you. Heaven is nonaction, therefore it is natural if it does not know. But how could the Creator not know?"

The Creator replied: "Have you seen me create anything? Things come into being of themselves and change of themselves. How could

I fashion things, and how could I know? I do not even know that you call me Creator."

Translated by Uchang Kim

Monk Sigyŏngam (fl. 1270–1350)

A RECORD OF THE BAMBOO IN THE BAMBOO TOWER OF WŎLTŬNG MONASTERY

[WŎLTŬNGSA CHUNGNU CHUKKI]

In the southwest corner of Wŏltŭng monastery on Mount Hwa is Bamboo Tower; on a hill to the west stand thousands of bamboo, girding the back of the monastery. An old abbot, the great master of meditation, used to love the grove. One day he gathered friends in the tower and, pointing to the bamboo, said, "Please tell me the good qualities of bamboo."

One said, "Bamboo shoots are delicious. When the buds sprout, the joints are close together and the inside is soon filled with meat. Then you chop them down, cut up the meat, boil them in a sacrificial vessel, and roast them on the stove. Their aroma is sweet, their taste crisp. They fill your mouth and stomach. You will lose your taste for beef and pork fed on grain and look askance at the strong smelling meat of wild game. Eat bamboo shoots every morning and you will never tire of them. Such is the flavor of bamboo."

Another said, "The bamboo is strong, yet not strong; pliant, yet not pliant. It is fit to be used by humans. Bend it, and you can make a basket, a hamper, and a box. Cut it fine and bind it, and you have screens for the door; cut and weave it, and you have a mat for the hall; split and sharpen it, you have a box for clothes, a basket for cooked rice, a strainer for wine, a fodder-tub for the ox, and a water bag for the horse, as well as a round or square basket, wine skimmer, and wattle. Such are the uses of bamboo."

Still another said, "When the young sprouts come up, they cluster in rows, the small ones, the large ones, the early, the late, all in due order. At first they are tender, then they become tapered. When their tortoise-shell skin peels, their jade-red stalks grow tall. Then they shed their powder, the skin becoming white, and the white nodes are distinct. Their leaves like emerald smoke do not scatter, but cold winds rise from them. Their branches seem to murmur; their shade is deep. By evening their shadows play in the moonlight, and their chill figures are crowned with snow—such is the best time to enjoy them. From spring until the twelfth month you can chant verses here every day, dispel melancholy, and play with zest. Such is the elegance of bamboo."

A fourth said, "A bamboo a thousand fathoms high is called *xin*; one whose girth is several fathoms round, *shi*; one whose top is speckled, *chi*; dark-bodied ones, *yu*; prickly ones, *ba*; and hairy ones, *gan*. The staff from Qiongzhou in Sichuan, the flute from Qizhou in Hubei, the large-leaved ones from the Yangzi and the Han, the *dao* from Ba and Yu in Sichuan, the winter-sprouting ones from Lipu in Guangxi, the speckled ones from the rivers Yuan and Xiang, and the large ones called *yundang* growing in the marsh, and the flavorless *moye*—the names and appearances may differ from place to place. But their leaves do not fall even if the sea freezes, or dry up when it is hot enough to melt gold. Green and luxuriant, they do not change with the seasons. Therefore, the sage praised them and emulated them. They do not alter their determination according to time and place. Such is the integrity of bamboo."

Sigyŏngam said, "If I love the bamboo for its flavor, its usefulness, elegance, and integrity, all I get is externals, not its essence. When I look at the grace and height of a shoot since its sprouting, I realize how the embedded seed, once awakened, makes sudden progress. I look at it growing tougher as it ages, and I understand how cultivated power increases gradually. Its hollowness indicates that nature is empty. From its upright appearance, it is possible to deduce the true form of things. The transformation of its roots into a dragon I compare to a man's becoming a buddha. And feeding the phoenix with its fruit is its way of benefiting humans. My love of the bamboo stems not from what the four gentlemen have said, but from my own observations."

The master remarked," How profound! You are indeed a devoted friend of the bamboo."

I hasten to write these remarks down on the board as a model for future lovers of bamboo.

Yi Chehyŏn (1287–1367)

RECORD OF THE CLOUD BROCADE TOWER

[UNGŬMNU KI]

One need not go to remote places in search of beautiful scenery among mountains and streams. There are places of great natural beauty even in the midst of a capital city or a large town where people crowd together. Even if Mounts Heng and Lu, Dongting Lake, or the Xiao and Xiang Rivers were right before their eyes, those who compete for a name at court or wrangle for profit at the marketplace would not recognize their beauty. For one who pursues deer does not see the mountain; one who carries off gold does not see others; and one who can discern the tip of a fine hair overlooks a cartload of faggots. If a man is preoccupied with one thing, his eyes have no time for other sights.

Amateurs and those who travel at their own leisure pass through guardhouses and river crossings and choose their abodes in country villages. Then, roaming over hills and valleys and content in themselves, they recall Xie Lingyun (385–433),[1] who opened roads and frightened people, and Xu Fan,[2] who sought out a place for a country

---

1. Father of the "mountains and water" school of poetry.
2. Unknown.

house but was shunned by brave men. I say that both men were elegant!

To the south of the capital, there is a small lake, its area about sixteen acres. Along the shore, the houses of the commoners are joined together like scales on a fish or teeth on a comb. On the road that loops around the lake there is no end of passersby—some with loads on their backs or heads, some on foot, some mounted. Looking at their comings and goings, few would suspect that in the midst of this hustle and bustle there is a place secluded and rare, affording leisure and a broad view.

In the summer of the year *chŏngch'uk* (1337), Lord Hyŏnbok, Kwŏn Yŏm (1302–1340), seeing the lotuses in full bloom on the lake, at once fell in love with the place, bought a piece of land on the eastern shore, and built on it a tower about sixteen feet high and thirty feet across. There are no cornerstones, but the pillars have been treated to keep them from rotting. The roof is not covered with tiles but thatched with grass, yet it does not leak. The roofbeams are light and unplaned, yet straight. The walls have no paint, yet they are neither gaudy nor shabby. Whatever the external dimensions of the tower, its distinction is that it embraces the lotuses of the whole lake in its view.

The lord invited his father, Great Lord Kilch'ang, his brothers, and other relatives to a feast in the tower, and they passed so pleasant a time that the lord neglected to return home after sunset. One of his sons was good at large sinographs, so the lord had him write two graphs, Cloud Brocade, which were then hung up as the name of the tower.

I went there to see for myself. The place is beautiful indeed and worthy of its name: the fragrance of pink flowers and the green shadows of leaves cover both the lake and its shore; dewdrops shaken by the breeze fall into the water, gently rippling it. Not only this. The peaks of Mount Dragon, now blue, now green, their shadows changing with the light of morning and day, come up to the eaves of the tower.

Sitting in the tower, one can also observe the various aspects of a commoner's life and enjoy the sight of passersby—the loaded and the unencumbered, pedestrians and cavaliers, those who run and those who rest, onlookers and those who bow to their elders. While all this can be viewed and enjoyed, the passersby see only the lake and do not suspect there is a tower, much less someone watching them from it.

Natural beauty is not found only in remote places, but it cannot be discovered easily by the eyes and minds of seekers after office and profit. Perhaps heaven makes natural beauty and earth hides it so that men cannot find it easily.

Lord Hyŏnbok carries the seal of a myriarch and belongs to a family that married into the royal house. He is still under forty years of age. Whether in deep sleep or a drunken dream, he will enjoy fame, wealth, and honor. But he delights in the good and the wise. He does nothing that would frighten the people or make gentlemen shun him. He always lives in a secluded and empty place where the eyes of courtiers and merchants cannot reach. He delights his parents, and their happiness is passed on to friends; he enjoys happiness, and his happiness gladdens others. This is indeed praiseworthy!

The retired gentleman Ikchae (Yi Chehyŏn) hereby writes this record of the tower.

Translated by Uchang Kim and Peter H. Lee

Lady Nam of Ŭiryŏng (1727–1823)

VIEWING THE SUNRISE

[TONGMYŎNG ILGI]

I was anxious lest I miss the sunrise, so I slept not a wink all night. I often called out to a servant and asked for the boatman. He reported that I was sure to have a view, but I was impatient and could not calm myself. At cockcrow I shook the kisaeng girl and servants awake. A petty official arrived and told us that a supervisor in the office thought it too early to leave. Undeterred, I pressed a maid to cook rice-cake soup, which I left untouched. Then hurriedly I climbed to the terrace.

All was bathed in the serene light of the moon. The sea was whiter than the night before, and a gale chilled my bones. Gusts of winds shook hills and valleys, but the stars gleamed brightly in the east. It seemed that daybreak was still a while off. A wakened child was shivering, and the teeth of the kisaeng and servants chattered. My husband was worried that I might catch cold. Uneasy, I remained silent and sat still, giving no sign that I was cold. Dawn was slow in coming, so I summoned a servant, who replied that I had to wait. Only the breakers pounded the shore. A cold wind slashed at us, and the attendants around me hung their heads and buried their mouths in their chests, shivering. After a while the star in the east began to fade, the moon grew dim, and I could make out a streak of red light. With a cry of joy, I alighted from my sedan chair. The kisaeng and servants about me did not look up.

At last day broke, and I observed a long red aura, rolls of red silk spread on the sea, myriad acres dyed crimson and filling the sky. The angry waves were majestic, and the water the color of a red carpet; the spectacle was magnificent! The color then turned dark red, dyeing the faces and dresses of the onlookers. The swelling waves last night had been jade white, but now they stretched ruby red to the horizon. What a splendid sight!

The red color spread and the sky and water were bright, but the sun had not yet risen. Clapping her hands, the kisaeng said anxiously, "Now the sun is behind the waves. The red will turn to blue, and clouds will appear."

Disappointed, I was about to leave, but my husband and daughter encouraged me. "Don't worry. You'll see it," they said. Then Irang and Ch'asŏm said derisively, "We're used to watching the sun rise, so we know. You might get a chill, my lady, so why don't you go in and wait?"

I went back to my sedan chair, but a maid stopped me: "The sun will be up any minute. How could you leave now? Those girls are only guessing." Irang laughed and said, "They don't know any better. Don't believe what they say. Please go back and ask the boatman again." When the boatman replied that today's sunrise would be spectacular, I came out of the sedan and noticed that Ch'asŏm and Pobae, who had seen me entering the sedan, were gone, as were the three maids.

The splendid redness seemed to leap skyward. When Irang cried out to me to look down, I saw a red skein pushing through the swirls of clouds underwater, and a strange object the size of my palm, glowing like a charcoal on the last night of the month. As its reflection rose in the water, it seemed round as a chestnut but amber like a jewel, only more beautiful and brighter.

Above the red sea the object spiraled in circles, casting a shadow about the size of half a sheet of paper. Then the chestnut turned into a fireball as large as a tray, square and level, bouncing about and spilling redness over the length and breadth of the sea. The color began to fade, and now the sun sparkled like a jar, gleaming in ecstasy, blinding my eyes. The air, tinged with red, was brisk and clear. I could count the first pink rays, and then the tray turned into a wheel of fire pushing skyward. No longer gleams from a jar, the rays that had earlier touched the sea now were like tongues of thirsty cattle about to leap into the ocean with a splash. The vast expanse of sky and water was dazzling, but the waves began to lose their hue, and the sun now was sharp and bright. Where else could one see such a spectacle?

When I think back, the first sight of the half sheet of paper came when the sun was about to emerge from the sea, its direct rays polishing the water. It resembled an amber chestnut when it was halfway above the horizon, seemingly half afloat, soaking up the red from the ocean. And when it was jar-shaped, the lovely object blinded me and more closely resembled a phantom. Ch'asŏm and Pobae, who had left earlier, came up to the sedan to congratulate me on viewing the sunrise at the hour of the hare (5–7 a.m.), while Irang, clapping her hands, was pleased that I at last saw what I had longed for.

When I was about to leave, village women milled around to bid me farewell, asking for parting gifts. I gave them some money to share among themselves.

On the way back to my lodging, I felt as if I had found a priceless treasure.

Lady Yu (n.d.)

LAMENT FOR A NEEDLE

[CHOCH'IM MUN]

On a certain day of a certain month in a certain year, a certain widow addresses a needle with a few words. To a woman the needle is an indispensable tool, though commonly people do not cherish it.

You are only a small thing, but I mourn you greatly, because so many memories are connected with you. Alas, what a loss, what a pity! It has been twenty-seven years since I first held you in my hand. How could a sensitive human being feel otherwise? How sad! Holding back my tears and calming my heart, I bid my last farewell to you by hastily writing down this account of your deeds, and my memories.

Years ago, my uncle-in-law was chosen as the head of the Winter Solstice Felicitation mission to China, and upon his return from Peking he gave me dozens of needles. I sent some to my parents' home and some to my relatives, and divided the rest among my servants. I then chose you, and got to know you, and we have been together ever since. How sad! The ties between us are of an extraordinary nature. Although I have lost or broken many other needles, I have kept you for years. You may be unfeeling, but how could I not love you and be charmed by you! What a loss, what a disappointment!

I was unlucky, I had no children, but I went on living. Moreover, our fortunes began to fail, so I devoted myself to sewing and you helped me forget my sorrow and manage my household. Today I bid you farewell. Alas, this must have come about through the jealousy of the spirits and the enmity of heaven.

How regrettable, my needle, how pitiful! You were a special gift of fine quality, a thing out of the ordinary, prominent among ironware. Deft and swift like some knight-errant, straight and true like a loyal subject, your sharp point seemed to talk, your round eye seemed to see. When I embroidered phoenixes and peacocks on thick silk or thin, your wondrously agile movements seemed the workings of a spirit. No human effort could have matched you.

Alas! Children may be precious, but they leave when the time comes. Servants may be obedient, but they grumble at times. When I consider your subtle talents, so responsive to my needs, you are far better than children or servants. I made you a silver case enameled in fine colors and carried you on the tie string of my blouse, a lady's trinket. I used to feel you there whenever I ate or slept, and we became friends. Before beaded screens in summer or by lamplight in winter, I used to quilt, broad-stitch, hem, sew, or make finishing stitches with double thread, and your movement was like a phoenix brandishing its tail. When I sewed stitch by stitch, your two ends went together harmoniously to attach seam to seam. Indeed, your creative energy was endless.

I intended to live with you for a hundred years, but alas, my needle! On the tenth day of the tenth month of this year, at the hour of the dog (7–9 p.m.), while I was attaching a collar to a court robe in dim lamplight, you broke. You caught me unawares, and I was stunned. Alas, you had broken in two. My spirit was numbed and my soul flew away, as if my heart had been pulverized and my brain smashed. When I recovered from my long faint, I touched you and tried to put you back together, but it was no use. Not even the mystic arts of a renowned physician could prolong your life, nor could a village artisan patch you up. I felt as if I had lost an arm or a leg. How pitiful, my needle! I felt at my collar, but no trace of you remained.

Alas, it was my fault. I ended your innocent life, so whom else could I loathe or reproach? How can I ever hope to see an adept nature or ingenious talent like yours again? Your exquisite shape haunts my eyes, and your special endowments fill me with yearning. If you have any feeling, we will meet again in the underworld to continue our companionship. I hope we may share happiness and sorrow, and live and die together. Alas, my needle!

Anonymous

THE DISPUTE OF A WOMAN'S SEVEN COMPANIONS

[KYUJUNG CH'IRU CHAENGNON KI]

The lifelong companions of a woman are seven: a yardstick, a pair of scissors, a needle, blue and pink threads, a thimble, a long-handled iron, and a regular iron. The lady of a household is in charge of them all, and none of them can keep a secret from the others.

A certain lady who often used to work with the help of her seven indispensable companions one day felt sleepy and dozed off.

Brandishing her slender body, the yardstick said, "Friends, listen. I am so perceptive I can measure the long, the short, the narrow, and the wide. It's because of me that my lady does not fail in her work. Don't you think my merits far exceed yours?"

Thereupon, the scissors grew angry. Shaking her long mouth, she replied, "Don't praise yourself so. Without my mouth, nothing could be shaped or formed. It is only through my services that your measurements become reality. Hence my merits exceed yours."

The needle reddened. "Don't argue, my two friends. However well you measure or cut, nothing is accomplished without me. So I am the first in merit," she retorted.

The blue and pink threads roared with laughter. "Don't talk non-sense. The proverb says, 'Three bushels of pearls have to be strung to become a treasure.' What could you accomplish without us?"

Then the old thimble laughed. "Don't quarrel, threads. Let me cut in. I cover tactfully the sore spot on the fingers of the old and young, so that they can finish their work easily. So how can you say I'm without merit? Like a shield on the battlefield, I help to get the work done, no matter how difficult it is."

The long-handled iron, fuming with rage, moved forward in a single stride. "You all want to show off your talents, but listen to me if you don't want to be called fools. My foot can smooth out wrinkles and correct what is crooked and bent. It's my work you're taking the credit for. Without me, you'd be ashamed to face our mistress no matter how hard you tried."

Choking with laughter, the iron said, "How true the word of the long-handled iron. Were it not for our service, who could talk about rewards?"

Their wordy warfare woke the lady, who suddenly rose up in anger. "What merits are you talking about? It is my eyes and hands that make you do what you do. How can you wrangle impudently behind my back and indulge in self-praise?"

The yardstick sighed and mumbled, "How unkind and unfeeling is humankind. How could she measure anything without me? As if this were not enough, she uses me to thrash the maidservants. I've held out this long only because I happen to be strong, and it saddens me that our mistress takes no notice of this."

The scissors joined in tearfully, "How unkind my mistress is. Day after day she forces open my mouth and cuts thick and hard fabrics just as she pleases. But if I am not to her liking, she strikes my two cheeks with an iron hammer, accuses me of having thick lips or blunt edges, and whets me. For her to talk like that, after all she's done to me."

The needle heaved a long sigh. "I was made from an iron stick belonging to the fairy Magu of Mount Tiantai and polished for ten years on a rock. She inserts thick and thin threads through my eye and make a hole with my leg through all kinds of dress goods. What an odious chore! Overcome with fatigue, sometimes I prick her under the fingernail and draw blood, but there's no relief."

The blue and pink threads chimed in, "How can we tell all our sorrow? Clothes of men and women, fine quilts, children's colorful dresses—how could one sew a single seam without us? When lazy ladies and girls pull us through the needle's eye too hard, or when we cannot pass through it easily, they curse us in unspeakable language. What is our crime, and how can we bear this grief?"

"My resentment is immeasurable," the long-handled iron complained. "For what retribution am I stuck in a brazier day and night throughout the seasons? After children have used me sloppily to iron the clothes for their dolls, they stick me in any old way until some woman picks me up and scolds me for not being warm enough, or for being too light or too heavy. They make me feel there is no place for me in the world."

"Your sorrow is like mine," the iron said, "so there is no point rehearsing it. They put burning charcoal in my mouth; it's like the tyrant Zhou's[1] cruel punishments of roasting and branding. Only because my face is tough and hardened can I bear it. And that's not all. Lazy women will put off their work for ten or even fifteen days. Then they blame me for the wrinkles that will not come out."

The old thimble leaped forward and waved her hand: "Listen, girls. I'm half dead from overwork, too; stop chattering on and on. If our mistress hears, all your sins will be visited on me."

"What if she does?" they replied. "She cannot manage without us."

The lady finally scolded, "You dared to criticize my behavior while I was asleep," and dismissed them all. They were withdrawing in despair when the old thimble fell prostrate. "The young ones acted

---

1. The last evil ruler of Shang.

thoughtlessly. Please calm your anger and forgive them," she begged the lady.

Thereupon the lady called all of them together. "I forgive you for the sake of the old thimble," she said. She promised the thimble never to be parted from her, and to this day she cherishes her as her most intimate friend.

Memoirs

Princess Hyegyŏng (1735–1815), the second daughter of the chief state counselor Hong Ponghan, was born on August 6, 1735. At the age of nine she was chosen to marry the crown prince, Sado (1735–1762), and she was officially appointed in the following year. Over the next decade and a half, the prince developed symptoms of mental illness, and his stern father, King Yŏngjo (1724–1776), finally ordered that he be sealed within a wooden rice chest, where he died seven days later—the only known filicide in the history of Chosŏn. Hyegyŏng's misfortunes did not cease when her son became king, succeeding Yŏngjo, and are recounted at some length in her memoirs, *A Record of Sorrowful Days* (*Hanjung nok*), written in the vernacular in four increments from 1795 to 1805.

As a witness and focal point of the political intrigue surrounding the court in eighteenth-century Korea, Hyegyŏng seeks to articulate and repossess the life and times she has known. Keenly aware of the destiny to which she was born, she searches for the meaning of her tormented existence throughout her experiences as a child, crown princess, widow, and queen mother. While she indicates that she wrote her memoirs to enlighten others, she must also have found it therapeutic. Her memories can be partial, faulty, and self-serving, but her voice captures the truth of her feelings and is rendered with attention to the language and rhythms of the eighteenth century, true to her time. She is at her happiest in the reconstruction of her all-too-brief childhood, as the following episode, written in 1795, shows.

Princess Hyegyŏng (1735–1815)

A Record of Sorrowful Days

[HANJUNG NOK]

That year (1743) an edict was issued requiring families with eligible daughters to register them for selection. Someone said, "There will be no harm done if you don't register your daughter. A poor family like yours should be spared the burden of preparing the clothing required for the process." "No," replied Father. "We have been salaried officials for generations. I receive a stipend from the court, and my child is the granddaughter of the Minister of Rites. I dare not deceive the court." Father then registered me.

At the time, we were so poor there was no way for us to have a new wardrobe made. My skirt was sewn from fabric that had been stored away for the marriage of my deceased elder sister, and old material was used for linings. Even so, we had to borrow money. The image of Mother making every effort to complete the preparations still haunts me.

The first of the three sittings was held on the twenty-eighth day of the ninth month (November 13). In spite of my inferior gifts, King Yŏngjo was extravagant with praise, and the queen gazed steadily on me. The mother of the prince, Royal Consort Yi, beaming with happiness, summoned me before the ceremony and was very affectionate. When court ladies scrambled for seats, I was so embarrassed I could hardly think. When it was time to bestow royal gifts, Royal Consort Yi and her daughter, Princess Hwap'yŏng, noted my deportment and tried to correct my clumsiness, and I followed their instructions. I then left the palace for home and slept that night in Mother's arms.

Early the next morning Father came in and spoke anxiously to Mother. "What shall we do? Everyone seems sure our daughter will be the one favored." "We shouldn't have registered her," Mother whispered, "the daughter of a poor, unknown scholar." In my sleep I overheard their worried words and woke up crying. Recalling the kindness I enjoyed at the palace, I was perplexed. Mother and Father tried to comfort me. "Do you think she understands?" they asked each other. I was deeply troubled in the period following the first sitting. Was it because I knew I would suffer many ups and downs at court? On the one hand I felt strange, but on the other this sensation seemed truly to forebode what was to come.

Word of my rating after the first sitting brought a large number of clansmen to our home. Servants we had not seen for years returned as well. This taught me much about our private and social life.

The second sitting was held on the twenty-eighth day of the tenth month (December 13). I was terribly frightened. Mother and Father too were worried; they hoped that by sheer chance I would not be selected. When I entered the palace grounds, however, I sensed that the choice had already been made; my temporary quarters had been refurbished, and I was treated with a new deference and respect. I lost my composure as I ascended to the royal presence. The king did not treat me as he did the other girls, but instead made his way past the beaded screen and began stroking me affectionately. "We've gained a beautiful daughter-in-law. We remember your grandfather well. When we had your father in audience, we were pleased because we knew we had gained a capable man. You are indeed his daughter!" His Majesty was most pleased. The queen and Royal Consort Yi were also pleased beyond words and showered me with affection. The princesses gathered around me, holding my hands, and they did not want to let me go. I remained a long while in a building called Kyŏngch'un Hall, and there a luncheon was served to me. A lady-in-waiting tried to remove my green jacket. I did not want to take it off, but she coaxed and cajoled me until I relented. After she took my jacket off, she measured my various parts. I was so startled I fought back tears of humiliation until at last I mounted the palanquin to leave the palace; then I cried. The palanquin was carried by palace servants. In the street the rows of black-robed women servants charged with delivering royal messages were an eerie sight.

When we arrived home, I was carried through the gate reserved for male visitors. Father raised the screen covering the palanquin and lifted me out. He had on his ceremonial robe and seemed uneasy treating me with deference. I clung to my parents and could not hold back the tears. Mother too was attired in her ceremonial robes, and the table was decked with a scarlet cover. Mother appeared somewhat awe-stricken as she kowtowed four times before accepting the missive from the queen, and twice before accepting one from Lady Yi.

From that day on my parents began to use honorific expressions with me, and the elders of the clan treated me with respect—all this made me feel uncomfortable and indescribably sad. Greatly apprehensive, Father gave me thousands of words of advice. I felt like a sinner who has no place of refuge. I did not want to leave my Father and Mother. My heart felt as though I would melt away—nothing seemed to interest me.

Close relatives and distant clansmen wanted to see me before I entered the palace. Not a single relative failed to visit us. Distant ones were entertained in the courtyard. The important ones included my great-great-uncle from Yangju. One great-uncle remarked, "The palace is very strict. Once you enter its confines, we may not have the chance to meet again. Always respect your superiors and act with prudence. The letter *kam* in my name means 'mirror' and *po* means 'help.' Keep this in mind after you have entered the palace." I seldom saw my great-uncle, so for some reason his words made me sad.

The third sitting was scheduled for the thirteenth day of the eleventh month (December 28). With the passing of each day my grief grew more unbearable and I slept each night in Mother's arms. Father's sisters and his sister-in-law tried to comfort me; they stroked me tenderly and were unwilling to take their leave. Father and Mother caressed me night and day, losing several nights' sleep. Even today my heart chokes when I think of those final days.

Two court ladies appeared at our home the day after the second sitting. One of them was Lady-in-waiting Ch'oe, governess to the prince, and the other was Kim Hyodŏk, an overseer of the attendants. Unlike the others, Lady-in-waiting Ch'oe had a stern and imposing mien. Her family had served in the palace for generations, so she was conversant with the intricate court protocol and never made a blunder. Mother was cordial and made the two ladies feel welcome. They measured me for clothing and left. Lady-in-waiting Ch'oe returned before the third sitting, accompanied this time by Mun Taebok, another overseer. They presented me a gift of clothing from the queen—a formal dress jacket of green brocade, another of pine-pollen yellow with grape designs, and a third of lavender silk, along with a crimson satin skirt and a summer jacket of fine cambric.

I had never before owned such fine dresses and had never coveted the clothing of others. There was a girl my own age among our close relatives. Her family was wealthy and provided her with every possible item of clothing and toilette, but I never envied her. One day she came to visit wearing a gorgeous deep-red lined skirt with elaborate seams. Mother watched for a while, then asked me, "Would you like to have a dress like that?" "If I owned one, I would surely wear it," I answered, "but I don't want one if we have to have it made." "You may be the daughter of an impoverished family," Mother said, "but when you marry, I'll make you a beautiful dress like that one as a remembrance of the maturity you displayed today." Before the third sitting, when it became evident that I was fated to marry the prince, Mother came to me in tears. "We couldn't afford to give you beautiful dresses, but I never forgot my promise to you. Though you will soon be entering the palace, where common costume is not allowed, I dearly wish to fulfill that promise to you." She made the skirt before the third sitting came, and grieved. When I wore it, I dissolved in tears.

I felt that it would be appropriate to bid farewell to the ancestors of my clan and to Mother's family, and I made my desire known. My wish was conveyed through the sister-in-law of Pak Myŏngwŏn, who was married to Princess Hwap'yŏng, King Yŏngjo's second daughter, to the mother of the princess, Royal Consort Yi. His Majesty was soon informed of my wish and commanded me to go.

Mother and I rode in the same palanquin and proceeded to the head house of the Hong clan, the house of a cousin of my father (Hong Sanghan). Because he and his wife had no daughter, they had often invited me to come and stay with them. Their love for me was known to His Majesty, who ordered Hong Sanghan to help with the preparations for my marriage. After I was selected, he came and stayed with us. When Mother and I arrived at his home, his wife was delighted to see me. I was led up to the ancestral shrine to perform obeisances. Though it was customary for younger generations to perform the kowtows in the courtyard, I worshiped the spirits in the main hall of the house. I was stunned by the perquisites of my new status.

We then went to the home of Mother's family, where we were received by the wife of Mother's brother. She was pleased to see us and reluctant to let us go. On previous visits, my cousins took joy in giving me great hugs and in carrying me around on their backs. This time, however, they took pains to maintain a decorous distance and treated me with deference, which made me feel sad. I was particularly fond of one of my cousins, who later married into the Sin clan, and I was very sorry to take leave of her. On our way home we stopped to pay our respects to Mother's two older sisters.

The days flew. Soon it was the twelfth day of the eleventh month. That night Father's sisters led me outside. "Take a good look at your home, for it will be the last time," they urged me, as they led me by the hand into the bright moonlight. The chilly wind blew over the snow, and tears coursed down my cheeks. I lay awake the whole night.

The command summoning me came by messenger early the next morning, and I donned the formal dress provided by the queen. The wives of clansmen came to bid final farewells, and close relatives gathered to accompany me to the detached palace. We all went up to the ancestral shrine and performed a special service to inform the spirits of the great honor being bestowed on the family. Father struggled to hold back his tears as he intoned the prayer.

Parting was more than we could bear. I cannot find words adequate to describe the sorrowful scene.

I entered the palace compound, resting first at the Kyŏngch'un Hall before continuing on to the T'ongmyŏng Hall, where I was received in audience by the Three Majesties—the king, the queen, and Queen Dowager Inwŏn. It was the first time the queen dowager had seen me. "This girl is beautiful and looks very kind," she said. "She is a blessing to the kingdom." His Majesty patted me affectionately. "Our daughter-in-law is bright. We made a good choice." I cannot express in words the delight of the queen and the sincere affection of Royal Consort Yi. Though of childish mind, I was grateful for the royal favor.

I freshened my makeup and changed into the ceremonial dress. After I had eaten, it was growing late; I performed the four kowtows to the Three Majesties and then left for the detached palace. His Majesty appeared in person at the place where I mounted my palanquin; he looked at me and took my hand. "We want you to be happy. We'll send you a copy of the *Elementary Learning*.[1] Study it with your father and be happy until you return again to us." He favored me with his tender love.

Dusk settled and the lanterns were lit as I left the palace. Being surrounded by ladies-in-waiting, I was unable to sleep; I wanted Mother at my side. I was unhappy without her and could easily imagine how sadness must weigh heavily upon her heart. Lady-in-waiting Ch'oe, however, was strict and bereft of human feelings. She had explained, "The laws of the kingdom do not allow you to stay on, my

1. *Xiaoxue* by Zhu Xi (1130–1200); see Kelleher, "Back to Basics," 219–251.

lady," and with that, had sent Mother away, so that I was unable to get any sleep. There was no human being as inconsiderate as she!

The following day His Majesty sent me a copy of the *Elementary Learning.* I studied it every day with Father. The head of our clan was with us, as were Father's brothers, Hong Inhan and Hong Chunhan, the latter a mere boy at the time. My oldest brother was also with us. The king sent a reader, too, for me to peruse in my spare moments, one which His Majesty had written for Princess Hyosun (1715–1751) when she married the former crown prince.[2]

My quarters were well appointed with furniture, curtains, folding screens, and toilette articles. Among these was a large Japanese pendant shaped like an eggplant. It was a gift from Royal Consort Yi and had once belonged to Princess Chŏngmyŏng—daughter of King Sŏnjo (1567–1608)—who had married my great-great-grandfather. She had presented the pendant to her granddaughter, who had married into the Cho clan. Either the family sold it, or it had fallen into the hands of the family of a lady-in-waiting who attended the royal consort. Now I, a descendant of the princess, was again in possession of a family heirloom that had once belonged to her. Surely this was more than mere chance.

My grandfather was a lover of art and had owned an embroidered screen in four panels. After he passed away (1740), one of his servants sold the screen. Later, Royal Consort Yi purchased it from a relative of one of her attendants, had it remounted, and gave it to me to put up in my bedroom. When my aunt visited me she recognized the screen at once. "This is most strange," she said. "An object owned by your grandfather has found its way into the palace and now stands in his granddaughter's bedroom!"

Another gift from the royal consort was her own eight-panel dragon screen. Father was astonished when he saw it. "The dragon

2. Yŏngjo's first son (1719–1728), temple name Chinjong, was appointed crown prince in 1725.

on this screen is just like the one that appeared in a dream I had the night before you were born . . ." The dragon's black scales were highlighted with gold thread so that the gold and black intermingled. Father mused, "This dragon is not completely black, but otherwise it's exactly like the dragon of my dream." Everyone marveled at the return of grandfather's screen and the similarity of the embroidered dragon to the one in Father's dream.

I stayed over fifty days in the detached palace. During that time I was often favored by visits from the lady-in-waiting sent by the Three Majesties to inquire after my welfare. On each occasion, at the wishes of the Three Majesties, my family was invited to visit me, and they were treated with hospitality. A visit by a lady-in-waiting was followed by the appearance of officials from the Ministry of Rites, who brought a table and wine cups. . . .

On the ninth day of the first month (February 21, 1744), I was invested as crown princess; the state marriage was scheduled for the eleventh. My separation from Father and Mother was nearing. I could no longer control my feelings and cried the whole day long. Father and Mother were sad and worried but managed to hold their composure. "When the daughter of a subject marries into the royal house," Father warned, "her family wins favor and her house flourishes. But when the family flourishes, disaster is sure to follow. Our house has enjoyed great favor for generations because my ancestor married a princess. Having enjoyed royal favor, I cannot shrink from boiling water or scorching fire. Still, for a lowly scholar to become overnight the father-in-law of the crown prince—this is not a portent of happiness but the beginning of disaster. From this day on I will live in fear and anxiety, not knowing when I will die." Father instructed me in even the smallest aspects of my daily conduct. "Respectfully serve the Three Majesties and discharge your filial duties. Be helpful to the crown prince with right actions and always be cautious in your speech. Add luster to the good fortune of your family and your kingdom." Though Father's exhortations on the last day ran to thousands of words, I listened with respect. But I could not keep back my tears. Even the trees and stones must have been touched by my grief!

After the marriage ceremony, Father and Mother continued their admonitions, which I heeded with respect. Father wore the deep-red official robes and cap of one who has passed the civil service examinations. Mother wore her large ceremonial wig and the dress with the lime top and violet collar. All our kinsmen came to bid me farewell, and the palace was surging with guests. Every movement of Father and Mother conformed to the rules of propriety, and their deportment was grave and correct. Everyone said, "The kingdom has gained exemplary in-laws."

Satire

"The Story of Gentleman Hŏ" (*Hŏsaeng chŏn*) is by Pak Chiwŏn (1737–1805), a champion of practical learning who wished to illuminate the workings of contemporary political, economic, and social institutions. Pak's objective was a vision of the independent, self-employed farmer as the foundation of a sound agricultural economy and a healthy society. In his story, the poverty-stricken Hŏ breaks out of the mores of his class to become a merchant. His aim, however, is not to make a profit but to show how money can be used. He pokes fun at the empty forms and pretensions of the literati class and dreams of a society that is able to stand alone.

"The Story of a Yangban" (*Yangban chŏn*), also by Pak Chiwŏn, is a delightful vignette on the same theme, which trusts the reader's intelligence. Chŏng Yagyong (1762–1836), another champion of practical learning and reform, casts a satirical eye on the psychology of the servant class in "On Dismissing a Servant" (*Ch'ultong mun*). "The Story of a Pheasant Cock" (*Changkki chŏn*), written in Korean, takes the form of a beast fable. The pheasant cock, the most loquacious and pedantic bird in Korean literature, represents the re-flexive male ego that demands conformity to the dominant culture. The pheasant hen, in rejecting the traditional role of a passive and servile wife, exposes the social forces that limit the choices open to women. A product of the times, this anonymous fable is a comment on the disparity and dilemmas of late Chosŏn life. References in it to the *Book of Songs, Historical Records,* and *Romance of the Three Kingdoms*—the most popular works of Chinese poetry, historiography, and fiction at the time—suggest the staple reading of the average educated person.

In these stories, the authors' views on the prospects for humans in the society they've created are not melancholy; they do not distort reality in an attempt to make human follies more ridiculous than they actually are. Characterized by comic detachment, these compact and indirect stories exude humor and laughter.

Pak Chiwŏn (1737–1805)

THE STORY OF GENTLEMAN HŎ

[HŎSAENG CHŎN]

Gentleman Hŏ lived in Mukchŏk village. Those who went straight up the valley beside Mount South came to a well in the shadow of an old gingko tree. The twig gate to Hŏ's house, which faced the gingko tree, was always open, and his small thatched cottage was exposed to the wind and rain. But Hŏ loved to read books. His wife eked out a living by taking in sewing.

One day, no longer able to endure her gnawing hunger, Hŏ's wife began to weep and pour out her dissatisfactions. "You've never taken the civil service examination. What's the use of reading?"

Hŏ laughed and answered, "I haven't finished my studies yet."

"Couldn't you then become a craftsman?"

"How could I? I've never learned any kind of skill."

"Well, then, what about becoming a merchant?"

"How can I become a merchant when I have no capital?"

Her patience spent, Hŏ's wife shouted angrily, "How can I? How can I? Is that all you've learned from the books you've been reading day and night? You cannot be a craftsman, nor can you be a merchant. How about becoming a thief?"

At this, Hŏ closed his book and stood up. "What a pity! It was my plan to study for ten years; I have studied only seven years now."

Hŏ went out of the house. But he knew no one else in town. He walked up and down Unjong Street before finally asking in the market for the name of the richest man in town.

He was told that this would be a certain Pyŏn. Hŏ went to Pyŏn's house. When he was presented to Pyŏn, he bowed low and said, "I am poor and have no money to start a business, but I would like to try out an idea that I have, if you would lend me ten thousand *yang* in cash."

"Fine," said Pyŏn, and he gave Hŏ the cash at once. Hŏ took the money and left without a word of thanks. To Pyŏn's sons and all the guests gathered around, Hŏ appeared to be a beggar. His belt was threadbare, the heels of his leather shoes were completely worn down, his hat was battered, and his coat was dirty. On top of that, his nose was running.

"Do you know this man?" Pyŏn's friends asked, astonished to see him giving money to someone like that.

"No."

"You have given away ten thousand to a complete stranger without even asking his name. What are you going to do?"

Pyŏn answered, "You wouldn't have understood. A man who is trying to get a loan usually speaks at great length. He says that he will not fail to keep his word, that there will be no cause for worry on his account, and so on. He usually looks shamefaced and tends to repeat himself. But this man we have just met—his clothes and shoes may have been tattered, but he spoke to the point with no trace of shame. He is a man who is not interested in material wealth; he is content with his life. Therefore, what he has in mind in the way of a business deal must be something big, and I am curious to see what he does. If I hadn't given him the money, I might have asked his name. But what's the use of asking his name when I have already given him the cash?"

Having so easily obtained the money, Hŏ thought, "Ansŏng is at the border of Kyŏnggi and Ch'ungch'ŏng provinces, and all the roads to the three southern provinces meet there." Not even stopping at his house, he went straight to Ansŏng and secured a place to stay. The next day he went to the market and began to buy all the fruit he could find—jujubes, chestnuts, persimmons, pears, pomegranates, oranges, tangerines, and pomelo. He paid double to buy them all up, gaining a monopoly in fruit.

Before long, no feasts could be held or sacrifices offered. Now the fruit merchants came running to Hŏ to buy back what they had sold him at ten times the price he had paid. Hŏ sighed and said to himself, "What a pity that a mere ten thousand in cash can jeopardize the country's economy! By this we may easily gauge the shallowness of the country."

After he had sold all the fruit, he bought knives, hoes, cotton, hemp, and silk. Then he crossed over to Cheju Island, where he bought all the horse tails he could find. "Within a few years, no one in the country will be able to cover his head," he said. Before long, as expected, the price of horsehair hats rose to ten times the usual.

One day, Hŏ asked an old sailor, "Do you know of any uninhabited island where a man could live without hardship?"

"Yes, sir. Once, long ago, I was caught in a storm for three days and three nights. Finally I landed on an island. I believe it was somewhere between Macao and Nagasaki. There were flowers and trees everywhere, and fruit and cucumbers were ripening with no one to look after them. Deer strolled in herds, and the fish in the sea were unafraid of men."

Hŏ was greatly pleased. "If you will take me there, I will share all my wealth with you."

The sailor agreed. On a day with favorable winds they sailed due southeast and reached the island. Hŏ climbed a peak and gazed all about, but he seemed dissatisfied. "This island is not even one thousand tricents wide. What can be done with it? But since the soil is fertile and the water is sweet, here I could live a life of seclusion like a wealthy man."

"On a deserted island like this, with not a soul to be seen, who would there be to live with?" the sailor asked.

"People will follow a virtuous man. I worry about my lack of virtue, not about the lack of people."

At the time, the area around Pyŏnsan[1] was being plundered by thousands of bandits. The provincial government mobilized troops but could not root them out. As defenses became stronger, however, it became increasingly difficult for the bandits to plunder the towns, and they were finally driven back, without provisions, to their remote fastness. Only starvation awaited them in the end.

Hearing this, Hŏ went alone to the bandits' hideout and began to speak persuasively to the leader. "If you stole one thousand in cash and divided it among the thousand of you, how much would each of you receive?"

"One *yang,* of course."

"Does any of you have a wife?"

"No."

"Do you own fields?"

"Why would we rob and endure hardships if we had wives and fields?"

"If you really mean that, why don't you marry, build a house, buy an ox, and till the land? If you do so, you won't be called a thief, you'll enjoy a happy marriage, and you'll be able to go where you please without fear of arrest. How nice that would be! You'll have clothing and food for the rest of your life."

1. Puan in North Chŏlla.

"Who doesn't want that? It's just that we don't have the money!"

Hŏ smiled and said, "Imagine bandits worrying about money! If all you need is money, I will provide it. If you go to the seashore to-morrow, you will see boats flying red flags. They will all be loaded with money. Take as much as you want."

With that, Hŏ made his departure. So fantastic had his words seemed to the thieves that they all laughed at him and called him mad.

Still, they did go to the seashore on the following day. There they saw Hŏ waiting with three hundred thousand in cash aboard his boats. Greatly amazed, they lined up and bowed to him. "We will do whatever the general orders us to do."

"Well then, try taking as much money as you can carry on your backs."

The bandits crowded around the money bags, but none was able to carry more than one hundred *yang*.

"How could you, who cannot carry more than one hundred *yang*, be robbers? Now that your names are listed as thieves by the government, you cannot return to civilian life. You have no place to go. I have a good idea. Each of you take one hundred *yang* and get a woman and an ox. I will wait here."

The thieves agreed and dispersed in all directions.

Hŏ waited with provisions sufficient for two thousand people for one year. All the bandits returned on the appointed day. When all were aboard, the ships set sail for the island. Since Hŏ had shipped out all of the bandits, life on the mainland became peaceful again.

The island's new inhabitants began at once to cut down trees, build houses, and erect bamboo fences. The soil was so rich that the crops flourished even when Hŏ's men neglected them.

So abundant was the harvest that a surplus remained, even after three years' worth of reserves had been laid away. Therefore Hŏ's men loaded the surplus onto the boats, sailed to Nagasaki, and sold it there. Nagasaki, a Japanese territory with 310,000 households, was at that time suffering from a great famine, so Hŏ's men were able to sell all that they had brought, and they returned home with one million in silver.

"Now I have seen my idea realized," Hŏ murmured. He called all his two thousand together and said, "When I came here with you, I planned to make you rich first, and then to invent a new writing system and new styles of clothing, including hats. But the land is small and my virtue is slight, so I am now going to leave this place. When you have children, teach them to hold their spoon in their right hand and to eat after their elders." Then Hŏ had all the boats burned. "If no one goes out, no one will come." Also, he threw five hundred thousand in silver into the sea. "Somebody will find it when the tide is out. Not even on the mainland could one spend a million *yang*. Of what use would it be in this small place?"

Finally, he called forth all those who could read and bade them board the boat. "I'm plucking the roots of strife from the soil of this island," he said.

Thereafter Hŏ went around the country, helping the poor. Yet there remained one hundred thousand in silver. "I shall repay Pyŏn."

Thus, Hŏ finally called on Pyŏn. "Do you remember me?" he asked.

Pyŏn was surprised. "Your complexion has not improved at all. You must have lost all of the ten thousand," he replied.

Hŏ smiled and said, "It is people like you who improve their complexions with money. How could ten thousand in cash nourish the way?" Then he paid back one hundred thousand in silver and said, "I did not finish my studies because one morning I could no longer endure the hunger. Your ten thousand *yang* has brought me only feelings of shame."

Pyŏn was so astounded that he jumped to his feet, bowed to Hŏ, and said that he only wanted one-tenth interest.

"How can you treat me as a merchant?" Hŏ said. Shaking his sleeves, he took his leave.

Pyŏn stealthily followed Hŏ, who went down the valley next to Mount South and entered a small cottage.

"Whose cottage is that?" Pyŏn asked an old woman washing clothes by the well.

"That is Hŏ's place. He was poor, but he always liked to read. One morning, he left home and did not return for five years. His wife lived alone and observed memorial services on the day of his departure."

Thus Pyŏn finally came to know the man's name. He sighed and turned back.

The next day, Pyŏn called on the cottage with all the silver he had received. Yet Hŏ would not accept it. "If I wanted to be rich, would I have thrown away one million to take one hundred thousand in its stead?" he asked. "Henceforth I shall rely on your supporting and looking after us. If you send enough grain for my family and enough cloth to clothe us, I shall be content all my life. Why should I wish to trouble my mind with money?"

Pyŏn tried in a hundred ways to persuade Hŏ, but Hŏ remained adamant. Pyŏn brought food and clothing to Hŏ ever after this, and always in good time. Hŏ was always glad to see Pyŏn, but if he brought too much, Hŏ would immediately show his displeasure and say, "Why do you wish to bring evil to my house?" If Pyŏn brought wine, however, he was given an especially warm welcome, and the two friends would raise cups until they were drunk. Thus the friendship of the two grew deeper over the years.

One day, Pyŏn asked calmly, "How did you make a million in five years?"

"This will make sense to you," Hŏ answered. "Our country has no trade with other countries, and everything we use is produced and consumed in the same province. With a mere one thousand, you can't buy up everything in sight. But if you divide that amount by ten, you can choose ten different items and buy a good amount of each. If the goods are light, they will be easy to carry, and even if you should lose one out of the ten, the remaining nine are bound to make you a profit. This is how small merchants make money. But with ten thousand *yang* you can buy the whole lot, whether you load it on a cart or on a boat.

It's the same with anything a country has a sufficiency of. You just get the whole lot with one sweep of your net. Say you choose something that's produced on land and buy it all up, or else you choose a sea product or something they use in medicine; not one merchant in the whole country will be able to turn up even a hint of that item. However, this method is a plague to the people. If someday some official were to employ it, it would be bound to injure the country."

Pyŏn took this in and then asked, "How did you know I would lend you the ten thousand *yang*?"

Hŏ replied, "You were not the only one who would have lent me the money. No businessman that had ten thousand could have refused me. I might easily make ten thousand through my own ability, but one's fate is up to heaven, and nobody knows for certain. Therefore, the man who trusts me is a lucky one. It must be because heaven has ordained it that a man who is rich already becomes even richer. If so, how could he *not* give me the money? Once I had the ten thousand, I was acting entirely under the aegis of that lucky man. And whatever I tried, succeeded. If I had gone into business with my own money, who can tell what the result might have been?"

"These days, officials wish to avenge the shame of Namhan Fortress, at the time of the Manchu invasion. Now is the time for wise and able men to arise and serve the country. Why would a gifted man like you wish to remain obscure all his life?" Pyŏn asked.

"Many have lived and died with their worth never recognized. Cho Sŏnggi (1638–1689),[2] who was worthy of being sent as an envoy to an enemy land, died in coarse hemp cloth. Yu Hyŏngwŏn (1622–1673),[3] an expert in military provisioning, idly whiled away his time at Puan. That will give you some idea of what sort of people are in charge of state affairs. As for myself, I had some talent in business,

2. A scholar and writer of fiction.
3. A pioneer of practical learning.

and I could have bought the head of Dorgon (1612–1650)[4] with the money I made. But I threw it all into the sea because I knew there was no way to use that money."

Pyŏn gave a long sigh and rose to depart.

Pyŏn had long been acquainted with Minister Yi Wan (1602–1674), who was then a commander in the Metropolitan Military Headquarters. The two friends were having a chat one day when the minister asked Pyŏn, "Do you know of an able and gifted man among the commoners whom I could work with on behalf of a great cause?"

Pyŏn mentioned Hŏ.

Yi was greatly amazed and said, "How strange! Could there really be such a man? What is his given name?"

"I have known him for three years, but I have never learned his given name."

"He must be a genius. Please take me to him."

When night came, Yi ordered his guards away and went on foot with Pyŏn to Hŏ's house. Pyŏn left Yi outside and went in alone to tell Hŏ the purpose of Yi's visit. Hŏ ignored him, saying only, "Open that bottle of wine you brought."

So they drank happily. Pyŏn was concerned for Yi, whom he had left outside, and mentioned Yi's business over and over, but Hŏ would not listen.

It was not until the night was far advanced that Hŏ asked, "Shall we see the visitor now?"

Hŏ did not budge from his seat when Yi entered. For a time Yi did not know what to do, but he finally announced that the government had been looking for wise men.

---

4. The fourteenth son of Nurgaci, founder of the Qing. He commanded the Manchu army that seized the fortress on Kanghwa Island.

Hŏ waved him to silence, saying, "The night is short and your words are long. It would be tedious to hear you out. What position do you hold?"

"I am a commander."

"Is that so? Then you must be a trusted officer of the state. If I were to recommend to you a reclusive sage comparable to Zhuge Liang (181–234),[5] could you ask the king to call on his thatched hut three times in person?"

Yi pondered briefly and then replied, "It would be difficult. I'd like to hear more of what you have in mind."

"I know nothing of second choices," said Hŏ.

When Yi begged again and again, Hŏ spoke: "Since Chosŏn was indebted to Ming in the past, the descendants of Ming generals and soldiers came eastward to our country, where they now live as vagabonds, homeless and unmarried. Could you ask the court to wed the daughters of the royal kinsmen to these men, and confiscate the estates of the meritorious and powerful to provide them with new homes?"

After a long silence with his head bowed, Yi said, "That too would be difficult."

"This would be difficult, that would be difficult! Well, what can you do? I have one rather easy proposal. Do you think you can do it?"

"I'd like to hear it."

"If one intends to rise up for a great cause, one must make friends with gallant men under heaven. If one plans to attack another country, one cannot hope to succeed without using secret agents. Now, the Manchu, as the lords of all under heaven, suspect that they have not been able to win the hearts of the Chinese. They regard us instead as their most trusted friends because we were the first to surrender. If we ask them to let our young men study in their country and serve in their

---

5. The great strategist of the state of Shu during the Three Kingdoms period.

government, as was done under Tang and Yuan, and to allow our merchants to come and go freely, they will be pleased with our gesture
and will consent. Then we select the country's youth, have them cut
their hair as the Manchu do, clothe them in Manchu dress, and send
them to China.[6] The learned will take the examination for foreign-
ers; the merchants will go deep into the region south of the Yangzi River
to gather information and make friends with the most gallant men
there. Only then will we be able to plan a great undertaking to wipe
away the country's disgrace. Afterward you can search for a member of
the Zhu clan of the Ming and make him emperor. If no heir of the Zhu
is left, you and the gallant men of China can select a person qualified
to be a ruler. Then our country will be a teacher to China, or we'll at
least enjoy the prestige of being China's elder uncle."

"With our scholar-officials adhering to the old ways as they are,
who would be willing to have his sons adopt Manchu hairstyles or
dress?" Yi said with a sigh.

At this Hŏ shouted wrathfully, "Who are these so-called scholar-
officials? How brazen they are to presume to call themselves so, when
they were born in the land of the barbarians Yi and Maek! The white
coat and white trousers you always wear are only fit for mourning,
and you bind your hair and wear it on your head like a gimlet—just
like the southern barbarians! How can you pretend to know about
good manners? General Fan Wuji (d. 227 BCE) didn't spare his own
head to avenge a personal grudge,[7] and King Wuling of Zhao wasn't
ashamed to adopt barbarian dress in order to make his country strong.
You say you want to avenge the Ming, but you still want to keep that

6. After conquering China, the Manchu required Chinese men to shave their heads and
wear queues, and to adopt Manchu dress. However, they did not subject the Koreans to the
same regulations. Even if the Korean upper classes despise the Manchu as barbarians and
dream of the restoration of the Ming, Hŏ is saying, the Koreans must adopt Manchu customs to achieve what they yearn for.

7. A Qin general who defected to Yan. Fan cut his own throat so that Jing Ke could
approach the object of his attempted assassination, the First Emperor of Qin.

gimlet-shaped topknot on your head. That's not all. You'll have to train yourself in horsemanship, swordsmanship, spear handling, archery, and stone throwing, yet you wouldn't part with those wide, flapping sleeves, and you speak only of good manners. I made you three proposals, but there is not one that you will carry out. How can you be a trusted officer'? Is this all there is to a 'trusted officer'? Men like you should be beheaded!"

Hŏ looked right and left in search of a sword, as if he were ready to kill Yi then and there. Yi was so terrified that he threw himself through the back window and ran home.

The next day, Yi called at Hŏ's cottage again, but it was deserted. Ho had disappeared.

THE STORY OF A YANGBAN

[YANGBAN CHŎN]

The word *yangban*[1] is an honorific term for scholar-officials. In Chŏngsŏn county there was a gentleman who was wise and loved reading books. A new magistrate went to visit him to pay his respects.

This gentleman, being very poor, had to borrow grain from the county office every year. Over the years he had come to owe a thousand bags.

One day the governor made a tour of inspection. When he reached Chŏngsŏn county and examined the lending of government grain, he grew very angry and said, "What kind of gentleman is he who borrows so much from military supplies?" He then ordered his imprisonment.

The magistrate pitied the gentleman, for he knew that he had no means to repay the grain. He could not bear to jail the gentleman but had no choice.

---

1. Throughout the rest of this translation, the term "gentleman" is used instead of *yangban*.

The gentleman wept day and night but could find no solution.

His wife abused him. "You always love to study, but you're no good at returning government grain. A gentleman, you say, but your kind isn't worth a penny."

A rich man in the village heard of this and discussed the matter with his family. "The gentleman may be poor, but his standing has always been high and prestigious. We may be rich, but we are always considered mean and low. We dare not ride horses, and when we see a gentleman we lose heart and tremble. We scrape and bow before him in the courtyard, dragging our noses and walking on our knees. We have always been disgraced like this. Now, because he is poor, that gentleman cannot pay back the grain. Being in great distress, he will not be able, despite his prestige, to keep his title. I want to buy his position for myself."

He then visited the gentleman and proposed to settle the account for him. The gentleman was very pleased and consented. Thereupon the rich man sent the grain to the county office.

Astonished, the magistrate went to the gentleman to find out how he had managed to repay the grain. Wearing a coarse felt cap and a hemp jacket, the gentleman prostrated himself in the mud, referred to himself as a "small" man, and dared not look up. Greatly astonished, the magistrate got down, raised him up, and asked, "Sir, why do you humiliate yourself like this?"

The gentleman became even more afraid, bowed his head, and prostrated himself once more. He said, "I am terror stricken. Not that I dare to humiliate myself, but I have sold my title to repay the loan. The rich man is now a gentleman. How can I use my former status to honor myself?"

The magistrate sighed and said, "How superior the rich man is! How gentlemanlike the rich man is! To be rich without being stingy is righteousness. To be anxious about another's difficulties is goodness. To despise the mean and desire the honorable is wisdom. That man is truly a gentleman. However, a private sale without a contract may lead to litigation. You and I will call together the people of the county as witnesses and draw up a deed. I will sign it as magistrate."

Thereupon the magistrate went to his office and summoned the gentry, farmers, artisans, and merchants to his courtyard. The rich man was seated to the right of the deputy magistrate, and the gentleman stood below the clerks. The magistrate then began to draw up a deed:

"On a certain day of the ninth month of the tenth year of Qianlong (1745), the following deed is executed because I have sold the title of gentleman to pay back the official grain I borrowed. Its value is one thousand bags.

"Now the term 'gentleman' has many implications. One who only studies is called a scholar; when he holds a court rank, he is called a great officer; when he has moral authority, he is called a superior man. The military corps stands to the west, the civil corps to the east; hence there are two corps. You may follow either of these courses, but from now on you must give up mean and base thoughts and imitate the ancients, always with a lofty aim. You must arise at the fifth watch (3–5 a.m.) without fail, light the oil lamp, focus on the tip of your nose and sit with your buttocks on your heels, and recite from the *Broad Discussion of the* Zuozhuan *by Mr. Donglai*[2] as smoothly as a gourd rolling on ice. You must tap your teeth and snap the back of your head,[3] swallow your spittle when you cough, brush your plush cap with your sleeves, and wipe away the dust that rises like waves. But you must not double your fists when you wash, or brush your teeth to avoid bad breath. You should summon your slave girls with a drawn-out voice and walk in a leisurely manner, dragging your shoes. You should copy the *True Treasures of Old Prose*[4] and the *Graded Collection of Tang Poetry*[5] with graphs like sesame seeds, one hundred to a line. Your hands should not hold cash or your mouth ask the price of

2. *Donglai xiansheng Zuoshi boyi* (1168).
3. To help circulation and invigorate oneself.
4. *Guwen zhenbao.*
5. *Tangshi binhui,* compiled by Gao Bing (1350–1423).

rice. However hot it is, you must not take off your stockings or loosen your topknot at the dining table. You should not eat the soup first or slurp when sipping. You shall not put down your chopsticks on the table with a thud. You must not eat raw scallions or lap your mustache when drinking wine or suck in both cheeks when smoking. You must not strike your wife in anger or kick utensils in irritation. You must not strike your children with your fists or swear at your servants or curse at your slaves. When scolding your oxen and horses, you must not insult their former owners. When ill, do not call a shaman; when sacrificing, do not invite monks. Do not warm your hands over a brazier; when talking, never splutter; and don't slaughter oxen or gamble. Should you act contrary to any of these precepts, the gentleman can take this document and initiate legal action to rectify the wrongs.

"The magistrate of Chŏngsŏn county signs and the deputy magistrate steward signs, as witnesses hereof."

Thereupon the attendant boy affixed the seals. The sound of stamping the seals was like the drumbeats announcing the king's procession; the paper looked like a sky strewn horizontally with the seven stars of the Big Dipper and vertically with the three stars of Orion's Belt. Then the clerk read it.

The rich man stood in disappointment for some time, but finally spoke: "Is this all there is to being a gentleman? I heard that a gentleman was like an immortal. If it means nothing more than this, I have been cheated. Please change it to read more profitably."

Thereupon the magistrate executed another deed that read: "When heaven gave birth to people, it divided them into four classes, and among these the most honorable is that of scholar-officials, also called gentlemen. There is no profit greater than this. They do not till the soil or engage in trade. With a smattering of classics and histories, the better ones will pass the higher examination; lesser ones will become literary licentiates. The red diploma of the higher civil service examination is no more than two feet long, but it provides everything one needs—indeed, it is like a purse. Even if a licentiate gets his first appointment at thirty, he can still become famous on account of his father's name and fame. If he wins the favor of a man of the Southern faction,[6] his ears will become white from sitting under a sunshade and his stomach full with the "yeses" of servants. The floor of his room will be strewn with the earmuffs left by female entertainers, and the grain piled in his courtyard will be enough for the cranes to feed on. Even a poor scholar in the country can decide matters as he wishes. He can have his neighbor's oxen plow his fields first, or use villagers for weeding. Who will dare behave rudely to him? Even if he pours lye into your nostrils, catches you by the topknot, or pulls your hair under your ears, you cannot show resentment . . ."

When the deed was half written, the rich man put out his tongue: "Stop, stop. How absurd! Are you trying to turn me into a robber?"

Shaking his head, he went away. And for the rest of his life he never again mentioned the word "gentleman."

Chŏng Yagyong (1762–1836)

ON DISMISSING A SERVANT

[CH'ULTONG MUN]

Once upon a time, Wang Bao (1st cent. BCE) drafted a labor contract for his slave. It was so severe and exacting that the slave could not sleep at night or rest during the day. Moreover, the rules were as numerous as the hairs on a cow, and Wang's nagging was as irritating as the droning of a mosquito. The slave toiled until his joints creaked and his bones ached. Tears and snivel flowed down his face, wetting his chin and chest. But to revile him because of momentary anger is not a gentleman's way.

---

6. A powerful political faction during the last quarter of the eighteenth century.

Now, in my servant's contract, I made the terms generous. Its contents follow:

"Get up at dawn, sweep the yard, and dredge the mud from the drain. Quietly cook rice—only wash the chaff off and cook it well; you don't have to make it sweet and soft. After breakfast, hoe the garden. Cut down the dead trees, separate the eggplants, thin out the scallions, pick mallows, pluck leeks, manure the taro patches, heap soil around the potato stalks, level the banks around the cabbage patch, and dry mustard seeds in the sun. Tend the cucumbers and water them, but take care not to hurt their stems. Sluice water through the tube to the lotus, plait straw mats to protect the plantains, and at times bank up the roots of the gardenia and pomegranate and water them. Mow the grass to clear the path and cut down trees to repair the bridge; chase away village urchins and keep haymakers away from my farm. But do not frighten them.

"You are not expected to do all this in a single morning, but to work at them throughout the seasons. In addition, you will at times deliver provisions to mountain temples, make trips to fishmarkets to buy fish and then dry them, go to town to get pills, or run to a neighbor's house to borrow ginger or dates. In most cases, the distance will not be more than five to ten tricents. When hungry, you may eat rice cakes and drink wine, but not to the point of falling down from drunkenness. If you have any energy left, you may go to the mountains to cut down ailanthus and mangrove and store them as firewood for the rainy season. I will give you a patch of dry field and paddy, where you can plant rice and beans. When harvest time comes, you must report to me promptly, but you are in sole charge of your own weeding and plowing. I will not take you to task if you have a bad crop. Also, if you don't follow my instructions, you will lose your job."

When I had read all this to him, the servant kowtowed, putting his hands to his brow, and said, "I am grateful to your honor for your favor." His face beamed with delight, and he repeated his oath of loyalty.

"I will not complain," he said, "even if I should become a pygmy or a cripple in your service. Flog my buttocks if I ever go back on my words."

His deeds, however, did not match his words, like those of an official who neglects his duties once he gets his position. Wherever he went, he raised dust. As if confused, he did nothing right. He never fertilized or watered. Mugwort grew thick and brambles ran wild. Snakes crawled about, and children ran away in fear. The vegetables and cucumbers rotted, and flowering plants failed to put forth their buds. He allowed woodcutters, with whom he was in collusion, to fell trees. After breakfast, he sallied out, only returning after dark. He prowled the markets, drank heavily, and when it was time to sober up, snored under the tree. He wore fine linen and ate minced and pickled meat. He was not only dull and stupid but also foolish and arrogant. He giggled when there was no cause, bragged, and told lies. He committed crimes every day. When admonished with kind words, he still did not reform.

At last, I, Master Yun, called him in and rebuked him in a stern voice: "According to our country's code, no one ranks higher than a minister. Yet if he does nothing to earn his salary, he must be removed so that the wishes of the people can be better served. If a magistrate is soft and weak, and unfit to uproot villains or wealthy bullies, or if he is greedy and petty minded and cannot comprehend the interests of the throne, he must be dismissed so as not to drain the fat and blood of the people. You are a mere servant in the kitchen. How dare you to think you could escape a similar punishment! Return your salary, and do not presume to covet what is not your due."

Upon hearing this, the servant bit his fingers in regret and pounded his chest with his fists. His snivel flowed three feet long and his tears fell as heavily as an autumn rain.

Anonymous

The Story of a Pheasant Cock

[CHANGKKI CHŎN]

When heaven and earth came into being, all things prospered. Man stood above the animals below. There are three hundred species of winged creatures, and three hundred hairy ones.

Observe the pheasant, plumed in five colors and called a gorgeous creature. In accord with the inborn nature of mountain birds and wild beasts, the pheasant lives far away from the world of humans. Its arbor is the tall pine tree by an emerald stream in the dense forest; it pecks at grain scattered in the fields. All alone, it is often caught by licensed hunters and hounds to fill the stomachs of high ministers and rich old men in Seoul, and its feathers are used to decorate army banners and dusters at the shops. Indeed, its contributions are many.

Young hawks fly up to the highest peak of White Cloud Terrace to scan the hidden valleys and soar over the magnificent scenery. Club-carrying hunters shout here and there, and hounds follow the scent between eulalia plants and oak leaves—alas, there is no escape. Byways too are encircled by hunters; where can this hungry bird escape the freezing cold?

In the hunting season, the pheasant cock is dressed in a purplish-red silk robe with yellow-green silk collar and white neckband, capped with a jade hairpin and twelve beautiful tail feathers. How grand he looks! Dressed in a finely quilted blouse and skirt, his mate walks behind her nine sons and twelve daughters, marching down the open field in a line.

"You peck in that row while we peck in this one. When we peck at beans, one by one, we need not envy what man provides. Living beings are not meant to starve. To eat our fill is only our fortune."

Then they espy a red bean in the very middle of the plain.

"It looks delicious," exclaims the pheasant cock. "How can I refuse heaven's gift? I shall have it—it's my luck."

"Don't eat it yet. I see the tracks of men in the snow. It looks suspicious," warns the pheasant hen. "Upon looking closer, I see that the ground has been swept clean. Please don't."

"How foolish! Now it is the coldest month of the winter, with snow piled up everywhere. Over a thousand hills, no birds are flying, and on myriad roads, no tracks can be seen at all.[1] How can there be any trace of a human?"

"Your reasoning may be sound, but last night I had a dream that portends disaster. Please consider the matter carefully."

"Let me tell you my dream. I flew up to heaven on the back of a yellow crane to greet the Jade Emperor. He conferred on me the title of Retired Gentleman of Mountains and Groves and granted me a bag of beans from his granary. This must be one of them. The ancients say that the hungry eat well and the thirsty drink easily. I shall fill my empty stomach."

"That was your dream, but I interpret mine as unlucky. At the second watch I dreamed that rain slashed the slopes of the North Mang hills,[2] and a double rainbow in the blue sky suddenly turned into a cangue and cut off your head. This must portend your death. Please don't eat it."

"Don't worry about your dream. It only predicts that I will come in first in the royal examination on the Ch'undang Terrace in Ch'anggyŏng Palace; I will parade through the streets of Seoul, with the two twigs of flowers that the king has granted me garlanding my head. I'll study hard for the examination."

"Let me tell you my dream at the third watch. You wore an iron cauldron weighing a thousand pounds and drowned in the deep blue

1. Allusion to "River Snow" by Liu Zongyuan (773–819); Watson, *Columbia Book of Chinese Poetry*, 282.
2. The graveyard in the hills of Luoyang.

sea, and I wailed alone on the shore. It must portend our death. Please don't eat it."

"That dream is even better. When the great Ming is about to be restored and calls for Chosŏn's help, I will be a general wearing a helmet and I will cross the Yalu, restore order in the central plains, and return home in triumph."

"That may be so; but listen to my dream at the fourth watch (1–3 a.m.). An old man sat in the high hall and a boy was offering a cup of wine when the poles supporting the twenty-two-foot-wide awnings collapsed over our heads, a sign of bad luck. I had another dream at the fifth watch: towering pines filled our courtyard and three stars guarded the purple forbidden enclosure, while the supreme sky god, the Great Unique, was surrounded by the Milky Way. Then one star fell before our eyes—it must have been a general's star. It is said that a similar star fell when Zhuge Liang (181–234) died on the Wuzhang plain."

"Don't worry. The collapsed awning means that you and I will sleep together tonight on a floor of grass, with screens of flowery trees, a stump for a pillow, arrowroot leaves for a bed, and oak leaves for a quilt. The fall of the star means that the old mother of the Yellow Emperor has conceived a son with the help of the seven stars of the Great Dipper, and the Herd Boy and Weaver Maid will meet again on the seventh day of the seventh month. Hence you will have a wonderful son. Dream such a dream often."

"At cockcrow I dreamed that, wearing a colorful jacket and skirt, I roamed the green hills and blue streams, when suddenly a shaggy blue hound bared his teeth, jumped on me, and clawed me. Dumbfounded, I fled into a cluster of hemp plants. Slender hemp plants fell down and thick ones flew about, all tangled around my slim waist. This portends that I shall be a widow in mourning. Please, for my sake, don't take that bean."

Fuming with anger and stamping and kicking, the pheasant cock retorts: "With your lovely face and graceful carriage, you will take a lover behind the back of your lawful husband. Hence the joints of your wings will be tied with a heavy orange rope, and you will be dragged through the streets and clubbed. That's what your dream forebodes. Never mention such a dream again, or I shall break your shins."

"A crying goose by the water carries a reed in its beak—that is the proper conduct of a gentleman. A phoenix that soars thousands of feet high does not peck a single grain of millet—that is a gentleman's sense of honor. Though a small creature, you should set your heart on noble deeds. Bo Yi and Shu Qi shunned the grain of Zhou, and Zhang Liang of the Han (d. 187 BCE) retired because of his illness and ate with strict caution. You too should emulate them and be careful not to touch that bean."

"How ignorant you are! As if I don't know the requirements of proper conduct, much less have a sense of honor. Yan Hui, a disciple of Confucius, died young, no more than thirty. For all their loyalty and integrity, Bo Yi and Shu Qi starved to death on Mount Shouyang. Because of his Daoist practices, Zhang Liang joined the Master of the Red Pine. What good is a sense of honor? At the Hutuo River, Liu Xiu, later Emperor Guangwu, ate a dish of cooked barley; at the Huai, Han Xin (d. 196 BCE), who later became general of the Han, was fed by an old woman bleaching coarse silk. Who knows but that I too will become like them after eating that bean?"

"I'll tell you what you will be. As a gravekeeper you will be appointed a magistrate of Hades, never to see the green hills again. Don't old books tell you how many stubborn men have brought ruin on themselves and on their families? The first emperor of the Qin never listened to the advice of his son Fu Su, and after forty years of disaffection and turmoil the dynasty was toppled by the time of his heir, Er Shi. Xiang Yu (223–202 BCE) didn't listen to his aide Fan Zeng and had eight thousand of his men killed. Chased by the Han army, he fled to Wujiang and could not bear to return home, so he cut his own throat and died. King Huai of Chu rebuffed the advice of Qu Yuan (c. 340–278 BCE) and decided to go himself to the land of his enemy, the Qin. When he reached the Wuguan pass, he was hemmed in by the

Qin army and eventually died there. How pitiful and shameful must his spirit have been when it met the loyal soul of his banished minister, who had drowned himself in the Miluo River out of despair. Your stubbornness is bound to be your ruin!"

"Do you mean to say that everyone who eats a bean will perish? Read the old texts, and you will find that those whose names carry the letter *tai*[3] all lived to a good old age and became famous. The Heavenly Emperor of remote antiquity (*tai*-gu) lived 18,000 years; *Tai*-hao Fu Xi's heirs continued for fifteen generations; Tang *Tai*zong quelled the rebels and helped found the Tang. Among the hundred grains, the bean is the first. Jiang *Tai*gong was sought out by King Wen of Zhou when he was eighty; the immortal poet Li *Tai*bo (701–762) went up to heaven on the back of a leviathan; and the *Tai*-i (the Great Unique) in the north is a star among stars. After feasting on this bean, I too will live long like Jiang Taigong, ride the heavens like Li Taibo, and become an immortal in the Great Unique."

Utterly listless, the pheasant hen withdraws.

Observe the behavior of the pheasant cock as he moves toward the bean. Spreading out his twelve plumes, head nodding, hesitating, he advances. With his crescent-shaped tongue he pecks—and two pulleys fall and strike his head, just as Zhang Liang and his assassins tried with an iron bludgeon to assassinate the First Emperor but mistakenly struck the carriage of his attendants. Crash! Bang! He's caught!

"Haven't you realized what will become of you? A woman's word might ruin a family or bring disgrace."

Observe the pheasant hen. In a flat field of gravel, she loses all composure and rolls about, striking her breast. Now she gets up, heart-stricken, plucks the grass, stamps her feet, and cries her heart out. Her nine sons, twelve daughters, and her friends all pity her and

---

3. *T'ae* in Korean. The author is punning on another Korean reading of the same graph as *k'ong* "bean" *t'ae* and cataloging those whose names contain the same graph.

offer condolences. Only wailing resounds among the empty hills and bare trees.

"The cry of the cuckoo among the moonlit empty hills quickens my sorrows," the pheasant hen says. "I read in the *General Mirror for Aid in Government*,[4] 'Good medicine is bitter to the mouth but benefits the sick, and loyal words offend the ear but are of benefit to one's conduct.' If only you had listened to my advice! How frustrating! What a pity! To whom can I reveal the deep love between us? My tears become nails; my sighs, wind and rain. My breast is ablaze. What am I to do with my life?"

Lying under the pulleys, the cock still mumbles, "Hush, you wretch! Who would climb a mountain if he knew what troubles lay ahead? If one is clumsy, one misses the opportunity. Have you ever seen anyone die without trouble? One can often tell by feeling the pulse if one is to die. Take my pulse and see."

"Your pulse on the spleen and stomach has stopped, that on the liver is chilly, the yin and the yang pulse are gone, and your life pulse is slow. How sad! Oh, you stubborn monster!"

"What about my eyes? Examine the pupils."

"Now you are done for. The guardian of one pupil left you this morning, and that of the other is about to abandon you. . . . I was born under an unlucky star. How often have I become a widow! My first husband was snatched away by a young hawk; the second was bit by a hound; the third, shot by a gunman. With you I have been happy, but before marrying off our nine sons and twelve daughters, you've been caught by the trap. Hunger drove you to your death. Am I possessed by evil spirits? How pitiable you look! Is it because of your age or illness? Or was it ill luck that brought you disgrace? The evil spirit of obstinacy? How can I make you live? Whom will our children marry? Who will help me deliver the one I am carrying? I planted magic herbs in a wide field thick with clouds and trees and hoped to

4. *Zizhi tongjian* (1067–1084).

share happiness with you for a hundred years. But before three years have passed, I must part with you forever. When will I find again one with your imposing stature? O sea roses on the stretch of beautiful sand, don't resent the fall of flowers. Next spring you will bloom again, but my husband, once gone, will not return. I'll be nothing but a widow, a widow!"

"Don't give way to sorrow," he says, half opening his eyes. "It was my mistake to marry one who keeps on losing husbands. The dead cannot return to life, so it is unlikely that you will see me again. But if you are determined to have a last look at me, tomorrow morning after breakfast, follow after the man who has trapped me. I might be hanging in the market of Kimch'ŏn or in some provincial storehouse or served on a magistrate's dinner table; I might even be a dried pheasant presented by a bride to her in-laws. Don't mourn my death, but keep yourself chaste so as to be honored by the court. How wretched is my lot, how terrible! Don't cry, beloved, my innards are melting. However sad you might be, dying is sadder."

He puts up his last struggle—planting his legs firmly against the lower pulley and tugging at the one above. There is no escape; he merely loses some feathers.

Master T'ak the trapper has been keeping watch. With a mouse-fur cap and a stick, he walks, swinging his arms, then jumps upon the trap and pulls out the catch. Rejoicing, he dances. "Hurrah, I'm happy. Did you come down to drink the blue-green water below Mount South? Or did you come to visit peach-blossom girls in the gay quarters beyond the mountain? Not knowing that greed invites death, you were driven by appetite. So I've caught you, who used to roam over blue waters and green hills. I'll offer a sacrifice to the mountain spirits and catch all your kin." He pulls out the bird's crooked tongue and places it on a rock. Pressing his hands together, he prays: "May that trap also catch a pheasant hen. I put my faith in Amitābha and the compassionate Bodhisattva Who Observes the Sounds of the World!" Bowing again and again, he goes downhill.

Immediately thereafter, the widow goes to the rock and gathers the tongue; crying bitterly, she covers it with arrowroot leaves and buries it with honeysuckle. She inscribes the pheasant cock's name and rank on a flag of day lily and hangs it on a small pine tree; then she digs a grave close to where two sides of a field meet, and buries her mate. Then she offers a sacrifice to the mountain spirits and buddhas. Offerings befitting the occasion include dewdrops from a fallen leaf, dishes made of Cheju chestnut shells, cups made of acorns, and spoons and chopsticks made of rushes. The well-dressed crane offers the first cup; the nimble swallow is the receptionist; the eloquent parrot is the protocol officer; and the crested ibis, kneeling, intones the prayer: "On a certain month of a certain year, your widow ventures to announce to you, my deceased husband, who was a retired gentleman, that your body has been buried and your soul has returned to become a spirit. I bow down and offer libations and hope that you will reject the old and follow the new. Please rely on this."

When they hesitate to clear the offertory table, a hungry black-eared kite looks down and asks, "Who is the chief mourner? I'll get you!" It pounces upon one of the young and flies up to the highest peak of the storied cliffs, but fumbles its prey: "I've been starving for more than ten days because of the cold. Today I have caught the favorite of humans. The steamed octopus, abalone, and sea cucumber are the favorites of a bachelor. The peaches of immortality that ripen every ten years are the fruit of the Queen Mother of the West; the wine from Mount Yak is the favorite of the Four Whitebeards of Mount Shang;[5] and chicks and puppies that have died a natural death are the favorites of the field marshal, the kite. Large or small, it is a pheasant. Let me eat it to abate my hunger."

5. Figures representing a high standard of integrity: the Four Whitebeards retired to Mount Shang in disapproval of the Qin tyranny; *Qian Hanshu* (History of the Former Han) 40:2035–2036.

Swaying to and fro, it looks around and behold, the pheasant chick has fled downhill, leaving not a trace. He heaves a sigh. "For the cause of justice and humanity, Guan Yu (d. 219) released Cao Cao in the narrow pass of Huarong, and out of kindness, even the suspicious kite has set his victim free. My children will enjoy a golden age."

The jackdaw from the T'aebaek mountains, after an excursion to the north peak, comes down to allay his hunger and offer condolences to the widow. After feasting on the fruit, he sighs and says, "With his stature and virtue, I thought he would live long. But because of a single red bean he met with an untimely death. Listen, if there is a hero, there will be a fleet steed; if there is a writer, there will be a famous calligrapher. I see that we are destined to enjoy marital harmony. Would a butterfly have time to ponder fire among the flowers, or a goose to dread an old fisherman when it sees water? You know my lineage and prospects, so why don't we make our fortune and enjoy bliss for a hundred years?"

"Even though you're a creature of no account, in which book of propriety have you read that a widow can remarry before fulfilling a three-year mourning? 'Clouds follow the dragon, and winds follow the tiger.' And 'a wife should follow a husband.' Am I to follow every suitor?"

"How ridiculous," the furious jackdaw retorts. "The *Book of Songs* says, 'We are seven sons, / Yet none could soothe his mother's heart.'[6] It suggests that the lady in question remarry even if she has seven sons. Much less should you, puny thing, talk about integrity and constancy. I've yet to see a chaste pheasant hen whose virtue is honored."

Then an owl, after expressing his condolences, turns to the jackdaw: "Your body is black and your bill grotesque. You don't even stand up before an elder."

"You bigoted and rude owl! If your eyes are depressed and your ears move, does that make you an adult? Don't laugh at my black

---

6. *Shijing* 32:4; Waley, *Book of Songs,* 73.

body. My outside may be black, but not my inside. I happened to fly over Shanyin and got smudged. Don't ridicule my bill. Goujian of Yue (d. 465 BCE), whose mouth had the look of a crow's bill, polished his sword for ten years and succeeded in vanquishing his enemy, Fuchai of Wu (d. 473 BCE). How could you, unlettered as you are, pretend to be an adult? I won't let you go unpunished."

As they quarrel, a lone goose happens to alight from among the clouds. Looking around, his body drooping, he attempts to cope with the situation. "Elders? When Su Wu (c. 143–60 BCE) of the Han was in captivity for nineteen years in the north sea, I carried his message and offered it to the Son of Heaven with my own hands. Take this into account; you'll know who the elder is."

A drake in the lotus lake in front, seven times a widower without an heir, has been seeking a mate for some time. Upon hearing the news, he intends to propose without a matchmaker—a honking goose carrying a pair of wooden geese,[7] an osprey bearing a box on its back, a lively stork following behind, and a graceful halcyon as a verbal messenger.

The halcyon asks, "Is the bride home? The bridegroom is here."

"You think you can handle a widow so easily, without even checking our fortune. Are you pressuring me?"

"What need to have a widow's and a widower's fortune told?" the drake asks. "A bride and bridegroom sharing the same bed—that's marriage. Let's choose an auspicious day. . . . Yes, tonight is the best. A union of two families is the source of all happiness. Cut out the chatter, let's go to bed."

"You think you can get away with such wicked words because you're a male?"

"Listen to what I can offer you. In the broad waters around fairy seamounts, with pink smartweed and white duckweed for our home,

---

7. At the marriage rite, the bridegroom presents a wooden goose to the bride at her parents' home as a symbol of conjugal love.

silver scales and jade bodies for our food, we'll wander about—the water is the best place to live between heaven and earth."

"How can you compare your life with mine on land? Listen. We stroll the flat plain and broad field, fly up to a high peak on a cliff, and view the four seas and the eight quarters. In late spring, when the willows' colors are new, green upon green, around the guest lodge,[8] golden orioles flit among them; and when peaches and plums open in the spring breeze[9] and the cuckoo calls sadly, even grass and trees and birds and beasts are moved to tears. In the season of yellow chrysanthemums, we pick a myriad of fruit and store it everywhere. The gorgeous attire and the belling of the manly pheasant are without parallel. How can your life match ours?"

The drake remains silent. By his side is a pheasant cock, another visitor bearing condolences. "A widower for three years, I have not been able to find a fit bride. Our ties are preordained by heaven, and by the grace of God we'll become a couple and beget and marry off sons and daughters till we're buried in the same grave."

"When I think about my late husband, it would be inconsiderate of me to marry again so soon. But I'm neither young nor old—I'm just at the age when I know the appeal of a man and how to keep house. When I look at your manliness, I've no desire to keep chaste, and lust stirs in me. I've rejected all other suitors. They say, 'Birds of a feather flock together.' Indeed, it is meet and just for us to unite. Let's live together in any way we please."

The pheasant cock billows and flaps his wings, and they are married. Ashamed, the crow, owl, and drake retreat, and the black bird, halcyon, green finch, parrot, peacock, goose, heron, stork, and crowtit all return home.

---

8. Allusion to "Farewell to Yuan the Second on His Mission to Anxi" by Wang Wei (699?–761).

9. Allusion to "Song of Everlasting Sorrow" by Bo Juyi (772–846).

With the new bridegroom in front and nine sons and twelve daughters behind, braving the snow and wind, they return to the emerald stream in the cloud-capped wood. The next spring, after marrying off their children and visiting famous hills and waters, on the fifteenth of the tenth month, they enter the great river and transform themselves into clams.[10]

10. An old Chinese nature myth.

FICTION

> Epic fiction is the sole epistemological instance where the I-originality (or subjectivity) of a third person *qua* third person can be portrayed.
>
> —Käte Hamburger, *The Logic of Literature*[1]

Early texts such as the *Stories of Marvels* (*Sui chŏn*, c. 11th cent.), *Historical Records of the Three Kingdoms* (*Samguk sagi*, 1146), and *Memorabilia of the Three Kingdoms* (*Samguk yusa*, 1285) are laden with myths, fairy tales, and folktales. In the anonymous *Stories of Marvels*, one brief tale is told about a Ch'oe Hang who dies while longing for his concubine and then comes back to visit her. Breaking a rhododendron branch in two, he puts one piece in her hair and the other in his. After he disappears again, the concubine goes with his family to inspect his coffin, where they find the rhododendron branch on his dead body. The story does not end there, however. Ch'oe returns to life, and the couple grow old together (no. 5). Other marvels in the same collection include Chigwi's infatuation with Queen Sŏndŏk of Silla, which sends out fire from his heart to coil around a pagoda, becoming a fire demon (no. 7); two ravishing wives emerging from and reentering a piece of bamboo carried by their husband in his bosom (no. 8); an old man transforming himself into a tiger, a cock, a falcon, and a small dog (no. 9); and Kim Hyŏn's lying down with a tigress, who has metamorphosed into a young girl (no. 11).

1. Quoted in Cohn, *The Distinction of Fiction*, 24. Hamburger's definition applies only to third-person fiction (105–109); see Cohn, 23 and 97. Hamburger's phenomenologically grounded theory is most useful.

The *Historical Records* contains biographies of eighty-six persons. That of an impoverished and foolish-looking woodcutter who marries a princess and later distinguishes himself as an exemplary warrior reads like a folktale.[2] Prophetic dreams herald the birth of Kim Yusin (595–637). At age sixteen, he goes to a stone grotto in the central peaks where he purifies himself and pledges that he will defeat the invading enemy. After four days of prayer, he meets an old man clad in rough garments who tests him with a series of questions. Kim repeatedly entreats his help in repulsing the enemy, and the old man gives Kim a secret formula and disappears.[3]

The *Memorabilia* offers a number of folktales associated with eminent Buddhist monks and laymen. For example, the Segyu monastery sends Chosin the caretaker to its manor. Upon arrival, Chosin falls in love with the daughter of the magistrate and prays to the Bodhisattva Who Observes the Sounds of the World to grant him his wishes. In a few years, she marries another man. Again Chosin goes to the bodhisattva, complaining that his prayer to her has gone unanswered, and he cries till sunset. Worn out with longing, he falls asleep and enters a dream: he sees himself marrying Lady Kim and they live together for fifty years, and have five children. Now they are old and sick and cannot provide for the family. Their fourteen-year-old dies of hunger on Haehyŏn Ridge and Chosin buries him by the roadside. Starved, the couple founders and cannot continue. Their nine-year-old daughter begs for food, is bitten by a stray dog, and collapses in pain. They decide to go their separate ways, each taking two children. When his wife says, "I'm going home, you go south," Chosin wakes up. He returns to Haehyŏn Ridge, digs up the ground where he had buried his child in the dream, and finds a stone image of Maitreya, the future Buddha who resides in the Tuṣita heaven. Chosin builds a Pure Land monastery on the spot and performs good deeds.[4] Dream time seems longer than real time, just as the story time and the discourse time do not coincide. Chosin lives an

---

2. SS 45:425–426.
3. SS 41:393–394.
4. SY 3:161–163.

entire life within the space of a dream. The narrator's comment frames this mystery as an element of the Buddhist worldview and a warning to those who covet what is unattainable.

These fairy tales and folktales were recorded in literary Chinese, the language of literacy and official culture, accessible only to those who obtained an education. Like Latin in the medieval West, literary Chinese was a prestige language that became supranational and supratemporal.[5] The motifs of well-known fairy tales and folktales, rooted in cultural memory, seem to have come originally from oral sources or their reimaginings, but were seldom transcribed verbatim. What we have, then, are written folktales descended from oral transmission that emphasize improvisation. They attempt to imitate an illiterate voice and pretend to appropriate that voice in the diglossic culture of Korea. The tales are for entertainment—the unrealistic or impossible as filtered through the minds of the educated, and created primarily by them. A growth of interest in wonder—the marvelous and magical—enabled writers to bring the folktales into literature. The process of literalization, with the introduction of dialogue, dream visions, and the emotional lives of characters, made the stories interesting. These tales must have been told by a real person at a particular point in history, and our three sources gave them a new lease on life. Although verbs representing perceptions, thoughts, and feelings are few, what the tales place in the foreground is desire, the ultimate sign of subjectivity.

Early Chosŏn Tales of Wonder

Kim Sisŭp (1435–1493) led a checkered life as an eccentric monk and writer of verse and prose. Sejo's usurpation of the throne from his young cousin Tanjong occurred when Kim was twenty; in the aftermath he shaved his head and became a wandering monk. From then on he was known for his odd behavior, which hid his brilliance. In 1465 he built a study on Mount Kŭmo near Kyŏngju, where he wrote the *New Stories from Gold Turtle Mountain* (*Kŭmo sinhwa*) in literary Chinese. The five stories in this collection are in the tradi-

---

5. Ziolkowski, *Fairy Tales from before Fairy Tales*, 35.

tion of the *chuanqi,* or tales of wonder,[6] and concern love affairs between mortals and ghosts and dream journeys to the underworld or to the Dragon Palace.

The story of Student Yi, set in the Koryŏ capital of Kaesŏng, shows a number of features common to the type: an exchange of poems—a common activity of characters in East Asian romance since the *Visit to the Transcendents' Grotto* (*You xianku*) by Zhang Zu; a ghostly wife; and a didactic comment at the end of the story. Kim's extensive use of literary allusions evinces his wide reading—especially of the *New Stories Told by Trimming the Lampwick* (*Jiandeng xinhua*) by Qu You (1341–1427), to whom he is indebted. The topoi of Ms. Ch'oe's lovesickness—tossing and turning, insomnia, lack of appetite for food or water, delirious speech, and lackluster skin—were repeated in later stories, with the addition of still more telltale signs such as darkened vision, sunken eyes, irregular palpitations of the heart, a whirring in the ears, pallor or a jaundiced color, sudden sweating, helplessness, stupor, and anorexia.[7]

Romance and Vernacular Fiction

Vernacular fiction bloomed in the seventeenth century when four major works in the vernacular appeared: "The Tale of Hong Kiltong" by Hŏ Kyun (1569–1618), *A Dream of Nine Clouds* and *Record of Lady Sa's Journey South* by Kim Manjung (1637–1692), and *Showing Goodness and Stirred by Rightness* by Cho Sŏnggi (1638–1689). Although it is still debated whether Kim and Cho's works were first composed in Korean or in literary Chinese, two records attest to the fact that they wrote for their mothers, who were literate, educated women. As their works circulated in Korean and Chinese versions immediately upon completion, they acquired a vast readership. Works of fiction gave emotional gratification, satisfied psychological

---

6. Also translated as "transmission of the strange" or "accounts of remarkable things"; *chŏngi* in Korean. See Ma and Lau, *Traditional Chinese Stories*, xxi–xxii and 385.

7. Beecher and Ciavolella, *Jacques Ferran*, 50; Wack, *Lovesickness in the Middle Ages*, 40 passim.

cravings, provided an alternate world, and offered a form of escape—
needs not met by patriarchal institutions or the longing for reform of
the social order. Why were such works—and of a quality that would
influence the fiction of later generations—produced at this time?

One reason is the new social reality that came into being after
the Japanese and Manchu invasions of the sixteenth and seventeenth
centuries. In this new environment a great number of commoners,
the main consumers of vernacular fiction, demanded a literary form
that corresponded to the contours of contemporary society. Satisfy-
ing this demand became the literary pursuit of certain members of
the ruling elite who not only discerned the social contradictions
within their world but felt the need to express them. A second reason
was the long tradition of fiction writing in literary Chinese, which
in turn had stimulated the introduction, translation, and adaptation
of popular Chinese fiction for a local audience. Around the beginning of the seventeenth century, four great works of Chinese fiction
were imported and widely read by the literati: *Romance of the Three
Kingdoms*, *Journey to the West*, *Water Margin*, and *The Plum in the
Gold Vase*.[8] The martial themes of the *Romance of the Three Kingdoms* were especially popular after the Japanese and Manchu invasions, and more and more readers began to seek out works of fiction.
The formation of a wide readership at that time coincided with the
rise of a commodity economy in which farmers produced items that
could be sold for cash. In this environment fiction was produced and
turned into a commodity for widespread consumption through commercial innovations such as the lending library and the printing of
woodblock editions.

Fiction writing was not an activity that authors could take pride
in, however. Indeed, in conservative precincts of the traditional culture, fiction was still despised as a corruptor of morals and a source
of social disruption. This is why the author and date of composition
of most early works of vernacular fiction remain unknown (Kwŏn
P'il and Cho Wihan adopt the pretense of basing their works on sto-

---

8. *Sanguo(zhi)yanyi, Xiyouji, Shuihu zhuan,* and *Jinpingmei.*

ries they have heard from a friend). It is difficult to imagine how
Korean literati schooled in the Confucian canon comprehended the
new genre of vernacular fiction. Chinese works of fiction had been
appraised in impressionistic terms—referring to the author but not
to the work itself. They were used to applying the criteria of history
to the reading of fiction and judging fiction by the standards of history
writing. Yet one is based on presumed facts, the other on invention.

Hŏ Kyun and Kim Manjung, who were avidly read by court ladies, did not openly profess to be writing fiction and seldom referred to their own works. Authorial disavowal or anonymity was a
convention that had been established to circumvent the Confucian
sanction against writing imaginative stories. This situation changed
by the nineteenth century, when translators of Chinese fiction did
not hesitate to sign their names to their work. Kim Chŏnghŭi (1786–
1856), a calligrapher, painter, and scholar of epigraphy, claimed his
translation of the northern Chinese variety play *Romance of the
Western Chamber* (*Xisiangji*). Hong Hŭibok (1794–1856), who defined fiction as a creation designed to give delight, not edification,
did the same with his translation of the hundred-chapter *Flowers in
the Mirror, a Romance* (*Jinghua yan*) by Li Ruzhen (c. 1763–1830).
As he was a secondary son, Hong's path to officialdom was blocked,
but he visited China several times, probably as an interpreter, and
bought and read Chinese fiction. He was sufficiently entranced by it
to read his Korean translations to his aged mother, his wife (when
she was ill), his daughter-in-law, and his daughters.

Among the new consumers of fiction were people who relied on
an oral storyteller (*chŏngi su*). These professional reciters often did
their job so well that they attracted huge crowds—the unlettered
now able to read with their ears. Some female auditors believed that
fictitious happenings were true and tried to imitate them, reinforcing the idea that fiction corrupts readers. On September 18, 1790,
an incident that occurred during a storytelling session in a tobacco
shop near Chongno in central Seoul caught the attention of King
Chŏngjo (1776–1800) and the townspeople alike. When the narration reached the point in the story where the protagonist is thrown

into despair, one unidentified listener in the audience rose up and stabbed the storyteller to death with a tobacco knife.[9] The indignant listener had not only identified himself with the character; he also mistook the storyteller for the author. In this situation, the storyteller's power to make his audience identify with the characters in the narrative cost him his life.

The consumers of vernacular fiction were mainly women of the upper and middle classes. Literate in Korean and having sufficient money and leisure, they were instrumental in the development of the lending library and the subsequent production of woodblock-printed fiction. Like music, oral narration had "no existence or continuity apart from its performance,"[10] and some members of the audience craved a manuscript or printed copy that they could hold in their hands and keep. Letters written in Korean by Queen Insŏn (1618–1674) to her daughter Sungmyŏng ask the princess to return *Water Margin* and two other works of fiction she had borrowed. When Princess Tŏgun, the third daughter of King Sunjo (1800–1834), married, she is said to have brought with her some five thousand books, including works of fiction. From these and other records, it appears that a large number of imaginative stories entered the palace—including multivolume works of fiction kept in the Naksŏn Study in Ch'angdŏk Palace, probably obtained through middlemen and the lending library.

An increase in the numbers of fiction writers—all anonymous—and readers in the late Chosŏn led to the rise of professional writers who could earn a living through their talent. Many were impoverished literati who had been the victims of factional struggle or political upheaval, or who lived in obscurity in the countryside for similar reasons. Yi Tŏngmu (1741–1793) reports that village schoolmasters also wrote fiction: "One would narrate a story and the second would write it down, while others carved woodblocks and sold

9. *Chŏngjo sillok* 31:6a.
10. Finnegan, *Oral Poetry*, 28.

them to a bookstore to purchase meat and wine."[11] Some fiction writers were literati who held official positions; others were members of literati families whose power had been eclipsed; still others were interpreters of Chinese who had literary talent as well as access to works of Chinese fiction. Some of these writers tried to recreate a distant and idealized past; some sought in their works the emotional satisfaction denied in ordinary life; some staged the conflict between good and evil, whether socially or morally; and some narrated the lives of national heroes, while others took a critical approach to social issues, demanding change in the social structure.

The object of greatest fascination was the story of the exemplary hero. Indeed, what proved most captivating for writers and readers of vernacular fiction was the career of the hero whose powers exceed those of normal human beings. The story typically has the following structure: a hero is born late to noble parents as a result of prayers offered to a mountain spirit or the Buddha; as a transcendent being relegated to the human world because of a minor misdemeanor in heaven, he is a man of unusual ability and spirit; because of a villain's persecution, he undergoes a series of trials and perils; an ally saves him and becomes his father-in-law; he meets an enlightened Buddhist monk and studies magical as well as martial arts; when a villain, in collusion with a foreign enemy, rises in revolt or even usurps the throne, the hero defeats the evil forces, attains high rank, and enjoys riches and honor with his wife; in the end, the couple ascends to a transcendent realm. This biographical pattern repeats the ritual passage of the mythological hero, recapitulating motifs that first appeared in foundation myths and reappear in shamanist narrative songs. Works such as "The Tale of Hong Kiltong" and *A Dream of Nine Clouds* transpose the hero tale into the realm of fiction.

Superimposed on this pattern were other elements devised to satisfy the new reading public. These include the separation of two lovers by the appearance of another suitor or by one lover's absence in the capital to take the civil service examinations; hairsbreadth escapes from appalling adversities; miraculous encounters at critical

---

11. Kim Chinse, "Kososŏl ŭi chakka wa tokcha," 56.

junctures; and a final reunion and happy ending. In the aftermath of the Japanese and Manchu invasions, writers were stimulated to set stories in distant China, whose Son of Heaven is on the verge of surrender to the invaders when the hero appears and saves him. In some stories, the arc of separation and final reunion takes a new direction with the introduction of a female hero, now empowered to follow the same biographical pattern as the male hero. This role reversal in favor of women was a powerful means to attract women readers.

The role of brokers or middlemen (*sŏk'wae, ch'aekk'wae*) in procuring manuscript copies and printed editions of fiction became increasingly significant. Since selling books had long been deemed a shameful act by Korean custom, it had to be carried out clandestinely—a situation that called for a middleman. He is said to have existed from the beginning of printing, say from the late Silla period onward, when the middleman played a role in the distribution of new or rare editions of Chinese books. In Chosŏn, the diary of Yu Hŭich'un (1513–1577) mentions a Pak Ŭisŏk in Seoul (November 18, 1567) and another *sŏk'wae*, Song Hŭijŏng, who brought a copy of the *Korean Gazetteer* to sell (September 11, 1568).[12] With the increase of manuscript or printed copies in circulation, books began to be sold by peddlers of women's items, by vendors of brushes and ink, and even by itinerant merchants as they visited their clients—a revolution in reading dissemination.

In addition, lending libraries loaned out manuscript or printed copies of stories for a fee. These libraries began to appear in the middle of the eighteenth century, making works of fiction accessible to a broad range of readers, especially women. Ch'ae Chegong (1702–1799) commented on the habits of women readers and their consumption of fiction, which in his day numbered a thousand or more available titles. To obtain a story from a lending library, he observed, women would sometimes sell their ornamental hairpins or bracelets or even secure a loan.[13] Maurice Courant (1865–1935), who lived in Korea from 1890 to 1892, mentions the existence of

---

12. *Miam ilgi ch'o*, 1:20, 325.
13. Ch'ae's preface to *Yŏ sasŏ*, quoted in Kim Chinse, 62.

many such libraries where women would bring pots and pans as security for the loan of a book.[14] These libraries collected, kept, revised, and circulated a significant range of vernacular fiction. The emergence of bookstores, which transferred ownership of books from seller to buyer, came somewhat later. Although the idea of a bookstore was a subject of discussion from as early as the beginning of the sixteenth century, it was not until the end of the eighteenth century that books began to be purchased as a commodity, and bookstores came into being.

Popular Literature

The nineteenth century was the heyday of popular literature and entertainment. The dominance of these vernacular forms reflected the impact of a number of economic and political changes taking place in the country. The consumers and supporters of popular literature, including rich farmers, merchants, moneylenders, interpreters, local functionaries, and clerks, were largely situated between the ruling elite and the common people. They frequented urban centers of amusement, where *sasŏl sijo* were sung and *p'ansori* performed, with a renewed emphasis on the dimensions of orality and performance in vernacular literature.

Woodblock-printed editions of vernacular fiction began to appear in the mid-nineteenth century; the *Samsŏl ki*, a collection of six short stories printed in 1848, was the first.[15] As a commercial product, it was a turning point in the production and diffusion of vernacular fiction. In order to sell copies, distribution had to be systematic. The author, publisher, and bookseller had to develop expertise and a sense of profession. Carved on woodblocks and printed by hand, the printed edition stimulated efforts to refine, improve, or abridge the manuscript version of stories; the printer also served as a writer. As a result, vernacular fiction began to appear in a more orderly and coherent for-

14. *Bibliographie coréenne*, 3 vols. (Paris: Ernest Leroux, 1894–1897), 1:22–26.
15. Yu T'agil, "Kososŏl ŭi yut'ong kwajŏng," in *Hanguk kososŏl ron* (Asea munhwasa, 1991), 353.

mat, an occasion for the social recognition of fiction as a literary genre. The complicated printing process kept the woodblock editions an artisanal product, however, and the price of a printed copy was often beyond the reach of women readers and commoners.

The three main venues of printing were Seoul, Ansŏng in Kyŏnggi, and Chŏnju—all commercial towns, close to the site of papermaking facilities, where fiction was in demand and smooth circulation could be guaranteed. The primary consumers were again women of the upper and middle classes who had sufficient time and money to cultivate the habit of reading, and male commoners. Initially, there were some forty titles of printed fiction (if we count different editions of the same title, the total comes to some two hundred). In general, Seoul editions ran to twenty or thirty pages; a longer story was normally divided into two or three volumes. Rich in Sino-Korean diction and literary language, more realistic in style and precise in the usage of vocabulary, elegant and logical in content, the Seoul editions were well received by the women. The Chŏnju editions, by contrast, ran to seventy or eighty pages (the size of the letters was larger than in the Seoul editions, which used a more cursive style). They are characterized by the use of the Chŏlla dialect with its four-syllable rhythms, their tendency to prefer description over explanation, and their wealth of humor and satire to suit the taste of commoners.

Stories of Marvels

SŎNGNAM WITH A BRANCH STUCK IN HIS HAIR

[SUSAP SŎNGNAM]

The polite name of Ch'oe Hang of Silla was Sŏngnam. He had a concubine whom he loved dearly, but his parents had intervened, and the two could not meet. After several months Ch'oe died suddenly. Eight days later he went to his concubine's house at night. She did not know that he had died and welcomed him joyfully. He had inserted a rhododendron branch in his hair. Sharing half of it with her, he said, "Since my parents will now allow us to live together, I have come for you."

He brought the concubine back to his house, leaped over the fence, and went inside. A light came on inside the house, but there was no further sign from him. When members of his family came out and saw her, they asked why she was there. The girl explained. Ch'oe's family said, "What you are telling us is very strange. Hang has been dead for eight days, and today is his burial."

The concubine replied, "My husband and I broke a rhododendron branch in two and inserted the two halves in our hair. That is the proof."

They went to the coffin, and when the family opened it, they found a rhododendron branch on Ch'oe's head. His clothes were damp from the dew, as were his shoes. But the girl realized that Ch'oe was dead, and she wept bitterly and wanted to die.

Then Ch'oe came back to life. The couple lived together for thirty years, into their old age, before passing away.

Heart Fire Coiling around a Pagoda

[SIMHWA YOT'AP]

Chigwi, a man from Hwalli Station in Silla, became infatuated with the beautiful Queen Sŏndŏk and was unable to stop weeping, because of his distress. His appearance grew haggard. Visiting a monastery to pay her respects, the queen heard about Chigwi and summoned him. Chigwi came to the foot of the pagoda in the monastery compound but fell into a deep sleep while waiting for the royal carriage to arrive. Seeing he was asleep, the queen removed a bracelet, placed it on his chest, and returned to the palace. Chigwi remained in a stupor for a long time after he awoke. Then fire leapt from his heart, coiled around the pagoda, and became a fire demon. The queen ordered a magician to write an incantation that read:

> The fire in Chigwi's heart
> Consumed his body, and he became a fire spirit.
> Let him be exiled over the ocean,
> Neither appearing here nor being intimate with me.

According to the custom of the time, this text was pasted on gateways and walls in order to ward off conflagrations.

Beauties in a Bamboo Stalk

[CHUKT'ONG MINYŎ]

When Kim Yusin (595–673) returned to the capital from Sŏju, there was another traveler on the road ahead of him. The traveler's head was enveloped in a supernatural nimbus. When the traveler went to rest under a tree, Yusin likewise stretched himself out there and pretended to sleep. The traveler waited until there were no passersby. Then he searched about in the bosom of his gown, took out a piece of bamboo, and shook it. Two beautiful girls came out. They sat together and talked; later they went back into the bamboo.

Yusin followed the traveler and asked him about what he had just seen. The traveler's speech was quiet and refined. When the two entered the capital together, Yusin took the traveler by the hand, brought him into the shade of a pine tree on Mount South, and arranged a banquet. The two beauties also appeared and took part in the feasting. The traveler said, "I live on the western sea, and I married these girls on the eastern sea. Now I am going to visit my parents-in-law together with my wives." When he finished speaking, the wind began to blow, and the clouds grew dark. Suddenly he disappeared and was seen no more.

Translated by Frits Vos

Tales of Wonder

Kim Sisŭp (1435–1493)

STUDENT YI PEERS OVER THE WALL

[YISAENG KYUJANG CHŎN]

In Songdo[1] there was a man named Yi who lived by the Camel Bridge. He was seventeen,[2] handsome, and cultured, with innate talents. As a student at the royal academy, he would read poetry even on his way to school.

In a nobleman's house by Sŏnjuk village there lived a Miss Ch'oe. She was about fourteen or fifteen, beautiful, skilled in embroidery, and she excelled in writing poetry. People used to praise the two young people:

Free and elegant, student Yi;
   lovely and virtuous, the Ch'oe girl.
Hearing of his talent and her face
   will sate your hunger.[3]

---

1. Koryŏ's capital, now Kaesŏng.
2. Seventeen by Western count (all ages given are in Western count).
3. *Shijing* 138:1; Karlgren, *Book of Odes*, 89.

Yi would pass by Ms. Ch'oe's house, books tucked under his arms. The north wall of her mansion was ringed with graceful drooping willows, under which Yi would rest.

One day he peered through the wall. Beautiful flowers were in bloom, and birds and bees were vying clamorously. To one side, through clusters of flowers, one could see a small tower. A beaded curtain was half raised, and silk curtains hung low. A beautiful girl sat within. Tiring of embroidery, she had halted her needle in mid course. Resting her chin in her palm, she hummed:

> Alone by the gauze window, my embroidery lags;
> in a clump of flowers, the oriole trills.
> For no reason I resent the eastern breeze;
> sunk in thought, quietly I stay my needle.
>
> Who is that pale young man on the road,
> among drooping willows, with his blue collar[4] and broad belt?
> Were I to turn into a swallow in the hall,
> I'd lift the beaded curtains and cross over the wall.

Hearing this, Yi became anxious to display his skill at verse making. But the walls were high, and the garden deep and secluded. He had no choice but to turn back, frustrated. On his return from school, he wrote three stanzas of verse on a slip of paper, tied the paper to a piece of tile, and threw it over the wall. The poems read:

> Twelve peaks of Mount Shaman[5] lapped in mist,
> their pointed edges emerge, purple and blue-green.

---

4. The student's uniform, as in *Shijing* 91:1; Waley, *Book of Songs*, 46.

5. Song Yu, "Gaotang fu." The goddess of the mountain, believed to dwell near the Yangzi Gorge in eastern Sichuan, came as an apparition to King Xiang (r. 298–265 BCE) at Sun Terrace and spent the night with him. Leaving, she claimed to be "cloud and rain," a euphemism for sexual intercourse. Song's "Shennü fu" celebrates her beauty; see Fusek, "The 'Kao-T'ang Fu,'" 392–425.

Don't prey on King Xiang's dream on a lonely pillow;
  let's meet on the Sun Terrace as clouds and rain.

As Sima Xiangru enticed Zhuo Wenjun,[6]
  so my love is already deep.
Pink peach and plum blossoms on the colored wall—
  where do they fall, strewn by the wind?

Will we be together, will we not?
  In vain my sorrow turns a day into a year.
You pledged love with your poems of twenty-eight.[7]
  When will I meet my fair love at Lanqiao?[8]

Ms. Ch'oe asked her maid, Hyanga, to retrieve the message. She read the poems over and over and was delighted. She then threw back over the wall a slip of paper bearing eight words: "Have no doubt, Sir! Let us meet at dusk."

Yi set out for the house at dusk, just as the girl had suggested. Suddenly he saw the branch of a peach tree beckoning to him over the wall. He drew near to examine it closely and found a bamboo chair suspended from a rope swing. He climbed over the wall.

The moon was rising over the eastern mountain; flowers cast shadows on the ground, and their pure fragrance was lovely. Yi thought he had entered a fairyland. Though he might chuckle to himself about the affair, he realized it had to remain a secret. He was apprehensive. When he looked around, he found the girl and the maid sitting on a mat in a secluded corner among the flower bushes; they

---

6. Sima Xiangru (179–117 BCE). In the *Shiji*: "Wen-chun ran away from home and joined Xiangru and the two of them galloped off to Ch'eng-tu and opened a wine shop" (Watson, *Records of the Grand Historian*, 2:299).

7. A heptasyllabic quatrain.

8. Where transcendents dwell, southeast of Lantian county in Shenxi; also where, in a play by Long Ying (fl. 1573–1620), Bei Hang of the Tang and Yunying (Cloud Bloom) meet.

wore flowers in their hair. Catching sight of Yi, the girl smiled and sang two leading lines:

> Between peach and plum boughs, brilliant flowers,
>> on the bridal pillow the delicate moonlight.

Yi capped the verse:

> If someday our secret leaks out,
>> how sad our love in the wind and rain.[9]

The girl grew pale and said, "At first my desire was to serve you, keep house for you, and be happy with you forever. But how could you say such a thing? Though I am a woman, my mind is calm. How could you, a man, compose such lines? If what happens in my room leaks out someday, my father will censure me. But I shall accept the blame myself. Hyanga, please go within and bring wine and fruit for our guest."

The maid went. There was quiet all around, no sound of voices anywhere. Yi asked, "What place is this?"

"We're beneath a small tower in the rear garden," Ms. Ch'oe answered. "Because I am their only daughter, my parents love me deeply. They built this tower by the lotus pond so that my maid and I might enjoy the lovely spring blossoms. My parents live apart, so they can't hear us talking and laughing." She then poured a cup of "green bubble" wine and sang a poem in the old style:[10]

> Over the curved rail I look down on the lotus pond;
>> among the pond flowers, lovers whisper.
> Light, light scented mist, mild mild spring.

---

9. Refers to the anger of parents.
10. Old-style as opposed to modern-style (regulated) verse (*jintishi*).

Let's write a new song, sing of white hemp.[11]
The moon shines through the flowers and onto the mat.
    Pull the long branch—a shower of pink petals.
Stirred by the wind, a pure fragrance seeps into my robe;
    Miss Jia[12] steps forward to do a spring dance.
Her silk blouse skirts a wild rose,
    rousing the parrot dozing among the blossoms.

Yi harmonized:

I stumble into Peach Blossom Spring,[13] flowers everywhere;
    I cannot express all that is in my heart.
The cloud of your hair, golden hairpin placed low;
    your cool spring blouse of green ramie cloth.
A row of lotus blossoms in the east wind;
    don't let them shudder in the wind and rain.
A fairy's sleeves whirl, shadows sway;
    among the cassia shadows the moon goddess[14] dances.
Sorrow always comes before a good thing is complete;
    don't teach the parrot new words.

The drinking over, Ms. Ch'oe said, "What happened today has certainly not happened by chance. Follow me, and let us embrace."

With these words, she entered through the north window, and Yi followed. There they climbed a ladder into the tower, which was lightly furnished with a stool and a desk with writing materials neatly arranged. On one wall was a painting, *Misty River and Tiered Peaks,*

---

11. Allusion to song by Wang Jian (768–833); see Cao Yin, *Quan Tangshi* (Complete Tang poems), 298:3371–3372.

12. Daughter of Jia Cheng (217–282), who stole exotic perfume from the Western Regions to give to her lover Han Shou. *Jinshu* (Book of Jin) 40:1172–1173.

13. *Locus amoenus* created by Tao Qian (365–427); see Hightower, *Poetry of T'ao Ch'ien*, 254–258.

14. Henge, the wife of Yi the Archer, who obtained the elixir of immortality from the Queen Mother of the West; Henge stole the elixir and fled with it to the moon.

and another, *Bamboo Grove and Old Tree*—both were famous paintings. Above each was an unsigned colophon. The first read:

> Whose brush has the uncoiled power
>   to paint myriad hills above the river?
> Majestic Fanghu,[15] countless fathoms high;
>   its peaks shimmer through haze and smoke.
> Hundreds of miles away, outlines are dim;
>   nearby, steep peaks are green coils.
> Boundless blue waves touch the far sky;
>   at dusk I gaze into the distance and think of home.
> This painting makes me lonely and desolate—
>   a boat on the Xiang[16] in the wind and rain.

The second read:

> The wind sighs through the lonely bamboo grove;
>   a tall old tree harbors tears of bygone days.
> The wild root is coiled and moss covered;
>   the old trunk, gnarled, resists wind and thunder.
> My heart treasures the Fashioner's[17] abode.
>   With whom can I talk about this wondrous place?
> Wei Yan[18] and Wen Tong[19] have long since gone;
>   how many can fathom heaven's secrets?
> Facing this painting by the bright window, forgetting care;
>   Its wondrous brushstrokes attain inner serenity.

15. "The waters of eight corners and nine regions, the stream of the Milky Way, all pointed to it, it neither shrinks nor grows. Within it there are five mountains . . . 3,000 miles high and as many miles round; the tablelands on their summits extend for 9,000 miles" (Graham, *Book of Lieh-tzu*, 97, under "Entry to the Void").

16. The Xiang, rich in legends, carries the waters of the Xiao into Lake Dongting in Hunan.

17. The old man who fashions creatures; also a metaphysical principle responsible for the particularity of the phenomenal world. See Schafer, "The Idea of Created Nature."

18. A Tang painter.

19. A Northern Song painter (1018–1079).

Another wall was covered with pictures of the four seasons, each with four quatrains. The writing was refined and elegant in the style of Zhao Mengfu (1254–1322).[20] The first scroll read:

> The lotus curtain is warm, its fragrance trails.
>   Outside the window, a rain of pink petals.
> My dream is broken by the bell of the fifth watch;[21]
>   on the magnolia-covered hillside a blackbird cries.

> On a spring day a swallow's warble swells—I close my door.
>   Weary and mute, I stop my sewing.
> Butterflies flit in pairs among the flowers,
>   chasing falling blossoms in the garden's shade.

> A chill passes through my green silk skirt,
>   heartbroken, I face the spring wind in vain.
> Who can measure the throbbing of my heart?
>   Among a hundred flowers mandarin ducks dance.

> Spring colors sink into the house of Huang the fourth lass,[22]
>   deep red and light green on the gauze window.
> Fragrant garden grasses suffer a spring sorrow;
>   I'll lift the beaded curtains and view the falling blossoms.

The second read:

> Thick ears on early wheat, a young swallow darts aslant;
>   over the south garden, the pomegranate tree blooms.
> Beneath the green window, a girl wields her scissors
>   To cut purple silk to make a new shirt.

---

20. Yuan poet, painter, and calligrapher.

21. 3–5 a.m.

22. Allusion to Du Fu, "Strolling along the River Bank, Looking for Flowers"; see Qian Qianyi, *Qianzhu Dushi,* 12:405.

The season of golden plums, a fine rain on the screen;
   orioles twitter in the shade, swallows fly in through the blind.
Again a year is gone, its view is old—
   beech flowers fall—the bamboo shoots sprout.

Should I hit the oriole with a green plum?
   The wind passes the southern eaves, the sun sets late.
Lotus leaves exude a fragrance, the pond is full.
   In deep green waves, cormorants bathe.

The pattern on the bamboo couch resembles waves;
   on the screen, the Xiao and Xiang and a wisp of cloud.
Unable to bear being lazy, she cannot wake from a daydream;
   through the half-opened window slant the rays of the setting sun.

The third read:

Chill chill the autumn wind; a cold dew forms;
   the moonlight is graceful, the jasper autumn water, blue.
Wild geese return cackling in ones and twos;
   at the well, a rustle of falling beech leaves.

Chirp chirp a hundred insects under the couch;
   on it a fair lady sheds jade teardrops.
Miles away, her lover fights at the front;
   in twilight at the Jade Gate Pass,[23] the moon is bright.

She wants to make new clothes—the scissors feel cold.
   She calls her maid to bring the iron.
Not noticing the fire is out,
   she plucks the zither and scratches her head.

---

23. West of Dunhuang, in Gansu, where the Chinese maintained patrols against incursions from the northwest over the wall.

The lotus falls in the pond; plantains turn yellow;
  The first frost coats the duck-painted tiles.
She cannot hold back old sorrow or new grief;
  And yet the crickets cry in her secluded room.

The fourth read:

A plum branch casts its shadow on the window;
  on the windy west veranda, the bright moon.
She stirs the fire in the brazier with tongs
  and calls for her maid to change a pot for tea.

Startled by night frost, the leaves shiver;
  the whirlwind chases the snow to the veranda.
In vain she dreams all night of her love
  as he wanders along the icy river, the old battlefield.

The sun in the window brings the warmth of spring;
  her grief-stricken eyes show traces of slumber.
A small plum branch in the vase half opens its buds;
  demure, silent, she stitches a pair of ducks.

Frosty winds ravage the northern forest,
  a cold crow caws at the moon.
Before the lamp, her lovelorn tears
  fall on her needle's eye—she stops her work.

To one side there was a small, separate room with curtains, a mattress, a blanket, and pillows, all neatly arranged. Outside the curtains there was musk incense and an orchid-oil lantern burning bright as day. Their lovemaking was delicious.

Yi stayed several days, then quoted Confucius: "'While father and mother are alive, a good son does not wander far afield. If he does, he should let them know where he goes.'[24] It has already been three days since I left home. They must be waiting for me at the entrance to the village. This is not the way of a son."

Ms. Ch'oe sympathized and sent him away over the wall. From that time on, Yi went to her every night.

One evening, Yi's father said to him: "You used to leave in the morning and return in the evening so that you could study goodness and the way of righteousness as taught by the sages of the past. But now you go out at dusk and return at dawn—what is this all about? You are behaving frivolously, climbing over people's walls and breaking their trees.[25] If this becomes known, everyone will blame me for not raising you strictly. And the girl—if she is of noble birth, your reckless behavior will sully her reputation and bring censure down upon her. This is a serious matter. Go at once to the southeast and take charge of the servants. And don't come back!"

The very next day Yi went south to Ulchu.[26] Ms. Ch'oe waited for him every evening in her garden, but he did not return for several months. Assuming that he had been ill, she sent Hyanga to make discreet inquiries of Yi's neighbors. One neighbor said, "Young Yi offended his father. It has been several months since he went south."

On hearing this, Ms. Ch'oe fell ill; she lay in bed tossing and turning and could not get up. She took no food, not even water; her speech grew delirious, and due to her grief, her skin lost its luster. Her parents were perplexed and asked what was wrong, but she would not speak. When they examined her writing box, they found the poems she had exchanged with Yi. "Who is this Yi?" they exclaimed, beating their breasts. "We have nearly lost our daughter!"

The matter had come to light, and Ms. Ch'oe could dissemble no longer. Her voice was unsteady and her speech halting as she said:

24. *Lunyu* 4:19; Waley, *Analects*, 105–106.
25. *Shijing* 76; Waley, *Book of Songs*, 35.
26. Ulsan in South Kyŏngsang.

"How can I hide my secret from my father and mother who have raised me with love? I believe that the love between man and woman is the most important human feeling. The *Book of Songs* says, 'The plum falls; let those gentlemen who would court me come while it is auspicious'[27] and the *Book of Changes,* 'The influence shows itself in the thighs!'[28] I am frail as the willow, and should have married before the 'falling mulberry leaves, yellow and sere.'[29] Now I have wet my clothes with dew[30] and betrayed those closest to me. Like creepers clinging to moss,[31] I am like the girl in a Chinese romance.[32] My guilt is undeniable: I have dishonored my family's name. But in coming to know that wayward man, I grew fond of him, and my sorrows have only multiplied. I tried to bear the loneliness, but in my weakened condition my longing grows deeper every day, and the pain from my illness is twice as intense. I am at death's door and soon will become a hungry spirit. If my father and mother will honor my last wish, my life may be preserved; but if you reject my plea, I will surely die. I know I will roam with my love again in the Yellow Springs[33] before I marry another."

Seeing the girl's determination, her parents ceased their questioning. Now warning, now cajoling, they tried to reassure their daughter. Then they secured a matchmaker to propose marriage to the Yi family.

The elder Yi asked about the lineage of the Ch'oe family. "My son may be young and dissipated, but he is well educated and carries himself like a man. Someday he will surely succeed in the examinations

---

27. *Shijing* 20:1; Waley, *Book of Songs,* 30.

28. Hexagram 31, which warns against acting impulsively; Rutt, *Book of Changes,* 254, 397.

29. *Shijing* 58:4; Waley, *Book of Songs,* 97 .

30. Lost her chastity. *Shijing* 17:1; Waley, *Book of Songs,* 65.

31. "To join with my lord now in marriage,/a creeper clinging to the moss" ("Nineteen Old Poems of the Han," in Watson, *Columbia Book of Chinese Poetry,* 99).

32. Alludes to the story by Qu You in which student Wang meets a girl at a pond by the Wei River; see Qu You, *Jiandeng xinhua,* 2:49–53.

33. Hades.

and become well known.[34] As yet, though, it is too early to think of finding him a wife."

When the matchmaker reported back to the Ch'oe family, the elder Ch'oe sent her back again with a message: "My friends all praise your son's surpassing talents. Even though he has not yet passed the examination, I know he will not be content to live in obscurity. I think it would be well to quickly set an auspicious date to unite our two families."

To this the elder Yi replied: "I too have studied the classics since my early years, but have grown old without achieving my goal. My slaves have left and my relatives are of little help. Life is hard for us, and we're not well placed. Why would a powerful family like the Ch'oe consider the son of a poor scholar as a possible son-in-law? This must be the work of some meddler who wishes to flatter my house and deceive yours."

Through the matchmaker the elder Ch'oe replied: "The wedding presents and robes are all ready. Please choose an auspicious day for the ceremony."

Only upon hearing this did the elder Yi reconsider. He at once sent for his son and asked his opinion. Beside himself with joy, the son wrote a poem:

> The broken mirror becomes round again at the opportune time;
>> magpies in the Milky Way[35] furthered this moment.
> Now the old man under the moon[36] ties the red knot—
>> How can I resent the cuckoo calling the east wind?[37]

34. *Shijing* 252:9; Waley, *Book of Songs*, 184.

35. The Herd Boy and Weaver Maid, fated to be separated on the east and west sides of the Milky Way, meet once a year when magpies build a bridge to allow them to cross over the vault of heaven.

36. Originally a god of marriage who uses red strings to tie the knots between a man and a woman that will bind them together through three lifetimes; the figure became a common term for a matchmaker.

37. Traditionally, the cuckoo is the herald of spring.

Ms. Ch'oe was relieved to hear the good news. She wrote:

> Bad ties have become good ones;
>> old vows are now fulfilled.
> When shall we pull a small cart?[38]
>> Help me rise to put the flowery comb in my hair.

An auspicious day was chosen, and at last the ceremony took place. Their love, once ended, began anew. After becoming husband and wife, they loved each other deeply but still accorded each other the respect that a host might accord a guest. None could equal in constancy these paragons of conjugal bliss.

The following year Yi placed first in the higher civil service examination and rose to high rank. His fame spread at court.

In 1361, the Red Turbans[39] occupied the capital, and the king fled to Pokchu[40] in the south. The bandits burned houses and massacred people and cattle. Defenseless families fled east and west seeking refuge. Although Yi hid his family deep in the mountains, one armed bandit followed them. Yi managed to escape, but his wife was caught.

When the bandit was about to have his way with her, she rebuked him: "Kill me and eat me, you tiger, you devil! I'd rather be food for a wolf than the mate of a dog or pig!" In rage the bandit killed her and hacked apart her body.

Yi hid in the wilderness and was barely able to survive. At last he heard that the bandits had been subdued and made his way to his parents' home, but it was burned to ashes.

---

38. Alludes to a story about the wife of Bao Xuan of the Later Han, who helped her husband's small cart to return home. *Hou Hanshu* 83: 2765–2768.

39. Chinese brigands who invaded from across the Yalu in the twelfth month of 1359 and the tenth month of 1361, when the capital fell. See Robinson, *Empire's Twilight*, 74–97 and 130–198.

40. Andong in North Kyŏngsang.

Next he went to his wife's parents' home. Every wing and corridor was deserted; only the sound of mice squeaking and birds' cries intruded on the stillness. Unable to bear his grief, he climbed the small tower and stifled his sobs with deep sighs. He sat there till dusk, thinking of the happy days that now seemed but a dream.

At about the second watch (9–11 p.m.), when wan moonlight shone on the roof and beams, Yi heard footsteps approaching down the corridor. He turned and saw his wife. He knew she was no longer of this world, but he loved her so much he did not doubt her presence. At once he asked, "Where have you gone to save yourself?"

Clasping Yi's hands, she wept profusely and poured out her tale: "As the daughter of a good family, I received instruction from childhood. I became skilled in embroidery and sewing, and I learned poetry and calligraphy and the path of goodness and righteousness. I knew only the ways of a woman: how could I know of the affairs outside? When you peered through the wall of red apricot blossoms, I offered you my love—a pearl in the jasper sea. Then we smiled at each other under the blossoms and pledged ourselves to a lifelong union. When we met again behind the curtain, our love could not be contained in a hundred years. To speak of these things brings unbearable sorrow and shame. How could they be overcome? I wanted to return to the countryside and live with you forever in our beloved garden, but I met calamity and found myself defiled.[41] I resisted the wolf and tiger's advances to the end, and chose to be torn to pieces and left abandoned in the mire. It was surely human nature to do so, but a human heart could not bear it.

"After we separated in that mountain valley, I sadly became a bird that had lost its mate. Our houses were destroyed; my parents were lost. I could only lament, a weary, homeless spirit. Integrity is precious; life is insubstantial. It was fortunate that my frail body escaped shame, but was there anyone who pitied my heart when it was torn to pieces

41. Lit., "facedown in the gutter." *Mengzi* 1B:12; Lau, *Mencius*, 70.

and reduced to cold ashes? Only my rotting entrails remain to harbor resentment. My skeleton lies exposed in the wilderness, and my insides have been abandoned to the earth. Were the joys of the past my only compensation for today's sorrow?

"Now that the warm spring wind has visited the deep valley,[42] the soul of Qian flees with her lover,[43] and I have come back to fulfill our vows for a time. Our pledge to meet after twelve years on Mount Penglai[44] is unbroken, and from the immortals' abode comes the sweet scent of our three lives. At this moment, recalling our long separation, I promise I will not forget our vow. If you remember that promise, I will serve you as long as I can. Will you let me?"

Deeply moved, Yi said, "That has been my wish from the beginning." He was overcome with joy.

Now they abandoned themselves to their feelings. When their talk touched on the family fortune, Yi's wife said, "Nothing was lost—it is buried in a mountain valley."

"What about our parents? Where are their remains?"

"They were abandoned, in no particular place."

When their talk had ended, they went to bed and took great pleasure in each other, as in the past.

The following day, they went together to look for the hidden treasure and found several ingots of gold and silver and other valuables. They gathered up the remains of their parents and buried them together at the foot of Mount Ogwan.[45] They planted trees, offered sacrifices, and completed the rites.

---

42. Zou Yan's flute was able to change the cold of winter to a warm spring. *Shiji* 74:2344–2345; Graham, *Book of Lieh-tzu*, 108.

43. Qian's soul fled with her lover, leaving her body behind. See Chen Yuanyou, *Lihunji* (Daibei: Yiwen, 1968).

44. In Chinese mythology, one of the sacred seamounts in the eastern sea, the dwelling place of transcendents.

45. Thirty tricents west of Changdan, east of Mount Pine in Kaesŏng.

From that time on, Yi did not accept any office and lived with his wife. The servants who had fled returned, but Yi took no interest in ordinary affairs and shut his gate to relatives and to acquaintances who came by on ceremonial occasions. He was always with her— exchanging cups, harmonizing lines of poetry, and enjoying only her company.

Some years later, there came an evening when Yi's wife said, "We pledged our love for three lives, but worldly affairs intruded. Before we can tire of our joys, I fear a sad parting must come." Then she sobbed.

Surprised, Yi asked, "Why do you say such a thing?"

"I cannot escape the pull of the underworld," she answered. "The Heavenly Emperor, knowing that we had not sinned in our previous life and that our ties were unbroken, allowed me to return to you to share your sorrow for a time. But I cannot tarry long in the world of humans lest I confuse them and lead them astray."

She called her maid to bring wine and bade Yi drink. Then she sang a new song to the tune of "Spring in Jade Tower":[46]

Arms in the battlefield as far as eye can see:
    jade smashed, flowers blown away, a drake has lost its mate.
Who will bury the scattered bones?
    A wandering soul, blood stained, has none to plead for her.

I cannot become a fairy on Mount Shaman.
    The broken mirror breaks again—O my grieving heart!
Once parted, we shall be apart forever,
    without a word passing between here and there.

Choking with tears at every phrase, she could not finish. Yi was also unable to contain his grief. "I would rather go with you to the

46. A *ci* tune title.

Yellow Springs than suffer this separation. After the invasion, families and their servants fled in all directions, and my parents' remains were abandoned in the wilderness. Who would have buried them had it not been for you? 'While parents are alive, serve them according to ritual. When they die, bury them according to ritual.'[47] You have fulfilled the ancient sage's teaching through your innate devotion and humanity. I am deeply moved and overwhelmed by shame. Why should we not live a hundred years here and become dust together?"

"Your life's allotment has several dozen more years," she answered, "but my name has already been entered in the roll of departed spirits, and I can remain here no longer. To persist in my love for a mortal would defy the underworld's laws. Then not only would I be punished, but you would be as well. My remains are still scattered outside. If you would favor me, please place them beyond the reach of the elements."

The couple gazed into each other's eyes as tears streamed down their faces.

"Take care, my love," she said, and gradually disappeared, leaving no trace.

Yi gathered her remains and buried them beside her parents'. The rites concluded, Yi became deeply despondent. He fell ill and died in a few months.

All who heard this story were moved by it, and by the couple's constancy in particular.

---

47. *Lunyu* 2:5; Waley, *Analects*, 89.

Romances

Kwŏn P'il (1569–1612)

The Story of Gentleman Zhou

[CHUSAENG CHŎN]

Among the works of fiction from sixteenth- and seventeenth-century Korea, "The Story of Gentleman Zhou" stands out as a romance written in literary Chinese. The story describes the development of a love triangle between a talented man and two charming maidens, Paidao and Xianhua. The male protagonist, Zhou, first becomes involved with Paidao, a female entertainer; the plot thickens when he falls in love with Xianhua, the alluring daughter of a noble family. Paidao, left bewildered and heartbroken, suffers a physical decline and succumbs to lovesickness. The ending of the story is dark—Zhou fails to consummate his relationship with Xianhua and faces grave peril, having been conscripted into the Ming army and transported to Korea, where he recounts his story to the author, Kwŏn P'il. Drawing on the rich sources available to fiction, the story shows the dual influences of Chinese tales of wonder (*chuanqi*) and local folk narratives. Also, it combines fictional with realistic elements, taking the form of a biographical record in which the author appears to be writing about an actual encounter with the protagonist.

Most romances and works of fiction from this period are anonymous. Yet scholars generally agree that "The Story of Gentleman Zhou" should be attributed to Kwŏn P'il (1569–1612), following Yi Myŏngsŏn's claim in his *History of Korean Literature* (*Chosŏn munhak sa*, 1947). The discussion of authorship still continues, however, because no edition of the story clearly indicated the author and date until a North Korean edition was discovered with a postscript signed by Kwŏn Yŏjang (the author's courtesy name). This translation is based on the North Korean edition (1963).

Kwŏn P'il, known as a gifted poet, was active from the late sixteenth to early seventeenth century. He is often described as an iconoclastic thinker who avoided mainstream literature and wrote from the standpoint of an outsider. Born in 1569 as the fifth son of Kwŏn Pyŏk (1520–1593), a high-level official at the Ministry of Rites, Kwŏn P'il learned classics and poetry at an early age from Chŏng Ch'ŏl (1536–1593). He was an active member of a literary coterie and shared close ties with Yi Annul (1571–1636), Hŏ Kyun (1569–1618), and Cho Wihan (1567–1649).

His mastery of poetry and other genres smoothed the way for Kwŏn into the ranks of the Royal Confucian Academy. At the age of eighteen, he passed the initial civil service examination and had the highest ranking going into the next level (*poksi*). He failed the exam in the capital, however, when he was found to have miswritten one sinograph. At thirty-two he took up his first official post as an instructor of juvenile education (*tongmong kyogwan*) but soon resigned. From that time on, he lived as a retainer of a powerful family until he was seized and accused of the crime of factionalism—a poem he had written, "The Willows of the Palace," was thought to have alluded to high-handed behavior by courtiers close to Prince Kwanghae (1575–1641). After being severely questioned by the prince, Kwŏn ended his life while on his way to the place of exile, at the age of forty-two. "The Story of Gentleman Zhou" is a sensitive portrait of an intellectual with a powerful and restless imagination as well as his own vulnerabilities.

Gentleman Zhou's name was Gui, courtesy name Zhiqing, and pen name Meichuan. Zhou's family had lived in Qiantang for generations, but since Zhou's father served as transport officer in the prefecture of Chu, his family settled there. Zhou was young and intelligent, and also composed verse well. At the age of eighteen, he entered the National Academy, and because he was respected by his colleagues, he believed he would succeed. However, he failed the civil service examination several times. One day he sighed and said, "A human being is like a speck of dust on a fragile and tender leaf. Why should I allow myself to be fettered by achievement and reputation? It would be meaningless to spend my whole life seeking mundane pleasures." He did not take the examination again. Instead, he collected all his fortune—hundreds in cash—and set off on a business venture. With half of the collected money, he bought a boat and traveled to sundry rivers and lakes; with the other half he bought goods in the local markets and made a small profit by selling them in distant prefectures. He made himself into a merchant, but in reality he was like an aimless, lonely wanderer, finding himself in Wu in the morning and in Zhou in the evening.

One day he anchored his boat at a dock near the Yueyang Tower and entered the gate of the town, where he met his friend Student Luo,

who was well known in town. He was delighted to see Zhou and offered him a drink. They shared several cups, and Zhou got so drunk
he lost his sense of time. It was already dark when he returned to the
boat, and the moon had risen. Zhou let his boat drift, leaned on the
oar, and fell asleep. Powered by the wind, the boat traveled as swiftly
as a flying arrow. Suddenly Zhou was awakened by the sound of a
temple bell far off in the fog. The moon was setting in the west. When
he looked up the grassy riverbank, he saw green trees dim in the distance and lamplight emanating from a red balustrade and a blue
beaded screen. He asked a passerby where he was and learned that it
was his hometown, Qiantang. Feeling nostalgic, he composed a poem:

> Leaving Yueyang, I leaned on the magnolia oar;
>> the wind brought me home drunk in a single night.
> An oriole twitters and the spring moon wanes at dawn;
>> surprised, I awakened to find myself in Qiantang.

In the morning, Zhou climbed up the bank and looked for his old
friends, but most of them had passed away or left town. Humming a
verse and wandering here and there, he hesitated to leave. There was
a woman, Paitao, with whom Zhou used to play in his childhood.
Paitao was endowed with talent and beauty and was widely known in
Qiantang as an outstanding female entertainer; many called her Lady
Pai. When she took Zhou to her house and gave him a warm reception, he presented her with a poem out of gratitude.

> Fragrant flowers at the sky's edge dampen her cloth;
>> As I return from far away, things have changed.
> Only Du Qiu[1] has cherished her reputation;
>> a beaded screen hangs in the tower in the sunset.

---

1. A concubine of Yi Qi in the Tang. After Yi died, she became a favorite of Jing Ling.

Deeply impressed by the lyric, Paitao said, "You have such literary flair. You are obviously qualified for a high position—why aren't you bending your back to seek office instead of floating like a weed in the river?" She also asked, "Have you married?" Zhou answered, "Not yet." Then Paitao smiled and said, "I beg you not to return to the boat. You can stay with me. On your behalf, I will find you a perfect match." She implied that she harbored affection for Zhou. Fascinated by her beauty, Zhou looked at her, smiled, and thanked her. "How dare I ask you to do that for me!" The sun was setting, and they were still talking. Paitao had a young servant girl escort Zhou to the guest room to rest.

When Zhou entered the room, he found a heptasyllabic quatrain hanging on the wall. He was struck by the originality of the poem. When he asked the servant girl about the poet, she replied, "Our lady composed it."

> Lute, please do not play a song of longing.
>   Your haunting melody wrings my heart.
> Shadows of flowers on the curtain, how lonely I am!
>   How many dusks have I spent in spring?

Zhou was already attracted by Paitao's charm, but her poem fascinated him even more. All kinds of thoughts went through his head. He wanted to test whether or not she was interested in him by capping her poem. He struggled to think of a line that would impress her, but failed to complete the poem until midnight.

The bright moon shed its light on the ground, casting shadows here and there. When he walked through the house, he heard the sound of human voices and the whinny of a horse, but they soon stopped. Zhou was curious about the noise, but there was no way to investigate. He found Paitao's room, which was not far away. He could see Paitao's shadow through the gauze window from the red lamplight illuminating the room. To steal a glance, Zhou crept closer. Paitao was sitting alone. She spread out a piece of colorful paper, perhaps to write a poem, and then began to recite the first lines of "A butterfly envying the flower." When he saw her grappling with the last lines, Zhou opened her window and asked without ceremony, "Do you mind if I add some lines to your lyric?" She pretended to be annoyed by the interruption: "The guest who has contrived to come here must be insane." Zhou answered, "The guest is an ordinary man; it is the hostess who drives him to insanity." Then with a smile Paitao allowed Zhou to complete the lyric:

In a deep and small courtyard, my mind is troubled.
    The moon hangs on a branch of blossoms;
an incense burner blows smoke into the sky.
    The beautiful one inside the window is afraid to grow old.
Awakened from a dream, she is drawn to the flowers and plants.
    Mistakenly I enter the twelve islands of the seamount Penglai.[2]
Fanchuan[3] did not know he'd found a fragrant plant.
    In an instant I awaken, as a bird sings in the tree:
There's no shadow on the blue screen when dawn reddens the terrace.

When Zhou finished the last line, Paitao arose from her seat and offered him a special wine in a jade cup. Zhou's mind turned to other thoughts, so he declined the drink. Paitao saw the sadness in Zhou's face and said, "I was originally from a renowned clan. My grandfather worked in the merchant shipping office in the prefecture of Quan. But he was implicated in a dispute, and my family was downgraded to the status of commoners. Since then, we have known poverty and been unable to regain our station. What is worse, my parents died when I was young, and I was raised by relatives. I wished to preserve my chastity, but I found my name already on the registry of female entertainers. From that time on, I had to accompany customers at banquets. When

---

2. The mythical dwelling place of immortals.

3. The pen name of a Tang poet, Du Mu (803–853), who had a love affair with a female entertainer he compared to a "fragrant plant."

I am at rest alone in my house, I shed tears when I look at the flowers and face the moon. But now I have met you. You have a noble presence and a kind mien, and you also possess talent and wit. Although I know my origins are obscure, I would like to spend this night with you and then to serve you as my husband in this life. My only wish is to see you establish yourself by winning a government post someday. Then I hope you will take my name out of the registry so that no further disgrace will befall my family. That is what I wish for. Even if you should abandon me afterward and spurn the chance to see me, I will thank you for your favor. How could I blame you?" Paitao shed tears after these words.

Touched by Paitao's declaration, Zhou put his arm around her waist and wiped her tears with his sleeve. "That is only what a man is supposed to do. Even if you had said nothing, I could never be heartless to you!" Upon hearing this, she dried her tears and changed her expression. "According to the *Book of Songs,* women are not at fault, but men have altered their ways.[4] Do you not know the story of Li Yi and Huo Xiaoyu?[5] But if you say that you won't abandon me, you must write out your vow." Paitao gave him a piece of fine silk from the state of Lu, and Zhou took a brush and wrote a poem in one stroke:

> Blue mountains never get old;
> > green water stays long.
> You may not believe my words,
> > but the bright moon is in the sky.

Paitao sealed the poem and put it inside the waist of her skirt. Then they spent the night together, reciting the "Rhymeprose on Gaotang." The pleasure they found was comparable to that of Student Jin and

---

4. *Shijing* 58:4; Waley, *Book of Songs,* 50.

5. The tragic love affair between a Confucian scholar and a female entertainer is recounted in a tale of wonder (*chuanqi*) by Jiang Fang (fl. 820); see Mair, *Columbia History of Chinese Literature,* 585.

Cuicui in the "Tale of Cuicui," and of Gentleman Wi Wei and Ping-ping in "The Return of Jia Yunhua's Soul."[6]

On the following day, Zhou heard a horse whinnying at the door and asked Paitao about it. She replied, "Not far from here, across the brook, there is a manor with a red gate. It is the house of a certain Minister Lu, who was once a prime minister. He passed away, and since then his wife has been living in the house with a son and a daughter, both unmarried. They pass the time singing and dancing and have often asked me to join them. She sent a horse last night, asking me to come, but I said I was sick in bed, as I wanted to be with you." Zhou was glad to hear it and put aside any thoughts of his friends or his business; he only wanted to stay, and to play music and drink.

One day they heard someone knocking on the door at noon. Paitao sent a servant to see who had come to visit her. It was a servant girl from the minister's house, carrying a note on behalf of the lady. The note said, "I am planning a banquet, and it wouldn't be right without you. If it is not too much trouble, I would like to ask you to come and join us." Paitao spoke to Zhou: "Again I have been asked by the noble woman to join her party. I don't think that I can decline her offer this time." She combed her hair and dressed herself beautifully, and when she left for the minister's house, Zhou saw her off at the door, asking several times for her to return before nightfall. Paitao rode away, looking like a slender sparrow; her horse seemed to be a flying dragon stirring up the flowers and willow leaves.

Zhou could not quiet his mind after seeing her go, so he decided to follow. When he reached the Yongjin Gate, he turned left toward the Chuihong Bridge. Just as Paitao had said, there was a tall house with curved terraces and a red gate fronting the water. Half of the façade was hidden among green willows and pink cherry blossoms, so

6. "Jia Yunhua huanhun ji" by Li Zhen (1376–1452); see Mair, *Columbia History of Chinese Literature*, 681.

that the house seemed to be floating in the clouds. He could hear laughter above the sound of the music coming from inside.

Zhou wandered about the bridge. Leaning against a pillar, he recited a classical poem.

> In the willows across quiet water, the tower rises high;
>> blue tiles on the azure roof display the color of spring.
> A refreshing breeze sends laughter and voices.
>> Flowers block the view; I cannot see people in the tower.
> How envious I am of a pair of swallows among the flowers,
>> darting now into the red-beaded hanging screen.
> Wandering aimlessly, I cannot bear to turn my steps toward home.
>> The golden waves in the sunset only deepen this traveler's sorrow.

While Zhou loitered, the sunset colors touched the sky, and soon dusk fell as the darkness gathered. Then he saw a group of maidens coming out of the house, all mounted on horses with golden saddles and embroidered bridles that dazzled the eyes. He thought that Paitao must be among them and hid himself in a vacant shop on the market street to watch for her. More than ten maidens passed, but not Paitao. He felt strange, so he walked back to the entrance of the bridge.

It became so dark that no one could have distinguished a horse from a cow. Zhou passed through the red gate and approached the tower but still found no one. In the moonlight he only saw a pond north of the tower, encircled by a mélange of flowers. There was a small curved path visible behind the flower bed, so he followed it, walking as quietly as he could. The path led to a large hall, and as he began to walk around it, he saw another, smaller hall covered with grapevines. It was nicely decorated, and its window, bright with candlelight, was half-open. Inside he could see maidens in red skirts and indigo jackets slowly moving. It was a picturesque sight.

Zhou hid behind the edge of the window and continued to peer inside. A golden folding screen and colorful blankets caught his eye.

There was an old woman in a red silk jacket, sitting on a white cushion. She looked to be in her fifties, but when she turned her head and winked at someone, Zhou could tell that she must have been gorgeous in her youth. Also, there was a thirteen- or fourteen-year-old girl sitting next to the older woman. The young girl was beautiful, with a blue tint in her cloudlike hair and rosy cheeks. When she glanced to the side, her enchanting eyes reminded him of sunshine in autumn, and her smile was like the early morning dew in spring. Compared to this girl, Paitao, sitting next to her, was an owl or raven alongside a phoenix, or pebbles or sand beside jade beads. Zhou was mesmerized, enthralled; he felt a great pull to give in to the insane urge to rush into the hall.

When wine cups were passed around, Paitao declined and excused herself to go home. The lady insisted Paitao stay longer, but as Paitao repeated her wish, the lady became more curious. "You used to stay up late at night; why do you wish to leave so early today? Do you have an appointment with someone significant?" Paitao, adjusting her dress, replied, "Since you have asked, I will not hide it from you." She spoke in detail about the encounter and the affair with Zhou. When the lady was about to respond, the young girl looked over at Paitao, smiling. "Why didn't you tell us beforehand? We nearly ruined your auspicious meeting tonight!" The lady laughed along with them and allowed her to leave.

On hearing this, Zhou rushed home and pulled up the bedclothes, pretending to be asleep. Paitao arrived and saw Zhou lying quietly. She wanted to wake him and said, "What kind of dream are you dreaming now?" Zhou opened his eyes and replied:

> In my dream I entered a jasper terrace in a radiant cloudbank,
> And within the nine-flowered raiment I met a Daoist fairy.

"Whom are you referring to as a 'Daoist fairy'?" Paitao asked with curiosity. Zhou became flustered, not knowing what to say, and came up with another poem:

> Awakened from sleep, I delight to see the transcendent by my side.
> What would I do with a courtyard filled with flowers and moonlight!

Zhou tried to clear away doubts by saying, "You are my fairy lady, aren't you?" and Paitao replied, "If so, you should be my fairy lad." They decided to call each other "fairy lady" and "fairy lad" from that moment on. Zhou also asked why she had come home so late. She said, "After the banquet, the lady had the other female entertainers go home but asked me to stay a little longer with her daughter, Xianhua. So we enjoyed a small party of our own, and that is why I was late." Zhou was curious about the girl, so Paitao added more:

"Her courtesy name is Fangqing. She is fourteen and so elegant and beautiful. She does not seem to belong to this world. She is also well versed in poetry and embroidery. I am not even qualified to envy her. Last night she composed a lyric to 'Wind among the Pines.' That song is usually accompanied by a zither, so they wanted me to play it since I know the melody." Paitao recited the lyric for Zhou.

> Outside the window, flowers bloom and spring days grow longer.
>   The house is silent, the beaded screen is drawn.
> A duck on the sandbank warms itself alone in the sunlight,
>   Envying a pair of ducks playing in the pond.
> It is foggy by the willow trees;
>   in the mist the branches are still subtle and green.
>
> The beauty awakened from a dream and leaned upon the balustrade,
>   Sadness welling in the corners of her eyes.
> The swallow sings and the nightingale warbles in their season;
>   how regretful it is to waste the dreams of youth.
> Carelessly I play my lute and dally;
>   who could know of the deep regret hidden in the song?

As Paitao recited each line, Zhou wanted to praise the remarkable talent of the poet. But he concealed his feelings and said to Paitao:

"This lyric seems to reflect the kind of feelings that arise in the women's quarters. If she did not possess at least the literary talent of a Su Ruolan,[7] she could not have composed a poem like this. However, her talent cannot match that of my fairy lady." Zhou had seen Xianhua, and now his feeling for Paitao was gone. Even when they exchanged cups of wine and laughed together, his mind was filled with Xianhua.

One day the lady called in her son, Guoying, and said, "Now you are turning eleven, but you still have not learned the classics. You will be a grown-up someday. If you do not acquire your scholarship, you won't be able to behave as a man should. Recently I heard that Paitao's fiancé, Zhou, is a man of erudition. Why don't you ask him if he will teach you?" The lady was quite strict with her son, so Guoying did not dare to go against her wish. The next morning, Guoying left home with his book under his arm to meet Zhou. After hearing Guoying's story, Zhou laughed in his sleeve, thinking, "This is what I have longed for." Even though he wanted to agree immediately, Zhou declined the request several times to show his modesty. Only when Guoying asked for the fourth time did Zhou agree to teach him, and he had a further idea. Paitao was away at the time, and he suggested to Guoying that he could take his lodging with the family: "It might not be so easy for you to go back and forth every day. I'm afraid it will wear you out. Your family has a guest room in the house, and if I move to your place, it would lighten the burden on you, and you wouldn't get exhausted by traveling. That would allow us to concentrate more on the teaching." Guoying was pleased to hear it and kowtowed to Zhou in gratitude. "I had been thinking that same thought for a while, but I didn't want to bother you." Guoying returned home and spoke with the lady about Zhou's proposal. The lady was pleased with the idea and sent an invitation to Zhou right away.

7. The courtesy name of Su Hui (fl. 4th cent.), a gifted female scholar and poet who composed "Xuanji tu," a palindrome to express her love for her husband in exile.

Paitao saw it when she came home later that day. It was a complete surprise. "Another secret lover? How could you have planned to move out and abandon me?"

"I heard there are over thirty thousand books in Guoying's house that the minister bequeathed to his family. Since the lady cherishes them so much, she does not lend them to anyone. They are supposed to be rare items that no one can easily find. All I want is to have an opportunity to see for myself."

"If you wish to devote yourself to your studies to that extent," said Paitao, "I will be glad to let you go."

Zhou moved into the minister's house without delay. From that time on, he spent his days teaching Guoying. When night fell, he ventured to unlock the gate and enter the private quarters. But the door was firmly bolted. He tried for ten nights in a row, but always in vain. He could not sleep and lay awake thinking: "I came here with one purpose: to meet Xianhua. It is almost the end of spring, but I haven't seen her even once. I can't just wait until the Yellow River turns clear. No one has a limitless life. I need to scale the wall immediately. If fortune is mine, the outcome will be favorable. I would rather be punished severely and die here than do nothing."

One night when the moon was hidden behind dark clouds, Zhou crept over the walls and found his way to Xianhua's room. Every pillar and corridor was partitioned by beaded screens and curtains. He looked around and saw no sign that anyone was there other than Xianhua, who was playing the lute by candlelight. Crouching behind a pillar, Zhou listened to the tune she was playing. After finishing the song, she recited "Greeting to the Bridegroom,"[8] one of Su Shi's lyrics.

Who is knocking on my window outside the screen,
    Waking me from a dream—I was in the jasper tower.
Alas, it may only be wind blowing through the bamboo.

8. "Hexinlang," by the Song poet Su Shi (1037–1101).

Instantly, Zhou replied from outside the screen:

> Don't say it's the wind passing through bamboo.
> The comely one has come to you.

Xianhua, pretending not to hear the voice, put out the light and went to bed. Then Zhou entered the room. He spent the night with her. She was so young and delicate that she could barely endure the pain during their intercourse. But light rain fell through light clouds; the willow branch seduced the flower. She sometimes whispered. Then she gently smiled and soon grimaced. As a bee looks for honey and a butterfly finds the flower, Zhou was so obsessed with her he did not even notice when day was breaking. Suddenly he heard an oriole singing outside the balustrade and ran out of the room. The pond and courtyard were quiet, shrouded in the mist. Xianhua sent him off at the door. Then she closed the door and spoke from behind it.

"You should never come back. If anyone finds out about this, we will be in great danger."

Zhou was nonplused. He was struck dumb. "I thought I had finally found my mate. How can you turn me away like this?"

"I was just joking. Don't be mad. I would like you to come back again, later tonight."

Zhou was so gladdened by Xianhua's reply that he shouted to himself, "Yes, yes!" in excitement. Then she composed a poem, "An Oriole Singing in the Summer Dawn," and hung it on the door.

> After the rain, light fog all around.
>> The green willows like a painting, and smoke.
> Spring sorrow does not go away when spring is gone.
>> An oriole followed the dawn and sings near my pillow.

That night Zhou sneaked into the courtyard. When he was about to climb over the ivy-covered wall, he heard the scuffing of shoes.

Fearing he had been seen, Zhou turned to flee. At that moment, someone suddenly threw a plum and it hit his back. He was perplexed but had nowhere to run, so he crouched down under some bamboo. Then the person walked up close and spoke to him.

"Don't be afraid. It's me, Yingying."[9] Zhou realized that Xianhua had tricked him. He stood up and encircled her waist with his arms.

"Why did you surprise me?"

Xianhua said with a smile, "How could I surprise you? How could you be surprised by your shadow?"

"I have stolen the perfume and pilfered the pearl.[10] How can I not be intimidated?"

Zhou held Xianhua's hands and drew her into the room. He found a poem hanging on the window. He became curious about the last couplet.

"It says 'a beautiful one has deep sorrow.' Why did you write this?"

"A woman is always concerned about such matters. Until she finds her mate, she feels anxious. After she meets him, she feels anxious again for fear of being betrayed. A woman lives her life with many anxieties. Even though I was fortunate to meet someone like you, you have become a thief who climbs over the wall and breaks the hardwood,[11] and I have become a disgraced woman on paths drenched with dew.[12] If our meetings ever come out, it will be a great shame to my family. Also, we will be disdained and derided by our neighbors. My only wish is to stand by you so we can grow old together, but it is unlikely to happen. Perhaps our destiny is like a rising moon among

---

9. Yingying is the heroine of "Yingying zhuan" (Story of Yingying) by Yuan Chen (779–831), which later was transformed into *Xixiang ji* (Romance of the western chamber), attributed to Wang Shifu (c. 1259–1300).

10. This phrase refers to fornication, especially an unmarried man's illicit liaison with an unmarried woman.

11. *Shijing* 76:3; Waley, *Book of Songs*, 65.

12. *Shijing* 17:1; Waley, *Book of Songs*, 16.

the clouds, a flower among fallen leaves. The greatest pleasure we can share will not last long. What should we do?"

Xianhua could not suppress her emotions or stop her tears. Zhou wiped her eyes and spoke to her.

"Born as a man, I can take any woman I wish as my wife. I promise that soon I will send the matchmaker and propose that you become my wife in a suitable manner. You needn't have any fear."

Xianhua stopped weeping and thanked him. "If you will do so, I, your Taoyao,[13] will be greatly pleased. I may lack the womanly virtue to bring harmony to your family, but if you marry me, I will gather wild herbs and serve the family shrine."

Then she took a small mirror out of a fragrant box and split it into two pieces. She kept one piece for herself and gave the other to Zhou.

"Please keep this until our wedding, and promise me that on the day we unite, these pieces will come together."

She also gave him a silk fan. "These are two very small gifts, but they represent my heart. I wish you never to abandon it like a summer fan in the autumn breeze, and to cherish me as bright moonlight even when I have grown dim like the moon goddess."

From that time on, they met every night and parted at dawn.

One day Zhou realized that he had not seen Paitao for a while and was afraid her doubts might have grown. So he went over to her place and stayed there for a night. That night Xianhua entered Zhou's room and happened to look into his bag. In it she found a poem written by Paitao. Xianhua turned green with envy. Then she took brush and ink from the desk and covered the poem in black. She wrote a lyric of her own on a piece of blue silk, gave it the title "Between Eyes and Eyebrows," and put it into the bag:

---

13. The name Taoyao means Peach Blossom. *Shijing* 6:1–3; Waley, *Book of Songs*, 8.

Outside the window, as the firefly's glow comes and goes,
    the waning moon hangs on the high tower.
The bamboo near the steps make a sound;
    the paulownia's shadow moves on the beaded screen.
When the night is quiet, my mind grows anxious,
    there's still no news of the prodigal one.
Where could he be, seeking his pleasures?
    You are not thinking of me.
This separation weighs heavily on my heart,
    and I sit alone, with endless thoughts.

The next day Zhou returned to the mansion, and Xianhua tried not to reveal her jealousy or her grief. She did not mention the poem in Zhou's bag because she wanted him to feel ashamed even longer. However, he hadn't noticed it and was nonchalant about his behavior.

One day the lady held a banquet for Paitao to express her thanks for introducing Zhou to Guoying. She had Paitao sit next to Zhou and serve him wine and food. Zhou drank himself into inebriation and fell unconscious. Paitao could not sleep. By chance she looked inside Zhou's bag, wondering if her poem was still there. She found it blackened out; she felt suspicious and found the lyric "Between Eyes and Eyebrows." She soon understood that it was Xianhua's doing. Paitao was upset but she put the lyric into her sleeve, returned the bag to its place, and waited for daybreak. When Zhou woke up, she addressed him slowly: "You have been staying at this mansion for quite a while. Why don't you come back to my place?"

"It is because of Guoying. He hasn't finished his studies yet."

"You must be extremely devoted to your job, since you are teaching your future wife's younger brother."

"What did you say?" Zhou said with embarrassment. Paitao stopped talking and took a seat without a word. Zhou lowered his head and looked down at the floor. Then Paitao tossed Xianhua's lyric at him and said, "A gentleman does not jump over walls or peep into holes in windows,[14] yet you did. I will see the lady and report everything."

Paitao was about to leave the room when Zhou seized her by the waist and told her the truth. Then he bowed to the ground and said, "You and I have already promised we will marry. You don't need to drive me into a corner." Paitao softened her voice and said, "If that is true, let's return to my place together. Otherwise I will take it that you want to break our vows. Why should I remain faithful to them?"

So Zhou made up a reason for the lady and returned to Paitao's house. But Paitao, having learned of his relationship with Xianhua, no longer called him a fairy lad. While Paitao harbored this resentment, Zhou could not stop thinking of Xianhua and grew thin and wan. For twenty days, pretending to be ill, he did not rise from his bed.

Around that time, Guoying died of a sudden illness. When he got the news, Zhou prepared himself to go to the funeral. At the mansion, he bowed to Guoying's coffin and prayed for him. Xianhua had also been seriously ill, because of Zhou, and could not stand on her feet. Hearing that Zhou had come, she sat in white mourning clothes behind a beaded screen. Zhou finished his prayer and wanted to see her, but he did not dare to look in her direction. In a couple of months, Paitao also fell ill and realized that she would not recover. On her deathbed, she rested her head on Zhou's lap and whispered her last words.

"I have become an abandoned branch on a tree, yet I always counted on you, as a bird takes rest under the shade of a pine tree. I did not know the oriole would sing while my flower was still fragrant. I bid farewell to you. The silk garments and the zither's melodies are all gone. My wish to grow old with you is also gone. After you marry

---

14. "When a man is born his parents wish that he may one day find a wife, and when a woman is born they wish that she may find a husband. Every parent feels like this. But those who bore holes in the wall to peep at one another, and climb over it to meet illicitly, waiting for neither the command of parents nor the good offices of a go-between, are despised by parents and fellow-countrymen alike" (*Mengzi* 3B:3; Lau, *Mencius*, 66–67).

Xianhua, please bury my body near the roadside you frequent. That is my last wish. If you could do that for me, it would be like living even after I am dead."

She fainted after these words. When she regained consciousness, she called Zhou's name. "Gentleman Zhou, Gentleman Zhou, please be good to yourself." Paitao spoke a few more words, and then her breath stopped. Zhou wailed, and buried her near the roadside that skirted the lake and hills, fulfilling her wish. He composed a prayer for her:

> On a certain day of a certain month, I, a retired gentleman, Meich'uan, would like to offer a sacrifice to your spirit with *jiahuang* and *lidan*.[15] Alas, your spirit! You had a flowerlike soul, and so refined was your manner it seemed like moonlight. You danced like a willow streaming in the wind, as light as a roll of silk. You looked like an orchid in a quiet valley, a pink blossom wet with dew. Jia Yunhua's complexion[16] could not compare with yours, and your ability in palindrome verse outstripped even a talent like Su Ruoyan's. Although your name was on the roll of female entertainers, your spirit was chaste and incorruptible. Unlike you, I was a lonely wanderer, a catkin in the wind, a floating weed on the river. I was fortunate to meet one like you, as if I could gather dodder in the village of Mei.[17] I promise I will be with you when we meet by the willows of the eastern gate.[18]
>
> In the bright moon, we made a vow to each other. The night was quiet and the courtyard was awash in spring color. We played the flute and shared good drinks, and never knew our pleasure would turn into deep sorrow before we could cover ourselves with a silk

---

15. *Jiahuang* and *lidan* refer to banana and lychee, exotic fruits from southern China.

16. Jia Yunhua is the heroine of "The Return of Jia Yunhua's Soul" by Li Zhen (1376–1452).

17. *Shijing* 48:1; Waley, *Book of Songs*, 40.

18. *Shijing* 140:1; Waley, *Book of Songs*, 109.

blanket, so like a cloud the color of jade.[19] But the dream of a pair of love birds[20] was shattered. Love was dissolved and our affections scattered like rain. I lift my eyes but your silk skirt is faded. I cannot hear the tinkle of your jewels. The Luo silk still bears your fragrance, but the red zither with twelve strings lies alone on your bed, and the old house near the Lan Bridge is managed by your servant.

O, how I long to see you again! I can't forget your singing, and I still feel your presence with me. But I can see you no longer, nor hear your voice, even though your jadelike spirit and flowery features are still clear in my vision. I've lost my beloved in this unfamiliar place, and have no one to turn to. I must pull my old boat, go over the roaring waves in the sea, and enter a harsh world, a lonely, dismasted vessel traveling thousands of tricents. On whom can I rely? Next year I will weep bitterly for you, but can I be sure in this vast world? The clouds on the mountains come around and the tide flows again, but once gone we scarcely know how to return.

For you I consecrate this offering with this cup of wine. I confess my inmost feelings with this piece of writing. Please take the cup that I now offer while facing the wind, flowery soul! May this offering be acceptable to you.

Zhou bade farewell to the two female servants and said, "Please take care of the household. I will be back when I achieve my goal, and fetch you." The servant girls all wept and said, "We served our lady like our mother. She also loved us like her own daughters. We are unfortunate to see her dying this early. You are the only one we can depend on. But you too have to leave. Whom should we lean upon?" They shed more tears.

After Zhou comforted them, he got into the boat but had no energy to row away. When his boat passed under the Chuihong Bridge that night, he sat up and looked up at Xianhua's mansion, wherein

19. Silk blankets the color of jade: traditionally, a newly married couple is provided with a luxurious blanket as a wedding gift, the token of a wish for conjugal harmony.

20. A pair of mandarin ducks stands for conjugal fidelity.

candles in blue silk covers could be seen blinking. The lights gradually sank into the shadows of the town. He feared that his promises with Xianhua must also have ended. Grieving over his misfortune, he recited "A Song of Longing."

> Flowers and willows are deep in the spring mist.
>   I thought good news would come.
> A beauty was in the inner room, curtains drawn;
>   Was it a good bond or not?
> The silver light in the hall wanes.
>   I return to the boat to follow the cloudy shore.

Zhou was lost in thought until dawn. If he left town, he wouldn't be able to see Xianhua. But because Paitao and Guoying were dead, he had no place to stay. So he had no choice but to keep rowing his boat. Xianhua's mansion and Paitao's grave gradually receded from sight. The boat passed by the mountains and went around the bend of the river. Everything was in darkness.

A relative on Zhou's maternal side, named Zhang, was a rich man in Houzhou prefecture. He was known to get along well with his relatives. The senior Zhang decided to do Zhou a favor and treated him well, so Zhou became comfortable with where he was. However, his longing for Xianhua deepened. During this time he suffered from insomnia, but soon it was spring.

It was the year *imjin* (1592). Zhang thought it strange that Zhou's face was growing pale, so he asked him the reason. Zhou could not conceal his love for Xianhua and told him the story. Zhang replied, "Why didn't you share this with me? My wife and Minister Lu share the same surname, and the two families are intermarried. I will make your wish come true."

The next day, Zhang had his wife write a letter to the minister's house in Quantang to arrange a marriage. Since being separated from Zhou, Xianhua had felt lonely and weak. When Zhang sent the letter to promote the marriage, she and all her family were glad to receive it. With the news, Xianhua got out of her bed, combed her hair, and dressed herself. Zhang and the lady agreed to arrange a marriage ceremony for Zhou and Xianhua in the ninth month of the same year.

Meanwhile, Zhou was sitting at the dock, waiting for news from Xianhua. In fewer than ten days, Zhang's servant came back with the betrothal date together with a letter from Xianhua, written in her own hand. When Zhou opened the letter, it exuded her perfume and showed the streaks her teardrops had left on the paper, revealing that she too had suffered a great deal.

Gentleman Zhou, after cleansing my body and mind, an ill-fated girl, Xianhua, is writing a letter to you. I was born with a delicate constitution and grew up in the women's quarters. Even after I came to harbor affection for you, I was too shy to express it. Whenever I saw a green willow on a roadside hill, I thought of my beloved. Whenever I heard an oriole, I saw the beloved of my dream at dawn. Then one morning a beautiful butterfly brought news, a mountain bird led the way, and the moon was in the east. Your footstep was on my doorstep.[21] When you crossed over the wall, what value could I see in my body's chastity?

But good things are always joined to bad, and I could not keep faithful appointments. My heart loved you always, but my body grew thin. After you left, the spring came again, but raindrops beat the pear blossoms down, fish hid in the deep, and the geese flew away. When it became dark, I closed my door and immersed myself in thought. I could not sleep and tossed and turned. It was because of you that my body became gaunt.

During the day, it was always empty inside the silk folding screen; at night, the candlelight in the silver lantern went out. In a single day I injured my body and learned that I loved you with all my life. Every time flowers fell, my longing for you mounted higher,

21. *Shijing* 99; Waley, *Book of Songs*, 22.

and when I saw a waning moon, I shed tears. My three spirits[22] were gone and my eight wings[23] were folded. Had I known this, it would have been better to die.

Now the matchmaker has come, and I need only wait for my wedding day. But living alone, I became sick and could not rise from my bed. My flowery face lost its luster, and my cloudy hair is no longer sleek. I am afraid you might be surprised or even turn me down because my appearance has changed. What if I should die like a morning dewdrop before our day comes? My grief is endless. But, as long as I can appeal to you with my sad heart even when I am in the grave, I will have no regrets. Because you are myriad tricents away beyond the cloud-capped mountains, I cannot send my news to you, so I stretch out my neck to glance at you, and that makes my bones break, and my soul flies away.

Hu prefecture is an isolated basin, so the humid air might do you harm. Please take care of yourself. I cannot express fully what is in my heart and only send this message with the help of a wild goose.

On a certain day of a certain month,
Xianhua

When Zhou finished reading this letter, he felt as if he had awakened from a dream and now was sober again after a long inebriation. He felt sad and happy all at once. He counted down how many days remained until the ninth month. It felt like too long. He wanted to move the date up, so he went and asked Zhang to send a servant to deliver his letter to Xianhua.

My beloved! Our ties through three lives are substantial. I was touched by your letter, which traveled more than a thousand tricents. I appreciated the hospitality your family offered to a wretch like me.

---

22. The three souls in one's mind/heart, according to Daoist philosophy.
23. This phrase is in the "Story of Cuicui," in the *Jiandeng xinhua* by Qu You, where Taokan dreams that wings grow in his armpits and he soars to the sky.

In the flowerbed in your courtyard, we made our vows under the moonlight. I cannot thank you enough for your grace and kindness. Yet the Fashioner of Things gets jealous of human beings when they have too many good things. Who could have foreseen that one night of separation would mean not seeing each other for a year! While we were separated by the layered mountains and meandering rivers, I shed so many tears thinking of you in a foreign land. The wild geese may cry in the clouds over the Wu and monkeys make noise in the Chu, but I sat lonely in a relative's house. Anyone with emotions would feel the same.

Ah, my beloved! You too know the sorrow of separation. An old saying has it that each day I do not see my love feels like three years. By my calculation, one month comes to ninety years. If we carry out the plan to marry in late autumn, you will find me lying among the weeds on a desolate mountain.[24] I am so frustrated that I cannot express my feelings in words. When I face the paper, I am choked with tears. What more can I say?

Zhou wrote this letter but could not have it delivered to Xianhua because war broke out: the Japanese army invaded Korea and the Chosŏn government sought reinforcements from the Ming. The Ming emperor viewed Chosŏn as a close neighbor that had served China with sincerity, so he dispatched an army in relief. If Chosŏn were defeated, the people west of the Yalu would be threatened. He also considered it his duty to help the Koreans and reinforce their trusted relationship. So he ordered General Li Rusong (1549–1598) to lead the Ming army and repulse the outlaws from Japan. In time, a spy came back from Chosŏn and reported to the Ming emperor: "The soldiers of the northern region are defending against the Manchu army while the southern people battle the Japanese outlaws. It would be best to send the southern army to Korea." Accordingly, soldiers were conscripted in the prefecture where Zhou was staying. A bureaucrat who

24. This implies that Zhou might die of lovesickness and would be in his grave.

served as an official messenger was well informed of Zhou's skills and hired him as a clerk. Zhou wanted to decline the job but could not avoid the duty. Before he left town, he went up to the Paeksang Tower and wrote a heptasyllabic poem. Here is the concluding part:

> A lone traveler mounts the high tower by the river.
>> Beyond the tower, how many layers of mountains!
> Even if they block my eyes from seeing my home,
>> They won't be able to cut off my heart, yearning for my homeland.

The next spring, in the year *kyesa* (1593), the Ming army advanced quickly into Kyŏngsang province in the south. Zhou kept thinking of Xianhua and became ill. He could not keep up with the military forces and stayed in Songdo. I had business to take care of there and by chance met Zhou in an inn. We could not communicate in each other's language, only by means of sinographs.

Zhou seemed glad to find that I understood literary Chinese and treated me well. I asked him why and how he had gotten sick. He did not reply, but sadness filled his face. It was raining that night, and we talked all night long. Then Zhou gave me a poem:

> The lonely shadow is helpless.
>> The sorrow of parting is hard to express.
> The homesick soul reaches the trees near the river.
>> I am restless by the dim light reflecting on the inn.
> I cannot bear to hear the rain in the sunset.
>> The clouds of fairy land are far away;
> Yingzhou is blocked by the sea.
>> Where is the beaded screen by the jade tower?
> Like a floating weed, I let myself drift on the water,
>> wishing to sail to the Wu River in a single night.

I became curious about this lyric and its unusual longing, so I asked him about it. Zhou shared his story from beginning to end. He also took out of his pocket a paperback entitled "Among the Flowers," which contained approximately one hundred poems, including those exchanged between Zhou and Xianhua and between him and Paitao, along with ten other poems exchanged among friends. He shed tears and asked me to write a poem, so I could not refuse. I used the rhymes of a poem by Yuan Chen (779–831) and attached mine to the postface of the collection. As words of consolation, I wrote: "A man is only concerned about his name and fame. How could there be no beauty to be matched in the world? Soon when the Three Han (Korea) is pacified, the Ming army will return and you will be able to go home. The east wind is already with you to return. Miss Jia said, please do not worry about being confined in another's garden."

The next morning, we bade farewell with tears. Zhou expressed his gratitude several times and said, "This is a trivial and banal story, so just keep it to yourself." At that time, Zhou was only twenty-six years old, and his face reminded me of a beautiful painting. I, Kwŏn Yŏjang (Kwŏn P'il), have written this story in the fifth month of the year *kyesa* (1593).

Translated by Janet Y. Lee

Hŏ Kyun (1569–1618)

THE TALE OF HONG KILTONG

[HONG KILTONG CHŎN]

The "Tale of Hong Kiltong," written in Korean, shares some features with English and French medieval romances in the vernacular. As a secondary son of Minister Hong and his seventeen-year-old maid, Kiltong cannot call his father *Father* or his brother *Brother*. He studies the military arts, astronomy, geomancy, and the *Book of Changes*. He uses magic and the power of mantras and can make himself invisible, shrink distances, and project replicas of himself (out of straw). He has the capacity to be other than he appears, vanish in a cloud of mist, and leap without a trace into the void—neither fetters nor a cangue can contain him. Thus the hero of this romance is superior to other men in skill, and to his environment by virtue of his ability to suspend the laws of nature. Near a stone portal at the base of a boulder, Hong finds a bandits' lair; he awes them with his physical power and valor and becomes the leader of the "Save the Poor" brotherhood bound by laws of friendship and solidarity. Hong is a self-conscious hero, however, his identity having been determined by birth. Although he wills adventures and overcomes obstacles, his external traits are largely passed over in his quest for legitimacy. Moreover, love plays only a small role in this story; the narrator suppresses it, unlike in Western romances. Instead, the hero is guided throughout by the vision of a just society without discrimination.

Hŏ Kyun (1569–1618), the author of "The Tale of Hong Kiltong," was the third son of Hŏ Yŏp (1517–1580), headmaster of the Royal Confucian Academy, censor-general, and an incorruptible and unsullied official. Hŏ Kyun passed the higher civil service examination in 1594 and rose to become third royal secretary (1615) and minister of punishments (1616). As a person and politician, he is said to have been frivolous, depraved, and treacherous. Accused of befriending a group of secondary sons (his teacher of poetry was one) and joining in their plans for a coup, he was executed with other members of the group on October 12, 1618. Hŏ Kyun never openly acknowledged that he was writing fiction and criticized *Water Margin* (*Shuihu zhuan*), the late fourteenth-century Chinese novel often identified as his inspiration, as "licentious, wily, cunning, and unsuitable for education."[1] In doing so, he might simply have wished to conceal his indebtedness to that work. In any case, Hong's story became the target of vituperation, and his execution was considered a condign punishment for the author of a lie—a maker of make-believe. By the end of the century, however, his work was avidly read, both within the court and outside it, and was widely recognized as Korea's first great achievement in vernacular fiction. Since then its influence, especially on popular culture, has never ceased.

During the reign of King Sejong in Chosŏn, there was a minister whose name was Hong. Scion of a long-established and illustrious family, he passed the civil service examinations at an early age and went on to attain the post of minister of personnel. He enjoyed a good reputation both in and out of government circles, and his name resounded

---

1. We do not know which edition he read, but because he was twice an envoy sent to Ming China (in 1610 and 1615), he could have obtained a copy while in Peking.

throughout the country as a man in whom loyalty and filial piety were combined.

Early in life he had two sons. The first son, named Inhyŏng, was born to his official wife, who was of the Yu clan; and the other son, Kiltong, was the child of his maid servant Ch'unsŏm. Minister Hong once dreamed of Kiltong's birth: sudden thunderbolts resounded and a green dragon with flailing whiskers leaped at him; he woke frightened, only to find it was but a passing spring dream. In his heart he was overjoyed; he thought: "Surely this dream must herald the birth of a lovely son!" And with this thought he rushed to the inner room where his wife rose to meet him.

In joy, he took her jade hands to draw her near to him and press his love upon her, but she stiffened and said, "Here, you, a minister of state, forget your dignified position and take to the vulgar antics of a giddy youth! I will not submit to it."

So saying, she drew her hands away and left the room. The minister, disconcerted and unable to endure his exasperation, returned to the outer room where he deplored his lady's lack of understanding, when the maid servant Ch'unsŏm came to serve him tea. Quietly, he drew the girl to him and led her to a room, where he made love to her. Ch'unsŏm at this time was seventeen. Having once given her body to the minister, she never left his gates again and had no thoughts of accepting another lover. The minister, delighted with her, made her his concubine. Indeed, from that month, she began to show the signs of pregnancy, and in the ninth month gave birth to a child of jade-fair beauty whose frame and vigor were like no other and whose mien and spirit foretold a brilliant hero. The minister was happy, but still saddened that the child had not been born to his proper wife.

Kiltong grew steadily, and when he was seven years old he could already grasp a hundred things from hearing only one. The minister was more devoted to this son, but owing to the boy's ignoble birth, felt compelled to rebuke him promptly whenever the child called him

Father, or his brother *Brother.* Even after Kiltong had reached the age of nine, he could not presume to address his father and brother as such. Moreover, he was scorned even by the servants. This grieved him deeply, and he could not still the turmoil within himself.

Once, at the full moon of the ninth month, a time when the bright clarity of the moon and the brisk coolness of the wind conspire to engage a man's passions, Kiltong in his study set aside his readings and, pushing the table away, lamented, "When one born to a man's role cannot model himself after Confucius and Mencius, then he had best learn the martial arts. With a general's insignia tucked into his waistband, he should chastise the east and subjugate the west, render meritorious service to the state, and illuminate the generations with his name. That's the glory of manhood. But why have I been left disconsolate, why is my heart rent that I may not name my own father and brother? Have I not cause for grief?" Kiltong stepped down into the garden and set about practicing his swordsmanship. The minister, also out enjoying the moonlight, caught sight of his son pacing the garden and called him over to ask the reason.

"What's gotten into you—not asleep so late at night?"

Kiltong answered respectfully, "I have always enjoyed the moonlight, but there is something else tonight. While heaven created all things with the idea that mankind is the most precious, how can I be called a man when such value does not extend to me?"

The minister knew what he meant, but scolded, "What are you talking about?"

Kiltong bowed twice and explained. "Though I grow to manhood by the vigor your excellency has passed to me, and realize the profound debt I owe for your gift of life and mother's upbringing, my life still bears one great sorrow: how can I regard myself as a man when I can address neither my father as Father nor my brother as Brother?" He wiped off his flowing tears with the sleeve of his jacket.

The minister heard him out, and though he felt compassion for his son, he could only rebuke him severely for fear an expression of sympathy might give him license. "You're not the only child born to a maidservant in the home of a minister. How dare you show such willful arrogance? If ever I hear such talk as this again, I will not allow you in my presence!"

Kiltong dared not utter a word but could only sink to the ground in tears. The minister ordered him away and Kiltong returned to his quarters, where he was overcome with sorrow. He was by nature uncommonly gifted and was a boy given to thoughtfulness and generosity. So it was that he could not quiet his heart or manage to sleep at night.

One day Kiltong went to his mother's room and in tears said, "We are in this world as mother and son out of the deep ties we had in a former life. My debt to you is immense. But in my wretched fortune I was born ignoble, and the regret I harbor is bottomless. When a man makes his way in the world, he cannot submit to the scorn of others. I cannot suppress this spirit innate in me and have chosen to leave your side, Mother. But I beg you not to worry about me and to take care of yourself."

Astonished, his mother replied, "You are not the only boy born humbly in a minister's home. How can you be so selfish? Why do you tear at your mother's heart so?"

Kiltong replied, "Long ago, Jishan, the secondary son of Zhang Zhong of Jin, left his mother when he was twelve. In the Yunfeng Mountains he perfected the way and left a glorious name to posterity.[2] Since I have decided to follow his example and leave the vulgar world, I pray you wait in peace for another day. From the recent behavior of the Koksan woman, it appears she has taken us for enemies out of fear that she might lose the minister's favor. I'm afraid she plots misfortune for me. Please don't let my departure worry you so."

But his mother was saddened.

2. For the story of Jishan, see *Jinshu* 94: 2451–2452.

The Koksan woman, originally a female entertainer from Koksan named Ch'oran, had become the minister's favorite concubine. Since she was extremely arrogant and quick to carry false tales to the minister about anyone who displeased her, she was at the center of countless difficulties in the household. Ch'oran had no son of her own and, having seen the affection shown Ch'unsŏm by the minister after Kiltong's birth, she plotted with all her spite to eliminate the boy.

Then one day, her scheme conceived, she called in a shaman and said, "I must have this Kiltong out of the way to find any peace in life. If you can carry out my wishes, I shall reward you handsomely."

The shaman listened and replied with pleasure. "I know of an excellent physiognomist living outside Hŭngin Gate who with only one look at a person's face can divine the good and evil of both past and future. What we should do is call the woman in, explain your desires to her, and then recommend her to the minister. When she tells him about events of the past and future just as if she had seen them herself, he is sure to fall under her influence and could be made to get rid of the child. Then if we only wait for the opportune moment and do thus-and-so, how could we fail?"

Ch'oran was very pleased. Straightaway she gave the shaman fifty *yang* in silver and then sent her off to call in the physiognomist. The shaman bowed low and left.

The next day when the minister was in the women's quarters talking about Kiltong with his wife, praising the boy's uncommon virtues and regretting his low birth, a woman suddenly appeared in the courtyard below and bowed to him. Thinking it strange, the minister questioned her.

"Who are you? What do you want here?"

"I practice physiognomy for my living and just happened to be passing by Your Excellency's gate."

This reminded the minister of Kiltong, for he wanted to know the boy's future. He called the boy immediately and showed him to the woman. She looked him over for some time, and in her astonishment almost blurted out, "I see in your son's face a hero, unchallenged by history and peerless in his own age! Only his lineage would be a drawback—there should be no other cause for concern!" But instead she only faltered and stopped.

The minister and his wife were puzzled and asked, "Whatever it is, we want you to speak directly with us."

The woman, feeling compelled, asked that the others retire. "From what I see, the boy cherishes elaborate and untamed dreams. The lustrous ether of the hills and streams radiates from between his eyebrows—a royal countenance. Your Excellency had best watch him carefully, for your household will surely be visited with ruinous misfortune when he grows up."

After a moment of stunned silence, the minister finally gathered himself and said, "Though I know man cannot escape his fate, I still forbid you to reveal this to anyone." With this command he gave the woman a little silver and sent her away. Not long after, the minister moved Kiltong into a cabin in the mountains where he could keep careful watch over his movements.

Unable to overcome the even greater sadness he felt at this turn of events and seeing no way out, Kiltong occupied himself with studying the military arts, astronomy, and geography. The minister was disturbed when he learned of this. "If the boy uses his native talent to further ideas that go beyond his station, the physiognomist will have been proven right. What am I to do?"

In the meantime, Ch'oran maintained her secret contacts with the shaman and physiognomist, and through them managed to keep the minister stirred up. Intent on getting rid of Kiltong, she secured at great expense an assassin named T'ŭkchae and explained the circumstances to him. She then approached the minister. "It was uncanny that day the way the physiognomist could perceive events. What do you think? What are you going to do now about Kiltong's future? Even I was surprised and frightened. Doesn't it seem the only choice is to have him put out of the way?"

The minister worked his brows as he listened. "The matter is in my hands, and I want you to refrain from involving yourself in it." He dismissed her but was left troubled and confused. Finding it impossible to sleep at night, he soon grew ill. His wife and son Inhyŏng—the latter now an assistant section chief in a ministry—were greatly worried and at a loss for what to do.

Ch'oran, who had been attending the minister, one day remarked, "The minister's critical condition is brought about by the presence of Kiltong. Now this is the way I see it. If we just do away with the boy, not only will the minister completely recover, but the whole household too will be assured of security. How is it you haven't considered this?"

"You may be right, but who could possibly do such a thing that violates the most solemn strictures of moral law?" the wife asked.

"I have heard there is an assassin called T'ŭkchae who claims he can kill a man as easily as picking something out of his pocket. Give him a thousand *yang* and then let him sneak in at night to do the job. By the time the minister finds out, there will be nothing he can do about it. I suggest, my lady, you give this serious thought."

The wife and son broke into tears as they replied. "Painful as it may be, such a move would not only serve the good of the country, but help the minister and indeed protect the Hong family. Yes, do as you have planned!"

Highly pleased, Ch'oran called T'ŭkchae in again and explained in detail what she had been told. Ordered to do his work with dispatch that very night, T'ŭkchae agreed and waited for the dark to come.

The story goes on: When Kiltong considered the sorrow and pain of his present situation, he had no wish to remain any longer, but his father's strict commands left him with no choice. He passed the nights without sleep. On this night, he had lit the candle and to steady his wits had turned to the *Book of Changes,* when suddenly he heard a crow cry three times as it passed. Kiltong thought this ominous and said to himself: "This bird usually avoids the night. Crying out in passing like this must surely bode ill." He spread out the eight trigrams and studied them and was alarmed at what they portended. He pushed his desk aside and, employing his knowledge of magic, made himself invisible and watched and waited.

It was during the fourth watch (1–3 a.m.) that a man carrying a dagger stealthily opened the door and entered his room. Kiltong, making sure he was unseen, chanted a mantra. A cold wind suddenly filled the room, and in a moment the house had vanished—in its place was only the fresh beauty of a vaulted mountain recess. Terrified by Kiltong's marvelous powers, T'ŭkchae concealed his dagger and sought to escape. But the road ahead was suddenly cut off when a lofty, bouldered cliff rose to block his way. Trapped, he groped frantically about him. Just then he heard the sound of a six-holed flute and, pulling himself together, looked up to see a young boy approaching astride a donkey.

The boy stopped playing the flute and began to rebuke T'ŭkchae. "Why would you want to kill me? Do you think you can harm a guiltless man for no good reason and still avoid the retribution of heaven?"

He chanted one more mantra, a black cloud formed, and sand and stones flew through the air. When T'ŭkchae managed to gather his wits and look about, he discovered Kiltong before him. "Even with his marvelous powers, how could this child be any match for me?" thought T'ŭkchae and flew at him.

"Though this is your death, bear me no malice! It was Ch'oran who swayed the minister through a shaman and physiognomist to have you killed. Don't hold it against me," he cried as he leaped, dagger in hand.

Kiltong could not control his rage. Blinding T'ŭkchae with magic, he snatched the dagger away and denounced the would-be killer under the blade of his own knife.

"If your greed allows you to murder so easily, then I can kill your brutish sort without a second thought," Kiltong said, and sent T'ŭkchae's head flying across the room with a single sweep of the blade. Still overcome by anger, Kiltong went that same night and seized the physiognomist and pushed her into the room with the dead T'ŭkchae. "What have you against me, to plot my murder with Ch'oran?" He chastized her, then slit her throat.

Was it not a terrible thing?

Kiltong had killed them. Now he looked up into the night sky where the Milky Way trailed to the west. Moved by the clarity of the moon's thin light, Kiltong, in his rage, thought to kill Ch'oran. But the thought of the minister's love for her dissuaded him; he threw away the dagger and resolved to seek an exile's life. He went directly to the minister's room to take formal leave of him.

Startled to hear the footfalls outside, the minister opened his window and discovered Kiltong there. He called him in and asked, "What are you doing up and about so late at night?"

Kiltong prostrated himself and answered, "I have always intended to pay back the life's debt I owe you and my mother, if only one-ten-thousandth part. But someone of evil design in the household has deceived your excellency and attempted to kill me. Though I have escaped with my life, I know I cannot remain here and serve your excellency any longer. So I have come now to bid you farewell."

The startled minister asked, "What calamity could have occurred that would force you to leave your childhood home? Where do you intend to go?

Kiltong answered, "By the time day breaks, you will have learned the circumstances as a matter of course. And, as for me, why worry about the whereabouts of this cast-off child? It's my lot to wander aimlessly as a cloud." In twin streams his tears poured forth; his words faltered. The minister was moved to pity at the sight and began to offer counsel.

"I can appreciate the grief you must be suffering. I am going to give you my permission to address me and your brother as *Father* and *Brother* from this day on."

Kiltong bowed twice and said, "Now that my father has cleared away this one small sadness of mine, I know I can die without regret. I sincerely wish you a long, untroubled life, my father." Again he bowed twice to take his leave, and the minister, unable to stay his son, could only ask him to take care.

Kiltong then went to his mother's room to inform her of his departure. "Though I am leaving your side now, there will be a day when I can come back to serve you. I pray you will take care of your health while I am away."

As she listened, it crossed her mind there might have been some calamity, but seeing him bow now in departure, she grasped his hands and cried, "Where will you go? Even in the same house it has always seemed difficult to accept the small distance that has separated our quarters. But now how am I to endure, having sent you off to an unknown place? I only pray you will return soon so we can be together again." Kiltong bowed twice in taking his leave and, passing through the gate of his home, headed aimlessly toward the shrouded mountain recesses.

Is this not a pitiful thing?

The story goes on: Extremely apprehensive at receiving no word from T'ŭkchae, Ch'oran inquired into what had happened. She learned that Kiltong had disappeared without a trace and that the bodies of T'ŭkchae and the woman had been found in the room. Stricken with terror, she flew to inform the minister's wife of what she had found out. The lady, equally alarmed, called in her son, the assistant section chief, to tell him what she had heard.

When all this was finally reported to the minister, he went white with shock and said, "Kiltong came to me last night and with heavy heart bade me farewell. I thought it was very strange at the time—but now, this!"

Inhyŏng dared withhold no longer what he knew of Ch'oran's involvement in the affair. Greatly angered, the minister had Ch'oran driven out of the house and the bodies quietly removed. He then called in the servants and ordered them never to speak of the matter.

The story continues: After leaving his parents and going out through the gates of his home, Kiltong wandered aimlessly until one day he happened upon a place where the scenery surpassed anything he had ever seen. He ventured farther, looking for a house, and discovered a closed stone portal at the base of a huge boulder. Opening the door with care, he stepped through it and saw hundreds of houses set out neatly across a wide and level plain. A great number of men were gathered before him, enjoying themselves at a feast; this valley was a bandit's lair. Suddenly they caught sight of Kiltong and were pleased to see from his appearance that he was a man of no mean quality.

"Who are you?" they questioned him. "Why have you sought out this place? The braves you see gathered here have not yet been able to settle upon a leader. Now, if you think you have courage and vigor enough to join our ranks, see if you can lift that rock over there."

Sensing good fortune in what he heard, Kiltong bowed and said, "I am Hong Kiltong from Seoul, the son of Minister Hong by his concubine. But when I could no longer endure the scorn I suffered there, I left and have since been roaming the four seas and eight directions until I chanced upon this place. I am overwhelmed with gratitude that you speak of my becoming your comrade. But what trouble should it be for a man to lift a rock like that?" With this, he hoisted the rock, which weighed one thousand catties, and walked some ten paces.

The assembled braves praised him with a voice. "Here is a real man among men! Not one man in all our thousands could lift that rock, but beneficent heaven has today given us a general!" They seated him at the place of honor and each in turn pressed wine upon him. Swearing oaths of fealty in the blood of a white horse, the assemblage raised its unanimous approval and celebrated the day long.

Kiltong and his men practiced the martial arts until, after several months, they had quite refined their tactics.

Then one day some of the men approached Kiltong. "For some time now, we have wanted to raid the Haein temple at Hapch'ŏn and strip it of its treasures, but we have been unable to carry out our plan for lack of a clever strategy. Now, as our general, what do you think of the idea?"

Kiltong was pleased and answered, "I shall send out an expedition soon, and you should be ready to follow my commands."

In black-belted blue ceremonial robes, Kiltong mounted a donkey and prepared to leave camp with several followers in attendance. As he started out, he said, "I am going to that temple now and shall return after looking over the situation." He looked every inch the scion of a high minister's family.

When he arrived at the temple, he first called the abbot to him. "I am the son of Minister Hong of Seoul. I have come to this temple to pursue my literary studies and shall have twenty bushels of white rice shipped in for you tomorrow. If you are tidy about preparing the food, I will be glad to join you and your people for a meal at that time." Kiltong looked over the temple and left its precincts, having made promises for another day with the overjoyed monks.

As soon as he got back, Kiltong sent off some twenty bushels of white rice and called his men together. "Now, on a certain day, I wish to go to the temple to do such-and-such." When the appointed day arrived, Kiltong took some tens of his followers and went ahead to the Haein temple. He was received by the monks, who all came out to meet his party.

He called an elder to him and asked, "With the rice I sent, were you able to make enough food?"

"Enough, sir? We have been overwhelmed!"

Kiltong took his seat in the place of honor and bade the monks to share his company, each having been given a tray of wine and savories. He then led the drinking and pressed each monk in turn to join him. All were filled with gratitude.

Kiltong received his own tray and, while eating, suddenly bit with a loud crack on some sand he had secretly slipped into his mouth. The monks, startled at the sound, begged his forgiveness, but Kiltong feigned a great rage and rebuked them, saying, "How could you be so careless in preparing my food? This is indeed an insufferable insult and humiliation!" So saying, he ordered his followers to bind the monks together with a single rope and sit them on the floor. The monks were in a state of shock; no one knew what to do. In no time, several hundred fearsome bandits came swooping into the temple and set about carrying off all its treasures. The helpless monks could only look on, screaming their laments.

Soon after, a temple scullion on his way back from an errand saw what had happened and hurried off to notify the local government office. When he heard about this, the magistrate of Hapch'ŏn called out his militia and charged them to capture the bandits.

The several hundred troops who dashed off in pursuit soon came upon a figure in black robes and a nun's pine-bark cap who called to them from a promontory: "The bandits took the back road to the north. Hurry and catch them!" Believing this to be a helpful member of the temple, the soldiers flew like the wind and rain down the northerly back road, only to return empty-handed at nightfall.

It was Kiltong who, after sending his men along the main road to the south, had remained behind to deceive the troops in this clerical disguise. Safely back in the bandit lair, he found the men had all returned and were already sizing up the treasures. They rushed out to meet him and shower rewards upon him, but Kiltong laughed and said, "If a man hadn't even this little talent, how could he become your leader?"

Kiltong later named his band the "Save-the-Poor" and led them through the eight provinces of Korea, stopping in each township to confiscate the wealth unjustly gained by magistrates and to succor the poor and helpless. But they never preyed upon the common people nor ever once touched the rightful property of the state.

So it was that the bandits submitted to Kiltong's will.

One day Kiltong gathered his men around him to discuss their plans. "I am told the governor of Hamgyŏng province with his rapacious officials has been squeezing the citizenry to a point where the people can no longer endure it. We cannot just stand by and do nothing. Now, I want you to follow my instructions exactly."

Thus the braves slipped one by one into the Hamgyŏng area and, on an agreed night, built a fire outside the South Gate of the provincial capital. When the governor, in a state of alarm, called for the fire to be extinguished, the yamen clerks and the city's populace all rushed forth to put it out. Meantime, several hundred of Kiltong's bandits poured into the heart of the city and opened the warehouse to uncover the stores of grain, money, and weapons, which they carried out the North Gate, leaving the city to churn in chaos. These unexpected events left the governor helpless. When at dawn he discovered the warehouses stripped of their grain, money, and weapons, he paled in consternation and bent all efforts toward the capture of the bandits. The notice he forthwith posted on the North Gate named Hong Kiltong as leader of the Save-the-Poor Party and responsible for looting the city stores. Troops were dispatched to bring in the outlaws.

While Kiltong, with his band, had made a good haul of the grain and such, he was still concerned lest they be apprehended on the road by some misadventure. Thus he exercised his occult knowledge and ability to shrink distances, bringing them back apace to the lair where they ended the day.

Another day, Kiltong again gathered his men around him to discuss plans. "Now that we have looted the Haein temple at Hapch'ŏn of its treasures and robbed the governor of Hamgyŏng of his grain and money, not only have rumors about us spread across the country but my name has been posted at the provincial offices for all to see. If I don't take steps, I am likely to be caught before long. Now, just watch this trick!"

Whereupon, Kiltong made seven straw men and, chanting mantras, invested them with such spirit that seven Kiltongs all at once sprouted arms, cried aloud, and fell into animated chatter with one another. From appearances alone, no one could tell which was the real Kiltong. They separated, each going to a province and taking several hundred men under his command. And now no one knew where the real Kiltong had gone.

Eight Kiltongs roamed the eight provinces, calling wind and commanding rain as they exercised their magic. In night sorties that left no trace, they made off with grain stores in every township and even managed without any difficulty to snatch a shipment of gifts bound for officials in Seoul. Every township of the eight provinces was in turmoil, sleep at night was impossible, and travelers disappeared from the roads. Chaos covered the country. At last one governor reported the situation to the throne: "There is an accomplished bandit known as Hong Kiltong, who strikes without warning and can with ease summon up the wind and clouds. He has looted treasures from every township and raised such a furor with his antics that even gift shipments cannot be sent up to the capital. If this bandit is not caught, the whole country will fall under his threat. Thus I humbly beg the throne to charge the police officials of the left and the right to capture this man."

When he heard this, the king was alarmed and summoned the captains of his gendarmerie. Reports continued to arrive from the rest of the eight provinces, and when the king opened and read each one, he discovered that the names of the bandits were all the same—Hong Kiltong—and that the raids had taken place all on the same day at the same time.

Astonished, the king said, "The dauntlessness and wizardry of this bandit are unchallenged even by the rebel Chiyou.[3] But still, no matter how marvelous the fellow is, how could he, with his one body, be in eight provinces and stage his raids in one day and at the same time? This is no common bandit—it looks as though he will be a difficult one to capture."

The captains of the left and right were to dispatch their troops with orders to apprehend the bandit, but Yi Hǔp, the captain of the right, memorialized, "Though your servant is without particular talent, he begs the throne rest assured that he himself can capture and deliver up the bandit. Why, then, should the police officials of both the left and right be dispatched?"

The king approved and pressed the captain to depart with all haste. Yi Hǔp took his leave and, commanding a host of government troops, deployed them widely with instruction to gather again on a certain day in the county of Mungyǒng. Yi Hǔp himself took only a few officials with him and scouted the countryside incognito.

Late in the afternoon of another day, the party sought out a wine shop where they stopped to rest. Presently a young man rode up on a donkey and, exchanging courtesies with the captain, sighed and said, "The *Book of Songs* says: 'Everywhere under heaven is no land that is not the king's.[4] To the borders of all those lands none but is the king's slave.' Even though living here so far out in the country, I am still concerned for the country!"

---

3. God of war, who fought the Yellow Emperor. See Birrell, *Chinese Mythology*, 50–53.
4. *Shijing* 205; Waley, *Book of Songs*, 320.

The captain feigned surprise and said, "What do you mean by that?"

The boy answered, "Could I not be sorely troubled when people are being victimized by that bandit Hong Kiltong? He roams the eight provinces and mounts raids at will, but no one has yet been able to catch the marauder."

The captain responded, "You impress me as a brave and spirited young man who speaks with directness; how about joining me in capturing that bandit?"

"I have long wanted to catch him but could not find a man of courage to share my purpose. How fortunate to have met like this! Still, I know nothing of your ability—why don't we find a quiet spot and stage a contest between us?"

They went together to another place, where they climbed to the top of a boulder and sat down.

"Kick me as hard as you can with both legs and try to knock me off this boulder," said Kiltong as he moved out to the very edge and sat down again.

The captain thought: "No matter how powerful he is, he is sure to fall off if I give him one good kick." And, summoning all his strength, he kicked Kiltong with both legs at once.

But the boy just turned to him and said, "You are indeed a strong fellow. Though I have tested a number of men, none has been able to move me. But you, indeed, have nearly shaken me. If you will come along with me, I know we can catch Hong Kiltong!" With this, the boy led him into the deep recesses of the surrounding mountains.

As he followed his guide, the captain thought: "Until today I had always thought my strength worth boasting about. Seeing this boy's prowess, could one remain unawed? With just his help alone, I am sure to capture Hong Kiltong." A moment later, the boy turned and said to the captain, "This cave leads into Kiltong's lair. I am going in first to take a look around—you should wait for me."

The captain was suspicious at heart, but he bade the youth bring his captive back quickly, so he sat down to wait. Suddenly many tens of screaming warriors descended on him from the hills around. The captain attempted to escape but was easily overtaken by the bandits and bound.

"Are you not Yi Hŭp, captain of the gendarmerie? We have come to arrest you under orders from the king of the underworld." Collared in chains and driven like the wind and rain, the captain was frightened beyond his wits. It was not until after they had arrived at another place, where he was forced to his knees amidst fierce cries, that he could begin to grope toward consciousness and take in his surroundings. It was a grand palace; he saw countless yellow turbaned warriors ranked to the left and right, and a sovereign sitting upon his dais in a hall beyond.

"Contemptible wretch!" the lord roared. "How dare you presume to capture General Hong? For this we are going to condemn you to the underworld!"

His senses nearly recovered, the captain pleaded, "Worthless though I am, I have been arrested for no real crime. I beg you, my lord, spare my life and allow me to leave."

But the response from the dais was a burst of laughter. "Take a good look at me, you knave! I am Hong Kiltong, leader of the Save-the-Poor Party, the very man you seek. Since you had set out to capture me, I decided to test your courage and determination. So I lured you here in the guise of a blue-robed youth, that you might have a taste of my authority."

Whereupon, Kiltong ordered his attendants to loosen the captain's bonds and seat him near at hand in the great hall. Pressing wine on his guest, the general said, "You can see how futile it is to scout around for me—you had better just report back. But do not let on that you have seen me, for they are sure to hold you responsible. I urge you not to say a word of this." After pouring another cup and offering it to his guest, Kiltong ordered his attendants to free the captain and send him off.

At this, the captain thought: "Whether this is real or a dream, I do not know. Yet somehow I have come here and have learned to appreciate Kiltong's marvelous powers." But no sooner did he turn to leave than he suddenly found himself unable to move his four limbs. When he calmed his spirit sufficiently, he considered his plight and discovered he was wrapped inside a huge leather sack.

After extricating himself with some difficulty, the captain found three more sacks hanging on the tree beside him. He opened them one after the other, and discovered there the three retainers with whom he had set out originally. "What has happened? When we set out we had agreed to meet at Mungyŏng—how did we get here?" So asking each other, they looked around and saw they were on Mount North, overlooking Seoul.

"We fell asleep back in the wine shop. Then we were suddenly carried here, shrouded in wind and rain. There is no way to account for it."

"No one is going to believe this absurd story—you must say nothing to the others about it. This Hong Kiltong really has powers beyond believing—how could we ever capture him by human means? But if we return empty-handed now, we could never escape punishment. Let's wait a few more months before reporting back."

With this they descended the mountain.

In spite of royal commands throughout the eight provinces ordering his capture, there was no second-guessing Hong Kiltong's strategems: now riding about the thoroughfares of Seoul in a one-wheeled chaise, and now—with solemn prior announcement—appearing in various townships in the guise of a royal inspector aboard a two-horse carriage. To top it off, after ferreting out and summarily executing corrupt and covetous magistrates, the self-appointed royal inspector was even making official reports to the throne.

At this, the king, now in a towering rage, demanded, "That cur can wander the provinces indulging in such antics and yet no one is able to capture him. Just what do you intend to do about it?" Even as he called his counselors and ministers into conference, reports continued to arrive at court from the various provinces—each of them about the work of Hong Kiltong. Examining each as it came in, the king became distressed. He looked round at his officers and asked, "Maybe this fellow isn't a human after all—his behavior is more like that of a demon! Does anyone among my ministers know something about his origins?"

One of the officers stepped forward and addressed the throne. "This Hong Kiltong is a secondary son of the Hong who was once minister of personnel, and is half brother to Hong Inhyŏng, now an assistant section chief in the Ministry of War. All the facts might be brought to light were you to detain the father and son for a royal interrogation."

Further incensed, the king responded, "Why is it only now that you tell us of this?" He forthwith ordered the father's arrest through the State Tribunal and meanwhile had Inhyŏng brought in for questioning. Pounding his writing desk with awesome rage, the king roared, "We have learned that the bandit Kiltong is your half brother! How is it you have failed to restrain him and are content to stand by while the state is thrown into turmoil? If you do not bring him in now, the loyalty and filial piety of you and your father will go for naught in our eyes. Apprehend him immediately and remove this affliction from Korea!"

Awe-stricken, Inhyŏng removed his cap and bowed his head deeply. "My low-born younger brother was with us until he killed a man and fled, some years ago now, leaving us unable to learn of his fate. As a result, my aged father has sunk into a critical illness and can reckon his remaining life only in mornings and evenings. Kiltong, with his disregard for mortality, has burdened Your Majesty with deep concern, for which we deserve death without mercy ten thousand times.

But if Your Majesty, in the warmth of your compassion, would grant
our humble petition and forgive my father for his crime, allowing him
to return home to recover his health, I intend, even at the risk of life,
to capture Kiltong and thus atone for the sins of this father and son."

The king, having heard him out, was deeply moved. He forgave
the old minister and appointed Inhyŏng governor of Kyŏngsang province. "If you, my minister, had not the power of a governorship, I fear
you would not be able to catch Kiltong. I am giving you a year's time
in which you should be able to apprehend him easily."

In taking his leave, Inhyŏng bowed over and over again, expressing his gratitude for the king's benevolence, and that same day he set
out for Kyŏngsang. Upon assuming his new office, he had notices
posted in every township urging Kiltong to turn himself in. They read:

> The life of men in this world is governed by the five relationships;[5]
> and these relationships are realized through the constant virtues of
> humanity, righteousness, propriety, wisdom, and faithfulness. But
> if one, ignorant of this, disobeys his sovereign's commands and be-
> haves in a manner disloyal and unfilial, how can he be countenanced
> by the world? Kiltong, my brother! You should be aware of these
> things; come to your older brother voluntarily and let yourself be
> taken alive. Our father is sickened to the bone because of you, and
> His Majesty is deeply anxious—so extraordinary is your sinfulness.
> I have therefore been especially appointed to the governorship with
> orders to apprehend you, in failure of which the fair virtue amassed
> by generations of the Hong family will overnight be brought to
> naught. Would this not be sorrowful? Kiltong, my brother! If you
> consider this and surrender straight off, as I pray you do, your crimes
> should indeed be lessened and you would preserve our family. I do
> not know your heart, but it is imperative that you give this serious
> thought and present yourself.

5. Between father and son, sovereign and subject, husband and wife, elder brother and
younger brother, and friends.

Posting this notice in every township, the governor suspended all other official activity, awaiting only the surrender of Kiltong. One day a youth astride a donkey followed by tens of attendants appeared outside his residence to request an audience. But when the youth entered the receiving hall on command and made his obeisance, the governor studied his eyes carefully: it was Kiltong for whom he had been waiting so long.

With joyful astonishment he dismissed his officers and, embracing the boy, said in a tear-choked voice, "Kiltong! After you left home, our father, not knowing whether you were alive or dead, was taken by an illness that invaded his very breast. Not only have you thus compounded your unfilial behavior, but you have become the cause of great distress to the state. What can you be thinking to behave in a manner so disloyal and unfilial and, more, by turning to banditry, to commit crimes that are without parallel in the whole world? His Majesty, enraged by this, has ordered me to bring you in. Your crimes are beyond denial. You must go immediately to Seoul and submit quietly to the royal judgment."

As he finished speaking, the tears rained from his eyes. Kiltong lowered his head and replied, "At this pass what else could I presume to say but that I am determined to save my father and brother in their peril? Yet, would we have come to this, I wonder, had his excellency, our father, in the first place allowed this humble Kiltong to address him as Father and you as Brother? But, at this point events of the past have become meaningless; now you must have me bound and sent up to Seoul." Kiltong said nothing further.

Though the governor, on the one hand, was saddened when he heard this, he nevertheless composed an official report to the throne. After having Kiltong shackled in fetters and cangue and locked inside a barred wagon, he assigned more than ten strapping officers as escorts to push on day and night for Seoul. The people of each township along the way, knowing of Kiltong's prowess and having heard of his capture, choked the roads to gape at the prisoner as he passed.

But by now, a different Kiltong had been arrested in each of the eight provinces and sent up to Seoul. The court and citizens of the capital were lost in helpless confusion—there was no one equal to the situation. When the astounded king convened his full court to conduct a personal interrogation, the eight Kiltongs were brought forward only to argue among themselves.

"You're the real Kiltong, not me!" So they fought on, making it impossible to guess which one was the real Kiltong. Puzzled, the king forthwith summoned the former Minister Hong and said, "The saying goes, 'No one knows his son better than the father.' I want you to pick out your son among these eight."

The old minister respectfully bowed his head in remorse. "My low-born son, Kiltong, can be distinguished by the red birthmark he has on his left leg." And, admonishing the eight Kiltongs, he said, "Remember that you are in the presence of His Majesty and that your father is here below. You have committed crimes unheard of even in remote antiquity: do not try to avoid your just fate." With this, he vomited up blood and collapsed in a faint.

The king, in alarm, commanded his royal physicians to save the minister, but they could effect no improvement. The eight Kiltongs, seeing the old man's condition and tears streaming from their eyes, each produced from his pocket a pellet of medicine and put it in the minister's mouth. The old man recovered his senses before the day was out.

The eight Kiltongs addressed the king. "In view of the many boons granted my father by the state, how could I dare give myself over to improper behavior? But in origin I am the child of a lowly serving woman who could not call his father Father or his brother Brother. To my lifelong regret, I chose to leave my home and join a party of bandits. Still, I never once abused the common people but confiscated only the wealth of magistrates amassed through exploitation of the people. And now, when ten years have passed, I shall leave

Korea, for I have a place to go. A supplicant at Your Majesty's feet, I beg you end your concern over me and rescind the orders for my arrest."

As they finished speaking, the eight Kiltongs tumbled over all at the same instant—close scrutiny showed them all to be only straw men. Astonished anew, the king reissued his orders, this time with the aim of capturing the real Hong Kiltong.

The story goes on: Divesting himself of the straw men, Kiltong continued to wander about. Then one day he posted a notice on the four gates of Seoul which read: "Wondrous is he, for there will be no capturing Hong Kiltong. Only if he be appointed minister of war can he be apprehended." When the king had read the text of Kiltong's notice, he called the ministers of his court into conference.

The various ministers chorused: "To appoint that bandit now as minister of war, after having failed in all attempts to arrest him! What an embarrassment if such news were heard in neighboring countries!" The king concurred in this and settled with pressing the governor of Kyŏngsang province, Inhyŏng, to capture Kiltong posthaste.

When the governor saw these stern royal instructions he was struck with fear and trembling, lost for a way out of his dilemma. But then one day Kiltong appeared out of thin air and, bowing before him, said, "This time I truly am your brother, Kiltong. I want you to worry yourself over me no longer: have me bound and sent up to Seoul."

At this, the governor tearfully grasped Kiltong's hands. "Oh, irresponsible child! As much as we are brothers, I cannot but grieve at your failure to heed the guidance of your father and brother, putting the whole country into chaos. But still, you are to be commended for having surrendered to me voluntarily." He quickly examined Kiltong's left leg, and when he found the identifying mark there, he promptly bound his prisoner—taking special care to pinion all four limbs—and put him into the barred wagon.

Even engirded tightly as an iron drum by tens of select and strapping officers, and driven like the wind and rain, Kiltong's countenance did not change an iota. After several days the party arrived in Seoul. But just as they reached the palace gates, the iron bands broke away and the wagon flew into splinters, while Kiltong, with a twist of his body, flew up into the air like a cicada throwing off its shell and disappeared in a flutter, wrapped in clouds and mist. The officers and soldiers were left dumbfounded, able only to gape mindlessly into the empty air.

They had no choice but to report these facts to the throne. Upon hearing this, the king responded in great consternation, "I have never heard of such a thing—even from greatest antiquity!"

Then one of his ministers proposed, "Since it is this Kiltong's expressed desire to serve one time as minister of war and then leave Korea, why don't we grant his wish this once? If so, he would come to express his gratitude and then, grasping the opportunity, we could capture him."

The king approved and immediately appointed Kiltong minister of war, posting notices to this effect on the four gates of Seoul.

Kiltong soon heard of this and promptly made an impressive appearance on the main thoroughfare of the capital, riding in high dignity on a one-wheeled chaise and wearing the silk cap and formal gown, and a belt of rhinoceros horn, appropriate to his new office. The officials of the Ministry of War, hearing that the new Minister Hong was arriving to pay his respects at court, presented themselves as his escort to the palace. Meanwhile, the ministers of state, in full convention, had resolved to have a hatchet man lie in ambush for Kiltong and cut him down the moment he came out of the palace.

Now Kiltong entered the court, made obeisance, and addressed himself to the king. "In spite of the grievous crimes I have dared commit, Your Majesty has bestowed his gracious benevolence on me, freeing me of my lifelong anguish. But now I must take leave of this court forever. I humbly pray Your Majesty may enjoy a long life."

So saying, Kiltong leapt traceless into the void and vanished, wrapped in clouds. At this sight, the king sighed.

"Indeed, Kiltong's marvelous talents would be rare in any age! Now that he has declared his intention to leave Korea, there will be no further cause for distress on his account. Although I may have had my suspicions, he has displayed the fine heart of a real man: there should be no cause now for worry." He then issued a command to the eight provinces pardoning Kiltong and ending the campaign to arrest him.

The story continues: Kiltong returned to his hideout and gave orders to his robber band.

"I must go somewhere for a while: I want you men to stay put here until I get back—no coming and going!" he commanded, and forthwith rose up into the air.

After traveling for a while in the direction of Nanking, he reached a place known as the state of Lüdao. Looking all about him, he saw that the mountains and streams were well formed and clean, the people prosperous, and the land capable of supporting comfortable life. From here he went on to see the sights of Nanking and thence to Ti Island, where he also toured about viewing the mountains and streams and examining the character of its people.

But when he reached Mount Wufeng, he pronounced this scenery truly the most beautiful he had ever seen. The island, seven hundred tricents around, abounded in fertile fields and rice paddies, an ideal place for men to live. Kiltong thought in his heart: "Since I have now quit Korea, this is the place for me to live on in hiding, wherein I can lay great plans." With this, he abruptly returned to his home camp and addressed his men.

"On a certain day I want you to go to the banks at Yangch'on on the lower reaches of the Han River and there prepare a good number of boats, whence you will proceed up the Han to Seoul on such-and-such day of such-and-such month and there await my further orders.

I shall ask the king to give us one thousand bushels of unhulled rice, which I shall bring to you. Don't fail me!"

Meanwhile, the story continues: Now that Kiltong had forsworn his banditry, the former minister Hong was recovering his lost health, and the king, for his part, found the passing days free of the old concern. One evening, at about the full moon of the ninth month, the king was taking a stroll in his palace gardens, enjoying the moonlight. Just then a cool breeze sprang up unexpectedly, and he was startled to behold, descending from the void, the figure of a young piper playing an elegant melody on his jade flute.

The boy prostrated himself before the king, who exclaimed, "Child of another world! Why this descent into the human realm? Of what do you wish to inform us?"

Still prostrate, the youth answered, "I am Hong Kiltong, sire, Your Majesty's former minister of war."

The startled king asked, "But why do you come here so deep in the night?"

Kiltong replied, "It would have been my wish respectfully to serve Your Majesty for eternity. But I was born the child of a lowly maidservant and was denied the career a civil officer might enjoy in the Office of Special Counselors or that of a military officer in the Liaison Office. So it was that I took to roaming the country as I pleased, and it was only by raising havoc with government offices and offending the court itself that I finally succeeded in bringing my plight to the attention of the throne. Your Majesty deigned to grant my petition, and so I have come now to pay my last respects before quitting this court and land. I pray, sire, that you enjoy long life without end."

As Kiltong rose into the air and flew swiftly away, the king honored his prowess with unstinting praise. Thenceforth, with bandit depredations at an end, there was perfect peace in all quarters.

The story continues: Kiltong bade farewell to Korea and settled on Ti Island in the area of Nanking, where he built thousands of houses and strove to develop agriculture. Having taught his people the various skills, he set up arsenals and trained the able-bodied in the military arts. Indeed, his troops were well trained and well fed.

One day it happened that Kiltong was traveling toward Mount Mangdang to obtain a certain herb to be applied to arrowheads when he arrived in the area of Luochuan. Now a man living there by the name of Bo Long (White Dragon) had a daughter who was of uncommon talent and dearly beloved of her parents, but who had been inexplicably lost one day when a wild wind arose and wreaked havoc among them. Though the grief-ridden parents had spent one thousand measures of gold in a search that extended in all direction, there was not a trace to be found. The sorrowing couple let it be known: "Whosoever may find and restore our daughter to us, with him we shall share our family fortune and regard him as our son-in-law."

Kiltong was deeply moved when he heard of this, but since there was nothing he could do for them, he continued on to Mount Mangdang to dig up the needed herbs. It soon grew dark around him, and he was just wondering where to head next when the sound of men's voices arose and the bright glint of lamplight caught his eye. When he sought out the place whence it came, however, it turned out they were not men but monsters sitting about chatting with each other—the kind of monster called *ultong,* a sort that lives for many years and passes through infinite changes.

Concealing himself, Kiltong let fly an arrow and struck their leader, causing the monsters all to flee screaming. He propped himself up in a tree and after sleeping the night there returned to his search for herbs.

Kiltong's work was suddenly interrupted by three or so of the monsters who asked, "What is it that brings you so deep into our mountains?"

Kiltong replied, "I happen to be skilled in medicine and have come to find certain healing herbs. I consider it my good fortune to have come across you."

They were delighted to hear this. "Having lived here for some time, our king has now taken a bride, but just when he was celebrating at a banquet last night, he was struck and seriously injured by some divine arrow. Since you are a knowledgeable physician, you would surely be rewarded handsomely if you could heal the king's wound with those wonderful herbs."

Kiltong thought to himself: "This king of theirs must be the one I wounded last night." When he had acceded to their request, Kiltong was led to a gate where he was made to wait while they went inside. Soon reappearing, the monsters asked Kiltong to enter. Lying abed within the spacious and elegant red and blue villa was the abominable monster, who groaned and twisted his body up in order to look at Kiltong.

"It has been my unexpected fortune to be struck down by a divine arrow and left so critically wounded. But having heard of you from my attendants, I bade you hither. This is a heaven-sent salvation. Do not spare your skill with me!"

Kiltong expressed his thanks for the high trust and said, "I think it best first to give you medicine that will cure your inner distress and then, after that, to use herbs to heal the outer wounds."

When the monster agreed to this, Kiltong extracted some poisonous herbs from his medicine pouch and, hurriedly dissolving them in warm water, fed them to the monster. As soon as the potion had gone down, the monster let out a great cry and fell dead. At this, the other monsters flew into the room, only to be met by Kiltong's unleashed wonders. With great blows he felled them all.

Kiltong was startled then to hear the pitiful supplications of two young girls. "We are not monsters. We are human beings brought here as captives. Please save what is left of our lives! Let us go back into the world!"

Recalling what he had heard about Bo Long, Kiltong asked where they lived: one was Bo Long's daughter and the other was the daughter of one Zhao Tie. He cleared away the bodies and took the two girls back to their parents, who were overjoyed to have their daughter back and received Hong Kiltong as their son-in-law. Kiltong took Bo's daughter as his first wife and Zhao's as his second.

Thus had Kiltong, in a day's time, gained two wives and two families—all of whom he brought back with him to Ti Island, to the pleasure and congratulations of all.

One day Kiltong was scanning the heavens and, startled by what he saw, broke into tears. People around him asked the reason for this expression of grief.

Kiltong answered with a sigh. "I have been divining my parents' health by reference to the heavenly bodies, and the configuration indicates that my father is critically ill. But I am saddened to think how far I am now from that bedside I cannot reach." Everyone was saddened by his plight. On the following day, Kiltong went into Mount Yuefeng to pick out a suitable grave site and had work started on building a tomb with stonework on the scale of a state mausoleum. He also had a large boat prepared and ordered it to sail for the banks of the West River and there await further instructions. Thereupon he shaved his head and, adopting the guise of a Buddhist monk, set out himself for Korea in another, much smaller, boat.

Meanwhile, the old minister Hong, who had suddenly fallen gravely ill, called his wife and son Inhyŏng to him. "I am about to die and that itself is no cause for regret. But what I do regret is to die not knowing whether Kiltong is alive or dead. If he is alive, I am sure he will seek out the family now. In that event, there are to be no distinctions between primary and secondary, and his mother, too, is to be properly treated." With these words, he expired. The entire family mourned grievously, but once the funeral had been carried out they were perplexed that it was so difficult to find a propitious site for the grave. Then one day the gatekeeper announced that a monk had come, asking to pay his last respects before the dead. The family was pleased to receive him, but when the bonze entered and began to cry in great wails, they did not understand any reason for this and exchanged baffled looks among themselves.

After the monk had presented himself to the chief mourner and performed more sad cries of lamentation, he finally spoke. "Inhyŏng, brother, don't you recognize me, your own younger brother?"

The chief mourner examined this monk carefully—it was Kiltong. He caught his younger brother by the hands and cried, "Is it you, dear brother? Where have you been all this while? Our father's final words were spoken in great earnestness—it is clear to me where my duty lies."

He led him by the hand into the inner chamber to greet the widow Hong and to see Ch'unsŏm, Kiltong's mother, who wailed, "How is it you wander about as a monk?"

Kiltong replied, "It is because I am supposed to have left Korea that I now shave my head and adopt the guise of a monk. Furthermore, having mastered geomancy, I have already selected a proper resting place for Father, so Mother need no longer be concerned over it."

The delighted Inhyŏng exclaimed, "Your talents are peerless! What further trouble could plague us, now that a propitious grave site has been found?"

The next day, Kiltong conveyed the old minister's coffin and escorted his mother and brother to the banks of the West River where, as instructed, boats were standing by. Once the party was all aboard, they sped off like arrows. Soon they arrived at a particularly dangerous spot where an army of men in tens of ships had been standing by for their arrival. As expressions of pleasure were exchanged, the flotilla and its new convoy proceeded on their solemn way. Before long, they had made their way to the mountaintop, and as Inhyŏng surveyed the majestic setting he was unrestrained in his admiration for Kiltong's knowledge and ability.

With the interment completed, they returned as a group to Kiltong's residence, where his two wives, Bo and Zhao, greeted their brother- and mother-in-law. Kiltong's mother, Ch'unsŏm, was unstinting in her praise of his choices and also marveled at the imposing stature to which he had grown. After several days had passed and it came time for Inhyŏng to take leave of Kiltong and Ch'unsŏm, he enjoined his younger brother to keep the grave meticulously tended, and then paid his own parting respects at the tomb before setting out.

When Inhyŏng arrived in Korea he went directly to see his mother, Lady Hong, and related every detail of the journey, all to her wonder and pleasure.

The story continues: Having conscientiously observed memorials both at the time of the funeral and on the two succeeding anniversaries of his father's death, Kiltong now once again called his braves together. He perfected them in the military arts and spared no efforts toward agriculture in order to create a well-trained and well-fed military force.

The island kingdom of Lüdao to the south, with its myriad tricents of fertile land, had constantly held Kiltong's interest and attention as truly a country of heaven-sent abundance. Calling his men together one day, he said, "It is now my intention to attack Lüdao and I am asking every one of you to give his all in this effort."

The army set out the following day, with Kiltong himself in the forefront and General Ma Shu commanding the secondary force. Leading his fifty thousand select troops, Kiltong soon reached the foot of Mount Diehfeng in Lüdao and there engaged the enemy. The local magistrate, Jin Xianzhong, alarmed at the unexpected appearance of Kiltong's cavalry, notified his king and, at the same time, led his troops out to give battle. But in the engagement Kiltong cut down Jin Xianzhong at the first encounter, took Diehfeng, and saw to the pacification of its citizens. Leaving one Chŏng Ch'ŏl to hold Diehfeng, he reassembled his main force and set out to strike directly at the capital city. First, however, he dispatched a declaration to the government of Lüdao: "General of the Righteous Army, Hong Kiltong, addresses this missive to the king of Lüdao. Let him be aware that a king is never the sovereign of one man alone but ruler of all men. It is I who have now received the mandate of heaven and so raise armies against you. I have already destroyed the stronghold of Diehfeng and am now surging toward your capital. If the king will do battle, let him join in it now. If not, then let him promptly surrender and look to his salvation!"

Upon reading the missive, the terror-stricken king said, "We had put all our trust in the Diehfeng fortress and now it is lost! What recourse do we have?" He led his ministers out to offer surrender.

Thus Kiltong entered the capital and pacified its people. When he ascended the throne he enfeoffed the former king as lord of Ŭiryŏng and appointed Ma Shu and Cui Tie as his ministers of the left and right. When Kiltong had honored each of his generals with appropriate rank and station, the full court convened to offer him congratulations and pray for his long reign.

The new king had reigned only three years, but the mountains were clear of bandits and no man touched even a valuable left by the wayside; it was a nation of great peace. One day the king called in Bo Long and said, "I have a memorial here I wish to send to the king of Korea, which I must ask that you, my minister, spare no efforts to deliver." In addition to the memorial, he also sent along a letter to his family.

Upon arriving in Korea, Bo Long first presented Kiltong's memorial to the king, who was greatly pleased to see it and praised its author, saying, "Hong Kiltong is indeed a man of splendid talents."

The king, furthermore, issued a warrant appointing Hong Inhyŏng a royal emissary. Inhyŏng made formal expression of his gratitude and returned home to relate these happenings to his mother. She, on her part, made clear her intention to join him on the return to Lüdao, and Inhyŏng had no choice but to set out again with her.

After some days they finally reached Lüdao, where the king came out to meet them and, ceremonial incense tables set before him, received the royal message. This accomplished, the king, rejoicing in the reunion with Inhyŏng and his stepmother, joined them in a visit to the old minister's grave and then spread out a grand feast that brought pleasure to all.

Not many day later, Kiltong's stepmother, Lady Yu, suddenly took ill and expired; she was buried together with her husband in the same tomb. Inhyŏng begged leave of the king to return to Korea and report to the throne. His Majesty, hearing of the mother's death, expressed his condolences.

The story goes on: When the king of Lüdao had completed the three prescribed annual mournings, the queen dowager, Ch'unsŏm, passed away and was laid to rest in the royal tombs. Three mournings, once a year, were again observed.

Of the three sons and two daughters born to the king, the first and second sons were by Queen Bo; the third son and the two daughters were by Queen Zhao. He designated his first son, Hyŏn, as crown prince and enfeoffed all the others as princes and princesses.

The king had reigned thirty years when he suddenly fell ill and died at the age of seventy-two. His queens soon followed him and were laid to rest in the royal tombs. Thereupon, the crown prince ascended the throne and great peace reigned for successive generations on end.

Translated by Marshall R. Pihl

The Japanese Invasions

Record of the Black Dragon Year

Among the tales inspired by the Japanese invasions of 1592–1598, the *Record of the Black Dragon Year* is generally regarded as the most interesting because it is rich in fiction and subversive in aims. Compared to other wars fought on the peninsula, the Japanese invasions were unparalleled in their brutality and devastation. Oral narratives about the invasions had already begun circulating during the war. Thereafter they went through the process of conflation, selection, and combination and were widely transmitted through oral performances and the subsequent circulation of manuscripts and woodblock-printed editions. The story's popularity is attested by the number of versions extant, especially those with regional variations, indicating that memories of the war were shared by almost every living Korean. The *Record* exists in some forty manuscript versions, mostly anonymous, long and short, both in the vernacular and in literary Chinese. The vernacular version begins with the phrase *kaksŏl* (now it is said that . . .), indicating that what follows is fiction.

The *Record*'s most conspicuous feature is its emphasis on action. There are few descriptive passages or accounts of psychological states, and numerous stock descriptions of the heroes' appearance and strength. Battle scenes and the accoutrements of war figure prominently. Another feature is the age of the major characters. Like Western epic heroes, they are portrayed as being in their late teens and early twenties—perhaps to underscore the "youthful inner compulsion" that drives them to perpetuate their fame. The narrator loves well-made heavy armor and long swords: the helmet weighs three thousand pounds, the sword is seven feet long, and the hero wields a mallet or mace that also weighs three thousand pounds. The tale abounds in verbal threats and taunts from heroes to their foes both before and after individual combat, reminiscent of the boasting contests in the primary epics of the West. Here is the Japanese general Madŭng taunting Yi Sunsin: "Yi Sunsin! Little boy! Come out at once! Let's test our skills in a sea battle." A frequent insult is to call an opponent a "day-old puppy," from the Korean proverb "A young puppy does not know enough to fear the tiger."

Given these characteristics, what is particularly striking is the narrator's construction of a meditation master as the real hero of the tale. Great Master Samyŏngdang's (1544–1610) mission is to exact Japan's submission not by strength of arms but by the power of

Buddha's truth. The master constantly prays with a rosary of 108 beads and recites the scriptures, but he can also summon dragons and guardian spirits and transform the burning copper cell in which he has been imprisoned simply by writing the sinographs "ice" and "snow" on his cushion and on the walls. It is his mastery of concentration that brings the Buddha's help. The belief that no fire, ice, or sword can harm a buddha or bodhisattva is a major motif in Buddhist hagiography, just as it is in the lives of Christian saints. Only when the master brings down a great rain to flood the Japanese capital does the ruler of Japan surrender. The master represents an ideal order invested with peace and justice, and his victory is the triumph of spirit over matter. In an age when Buddhism was officially proscribed and monks were held in low esteem, the *Record*'s reliance on a great master to redress the wrongs inflicted by Japan invokes a belief that history is subservient to providence.

The *Record,* therefore, embodies a popular form of historiography that not only favors those from the periphery (most Korean generals and the great master himself are said to have come from the provinces) but inscribes, in its choice of vernacular prose, an ideologically motivated assertion of the commoner's place and power in Korean society. It competes with the official annalists and proves itself more comprehensive and efficacious in spreading the news of historical events in an unofficial but subversive way. This nationalistic text is a record of collective suffering, collective reflection, and collective expectations for moral and spiritual recovery.

Journals and a Journey to Japan

Reflecting the collective memory, literary works produced after the war continued to register indignation against the Japanese. Augmenting descriptions of the ravaged countryside were the indignities recorded in the journals of three Korean captives in Japan and the records of Korean envoys. These journals offer moving stories of hardship, perseverance, and resourcefulness, as well as other matters of interest to modern readers.

One captive, No In (1566–1622), was wounded in the decisive battle at Namwŏn (about October 5, 1597) and taken captive.[1] The ship carrying him and other captives arrived in Ukena, Iyo, around the end of January 1598. There No In met many detained Koreans, including one who had been in Japan for three years. From them he learned that Korean captives were bought and sold as a matter of course. Because of his classical education, however, he became something of a celebrity: young samurai would come to him with fans for poems, for which they paid him in silver coin. On the night of February 10, 1599, he attempted escape but failed, and was then transferred to Sakai, where he was placed in the custody of a subordinate of Shimazu Yoshihiro, lord of Satsuma, who had heard of him during his campaign in Korea and treated him with respect as a Confucian scholar. Learning of the presence of Ming messengers in Sakai, No contacted them and entreated them to take him along on their return voyage to China. On April 11, he boarded the Chinese ship with seven other Koreans and eventually reached Jangzhou. He then went to Fuzhou and met local officials and scholars, to whose homes he was invited and whom he impressed with his poems and prose pieces. Taken to the shrine for Zhu Song (1097–1143) and his son Zhu Xi (1130–1200), he met the instructor who lectured at the Wuyi Academy and answered questions put to him by young scholars and officials in writing. In these encounters, he gained respect as a Neo-Confucian scholar of erudition, loyalty, filial piety, and integrity— it was known, for example, that he had become a vegetarian since his capture by the Japanese, refusing to touch meat because he did not know the fate of his parents. His life while awaiting permission from Peking to return home was one of leisurely reading and writing. He often dreamed of members of his family. The extant portion of his *Diary of Kŭmgye* (*Kŭmgye ilgi*) covers the period from March 18 through August 13, 1599, when he was praised for the eight quatrains he had written on a screen in Fujian. Having received

---

1. Naitō Shunpo, *Bunroku Keichō eki ni okeru hirojin*, 329–440; *Haehaeng ch'ongjae* 9, 5–58 (original), 13–137 (translation).

his permission to return home, he then went to Peking via Shandong, where he worshiped at the Confucian shrine. In Peking, Emperor Shenzong (1573–1620) granted him a horse and ordered an escort to accompany him to Shanhaiguan, where the young graduates he had met in the south were on hand to bid him farewell. Then, via Liaoyang, he returned home to learn from his wife that his parents had died two years before.[2]

Kang Hang (1576–1622), who was even better known as a Neo-Confucian scholar in Japan than No In, was fleeing the war when on November 2, 1597, his boat was intercepted by Tōdō Takatora's soldiers off the coast of Yŏnggwang. He and his family all threw themselves into the sea, but the water happened to be shallow and they were captured. One of his sons and a daughter were abandoned by the Japanese, to be swept away by the incoming tide before Kang's own eyes. On the way to Japan, his six-year-old nephew fell ill and was thrown into the sea by the Japanese. On the beach near Ozu, his family members were so exhausted and starved that they fell at every step; his four-year-old daughter had to be carried alternately by his wife and his mother-in-law. Only when someone on the shore brought them food and tea did they regain their sight and hearing, but in February his nephew and niece died from an illness. After an unsuccessful attempt at escape (May 29, 1598), Kang was transferred to Osaka, then to Fushimi in Kyoto, where he found many compatriots and met Fujiwara Seika (1561–1619) and his friend Akamatsu Hiromichi (1562/3–1600), who hired him as a copyist of Confucian canonical texts and Zhu Xi's works.[3] In his journal *Record of a Shepherd* (*Kanyang nok,* published in 1656),[4] he mentions the presence of more than a thousand Korean captives in Japan and the existence of nose mounds.[5] Kang returned to Pusan

---

2. This portion is supplemented from *Kŭmgye chip* 2, in Naitō, 429–430.

3. Abe, *Nihon Shushigaku to Chōsen*, 62–125, 131–134.

4. *Haehaeng ch'ongjae* 2, 15–34 (original), 113–232 (translation). The diary portion is titled *Sŏmnan sajŏk* (My experience during the war). Naitō, 14–34.

5. Hideyoshi ordered his commanders to cut off the noses or ears (rather than the head) of every Korean killed, preserve them with salt, and send a fixed number to Kyoto for

on June 25, 1600, his passage on a ship procured by his earnings as
a copyist in Kyoto.

To escape the Japanese troops marching north to attack Namwŏn,
Chŏng Hŭidŭk (1575–1640), the author of *Record of a Voyage on the
Sea by Wŏlbong* (*Wŏlbong haesang nok*, first published in 1786),[6]
tried to flee with his family by boat, on November 6, 1597, but was
caught off the coast of Yŏnggwang, near Ch'ilto. His mother, wife,
sister-in-law, and younger sister all jumped into the sea rather than
be captured and later were officially honored as Confucian martyrs.
His infirm father and children were released, but Chŏng and his
brother, together with some one hundred captives to be sold as
slaves, arrived in Inotsu, now Tokushima, in Shikoku on January 26,
1598. He found there a number of Koreans, including members of
the literati.

In his life of captivity, Chŏng describes a poor shelter exposed
to rain and winter storms, and being beset with hunger, mosquitoes,
and typhoid fever or some other epidemic disease, from which he
suffered for several weeks. He dreamt constantly of his parents, wife,
and the two small sons left at home. He also met two servants from
his household who had arrived as captives on a separate ship, as well
as two Chinese captives. On the roads he met many other Korean
captives who had arrived earlier; and whenever they gathered, they
sang Korean songs to console themselves. He was given a degree of
freedom by the authorities and recorded poems he exchanged with
his captors. He also describes copying books and working as a ghost-
writer to earn enough money to obtain his return passage on a boat.
When he finally reached home on September 9, 1599, he found that
his whole village had been reduced to ashes.

It appears that these three Koreans, because of their knowledge
of the Confucian canon and their ability to write poetry and prose

---

his inspection and burial. The official recognition of distinguished service depended on the
number of noses dispatched to him. Kitajima, *Chōsen nichinichi ki*, 208, 289–322; Nuki,
Hideyoshi ga katenakatta Chōsen bushō, 164–166.

6. Naitō, 39–54; *Haehaeng ch'ongjae* 8, 67–140 (original), 193–446 (translation);
Naba, "*Geppō kaijōroku* kōshaku."

in literary Chinese, received better treatment than others. For them, writing poetry was a part of everyday life, and through this medium they created a community by speaking to their friends, captors, and future readers. They also seem to have been able to communicate by letter among themselves. For example, Chŏng Hŭiduk learned of Kang Hang's presence in Kyoto and responded to one of No In's poems with his own; No In responded to Kang Hang by means of a courier.[7]

Frequent expressions of sorrow, nostalgia, and mortality call for a special response. Kang Hang fasted for nine days without taking a drop of water but failed to die. Chŏng Hŭiduk attempted to jump overboard into the sea but pulled himself back because of his filial duty to his parents and family. Kang lamented the death of many Koreans, including his own family members and the slaves killed or fallen overboard whenever the ship hit a rock. Phrases such as "weep bitterly" (*t'onggok*), "tears of blood" (*hyŏllu*), "how sorrowful" (*ch'amŭi*), "defy description" (*pulga hyŏngŏn*), and "tears flow in spite of oneself" (*pulgak nuha*) recur repeatedly[8]—the sheer amount constitutes a discourse unique to these texts. Chŏng Hŭiduk especially, who was twenty-two at the time, is prone to weep bitterly when thinking of his dead wife, his parents, and his home. These accounts all register the impossibility of adequately expressing the experiences laden within them—the inexplicable presence of sorrow and anger not always named but nevertheless present. Indeed, they provoke a response quite in keeping with collective memory and a shared cultural grievance. It is not a secret that responses are shaped by material and ideological conditions outside the realm of language, a pretextual historical reality.

In what sense does the repetitive intrusion of heartrending crying in the journals of Korean captives constitute a unique discourse? Those cryptic but naked verbs are not deliberative language, as in a poem, but a record of inconsolable memory and uncommunicable

7. Naitō, 471–493.
8. *Wŏlbong haesang nok*, 2:3b, 4a, 4a–b, 10b, 32b.

grief by the disconsolate survivors. The instrumental value of those words—as the saying "words do not exhaust meaning" adumbrates—cannot possibly capture their grief. These notations inscribe a crisis of thought, speech, and representation and indicate a textual itinerary of trauma: "the response to an unexpected and overwhelming violent event or events that are not fully grasped as they occur, but return later in repeated flashbacks, nightmares, and other repetitive phenomena,"[9] "an event that is experienced too soon, too unexpectedly, to be fully known and is therefore not available to consciousness until it imposes itself again, repeatedly."[10] Weeping and dreaming point to the impact of traumatic experiences on the mind—incomprehensible catastrophes that befell the narrators' beloved ones as well as their own encounters with death. They themselves did not understand their own traumas because they had no language adequate to express them. The effects of those experiences were not apparent to them until they were interned. Then they began to see "the unbearable nature of the events and the unbearable nature of themselves as survivor(s):"[11] the tragedy of the father surviving two of his children (Kang Hang), and the tragedy of the son surviving his mother, the husband surviving his pregnant wife, the brother surviving his younger sister, and the brother-in-law (Chŏng Hŭidŭk) surviving his sister-in-law. The uncontrollable weeping and the frequent appearance of their loved ones in the survivors' dreams show the impact of trauma and registers the impossibility of comprehending their death. Kang and Chŏng do not tell us whether their family members appeared dead or alive in their dreams, nor do they indicate what they said. Dreams not only mourn the dead but are acts of homage to them. Because Kang and Chŏng could not betray the past, the freedom of forgetting was denied them. Deprived of freedom and dignity, surrounded by the invisible landscape of death, both could only silently shed "tears of blood."

9. Caruth, *Unclaimed Experience*, 91.
10. Ibid., 4.
11. Ibid., 7.

By notations of such weeping, Kang and Chŏng bear witness to an unprecedented historical occurrence—the destruction and suspension of civilization—"in excess of our normal frames of reference."[12] Chŏng provides only a minimal narrative context for the death of his mother and his wife and the last words they spoke (139 graphs):

My mother, born Yi, said to her old daughter-in-law, born Pak, and my wife, born Yi, and my unwed younger sister: "Now that hideous outlaws have closed in on us, we can't predict what calamity will befall us. Alas, the only path for four women is a death that will not disgrace us."

My wife then added: "When the invasion took place while we were at home, I vowed to die with my husband. In this I am fully determined." She bid farewell to my parents and turned to me and said, "I hear sincerity will move heaven. I beseech you, then, to be prudent in your action and, together with your brother, protect your father and come back alive. That's what the adult man should do."

Finally, striving to be first, my wife, together with my mother, sister-in-law, and sister, threw herself into the sea. My brother and I were bound and left in the ship, so we could not die when we wanted. What inexpressible grief! What inexpressible grief! Bitterly I weep. Bitterly I weep.[13]

As an educated Korean man of the time, Chŏng translates their last words into literary Chinese, hence far removed from the actual words spoken in Korean. Nor do the words capture the tone, voice, intensity, and other linguistic features of the speakers. They are from Chŏng's memory, belatedly, as he reenacts the overwhelming event he experienced. Chŏng's account conveys both "the truth of the event and the truth of its incomprehensibility," a "catastrophic

---

12. Scarry, *The Body in Pain*, 21; Felman and Laub, *Testimony*, xv, 5, 104.
13. *Wŏlbong haesang nok*, 1:1b–2a (cf. 2:36b).

knowledge" that he cannot express to others.[14] However, he vows to tell about it as a "mode of access to that truth."[15]

Overwhelming loss demands a witness, and the cryptic language at the end enacts his massive psychic trauma. The act of remembering becomes the moment of irrevocable loss, and the repetition of spasmodic cries and bitter weeping inscribes death and mourning. So long as Chŏng retains the memory of that moment of separation and loss, mourning is necessarily insistent and unfinished. Bearing literary witness is a "re-externalization of the evil that affected and contaminated the trauma victims,"[16] the process by which the survivors reclaim their position as witnesses speaking for the victims, "whose voicelessness no voice can represent."[17] As historical participants in these events, both Chŏng and Kang transmit the direct experiences of eyewitnessing. They must survive in order to bear witness; they must bear witness in order to affirm their survival. They ask history to look at the truth: it should not be a story of forgetting, but one of remembering how many innocent men and women, old and young, perished. Chŏng affirms the possibility of placing feminine subjects in history: their story should be differentiated from all others and recalled, internalized, and memorialized. They ask us to be second-degree witnesses and participants in the event. Their diaries are an "act of urgency."[18]

To bear witness is "*to bear the solitude of* responsibility, and *to bear the responsibility,* precisely, of that solitude."[19] Their solitude, silence, and anticipatory terror were broken by the captors, by their request. But when the captor and captive have a common language, it is a foreign one, a language other than their own. Often Kang and Chŏng write poems in Chinese at the request of their captors, who send them their own work asking them to harmonize with it, ask for

14. Caruth, 153, 256.
15. Felman and Laub, 16.
16. Ibid., 69.
17. Ibid., 197.
18. Ibid., 114.
19. Ibid., 3 (author's emphasis).

impromptu poems on their fans, or accompany their gift of sauce, fish, fruit, rice, medicine, and the like with similar requests. The captors say, as the Zen priest Tōgaku says to Chŏng: "Show me what kind of Chinese poetry you can write, and I'll help you return home alive."[20] Of concern here is the degree of appropriation of literary Chinese and the acknowledgment of the privileged status of written Chinese as the only mark of education and culture. While some Japanese are monstrous in their brutality, others present themselves as members of a large civil community in East Asia by expressing their reverence for Chinese poetry. Poetry matters, and so does the importance they grant it. Indeed, the captors are telling the captives that they too participate in the elite culture of sixteenth-century East Asia.

Hwang Sin (1560–1617) recorded his journey to Japan as an envoy during the war, in 1596, to join the Ming envoy there to discuss peace with Hideyoshi. He mentions as a fact the presence of more than 5,000 captives on one island, some of whom came to his residence begging for help.[21] Travel records written by subsequent envoys, beginning with the first postwar mission of 1607 and continuing until that of 1624, still mention the existence of nose or ear mounds, the sale of Korean captives at Nagasaki and elsewhere, and the reckless murder of captives and those kept against their will many years after the end of hostilities. The repatriation of captives was the main objective of these missions. Some captives, however, had married Japanese; some eunuchs served Hideyoshi; some men had become adopted sons; some females had become waiting women, wives, or concubines of samurai; some were settled there as potters,[22] physicians, Buddhist monks, beancurd makers, paper manufacturers, or landscape artists. According to the official record,

---

20. *Wŏlbong haesang nok*, 2:9a–b.

21. *Ilbon wanghwan ki*, *Haehaeng ch'ongjae* 8, 43–59 (original), 131–191 (translation).

22. For a moving story of a community of Korean potters who were brought by Japanese troops to Naeshirogawa in Kagoshima, Kyūshū, in 1597, see Shiba, "Kokyō wasurejigataku sōrō," and a translation in Kato, *The Heart Remembers Home*, 15–62. See also Kitajima, *Chōsen nichinichi ki*, 385–386, and Ch'oe Kwan, *Bunroku Keichō no eki*, 70–78.

7,500 Koreans were returned by 1643, but Japanese records mention many more (about 30,000) still detained against their will.[23]

In his poem diary covering July 29, 1597, through March 8, 1598, Keinen (d. 1611), the Japanese priest-physician and noncamp follower of the 1597 campaign,[24] provides an eyewitness account. He describes butchery, atrocities, plunder, arson, hard-fought battles, and heaps of dead everywhere. He saw at Pusan and elsewhere the Japanese slave traders (*hito akinaiseru mono*) hauling the bound Korean captives to their ships to be transported to Japan. The wrenching cries of the old and young, men and women, forcibly separated by the captors and calling the names of their loved ones, brought Keinen to recall pictures of hell, a simile repeated several times in his text.[25] Japanese peasants were pressed into service to accompany the troops, and Koreans were used to fill their places—indeed, the bodies of Koreans were considered labor power in Japan.[26] At the siege of Ulsan by the Chinese-Korean army (January 19–31, 1598, according to the diary), Keinen relates that the three hardships were cold, hunger, and thirst. The true meaning of war, he avers, is human greed. He adds that he himself has had to suppress his own desires.[27]

The captives in Japan and the narrators of the works of fiction presented below had been through hell. They bore witness to a barbaric war, an epidemic of evil, a tragedy of unalterable fate. The modern reader cannot forget certain scenes that flicker before his eyes, either singly, in pairs, or one superimposed on another: aristocratic Korean women hurling themselves into the sea to keep their virtue unsullied (or simply to avoid rape, torture, and painful death), for example, and women servants from the literati or peasant families transported against their will to a life of bondage in a foreign

23. Naitō gives a total of twenty to thirty thousand captives (57–196); Kitajima (360) says the figure is merely "a drop in the ocean."

24. Naitō, 561–706, provides the text and an interpretation of the diary.

25. Ibid., 654–655, 668–669.

26. Ibid., 667, 684.

27. Ibid., 653.

land. The heroic self-sacrifice of the former is morally powerful, and they are rightly commemorated for their integrity;[28] as for the latter, we know almost nothing more because none of them left any writing. Then there are Japanese troops massacring the population of walled towns such as Namwŏn and Chinju, juxtaposed against a select few in their own country exchanging poems in literary Chinese with the Korean literati captives. The knowledge and ability of these captives brought them a measure of respect. They spent their days in self-cultivation and reflection and strove to live up to the highest Confucian ideals. As their works attest, they tried to emulate their precursors, who preferred death to shame. Willing to suffer for the sake of their country, Kang Hang, Chŏng Hŭidŭk, and No In remained loyal to their principles. Kang, for example, deemed it shameful to remain alive as a captive in the enemy's land rather than die a righteous death. Hence he first titled his journal *Kŏngo rok*, a record of a criminal; later his colleagues renamed it *Kanyang nok*, comparing his loyalty to that of Su Wu (c. 143–60 BCE) of the Han, who refused to compromise his principles during nineteen years of captivity among the Huns.[29] These authors' sincerity and integrity— like that displayed in Ch'oe Ch'ŏk's odyssey—assure them a continuing power to interest readers today and in the future.

Anonymous

RECORD OF THE BLACK DRAGON YEAR

[IMJIN NOK]

One day, the king had a dream: From the east came a girl with unkempt hair, carrying a broomcorn millet sack on her head; she entered the palace in tears and placed the sack on the stone step. Soon in the

---

28. Ki and Yun, *Tongguk sinsok Samgang haengsilto*, 8:60a–b (p. 829).
29. *Kanyang nok*, *Haehaeng ch'ongjae* 2, 2:34.

eight provinces flames pierced the sky, and the people were in turmoil. When the king woke up in shock, he realized that it was an evil portent, cruel and distressing. The next day he was still troubled by the omen. And when the hundred officials at court convened to discuss it, all were silent. Thereupon, Third State Counselor Ch'oe llgyŏng spoke: "The girl had a broomcorn millet sack on her head; likewise the graph that contains the human radical with those for rice and girl make up the graph for *wae*, Japan.[1] So I fear there will be a Japanese invasion like fire in the eight provinces. As Japan is strong and prosperous, disaster will soon be upon us."

The king asked, "When this will happen?"

Ch'oe stated, "After three years, in the Black Dragon year, summer, after the fifteenth of the fourth month, they will land."

The hundred officials were silent. But the king became angry and declared: "During such a peaceful reign you disturb the court with your foolish talk! Divest him of his official rank and exile him to Tongnae!"[2] Thereupon Ch'oe went at once to the place of exile.

The story resumes: On the twenty-eighth of the lunar month, summer, of the Black Dragon year (June 7, 1592), it so happened that as an astrologer was gazing eastward, the sun's rays dimmed, the air filled with death, waves touched the sky, and black clouds covered the water as they approached. Countless thousands of Japanese ships covered the ocean, their three-tiered masts wrapped with blue awnings, the beat of drums and battle cries shaking the waves as they came.

In an instant, they landed and killed the magistrate of Tongnae. Like thunder a man roared: "With this sword I'll cut off the heads of the people of Chosŏn." All looked upon him and saw that he was the commander-in-chief. After three days' rest, Supreme Commander

1. The sinograph *wae* is divided into its three components, a method used in divination.

2. A town in South Kyŏngsang province, north of Pusan; its scenic spots include Haeun (Sea Cloud) Terrace.

Chosŏp planted the general's standard, allotted soldiers for each of the eight provinces, summoned Ch'ŏnch'ang and Manch'ang,[3] and said: "Assemble the unit commanders in columns, complete the number in each unit, and take a roll call."

The two generals obeyed the order and reported: "Renowned generals number over two hundred. There are two million armored soldiers, three million cavalry, one million advance soldiers, and twenty-eight thousand infantry scouts for each province."

Supreme Commander Chosŏp and Deputy Commander Kiyomasa mounted the general's platform and summoned Madŭng and Mahŭng. They gave them eight hundred commanders and fifty thousand soldiers and said, "Attack the twelve districts of Chŏlla, annihilate the whole province, and hold and defend the walled town of Chŏnju."

They summoned Mugyŏng and Pugyŏng and said, "Take eight hundred renowned commanders and fifty thousand soldiers. Destroy North Chŏlla province, cross Autumn Wind Ridge,[4] and destroy the fifty districts of Ch'ungch'ŏng province."

They also summoned Kyŏngch'ang, gave him two hundred renowned commanders and thirty thousand soldiers, and said, "Destroy West Kyŏngsang province and the districts east of the Great Pass Ridge[5] and hold the walled town of Wŏnju."

They also summoned Hosŏp, gave him two hundred commanders and fifty thousand soldiers, and said, "Destroy the twenty districts

3. These and other Chinese and Japanese names are mostly fictitious, with the exceptions of Kiyomasa and Li Rusong. So are some Korean names, such as Ch'oe Ilgyŏng. Fictitious Japanese names in Korean cannot be rendered in Japanese, because they are merely a combination of sounds without corresponding sinographs; even when the sinographs are given, they do not yield the Japanese reading; hence they are given in Korean as in the text.

4. A ridge between Kimch'ŏn, in North Kyŏngsang, and Hwanggan, in North Ch'ungch'ŏng; as the highest spot along the Seoul-Pusan railway, it demarcates a border between central and southern Korea.

5. A ridge between Kangnŭng and Chŏngsŏn in Kangwŏn, about 18 km long and 865 m high.

in Kangwŏn province, cross Bamboo Ridge,[6] and crush the twenty-one districts of Hamgyŏng province.

They also summoned Sŏch'olgŏl and Sŏch'ŏlbae and said, "Cross Kangwŏn province and destroy Kyŏnggi province. If you seize the capital city, send news of victory."

"Chosŏp will cross Bird Ridge[7] and destroy the twelve districts of Kyŏnggi province. You must rush your cavalry to assault P'yŏngan province, cut off its forty-two districts, enter the walled city of P'yŏngyang, and await Kiyomasa. Deputy Commander Kiyomasa will command six hundred generals and fifty thousand soldiers. He will destroy East Kyŏngsang province, enter Kyŏngju, hold and defend Taegu, destroy Sangju, wipe out the seven towns of Yŏngye, cross Bird Ridge, annihilate Kyŏnggi province, ambush Seoul, cut off the heads of Chosŏn's generals, and offer them to those under our generals' command. If among the generals there is one who is negligent, execute him on the spot and report it later."

All the generals and soldiers formed into units and began to march. The standards, spears, and swords mocked the sun and moon. The beating of drums, blare of bugles, and shouts of men shook heaven and earth. The sight was imposing and stern. Alas, the corpses of the people of Chosŏn were piled as high as mountains; blood flowed and formed rivers. It was impossible to guess the number of deaths. At dusk, flames everywhere pierced the sky. By day, plundering thieves killed countless innocent people, and weeping shook the Nine Springs.[8] The sight was unbearable.

Continuing with our story: At this time, in Sakchu of P'yŏngan province, there was a person with the family name Yi and the given name

---

6. A ridge between Yŏngju in North Kyŏngsang and Chŏngsŏn in Kangwŏn, 689 m high.

7. Either a ridge between Mungyŏng, in North Kyŏngsang, and Koesan, in north Ch'ungch'ŏng, 1,017 m; or one in Songhwa, Hwanghae, 151 m.

8. The underworld.

Sunsin. His other name was Lord Ch'ungmu (Loyal Warrior). He had lost his parents at an early age and was now twenty years old. He was a person of magnificent body and spirit; he could lift three thousand pounds; and he daily practiced horsemanship and archery.

He said with great joy, "This is an opportune time. With my talent I will deliver millions of people." He left home and endeavored to build a boat by the sea, waiting to be summoned by the court. The boat was ten thousand feet in length and ten fathoms in height, and its four sides were rounded so that no water could enter. Seen from afar, it looked like a large turtle floating on the water. He built several thousand and called them *kŏbuksŏn* (turtle ships).

He then went to various bureaus, pressing for military provisions and horse fodder. He went down to Chŏnju to see the provincial intendant Paek Naesu and said, "Now the Japanese outlaws are everywhere, so please send a message to the king quickly. If the king summons me, I will repel the enemy with my own sword."

The intendant replied with great joy, "I have already sent several dispatches, but there's been no news. It must be because the roads are blocked. General, please take action against the marauders at once. There are twenty thousand soldiers assembled from seven villages. Achieve merit and protect the altars of soil and grain."[9] Yi Sunsin readily agreed to put Paek Sŭngsu in charge of transporting military supplies and launched an attack against the Japanese invaders. Mahŭng invaded the seven villages south of Chŏlla province. Entering a large river, he sent a dispatch ahead. Yi Sunsin, with a helmet that displayed the sun and moon, wearing star-studded armor,[10] carrying a seven-foot-long sword in his hand, and riding a Mongol horse, came out surrounded by soldiers ready to fight.

9. Where the ruler offered sacrifices in spring and autumn; emblematic of the state. See Hucker, *Dictionary of Official Titles*, 5133; and Peter H. Lee, *Songs of Flying Dragons*, 125–128.

10. In the original, *mansŏng,* which can also mean "myriad stars."

The Japanese general Madŭng, who had led a naval force of a thousand soldiers waiting at sea, cried: "Yi Sunsin! Little boy! Come out at once! Let's test our skills in a sea battle!" So Yi Sunsin, over-joyed, deployed his boats in the *myo* (rabbit) formation, killed fifty thousand Japanese bandits beneath the waves, and then surfaced.[11]

Mahŭng, who had been in the base camp, came running and said, "Sunsin, do not harm my soldiers." As columns of flames arose from somewhere, Yi Sunsin looked away in surprise. Mahŭng, taking out an arrow, shot Yi Sunsin in the left chest. With a sigh he said, "Because of this single child, tens of thousands of generals and soldiers are now lonely underwater spirits."

The story resumes: When the Japanese general Kiyomasa surrounded the capital, the people in it suffered greatly from hunger and thirst. Many died and the people became panic stricken. One day a cold wind arose from outside the South Gate; sand and stones flew about, thunder filled the air, the ground seemed to sink, and the Han River boiled. In the enemy camp the generals and soldiers were terrified and broke formation, racing helter-skelter like breaking waves.

Kiyomasa looked in the air and saw a general wearing a red-gold helmet and a thousand-pound suit of armor. Brandishing a Blue Dragon sword and wearing a three-point beard, the general glared with the eyes of a phoenix and said:

"I am the marquis of Shouding, Guan Yunchang (d. 219), of the Three Kingdoms of the past. To avoid wind and rain, I am now en-trusting myself to the state of Chosŏn. Barbaric Japanese outlaws, how dare you invade Chosŏn! When I beheaded the commanders of five passes,[12] hundreds of thousands of heroes all died at my hands.

---

11. In the original, *mulsok* 'under water' is repeated twice, hence "surfaced." The nar-rator probably understood the turtle boats to be submarines.

12. The story of how Lord Guan Yu, on his way to rejoin Liu Xuande, beheaded six pass commanders at five passes is told in chap. 27 of *Sanguozhi*; see Roberts, *The Three Kingdoms*, 206–212.

I am from the other world. And if I enter into battle, you will be erased in an instant. If you do not wish to meet sudden death, evacuate your position and retreat at once. If you are arrogant, I will pulverize the Japanese people."

Kiyomasa was stunned, for it was indeed the famous general of the Three Kingdoms. Then, still speechless, Kiyomasa saw that Lord Guan's horse had vanished. He faced the sky with measureless gratitude and evacuated his position at once, retreating to Kangwŏn province.

The story resumes: Li Rusong swept through the eight provinces, severing the veins of mountains and rivers. When he arrived at this place, an old man riding a black ox passed in front of him, and Li said to him angrily, "Frivolous one, you treat me with contempt!" With his sword, he spurred on his horse, but though he struck it twice, the old man on the ox kept ahead and unaffectedly rode on, slowly penetrating the steep mountains. Li Rusong, still more enraged, whipped his horse on, but he could not keep up.

The old man crossed a large mountain and then a steep ridge and gradually went deeper, where the peaks and ravines touched the sky. Atop a cliff where trees formed a dense forest was perched a small thatched cottage of a few *kan*.[13] The old man went into the house and Li followed him. Looking left and right, he beheld such magnificent scenery that it was truly like a mansion in heaven. But because the distance still to be covered was boundless, he sought the owner in front of the gate. When an azure-clad boy came out to lead him into the guest room, Li tied his horse outside the gate and entered.

The old man was delighted to see Li. After they exchanged greetings, he said respectfully, "General, where is your home? I disgrace you by making you come to my lowly place. I cannot overcome my awe."

---

13. The unit used to measure the area of a room: about 8 feet.

"One who travels all over comes and goes everywhere," Li Rusong replied. "The time is late and I have far to go, so I would like to put up here for the night."

The old man sighed and began to lament: "I am unfortunate. Although I have eight sons, seven are gathering medicinal herbs and have gone south of the river to sell them in Shu.[14] My youngest is here, but he is unfilial and getting worse. He does not understand human relations and has severed the father-son relationship between us, so how can he be considered a person? Since we have now met, it is opportune that I should ask you to kill this unfilial son."

Li Rusong's anger exploded as he listened, and he said, "How can I allow a son who does not know his parents to live?"

The old man was greatly pleased. He opened the gauze window and said, "He went over there to the highest peak to gather medicinal herbs. He will return soon."

Li Rusong asked, "What is the name of this mountain?"

The old man answered, "To the west it is called T'aebaek Mountain and to the east it is called Sobaek Mountain."[15] The old man brought out some wine and refreshments.

Shortly after Li Rusong had eaten, the azure-clad boy came in, wearing an octagonal belt and holding five-colored flowers in his hand. When Li Rusong returned his greeting, the old man said to his son, "Entertain our guest well." So saying, he went inside.

"I hear that you are unfilial and have no respect for human relations. Scoundrels like you should be killed as a lesson to posterity," Li said.

14. Here the description seems to refer to China, "south of the Yangzi and Shu," the latter referring to modern Sichuan.

15. T'aebaek is the mountain range that constitutes the backbone of the Korean peninsula, about 600 km long; or the name may refer to a mountain between North Kyŏngsang and Kangwŏn, the seventh highest in Korea. The name Sobaek is shared by two mountains, one in North Kyŏngsang and the other in South Hamgyŏng, on the border between North and South Hamgyŏng.

"Who are you to mock an adult? I will do away with you," the boy answered.

Further enraged, Li Rusong drew his sword and struck at the boy. The sword broke. Unaffected, the boy sat down and said in reproof, "I've known you for a long time. Although I intend to pulverize you, for the moment you are a guest in my house. To render meritorious service and leave a beautiful name behind is what every grown man wishes. But you, with perverse notions of usurpation, have been smashing the faults in our mountain ranges. How can I not be furious?" He grabbed Li Rusong with one hand, threw him out the door, and roared: "Dirty general! Leave this mountain at once!"

In resignation, Li Rusong looked up at the sky and lamented: "I cannot stay here for long." As he was leaving the compound, he heard the clear sound of a bamboo flute coming from somewhere. He looked in all four directions, and on the pine-crested cliff there stood a thatched cottage that was bright and clean. There was the old man, wearing a coarse yellowed turban and hemp clothes and a black belt, sitting on the railing. The azure-clad boy rode a crane and danced with jasper flowers on his head. In his hand was a jade flute, which he played as he sat neatly upright.

Li Rusong found his way there little by little, relying on the shadow of the pine arbor. To the melody of the bamboo flute the boy sang:

Stout man, stout man, stout Chinese man,
Cross the Yalu River quickly.
Hurry, hurry, hurry, crossing the river.
Xiang Yu cannot forget the beautiful Lady Yu at the O River by the still full moon,[16]

16. Xiang Yu (233–202 BCE), the warlord who led the revolt against the Qin in 209, was eventually defeated by Liu Bang, founder of the Han. On the eve of his last battle: "With him were the beautiful Lady Yu, who enjoyed his favor and followed wherever he went, and his famous steed Dapple, which he always rode. Hsiang Yu, filled with passionate

And the spring wind cannot forget Precious Consort Yang at Mawei,[17]
Liu Bang of Pei Marsh entered the pass first,[18]
How can the wicked tiger of Mount Ch'o not know the rise and fall of
  states?
Xiang Yu's piebald horse is nowhere to be seen,
And at age sixteen he crossed the O River.
Stout Chinese man, cross the river quickly.

Li Rusong heard the song and said with a sigh, "This mountain spirit
wishes me to return to my home country. This earth spirit will weaken
my resolve. Every good objective has obstacles." He whipped his horse
and on his return home stopped by the capital. His Majesty came out
to greet Li, who took his leave, saying, "Chosŏn is my homeland, and
our family burial sites are here. How could I ever betray you? I humbly beseech Your Majesty to keep well for myriad years."[19] When he
was leaving for Ŭiju, His Majesty received him with humble words
and rich presents, came out forty tricents, and saw him off.

The story resumes: It was the third month of spring, thirteen years
after the Black Dragon year. There was a Buddhist monk named Great
Master Sŏsan at Naksan monastery in P'yŏngan province. At eighty,
he read the Buddhist scriptures daily. One day, after burning incense
and lighting candles, he was invoking the name of the Buddha when
a buddha with a gold embroidered cassock said to him: "In the year

---

sorrow, began to sing sadly, composing this song" (*Shiji* 7:295–339; Watson, *Records of the
Grand Historian*, 1:70).

  17. The favorite concubine (718–756) of the Tang ruler Xuanzong was strangled to
death at Mawei slope in Shensi, at the demand of the imperial troops. Bo Zhuyi (772–846)
captured the emperor's love for his lady in "A Song of Everlasting Sorrow," in 120 heptasyllabic lines.

  18. Liu Bang (r. 206–195 BCE), founder of the Han dynasty, was born in the district
of Pei.

  19. Goodrich and Fang, *Dictionary of Ming Biography*, 1:830a–b.

of the Black Dragon, the Japanese raiders burned every Buddhist hall. Once more, the Japanese bandits face their troops eastward to avenge their enemy. They seek to annihilate Buddhism. Having received instruction from Śākyamuni, the Thus Come One, I transmit it to you, the master of meditation, to dispatch your disciple Yujŏng to cause Japan to surrender."

When he awakened, the words of instruction were still ringing in his ears. As the great master came out and observed the heavenly ether, Japan's main star and Chosŏn's main star were locked in deadly combat, and death was in the air. He called his disciple Yujŏng and informed him of his vision. The following day he made preparations for a journey. Arriving at the capital, Great Master Sŏsan presented himself before the king, prostrated himself, and said, "This humble monk is a monk of Naksan monastery at Yŏngbyŏn in P'yŏngan. Śākyamuni, the Thus Come One, saying that Japan is again raising an army and our state is in danger, asked this humble monk to go to Japan and come back with Japan's surrender. This is the reason I am here."

The king replied in great surprise: "Even though you are a monk, you are also my subject. Go to Japan and prevent them from raising an army. Receive their written surrender and ease my distress."

"I am eighty and lack the physical strength," the great master replied. "But I have a great disciple, Samyŏng, who is capable of going to Japan. If you send him in my place, he will ease Your Majesty's distress."

The king summoned the disciple at once, and Samyŏng followed the messenger into the capital and came before the king.

His Majesty asked, "How old are you?"

Samyŏng replied, "I am nineteen. My name is Yujŏng."

Everyone saw that his face was like a white gem and his mind was as clear as water flowing in autumn. He was indeed a living buddha.

"I have heard the words of your teacher," His Majesty said. "After undergoing defeat in the Black Dragon year, Japan is again raising an

army. This is our state's great concern. Go to Japan, receive their surrender document, and ease my distress."

Samyŏng prostrated himself, saying, "Would I not go through fire
and water at Your Majesty's command and my mentor's directive?"

The king was pleased and immediately designated Samyŏng as an
envoy. In a dignified manner he presented him with a long baton and
a hatchet representing his authority. As Samyŏng bid him farewell, the
king personally urged on him three cups of wine and sent him off with
provisions for the journey. The procedure was solemn.

When Samyŏng arrived in Tongnae, the magistrate So Wandŏk
expressed contempt for him because he was a monk. Using the excuse
of illness, he would not come to meet him.

Samyŏng said in great anger: "I have received a royal command
and am on my way to a long sea voyage. Since you make light of my
words, you must not care for your country." So saying, Samyŏng had
him beheaded and exposed his head. Reporting this to the court, he
boarded his boat and headed for Japan.

The story resumes: The ruler of Japan heard that Chosŏn's living buddha was coming and assembled the entire court to discuss the matter:
"It is said that Chosŏn's living buddha is coming. We must devise
an ingenious scheme. What should we do?" Grand Councillor
Honggult'ong suggested: "The living buddha is a manipulator of nature. So I have a scheme. On the Chosŏn envoy's way, write and post
18,900 graphs of poetry and prose on a 18,900-panel screen, and have
him recite it from memory. If he does not forget a word, it must be
magic. Then we will know if he is a genius or a charlatan."

The ruler of Japan approved the plan and ordered the court to
welcome Chosŏn's living buddha. Then he came out with attendants
to receive Samyŏngdang. After finishing the ceremony, the ruler of
Japan said, "It is said there is nothing that the living buddha does not
know. There is a screen in the entranceway. Do you remember the
number of panels?"

Samyŏngdang said: "King, you are fit to be mocked by a knee-high boy! What is the point of asking? The folding screen has 18,990 panels."

"Can you recite from memory the poetry and prose written on them?"asked the ruler.

Samyŏng, who was holding a rosary in his left hand and wearing a cassock and gold crown on his head, recited 18,989 panels of poetry and prose until the hour of the horse (11 a.m.–1 p.m.) the next day. The Japanese ruler and all his subjects were astonished and said, "He does not know one panel. How can that be?"

Samyŏngdang replied, "How can I know the writing I did not see?"

The Japanese ruler sent someone to check if there was a mistake and, indeed, a panel had been covered by the wind.

All the more surprised, they set about to find another ingenious scheme. Then a subject proposed: "Outside the South Gate there is a lake more than a myriad fathoms deep. Arrange a great banquet and fashion a thousand-pound cushion of copper. Give it to the living buddha that he may ride the cushion and enjoy a boat ride on that water. If he does not carry it out, how can he expect to live?"

The ruler of Japan appoved the idea, arranged a banquet, and raised the tents. While he was enjoying the feast with Samyŏng, he took out the thousand-pound cushion and said: "Living buddha, please ride on that cushion and float on the water. Then we will know the power of the living buddha."

Samyŏng laughed in his heart. Summoning the Dragon King of the four seas, he invoked a divine general and rode on the cushion that was floating on the water. If the east wind blew, he went west; if the south wind blew, he went north. Then Samyŏng commanded: "Ruler of Japan, listen. I am a disciple of Śākyamuni, the Thus Come One. As I am boating on water like this, provide some music and come out yourself and dance. If you do not, you will suffer a great calamity."

The ruler of Japan, greatly astonished, rose and danced. After enjoying himself all day long, Samyŏng then returned to the detached palace and said, "Ruler of Japan, come out at once and surrender. I intended to enter your country in the Black Dragon year to exterminate your seed, but Śākyamuni the Thus Come One held me back until the next opportunity. But now I am here. Ignorant of the power of heaven, you arrogantly invaded Chosŏn. Our king was troubled, and eight thousand living buddhas exerted themselves to serve their country with utmost loyalty. How can you possibly resist? If you treasure your life, present a surrender letter. Otherwise I will lay waste to Japan."

The ruler of Japan was awestruck and could not dine or sleep comfortably. Again a subject informed him: "I have an ingenious scheme. Make a copper cell to imprison him. Make Samyŏng sit in the room, seal the door, light a charcoal fire, and work a pair of bellows. However much he says he is the living buddha, his bones will melt."

The ruler of Japan approved this idea, so they built a copper house, assigned it as the residence of Samyŏng, sealed the door when he was inside, and stacked up charcoal. When they blew on huge bellows, Samyŏng wrote the graph "ice" on his copper cushion and the graph "snow" on the walls. Sitting upright, he recited the Buddhist scriptures from memory, and the cushion became cool. For two days and nights, the Japanese worked the huge bellows, the copper posts melted, and the ruler of Japan said, "However much of a living buddha he says he is, all of his spirit will melt."

Then he had a soldier open the door and looked inside. Samyŏng, dressed in a cassock and sitting calmly, shouted: "They say it is hot in the south. Why is it so cold here?" Looking carefully, they saw that the place where he sat was covered with ice, and snow was falling on the walls in all four directions. The ruler of Japan was greatly astonished and again placed Samyŏng in the detached palace. The ruler was greatly distressed, and another subject said, "All stratagems have proved useless. So I entreat you to try another plan to escape calamity. Make a metal horse from copper, heat it with charcoal, and force him to go about riding the horse."

The ruler of Japan said: "Why would a living buddha who spreads ice in a red-hot room be afraid of fire? But try it anyway."

So they heated a copper horse with bellows and transformed it into a fiery horse and said, "Ride this, living buddha of Chosŏn." Samyŏng laughed wryly, faced west toward Chosŏn, bowed four times, spat three times—and from the west a speck of black cloud came floating. In an instant, heaven and earth were overturned. Thunder sounded from all four directions, startling everyone out of their wits, torrential rain poured down, the ocean overflowed, and the Japanese capital was nearly engulfed. The ruler of Japan was terrified. He unfastened his royal seal and hung it on his neck, took off his royal robe, fastened it to his neck, bowed his head to the ground, and apologized: "Divine living buddha, please spare my life."

Thus he did beg. And only then did Samyŏng stop the rain and say, "Will you ever again harbor treacherous aims and oppose Chosŏn?"

"Henceforth I will have no such presumptuous intentions," said the ruler of Japan, as he prostrated himself and begged for mercy. He bowed a hundred times and apologized: "If you spare my life, I will forever repay your kindness."

Samyŏngdang granted his wish and said, "Every year you must submit as tribute three hundred human skins, three thousand pounds of bronze, three thousand pounds of peony bark, and three thousand pounds of other Japanese goods."

When the ruler of Japan had written an acknowledgment of surrender on these terms, Samyŏngdang said, "There are a thousand living buddhas in each of our provinces. If you ever again harbor treacherous designs, eight thousand living buddhas will rise as one and lay waste to Japan. Be careful." The ruler of Japan touched his head to the ground a hundred times.

When Samyŏngdang returned to Chosŏn, the ruler of Japan bade him farewell with great ceremony and lavish presents. Arriving in Chosŏn, Samyŏngdang presented the Japanese ruler's letter of surrender and the list of tribute goods to His Majesty, went down to P'yoch'ung monastery in Miryang, Kyŏngsang province, and passed away on the fifteenth day of the seventh month, the day of the full moon. His Majesty grieved and built a private academy at P'yoch'ung monastery, ordered memorial services to be held in spring and autumn, and ordered the monks of eight provinces to perform a vegetarian feast for Samyŏngdang every year on the fifteenth of the seventh month and to transmit these rituals down through the ages. With that, His Majesty became more devout and felt deep reverence for the path of the Buddha.

Cho Wihan (1558–1649)

THE STORY OF CH'OE CH'ŎK

[CH'OE CH'ŎK CHŎN]

"The Story of Ch'oe Ch'ŏk" is a fictional narrative written in literary Chinese by Cho Wihan in the mid-seventeenth century. In the late sixteenth and early seventeenth centuries, the Chosŏn state was invaded first by the Japanese to the east (1592, 1597) and then by the Manchu in the north (1627, 1637). Although Chosŏn did not see a dynastic change from these invasions, its society underwent profound shifts with social and economic dislocations and unpredictable transformations of identity.

Displacement and transformation of identity during the wars are two of the most prominent themes in Cho's story. Against the background of the "transnational" war, the characters are forced to cross borders, change their national identity, adopt foreign languages, and even change their gender identity. In exploring individual lives, Cho reconstructs the war experience from the perspective of the common people.

The complete version of the story is in the library of Seoul National University. It has appeared in a number of editions—for example, under the title "The Story of Hongtao" in *Ŏu's Unofficial Histories (Ŏu yadam)*, editd by Yu Mongin (1559–1623). Abridged records concerning the character Ch'oe Ch'ŏk, written in a more factual manner, appear in the collected works of writers such as Yu Manju (1755–1788) and Kim Chinhang (d.u.).

Ch'oe Ch'ŏk, courtesy name Paeksŭng, was born in Namwŏn.[1] He lost his mother at an early age and lived alone with his father, Suk, east of the Manbok temple, outside the western gate of the city. As a child he was high-spirited, sociable, trustworthy, and mindful of the most important rules.

One day his father admonished him, "You still lack education and refinement. What kind of person are you going to be? The country is now afflicted by war and the towns and villages are recruiting soldiers. Don't make your old father sick with worry by wasting your time hunting. You should keep your eyes on your books so that you can concentrate on preparing for the civil service examination. Even if you don't pass, you can still avoid packing a quiver of arrows on your back and serving in the army. On the south side of the city there is a literatus, Chŏng, one of my old friends. He is studious and skilled in composition; he might be a good teacher for a beginner like you. You should go to him and learn from him."

Ch'oe immediately went to Chŏng's house with his books. He asked Chŏng to become his teacher and continued to study hard. Within a few months, his verses grew so fluent that they surged like a river that has overflowed its banks. All the people in the village praised his exquisite talent.

Every time Ch'oe had a lesson, a certain girl hid in the shade under the window and secretly listened to him as he recited. She was sixteen or seventeen years old. Her eyebrows were beautifully shaped like a painting and her black hair shone like lacquer.

---

1. A city in North Chŏlla.

One day his teacher was away for lunch and Ch'oe was sitting alone, reciting his lesson. All of a sudden, someone threw a small piece of paper through the window into the room. He picked it up and read it. It contained the last stanza of "Plop Fall the Plums."[2] Ch'oe felt his spirits so uplifted that he couldn't remain calm. He wanted to find the girl's room and embrace her that night. But he quickly thought better of it. He tried to chasten himself by contemplating the model conduct of Kim T'aehyŏn (1261–1330),[3] but he wavered between righteousness and desire. In a while he saw his teacher coming in and hid the letter in his sleeve. When he departed after his lesson, he saw a maidservant standing outside the door. She followed him and said, "I have something to tell you." His heart having been stirred by the poem, he was more than curious when he heard those words. He gave her a nod to follow him to his house, where he asked her what the matter was.

She answered, "I am Ch'unsaeng, Lady Yi's maid. I came because she sent me to ask you for your response to the poem."

Puzzled, Ch'oe asked, "Aren't you a maid of the Chŏng family? Why do you call her Lady Yi?"

She answered, "My master's house was originally in Ch'ŏngp'a, a village outside the South Gate of Seoul. My master, Yi Kyŏngsin, died young, and the widow, Lady Sim, was left alone with her daughter. Her daughter, Ogyŏng, is the one who sent the poem to you. Fleeing the war last year, they boarded a ship on Kanghwa[4] and went to Hoejin in Chŏlla province.[5] This autumn, they left Hoejin to come here. Master Chŏng, a relative of Lady Sim, has been generous in accommodat-

2. *Shijing* 20:3; Waley, *Book of Songs*, 30.

3. A scholar-official of Koryŏ who is said to have never gone back to his teacher's home after receiving a poem from a widow in his neighborhood.

4. An island near Seoul.

5. A town to the southeast of Naju.

ing us. Now he is seeking a good husband for Lady Yi, but he has yet to find a worthy son-in-law."

Ch'oe responded, "How did your Lady Yi learn to read and write, being a widow's daughter? Are you saying that her talents are a gift from heaven?"

"She had a brother named Tŭgyŏng. He was gifted in writing but died a bachelor at the age of seventeen. Lady Yi picked up a bit of skill in writing while listening to her brother reciting his lessons. Thus she can only write her own name, and poorly at that."

Ch'oe gave her food and drink and then brought out a small piece of paper on which to write his response:

> Your letter this morning has captured my heart. Having met the bluebird, I cannot suppress my happiness. Like a bird that looks in the mirror and sobs in grief, having lost its mate, or like a widower who calls to his wife while looking at a painting of her, I long for my soul mate. I am not unaware of the story of how Sima Xiangru[6] lured Zhuo Wenjun by playing the zither and of how Jia Yun presented precious incense to Han Shou.[7] And yet I cannot figure out how high Mount Penglai[8] is or how long the Weak Water[9] might be. Contemplating these, my face has turned yellow and my neck grown thinner. What has happened today feels as if the rain of Sun Terrace[10] were pouring down on me in a dream and the letter from the Queen Mother of the West[11] has unexpectedly reached me. If we should

---

6. The most famous poet of rhapsody in China.

7. Daughter of Jia Cheng (317–352), who stole exotic perfume from the Western Regions and gave it to her lover Han Shou. *Jinshu* 40:1172–1173.

8. A mythical seamount in the eastern sea where transcendents dwell.

9. The name of a magical stream on which not even a feather can float; see Needham, *Science and Civilization in China*, 3:608–611.

10. The place where the goddess of Mount Shaman is believed to have appeared to a king of Chu.

11. Believed to rule the land of transcendents in the Kunlun Mountains; see Birrell, *Chinese Mythology*, 171–175.

bind ourselves with the threads of the old man under the moon[12] just as Qin and Jin did,[13] we would fulfill our wishes over three lifetimes without once breaking our vow to be buried together in the same place. This letter cannot express all I want to say. Even if I did put it all into words, how could they convey the depth of my feelings? Yours truly,

Ogyŏng was overjoyed to receive the letter. The next day she sent Ch'oe her response:

I was born and grew up in Seoul. Early in my education, I had the misfortune of losing my father. After the war, I had to look after my mother all by myself. Having no other family members, she and I made our way to this southern province and found a place to stay here in my relative's home. I have just turned fourteen, but I am not yet married. I am afraid, with the outbreak of war and the presence of looters, it will be hard to keep the precious jade beads from being broken or my honor intact. That is why my old mother is exhausting herself, worrying about me. My only concern is that a vine must pick a tall tree to rely on. My happiness for a hundred years will be determined by whether I find the right person. If I do not, I won't be able to respect and devote my whole life to him. I have watched you closely and can tell your words are gentle and your manners elegant. Your sincerity and truthfulness shine forth from your face. If I were looking for a wise husband, whom should I choose but you? I would rather become your concubine than marry a man with no talent. I am only afraid that my wretched fate will not allow me to fulfill this wish. I sent a song yesterday, but I did not mean to stir up your desires. I just wanted to see how you would respond. Although I am not an overly proud woman, I am not one of those who sell themselves in the marketplace. Why would I take a risk to commu-

12. The old man who uses red threads to tie the marital knots.

13. Two kingdoms in the Warring States period that maintained alliances sealed by marriage over several generations.

nicate with you through a hole in the fence? We should inform our parents and in due time have a proper wedding. Until then I will remain chaste and faithful. How could I tire of being respectful toward you! Since I was the first to send a poem, I have committed the disgraceful act of matchmaking for myself. Again, by exchanging clandestine letters, I have lost my purity as a lady of the inner chamber. Now that we are aware of what is in each other's heart, we should no longer be so impetuous as to exchange letters. From now on, you must go through a matchmaker, so that you do not make me commit this disgraceful act again. I beseech you with all my heart.

Receiving this letter with happiness, Ch'oe said to his father: "I have heard that a widow who came from Seoul to stay at Chŏng's place has a daughter who is young and attractive. Why don't you consult with Chŏng about a marriage with her, so that someone with quicker feet does not get her first?"

His father said, "They are of the upper class, despite being far from their home. They must be looking for a bridegroom who is from a wealthy family. Our family is humble and poor. They will not welcome us."

Ch'oe persisted in trying to persuade his father. "Just go and talk to them. It is up to heaven alone whether they will accept me."

The next day, his father went to Chŏng, who said, "I do have a cousin who fled from Seoul during the war and is now staying with me. Her daughter's appearance and manners make her exceptional compared to the other women of the inner chamber. I am trying to find a son-in-law who can support her family. I do know that your son is so extraordinarily talented that he will not fail to meet my expectations. My only concern is that he has no fame or wealth. I will consult with my cousin and then talk with you again." Ch'oe's father returned to inform his son of their conversation. With great anxiety, Ch'oe waited many days for a response.

When Chŏng went to discuss the matter with Lady Sim, she too was troubled: "Being far away from my hometown, I am by myself with no one to rely on. I only have a daughter, and I want to marry her off to a wealthy man. I don't want the son of a poor man, no matter how talented he may be."

That night, Ogyŏng came into her mother's room. She seemed to have something to say but hesitated to speak.

Her mother said, "Whatever you have on your mind, please do not hide it from me." Ogyŏng remained undecided, blushing the whole time. She spoke only because she felt forced to do so. "You are trying to find a husband for me, and you must be looking for someone from a wealthy family. I sympathize with your concerns. If I were to marry a man from a wealthy family who has admirable talent, how fortunate that would be! But if a man from an affluent family has very little talent to speak of, he would hardly be able to support his own family. Suppose I chose a miserly man to be my husband. Even if my family had enough rice, would I be allowed to eat until I was full? I have watched Student Ch'oe, who comes here to study with my uncle every day. He is reliable and faithful, definitely not frivolous or licentious. If I were to marry him, I would wish for nothing else for the rest of my life. Besides, poverty rather befits a scholar. A man who has gained his wealth in an unjust way is not someone I would want. I plead with you to marry me to Ch'oe. I know this is not something I should be discussing, but it's a serious matter. How can I restrain myself and remain silent? If I were to marry a mediocre man and ruin my life, that would be like a broken tile that cannot be put back together again, or like colored thread that can never be made white again. What use, then, in crying all night long? Belated regrets fix nothing. My situation is different from that of others. I have no father to protect me; even worse, everyone in the neighborhood is an enemy. If my husband is not faithful and reliable, how can he support you and me? I would rather be like Lady Yan, who asked to get married on her own, and would not refrain from choosing a mate for myself, as Lady Xu[14] did. How can I hide myself deep in the inner chamber, only to watch as others speak, and leave myself open to all manner of peril?"

Her mother had no choice but to tell Chŏng the next day, "I thought about it again last night. Although Ch'oe is poor, I can see that he is an admirable scholar. Being wealthy is entirely up to heaven and cannot be brought about by human intentions. Rather than pursuing the marriage of Ogyŏng to someone I don't even know, I would prefer to have Ch'oe as my son-in-law."

Chŏng said, "If you feel this way, I am totally in agreement with you. Although Ch'oe is as yet an unknown scholar, he is like a jade in quality. Such a man is hard to find, even if you search all over Seoul. Once he begins to act on his desire to succeed, he will not remain in a small pond." That same day, Chŏng sent for a matchmaker to arrange for the engagement. Finally, the fifteenth of the ninth month was set as the wedding day. Ch'oe was so excited that he counted the days on his fingers while awaiting the wedding.

Sometime later, a former *ch'ambong* (rank 9b) in Namwŏn, Pyŏn Sajŏng (1529–1596), raised a Righteous Army to march to the southeast to repel the Japanese.[15] Since Ch'oe was good at archery and horseback riding, he was forced to join the army. In camp, Ch'oe was so despondent that he fell ill. On his wedding day, Ch'oe petitioned to go on leave.

The commander was furious. "At a time like this, how dare you think of your wedding! When the king is begrimed with dust and out in the field, his servants cannot afford even a moment of sleep while carrying a spear. Moreover, you aren't of marriageable age yet. Take

14. In the state of Zheng, the sister of Xu Wufan selected her own husband from two eligible candidates. *Zuozhuan* (Zuo commentary, 540 BCE), Zhao 1.7.

15. Pyŏn raised an army in Sunch'ŏn in 1592 that is said to have killed two thousand Japanese soldiers.

up the matter after you defeat the enemy. It won't be too late." He did not allow him to leave.

When Ch'oe did not return from the army, Ogyŏng could do nothing but watch helplessly as the wedding date came and went. She could hardly eat or sleep. Meanwhile, there was a student in the neighborhood named Yang. His family was wealthy. Having heard that Ogyŏng was clever and wise, he tried to take advantage of Ch'oe's absence to marry her. Yang passed some money to Chŏng and his wife and pressed them every day. Chŏng's wife said to Lady Sim: "Ch'oe the student is so poor he has to worry every morning about what he will eat for dinner. He has so many difficulties supporting just his father that he is already in debt. Is he capable of supporting a family with no worries? Moreover, he is serving in the army and hasn't yet come back. We don't even know if he is alive or dead. The Yang family has been long admired for their wealth, and Student Yang is no less intelligent than Ch'oe." Chŏng and his wife were in agreement. They constantly spoke in favor of Student Yang.

Lady Sim was finally persuaded and chose an auspicious day in the tenth month for the wedding. Her resolve was firm, she said, and it would never be broken.

One night Ogyŏng appealed to her mother. "Ch'oe is serving in the Righteous Army, so his comings and goings must be up to the commander. He would not break his promise intentionally. If I break our vows too hastily and fail to wait for news from him, who will be the faithless party? If you try to discourage me from waiting, I still would sooner kill myself than be married off to another man. Please do not betray the will of heaven. I beg you, don't destroy me!"

Her mother said, "Why are you so stubborn? You are supposed to obey the head of the household. What could a little girl like you know?" And she went to bed.

That night she was deep in a dream when she suddenly heard someone choking. She woke up and felt for her daughter but could not find her. Alarmed, she got up to search. Ogyŏng was lying facedown under the window with a towel tangled around her neck. Her hands and feet were already cold. The faint breath coming from her mouth was fading away. Frightened, Lady Sim undid the knot and woke up the maid Ch'unsaeng to have her bring a light. She wept bitterly, holding her daughter in her arms. She put a spoonful of water into Ogyŏng's mouth, and Ogyŏng's breath came back after a while. The Chŏngs also came to help. They were greatly frightened, and after that night no one mentioned the Yang family again.

Ch'oe's father's letter to his son recounted all that had happened. Ch'oe was already suffering from a serious illness, but now, alarmed at the news, his condition worsened. When the commander was informed, he immediately let Ch'oe return home. Within a few days Ch'oe shook off the illness and recovered fully. The wedding was finally held on the first day of the eleventh month. The two radiant ones were joined together in the Chŏng household. You can imagine how happy they were. Ch'oe then returned to his own house with his wife and his mother-in-law. All the servants rejoiced as they entered through the gate, and their relatives waiting in the house offered their congratulations when they entered.

News of their happiness spread, and the regard in which they were held soared in the neighborhood. Ogyŏng did not look down on chores and she kept herself busy drawing water from the well, pounding grain in a mortar, and weaving cloth on a loom. She was devoted to the care of her father-in-law and her husband, and she carried it out with utmost sincerity. People in the area who knew of her said that neither the wife of Liang Hong nor the wife of Bao Xuan could exceed Ogyŏng in her devotion.[16] What is more, she treated people of all classes in the proper manner.

---

16. Liang Hong was a poor scholar of the Eastern Han (25–220), and Bao Xuan, of the Western Han (202 BCE–23 CE). Their wives were famously respectful and devoted to their husbands.

Once Ch'oe was married, everything he tried went well and his family grew more prosperous. His only concern was that he was now of age and not yet a father. On the first day of every month, Ch'oe and his wife went to the Manbok temple to pray for children. It was on the first day of the first month of the following year that a golden buddha, six fathoms tall, appeared in Ogyŏng's dream. "I am the buddha of the Manbok temple," he said. "I am moved by your kindness and sincerity and will bestow upon you an extraordinary son. When he is born, he will bear a particular mark." In time, Ogyŏng gave birth and the baby had a red mark on his back, as large as his palm. They named him Mongsŏk (dreaming of Śākyamuni).

Ch'oe enjoyed playing the flute. He would play every night when the moon rose and every morning when the flowers opened their petals. On a clear night late in spring, a gentle breeze was blowing and the bright moonlight was white. A delicate fragrance tickled the nose while falling petals clung to one's sleeves. Ch'oe brought out a wine jug, filled the glass, and drank. Leaning on the reading table, he played three songs on the flute. The resonance rippled away. Ogyŏng remained silent for a while and said, "I usually dislike it when women recite poetry. But being in this mood, I can't resist." She recited a poem:

> Wang[17] plays his flute as the moon begins to set.
>   The azure sky, like an ocean, is misty with dew.
> Let us fly together on a bluebird,
>   On the misted road to Mount Peng, we'll never be lost.

Ch'oe had been unaware of Ogyŏng's talent in poetry and was astonished now. He praised her poem repeatedly and then harmonized with one of his own:

---

17. A son of King Ling of Zhou (6th cent. BCE) and a noted player of the *sheng* (mouth organ made from thirteen bamboo pipes).

Jasper Terrace[18] floats far off in dawn's crimson cloud.
  The flute is silent but the song still remains.
Its resonance fills the sky while the moon sets over the mountain.
  Flowery shadows in the garden sway in the fragrant wind.

During the recitation, Ogyŏng's delight was boundless. But as her joy ebbed, she was overcome by sadness. "Human life is filled with unpredictability," she sobbed. "Good news is followed by bad, and in our short lives we can never stop meeting and parting. Will I ever be without cares?"

Ch'oe pulled up his sleeves to wipe away her tears. "When heaven contracts, it is ready to expand. Once it is full, it can only be emptied. That is heaven's law. If an event is good, a bad one is already on its way. We can never be free from worries and regrets. That is what human life is about. If we meet with misfortune, we should say it is our destiny and stay calm. Let's not be sentimental. As the old saying has it: 'Talk about fortunes and never about misfortunes.' And the proverb repeats: 'Do not spoil your happiness with your concerns.' "

Thenceforth their love and affection grew stronger. They knew they were soul mates and were never apart even for a day.

In the eighth month of 1597 (September 25), Namwŏn fell to the Japanese army. All the people in the village were scattered. Ch'oe's family members fled to Yŏngok on Mount Chiri.[19] Ch'oe made Ogyŏng put on men's clothing and hide herself in the crowd. People who saw her never realized she was a woman. At last they entered the mountain cave, and a few quiet days passed. But when the rice supply was entirely eaten, they knew they were going to starve. Ch'oe and a few other stout men decided they had to go down from the mountain to get more rice and to scout the enemy. When they reached

---

18. The name of the tower where Jian Di, the first ancestress of the Shang, was shut away; see Birrell, *Chinese Mythology,* 114–116.

19. A mountain range between South Kyŏngsang and North Chŏlla, 1,915 meters high.

Yŏngok,[20] they ran into the enemy troops unexpectedly. Ch'oe hid himself among the rocks and bushes and then fled. That day, the enemy entered Yŏngok. All over the mountain and through the valleys, they plundered. Ch'oe's escape route was blocked and he could not move ahead. After three days, the enemy withdrew and Ch'oe returned to Yŏngok. There he saw the dead bodies piled up and blood still flowing like a river. He heard the sound of wailing coming from the woods. Ch'oe approached and found some of the old people and children there; severe wounds could be seen all over their bodies. They said to Ch'oe: "The enemy entered the mountain cave, and for three days they looted, killed people, and took away the children. They withdrew to a camp by the Sŏmjin River[21] yesterday. If you want to find your family, go and search the river."

Ch'oe cried out to heaven, beating the ground. He threw up blood. Setting out for the Sŏmjin River, he walked a few tricents before he noticed someone moving in a pile of dead bodies. Her face was covered with blood, and her intermittent groans seemed to be coming from the threshold of death. Ch'oe did not recognize her but when he saw that her clothes seemed to resemble those of Ogyŏng's maid, Ch'unsaeng, he called aloud, "Are you Ch'unsaeng?" Ch'unsaeng strove to open her eyes and her voice came from deep within her throat.

"Young master! Young master! Your family was all taken captive by the Japanese. I was carrying your son, Mongsŏk, on my back, so I could not run fast. The enemy hit me and went away. I fell to the ground as if dead and woke up half a day later. I don't know if the baby is all right." Her breath became labored. Her eyes closed and she did not speak again. Overcome, Ch'oe beat his chest, stamping his feet on the ground. He felt waves of despair mounting ever higher until he fainted and fell to the ground.

20. A town in South Chŏlla.

21. Begins at Chinan in North Chŏlla and passes through Namwŏn, Kurye, and Hadong before emptying into the South Sea, a distance of 212 km.

When he woke, not knowing what else to do, he continued heading toward the Sŏmjin River. On the riverbank were a number of the wounded, old and weak, who had gathered to lament. When Ch'oe questioned them, they said, "We were hiding in the mountain cave when the Japanese attacked. They selected the strongest young men and dragged them to their ships. They beat us terribly." Ch'oe wept bitterly. Feeling totally alone, he no longer wanted to live. He tried to throw himself into the river, but the people nearby stopped him. He wandered away from the river, not knowing where to go. He began to search for the road that would take him back to his old house. After three days, he reached it. The fence was broken and the roof had fallen in; little flames were still burning here and there in the house. Corpses were piled up in front, a small hill. He could not even find a place to stand.

Ch'oe finally sat down to rest beside the Kŭm Bridge. He had not eaten for several days and he was drained of energy. When dawn came, he could not stir. At that moment, a Ming commander leading a dozen cavalrymen came up from the village to wash their horses under the bridge. Ch'oe knew some Chinese since he had been in charge of the reception of Chinese soldiers and had exchanged poems with them when serving in the Righteous Army. He told the commander that his entire family had been massacred and that he had nowhere to go. He said that he wanted to accompany them to China, where he would live in seclusion. The commander took pity on him and was sympathetic to his plan.

"I am Company Commander[22] Yu Youwen, under Regional Commander[23] Wu. I am from Yaoxing in Zhejiang province. My family is not wealthy, but we are able to support ourselves. What is important in life is meeting people who truly understand. To do so, we must be able to travel as we please, regardless of the distance. You have no family

22. Hucker, *Dictionary of Official Titles*, 927.
23. Ibid., 7146.

ties holding you back anymore. There is no reason you should not travel." The commander called for a horse for Ch'oe to mount and brought him to his camp.

Ch'oe had always been gifted with keen insight. He was also skillful in archery and horseback riding and he had some knowledge of writing. The commander liked him. He shared his table with Ch'oe at meals and insisted that Ch'oe sleep in his tent. Not long afterward, the Ming army returned to China. Yu listed Ch'oe as a Chinese soldier in the roster, and Ch'oe crossed the border without incident, to settle in Yaoxing.

When Ch'oe's family members were captured and brought to the riverbank, the Japanese paid little attention to his father and mother-in-law, seeing them as old and weak. They were able to sneak into the bushes, and when the Japanese withdrew, they went begging from village to village. At Yŏngok temple[24] they heard a baby crying inside the Buddhist monks' residence. Lady Sim said to Ch'oe Suk with tears in her eyes, "Whose baby is crying? It sounds like my grandson." Suk hurried to open the door into the compound and found that it was Mongsŏk. They held the baby to their bosoms and cried for a long while.

"Where did you find this baby?" they asked. The monk Hyejŏng replied, "I heard a baby crying among the dead bodies lying beside the road. I brought it here in the hope that its parents might come. My hope is realized today. It is nothing but the will of heaven."

Ch'oe Suk and Lady Sim took turns carrying the baby on their back and made their way back to his old house. He gathered some of his former servants together and strove to reestablish the household.

Ogyŏng had been captured by an old Japanese soldier named Donu. He was a devout Buddhist who did not wish to kill living beings. Originally a merchant, he was an experienced helmsman who had

---

24. On Mount Chiri in Chŏlla province.

been selected by the Japanese general Yukinaga[25] to captain a warship on the expedition to Korea. Donu, who had taken a liking to Ogyŏng, was afraid she would try to run away, and he tried to please her by providing her with good food and nice clothes. Ogyŏng, however, threw herself into the water over and over again, trying to kill herself. But each time she tried, she was discovered and stopped.

One night a golden figure six fathoms high appeared to Ogyŏng in a dream and said, "I am the buddha of the Manbok temple. Please do not think about dying. You will without doubt experience happiness in the future." Ogyŏng woke up and the dream was still vivid in her mind. She understood that things might not be totally hopeless, so she forced herself to eat and tried not to think of killing herself.

Donu's family lived in Nagoya. His wife was old and his daughter young. There were no other male members in the family besides Donu. He kept Ogyŏng inside his home but never allowed her to enter the inner quarters. Ogyŏng told him, "I have a weak body and was often sick. In my native land, I could not do the work that young men typically did. What I could do was sewing and cooking. I cannot do anything else." Donu felt pity for her, and named her Sau. Whenever he went on a trading voyage, he took Sau along as a crew member to manage the compass. They sailed as far as Fujian and Zhejiang.

At that time, Ch'oe was living in Yaoxing. He had become sworn brothers with Yu, who wanted to give him his younger sister in marriage. Ch'oe declined: "All my family fell into the hands of the enemy, and I do not know whether my old parents and poor wife are alive or not. I can't even conduct funeral services for them. How could I dare to even think of marriage and my own happiness?" Yu understood and dropped the idea.

In the winter of that year, Yu became ill and died. Ch'oe once again was on his own. He wandered along the Yangzi and the Huai

25. Konishi Yukinaga (1555–1600), a Christian daimyō under Hideyoshi who had been baptized under the name of Agostinho.

rivers. He traveled to famous places: he viewed the waterfalls at Dragon Gate in Shanxi, explored the remains of Yu the Great in Chejiang, followed the courses of the Yuan and the Xiang rivers, boated on Lake Dongting, and climbed the Yueyang Tower[26] and the Gusu Terrace.[27] He whistled long beside the river and at the top of the mountain. He flew between the clouds and the water. As he did so, he became increasingly willing to give up the human world.

He had heard that the Daoist monk Haichan, formerly Wang Yong, was living in seclusion on Mount Jingcheng in Sichuan. Haichan practiced alchemy in order to compound Daoist medicines and he was reputed to know how to become a Daoist transcendent. Ch'oe longed to go to Wang Yong and learn the secret. At that time Song You, with the pen name Hechuan, lived inside the Yongjin Gate in Hangzhou. He was well versed in the classics and history but did not aspire to worldly fame. He was solely devoted to writing. He also had a righteous spirit and was content to be helpful to others. He regarded Ch'oe as a friend to whom he could pour out his innermost thoughts. Knowing that Ch'oe was going to Wang Yong, Song You came to visit, bringing wine with him. When he started to feel its effects, he began to call Ch'oe by his courtesy name and said, "Paeksŭng! Among those who live in this world, who would not wish to live a long life? From ancient times to the present day, all over the world, where have we not searched for the key to long life? We do not know how long we will live. Why take Daoist medicine and endure starvation? Why abuse yourself and live among the mountain ghosts? You should follow me. If we take a ship to the provinces of Wu and Yue with tea and paintings to trade, we will be able to enjoy the rest of our lives. Isn't that what a man of true understanding would do?" Ch'oe realized the truth of his words then and there and set off with him.

26. The gate tower in the walls of Yozhou, looking westward across Dongting Lake.
27. A pavilion in the state of Wu, the residence of the famous beauty Xishi from Yue.

In the spring of 1600, following a trader named Wu from the same village, Ch'oe went to Vietnam by ship to trade. At that time, a dozen Japanese trading vessels were anchored in the harbor. They stayed there for around ten days. On the second of the fourth month, the sky was cloudless and the sea like silk. The wind stopped and the waves calmed. No sounds were heard and no shadows could be seen. All the sailors were sleeping; sea birds were heard from time to time. The sound of prayers to Amitābha[28] was coming from a Japanese ship, and its effect was profoundly sad.

Ch'oe was leaning on the windowsill by himself and reflecting on his situation. He took a flute out of his luggage and played a tune in the *kyemyŏn* mode[29] to release the cares and sorrow from his mind. With the song, the sky and sea changed color, and the clouds and fog altered their shapes. The sailors were startled awake, overwhelmed with sorrow. The prayer to Amitābha from the Japanese ship ceased at that moment. In a little while, a voice began to recite a heptasyllabic quatrain in Korean:

> Wang plays his flute as the moon begins to set.
>> The azure sky, like an ocean, is misty with dew.
> Let us fly together on a bluebird,
>> On the misted road to Mount Peng, we'll never be lost.

The poem was followed by the sound of lamentation. Thunderstruck, Ch'oe's mind stopped. He dropped his flute on the floor without realizing it and turned deathly pale. "What's the matter?" Hechuan asked. Ch'oe did not answer. Hechuan asked again, and this time Ch'oe tried to answer, but his voice was choked with tears. In another moment, he was able to say, "That poem is my wife's. No one else has

---

28. "Infinite Light," the buddha who presides over the western paradise.
29. A pentatonic mode.

ever heard it. And the voice sounds just like her. Is my wife on that ship? Impossible!"

Ch'oe then related what had happened during the war. All the crewmen were stunned. Among them was a boy named Du Hong, who was young and brave. Hearing Ch'oe's story, he appeared agitated. He grabbed an oar, stood up, and said resolutely, "I will go and find her."

Hechuan stopped him. "If you cause a disturbance in the middle of the night, I am afraid you will end up making a great deal of trouble. It would be better to do something quietly tomorrow morning." Everybody said, "He is right." Ch'oe sat down and waited for morning.

No sooner had the first light entered the eastern sky than Ch'oe went down to the harbor to find the Japanese ship. Ch'oe asked in Korean, "Somebody recited a poem last night who must be from Chosŏn. I am from Chosŏn. If I could meet this person, I, a wanderer from Yue, would not be the only one to rejoice at meeting someone from his country."

Ogyŏng, who had been on board the ship the previous night, had heard a Chosŏn song being played on the flute. The song sounded like a tune she knew well from the past. Had her husband come there? She had tried to find out by reciting the poem. Hearing Ch'oe's words, she was overcome with emotion and rushed off the ship immediately. They embraced with a loud cry, and tumbled down onto a sandbar. It was as if they had stopped breathing and could not say a word. Their tears poured down, blinding them. People from the two ships gathered around. At first, they were not sure if they were watching two relatives rejoicing at meeting each other. Only after a while did they realize that the two were husband and wife. Everyone marveled: "How strange! How strange! This has come to pass through the will of heaven. Such a thing has never happened before."

When he could speak, Ch'oe asked Ogyŏng about his parents. Ogyŏng said, "When we reached the riverbank, after being driven from the mountain, they were fine. Later, however, when we were boarding a ship, we were separated, swept up in the turmoil." They cried again in unison, embracing each other. Everyone hearing them could not help but shed tears.

Hechuan asked Donu if he could purchase Ogyŏng for three lumps of white gold. Flushed with anger, Donu said, "It has been four years since I got him. I have loved him for his decency and sincerity. I have thought of him as my brother. We were never apart, whether sleeping or eating. However, I never realized that he is a woman. Having seen this today, I know that this must be the work of heaven and earth and their spirits. I am stupid, but not a tree or a rock. How could I dare profit from this?" He drew ten *liang*[30] of silver from his luggage and offered it. "We have lived together for four years. Now we are going to part all of a sudden. My heart is filled with sadness and grief. But you have met your husband again after a hardship equal to ten thousand deaths. This is something that has never happened before in the human world. If I stand in your way, heaven will surely reprimand me. Please go, Sau! Take care of yourself, take care of yourself!"

Ogyŏng declined the money. "Thanks to your protection, I was able to survive. Now that I have met my husband again, I am indebted to you for so much. If I take this, how can I repay my debts?" Ch'oe expressed his appreciation over and over again, and brought Ogyŏng to his ship. People from neighboring ships came to see them every day. Some congratulated them by offering pieces of gold and silver and silk. Ch'oe received all of the gifts with deep gratitude. Hechuan went home and cleared out a room. He invited the husband and wife to stay there, where they would be comfortable.

Ch'oe was overjoyed to be with his wife again. But having settled in a foreign country far from his native land, he had failed to find any of his family members even though he had searched everywhere. He was concerned about his parents, and it pained him to think of his

---

30. Equivalent to ten taels, or approximately ten ounces.

son. Day and night he continued to worry, and to pray silently that they would return home alive. A year passed and another son was born. In the evening just before the birth, a six-fathoms-tall buddha again appeared to him in a dream. When the baby was born, he also had a mark on his back. The husband and wife believed that Mongsŏk had returned to them, and they named him Mongsŏn (dreaming of a transcendent).

When Mongsŏn was grown, his parents wanted to find a good wife for him. In the neighborhood there was a girl of the Chin family, named Hongtao. Less than a year after she was born, her father, Wei-qing, had gone to Chosŏn in the army led by Regional Commander Liu and had not returned. Later, as a young woman, Hongtao lost her mother as well. She was raised by her aunt's family. It was a source of constant pain for her that her father had died in a foreign country and that she did not even know what he looked like. She wished that just once she could go to that country and call back his soul, so that she could release the burden in her heart. However, as a woman, she could not figure out how to make this come about. Hearing that Mongsŏn was interested in finding a wife, she said to her aunt, "I would like to marry into the Ch'oe family so that I might have an opportunity to go to Korea." Her aunt knew of Hongtao's wish. She straightaway met with Ch'oe and related the story. Ch'oe and his wife were moved. "It is praiseworthy that such a woman exists. Her resolution is admirable." Eventually Hongtao was married to Mongsŏn.

In the following year, *kimi* (1619), Nurgaci (1539–1629) invaded Liaoyang. His forces captured many military camps and killed many soldiers. The Ming emperor was enraged. To defeat Nurgaci's army, he conscripted soldiers from the entire country. Wu Shiying of Suzhou was serving as a company commander in the army of Qiao Yiqi, the mobile corps commander.[31] He had heard from Yu Youwen that Ch'oe

---

31. Hucker, *Dictionary of Official Titles*, 8037.

was wise and brave. Accordingly, he made Ch'oe his secretary and conscripted him into the army.

As Ch'oe was about to leave, Ogyŏng held his hands and said: "I was born with an ill fate, and so I experienced all those terrible things before. I escaped death many times while undergoing many afflictions and great suffering. And then I found you again, because of heaven's grace. It was as if the cut string of the black zither was joined anew and the broken mirror had become round again. Since our broken threads were healed, we fortunately had a son who will now take care of the ancestral rites, and we have lived together happily for twenty years. Recalling what we endured, I would not be sorry to die right now. I have long been aware that I will return to the other world before you and repay what I owe you. It was the furthest thought from my mind that I should have to be separated from you again, like Orion and Antares,[32] in our old age. Since the distance from here to Liaoyang is myriad tricents, it will not be easy for you to return. How can we promise to meet again? I would rather end my useless life here, in this place of parting, so that you will not worry about me staying alone in the inner quarters and I will not worry day and night about you. Please go, my dear! Bid me farewell forever! Bid me farewell forever!"

She wept as she finished speaking and pulled out a knife to end her life. Ch'oe snatched it away and consoled her: "How can that feeble enemy leader stand a chance against this mighty army of ours? The imperial army will sweep away everything in its path,[33] and defeating the enemy will be like crushing an egg. Serving in the army will only entail a few months of suffering. You should not do anything as drastic as taking your own life. You need only wait until I come back, and we will exchange wine cups to celebrate. You can rely on our son, Mongsŏn, who is strong and robust. Please take good care of yourself

---

32. Since one is located in the east and the other in the west, they cannot see each other.

33. *Shijing* 263:5; Waley, *Book of Songs*, 137: "The king's hosts swept along / As though flying, as though winged, . . . / innumerable, unassailable."

and do not give me cause for more worry." He gathered his kit and left.

The imperial army arrived in Liaoyang and marched hundreds of tricents, deep into the land of the barbarians. They met the army from Chosŏn and built a camp together at Umo Ridge. But the Ming general underestimated the enemy and his army was decimated. Nurgaci killed every soldier in the imperial army he could find. As for the Chosŏn army, he alternated between threatening them and treating them well, and in consequence some of the soldiers under the mobile corps commander were able to escape death. Qiao, leading a dozen soldiers, had snuck over to the Chosŏn army and begged that they be given Chosŏn uniforms. General Kang Hongnip (1560–1627)[34] gave them spare uniforms and helped them for a time. But a junior officer, Yi Minhwan (1573–1649),[35] was afraid of angering Nurgaci and took away their uniforms, sending them to the enemy camp. In the confusion, Ch'oe remained in the Korean camp and saved himself. When Kang Hongnip surrendered, Ch'oe was detained as a prisoner of war along with the other Chosŏn soldiers.

At that time, Mongsŏk from Namwŏn was serving as an army officer in Kang's camp. When Nurgaci moved the captured enemy soldiers, Ch'oe happened to be imprisoned in the same place as Mongsŏk. Father and son met, but did not recognize each other. Mongsŏk, noticing that Ch'oe did not speak Korean well, thought he was a Chinese soldier who had picked up some Korean and was pretending to be a Chosŏn soldier to avoid death. When Mongsŏk asked where he was from, Ch'oe for his part suspected that Mongsŏk might be a spy sent by Nurgaci. Therefore, he gave several different accounts of his background, at one time saying he was from the province of Chŏlla,

34. A scholar-official of Korea who led the army in support of the Ming against the Late Jin but surrendered and became a prisoner of war.
35. A scholar-official serving under Kang Hongnip.

and another time, from the province of Ch'ungch'ŏng. Mongsŏk thought it strange but could not unravel Ch'oe's story.

As days passed they became closer. Eventually they felt so well disposed toward each other that there was no reason to hide anything. Ch'oe related all that he had gone through. Mongsŏk felt his face changing and his heart pounding. Suspended between doubt and belief, he asked how old the lost baby would be now and what he looked like. Ch'oe said, "He was born in the tenth month of 1594 and died in the eighth month of 1597. He had a red mark on his back that looked like a baby's palm."

Mongsŏk lost his composure, almost collapsing in surprise. He rolled up his shirt and showed his back. "I am that boy!" Ch'oe instantly realized that Mongsŏk was his own son. They did not stop crying and embracing and asking about each other's family for days on end.

There was an old Manchu who was often around when they talked. It appeared that he could understand some Korean, since he often had a sympathetic expression. One day when all the other prisoners went out, the old man snuck into the place where Ch'oe was staying. He sat beside him and asked in Korean, "The two of you keep wailing, which is not how things were in the beginning. You must have unusual stories. I would like to hear them." Ch'oe feared getting into trouble, so he hesitated. The old man said, "Don't be afraid! I am also a soldier from Sakchu.[36] The local official in my village was so greedy and cruel that there was nothing he would not do. I could no longer endure such suffering. It has been ten years now since my whole family moved to the Manchu land. The Manchu possess such a high degree of integrity that as rulers they do not exploit their subjects. Life is like a morning dew. Why should we be loyal to a hometown that only offers us a whip? Nurgaci ordered me to lead eighty soldiers and to stay close to the Chosŏn people to prevent them from fleeing. Now that I

36. A town in the northwest of P'yŏngan province.

have heard your story, I must say that it is unusual. Nurgaci may reproach me, but how can I keep you prisoner?" The next day he provided them with food and had his own son show them an escape route.

Thus Ch'oe returned to his homeland with his son after an absence of twenty years. Anxious to see his father, he fasted on his way to the southern province. Although he had a boil on his back, he did not have time to treat it. When they reached Ŭnjin,[37] he could no longer ignore the danger presented by the boil. He had used up all of his energy on the road. He began to choke, as if death were near. Mongsŏk was alarmed and tried all kinds of medicine, but nothing seemed to help his father. Fortunately a Chinese deserter passed by, on his way from the Honam region to Yŏngnam. Looking at Ch'oe, he said, "Your condition is dire. If you let today pass without treating it, your life will be forfeit." He pulled out an acupuncture needle from his luggage and broke Ch'oe's boil. Ch'oe recovered that same day.

Two days later, he reached his family, limping with a walking stick. All the people in his house were astonished—it was as if they had seen a dead man. Father and son embraced and could not stop crying until dusk. They felt as if they were in a dream. Lady Sim had become extremely distraught since losing her daughter. She had relied totally on Mongsŏk. But believing that Mongsŏk had died in the war as well, Lady Sim had kept to bed for several months. Seeing Mongsŏk returning with his father and hearing that Ogyŏng was also alive, she cried as if she were out of her mind. Those who saw her could not tell if she was elated or distraught.

Mongsŏk felt so grateful to the Chinese deserter who had saved his father that he brought him along as well. He wanted to compensate him for what he had done. Ch'oe asked, "You are a Chinese. Where is your home and what is your last name?"

37. A county of Nonsan in South Ch'ungch'ŏng.

He replied, "My last name is Chen, my first name Weiqing. My home is inside the Yongjin Gate in Hangzhou. In the twenty-fifth year of Wanli (1597), I was stationed at Sunch'ŏn while serving in the army led by Area Vice Commander Liu Ting (c. 1552–1629).[38] One day I was spying on the enemy. I violated an order and was supposed to be punished according to military law, but I escaped from the camp and wandered away, ending up where I met you."

Hearing this, Ch'oe was surprised and asked, "Do you have parents and a wife and children?"

He replied, "I have a wife who gave birth to a daughter only a few months before I left."

Ch'oe asked, "What did you name your daughter?"

"On the day she was born, a neighbor presented us with a peach. Therefore I named her Hongtao, meaning 'red peach.'"

Ch'oe suddenly took hold of Weiqing's hands and said, "How strange, how strange! When I was in Hangzhou, I lived in the neighborhood where your family lived. Your wife died of an illness in the ninth month of 1611. Hongtao grew up in the house of her aunt, Wu Fenglin. I made her my daughter-in-law. I never imagined that I would meet her father here."

Weiqing was so surprised that he could not stop exclaiming for some time. He said sadly, "I have been part of the household of the Pak family in Taegu. I have an old servant there and manage to make a living by practicing acupuncture. Now that I hear your story, I feel as if I am at home. I would like to rent a room if you will have me."

Mongsŏk stood up and said, "Not only did you save my father's life, but also my mother and brother rely on your daughter. You are already a member of our family. What could stand in the way?" He immediately had Weiqing move in. Once Mongsŏk heard that his mother was alive, he was full of concern. He wanted to go to China

38. Goodrich and Fang, *Dictionary of Ming Biography*, 1:964–968.

and bring her back, but was unable to do as he wished. All he could do was cry.

At the same time, the news came to Ogyŏng in Hangzhou that the imperial army had been completely defeated. She had no doubt that Ch'oe had been killed in battle. She cried day and night. Having decided to kill herself, she did not drink a drop of water. One night, a six-fathom-tall buddha appeared to her in a dream. He stroked her forehead and said, "Please do not succumb to death! You will definitely have happiness in the future."

She woke up and said to Mongsŏn, "When I was captured by the Japanese, I wanted to throw myself into the sea. But a six-fathom-tall buddha from the Manbok temple of Namwŏn appeared in a dream and said, 'Please do not die! You will definitely have happiness in the future.' Four years later, I met your father again in a harbor in Vietnam. Now I wanted to die again and just had the same dream. Does that mean your father might have escaped death? If your father were alive, I would not be sorry even if I were to die. How could I have any regrets?"

Mongsŏn cried, "I have heard that Nurgaci killed all the Chinese soldiers but released all Chosŏn soldiers. Since my father is from Chosŏn, he may have survived. How could your dream of the buddha be misleading? I beg you not to take your life so that you can wait for my father's return."

Ogyŏng changed her mind and said, "Nurgaci's den is only four to five days' walk from the border with Chosŏn. If your father is alive, he would have fled to Chosŏn. Would it be possible for him to walk myriad tricents and come to us? If he has died, I should go to Ch'angju[39] and call to the wandering spirit so that he will return and remain in the hills with the ancestors and not starve on the edge of the desert. I would thereby fulfill my conjugal responsibility. Even a bird of Viet (Yue) builds its nest facing the south, and a Mongol horse leans toward

---

39. Ch'angsŏng kun in North P'yŏngan.

the north. Now that I am approaching death, I cannot help but turn my head toward home, as a fox does when he dies. My only father-in-law, my only mother, and my little baby—all of them lost on the day the Japanese invaded. I do not know whether they are alive or dead. I have only heard from Japanese merchants that the Chosŏn prisoners of war were all taken to Japan. If they are right, the prisoners would have been sent back to Korea. If the dead bodies of your father and your grandfather remain as bare bones in a foreign land, who will take care of the tombs for the ancestors? Not all of your relatives died in the war. If I could find just one, that would be a great blessing. Hire a boat and prepare some provisions. It is around two or three thousand tricents from here to Chosŏn. If heaven helps us and with fair winds, it will not take more than ten days to get there. My plan is settled."

Mongsŏn implored, "Mother, why are you proposing this? It would be wonderful if we reached Chosŏn. However, such a long voyage across the sea is not for a small boat. We cannot predict what harm the wind and waves and dragons and crocodiles may do to us. Pirate ships might appear at any time. If both of us end up in the stomach of a fish, what good will it do for my dead father? Although I am not very sensible or smart, I dare not follow such a risky plan considering the danger."

Hongtao, who was beside her son, said, "Don't be afraid! Mother will plan carefully—there is no need to worry about something that has not happened yet. In any case, should we remain on dry land, is there any way to ensure that we will not be harmed by fire or water, or pirates?"

Ogyŏng went on, "Even though the sea route is difficult, I am prepared for it. When I was in Japan, I considered a ship my home. I went by ship to Fujian and Guangdong in the spring to trade. In the autumn, I went to Ryukyu. I have been under sail while beset by fierce waves. I am also familiar with reading the constellations and measuring the tides. I can withstand wind and waves, rough or easy. I can steer the boat, be it safe or risky. If we meet with some misfortune, why wouldn't we have a means of escape?"

Ogyŏng straightaway set to making clothing of both countries, Chosŏn and Japan. Every day she made sure her son and daughter-in-law were learning the languages of both countries. And she warned Mongsŏn, "Sailing totally depends on the oars. They should be strong and rigid. Another thing we cannot do without is a compass. As for choosing a date to embark, do not argue with me."

Mongsŏn went away in silence and in private criticized Hongtao: "My mother came up with a plan that will result in death for us all. Even though she is taking such a risk, my father has already lost his life. What kind of situation are you putting my mother in by agreeing to go along with her plan? You are utterly thoughtless."

Hongtao replied, "Your mother put a great deal of careful consideration into her plan. We should not argue with her. If we prevent something now that we should not, I am afraid we will regret it in the future. It is better to go along with the plan obediently. Although you have no regard for my person, at least pity my brood.[40] I beg you to consider my own personal situation as well. Only a few months after I was born, my father died in the war. His bones were discarded in a foreign land and his spirit wanders in a bare field. Turning my gaze to the heavens, how can I call myself a human being? Recently, I heard a rumor that many stragglers got off the troop ship and escaped to Chosŏn. Feeling the deep love of a daughter, I cannot but wish for even the smallest bit of fortune. With your help, I might be able to reach Korea and walk through the battlefield so that I can release a bit of my debt that will otherwise last until the world comes to an end. Then I will be happy—even if I arrive in the morning and die that same evening." And then she shed tears.

Mongsŏn realized that he could not prevent his mother and his wife from carrying out the plan. He promised to make preparations

40. *Shijing* 35:3; Waley, *Book of Songs*, 100.

for their departure. On the first day of the second month of 1620, they set out in the boat.

Ogyŏng said to Mongsŏn, "Chosŏn is to the southeast. You must wait for the wind from the northwest. You should seat yourself firmly and grip the oars tightly. And listen to what I tell you to do."

They set the sail on the mast and mounted a compass on the bow. They checked the boat thoroughly and found there was nothing lacking. After a while, they saw fish joyously jumping and the sail was filled steadily, pushing them to the southeast. They struggled to keep the sail aloft but sailed at full speed, day and night. As if lightning were striking the waves and thunder shaking the sea, they sped in no time to Deng and Lai, and then to Qing and Qi.[41] Islands seen from far away went by and disappeared in a blink. One day they encountered a Chinese reconnaissance vessel. A soldier on the boat asked, "Where are you coming from and where are you heading?"

Ogyŏng answered, "We are from Hangzhou. We are heading for Shandong to sell tea." The Chinese ship sailed away.

The next day a Japanese ship approached. Ogyŏng changed into Japanese clothing and received the Japanese captain. The captain asked, "Where are you from?"

Ogyŏng answered in Japanese, "We set out to fish. Having been swept away by the storm, we have lost our original boat and oars. We picked up this ship in Hangzhou. We are on our way back home."

The Japanese said, "How sad! The way from here to Japan is difficult. Keep to the south and keep going." The captain returned to his ship.

That evening the south wind was fierce and the waves practically reached the sky. The fog was so thick it was hard to make out objects at an arm's length. The mast broke and the sail tore away. They could not determine where they should try to anchor. Mongsŏn and Hongtao

---

41. Dengzhou, Laizhou, Qingzhou, and Qizhou in Shandong.

were exhausted from seasickness and terror stricken. Ogyŏng sat alone praying to Amitābha.

At midnight the waves died down. They anchored off a small island and repaired the ship, staying there a couple of days. Across the wide sea, they could see a ship coming closer, little by little. They had Mongsŏn remove their equipment from the boat and hide it in a crack between some rocks. A short time later, the ship's sailors disembarked boisterously. Their language and clothing were neither of Korea nor of Japan—the sailors most closely resembled the Chinese. They were not armed. The sailors beat them with a cudgel and ordered them to bring out anything of value.

Ogyŏng said in Chinese, "We are from China. We came out to fish and drifted here. We do not have anything precious." She cried and begged for their lives. The sailors did not kill them, but they did take the boat in which they had been sailing. They tied it up to their stern and pulled it away.

Ogyŏng said, "They must have been pirates. I have heard that there are pirates between China and Korea. They appear and plunder, but do not harm people. Because I did not listen to my son's advice and insisted on this voyage, heaven has turned away; or rather, it has brought about this disaster. What can we do now that we have lost our boat? The broad sea touches the expanse of the sky; we cannot fly across it. We cannot sail on a raft of logs. We cannot sail on bamboo leaves. Nothing but death awaits us. I am dying too late, and my poor children are going to die because of me."

She cried, embracing her son and daughter-in-law. Their crying shook the cliff and their sorrow appeased the high waves. The sea gods cowered and the mountain ghosts frowned. Ogyŏng climbed up the cliff to throw herself into the sea, but her son and daughter-in-law stopped her—she must not kill herself. She said to Mongsŏn, "You have stopped me. But what do you think will happen? The food we have will sustain us for no more than three days. As we wait helplessly, what can we expect other than death?"

Mongsŏn said, "If we die when the food has run out, it will not be too late. If we can find a way to survive until then, we may not regret it." He climbed down, helping his mother. At night they lay in the crack between the rocks. As the sky was brightening, Ogyŏng said to her son and daughter-in-law, "When I fainted from exhaustion, the six-fathom-tall buddha appeared to me again. He said something. How strange it is!" The three of them gathered and chanted a prayer to Amitābha. They prayed: "World-Honored One, please condescend to help us."

Two days later, a ship appeared on the horizon and approached. Mongsŏn was puzzled and said, "I have never seen this kind of ship before. I am afraid." Ogyŏng looked at it and said, "We are saved! That is a Korean ship." She put on Korean clothing. She had Mongsŏn go up the hill and wave a jacket. The sailors stopped the ship there and asked, "Where are you from? How did you come to be on this remote island?" Ogyŏng replied in Korean, "We're originally from one of the literati families in Seoul. We got on a boat at Naju, but it encountered a fierce storm. The boat capsized and everyone perished, except for the three of us, who grabbed the sail and floated here. We were just now taking our last breaths."

Listening to the story, one sailor was filled with sympathy. He anchored and brought them up. He said, "This is the trade ship of the commander general. We need to get back in time, so we cannot go farther." Arriving in Sunch'ŏn,[42] the ship anchored and let them disembark. It was the fourth month of the year *kyŏngsin* (1620).

After crossing hills and waters for five or six days, Ogyŏng, her son, and her daughter-in-law finally reached Namwŏn. She assumed that all of her family members had died. She only wanted to see her husband's old house. She went in search of Manbok temple. Arriving at Kŭm Bridge, she looked ahead. The fortress wall looked clear. The village was unchanged.

---

42. Port town in South Chŏlla.

Ogyŏng pointed to a house and said, "This is your father's shabby cottage. I do not know who is now living in this place. Why don't we just go in and ask if we can stay a night in order to decide what we should do next?" When they got to the door, Ch'oe was visible, seated under the willow tree and talking with his guest. Ogyŏng came closer and looked at him carefully. It was her husband. She and her son cried out at the same time. Ch'oe recognized them as his wife and son.

"Mongsŏk's mother has come back!" he exclaimed. "Who brought them? Is it real or is it a dream? Are they gods or humans?" Hearing this, Mongsŏk came out barefoot, almost falling down in his haste. Mother and son met again. We can imagine what the scene was like. They came into the room holding each other, pushing and pulling. Lady Sim, who had been quite ill, heard that her daughter had returned. She was so surprised that she fainted. She looked inert, practically dead already. But Ogyŏng embraced her and she revived. Ogyŏng consoled her mother for a long while. Ch'oe said to Weiqing, "Your daughter has come as well." He had Hongtao tell Weiqing the whole story. Each family had reunited with its own son and daughter. The sound of their calling and crying moved all the neighbors. Those who were watching were curious at first. As they heard the story of Ogyŏng and Hongtao, however, there was no one who was not clapping and weeping. They eagerly retold the story to people all around.

Ogyŏng said to her husband, "It is all because of the bliss bequeathed by the six-fathom buddha that we have this day. I have heard that the golden statue has been destroyed and we do not have anything to worship anymore. Yet the spirit is still in heaven and it allowed us to survive. We should find a way to express our gratitude." They prepared the necessary items and went to the destroyed temple. They cleaned up a room and performed the ritual. They performed ablutions, abstained from meat, and offered a sacrifice.

Ch'oe and Ogyŏng supported their parents and took care of their son and daughter-in-law. They continued to live in the old house outside the West Gate of Namwŏn.

Ah! Father and son, husband and wife, father-in-law and mother-in-law, older brother and younger brother, they had all been scattered across four countries and missed one another for three decades. They had gone into the enemy's land. They went to and emerged from the place of death. At the end, nothing was left unsolved. Could all this have come about through human efforts? Heaven and earth must have been moved by their devotion to cause such strange things to happen. If an ordinary woman has a sincere wish, even heaven cannot ignore it. Sincerity like this can never be denied. When I came to live in Chup'o, south of Namwŏn,[43] Ch'oe sometimes visited me and related this story. He asked me to record it so that it would not be forgotten. Not being able to refuse, I record its outline. In the intercalary second month of the first year of Tianqi (1621), Soong[44] writes.

Translated by Hyunsuk Park

The Manchu Invasions

Historians attribute the 1626–1627 invasion to the Korean scholar-officials' contempt for the barbarian Manchu, whom they considered far inferior to the Ming in China, seen as the source of the Confucian classics in verse and prose and of literacy. The invasion may have been prompted as well by immediate provocations such as the Korean court's protection of the Chinese general Mao Wenlong (1576–1629), who had used the Korean island Ka, near the mouth of the Yalu, as a military base to harass the Manchu. Another factor may have been the inflammatory pressure of Korean rebels who had fled to Manchuria, where they agitated for an invasion of Korea,

43. The author's temporary abode, having left the capital.
44. A pen name of Cho Wihan.

following the collapse of an ill-starred insurrection led by the turn-coat general Yi Kwal (1624).

In any event, the Manchu army crossed the frozen Yalu in February of 1627 and captured several northern towns. Escaping to Kanghwa Island, King Injo (1623–1649) sued for peace in exchange for a pledge to honor the Manchu throne as a younger brother would respect an older brother (March 19, 1627). The Manchu then withdrew. But when Abahai (Hong Taiji, 1592–1643)[1] changed the name of his state to Qing, in 1636, Chosŏn refused to acknowledge his suzerainty. Diplomacy with the Manchu had continued up to this juncture, as witnessed by the exchange of state papers, the establishment of common markets at Anju and Ŭiju, and the transmission to the Manchu court, on request, of Confucian texts such as the *Spring and Autumn Annals, Book of Changes, Book of Rites,* and the *Comprehensive Mirror for Aid in Government,* a history of China from 403 BCE to 959 CE. Korea had also sent shipments of grain. Yet the Korean court's contempt for the Manchu had not diminished, and it continued to maintain close ties to the declining Ming, going so far as to use the Ming reign title even after the dynasty's demise.

Inevitably the second invasion came, in January of 1637, with Abahai himself at the head of a large force, said to be 300,000 strong. It soon reached Kwangju, north of Seoul. This time King Injo sent his family to Kanghwa Island while he himself fled to the mountain fortress of Namhan, south of Seoul. On February 16, Kanghwa fell to the Manchu under the command of Dorgon (1612–1656),[2] and the royal party was taken prisoner. Abahai then requested that the king leave his fortress, which he at length, after much debate among his advisors, decided to do, capitulating at Samjŏndo, the Songp'a crossing on the southern bank of the Han.

In an indigo garment and riding a white horse without an honor guard, the king left the fortress from the west gate, accompanied by the crown prince and some fifty attendants. The Manchu emperor,

---

1. Founder of the Qing dynasty; see Hummel, *Eminent Chinese,* 1:1a–3b.
2. The fourteenth son of Nurgaci; Hummel, *Eminent Chinese,* 1:215b–219a.

camped at Majŏn Cove, had built a platform on the cove's south side, bedecked with yellow curtains. When the king arrived, a Manchu general asked him to sit below the platform, facing north, where he performed the Manchu rite of surrender. At the east side of the platform stood the crown prince together with the prisoners captured on Kanghwa Island. Then the king was asked to mount the platform. Abahai sat facing south; the king faced west. Refreshments came first, served with wine. Then the Manchu general brought a white horse with a gem-studded saddle and a sable robe, the emperor's gift. The general relayed the emperor's message: "I have brought the robe as a present, but I observe that your system of clothing is not the same as ours and I am not forcing you to put it on. It expresses only our goodwill." The king received it and put it on. The same gift was made to the crown prince and to his immediate family, ministers, and secretaries.

King Injo then boarded a ship at Songp'a ford, escorted by a military guard. The royal party arrived in Seoul around 10 p.m., and the king retired to the Yanghwa Hall at Ch'anggyŏng Palace.[3] On the third of March, Abahai returned some 160 captives, men and women. The next day, the crown prince, his brother, and their families began their journey north as hostages, arriving at Shenyang (Mukden) on May 4. On March 25, Abahai returned to the north, and King Injo saw him off. On September 15, the Qing reign title was used in the royal calendar for the first time. Crown Prince Sohyŏn (1612–1645), Injo's first son, was a hostage for seven years and took part in the Manchu expedition to Peking, where he met Adam Schall (1591–1666), a German Jesuit and astronomer. Sohyŏn returned to Korea in 1644 with books on Catholicism and astronomy, a map of the world, and an image of Christ.[4]

The Manchu invasions inspired two popular narratives, "The Story of Lady Pak" and "The Story of General Im Kyŏngŏp."

3. *Injo sillok* (Veritable records of King Injo) 33:41a–49a, esp. 23a–24b, and *Chōsen shi* 26:445–446.

4. *Injo sillok* 46:1a.; *Chōsen shi* 26:222.

Anonymous

THE STORY OF LADY PAK

[PAK-SSI CHŎN]

The Story of Lady Pak is the legend of a heroic woman of Chosŏn who took charge of military affairs during the Manchu invasion of 1636–1637, during the reign of King Injo. The hero of the story is the noted Confucian scholar Yi Sibaek (1592–1660), and the heroine is his wife. The actual name of Yi Sibaek's wife was Lady Yun, yet in this fanciful historical tale (preserved in an old moveable type edition), she is known as Lady Pak.

Lady Pak had been born as the most hideous creature under heaven. The daughter of the enlightened Daoist hermit Pak Saek, she was married to and then mistreated by Yi Sibaek from the first night of their marriage. She herself, however, was adept in Daoist magic and in the event became a heroic woman known for her wisdom and foresight.

Transformed by her father's alchemy into a beautiful woman, Lady Pak overcame her initial fate to enjoy a life of marital harmony. She foresaw the Manchu invasion of 1636, helped to organize the country's military preparations, and exposed the true intent of a Manchurian princess sent to assassinate both Yi Sibaek and General Im Kyŏngŏp (1594–1646). By means of a message sent in secret to King Injo, who had taken refuge at the mountain fortress of Namhan, she was then able to clear the way to a peace treaty with the Manchu. Lady Pak went on to kill the Manchurian subordinate commander Yonggoltae, unnerving the commander-in-chief, Yonggultae, to such an extent that the Manchu troops soon departed from Korea. Through her exploits, Lady Pak showed that Chosŏn indeed had women who could be of use in national crises. Sections 9–12, the dramatic conclusion of her story, follow.

Section 9. The Manchu army rushes in like the tide. Yonggoltae makes a surprise attack on P'ihwa Hall and is surprised himself.

When Ki Hongdae came back, she informed the Manchu emperor of her return.

The emperor asked, "How was your journey to Chosŏn?"

"When I received your order, I went to the far foreign land to carry out our plan. But there I met a heroine without equal, a Madam

Pak. I barely managed to save my own life, much less accomplish the mission. I would have died a stranger in a foreign land had she not forgiven me when I pleaded for my life. She gave me a good scolding. She called me a disgrace, and said that you, Your Majesty, was no more than a common beast for having such a preposterous scheme."

Listening to the account, the Manchu emperor became angry. "How can I not be displeased when one such as you has gone out and returned, only to expose my plot and render all my planning useless?"

He beckoned to his consort. "Ki Hongdae has brought me the ill tidings of her journey to Chosŏn. She failed to kill both the general and the transcendent woman. My scheme against Chosŏn has failed; how should I now vent my anger?"

The consort replied, "There is still a way. If you wish, try it and see if it works."

"What plan is this?"

"Granted, Chosŏn has the transcendent woman and a brilliant general. But there are traitors who can dissuade the king from listening to the woman, and they do not have the skill required to utilize the general effectively. Your Majesty should have his army attack, but not by the land route in the south; rather, go over Mount Paektu in the north and pass through Hamgyŏng province to the east. No defenses exist there, and the capital will easily fall if it is attacked through the east gate."

Hearing this, the emperor was overjoyed and immediately gave commands to Hanyu and Yonggultae. "Gather one hundred thousand men and march, as the consort has directed, to the east. By crossing Mount Paektu, you can come straight from the north and invade the capital by the east gate."

The consort added: "As you enter their country, post sentries on the routes to the capital, specifically from Ŭiju,[1] to prevent any warning from reaching Seoul. Upon entering the capital itself, do not breach

---

1. Northwest of P'yŏngan province on the left bank of the lower Yalu.

the backyard of the house of the third state counselor. In that yard is the small cottage of Pak, called P'ihwa (Escaping Calamity) Hall. On both sides are marvelous trees that are quite abundant. If you do enter the backyard of that house, forget success, for you will not have the strength even to save your own lives, much less return home. Remember my instructions."

The two generals listened to her counsel and marched east, leading one hundred thousand men. They crossed the Eastern Sea and then headed for the capital. When they attacked, they put out the signal fires so that no one in faraway Seoul knew of their approach.

At that time, Lady Pak, who had been sitting in P'ihwa Hall, suddenly saw a vision in the heavens. Quite alarmed, she called out to her husband. "Outlaws have invaded from the north! Since they are coming, let us call for the mayor of Ŭiju, General Im Kyŏngŏp, to reinforce our army so they can repel the invaders in the east."

The minister, becoming irritated, replied, "I think if the outlaws invade our country, they, being from the north, will attack from the north into Ŭiju. If we call the mayor of Ŭiju to come to our aid, it will leave the north unprotected. It would be perilous to let the Manchu take the north. On what grounds would you choose to disregard the threat from the north and defend the east?"

"The Manchu are crafty. They will come from the north but do not want to encounter General Im by going through Ŭiju. They plan to cross over Mount Paektu, skirt the north, and smash through the Great East Gate. They will reduce our capital to rubble. How can you not be alarmed? I beg of you, stop this chatter and go quickly to warn the king."

Upon hearing her words, the minister realized their predicament. He quickly went to the palace and related everything that Lady Pak had said to the king.

Now quite distressed, the king gathered the court to discuss the situation. The second state counselor Wŏn Tup'yo (1593–1664) said, "The northern barbarians are certainly clever. I agree that we should order the mayor of Ŭiju, General Im, to rebuff the invaders from the east."

Opinions varied. One voice cried out: "I believe the forecast of the second state counselor is exceedingly unlikely. Having already been defeated by General Im, what strength do the northern barbarians have to come against our country? And even if they have raised an army, it is not certain they would bypass Ŭiju. Furthermore, if Your Majesty orders General Im to protect the east, leaving Ŭiju defenseless, the northern barbarians could make a surprise attack there, which would expose us to great danger. There is not a moment to lose. How can you listen to a fickle woman and choose to defend the east like a senile old man? How can you say this is wise? This is a grave attempt to harm our country. I beg of you to consider carefully."

"Having personally experienced the transcendent powers of Lady Pak, I know that they outstrip human wisdom," said the king. "How can I consider her fickle? I am convinced that, just as she says, defending the east is correct."

The voice again countered: "At present the season is peaceful and the harvest has been rich. With the country enjoying prosperity, the people sing the 'Ground-Thumping Song.'[2] In a peaceful world like this, relying on the words of a fickle woman will cause unrest, alarming everyone. Therefore, listening to her would be to disregard all the other citizens of our country, those whose welfare should be Your Majesty's chief concern. Thus, I would urge that this woman be punished according to our laws, so that public unrest can be brought under control."

As he spoke, adamantly opposing the king's view, everyone looked around in puzzlement and found that it was not some newcomer but the chief state counselor Kim Chajŏm (d. 1651).[3] He was renowned as one who not only kept company with lowly men, avoiding the

---

2. Watson, *Columbia Book of Chinese Poetry*, 70.

3. A traitor who spied for the Manchu and was executed for his treason in 1651.

nobility, but did as he pleased concerning affairs of state. Now he was intent on ruining the country, but all the ministers who had gathered were cowed by his influence and dared not speak. Minister Yi, also unable to contend with him, returned home with a heavy heart and told his wife about the proceedings.

Lady Pak listened to his report and cried to the heavens, "Oh, we are undone! How can our country not be doomed when a fool like that is called a man of ability? He only enters the court to work our ruin. The northern barbarians are not far away, and they will invade our capital. As a loyal official, how can you sit and watch? Please emulate Bi Gan[4] and try to save our altars of soil and grain."[5]

The minister heard her cry and was saddened. Although righteous indignation welled up in his heart, he could not overcome the despair he felt. Looking to the heavens and lamenting, he returned to the palace.

All of this came to pass on the last day of the year 1635.

The northern barbarians smashed the Great East Gate and surged forward like the sea. Their war cries shook the heavens and earth. It is hard to describe the scene of carnage. The enemy commander exhorted his army to seize the people and slaughter them. The bodies piled up like a mountain and their blood flowed like a river.

The king was greatly bewildered, not knowing what to do. He met with his ministers to consider the situation. Looking to the heavens, he implored, "Now, before our very eyes, the city overflows with northern barbarians. Our citizens are being slaughtered without reason, and the altars of soil and grain are in peril. What are we to do?"

---

4. A loyal advisor to Zhou, the last evil ruler of the Shang (1766–1222 BCE). *Shiji* 32:1479.

5. Altars where emperors and kings offered ritual sacrifices in spring and autumn; "soil and grain" thus became a common metaphor for the state. Hucker, *Dictionary of Official Titles*, 5133.

Yi Sibaek answered, "The situation is grave indeed. I believe it would be best to leave the capital and flee to the fortress on Mount Namhan."

The king agreed and summoned his palanquin. As they fled through the South Gate toward the walled fortress of Namhan, a group of soldiers surrounded the party.

In alarm, the king cried out, "Who will repulse these adversaries?"

Hearing this, the third state counselor wheeled his horse around, shouting, "I will cut them down!" He lifted his lance and charged forward. Dispatching the enemy with a single thrust, he then escorted the king's palanquin to Mount Namhan.

The commanders of the northern barbarians, Hanyu and Yonggultae, led their army of one hundred thousand men into the capital and seized it. Seeing the palace empty, they realized that the court had fled to the mountain fortress. Yonggultae ordered his younger brother, Yonggoltae, to secure the capital and to rape any beautiful women.

Hanyu, meanwhile, left one thousand soldiers there and led the remainder on a march to the fortress on Mount Namhan. They surrounded the fortress and laid siege to it for several days. The king and his ministers were confronted again by peril.

At that time, Lady Pak had brought all her close relatives to P'ihwa Hall, where they stayed. The women who had taken refuge there, hearing that Yonggoltae was seizing both booty and beautiful women, wanted to flee. Lady Pak tried to comfort them, saying, "Now that the outlaws are in the city, it is not safe for you to move around." But the women were not comforted and grew doubtful about Lady Pak.

It happened then that the Manchu general Yonggoltae, while leading a war party of nearly one hundred men about the capital, discovered the house. Upon closer examination, he saw a tidy cottage standing apart from the main house. A large number of women could be seen in and among the trees surrounding it. But on the right and left, the trees became dragons and tigers, while their branches turned into birds and snakes. The transformations were astounding, and the smell of death was in the air. Yonggoltae and his men looked at each other, dumbfounded.

Nonetheless, knowing nothing about the transcendent powers of Lady Pak, Yonggoltae determined to pillage the property and abduct the women. But as his men entered the grounds, the previously clear sky suddenly filled with black clouds, and lightning and thunder poured from the heavens. The hall was instantly surrounded by mountains, layer upon layer.

Section 10. Lady Pak, possessor of transcendent magical powers, kills the enemy general. Yonggultae makes a surprise attack on P'ihwa Hall.

As Yonggoltae stared ahead in a muddled state, a woman, sword in hand, solemnly came forward. "What kind of thief are you?" she said with scorn. "You must want to die right away."

Yonggoltae replied, "I entered these grounds not knowing whose house it was. With your assent, I hope I can be spared and depart safely."

The woman roared with a voice like thunder: "I am Kyehwa, the maid of this house. Relying solely on your meager strength, what manner of hoodlum are you to brazenly enter? My mistress has commanded me to bring your head to her. So I have come for you. Prepare to die!"

Hearing this, the Manchu general became infuriated and drew his sword. But as he lifted his arm to strike, his strength failed and he was powerless to fight. In great astonishment, he looked to the heavens, lamenting, "I, born a man and a general of a mighty army, have come a great distance from a faraway land—only to die before my great achievement can be accomplished. How could I have known that I would die at the hands of a woman?"

At this, Kyehwa laughed. "You fool! You are pathetic! Calling yourself a hero. You came to this foreign land and cannot overcome even a fragile woman like me. All you can do is lament over your misfortunes. How could a weakling like you become a military leader and hope to invade a foreign land? Heed what I say. Your lawless king ignored the will of heaven, unjustly seeking to conquer a land known for its civility. Then he sent a whelp like you? Considering your king's ignoble actions, all I can do is laugh at your predicament. I feel compassion toward you, but my sword knows no compassion and will remove your head regardless. Prepare for death. How could an ignorant common man like you act against the will of the gods? As a spirit, do not hold a grudge against me after your death." When she finished speaking, she took her sword and struck off the Manchu general's head, the sword flashing as the head rolled off the horse.

With the head of Yonggoltae in her hand, Kyehwa entered P'ihwa Hall and presented it to Lady Pak. The lady took the head and threw it out the door. Only then did the wind stop and the clouds clear to let the peaceful moonlight through. The lady then went out to pick up the head and hanged it from the tallest tree on the hill behind the house for all to see.

Meanwhile, the Manchu army rushed like an angry wave at the fortress on Mount Namham, where the king had fled. They relentlessly fell like frost and snow. The country's fortunes had turned ill. Ch'oe Myŏnggil (1586–1647), a chief state counselor, suggested, "Perhaps it is better to now make peace."

At those words, the king looked to the heavens and lamented. He then wrote a letter and sent it to the Manchu camp. The enemy responded by quickly locking up the queen, the crown prince, and the three other princes, royal concubines, and ladies-in-waiting in the fortress. The soldiers were commanded to treat them like criminals. The Manchu army then marched back to the capital. Witnessing all of this, the king grieved all the more. All the officials also sighed to the heavens. They tried to comfort the king: "We pray endlessly, Majesty, that you will be safe."

The people wanted Kim Chajŏm drawn and quartered. "Chosŏn's misfortunes must be the will of heaven," they cried. "That small man,

Kim Chajŏm, helped the enemy and brought us destruction of this magnitude. How could things be any worse?"

In the meantime, after receiving the terms of the settlement, Yonggultae had marched on the capital. A sentry, making his rounds, reported, "General Yonggoltae died at the hands of a woman."

At the report, Yonggoltae's older brother was greatly shocked and wept bitterly. "I came only after receiving the Chosŏn king's peace treaty. Who would dare to kill my younger brother? It is my duty to avenge his death. Take me to the house," he commanded his soldiers.

When they reached the house of the third state counselor, they looked around and saw Yonggoltae's head hanging from a tree in the back garden. Yonggultae could no longer control his anger. He drew his sword, intending to ride in on horseback.

But Hanyu, the chief military commander, stopped Yonggultae. After peering in, he had been startled by the appearance of the trees in the garden. He said, "General, calm down. Listen to me and do not go in. Look at the trees in the garden—they are not normal trees. Knowing that these houses of old might conceal a Zhuge Liang,[6] how can we not be apprehensive? Your brother did not have the ability to recognize a dangerous situation in this land of peril. He underestimated his opponent, and because of that, he lost his life. What is there to begrudge? Reflect on the time of the Three Kingdoms. Do you remember when General Lu Sun advanced on Zhuge Liang's Eight Formations and suffered great losses?[7] Do not enter."

Yonggultae's wrath was terrible, and he struck the ground with his sword. "If that is so, how can I avenge his death?" he cried. "We came together to this distant land and accomplished a great feat. How

6. The foremost strategist of the Three Kingdoms period, Zhuge Liang (181–234) was renowned for his cunning as a tactician and his brilliance as a statesman and scholar.

7. *Sanguozhi* (Records of the Three Kingdoms) 58:1343–1361. The Eight Formations was a maze of great stones arranged in regular formations beside and partly in the river near Kuizhou. They were one of three stone mazes constructed by Zhuge Liang to demonstrate the uses of different military formations. See Hawkes, *Little Primer of Tu Fu*, 186.

could he be killed so suddenly and I not avenge his death? It is unthinkable that the nation's general should give in to a woman. Will I not be mocked by posterity if I just do nothing?"

"General, you must calm yourself," Hanyu replied. "If you enter this dangerous place, trusting only in your own valiant efforts, it will be difficult for you to stay alive—let alone avenge your brother's death. Ease your heart and perceive the mysterious tactics that surround you. Should you take even a myriad of soldiers with you, none would survive, and you would not be able to set foot in the house. And you want to go in by yourself? You cannot expect to return alive."

Yonggultae considered what Hanyu had said and was unable to enter the grounds. Instead, he ordered that the troops burn the cottage. His men, working together, started the fires. But amid the smoke the trees turned into countless soldiers. And to the beat of a drum and the battle cry of countless warriors, swarms of dragons and tigers butted heads. Winds gusted and great clouds arose, surrounding everything in thick layers. Celestial soldiers bearing swords, spears, shields, and armor descended, killing the enemy soldiers as they entered the gate. The sound of the drum and the warriors' battle cry seemed to cleave the heavens.

The noise was so great that the Manchu soldiers became confused and could not reassemble into formation. Many were trampled in the mêlée. The Manchu generals retreated, and the sounds of bloodshed finally ceased. The celestial soldiers had vanished without leaving a trace.

Seeing no sign of their assailants, the Manchu generals could hold back their anger no longer. But when they drew their swords and rushed into the grounds, the clear air suddenly turned foggy, and no one could see. Yonggultae shrank from entering P'ihwa Hall. All he could see was his brother's head, and he lamented to the heavens.

A woman suddenly emerged from the trees and announced, "Yonggultae, you ignorant fool. Your ill-fated brother died by my sword. Do you wish to suffer a similar fate?"

Yonggultae, angered by her words, replied, "What manner of woman are you to taunt a man? My brother was killed due to his ill fate, but I hold your king's letter of surrender. Your country is subject to ours. How dare you harm us? You are clearly an ignorant woman who does not understand affairs of state. Your life is truly worthless. Come quickly and die by my sword, and atone for your crime."

Kyehwa pretended not to hear him, reviling him instead. Pointing at his brother's head, she said: "I am the servant of the lady of unswerving loyalty. Consider your state, which I find pitiful. Your brother, Yonggoltae, was killed by me, a mere woman. You cannot defeat me. Your anger only grows because you cannot control this situation. You are pathetic!"

Yonggultae, his anger mounting, stood up to put an arrow in his iron bow. He shot at Kyehwa, but it fell six or seven steps away. His anger overflowing, Yonggultae ordered his soldiers to shoot their arrows at her. They obeyed, but without success. After wasting all their arrows, Yonggultae was choking with anger. He did not know what to do. He was confounded by this marvelous power and could not bear it any longer.

He shouted to Kim Chajŏm: "You are a citizen of Manchuria! Quickly collect all the soldiers within the walls and destroy the enemy's formation! Capture Lady Pak and Kyehwa! If you do not, you will find yourself subject to martial discipline!"

Kim Chajŏm, not knowing what else to do, replied, "How can we disobey your command?" He fired a shot into the air and commanded his men to surround the formation and advance from all directions. But how could they destroy the formation?

At that moment, Yonggultae came up with an idea and commanded his soldiers to advance on the encampment with gunpowder.

"No matter how many skills you possess, I'm sure you want to live!" Yonggultae shouted. "If you deem your lives precious, come out and surrender!" He yelled and swore some more, but no one responded.

Section 11. Yonggultae heads for home with the crown prince and numerous palace women as hostages.

Commander-in-chief Yonggultae ordered the soldiers to kindle their sparks all at once, and the sound of gunpowder exploding made it seem as if the earth itself were collapsing. Tongues of fire blazed in all directions, and the flames reached up to the heavens.

Lady Pak ordered Kyehwa to throw out a talisman. Then the lady raised a red flowered fan in her left hand and a white flowered fan in her right. She tied a five-colored string between the two fans and tossed them into the fire. A great wind suddenly arose out of P'ihwa Hall and pushed the flames into the Manchu camp. Many suffered death by fire. The sky and earth seemed to meld together, and the army was consumed.

An incredulous Yonggultae quickly retreated. He cried to heaven: "We raised an army and captured Chosŏn in one fell swoop. Yet here we've only come up against a woman, one who has killed my poor brother. How can I face the emperor and his consort?"

The soldiers, realizing the import of his statement, gathered to consult even while his lamenting continued. They concluded that since they could not retaliate against Lady Pak, they should withdraw. The army gathered the queen and crown prince, together with many palace women, and began to leave Seoul. As they departed, the people's anguish was deeply felt, a mourning that seemed to tear the land.

Lady Pak ordered Kyehwa to shout to the outlaw camp: "Listen, you foolish barbarians! Your emperor, ignorant of our country's civility, sent you who are still wet behind the ears to invade Chosŏn. It was our country's misfortune, and we suffered defeat. But why do you carry off our people? If you should even try to take the queen away, we will see you all dead. You will be annihilated."

Hearing this, the Manchu general laughed. "Your words have no meaning. We already have the king's surrender. What we take and what we leave behind is up to us. It is none of your concern."

At this boundless insult, Kyehwa rose up and exclaimed: "Since you will not change your attitude, witness now my power!"

At the sound of her mantra, two rainbows appeared and hail began to pour down. In the blink of an eye, cold rain and snow blew in, and frozen ice trapped the entire Manchurian camp from the generals to the horses.

The Manchu general, realizing that no one could break free, finally spoke up: "When the imperial consort first issued our commands, she warned us that there is a transcendent person in Chosŏn, and that we should not invade Yi Sibaek's backyard. We did not understand. In an instant we forgot the advice, and coming here, we suffered calamity. With one hundred thousand men and poor Yonggoltae all dead, how can we now face the imperial consort? There is nothing we can do but extend our apologies to you, Lady Pak."

The soldiers took off their armor and strapped it to their horses. With clasped hands they prostrated themselves on the ground in front of the camp, in supplication and earnest entreaty.

"I have been humbled," Yonggultae said. "Until I came to Chosŏn, my knee had never once bent, but now, before Lady Pak, I bend my knee and pray that you will release us and allow us to go; we will not take your queen hostage."

Lady Pak drew back the curtain and loudly proclaimed: "We could slay both you and your seed in great measure, but as we do not wish to take life, you are pardoned. According to your word, you will not take our queen, but yet you say you will take our crown prince? That too is the will of heaven, so you cannot go against it. But be sure to treat him with great care. Though I sit quietly, I know everything. If you choose to defy heaven's will, I will assemble transcendent forces and armaments and execute every one of you. Then I will proceed to Peking, where I will capture your ruler and exterminate your entire race, sparing none. Heed my words and do not disobey."

Yonggultae implored Lady Pak: "If you could return Yonggoltae's head to us, we will return to our homeland with your blessing."

Lady Pak laughed. "In wartime of old, Zhao Xiangzi lacquered Jibai's skull and made it into a wine cup.[8] To repay an enemy, I too, as in ancient times, will have Yonggoltae's head lacquered. This will ease my mind over our losses at the fortress on Namhan."

Hearing this and seeing Yonggoltae's head, Yonggultae's heart was stricken, but he could do nothing but cry bitterly. His only recourse was to take the troops and leave.

Lady Pak now commanded: "March on, and proceed to Ŭiju, where you will meet General Im."

Not knowing what was in Lady Pak's mind, Yonggultae thought: "We have already received the Chosŏn king's surrender. I look forward to meeting him."

So he departed, carrying away treasures from the royal family and plunder from the capital. He also abducted a number of beautiful women.

Looking up to heaven, the women cried out: "Through her own good fortune, Lady Pak has escaped our troubles and takes her ease in our native land. But what did we do to deserve to be carried away to a foreign country?" They appealed to everyone they saw: "Will we ever see the mountains and streams of our native land again?" Tears flowed from countless citizens.

Lady Pak instructed Kyehwa to tell them: "It is our common lot to experience both joy and pain. Do not be overly sorrowful. There will be one who will protect both the royal prince and all the women. May peace surround you, and may they arrive safely."

Section 12. General Im Kyŏngŏp assuages his anger on the way. The ministerial couple lives happily to age eighty and ascends to heaven.

Because the Manchurian army had been hidden between Seoul and Ŭiju at the time the defending army arrived, the two cities were cut

8. *Shiji* 43:1794ff.

off from one another, and tension was high. Looking into the face of great misfortune, the king had dispatched a letter to Ŭiju calling for General Im Kyŏngŏp's assistance, but the letter was intercepted. Im Kyŏngŏp was completely unaware that the country had fallen. When he finally heard the news, he galloped all day and night toward Seoul even though it was too late.

On his way there, he found a group of soldiers and their horses blocking the road. When he saw they were Manchurians, his fury swelled, and in spite of their overwhelming numbers, he drew his sword, galloped toward the enemy, and instantly slew everyone in sight. His anger unrestrained, he whipped his horse and raced on to the capital.

Seeing another unit of the enemy army marching along in high spirits over their victory, General Im Kyŏngŏp became so enraged that he rushed to the leader of the advance guard and severed his head with a single stroke of his sword. Then he dashed hither and yon, scattering the enemy cavalry into the autumn wind. As the bodies piled up on top of one another, the Manchu army seemed incapable of defending itself.

The Manchu generals Hanyu and Yonggultae, lifting their eyes to heaven, realized they had fallen into Lady Pak's plan. They immediately dispatched a letter to the capital, producing a hasty letter from the king commanding Im Kyŏngŏp to permit the Manchurian army to pass.

Im Kyŏngŏp held out his sword in homage, turned in the direction of the king, and bowed four times. Then he opened and read the king's message.

It said: "The misfortune of our kingdom is so great that on a certain day of this month the Manchu outlaws invaded from the north. They destroyed the Great East Gate and reduced the capital to ruins. I sequestered myself behind the walls of the fortress at Namhan, but one hundred thousand enemy troops surrounded the mountain for days on end. The attack was sudden, you were many tricents away, and we had no worthy commander. We could not match up against the enemy and had no choice but to lay down our arms. Our plight was truly grievous. However, this situation now cannot be meritorious and gains us nothing. If the enemy soldiers march by, do not block their way and allow them to pass."

When Im Kyŏngŏp finished reading the letter, he threw his sword to the ground and wept bitterly. "How lamentable! So a small man has brought our country to ruin! How could the clear vault of heaven be so indifferent?"

He continued to weep as he picked up his sword and ran to the enemy line. Grabbing the Manchu general, he threw him to the ground. "You came to this country not knowing of our might," he shouted. "You ignorant barbarians resolved to offend heaven by coming to this land and committing unspeakable harm. I would slaughter you in an instant, but because of our country's misfortune and the king's command, I will instead allow you to live and to pass through. Watch yourselves, and be sure that you escort our crown prince safely." Im Kyŏngŏp grieved a moment longer, then bade them go through.

The king, meanwhile, deeply regretting that he had not listened to Lady Pak, lamented with all the officials: "If we had followed her advice from the beginning, nothing like this would have happened."

Sorrowing all the more, the king said, "Had Lady Pak been born a man, we would never have feared the Manchu outlaws. But even as a woman, alone and unarmed in the women's quarters, she has glorified the majesty of Chosŏn by subduing the fighting spirit of countless Manchu thieves. This event is unprecedented."

At this, the king bestowed on Lady Pak an office of the first rank, gave her the title of Lady of Unswerving Loyalty, and granted her an immense reward. He ordered a woman from the palace to carry the decree to her.

When the Lady of Unswerving Loyalty received the decree, she faced the north and bowed four times. Then she opened the letter and read the contents.

"Because I was imprudent, I did not listen to the faithful counsel you gave on behalf of the country. Because I did not heed your gift of prophecy, our nation has suffered immeasurable grief, bringing us to this lamentable situation. I am, therefore, all the more ashamed to send you this poor decree. I am already aware of your virtue, loyalty, and piety. Even while confining yourself to the women's quarters, you have rescued the queen from peril and glorified the majesty of our country. I will not belabor the magnitude of your loyal devotion, and sincerely desire that you should share in the prosperity, joys, and sorrows of our nation."

Lady Pak understood the decree and gave thanks to heaven.

When she had first come to her husband's house, her face was so ugly that a person desirous only of feminine charm could not be captivated; by transforming her outward appearance to achieve conjugal harmony, she revealed her original face; she designed the eight gate-defense formations and kept the Manchu outlaws from entering P'ihwa Hall; she refused to allow the Manchu to carry off the queen, lest she suffer unspeakable atrocities at their hands; she allowed the crown prince to be escorted north because it was the will of heaven; and she made the enemy army retreat along the road to Ŭiju so that they would meet Im Kyŏngŏp, thus relieving the hero's indignation.

After that juncture, Lady Pak devoted herself to whatever the country needed. She ruled her male and female servants according to righteous principles and promoted harmony among her relatives. Her virtue was known throughout the country, and her name was bequeathed to posterity.

Lady Pak and the minister Yi Sibaek had many children. They enjoyed a long life together as a couple, and were surrounded with wealth and honor. Yi Sibaek, in living a happy life of some eighty years, became known as the Minister of Peace and was respected by all the officials as well as the entire country.

It is not uncommon for sad times to come when joyful times have ended. Lady Pak and the minister, as fate would have it, grew ill one after the other. All kinds of remedies were tried, but none was effective. So the couple gathered their descendants together to discuss what was to be done after their deaths.

Their instructions were: "The ancient sage said, 'We are put on this earth to live, but death will return.' Although good luck might seem endless, it is natural that first we live and then we die. After we pass on, do not grieve unduly."

Then they both took in their last breaths and died one after the other. The elders and the young of the family followed the mourning rite rigorously and carried them to their ancestral burial ground. At the news of their deaths, the king was saddened, and he sent bolts of cotton, gold, and silver to cover the expenses of the funeral. Thereafter, as the descendants from generation to generation carried on in making offerings to their forebears, their ranks and rewards continued to increase, generation after generation. Great was their clan!

Translated by Mark Peterson

Vernacular Fiction

Kim Manjung (1637–1692)

A DREAM OF NINE CLOUDS

[KUUN MONG]

A Dream of Nine Clouds, a romance that circulated in Korean and Chinese versions simultaneously, was written by Kim Manjung to console his mother at the time of his exile. Set in ninth-century Tang China, it belongs to a tradition of stories bearing the word "dream" in their titles, suggesting that even at its best life is no more than a dream.

Richard Rutt (1925–2011) comments: "The prologue tells how a Buddhist monk came to transmigrate into a brilliant young Confucian scholar, and the epilogue tells how he became a monk again. The bulk of the story is the 'dream' of the successful career of his Confucian manifestation. The dream itself falls into two halves; in the first the hero meets eight women, in the second he marries them. He meets the women in different places, and the changes of locality, with a different woman as the center of interest in each place, give the first half a lively variety. The second half of the dream is an account of happiness and honor after the winning of glory and success. In contrast to the first half, there is little movement, but much conversation. Such psychological interest as the characters evoke is developed in this section, where the personalities of the women become more distinct. The fact that the book is good entertainment does not detract from its transcendental values, but transforms what might have been a philosophical parable into a genuine work of creative literature."

A Dream of Nine Clouds shares a number of features common to the romance—the vision of life as a quest, episodic structure, themes of descent and ascent, cases of coincidence, elements of fantasy and adventure, characterization by synecdoche, and a high degree of stylization and structural patterning. Our extracts give the prologue and epilogue of the story.

Xingzhen Becomes Shaoyou

The five sacred mountains of China are Mount Tai in the east, Mount Hua in the west, Mount Heng in the south, another Mount Heng in the north, and Mount Song in the center. Mount Heng in the south is the highest of them. It has Mount Jiuyi to its south, Dongting Lake to its north, and the Xiao and Xiang Rivers flow round it. Its five peaks, Zhuyong the Fire Spirit, Zigai the Violet Baldachin, Tianzhu the Pillars of Heaven, Shilin the Rock Granary, and Lianhua the Lotus Peak, have their tops hidden in the clouds and wreaths of mist around their shoulders; on a hazy day it is impossible to make out their shapes.

In ancient times, the great Yu, after he had controlled the floods, climbed this mountain and set up a memorial stone on which he recorded his feats; the superb graphs in seal script are still clear and easy to read. In the time of Jin, Lady Wei became a Daoist and by divine appointment came to live on this mountain with a troop of fairy boys and girls; that is why she is called Lady Wei of the Southern Peak.

Here there is not space enough to tell of all the wonderful things that happened on the mountain.

In the time of the Tang dynasty, an old monk from India came to China, took a liking to the Lotus Peak on Mount Heng and built a monastery for his five or six hundred disciples, to whom he expounded from his copy of the *Diamond Scripture*. He was the venerable Liuru, known as the Great Master Liuguan. He taught the people and dispersed evil spirits; men said that a living Buddha had come to live on the earth.

Among his hundreds of disciples some three hundred more were advanced adepts. The youngest of them was called Xingzhen. His complexion was as pure as the driven snow and his soul was as limpid as a stream in autumn. He was barely nineteen years old, but he had mastered all the scriptures, and Liuguan loved him so much for his grace and wisdom that he intended him as his successor.

When Liuguan expounded the dharma to his disciples, the Dragon King from Dongting Lake used to transform himself into an old man dressed in white and sit in the lecture hall to hear the sermons. One day Liuguan said to his pupils: "I am growing old and feeble. I have not left the monastery gates for over ten years. I am no longer able to go out. Will one of you volunteer to go to the Dragon King's water palace and return his compliment on my behalf?"

Xingzhen at once asked if he might be allowed to go. Liuguan was delighted and sent him off with his order. He was dressed in a heavy robe and carried an official staff with six jangling rings attached to the top. Thus with high spirits he made his way toward Dongting.

Just after Xingzhen had set out, the gatekeeper of the monastery came to the master and told him that the Lady Wei had sent eight of her fairy maidens, who were waiting outside the gate. He ordered them to be admitted. They presented themselves in due order where he was sitting and circled him three times, scattering fairy flowers, before they delivered Lady Wei's message:

"Sir, you live on the west side of the mountain and I live on the east. We are near neighbors, but I am so busy that I have never once had the opportunity to attend the monastery and hear your teaching. So I am sending some of my maids to greet you with gifts of celestial flowers and fairy fruit and silk brocade as tokens of my respect and devotion."

Then each girl knelt down and raised the gifts of flowers and fruit and silks high over her head as she presented them to the old man. He handed them to his disciples, who set them out as offerings before the image of Buddha in the monastery.

Liuguan joined his hands in reverent greeting and said: "What has an old monk like me done to merit the favors of a transcendent?" Then he entertained the girls appropriately and dismissed them.

They took their leave of him and left. Outside the monastery gate they began to talk among themselves about how the entire mountain had originally been their domain, but since Liuguan had established his monastery with its enclosure, there were parts where they could not go freely. It was a long time since they had had a chance to see the Lotus Peak. "Now that our lady has sent us here on this lovely day and it is still quite early, let's go to the top of the peak and loosen our robes, wash our cap strings in the waterfall and make up a few poems. Then when we return home to the palace we can tell our companions all about it!"

Joining hands, they strolled up to the ridge to see the source of the waterfall. Then they followed the watercourse down as far as the stone bridge, where they decided to rest for a while.

It was spring. The valley was filled with all kinds of flowers, surrounding them like a pink mist. A hundred species of birds sang as in an orchestra of pipes and piccolos. The vernal air was intoxicating. The eight girls sat on the bridge and looked down into the water. Streams from several ravines met there to form a wide pool under the bridge. It was as clear as a polished mirror, and their beautiful dark eyebrows and crimson dresses were reflected there like paintings from Zhou Fang's hand.[1] They smiled at their reflections and gaily chatted to-

---

1. A Tang painter.

gether with no thought of returning home and did not notice when the sun began to slip behind the hills.

At the same time, Xingzhen had reached Dongting Lake and passed through the waves to the Crystalline Palace. The Dragon King had heard that a messenger was on his way from Liuguan and he appeared outside the palace gate with his entire retinue of courtiers to meet him. After they had gone into the palace, the Dragon King sat on his throne and Xingzhen kowtowed before him and presented his master's message. The Dragon King replied graciously and ordered a banquet. Xingzhen observed that the food, all made from fantastic delicacies, was entirely unlike what humans eat. The king himself offered a cup, but Xingzhen declined it: "Wine inflames the mind. It is a strict law of Buddha that monks should not drink it. Please do not force me to break a vow."

But the Dragon King replied: "Of course I know that wine is one of the five things that Buddha forbids; but my wine is quite different from the wine made by men. It neither arouses the passions nor befuddles the mind. Please do not refuse it."

Xingzhen was not able to hold out against this, and he drained three cups before he took leave of the Dragon King and left the palace, riding on the wind to the Lotus Peak. When he came down at the foot of the peak, his face was burning and he began to feel dizzy from the wine. He thought to himself: "If my master sees me in this condition, there will be no end to his anger."

So he went to the stream, took off his robe, and laid it on the white sand while he swirled his hands in the water and bathed his flaming face. Suddenly a strange fragrance was carried to him on the breeze. It was like neither incense nor flowers. It entered his mind and intoxicated his spirit, like something he had never before imagined. He thought: "What wonderful flowers have bloomed upstream? Their scent has come down with the current. I must go and see what they are."

He put on his robe again, arranged it neatly, and then began to walk up the river. So it happened that the eight fairies sitting on the bridge came to face Xingzhen. He at once put down his staff, joined his hands, and bowed deeply: "Gracious ladies, I beg your pardon. I am a disciple of the master Liuguan of Lotus Peak, and I have just been on an errand for him. Now I am on my way back. This bridge where you are sitting is very narrow, and there is not room for a man to pass by if ladies are sitting there. Will you kindly step down for a moment and allow me to cross over?"

The fairies replied: "We are attendants of Lady Wei, and we are just on our way back from delivering a message to your master, Liuguan. We stopped here to rest for a little while. The *Book of Rites* says that men should pass on the left and women on the right, but this bridge is extremely narrow. Since we were here before you came, we suggest you find another path."

Xingzhen said: "The stream is deep and there is no other path. Where else do you suggest I should do?"

The fairies said: "Bodhidharma (fl. 470–520) is said to have crossed the sea on a reed. If you have really studied with Liuguan, you must have great powers too. Why do you dispute the right of way with a group of girls, instead of passing over this little stream?"

Xingzhen laughed. "I see what you are after. You want me to pay some sort of toll. A poor monk has no money, but I have eight pearls and I will offer you those as a payment."

He snapped off a branch of peach blossoms and threw it to the girls. Eight flowers fell to the ground and immediately became sparkling jewels. The eight fairies each picked up one of the jewels, looked at Xingzhen and, laughing gaily, at once rose in the air and rode away on the wind. Xingzhen stood for a long while on the bridge looking in all directions, but he could not see where they had gone, and soon the shimmering mists had dispersed and the fragrance had faded away.

Xingzhen was deeply troubled and could not quiet his soul. He returned and told Liuguan what the Dragon King had said. Liuguan upbraided him for taking so long to get back. Xingzhen said: "The

Dragon King detained me with his kindness and I could not refuse and get away. It made me late in leaving." Liuguan asked no more questions, but sent him away to rest.

Xingzhen went to his cell. As he sat alone in the twilight, the voices of the eight fairies kept sounding in his ears, and their beautiful forms kept appearing before his eyes as though they were there in the room with him. However hard he tried, he could not collect his thoughts as he sat distractedly trying to meditate. He thought: "If a man studies the Confucian classics while he is young then serves the country as a general or a minister, he gets to wear a brocade coat and hang a seal of office on his jade girdle; he sees lovely things and hears wonderful things, he takes pleasure in beauty and leaves an honorable name for his descendants. That is the way for a man worthy of his name. We poor Buddhist monks have only a bowl for rice and a bottle for water, volumes of scriptures, and a hundred and eight beads to hang round our necks. All we can do is expound doctrine. It may be holy and profound, but it is terribly lonely. Suppose I do master all the doctrines of the Great Vehicle and succeed to the chair here on the Lotus Peak to carry on Liuguan's teaching, once my spirit and body have been parted on the funeral pyre, who will know that Xingzhen ever existed?"

His troubled mind kept sleep at bay until deep into the night. If he closed his eyes, he saw the eight fairies; if he opened them, the girls would disappear without a trace.

Then he pulled himself together: "The way of Buddha for purifying the heart is the highest course in life. I have been a monk for ten years and have avoided even the smallest fault. These deceitful thoughts will do my progress irreparable damage."

He burned some sandalwood, composed himself on his prayer mat, and was concentrating quietly on the Thousand Buddhas while moving the beads of the rosary round his neck when one of the boys called from outside: "Have you gone to bed, brother? The master wants to see you."

Xingzhen was alarmed and thought: "It must be something serious for him to call me at this time of night." He went with the boy to the lecture hall.

Liuguan had gathered all his disciples. He was sitting on the lotus seat, looking fearful and solemn. The lanterns and candles filled the hall with light. He rebuked Xingzhen harshly: "Xingzhen! Do you understand your sin?"

Xingzhen, frightened, knelt at the foot of the dais and answered: "I have served you for more than ten years and I have never willingly disobeyed you. Now that you accuse me, I do not wish to hide anything from you, but truly I do not know what I have done wrong."

Liuguan said: "A monk has three things to study: his body, his speech, and his will. You went to the Dragon Palace and drank wine. That was sin enough. On the way back you lingered at the stone bridge and dallied in idle chatter with eight girls, then threw flowers at them and toyed with jewels. After that, when you got home you dwelt on their beauty and thought about worldly riches and honor and mentally rejected the pure way of life of a monk. You have sinned in all three respects at once. You cannot stay here now."

Xingzhen wept and beat his head and begged: "Master! I have sinned, I know. But I drank wine in the Dragon Palace because I could not refuse my host's insistence. I talked with the fairies in the bridge because I had to ask them to get out of the way. I was tempted in my cell, but I repented and controlled myself. I have no other sins! If I have committed other sins, please instruct me and set me right. Why do you drive me away so cruelly and give me no chance to correct myself? I left my parents when I was only eleven years old to come to you and be a monk, and you loved me like your son. I respect and serve you as my father. The relation between teacher and disciple is sacred. Where can I go if I leave the Lotus Peak?"

Liuguan said: "I am making you go because you want to go. Why should I send you away if you wanted to stay? You say 'Where shall I go?' You must go where you wish to go."

Then he shouted: "Mighty Ones!" Immediately the commander of the yellow-turbaned constables of the underworld appeared and bowed to receive his orders. Liuguan said to him: "Arrest this sinner, take him to the underworld, and hand him over to Lord Yama!"[2]

When Xingzhen heard this, he broke out in a sweat of terror. Tears streamed from him as he put his head to the floor and implored: "Father, father! Hear me, please! When the holy Ānanda slept with a prostitute,[3] Śākyamuni did not condemn him, but admonished him. I sinned through carelessness, but I did not go so far as Ānanda. Why are you sending me to hell?"

Liuguan spoke severely: "Although the holy Ānanda slept with a prostitute, his mind was never shaken; you set eyes on female beauty only once and completely lose your heart. You cannot escape the suffering of transmigration."

Xingzhen still wept, and did not want to move. Liuguan spoke to comfort him: "If your mind is not purified, even though you stay in a mountain monastery, you will never attain perfection. But if you remain faithful to the way of Buddha, even though you are buried deep in the red dust of the world, you will surely come back one day. If ever you want to come, I will fetch you back. Go now, and trust me."

Xingzhen then bowed to the image of Buddha, took leave of his master and brethren, and went with the constables to the underworld, past the gate and then the terrace of "Looking Back in Regret," till they reached the city walls of the underworld, where sentries asked why they had come. The constables answered: "We have brought a sinner according to the orders given by Master Liuguan."

The demon soldiers opened the gates to let them in, and they went to the audience chamber where the reason for Xingzhen's arrival was announced. Yama dismissed the constables and spoke to him:

2. The lord of death and king of hell.

3. "The daughter of a woman named Mātaṅgī attempted to seduce him with the help of her mother's magic powers, only to come to realize her wrongdoing with the intervention of the Buddha" (*PDB*, 39).

"Although you lived on Lotus Peak, your name was already written in the roster on the table before King Kṣitigarbha,[4] Guardian of Earth and Deliverer from Hell. I understood from this that you had already achieved perfection and would win grace and salvation for many souls. What is the reason you have come here?"

Xingzhen was bitterly ashamed and hesitated before he replied: "I have sinned against my teacher by letting myself be misled by the South Peak fairies when I met them on the road, so I have been sent here. Do as you must."

Yama sent some of his attendants to Kṣitigarbha with the message: "Master Liuguan of the Lotus Peak has sent his disciple Xingzhen to the underworld for punishment, but he is not like other culprits. What should I do with him?"

The bodhisattva replied: "A man seeking perfection must find his own way. Why do you ask me?"

But Yama was intent on judging the matter properly. At that moment, however, two demon soldiers came in and said: "The yellow-turbaned constables have come again at Liuguan's order, with eight fairies under arrest."

Xingzhen was amazed at this news. Then he heard Yama say: "Bring them in!"

The constables brought the eight women in, and Yama made them kneel before him and asked: "Fairies of South Peak, indeed! You fairies have a boundless world of ineffable delights. How is it that you have come here?"

The fairies answered shamefacedly "Lady Wei sent us to Master Liuguan with a message, and on the way back we stopped to talk with the novice Xingzhen at the stone bridge. This made the master angry. He said we had defiled Buddha's demesne, and sent a letter to Lady Wei telling her to send us to your Majesty. We implore you to be compassionate and send us to a pleasant place to live."

4. "Earth Store" bodhisattva (*PDB*, 448).

Lord Yama called nine messengers to stand before him and commanded them: "Take each of these nine people and lead them back to the land of the living."

Yama had barely finished speaking when a great wind suddenly arose in front of the palace and swept the nine people into the air and whirled them away to different corners of space. Xingzhen was carried hither and thither on the wind behind his messenger until he touched down on firm ground. The noise of the wind died down and both his feet were steady. When he had collected his wits and looked about, he found he was closed in by thickly wooded mountains with clear streams flowing peacefully by. Here and there between the trees he caught glimpses of bamboo fences and thatched roofs, about ten houses together. The messenger made him wait outside one of the houses while he himself went in. While waiting, Xingzhen heard someone in the next-door house say: "The wife of the hermit Yang is pregnant. She's over fifty years old. It's amazing! It's past her time, but I haven't heard the baby crying. I'm worried."

Xingzhen realized he was to be born again in Yang's house and thought to himself: "I am going to be born into the world again. I have no body now, only a spirit. My flesh and bones have been cremated on the Lotus Peak, where I left them. I was too young to have any disciples, and so there will be no one to keep my relics together."

He fell to thinking like this in considerable distress when the messenger came out and beckoned him to follow, saying: "This is the township of Shouzhou in the province of Huainan of the empire of Tang. His wife's surname is Liu, and she is to be your mother. You were destined from your previous life to be the son of this family, so go in quickly and do not lose this good opportunity."

Xingzhen went in and saw the hermit, wearing a kerchief of coarse hemp and a rough coat, seated on the wooden floor by a brazier stirring a concoction of medicinal herbs. The smell of it filled the house. The woman's moans could be heard coming quietly from the inner room. The messenger urged him to go into the room, but Xingzhen hesitated, so the messenger pushed him from behind. Xingzhen fell over and lost consciousness, calling out for help as he fainted. The sound stuck in his throat and would not come out as words: it was only the crying of a newborn babe. The midwife said, "It cries so loud, it must be a boy."

The hermit Yang was carrying a bowl of medicine for his wife when he heard the baby cry. With mingled alarm and joy he hurried into the room, to find that she had already given birth to a son. Overcome with happiness he bathed the child in scented water, put it to rest, and then attended to its mother. When Xingzhen cried because he was hungry, they gave him milk, and as soon as his stomach was full, he stopped wailing.

While he was very tiny, he still carried traces of memory about the Lotus Peak in his mind, but as he grew and came to love his parents, he completely forgot all about his previous life. The hermit saw that his son had fine bones, and one day, stroking the child's forehead, he said to his wife: "This child is a heavenly being come to live among men." So he named him Shaoyou, which means "brief sojourner," and gave him Qianli, which means "a thousand tricents," for his courtesy name.

They loved him dearly, and by the time he was nine years old his face was as pretty as a piece of jade, his eyes shone like stars, his character was gentle and strong, and he was wonderfully intelligent and excelled in writing. He was a model child, destined to become a great man.

The hermit said to his wife: "I was not originally a man of this world, but because I was joined to you by our karma, I have stayed a long time in this world of dust. A long, long time ago I had a letter from my friends, the transcendents of Mount Penglai, asking me to go to them, but I could not go and leave you alone. Now that heaven has helped us and given you a brilliant son of more than ordinary ability, you have someone else to look after you. You will have riches and honor in your old age. So do not grieve when I leave you."

One day a group of transcendents came to the house, some riding white dragons, some on blue cranes. Then they departed toward the deep mountain valleys. The hermit Yang made a sign with his hand toward the sky, to summon a white crane that he mounted, and flew happily away. He had gone before his wife could utter a sound.

She and her son grieved beyond words. The hermit occasionally sent a letter through the air, but he never again returned to his home.

Shaoyou Becomes Xingzhen

So several years passed by. The twentieth day of the eighth month was Shaoyou's birthday, and his family prepared a banquet in his honor. It lasted more than ten days. The business and bustle beggared description; when it was over everyone returned to his own home and peace reigned again.

Soon the ninth month came, the first buds of the chrysanthemums began to open, and the dogwood berries appeared. Autumn was in full splendor. To the west of Cuiwei Palace there was a high peak; from the top of the pavilion eight hundred tricents of the Qin River could be seen like the palm of one's hand. Shaoyou particularly liked this view. On this occasion he had gone up there with the two princesses and the six concubines. Each had stuck a spray of chrysanthemums in her hair; they drank wine together as they enjoyed the autumn landscape. Gradually the setting sun made the shadows run down the mountain until they reached the wide plain. The brilliant colors of autumn were like a scroll painting unrolled. Shaoyou took out his jade flute and played a plaintive tune, as though composed of resentments or longing, of laments or protesting. . . . The women were all overcome with sadness; they did not like it. The two princesses said: "You have attained every honor, you have enjoyed riches for a long time, and everyone acknowledges it. Such a thing has hardly been seen before. Now in this lovely autumn weather, with a beautiful landscape before you, chrysanthemum petals floating in the cup, surrounded by beautiful women—what man could be happier? Yet the tune of your flute is so melancholy that it makes us all weep. You never played like this before; what is the matter?"

Shaoyou put the flute down, moved over to where they were, and sat down by the balustrade of the pavilion. He pointed and said: "Look over there to the north. In the midst of the flat plain stands a single rugged peak. You can just see in the fading evening light where the ruined Epang Palace, the vast palace of the first emperor of the Qin, stands among the weeds. Now look over to the west. A mournful wind stirs the woods where the mountain mist hides Maoling, the tomb of Emperor Wu of the Han. Over to the east, a whitewashed wall circles the green hills, where a red-tiled roof stands out against the sky and the bright moon comes and goes between the clouds. Nobody leans now on the jade balustrade, because that is the Huaqing Palace where Emperor Xuanzong of the Tang dallied with the Precious Consort Yang.[5] How sad: these three kings were all men of great renown in their time, but where are they now?

"I was a poor young scholar from the land of Chu but received the imperial favor and rose to the highest rank of the empire. I have married you all, and we have lived together in peace and harmony until our old age, and our affection continues to increase. How could this have been were it not a matter of karma fixed from our previous existence? After we have died, these lofty terraces will crumble and the lotus pools will silt up. The palace where we sang and danced today will be overgrown with weeds and wrapped in cold mists. Woodcutters and cowherds will sing sad songs, saying: 'This is where the Grand Preceptor Yang sported with his wives and concubines. All his

5. Xuanzong's undying love for Yang Guifei was immortalized by Bo Juyi in his "Song of Everlasting Sorrow" (806).

honors and pleasures, all his wealth and elegance, all the pretty faces of his women have gone, gone forever.' Those woodcutters and cowherds will look on the place where we have played just as I look on the palaces and tombs of the three emperors. Think of it—man's life is no more than a moment of time.

"There are three ways of thought on Earth: the way of Confucius, the way of the Buddha, and the way of the Daoists. Buddhism is the best of the three. Confucianism explains the working of nature, exalts achievement, and is concerned with passing on names to posterity. Daoism is close to meaninglessness, and even though it has many devotees, there is no proof of its truth. Think of the first emperor of the Qin and Emperor Wu of the Han and Emperor Xuanzong of the Tang. What happened to them is enough to make us understand. Since I gave up office, every night I have dreamed that I was studying meditation on the prayer mat. This is clearly a matter of karma. I must do like Zhang Liang,[6] who followed the immortal Master of the Red Pine to the abode of the blessed. I must go to seek the Merciful Bodhisattva who Observes the Sounds of the World beyond the Southern Sea. I must ascend Mount Wutai and meet Mañjuśrī.[7] I must put off the trammels of worldly life and obtain the way that has no birth or death. But because this means I must now say farewell to all of you, with whom I have spent such long and happy years, I feel sad. My sadness showed in my tune on the flute."

The women were deeply moved and said: "If you feel like this in the midst of your prosperity, it must be due to heavenly inspiration. We shall retire to our inner quarters and pray before the Buddha night and morning while waiting for your return. We shall pray that you will meet a great teacher and generous friends, so that you can attain the way, and return to teach it to us."

6. Minister under Gaozu of the Han, who later followed Daoist practices. The Master of the Red Pine is lord of the rain.
7. "Great Glory" bodhisattva.

Shaoyou, greatly delighted, said: "Since we are all agreed, there is nothing to worry about. I must leave tomorrow, so let us be merry tonight."

They all said: "We shall each offer you a farewell cup."

The cups were brought, and they were about to fill them when suddenly the sound of a staff striking the stone pavement was heard. Greatly surprised, they wondered who had come up there, when suddenly an old monk with long white eyebrows and eyes as clear as the waves of the sea, a man of strange bearing, stepped onto the terrace and greeted Shaoyou: "An old rustic monk craves audience."

Shaoyou realized that this was no ordinary person, so he rose quickly and replied: "Where have you come from?"

The old man smiled as he answered: "Don't you remember an old friend? I have heard that people in high rank have short memories; it seems to be true."

Shaoyou looked more closely and thought he knew who it was, but was not quite sure. Suddenly it came to him; glancing at Bo Lingpo, the daughter of the Dragon King, he said to the old monk again: "After I had defeated the Tibetans, I had a dream in which I went to the banquet of the Dragon King of Dongting Lake, and on the way back I climbed Mount Heng, where I saw an old monk lecturing on the scriptures to his disciples. Are you not that teacher whom I saw in my dream?"

The old monk clapped his hands and said with a great laugh: "Right! Right! But you only remember seeing me in your dream; you do not remember the ten years when we lived together. And they say you have such a good memory! What a scholar!"

Shaoyou was perplexed: "Before I was thirteen or fourteen years old, I never left my parents' house. At fifteen I passed the civil service examinations, and ever since then I have held office in the state continuously. I went east as an envoy to Yan, and west to subdue the Tibetans; otherwise I have scarcely left the capital. When could I have spent ten years with you?"

The old monk said, still laughing: "So you still have not woken from your spring dream."

Shaoyou asked: "Do you know how to awaken me?"

The old monk said: "That is not difficult," and raising his metal staff he struck the stone balustrade two or three times. Clouds arose, and enfolded the whole terrace, obscuring everything from view.

After a time, Shaoyou, bewildered as though he were in a drunken dream, called out: "Why don't you show me the true way, instead of playing tricks?"

He was not able to finish his question. The mist disappeared. The old monk had gone. Shaoyou looked round, but the eight women had vanished. The whole terrace and its pavilions had gone too. He was sitting in a little cell on a prayer mat. The fire in the incense burner had gone out. The setting moon was shining through the window. He looked down at himself and saw a rosary of a hundred and eight beads around his wrist. He felt his head: it was freshly shaven. He was no longer Yang the Grand Preceptor, he was once more a young monk. His mind was entranced, until at last he realized that he was Xing-zhen, the novice at the Lotus Peak monastery. He remembered: "I was reprimanded by my teacher and was sent to the underworld. Then I transmigrated and became a son of the Yang family. I came to the top in the national examination, and became vice chancellor of the Imperial Academy. I rose through various offices and finally retired. I married two princesses and was happy with them and six concubines, but it was all a dream. My teacher knew of my wrong thoughts, and made me dream this dream so that I should understand the emptiness of riches and honor and of love between the sexes."

He washed himself quickly, straightened his robe and cap, and went to the main hall, where the other disciples were already assembled. The master called with a loud voice and asked: "Xingzhen, did you enjoy the pleasures of the world?"

Xingzhen opened his eyes and saw his master, Liuguan, standing sternly before him. The lad bowed his head and wept as he said: "My life was impure. No one else can be blamed for the sins I have committed. I should have suffered endless transmigrations and pains in the vain world, but you have made me understand through a dream of the night. Even in ten million eons I could never repay your kindness."

The master said: "You went in search of pleasures, and came back having tasted them all. What part have I played in this? And you say that the dream and the world are two separate things, which proves that you have not yet woken from the dream. Zhuangzi dreamed he was a butterfly, and the butterfly dreamed it was Zhuangzi: and which was real, Zhuangzi or the butterfly, he could not tell.[8] Now who is real, and who is a dream—Xingzhen or Shaoyou?"

Xingzhen replied: "I am confused. I can't tell whether the dream was not true, or the truth was not a dream. Please teach me the truth and make me understand."

The master said: "I shall teach you the doctrine of the *Diamond Scripture* to awaken your soul, but there will shortly be some new pupils arriving and you must wait till they come."

Before he had finished speaking, the monk who kept the gate came, announcing that the eight maids of the Lady Wei had arrived. The master allowed them to come in and they at once entered and bowed before him, saying: "Although we have been attending Lady Wei, we have learned nothing and are unable to control our wayward thoughts. Our desires go after sinful things and we dream the dreams of mortality. There is no one to waken us. Since you accepted us, we have been to Lady Wei's place and yesterday took our leave of her. Now we have returned and beg you to forgive our misdemeanors and enlighten us with your teaching."

The master answered: "Your desires are good, but the Buddha's truth is deep and difficult to learn. It requires steadfast and persistent effort before it can be attained. Think carefully before you decide."

The eight girls withdrew and washed the powder from their faces and showed their determination by cutting off their clouds of black

---

8. Watson, *Chuang Tzu*, 49.

hair. Then they returned and said: "We have changed our appearance and we swear that we will be diligent in obeying you."

Liuguan said: "Very well. I am deeply moved that you have made up your minds."

Then he went up to the lecture seat and began to expound the scripture. Once again the light from the Buddha's brow shone forth on the world and celestial flowers descended like rain. And he taught them the mantra from the *Diamond Scripture:*

All is dharma, illusion:
A dream, a phantasm, a bubble, a shadow,
Evanescent as dew, transient as a lightning flash,
So should one view what is conditioned.[9]

Eventually he finished his teaching. In due time Xingzhen and the eight nuns all awakened together to the truth of the way without birth and death. Liuguan, seeing the faithfulness and spiritual maturity of Xingzhen, called a general assembly of his disciples and announced: "I came to China in order to teach the way. Now there is someone else who can hand on the dharma, and I shall return whence I came."

He took up his rosary, his wooden rice bowl, his water bottle, his ringed staff, and his volume of the *Diamond Scripture,* handed them all to Xingzhen and set off toward India.

From this time onward, Xingzhen governed the community at the Lotus Peak monastery, and taught with great distinction. Immortals and dragons, men and spirits revered him as they had revered Liuguan. The eight nuns followed his teaching till they all became bodhisattvas, and all nine entered together into the world of utmost joy, the Pure Land of Amitābha in the West.

Translated by Richard Rutt

9. See Conze, *Buddhist Wisdom Books*, 68–71.

Cho Sǒnggi (1638–1689)

SHOWING GOODNESS AND STIRRED BY RIGHTNESS

[CH'ANGSǑN KAMǓI ROK]

Written in both literary Chinese and the vernacular (some 260 versions exist), this story involves a power struggle within the royal court, in the midst of which a war with pirates breaks out. The story's main theme is concerned with the moral values within the family of an official named Hwa Chin. This version is based on the Singu sǒrim edition in the old moveable type.

The minister of war, Hwa Uk, had three legal wives, all of equal standing: Lady Sim, Lady Yo, and Lady Chǒng. Lady Yo had an untimely death, leaving a daughter named T'aegang. Lady Chǒng bore a very gifted son named Chin and died while he was still a child. Lady Sim bore a son named Ch'un, who was the eldest of Hwa Uk's children. Because of Ch'un's foolishness, Hwa Uk favored Chin, causing Lady Sim and Ch'un's discontent to grow.

One day, tiring of the infiltration of corrupt officials into the court, Hwa Uk decides to resign from his post and return home. He then sees to the marriage of Ch'un and also arranges for the marriages of T'aegang and Chin. However, Hwa Uk passes away before those marriages can take place. After his death, Lady Sim and Ch'un devise many ways to tyrannize Chin and his wives.

Chin achieves the highest ranking on the civil service examination and becomes an official. Ch'un is jealous of his younger brother's rise to power and in a wicked conspiracy brings false accusations against Chin, causing him to be exiled. In like manner, his wife is also falsely accused and cast out. However, Chin and his wives do not hold the least grudge against Lady Sim or Ch'un. While in exile, Chin meets the Daoist monk Kwakkong, who teaches him the ways of war.

Meanwhile, the pirate Sǒ Sanhae leads a rebellion, which inspires Chin to become a soldier. The pirates are subdued, and Chin receives recognition for his valor. The court recognizes his strength and makes him commander over the whole southern region. Chin establishes peace in the south, and at his triumphant return the emperor makes him Lord of Chinguk. In another part of the saga, Lady Sim and Ch'un make amends for their evil deeds and become good people. Chin forgives them for exiling him and his wife and returns to serve Lady Sim with all his heart, restoring peace in the family.

The following segment of the story relates the entrance of Ch'un's mistress, Cho, into the Hwa estate; Cho's harsh treatment of Chin's two wives, Lady Yun and Lady Nam; and Cho's poisoning of Nam and her narrow escape from death.

Thereafter Lady Sim breathed a sigh of relief, and from that day forth began to devise a sinister scheme with Ch'un: "In days past it was Lady Chŏng who received all the praise for her grace and beauty, not to mention her gifted child. Her power grew daily, while the noble and lowly alike saw us as nothing more than mere straw. But now Chin's two wives have surpassed Lady Chŏng in virtue and talent, and Chin himself has such honor and glory that the townspeople and our relatives all adore him. Even the servants submit to them more gladly than before. In the event that Chin should go to the capital, he may find favor with the emperor and gain the support of his fellow officials. He would then be as unstoppable as a dragon that has obtained the wish-fulfilling gem[1] or a tiger riding the wind. Our only option is to press him severely."

"Surely we must!" Hwa Ch'un replied.

One day Ch'un came to Chin and said: "When our beloved father was with us, there was peace in the land. However, he resigned his post, partly due to your encouragement, and returned to his homeland. Day by day the state of the country is becoming increasingly unstable, and disaster lurks on the horizon. And now, what have you to say about going off to court yourself, flaunting your greatness and glory in such a manner?"

"My elder brother has spoken wisely. Who am I that I should not carry out what you have said?" After making this humble reply, Chin immediately sent a memorial declining his position in order to help care for his elderly mother. After careful consideration, the emperor granted him leave for one year. From that time forth, Chin confined himself to Chugu Hall, where he enjoyed poetry and the classics.

However, Lady Sim had commanded her servants, Kyehyang and others, to make false accusations against Chin and to plague him with endless tormenting and insults. She also made sure to feed him spoiled rice and bitter herbs that no one could possibly eat. But Chin showed

---

1. *Cintāmani* in Sanskrit; *PDB*, 193.

no signs of despair. Lady Sim also forced Hwa Chin's two wives, Yun and Nam, to toil at sewing, weaving, embroidery, and all manner of laborious tasks. Nevertheless, the two women responded with all the grace and elegance of heavenly angels. Even the wicked Lady Sim could find no fault in that.

One day Ch'un informed his mother of his intention to take Miss Cho as his concubine. Outside the family, Ch'un's fellow conspirators Pŏmhwan and Changp'yŏng had become intimate friends, while within the family Lady Sim had proclaimed herself head of the household and the only person who should carry out the ancestral rites. In keeping with his wish, Ch'un presented Miss Cho with all sorts of fine linens and jewelry. She adorned herself until her beauty pierced the eye and her sweet fragrance filled the nose. As Ch'un looked upon her, she smiled cunningly and worked on him until the prodigal's heart could not resist.

That night Hwa Ch'un and Miss Cho slept together. The relentlessness of the lewd sounds they made and their foul deeds were enough to cause all the maidservants to blush. Meanwhile Lady Sim had discovered some jade trinkets under the eastern wall. Greatly astonished, she quickly hid them again.

The conceited Miss Cho habitually viewed the world as though she were a frog at the bottom of a well. She fancied herself a matchless beauty who could topple the empire. She dismissed the merits of Xi Shi[2] and laughed scornfully at Precious Consort Yang.[3] But when she first saw the young ladies Yun and Nam, Cho's countenance fell, fearing that another's beauty might surpass her own. As when she beheld her own face, she was angered by the honesty of the mirror.

The designs of Lady Sim alone would have been sufficient to spoil any household, but now with Miss Cho in the home, the chances

---

2. A famous beauty, of peasant origin, who lived in the fifth century BCE. She was used by the king of Yue to distract Fu Chai (d. 473 BCE), the king of Wu, from affairs of state.

3. Yang Guifei, the favorite concubine of the Tang emperor Xuanzong (712–756).

for destruction were even greater. Cho wearied Ch'un night and day with her appeals for him to get rid of his legal wife, Im. Finally Ch'un replied: "The faults of young Lady Im are evident to me, but my brother will inevitably object. One side of her is calm and immovable, and I don't know what trouble the two of them together could make for me."

Cho clapped her hands and shouted: "Chin is the younger brother of my lord. How would he dare to intervene in the expulsion of your wife? And if Im should happen to die on her own, that would surely bring no harm to my lord. However, I will go into seclusion, to weep at the faintness of heart in my lord should he allow his wretched wife to stand in the way of the fulfillment of our design."

Ch'un hesitated for a time, and then one day, after talking things over with Pŏmhwan and Changp'yŏng, he went into Chugu Hall, ostensibly to look into a chapter from the *Historical Records* of Sima Qian. After reading for a moment, he closed the book and posed this question to Chin: "In ancient times Emperor Wu of the Han, when he discovered the whole truth of his wife's jealousy, went ahead and divorced her. What do you think of that emperor's decision?"

Chin, blind to Ch'un's evil stratagem, answered straightforwardly: "Inasmuch as man is light and woman is shadow, only after the light overcomes the shadow can order in the home be established. Although Emperor Wu turned aside from his first wife, because of her sensual nature, it was because she was guilty of jealousy, one of the seven grounds for divorce,[4] that she was cast out."

Ch'un, greatly pleased at what he heard, ran to find his mother, Lady Sim. He said: "I can't help but be aware of Im's faults, and they have been a source of great vexation. I've refrained from casting her out only because my dear aunt adores her and because Chin would take her side. But Chin has spoken in my favor, and my dear aunt has

---

4. Disobedience toward parents-in-law, failure to produce a son, adultery, theft, undue jealousy, grave illness, and extreme talkativeness.

gone to Fujian. Is it not the time to rid myself of Lady Im and make Miss Cho my legal wife?"

"Lady Im has no faults, save not sleeping in your bed. How can she be guilty of jealousy?" answered Lady Sim with surprise and resolution. "Furthermore, my feelings for Lady Im remain the same, and I am not going to change my mind." Ch'un pleaded again and even a third time, but Lady Sim refused to listen.

Then Miss Cho had her maidservant Nansu conspire with Pŏmhwan, and she assisted him. She also had her maidservant Kyehaeng place a few evil tokens in Lady Sim's bedroom. Pretending to have just found the evil tokens, Kyehaeng then proclaimed to Lady Sim: "These belong to Lady Im!"

Lady Sim fell into a rage when she heard this, and she banished Lady Im from the region. The other servants were sorely grieved by this, and Lady Yun and Lady Nam raised their voices in grief. Chin threw off his hat and, unaware that he was shoeless, ran to the bottom of the stairs, wailing. Lady Sim, further outraged, shouted after him: "That woman Im's crimes exceed even those of Empress Wei.[5] She incessantly refuses her husband and will not allow him into her bed. You have already given up your charge in the government, so what is the reason for this show of indignation? Lady Im's jealousy has worsened daily since Miss Cho entered our household, and a curse such as has never been seen before has come into my own bedroom. Why should I suppress my anger and not banish her at once?"

Chin pleaded in desperation, striking his head upon the ground until it bled. Rebuking him for his frenzied behavior, Lady Sim exclaimed, "What concern is it of yours if I cast out my daughter-in-law?" Lady Sim then summoned her servants to escort him from the room.

While Chin grieved in the Paekhwa Hall courtyard, the treacherous Pŏmhwan continued sitting in the main hall. Suddenly he hastened

---

5. Tang Zhongzong's wife, who murdered the emperor and usurped the throne for twenty years (684–705).

over to Chin. Prostrating himself, he asked, "What ails you so, Master?"

Chin became enraged, and he ordered his strongest servants to seize Pŏmhwan and swing him around. He shouted, "It is because of traitors like you that order in the family of the minister of state has disintegrated!"

Pŏmhwan, realizing his peril, mustered only a weak grin because he was unable to speak. He was dragged out and driven from the estate. That same day, Lady Im took leave of the house and made her way to the sedan chair. She stopped to look back at the family shrine and with tearful eyes bowed twice, and said farewell. Filled with sorrow, she stepped into the sedan chair. Her wet nurse and the other servants wept as they followed after her.

At that time, there was not one in the entire Hwa household save Lady Sim, Ch'un, and Miss Cho who was not weeping. Lady Im's elder brother, Im Yun, had recently been removed from his government position and had returned to his home at Hejian, so she too went there. With a great show of dignity, Ch'un called all of his kinsfolk together and claimed Miss Cho as his own, which would make her his legal wife.

But Chin admonished Ch'un, saying: "Duke Huan of Qi (r. 685–643) said in his proclamation, 'Never take a concubine and make her a legal wife.'[6] Never has there been a greater profanity than for you to cast out your good wife when there were no grounds, and then take this lowly creature in her stead and have her attend to the ancestral rites! Preposterous!"

Ch'un shouted back in fury: "You have two wives; am I forbidden to take one?"

Ch'un then proceeded to take Cho as his legal wife. With her vanity, her violent mood swings, and her feminine persuasion, she played her foolish husband like a puppet. She took pleasure in cunning coquetry and in venting her quick temper, and Ch'un seemed to be

6. *Shiji* 32:1487–1493.

constantly in flight, carrying out her every wish. The household servants, on the other hand, were embarrassed. Everyone longed for Lady Im's return. Because of this, the servants began to slacken in their responsibilities, and order and discipline gradually disappeared.

One day Lady Cho went into Pich'un Hall, where Lady Nam stayed. Approaching Lady Yun, Lady Cho said: "This family has two heirlooms that are to be passed on only to the wife of the firstborn. Our honorable parents-in-law perceived that Lady Im was unworthy and on that basis denied her the treasure. They thought to divide it among the other wives, but you two, being the wives of the second son, cannot presume to be worthy of possessing the treasure. It defies all reason. Because of Im's perverted ethics and the disruption of the household, this family's name and reputation have been sullied. Yet the family has now been purged of the encroaching darkness, and order is beginning to return to all of its affairs. Since the relationship between the wife of the firstborn and the wives of the second son is like that of heaven and earth, surely it is improper for you to have the family inheritance."

"Has it always been that way? Lowly mistresses are not informed of such things. Is there a name for this treasure?" Lady Yun truly did not know and therefore inquired in this manner.

"One of the treasures is the Red Jade Bracelet. Empress Ma (1332–1382) of Ming Taizu (1368–1399) gave it to the Hwa ancestors in return for subjugating Nanjing. The other is the Green Jade Pendant—the most precious gem of all the treasures belonging to the King of Annam. He gave it to our great-great-grandfather when he established peace in the southern region. Accordingly, it was passed down from generation to generation, and it is imperative that it be passed on to the virtuous wife of the firstborn. How tragic that it should be mistakenly bequeathed to you and not our beloved Lady Sim, who is of such exquisite virtue."

Lady Yun immediately opened the chest and said as she conferred the Red Jade Bracelet upon Lady Cho: "As it should be."

Lady Cho's face was all aglow as she played with it like a toy. Lady Nam remained silent, staring sternly at Lady Cho. She saw no reason to surrender her own jewel in the same manner. Eventually Lady Cho left, disappointed that she was able to obtain only the Red Jade Bracelet.

Lady Nam then said to Lady Yun: "These jewels were esteemed gifts presented to our ancestors. How could you give yours away so quickly, without consulting our lord?"

Lady Yun responded solemnly: "If our lord were unable to preserve his position, would he not worry first about us? And if something were to happen to us, would we not try all we could to protect the jewel? In the *Book of Songs*, we read of how Lady Si of Pao caused the downfall of the grand and glorious state of Zhou.[7] Truly this is what is happening here!"

A few days later Lady Cho entered the main hall and began to speak of Lady Im's faults. Lady Yun paid her no attention, but Lady Nam became angry and said, glaring at Lady Cho: "The young lady has found favor with the firstborn son, but she has difficulty keeping a civil tongue. The sage has said, 'If an epidendrum burns, the fragrant species of orchids that grows in the marsh laments; no less does the fox mourn the death of a rabbit.' Young lady, are you the only one who has not heard of the time a palace woman ridiculed Lady Ban Jieyou[8] when she was cast out?"

Lady Cho's face turned pale with astonishment, and Lady Sim's temper flared as she scolded Nam. "Cho's status has changed from before. How dare you refer to her as 'young lady'!"

"A thousand pardons, my lady. I'm not yet accustomed to using the new title; forgive me."

---

7. *Shijing* 192:8; Karlgren, *Book of Odes*, 136.
8. A favorite concubine of Emperor Cheng of the Han (r. 32–7 BCE). When she lost favor, she composed a rhymeprose and a song: *Hanshu* 97B:3983–3988; Watson, *Columbia Book of Chinese Poetry*, 75–78.

How sad! Lady Nam's uncompromising nature was a trait inherited from her father. Her blunt speech and her intolerance for insults, unlike Lady Yun, made her scoldings by Lady Sim seem even more cruel.

One day as Lady Sim was overseeing Lady Yun and Lady Nam's embroidering, Chin's wet nurse, Kyehwa, cried out in agitation, "The court is going to strip our lord of his position and lower the status of Lady Nam to concubine. Look, the county clerk has come to take his appointment paper away!"

Lady Cho was overjoyed at the news. She then said to Lady Nam: "The straps of the young lady's heavy purse have just been cut. Oh my, what will ever become of your precious Green Jade Pendant?" Without changing her complexion, Lady Nam continued to embroider, and Lady Yun was unable to stop the flow of indignant tears.

Then Hwa Ch'un entered the room and said: "The court officials have brought the unfilial Chin's idleness to the emperor's attention and discharged him, dishonorably, from his post. They also believe it to be unfitting for the daughter of an executed criminal to be the legal wife of a son of the minister of state, so they have taken away her status and made her a secondary wife."

Lady Sim responded to her son's report: "It would seem that Chin's pomp and pride have led to his demise. A fitting end."

The villain Pŏmhwan, after suffering such harsh treatment from Chin, had felt the indignity sinking deep into the marrow of his bones. Since Lady Cho already loathed Chin and his wives, Pŏmhwan gathered his friends from far and wide and contrived a diabolical scheme. He went forthwith to the palace and was not heard from for some time. Ch'un began to question his whereabouts and then, accusing Chin, he shouted: "You are to blame for Pŏmhwan's disappearance!"

In those days, a dark and corrupt official named Yan Sung (1480–1565) wielded power, and few could keep from falling into his clutches.[9] Xing Mouqing[10] was a confederate of Yan Sung. Pŏmhwan sent Mouqing a message asking to see him, but Mouqing refused. So Pŏmhwan took eighty pieces of silver and some dates that Lady Cho had given him and took them to Mouqing's wife, Lady Geng. Only then did Mouqing send for him. He whispered, "What's the meaning of this? I see that you consider it not too far when you have come a thousand tricents to see me."

Pŏmhwan told him all about Chin's unfilial behavior and then, stating his true intention, said, "Hwa Chin has taken the daughter of the condemned criminal Nam P'yo as his wife. In addition, he has repeatedly expressed his bitterness toward our country and has even likened the noble Yan Sung to Jia Sidao."[11]

"You speak of the atrocities that Hwa Chin has committed. If this man means nothing to you, what is the reason for this animosity?" asked Mouqing with a grin.

"I . . . have my reasons."

"So that's it. I have a way to rid you of him permanently. All you must do is go and wait."

Pŏmhwan expressed his gratitude and left. However, he heard nothing for many days, and it only seemed odd because it was the first time that Lady Cho had attempted bribery with money and jewels. But Yan Sung had always hated Chin, so Mouqing told him about everything including the bounty from Lady Cho. When Yan Sung learned that Chin had taken the daughter of the former inspector Nam P'yo as his wife, he grew angry and immediately drafted a proposal to have Chin removed from his position. He gave it to Pŏmhwan, and two days later it came before the council.

---

9. A Ming politician denounced for his misgovernment; see Goodrich and Fang, *Dictionary of Ming Biography*, 2:586–591.

10. In the Chinese version, Yan Mouqing. Yi Chiyŏng, *Ch'angsŏn kamŭi rok*, 347–357, covers the translated part.

11. Late Song agrarian reformer (1213–1275), who was blamed for his treacherous negotiation with the Mongols in 1259.

After examining the entire document, the emperor said in astonishment: "How could Hwa Chin be guilty of such behavior?"

Yan Sung, who was seated next to him, spoke out: "I have already heard about it, and it is no lie." After he had completely slandered Chin's character, the emperor had no alternative but to heed the council, discharge Hwa Chin, and demote Lady Nam to the status of concubine. From then on, Nam was compelled to wear a servant's clothing, and she also had to wait on Lady Sim. For her part, Lady Cho seized the Green Jade Pendant and locked it up in the Hall of Treasures.

Lady Nam accepted her situation as the workings of fate and showed no emotion, even though the revilings and the beatings grew more severe. Finally, Lady Yun and Lady Nam met together in a remote, secluded place, and Lady Yun wept over Lady Nam's misfortune. Lady Nam tried to comfort her by saying: "We must not allow a small thing like this to discourage us. We came into this household as a consequence of a transgression in a previous life. We can only follow the will of heaven, and in due course we will return to the place whence we came. What reason have we to fear any kind of dishonor or disgrace? Furthermore, how fortunate we sisters are to have been given to our noble husband, who has never cursed heaven or accused anyone, even though he is continually oppressed day after day!"

Lady Yun took Lady Nam by the hand and wept all the more. "How admirable is my wise sister's dignity and ability to endure abuse that others could not possibly bear. Since our parents nurtured us, we have had an ocean of love and a mountain of compassion. If we did not eat of all our meal, they would inquire as to what was wrong; if we overslept, they would look after us. They could not bear our departure, and their tears streamed down on the day we entered this household. Surely they must still be thinking of our well-being. But we fall far short of their greatness, and we can never repay their kindness. And now, we have encountered misfortune in our husband's household. In a moment's breath you have found yourself locked in the gaping jaws of a tiger, and yet you show no indignation."

Lady Nam too began to weep as they silently made their way back. Meanwhile, Lady Cho, who had been eavesdropping on Lady Yun and Lady Nam from behind a wall, went to recount everything to Lady Sim, who cried out in anger: "How dare those two blemishes speak of us that way!"

So they confined Lady Yun in a small building in the north garden and Lady Nam in a corridor in the Middle Hall. Their servants were expelled from the premises, but Kyeaeng refused to let go of Lady Nam's dress. She fell to the ground, and as she lay sobbing, unable to get up, Lady Cho screamed in a terrifying manner, "Does your slave wish to die?"

Looking up, Kyeaeng laughed. "Why should I fear death? Though I am low born, at least I don't play with any treasures of the family I might find by the eastern wall as if they were toys!" Lady Cho's face turned pale with astonishment, and she beat Kyeaeng and chased her out of her sight. Lady Sim also joined in, scolding Kyeaeng as they chased her away. Then Lady Cho and Lady Sim locked the inner and outer doors of Chugu Hall, leaving Chin in solitary confinement. He did not utter a complaint even when they withheld his food.

One day Lady Cho sent her servant Nanhyang with some porridge for Lady Nam. "The gracious Lady Sim sent this porridge for you. Inasmuch as you have been cast out forever, it is fitting that you take this, that you may die an early death!"

Lady Nam looked at the porridge. It was a bluish color with a tint of yellow. She put the bowl to her lips and let out a sorrowful moan: "I have vainly striven to live my life, but alas, it seems that death is all that is left."

After she drank the poisoned porridge, Nanhyang ran back to tell Lady Cho. She jumped for joy and commanded Nanhyang to wrap the body in a mat made of reeds. Lady Cho then gave her trusted servant Maktong one hundred pieces of silver and told him: "Take the mat and cast it into the river. Do not tell a soul!"

In the third watch (11 p.m.–1 a.m.), Maktong hefted the mat-wrapped body and crept out the back of the north garden. He had scarcely gone one hundred paces when suddenly he became disoriented and began to make his way to a ravine in the mountains. Stopping, he realized he could neither see nor hear anything.

A Buddhist nun named Ch'ŏngwŏn, from the Chahyŏn hermitage on Mount Hua in Sichuan, had once come to Inspector Nam's house to obtain a painting of the Bodhisattva Who Observes the Sounds of the World. On that day the bodhisattva came to her in a dream and gave her three capsules of medicine, saying: "On an appointed day, Lady Nam will suffer an untimely death. In the third watch on that day, under a pine tree at Paolin monastery in Shaoxing, you shall restore her life by giving her this medicine." When she awoke, there beside her were the three capsules that she had seen in the dream. She immediately put on her robes and, taking her walking staff with metal rings, went to the Myŏngju hermitage at Paolin monastery, located just outside the north garden of the Hwa estate.

This was where the servants of Lady Yun and Lady Nam had gone to hide when Lady Cho chased them out. The servants each wept and cried out for their masters. Ch'ŏngwŏn pretended not to notice, but that night she spoke with Kyeaeng and the others, saying: "The afflictions of your mistress are indeed grievous. I intend to save her. All of you follow me!"

The nun quickly made her way toward the village entrance. The servants were skeptical, but followed anyway. When they came to the Ch'angsong River in Nangok, she suddenly stopped and, pointing across the way, exclaimed: "Here is the place!"

Suddenly the mighty servant who was carrying the large mat bundle set it down and cleared away the rocks to make a place to sleep for the night. Ch'ŏngwŏn approached the small encampment. She felt the mat and told Kyeaeng to lift it. Overwhelmed, Kyeaeng's legs trembled under the weight, and she realized she could not possibly do so.

"If we do not act quickly, it may be too late to save her. Lift!" said Ch'ŏngwŏn with determination.

The discouraged Kyeaeng began to cry and fell to the ground because of the seemingly impossible task. Ch'ŏngwŏn quickly ran to her side and said: "There is no time for this." As she tried to lift it herself, she saw that there was still some life in Lady Nam's pale face. At this, she gasped with joy and quickly reached into her bag, from which she pulled the three capsules. She dropped the first into some warm water, and as she poured it into Lady Nam's mouth, its heat began to spread throughout her body. The nun did the same with the second capsule, and Lady Nam opened her eyes, took a deep breath, and rolled over. After Ch'ŏngwŏn repeated the process a third time, Lady Nam spit out the noxious potion and sat up as she regained consciousness. Ch'ŏngwŏn exclaimed with joy: "You have nothing to fear now, my lady."

"O venerable master, what manner of being can restore life to one who was dead?" said Lady Nam. She then took a closer look and asked: "Are you not the nun who came to my father's home seven years ago to receive the picture of the bodhisattva?"

"It is so. When I saw you then, I saw your moral cleanliness. Your majesty and splendor made you appear as someone not of this world. Furthermore, your temperament, like silk thread streaming down, was as though it came from the heavenly courts. I knew that this misfortune would befall you and that there would be nothing you could do to stop it. All life is precious, no matter how wretched a creature may seem. It would have done no good to tell you then, so I said not a word. You could do nothing but follow the goodwill of the Dragon King, protected by the spirits, so no evil spirit would dare harm you."

Lady Nam then referred to the disastrous incident at Dongting Lake.[12] She said, "Because I did not follow my parents to death, the

---

12. Reference unclear. It may be to her own family's incident at the lake.

underworld hates me and brought this curse upon me. Wise one, you have extended compassion to one who had passed on, bringing her back into this world of suffering. Is this kindness? No, it is regret!"

"You do not understand the will of heaven. The saints and sages of old have only been able to achieve enlightenment after passing through trial and affliction. It was so with the World-honored Śākyamuni when he suffered afflictions atop the snow-covered Himalayas, and with Confucius when he was opposed by the people of Chen and Cai.[13] Posterity will not know your afflictions. Hence heaven wishes to demonstrate your wisdom and benevolence, so that the underworld may manifest your moral influence. Did you not see the paulownia tree by the stone image? The strong, sturdy trunk and branches remain steadfast when the winter winds blow. But we can cut, carve, and make the wood into a zither that makes a sound that all from both past and present would recognize. Know that it is not only man whom heaven can shake from mental lassitude to toughen his nature,[14] but you, my lady, as well."

Ch'ŏngwŏn then conveyed the words of the bodhisattva that she had received in her vision. She also said: "You still have several more years of tribulation. That is your fate. Now come with me. If we trust in the bodhisattva and can just endure for but a few more years, you will enjoy eternal blessings and rid yourself of tribulation forever."

Lady Nam sighed and did not respond gladly. That night she had a dream in which the Bodhisattva Who Observes the Sounds of the World came to show her an omen. The next day, Lady Nam and her servant Kyeaeng dressed in men's clothing so that they could travel in safety, and followed Ch'ŏngwŏn into Sichuan.

That same day, Maktong awoke from his slumber. It was a bright, beautiful day and the stream trickled down gaily. He looked all around

13. Confucius was in difficulties in the region of Chen and Cai because he had no friends at court, according to *Mengzi* 7B:18; Lau, *Mencius*, 197.

14. *Mengzi* 6B:15; Lau, *Mencius*, 181.

and stopped for a moment. He then cried out: "Is this a dream or is it real? How did I get here and where is the corpse? Ah, this is very strange. This is clearly no dream. It must be the work of a goblin! That wicked Lady Cho has already employed me to do her evil deeds, so what is the use in telling her the truth?"

He returned to the estate, concocted a lie, and explained the situation to Lady Cho. "I carried the mat, climbing over hills and crossing streams. Under the boundless night sky I came to some rugged terrain and stood upon a ledge, below which there must have been a ten-thousand-foot drop. At the bottom there was a clear blue pond, so I fastened the mat to a big rock and pushed with all my might. The rock and the mat tumbled to the bottom, and I heard a great splash."

Lady Cho was greatly pleased at what she heard and rewarded him with a large cup of wine.

Translated by Mark Peterson

Anonymous

THE STORY OF QUEEN INHYŎN

[INHYŎN WANGHU CHŎN]

Also known by the longer title *Inhyŏn sŏngmo Min-ssi tŏkhaeng nok* (Record of virtuous deeds of the sagely mother Inhyŏn, née Min), this account was written by an anonymous court lady close to the queen, as attested by a manuscript version written in elegant cursive calligraphy in the vernacular. The story focuses on the crucial events in the queen's life—her birth (1667), her investiture as queen (1681), her expulsion (1689), her return to the palace as queen (1694), and her untimely death (1701), caused by the malicious schemes of Lady Chang. These events are foregrounded and described in detail, the style heightened by the inclusion of polysyllabic words of Chinese origin. The narrator does not suppress disturbing facts.[1] At a critical turn, the authenticity of the narrator's account is

---

1. Kim Manjung's *Lady Sa's Journey South* (*Sassi namjŏng ki*) is a work of fiction about Queen Inhyŏn.

reinforced through the device of a dream, a fictive element that might have earned a charge of frivolity from educated readers were it not for the story's evident moral commitment.

The story turns on a sudden reversal of fortune for the queen, illustrating how adversity is the supreme test of human quality. The queen is able to oppose fortune's blows with goodness—she shines amidst undeserved suffering, like a jewel. She is exiled to her own home, a place of endurance, and endures what is unendurable, a model of patience. Contrary to the disdain for decorum shown by Lady Chang, the queen's behavior remains impeccable—she is a connoisseur of exquisite manners.

Lady Chang, the concubine of obscure origin, wins the favor of the king with her physical allure. She affects a pretentious manner to disguise her humble background, and her envy of the queen drives her to morbid jealousy. Her base purpose, to kill the queen, is a sign of evil incarnate.

Sukchong (1674–1720), the nineteenth king of Chosŏn, is generally accounted a good ruler, although he was not immune to error: he did become infatuated with Lady Chang and elevated her to the throne. Embroiled in factional conflicts, he had little choice but to side with groups that would support his decisions, uniting with one, for example, to remove the queen.

The story begins. The clan site of Queen Inhyŏn, the second consort of King Sukchong of Chosŏn, née Min, was Yŏhŭng, and she was the daughter of Min Yujung (1630–1687), pen name Tunch'on, the minister of defense and great lord of Yŏyang, and maternal granddaughter of Song Chungil (1606–1672), pen name Tongch'undang, the chief state counselor. It was said that her mother, née Song, had a wondrous dream, and the future queen was born on the twenty-third day, *chŏngmi*, of the fourth lunar month (May 15, 1667). At that time, auspicious air hovered over the house, and fragrance filled the delivery room for a long time. Knowing about the auspicious omen, her parents forbade the family to speak of it.

The child grew fast by any standard. She was as bashful as a flower, or the delicate moon; yet her face shone bright, making the white sun almost lose its luster. Everyone gazed upon her with a singular rapture. She was adept at weaving and sewing, as if a hundred spirits had come to help her, and she never betrayed her emotions. She was steadfast, discriminating,[2] imperturbable: others could not fathom her inmost thoughts and feelings. Her wholesome habits were innate and gentle, and she was exceptional in deeds of altruism and filial piety. Her fine manners—so natural and harmonious—and her virtue were simply remarkable. Modest in disposition, upright and reserved, she was broad-minded—indeed, she towered over everyone in all aspects. All day she sat composed, as if enveloped by auspicious clouds and harmonious airs—others could not aspire to her level. Her frame and fragrance recalled the high sky and the waters of autumn. Her integrity was like gold and jade, or pine and cypress. From early childhood, she disliked luxury and did not enjoy badinage. Outstanding in every accomplishment, including literary composition and calligraphy, she was well versed in history. In her leisure she sometimes took up a brush but never wrote anything florid.[3] Her parents, paternal and maternal uncles, and kin near and far all loved her, and the beauty of her name was known throughout the country.

Her father had sometimes observed a red rainbow shining in her washbasin and from it guessed that she was destined to become noble, so he paid special attention to her upbringing. Her uncle Min Chŏngjung (1628–1692),[4] despite his strict personality and mastery of Confucian learning, loved her too and once remarked: "If water is too pure, ghosts will shun it. This child is beautiful and wise, but her life span may not be long."

She lost her mother, Lady Song, at an early age, and during the long period of mourning, emaciated with grief, she still comported herself with decorum. She then served her stepmother, Lady Cho, with utmost devotion. Her maternal grandfather, Song Chungil, loved her and brought her under his care, and every day he would quietly say: "She has the virtuous conduct of Tairen, the mother of King Wen of

---

2. *Shangshu* (Book of documents) 2:4a; Legge, *Chinese Classics,* 3:61.
3. Something flowery, frivolous, or fictional.
4. A Westerner in politics.

Zhou, and of Taisi, mother of King Wu of Zhou." He schooled her in the clan's great tradition of Confucian learning and in the conduct of a virtuous woman: for such a one, even if her nature were not especially gifted, her name would surely still be known. How much more so with her—just as a high mountain produces jade, and seamoss grows in the deepest ocean. Any wise person, born to a renowned family—how could he remain inattentive to her?

In the year *kyŏngsin* (1680), Queen Ingyŏng (1661–1680)[5] passed away. The lack of a royal consort worried the queen mother, Myŏngsŏng (1642–1683),[6] and she ordered the selection of a virtuous young lady as a successor. The great lord of Ch'ŏngp'ung, Kim Umyŏng (1619–1675), the king's maternal grandfather, had heard of the virtuous young lady named Min and spoke to the queen mother about her. At the same time, Chief State Counselor Song Chungil presented his opinion to the king: "A queen is the mother of her people. Now your subject knows that the daughter of Minister of Defense Min is a woman of virtue. I hope that Your Majesty will avoid the complex selection procedure—requiring families with eligible daughters to register them for evaluation over three interviews[7]—and instead select the royal spouse directly." The queen mother was delighted with this suggestion, and the king gave his secretary the order to let it be known. The awestruck Lord Min immediately sent a memorial earnestly declining the honor. The king, however, had already made up his mind. He summoned the second state counselor Lord Min Chŏngjung to the palace and through him reprimanded the Min family for their disrespect. As a loyal subject, the minister could not find a way to decline and returned home. At a meeting, the Min family was moved to tears by the august royal favor.

5. Sukchong's first queen, who died on December 16, 1680, at the age of nineteen.
6. King Hyŏnjong's wife, née Kim.
7. The procedure to select the crown princess, in which candidates are screened through three sittings. For a glimpse of this ordeal, see Princess Hyegyŏng's memoir, *A Record of Sorrowful Days*.

A party of eunuchs and court ladies was sent to escort Lady Min to the palace at Ŏŭi-dong.[8] After meeting her, a court lady, filled with admiration, told her stepmother, Lady Cho: "By royal favor I have had the honor of serving three kings—Hyŏnjong (1659–1674), Hyojong, and Sukchong. I have also had the opportunity to be in contact with some eighty exceptional ladies. But I have never met a lady of virtue with such beautiful features—a great blessing to the state and the people. I count it my good fortune to have lived long enough to see her." Lady Cho replied with a humility and propriety that deeply moved the court lady, who related everything to the queen mother. She was greatly pleased and eagerly awaited the day of the royal wedding.

On the auspicious day, with a solemn manner, Lord Min conducted the ceremony. The king was then twenty-one years old. Attended by civil and military officials, the king went to the Ŏŭi-dong palace, where the bride was waiting, presented the goose on the jade table,[9] and urged the queen's sedan chair bearers to hurry. He himself sealed the door of the gold phoenix-adorned chair to hasten it on the way to the palace.

Unlike the weddings of crown princes, an event in the royal palace called for a different turnout: flags and pennons with embroidered dragons and phoenixes; halberds and battle-axes; a hundred officials lining the streets; well-dressed court ladies adorned with seven jewels and attended by ladies-in-waiting covering the road ten tricents long. Burning incense and dulcet tones filled the air—the splendor and grandeur of the wedding truly defied description. At the exchange of wine cups, the new queen's movements were dazzling, as if the bright light of a harvest moon shone on the palace, putting golden halls and jeweled terraces with all their treasures in the shade. Two queens,[10]

---

8. A building where King Hyojong (1649–1659) lived before becoming king.

9. Part of the wedding ceremony in which the groom places a wooden goose on the table to symbolize conjugal fidelity.

10. King Injo's second queen and Hyŏnjong's queen.

greatly pleased, took her to their hearts and prized her. All those who attended the ceremony rejoiced and loved her.

That same day, the queen was invested and gave audience to the princesses and consorts and three hundred ladies-in-waiting. The weather was balmy; the breeze blew gently, and auspicious clouds were entirely devoid of threat, as if nature knew it was the day the mother of the state ascended her throne. She had won the hearts of myriad people, and they all rejoiced.

After the accession, the queen's filial devotion to the queen mother and the dowager queen was exemplary. She helped her king and guided her people with harmonious virtue. She governed princesses and consorts and ladies-in-waiting with benevolence, dignity, and impartiality. Her love for them was like a warm spring hill where everything seems to flourish again. At the same time, her bearing and her commandments were solemn; people could not but look up to her. Those at court praised her qualities, and after a couple of months it became evident that she had transformed the manners at court. Everyone respected and received her warmly, which pleased the queen mother and the dowager queen, who prized her as a blessing to the state. The king too respected and received her warmly, and everyone in and out of court held her in the highest esteem. The queen mother and dowager queen wrote a letter to Song Siyŏl (1607–1689), first minister without portfolio, and praised the queen's virtue, bestowing special favor on the queen's mother. The Min family was overwhelmed by these favors.

In the winter of the year *kyehae* (1683), the king contracted smallpox, and at times his condition was critical. Greatly worried, the queen devoted herself to nursing him, denying herself food and sleep. The queen mother too agonized, and together with the queen bathed in cold water, set up an altar in the rear garden, and prayed day and night. Apprehensive for the queen mother's health, the queen implored that she be allowed to perform the prayers alone, but the queen mother would not listen. Both continued their prayers day and night. Blue heaven was moved by their devotion, for the king recovered. The people's joy was immeasurable.

But the queen mother[11] had exhausted herself during the king's illness that winter, and now she herself fell ill. The anxious king and queen cared for her day and night, employed herbal medicines, ordered the ministers to pray for her recovery at the ancestral shrine and the altars of soil and grain,[12] and granted amnesty to many prisoners. Despite the efforts of the royal physicians, there was no improvement, and the anxious king and queen were at their wit's end. On the fifth of the twelfth month (January 21, 1684), at the hour of the tiger (3–5 a.m.), the queen mother passed away at Chosŭng Hall, Ch'anggyŏng Palace, aged forty-one. The court and all its subjects trembled in sadness, the sound of wailing rose to heaven, and the king and queen mourned with inconsolable grief. Refusing meat dishes, they gained the admiration of the court for their exemplary filial piety. After three years of mourning,[13] the hall containing her tablet[14] was closed, as both majesties grieved beyond expression.

Two years later, Lady Chang (d. 1701), a maid, was given the rank of *hŭibin,* the highest a court lady could obtain. A crafty girl, she was quick-witted and shrewd, attracting the king's attention and then his favor. In the first month of the year *mujin* (1688), the king was almost thirty[15] and was concerned that he had no son. The queen shared his distress, and one day quietly suggested that he select a good girl from among the palace women and try to have a son by her. At first the king refused, but the queen admonished him daily that he could not wait for her to bear a son to continue the royal line. Her gentle words and lofty bearing evinced her true concern, and the king was moved. He ordered the court to select a consort. When Princess Myŏngan

---

11. Queen Myŏngsŏng, Hyŏnjong's wife.
12. National altar representing the state; Hucker, *Dictionary of Official Titles,* 5133.
13. Effectively twenty-seven months.
14. Made usually of the chestnut tree, 8 inches (*ch'i*) in length and 2 inches wide.
15. Actually twenty-seven years old.

(d. 1687), the third daughter of King Hyŏnjong and the king's sister, heard of this, she together with her aunt requested an audience with the king and the queen and said: "The queen is still young and should be able to bear a son." But the queen serenely replied: "Having little virtue and a weak constitution, I still presumed to be queen, but day and night I have walked as if on thin ice lest I not repay the kindness of the royal family. Again, with little virtue, I have not been able to bear a son. How can I not worry about the country's future and prosperity?" She was calm and collected, and they left the palace with a still deeper admiration for her. Eventually Lady Kim, with a rank of *sugŭi* (2b), was chosen as a secondary consort, and the queen treated her with respect and bestowed favors upon her, recalling again the examples of Tairen and Taisi. She was deeply admired. But the times were unpropitious, and life and fortune are preordained by heaven. From old, a beautiful woman is ill fated and a sage suffers calamity—hence people doubt the way of heaven.

In the eighth month of the year *mujin* (1688), King Injo's queen (Changnyŏl, 1624–1688)[16] passed away in the inner hall of Ch'anggyŏng Palace. Both the king and the queen lamented morning and evening and offered sacrifices and libations, almost excessively.

That year, the fourteenth year of King Sukchong's reign, on the twenty-eighth day of the tenth month, in winter (November 20, 1688), Lady Chang gave birth to a son. The king was overjoyed, and the queen too loved the child as if he were her own. If Lady Chang had understood her place, she would have enjoyed great glory, but she was impudent and presumptuous. While the virtuous queen enjoyed a high reputation, Lady Chang gave way to her jealousy and plotted to usurp the throne. She began to slander the queen, saying, "She intends to kill the newborn prince with poisoned wine," or "She always curses the consort." Concocting a scheme, she solicited help from some malicious court ladies to spread even more vicious rumors and planted false evi-

16. She became queen in 1638 but had no heir.

dence for the king to see and hear. The old saying is that the evil one never lacks helpers. The accusations that the queen was wicked increased every day, and suspecting the queen, the king began to treat her badly. Lady Chang's malevolent scheme, using her son as a pawn, weakened the king's mind, making him an easy victim. The king became partial and could not distinguish between right and wrong. He whose mind had once been strict and fair began to reject what was good and wise and to retain villains in his service. His misdeeds became an outrage to the upright people at court, and the queen realized that Lady Chang would soon cause some catastrophe. But the good fortune embodied in the presence of a regal prince overrode these concerns, and she continued to be faithful and earnest.

In the year *kisa* (1687), Great Lord Yeyŏng (Min Yujung) passed away, and the queen mourned her father's death, refraining from eating meat. At about this time, the king seemed to make up his mind, and a rumor ran wild among the people that the king was going to depose the queen. The twenty-third day of the fourth month was the queen's birthday,[17] and the palace supply office submitted a list of gifts to the court. The king, however, threw it away and ordered all the food to be removed. Then he gathered the ministers and all the officials above the second rank to announce his decision to depose the queen. Second Royal Secretary Yi Iman (fl. 1650–1709) remonstrated with the king, who, in a burst of anger, dismissed him from office. Yi Manwŏn (b. 1651), sixth advisor in the Office of Special Advisors, also remonstrated with him, and the enraged king banished him to a distant place. Some forty officials were exiled to border regions,[18] and the king issued a memorandum to confirm his decision. Duplicity now

17. This corresponds to May 15 in 1667, the year of her birth.

18. A lengthy digression on Pak T'aebo (1654–1689) occurs at this point in the narrative. Pak, who held the fourth rank in the Office of Special Advisers or Royal Decrees, pointed out the king's error, but his advice was spurned by the king, who inflicted heavy punishment by having Pak tortured to death.

plagued the court: the officials gathered in the palace to present a petition to the king, but that was not their true intention.

The following day, a bailiff in the Office of the Inspector General accompanied by a court lady came to the queen's quarters to deliver the king's decree. The queen removed her robe and hairpin and walked down the steps. She left her quarters and began to make preparations for her return to her natal home. But the king, angered by the wailing of her attendants at court, urged the queen to leave at once—an order without precedent since the beginning of the Chosŏn dynasty—and ladies-in-waiting were sent to her family to fetch a sedan chair. Many court ladies who always followed the powerful wished to curry favor, and their language on this occasion was impudent, their actions vainglorious and arrogant. The queen ignored them. Her own ladies-in-waiting were unable to bear their indignation but dared not displease the king, and they shed tears in corners where they could not be seen. One lady, instructed by Lady Chang, was about to open the departing queen's wardrobe when the queen complied with a smile, looking askance at her. Her bright countenance, like sunlight, seemed to penetrate their designs. She was silent, but her spirit, like an autumn frost, was silvery and luminous. Fearful, the ladies hung their heads in shame.

Repeated orders for the queen to hasten her departure arrived from the angry king. . . .

Finally the queen reached her home in Anguk-tong. When she arrived, her stepmother held her hands and wept. This revived the queen's mourning for her late father, and she said: "I am at fault, and we will not be able to live together in peace. I'm sorry, but it's best that you not stay here."

She gave orders to close all the gates of the house and seal them. Then she told the maids attached to the house to leave, shut down the main wing of the house, and settled in the servants' quarters, keeping only the ladies-in-waiting—the three who had left the palace, risking their lives.

The queen said to them: "You once belonged to the palace; it would be presumptuous of me to keep you in my service. You must return to the palace."

But they replied: "All our lives, we will never be able to repay you. How could we think of leaving you? We will follow you, even to death."

Moved, she allowed them to remain. With many rooms sealed off, the large house seemed desolate to those who had been accustomed to the pomp and splendor of the palace. The ladies found it difficult to bear the sadness and disappointment, but they served the queen sincerely, and seeing her inborn virtue and modesty, they never betrayed their sorrow.

When the queen's relatives called, she declined to see them. . . . She ordered the windows and four walls of the servants' quarters papered, and the grass on the hillside and in the garden cut. But in time the grass grew tall in the unweeded garden,[19] and at night the house was visited by ghosts and evil spirits. Frightened, the ladies tried to keep still. One day a stray dog wandered into the garden. The ladies wanted to chase it away, but it would not leave.

The queen said, "We don't know where it came from, but it refuses to go away. Its behavior is strange. Let it stay."

After some ten days, the dog gave birth to three healthy puppies, and the four of them would bark at the elf fire, causing the goblins to flee. Even animals know how to help; the wicked people in the palace who rejoiced at the queen's expulsion—were they not less worthy than these beasts?

The queen was by nature upright and unshakable, but she feared the wind and rain when it was accompanied by thunder, and she would escape indoors. To alleviate the tedium, she turned her attention to her brother's seven-year-old daughter and began to teach her the

19. Weeds, symbols of vices of human nature or disorder in humanity.

Elementary Learning[20] and *Lives of Chaste Women,*[21] along with weaving and sewing. The measure of her days was ignoble and humiliating, and her life seemed dreary, but she never blamed either people or ghosts. She was composed, and those around her submitted willingly. As the end of the three-year mourning period for her father drew near, her unassuaged grief had already weakened her health.

When the mourning period ended, her stepmother sent her colored dresses, but she declined: "How can an offender wear colored dresses? I will make my clothes, quilt, and pillow with cotton." She continued to wear white cotton garments and refused all personal ornaments, jewelry, and delicacies.

Earlier, after the queen's expulsion, the king had formally invested Lady Chang as queen (1690). When she gave her first audience, there were no upright officials in attendance. The court missed the deposed queen and was indignant at Lady Chang's vanity and cunning. But in the absence of loyal subjects, who would speak out? Lady Chang had the king name her father Great Lord Oksan, and her brother Chang Hŭijae became head of the military training administration. Deplorable affairs of state, lack of discipline, and loss of trust—the public was confused and rumors were rampant. Even the wisest rulers may become prey to slander. King Sukchong, proficient in arms and letters, should not have been deceived by Lady Chang, and he risked the honor of the dynasty. In the following year, *kyŏngo* (1690), Lady Chang's son was invested as crown prince. This increased the lady's haughtiness, and she dominated the palace with her insolence, reviling and severely punishing the court ladies. She was foul-mouthed and her overweening behavior defied description. Her brother too was treacherous and corrupt, the cause of disturbances in eight provinces, but no one dared say a word.

20. *Xiaoxue* by Zhu Xi.

21. *Lienu Zhuan* by Liu Xiang (c. 18 BCE). See Mair, *Columbia History of Chinese Literature,* 197–198.

Three or four years passed this way. After joy come tears, no gains without pains. The will of heaven changed; the clouds cleared and the sun began to shine again.[22] The king began to understand the error of his ways and realized the injustice that had been done to Queen Min and the wickedness of Lady Chang. He was filled with remorse, and his appearance changed. When small men and thick-skinned toadies appealed day after day to punish Queen Min's cousins and nephews, the king did not listen. Thus the Min clan survived. Lady Chang sensed this change of heart in the king and became terrified. She schemed with her brother to revive the 1680 conspiracy and purge,[23] and they began to murder the upright while plotting to poison Queen Min. The king saw through these evil plots and reversed the course of the conspiracy. He removed the treacherous officials and reinstated the loyal ones.

In the third month of the same year (1694), a messenger in the palace service went to observe Queen Min's house three times. On the ninth day of the fourth month (May 2), the king issued a memorandum to make the queen's innocence known, ordered her transferal to a separate palace, and dispatched a lady-in-waiting accompanied by a eunuch to transmit his own letter to her.

The queen declined to receive them: "How can an offender meet anyone from outside to receive a royal message?" and ordered the servants not to open the gate. For three days the messengers waited outside, but the queen did not relent. They returned to report her modesty to the king, and the king praised her reticence but was disquieted. He next sent an official from the Ministry of Rites, but to no avail. Another group comprising a royal secretary in addition to an official

---

22. In the king-sun metaphor, evil officials at court are the clouds that block the sunlight.

23. The Westerners' accusation that the Southerners plotted to enthrone Prince Poksŏn (d. 1680), King Sŏnjo's grandson and Prince Inp'yŏng's son. He was accused of rebellion and ordered to commit suicide. Chang perhaps tried to dig up dirt on the Westerners in order to impeach and exile them.

from the Ministry of Rites conveyed a message explaining the protocol to her, but again without success.

Then the king sent a stern message to the Min family: "This obstinate refusal can be construed as a personal reproach to the king. Open the gate at once!" The family submitted this message to the queen and urged her to comply, also to no avail. Several days later, the king dispatched another high official to ask that the gate be opened. He explained that it was not right for her not to open it.

At last the queen transmitted her reply through a lady-in-waiting: "This offender was only able to preserve her life through royal favor. Indeed, she is deeply grateful. But how can she now receive visitors and a royal command? The repeated requests make her uneasy."

Deeply troubled, the king issued another stern message to the Min clan, and Minister Min went to implore the queen. Finally she had the front gate unbarred, but it was not until the twenty-first of the fourth month that all the gates were opened. Those who entered now saw grass as tall as humans engulfing the garden. Workers were immediately sent to cut the grass, by royal command. Then messengers were perplexed to see stepping-stones hidden by moss, and windows indistinguishable from the walls. While officials shed tears, soldiers moved into the outer hall, which was repaired. The desolate house at once became livelier. The ladies-in-waiting, peering out through chinks in the windows, felt their sadness turn to joy in quick succession. The queen alone, without any sign of satisfaction in her words or countenance, felt uneasy.

Now that the outer gate was open, a line of family sedan chairs streamed into the house. The king sent four ladies-in-waiting bearing his personal letter, and messengers came one after another to urge the queen to accept the letter, but the queen did not open the middle gate for half a day. Only when the Min family pleaded that her actions were being interpreted as irreverence to the state did the queen concede and open the middle gate. Kowtowing at the foot of the steps, the court ladies were struck by the queen's emaciated appearance and lowly attire when they looked up, and they wept in spite of themselves. The queen pretended not to notice them. When they offered up the royal letter, she bowed four times, facing north. Then, after a moment, she opened it. The letter was filled with expressions of remorse and apologies for past injustices and asked her to return to the palace.

After reading, she sat in silence. One of the ladies-in-waiting, falling on her knees before the queen, said: "His Majesty ordered us to bring back your reply. I beg you to favor us with it." The queen, after a long pause, replied: "Return to the palace and report that the offending woman dares not submit a reply." Helpless, they returned to the palace and reported the queen's words. Filled with renewed anxiety, the king now regretted his past deeds. On the following morning, he decided to send another letter together with gifts of clothing, bedding, and tableware. The ladies-in-waiting carried out his order but wept, recalling the past. Receiving them, the queen was neither pleased nor inconsiderate. Her mind resembled the surface of a broad, deep body of water, without change.

The ladies-in-waiting explained: "His Majesty received us yesterday and asked if you had proper dinnerware; we answered that you did not. He replied, 'I may have been in the wrong, but it was the anger of the moment that caused my mistake.' He was displeased, and added, 'How careless of you to allow her household to remain so unprovided.' Then he ordered us to prepare these articles right away.

"But the Palace Supply Office said, 'We can prepare clothing and bedding, but the tableware cannot be made in time.' So the king ordered them to send the set that had been prepared for royal visits to the ancestral tombs. Then he inspected each item personally, complaining about the slowness in preparing bedding. He approved the new bedding and the pillow with embroidered lovebirds. One skirt in blue silk had to be remade because its color was somber, and he examined it himself before his meal."

With a short bow, the queen said: "I am deeply grateful for the royal favor, but presents that properly belong to the palace cannot be kept in a private residence. I dare not accept them. Please take them back."

When the ladies-in-waiting related what had happened, the king was moved by the queen's propriety and wrote another letter with comforting words. He also pointed out that her correctness could be read as a reproach, even a resentful one, to expose his mistake. He sent the presents back and warned the messenger: "You will be punished if you fail in your mission." Knowing what the king intended by sending the presents back, the queen put the letter away unopened and unanswered. But after the repeated entreaties of the court ladies and her family members, she read the letter and wrote a reply of five or six lines, full of gentle and courteous words, blaming herself for what had happened. Greatly moved, and especially because the twenty-third day of the fourth month was the queen's birthday, the king sent a reply with gifts of food and ordered the palace worthies to offer their tributes to her. With her glory being proclaimed in all quarters, the Min clan shed grateful tears and the people in the capital rejoiced.

But the queen was again resistant and declined the honors: "How can an offender in a private dwelling accept these tributes?"

Despite the efforts of the king and his officials to persuade her, she remained firmly set against receiving the admiration of the people. During that time a eunuch sent by the king and the palace officials to guard the house asked to inspect visitors, but the queen ordered him not to do so and freely welcomed her relatives without partiality.

An auspicious day—the twenty-seventh of the fourth month (May 20, 1694)—was chosen for the queen's return by the royal observatory. The king dispatched a eunuch official to inform her.

Surprised, the queen said: "The royal favor has enabled me to look at the sun and meet my family members. But how could I dare to enter the palace and present myself before His Majesty?" She declined and did not accept the presents.

Again the king sent a stern message to the Min family and ordered a senior official to admonish her. He sent four or five letters urging her to make up her mind—he thought it was her gentle nature that kept her from deciding. Reluctantly she once again put on royal robes. Her brother's daughter, whom she had taken in at age seven, had turned twelve and could not control her sobbing. All those present tried to console her, but their tears flowed as well. "Give me one of our sedan chairs," said the queen. The eunuch and her family members urged her to acquiesce, saying, "The king will not be pleased." So she finally stepped into a royal sedan chair. . . .

Meanwhile, at the palace the king personally inspected all her toiletries, including the comb box. When the sedan chair entered the palace gate, the king ordered a court lady to have the queen dismount at the balcony. When the court lady informed the queen that His Majesty was present, the queen said: "How can an offender dare to face the royal countenance?" By this time the king was approaching the chair. When he saw the queen's hesitation, he opened the door himself, lifted the beaded curtain, and used his fan to waft a puff of air into the compartment. The queen dismounted and prostrated herself on the balcony. The king felt the tension and ordered the court lady to lead the queen to her quarters. Refusing to sit on the royal cushion, the queen prostrated herself. As her mind took in the past and present, with mixed feelings of joy and sorrow, a fine mist rose over her eyebrows and unbidden tears glistened in the brilliance of her eyes. . . .

Recalling the past, the king could not control his feelings of remorse. Nobody present dared to look up.

At that time, the crown prince (b. 1688) was six but seemed almost like a young man. He bowed four times before the queen and sat before her. The queen noticed how big he was for his age. She held his hands in hers and breathed a deep sigh.

The king sat close to the queen and made amends for his past injustices in words sincere enough to melt even gold or stone. Far from being haughty or complacent, the queen was gentle and sincere; the king was filled with admiration, and the attendants were moved.

After her return to the palace, the queen's mental and physical condition were such that she touched no food. At meals the king ate but the queen did not.

When the king asked the lady-in-waiting how the queen was doing, she answered: "Her Majesty has not been well since her return to the palace and has eaten nothing." Alarmed, the king himself put a spoon in her hand and urged her to eat. Touched by his kindness, the queen tried to comply but was too weak to eat more than two spoonfuls. In those circumstances, how could she keep her health?

It was Lady Chang who had usurped the queen's position, and she believed that she would enjoy it forever. But when the king abruptly changed his mind and restored Queen Min, the change struck Lady Chang like a lightning bolt—she felt as if she were falling headlong over an ice-covered chasm. The fluctuation in her emotions made her heart jump like a cage of frolicking monkeys. Unable to control her wrath, she had one of the ladies-in-waiting deliver a message to Queen Min: "Officially I am still the queen. Why does the deposed queen not send her regards to me? Her conduct is impudent." Queen Min was speechless when she heard this message and ignored it. The king, who greatly repented his past injustices, was present when the message was delivered, and he was offended by Lady Chang's audacity. The king ordered the royal secretary to effect the reinstatement of Queen Min and to posthumously honor Great Lord Min with his former office. He also had the second state counselor Min Chŏngjung (1628–1692, the queen's uncle), who had died in exile in South P'yŏngan province, reinstated in his former position, and he destroyed the eulogy given to Lady Chang when she was invested and ordered her father to be removed from office and her brother to be confined in the place of exile.

"Evict Lady Chang and move her to lesser quarters!" came the royal order, and a court lady and eunuch were sent to tell her to hurry.

Lady Chang screamed at them, snarling: "I am still the mother of the people and of the prince. How dare you be so rude! I *will* receive the deposed queen's bow!" Hearing this, the angry king hastened to her chamber as Lady Chang was sitting down to dinner. The moment she saw him, her face turned blue and she said: "I am still the queen. Why does the deposed queen not pay her respects to me, and for what crime have you ordered me to leave?"

"What makes you think you should receive kind regards, or even retain your position?" replied the king.

Lady Chang overturned the dinner table, with food flying all over the room. "I am the mother of the prince, and that justifies keeping my position. I insist that I will receive Lady Min's bow."

In a towering rage, the king shouted: "Drag her out of here!" A lady-in-waiting carried Chang on her back to another building while the disparagement of Queen Min continued. The king was ready to expel her on the spot but decided to be discreet for the sake of the prince.

A favorable day was chosen for enthroning the queen. Three times she tried to decline the honor, but finally she put on the ceremonial robe and, facing south, acceded to queenship. Descending from the platform, she bowed to the king to express her gratitude. The dignity of her performance was a model of decorum twice over. The happy king led the queen to the throne to sit with him side by side. There he received the homage offered by the court and by the ladies-in-waiting. Harmonious breezes blew and auspicious clouds enfolded the palace wherein the people rejoiced, and every subject submitted willingly.

By nature strict and understated, the king exiled those ladies who had behaved badly and gave stipends to those who had followed Queen Min so that they could spend the remainder of their lives in peace and comfort, to the envy of other ladies in the palace. The officials who had been exiled because they resisted the king's decision to dethrone the queen were recalled by courier and promoted in recognition of their loyalty. Those who had died in exile were posthumously honored, and private academies were built where memorial rites could be offered in spring and fall. The king also praised their deeds so that their names would be transmitted to posterity, granted offices to their sons and grandsons as well as pensions for life for their families, and contacted them himself with messages in his own writing. The whole country expressed its heartfelt thanks for his justice and generosity.

Although Lady Chang was impudent and wicked, the king allowed her to remain a royal concubine with privileges second to those of the queen so that the prince should not suffer humiliation. Assigned to Ch'wisŏn Hall in the Yŏngsuk Palace, she would have been grateful for this royal consideration had she been capable of appreciating normal decency, but that was not in her nature. She blamed all her misfortune on the queen and persisted in abusing her in offensive language. In her fits of anger, she would beat her own son every time she saw him, and he eventually became impotent and an invalid. The king had no choice but to forbid the prince to go to his mother's chambers. The boy would ask the king tearfully: "Why am I not allowed to see my own mother?" The king comforted him but made sure that he would live with the queen in the inner palace. The queen was so fond of the prince that in time he forgot his real mother.

Lady Chang had been using the prince for her own advantage all along, but now she had lost him. The king never visited her quarters, and few in the palace pitied her. Although she was allowed to remain in the palace, her predicament was actually much worse than that of Queen Min when she was sent home. Queen Min had suffered hardships, to be sure, but the whole nation grieved for her, and her name shone forth. On her restoration the entire nation rejoiced, and the members of the Min family enjoyed both royal favor and the respect of the people. By contrast, no one sympathized with Lady Chang; they only sneered at her. When she wandered around the inner palace at night, she would hear the happy sounds of family life through the windows. As she stood listening, hearing the voices of the king, the queen, and the crown prince, she would boil with the desire for vengeance. She understood that the members of the Min family now enjoyed royal favor and the respect of the people, but there was no one who pitied her and her exiled brother on Cheju Island. Whatever she saw and heard made her furious; she was consumed with malevolent wishes. What did the future hold for her? No one could know. She decided on a plan, squandering the wealth she had hoarded while she was queen. But Queen Min was cautious enough to assign to kitchen duty only those whom she could trust, so Lady Chang's repeated attempts to bribe a lady-in-waiting to poison the queen went for naught.

Then she resorted to sorcery—her scheming had no end. If only she had stayed submissive and relied on the generosity of Queen Min, she could have shared in the power of the prince while enjoying the comfort and splendor of the palace. After all, she was the mother of the crown prince. But her insatiable lust for power was such that she entertained even more heinous and atrocious ideas—high treason. How horrible the retribution for her scheme!

In the year *pyŏngja* (1696), the crown prince turned eight. A capping ceremony was held and arrangements were made for the selection of his bride. The king and queen screened the candidates and chose a daughter of Sim Ho of Ch'ŏngsong. The wedding ceremony was held, and Lady Sim became crown princess. . . .

Lady Chang was irredeemably wicked. Intent on vengeance, she set up a shrine west of the Yŏngsuk Palace, recruited shamans and adepts,[24] and put up demonic effigies dressed in colored silk. The queen's family name and the hour and date of her birth were written on a piece of paper, along with prayers for her death; the queen's likeness had also been painted and hung on the wall, and Lady Chang's maids had been instructed to shoot arrows at it three times a day. When the portrait was finally punctured, she dressed it in silk, saying it was the queen's corpse, and buried it by the lake. This ritual went

24. In the original, *sulsa:* strategists, conjurers, necromancers?

on for three years, but the queen's health remained steady like a rock. Disheartened, Lady Chang decided to enlist the aid of Sukchŏng, her brother's wife. Birds of a feather flock together. They procured a human skeleton, dressed it in colored silk, and buried it under the stairs on the north side of the inner palace. They pulverized another skeleton and put the powder inside a padded dress and presented it to the queen. When the queen declined to accept it, they could only continue to throw up prayers at their shrine while devising a string of other blasphemies. It is said that evil cannot violate the just and that vileness cannot outdo virtue.[25]

The queen's life span was fated to be brief and she fell victim to a calamity brought by an evil spirit. In the fall of the year *kyŏngjin* (1700), the queen was suddenly taken ill with a strange sickness: a physical debility aggravated by chills and fever, with pains in the joints at midnight. Her condition being changeable, the king was worried and had Lord Min supervise the medicines used to treat her. The following spring, a yellowish rash kept erupting and disappearing, and physicians could not diagnose her symptoms. The king was afraid that the hardships she had endured during her exile, for which he was responsible, might be the cause of her illness. To ease his conscience, the queen pretended to feel well. When Lady Chang came to know of the queen's illness, she rejoiced secretly but thought that it was only luck, and persisted in her evil intrigues. The twenty-third of the fourth month was the queen's birthday. The king issued orders to prepare a great feast in her honor and to invite all the women of the Min family. The queen was reluctant, but the king insisted.

On her birthday, all the women of the Min family came, but they were concerned about the queen's sickly appearance.

---

25. At this point the narrator (or someone else) inserts the following: "Sun Bin and Pang Quan studied under the same teacher, but Pang, jealous of Sun's brilliance and superior strategy, had his feet cut off. When Sun's forces encircled Pang's army, Pang committed suicide. Sun was victorious." Its relevance here is unclear. *Shiji* 65:2162.

With tears in her eyes, the queen confided: "Without talent and virtue, I have been unable to repay the royal favor. Lately my mind is dim, and I feel as though I were surrounded by clouds and mist. I suspect that the end of my days is near. My only regret is that I have caused the king to worry. If it comes, it may not be easy to contact my family members. I beg you to teach your children to accumulate virtue. You must always invoke a blessing on them, so that they will prosper." The queen gave way to tears when she had finished speaking, and the ladies present wept together.

One lady thought: "Your Highness is still young and will surely recover from this little illness. Why must you give us these instructions?" Then they all left. The queen let out a long sigh as she saw them off, and the ladies continued to weep in their sedan chairs.

The princesses and royal concubines presented dresses to the queen on her birthday. Though she preferred to decline, their insistence made it impossible for her to refuse without hurting their feelings. But when Lady Chang presented a dress, the queen refused it. The crown prince, who happened to be present, appealed to her to accept the dress. How unfortunate! How could one know of the evil present in the accursed gift? Had the crown prince been aware of its true purpose, he would never have concealed his mother's scheme. The queen did not wear the dress, but she kept it in her room, where its malign influence could spread, and at night death was present in the air. In the fifth month her illness became worse, and she was no longer able to leave her bed. The best physicians were called in, at the king's insistence, and the Min brothers supervised her treatments and stayed with her. Whenever she saw them, she wept.

Admonishing her brothers and her nephew, she said tearfully: "I am concerned about your position and your reputation. You must always maintain your father's rectitude, and you must endeavor to serve the king loyally and to preserve your lives." The cause of her suffering was not a physical illness: the poison in evil imprecations cannot be cured by medicine. During the day she was well, but every night she ran a fever and babbled in delirium. No one could identify her illness from these symptoms.

In the seventh month, her condition became critical in the mornings and evenings. The entire court, including the crown prince, prayed to heaven and the northern constellation. But her health continued to decline, and she was unable to eat and sleep. The king, who now went without food and sleep while seeing to her every need, looked exhausted, and this weighed heavily on the queen's mind. Feeling that death was near, she stopped taking all medicines and refused to receive her female physicians. The king hurried to her room to persuade her to continue the treatment and held out the medicine to her himself. At the least, he was able to induce her to take some thin gruel.

In a day or two, the queen asked the ladies-in-waiting in charge of her medicine to come to her room. "I know I shall not live much longer and do not know how to repay you for your loyal service. When the three years of mourning are over, you will all return home to live happily with your families. Let's promise to meet again in the Nine Springs."[26]

The queen ordered them to clean the inner palace and light some incense. Then she washed her face, changed into new clothes, and sent for the king.

The king inquired: "Why aren't you taking care of yourself?"

"By your favor," she replied, "I have enjoyed the august position and glory of being your queen. However, I've not given you an heir, nor have I repaid even a hundredth of the favors you have bestowed on me. These are my regrets at this moment when death seems so near, and I shall not forget them even in the Nine Springs. Do not grieve because of my early death, Your Majesty; you must enjoy a long happy life."

"How can you say such dreadful things?" The king's words faltered. He wept and could not continue.

---

26. Hades.

How could the queen, even when her spirit was confused, not know of the king's sorrow?

"I pray Your Majesty will preserve your health, and please allow the one who departs to peacefully go."

Then she called into the room the crown prince and princess, together with the young prince and the royal concubines, and said: "By His Majesty's favor I have had the inestimable honor of being enthroned as queen again after five years of hardship. I had hoped to fill my remaining years with the loyalty and devotion of the crown prince and the young prince, but today I know that I must depart from this life. Please live long lives, devoted to His Majesty's service."

She held Prince Yŏning's[27] hand. "This child is exceptional and sagacious. I regret that I shall not be able to see him grow up."

Then she asked for her brothers and nephew. Overwhelmed by sorrow, they could not speak. The king had witnessed all this and his heart sank. Then he held up some thin gruel, offering it to the queen, who took two sips, breathing heavily. The king lifted her body, adjusted her pillow, and settled her down again. In a moment, she passed away in the Kyŏngch'un Hall in the Ch'anggyŏng Palace. It was the autumn of the year *sinsa,* the fourteenth day of the eighth month (September 16, 1701), at the hour of the snake (9–11 a.m.), in the sixth year after her return as queen. She was thirty-four. Her posthumous epithet was Inhyŏn (Manifesting Perfect Virtue), and her tomb, in Koyang, was called Myŏngnŭng. The memorial hall was named Kyŏngyŏn Hall.

The funeral was held on the eighth day of the twelfth month (January 5, 1702). The king directed that after his death he would be buried beside her.

The story continues. On the seventh day of the ninth month (October 8, 1701), the autumn air was chilly and the waxing moon faint. The

27. In his maturity, King Yŏngjo.

king shed silent tears as he watched the candle burn away. For a brief moment leaning against a cushion, he dozed off, and in a dream he beheld a deceased eunuch from the court, who said to him: "Wicked and abhorrent spirits are plaguing the palace. The death of the queen was their doing. They will beget great calamities in the future. Please, Your Majesty, be careful." The eunuch pointed toward Ch'wisŏn Hall and motioned to the king to follow him. It was where the queen's tablet was enshrined. In the upper part of the hall, the queen was sitting with her ladies-in-waiting.

Her face pallid, she broke into sobs, and said, "Mine might have been a short life even without the workings of evil spirits, but Lady Chang's evil incantations were the cause of my affliction. She is a mortal enemy, and my spirit grieves while harboring resentment. I could destroy her myself, but hope that you will look into this and settle the matter so that peace within the palace can be restored."

The king was clutching after her gown when he awoke—it was an empty dream.[28] The candle flames were iridescent, and eunuchs were in attendance outside. The king moaned and asked the time. It was the first watch (7–9 p.m.). The king quietly ordered a sedan chair to take him to Lady Chang's quarters. It was his first visit in six or seven years. Could anyone expect him unannounced?

That day was Lady Chang's birthday. Sukchŏng (her sister-in-law) and her followers congratulated her on the queen's demise, each claiming credit for the role she had played. Shamans and necromancers were chanting in front of a shrine. The sudden appearance of the king caused great confusion and consternation. He had overheard their words and he now examined their faces. Thinking his visit meant the restoration of their lady to favor, the maids ordered that food be brought, but the king spurned it. He noticed that the shrine in the yard,

28. Refers to Li Gongzuo (c. 770–848). "The Story of the Prefect of South Branch" concerns the ultimate vanity of striving for worldly fame and fortune. The dream world was identified as an ant colony beneath the south bough of a nearby locust tree.

which had been brightly lit a moment ago, was now dark. He stepped outside and on the opposite side of the yard found a folding screen. He ordered it to be removed. The maid hesitated but was obliged to remove it, revealing a portrait pasted on the wall. Careful examination confirmed that it was a picture of Queen Min. Countless arrow holes had left the portrait in tatters.

"What is this?" the king inquired.

When no one dared answer, Lady Chang spoke: "I had it put up so that I could admire her virtues."

In a rage the king said: "Then explain the arrow holes!" Chang had no answer. The king ordered a eunuch to light the way and proceeded to the shrine. It was indeed evil. Aghast, the king called the servants to seize and bind all who were present.

"I thought all along that you might be fomenting evil. Now here is the evidence. You will all die immediately unless you confess everything!" How could anything be hidden? When the guards began to beat them, they spat out all the hideous details of their abominable scheme.

With his flesh crawling and his hair on end, the king said: "Rearing a tiger will only cause calamity. I should have expelled Lady Chang long ago, but I kept her in the palace, inviting this monstrous end. This story must not spread."

He ordered the guilty to be held in the state tribunal and interrogated them himself the following day. Then he went to the outer palace but was unable to sleep all night. The next day he issued a decree, describing how the queen had died before her time. He did not omit Lady Chang's treason and evil scheme. Chang Hŭijae was brought back to Seoul from his exile on Cheju Island for a royal inquisition. Ch'unsang and Ch'ŏrhyang of the palace supply office were put in prison and beheaded at the Injŏng Gate. Yun Inji, the royal secretary, ventured to suggest that even though her treason was grave, Lady Chang's punishment might be reduced for the sake of the crown prince.

The king angrily replied: "It was for the sake of the crown prince that I let her remain in the palace. Yet she built a malignant shrine on the palace grounds and plotted against the queen, casting evil spells. I have opened an inquiry into this matter so that justice can be done to appease the queen's spirit. Is it at all proper for a subject to try to shield the very criminal who brought about the queen's death? Let Yun be stripped of his title, and banish him from the capital!"

Three flogs with a club made Ch'ŏrhyang confess that the shamans and adepts had been gathered and the construction of the shrine begun in 1695. The shooting and burying of the queen's portrait had started at about the same time. She gave a detailed account and ended by saying that was all she knew, because Sihyang and others had been responsible for other actions.

Accordingly, Sihyang, then twenty-two, confessed: "At first I acted as a messenger between Lady Chang and Sukchŏng. The only thing I witnessed then was Lady Chang's pleasure in receiving letters from her. Then she moved into the palace to live with the lady. They often ordered Ch'ŏrhyang and me to follow them at night with a basketful of something that they buried on the left side of the lake, and something else in small sealed packets under the steps of Sangch'un Pavilion. What they buried beside the lake was placed under the north wall of the queen's residence. Once I overheard Ch'wiyŏng reporting to the lady that the work was finished. To this the lady said, 'Do Siyŏng and Ch'ŏrhyang know what we have been doing?' Ch'wiyŏng replied, 'We did everything together, so they must know. They're faithful and it's better not to deceive them.' I was never let in on the secret, but there was some plot between the two women."

Then Siyŏng, a woman of forty, was questioned. Although crafty, she was forced to tell the truth: "We wrapped a skeleton in silk cloth of five colors and buried it with a piece of paper with the queen's name and birth date on it. We also prepared a dress with a cotton lining dusted with pulverized human bones as a present for the queen on her birthday. The queen declined it the first year. The following year she declined again, but at the repeated entreaties of the crown prince, she finally accepted it. The actual wording of the curse was prepared by Sukchŏng."

Then Sukchŏng was interrogated together with the shamans and necromancers. "We were originally in the service of Chang Hŭijae while he was in office," said a shaman. "And when he was exiled he gave us a large quantity of silver, asking us to help the lady when the need arose. Thus out of ignorance and greed we came to be involved in this treasonous crime. Lady Chang often asked me to make children's clothes for her and sent precious gifts in return, so it became my habit to comply. Once Lady Chang sent me a letter saying she was not feeling well. She said the building where she resided often rocked at night, and for that reason she felt the need to have a shamanic rite performed to exorcise its evil spirits. That's how I came to move into the palace with the other shamans. The lady confided to me her secret wish to kill the queen with evil spells, and I was forced to take part. I prepared the cursed dress, but the skeleton was obtained by my husband's former steward, Ch'ŏlmyŏng."

Ch'ŏlmyŏng was arrested, and he confessed that there was a blood pledge between himself and Hŭijae. While Hŭijae was in exile, Ch'ŏlmyŏng had been asked to help Lady Chang. Because of his oath to Hŭijae, he had searched all the provinces to obtain skeletons.

When the interrogators excavated the spot, the skeleton was found; and the cotton lining ripped out of the queen's dress shed bluish powder when it was shaken. With a deep sigh, the king remarked: "I cannot blame anyone, for the seed of this calamity was sown by me. How can I face the queen when we meet in the Nine Springs?"

A dozen evildoers were beheaded at the armory that day, and about the same number of ladies-in-waiting and servants were exiled to distant places. The king said: "Murdering a queen by calling down evil upon her is a treasonous crime. Perhaps even more serious is the crime of those high-ranking officials who have in the name of propriety counseled me against presiding over the inquisition. I have decided they must be punished, for their presence in my court will only invite graver calamities to come." All were deprived of rank and title and relieved of their offices; some were exiled.

Meanwhile, the king's blood boiled with rage against Lady Chang, who had been confined to her room. Had it not been for his concern for the crown prince, he would have had her killed instantly. He said: "She deserves the severest form of execution, but I will mitigate the punishment to save the crown prince from humiliation. Let her die by taking poison—that way her body will not be scarred at death."

Thereupon a lady-in-waiting went to Lady Chang's room. She took a bowl of poison and a royal message: "The magnitude of your crime has been disclosed, so you should have chosen to end your own life. But you still have not done so, hoping to evade your certain death. This makes you even more abominable in my sight. To save the crown prince from disgrace, I will mitigate your punishment and allow you to die peacefully. Take this poison and leave this world at once."

Lady Chang showed no sign of repentance. Rather, she had savored the queen's death and trusted in the power her capacity as mother of the prince gave her. Now the bowl of poison made her fly into a rage, and she screamed wildly: "What have I done to deserve poison? If you must kill me, kill the crown prince first." She threw the bowl into a corner of the room. Panic stricken, the lady-in-waiting fled back to the outer palace and reported to the king what had happened.

The infuriated king said: "Although I long to see her die, I did not think I could bear the sight of her evil face, so I sent the poison. She should not have resisted, and is only making more trouble trying to shelter behind the crown prince. This makes her crime even worse. Now take another bowl of poison and tell her to drink it. It is the last favor I shall grant her."

When Chang heard the royal command, she stamped on the ground, screaming: "Lady Min died young because it was her destiny!

By uniting against me, you may kill me now, but do you expect to be safe when my son succeeds to the throne?" She continued to shout abuses and again dashed the bowl to the ground. When this was reported, the king ordered a sedan chair and went to Chang's residence. He made her sit on the ground and roared: "Your crime against the throne warrants the most extreme form of execution. After I kill you, I will have your limbs cut off and exposed to public view! Yet, for the sake of the crown prince, I have been willing to favor you with the mildest form of death. Do you still dare to disobey my command and multiply your wrongdoings?"

Looking right back at the king, Chang protested in a shrill voice: "Lady Min's death was nothing but retribution for the wrongs she had done to me. In what way am I responsible? You abuse the power given to you as king by doing this."

Turning back his sleeves, the king raged: "What wickedness! Make her drink the poison!"

Chang kicked and lashed at the ladies-in-waiting who came to her with the bowl, screaming: "I am innocent! I will die with the crown prince!"

The king would have none of it and commanded that she be forced to drink the poison. When the ladies-in-waiting grabbed her arms and waist, she flew into a frenzy, refusing to open her mouth. In a fit of passion, the king ordered the ladies-in-waiting to pry her mouth open with a stick. Chang's attitude changed suddenly. In a panic, she began to entreat the king for mercy. "Think not of my crime, but of the love that existed between us. That and the crown prince—are they not reason enough to spare my life?"

The king refused to listen. With tears streaming down her face, she implored: "I'll drink the poison if you insist, but before I die, grant me a final wish. Let me have one last audience with the crown prince." These words were spoken in a tone so pitiful that the onlookers were touched in spite of themselves. The king, however, remained firm.

Finally, three bowls of poison were poured into her mouth. She screamed and fell down at the foot of the steps, dark blood streaming out from the seven apertures of her head.[29] Normally, one bowl is potent enough to cause death; three bowls killed her instantly. She had begun as a lowly maid at court and risen to a prominent position enjoying great honor and glory; but she overreached with an insatiable need to bring about the death of the queen. As a result, many were executed.

Glancing at the body before he rode away to the outer palace, the king said: "Get it out of the palace at once."

The following day, the king sent this command: "Although her crime was wicked in the extreme and treasonous, we must give her a proper funeral to save the crown prince from humiliation."

Did anyone mourn the death of Lady Chang? Her body decayed overnight, giving out a putrid odor that was taken as a sign of heavenly justice.

About the same time, Chang Hŭijae, Lady Chang's brother, was executed and his body torn to pieces and exposed at the execution site. The citizens of the capital came to see the sight and believed that he had at last been given his due. Greed and ambition were the causes of his fall. Is not his end a lesson for us all?

In the twelfth month of the year *sinsa* (1702), Queen Min's funeral took place.

The ministers of course urged the king to find a new consort. Although he would not hear of it at first, he reluctantly agreed, and in 1702 the daughter of Kim Chusin (1661–1721) was chosen.

On the eighth day of the sixth month (July 12, 1720), at the hour of the hare (5–7 a.m.), King Sukchong passed away in the Yungbok Hall of the Kyŏnghŭi Palace. It was the forty-sixth year of his reign, and he was fifty-nine. The crown prince succeeded to the throne. The new king was heirless, so his younger brother, Prince Yŏning, was

29. Eyes, nostrils, ears, and mouth.

made crown prince. The king, known as Kyŏngjong (1688–1724), died in the fifth year of his reign. He was thirty-six. Prince Yŏning (1694–1776), known by his temple name, Yŏngjo, succeeded in the same year.

More than anyone else, Yŏngjo realized the extent of his debt to his father, Sukchong. Above all, he never forgot the affection he had received as a child from Queen Inhyŏn. Soon after his enthronement, he visited the mansion in Anguk-tong where the queen had borne five years of hardship and cried aloud in grief. He then put up a plaque inscribed with his own calligraphy: "Kamgodang, Hall of Reminiscence." He also visited Min Yujung's brother's (Min Chŏngjung) home in Surekkol, where the queen was born. To this day the family has not sold this house.

The virtues of Queens Tairen and Taisu of the Zhou shine forever in the history of China. In our dynasty of Chosŏn, the august virtue of Queen Inhyŏn is the greatest. How beautiful! How admirable!

THE REUNION ON MOUNT HWA

[HWASAN CHUNGBONG KI]

"The Mysterious Reunion," or "The Reunion on Mount Hwa," has the characteristics of a detective story or a courtroom drama. The story illustrates both seventeenth-century Korean society and the judicial framework of that time. The plot is similar to that of the classic French story of mistaken identity "Beau Geste," or the British story "Southworthy." In outline, the story goes as follows.

During the reign of King Ch'ungnyŏl (1274–1308) of Koryŏ, the director of the chancellery was Kim Wanguk. He came from an influential family that over many generations had held important positions in the government, and his strength of character and writing skills were unsurpassed. However, a corrupt royal inspector, Yi Inch'ŏl, issued a false indictment against Kim Wanguk, and the king banished him to Cheju Island. Entrusting the management of family affairs to his son, Kim Sujŭng, Wanguk departed for his place of exile. Soon both his son and his wife, Lady Chin, beheld his image in dreams that foretold the news of his death.

Lady Chin and Sujŭng returned to their hometown of Andong. After the three-year mourning period, Sujŭng married Chinju, the daughter of Chang

Chihyŏn, and soon thereafter his mother, Lady Chin, also died. Sujŭng was called "the retired gentleman of the cloud-covered forest" because he rejected all government offices and lived with his wife in seclusion. For that reason, he was esteemed as a man of high values and principles. At the age of forty, Kim Sujŭng and his wife began to regret that they had no children. While the couple was grieving, a monk came by to solicit alms to repair the Haein monastery, and they donated one thousand *yang*. In a dream, Sujŭng was then told by a disciple of the Great Unique[1] that his wife would conceive and have a son of extraordinary talent. They named him Sŏnok. Before reaching age nine, Sŏnok had already acquired an extensive knowledge of the Four Books[2] and the Three Classics[3] and the books of ancient scholars. Also well versed in the martial arts, he had the ambition to become a statesman.

At that time, a judge named Yi Sŏngil resigned from his position and moved back to Kyŏngju. There he and his wife lived a contented life except for the fact that they had no progeny. He too had a dream, in which a servant of the moon goddess informed him that a child would soon be born. His wife then gave birth to a daughter of unsurpassed beauty and grace. They named her Nongok.

Kim Sŏnok and Yi Nongok were married by recommendation of the matchmaker Ch'unim, a good judge of character, and through the arrangement of servants from the two families. After the marriage, Kim Sŏnok followed the advice of his father and went to Anguk monastery to study for the civil service examinations. On one occasion, Sŏnok came down from the mountains to visit his wife, but when his father found out, he prohibited any further contact between them. When Sŏnok came home a second time, he was startled to see the shadow of a man in robes and a scholar's cap on the window of his wife's bedroom. Enraged, he was just able to restrain himself, and full of anguish, he abandoned the path he was on and took up the life of a homeless wanderer.

Kim Sujŭng's face turned pale when he learned of his son's disappearance, and he offered half of his wealth to the person who could find him. It happened that the son of Kim Sujŭng's third cousin was covetous of Sujŭng's possessions, so Kim Hyŏngok went in search of Sŏnok. He looked in every part of the country to no avail. But instead of returning empty-handed, he came back with a man he had found who looked like Sŏnok, named Kim Hŭngnyong. Sujŭng was then in mourning because of a gruesome dream that had conveyed to him the news of his son's death. It was at that juncture that Hyŏngok brought the false Sŏnok home.

Whe Kim Sujŭng and his wife saw him, they were overcome with joy. Only Sŏnok's wife, Nongok, knew he was an imposter, and she refused to share her bed with him. She then applied to the magistracy in an effort to expose the counterfeit

---

1. The supreme being, also known as Great Unity, in Daoism.

2. *Lunyu* (Analects), *Daxue* (Great learning), *Zhong yong* (Doctrine of the mean), and *Mengzi* (Mencius).

3. *Shijing* (Books of songs), *Shujing* (Book of documents), and *Yijing* (Book of changes).

Sŏnok, but the court ruled against her. Kim Sujŭng now rejected his daughter-in-law and disowned her. Judge Yi Sŏngil, in turn, demanded that his daughter, who had been expelled from her husband's house, kill herself. She was able to persuade her parents of her fidelity, however, and appealed to the highly reputed ethics of the Kim family to put the demand aside. Kim Sujŭng tried to quell the uproar by having his son remarry. When a delegate of the court began to make the arrangements, he entreated the king to look into the matter. The king then appointed Chin Yŏnsu, inspector of the eight provinces and an official of the Hallim Academy,[4] to investigate.

As it happened, Chin Yŏnsu was able to find the real Sŏnok in a Buddhist monastery in the Tanch'ŏn area in the northeast and brought him back to Andong, where eventually all the facts were made known. Chin Yŏnsu adopted Nongok as his daughter, and the court sentenced Hŭngnyong and Hyŏngok to a painful death and banished Kim Sujŭng and his son. Nongok was acknowledged as a woman of chastity, and a commemorative gate was erected in her honor. To celebrate the birth of the crown prince, the king then released Kim Sujŭng and Sŏnok from exile.

Kim Sŏnok placed first on the civil service examinations and became a scholar of the Hallim Academy. The king made an official apology for banishing Kim Wanguk and appointed Kim Sujŭng as a minister of state and Kim Sŏnok as minister of war. He later appointed Sŏnok as the commanding general of the southern provinces. Sŏnok led his army against the Japanese invaders and defeated them at the border. General Sŏnok then became director of the chancellery, which brought him glory and wealth. He and his wife died at the age of eighty.

The segment that follows is the courtroom showdown in which Nongok rejects the imposter Sŏnok and the real one is revealed—the story's climactic episode.

Kim Sujŭng honored the orders of the king not to discuss the remarriage of his son, but he was anxious for the king to make a decision. One day it was announced that the royal inspector was coming, and Sujŭng thought, "I was ordered to wait for a royal command regarding Sŏnok's remarriage. Now he is sending the royal inspector to confirm my son's authenticity and order his remarriage."

---

4. The academy members were the kingdom's foremost writers, who did the drafting, editing, and compilation of literary and historical works.

He took Sŏnok to the court and presented his case. The inspector responded, "You, Kim Sujŭng, have already declared this man to be your son. However, I cannot judge between truth and falsehood without listening to both sides. Bring to the court your wife, your son, and your nephew, as well as Yi Nongok, her parents and relatives, and the servants of both houses."

Sujŭng left the court and informed the Yi household of the royal inspector's orders. Judge Yi brought his wife and daughter to the court, and Sujŭng brought his family and their servants. All the people in both families came to the court out of obedience to the royal inspector.

The inspector first asked for Sŏnok and said, "In a moment we will call Nongok and demand an explanation of the allegations that have been brought against you. At that moment, you will go to the veranda, turn and face Lady Yi's sedan chair, and await my command." He then ordered Sŏnok to take an oath.

Turning to Kim Sujŭng, he asked, "Is that man really your son?"

Sujŭng replied, "Could I disguise such a relationship? He is clearly my son."

The inspector then asked Lady Chang the same question, and she answered, "He was in my womb for ten months. I have nurtured him from the time he came into this world, when I wrapped him in his blanket, until now, some twenty years later. How could I be deceived and not know something that has come out of my own body?"

The inspector addressed Hyŏngok, and he replied, "I encountered many hardships while searching for Sŏnok, leaving nothing to chance and not a single mountain or stream unsearched. I do not know how many times I nearly died, but I would rather have died than not found Sŏnok and seen the devastated look on my uncle's face. On my journey, I went up north to the Kyŏnghŭng[5] area, where I found him,

---

5. In North Hamgyŏng, an important base of defense against the Jurchens in the past.

and I brought him back. This is clearly Sŏnok. In addition to all the evidence, his own father calls him his son. How can there be any doubt?"

The inspector asked the false Sŏnok the same question, and he answered, "Could I call a stranger my own father? It is unthinkable."

The inspector spoke, "If you are truly who you say you are, the son of Kim Sujŭng, why did you leave your family, and what caused you to go to Kyŏnghŭng?"

The man who called himself Sŏnok responded, "There was no particular reason I left, and I did not think to consider the distress it would cause my family. Being young, I was bored with studying and went off to explore the world. I just started walking and did not realize that I had gone all the way to Kyŏnghŭng."

The inspector suppressed a chuckle and asked Yi Sŏngil and his wife if they believed Sŏnok was their son-in-law. In response, they answered together: "Indeed, he does look like our son-in-law, but according to what our daughter has to say, he is not."

Then the inspector asked the relatives and servants of both households the same question, and they all replied, "Clearly he is Sŏnok."

Then the inspector called Nongok, and as he watched, Sŏnok went to the veranda, faced Lady Yi's sedan chair, and waited. The inspector said to Nongok: "Your mother-in-law and father-in-law say that he is their son, but you alone say that he is not. You claim that your closeness to your husband is infinite, but how can it surpass the closeness between him and his parents? Your parents also say that he is their son-in-law, but you firmly maintain that he is not. You may be a good judge of character, but can you surpass that of your own parents? Furthermore, you claim to have the ability to perceive this man's true identity, yet you dispute your parents' judgment. They appear to be telling the truth; why do you contradict what they are saying? Everyone in your husband's home, including the servants, is certain that he is your husband. How is it that you are so stubborn as to insist on your own opinion? In the ancient texts it is said that 'the testimony of three people outweighs the testimony of two.' The Kim family and their relatives, the Yi family and their relatives, and the servants of both families amount to over one hundred people. The testimony of over one hundred people cannot be set aside by one person's word alone. You must either be crazy or devising some pernicious scheme. There has been civil unrest in the capital and provinces because of this incident in your family. The king has been troubled and he has asked me, the inspector of the eight provinces, to quickly determine who is the true Kim Sŏnok. If you have any fear of the penalty of death, you will change your testimony and conform to the judgment of these one hundred people. And from this day forth, you will serve him as you did before. Once you do this, you will have made restitution and His Majesty's concern regarding this case will cease. You will not be sentenced to death, and the anger of Sŏnok's parents regarding this situation will be appeased. Love and peace will reign in your relationship like before. Harmony once again will pervade your home, and you will be blessed with sons and daughters. As you grow old with your husband, you will be able to enjoy the riches and honor sent from heaven."

Lady Yi responded: "To be husband and wife means that two people from different families enjoy intimacy, one of the five relationships.[6] Confucius said that the way of a gentleman begins with the relationship between husband and wife.[7] Therefore, this relationship between husband and wife is crucial; it cannot be considered secondary to that between father and son. Even passersby can recognize its unique character. How can a woman who observes the three obediences,[8] remaining faithful to her father in her younger years, to

6. Between father and son, sovereign and subject, husband and wife, elder brother and younger brother, and friends.
7. Love as an inborn moral quality and practice must start in the family.
8. To her father, husband, and eldest son.

her husband when she is married, and to her son when she is older, not know her own husband? That imposter is not my husband. All of you, both sides of the family and the court, say that he is, but I, his widow, stand alone and say that he is not. Not only are you unable to recognize the truth; you say that I must be crazy. As a result I have been cast aside by my own in-laws. Heaven ignites my innermost feelings, and I know that I could not possibly invent such a vicious lie. You say that if I have any fear of death, I must conform, but I will do no such thing. Would this court tell me, an ignorant country girl, that I should sacrifice my honor in order to preserve my life? There is an old saying: 'It is easy for the ruler of a kingdom with ten thousand chariots to plunder, but even he cannot spoil the relationship of an ordinary husband and wife.' And now if you insist on executing me by the king's order, I will submit to it; and if I should die without seeing my husband ever again, no one will take pity on my soul. Even if my husband should return one day, no one here who would know who he is, and he would be condemned to the life of a beggar." Nongok ended her statement by saying that she was ready to be put to death.

Furious at her words, the inspector exclaimed: "How can you, an insane woman with evil intentions who is raising doubts regarding Sŏnok's true identity, dare to abuse the court in such a lowly, vile way? You have upset the king's tranquility by bringing discord and turmoil to the court and to the countryside. For this, you should be hanging by the neck out in the street as a warning to the people. But the king has sent me, out of his mercy and regard for human life, to conduct a thorough investigation. Even when everyone knows of the evil intentions in your heart, the king, out of his great benevolence, says that I should not mete out harsh punishment, because you are not an inanimate object. Even if you are obstinate, I am to reprimand you as if you were my own child."

Then he shouted: "Take her out and continue the interrogation!"

At that moment, another voice shouted out: "Punish that sick woman!"

As the guards began to take her away, Nongok said, "The inspector, who is sent directly from the king, is like a parent to us, and all the court officials are like servants in this house!"

Then she ran back to the court and grasped the person who had spoken out. It was the real Sŏnok, disguised as a servant. "Oh my husband," she cried, "where did you go, and why only now have you come back?" Then she fainted from the shock of seeing him. Nongok's father turned pale with astonishment and ran to where she lay. He quickly ground some medicine and put it to her lips. Rubbing her arms and legs, he wept. Nongok opened her eyes and looked again at her husband. He too had fainted. With her father's help, she began to revive him.

Everyone in the court was bewildered. Sŏnok's mother and father, along with their servants, looked at one another, not knowing what to do. The faces of Hyŏngok and the imposter Sŏnok had turned ashen, and they could not keep from trembling.

The inspector now praised Nongok for her fidelity and devotion. In his heart he admired her sagacity in knowing who the real Sŏnok was. As he walked to the inner court, showing Nongok and Sŏnok the way, he announced his intention to adopt Nongok as his own daughter. Nongok welcomed the relationship, and the inspector now made them sit next to him. He first inquired of Nongok, "How did you know who was real?"

"On one of my husband's front teeth, there is a blue spot the size of a sesame seed," Nongok replied. "Because of that one thing, I knew that the other man was an imposter. Otherwise, my husband looks identical to that villain."

The inspector extolled her cleverness and then said to Sŏnok, "I am adopting your wife as my daughter, which makes you my son-in-law. Now that I have met the two of you, I would like to become better acquainted. First of all, there are still some questions about why you left the monastery. Please tell me why you left so that I can resolve these concerns."

Sŏnok hesitated. Nongok broke in, saying, "When the inspector speaks, it is always true and sincere. Why do you hesitate to answer him?"

Only then did Sŏnok look at his wife and say, "Several years ago, I came down from the monastery. As I approached the house, I saw a shadow cast by a man dressed in robes and a scholar's cap on the bedroom window. I was enraged and wanted to kill you both. But I thought, 'If I do this, there will be a scandal and my family's name will be ruined. I would rather die instead.' So I left immediately and in my despair went to look for Qu Yuan (c. 343–278 BCE)[9] by the riverside, but I could not bring myself to jump into the water. I went back to the monastery, but all the time I was thinking, 'I can never forget the horror of seeing that man through the window in my bedroom. How can I ever enjoy being with my wife again?' I decided to bid farewell to the world and go into hiding. I would spend my days in seclusion. That was a hopeless time. While wandering about, I passed by Mount Cloud and ended up near Tanch'ŏn, in Hamgyŏng province, where I stumbled upon a cloister called Sangwŏn. There I became a student of the Great Master Suun, but then I met you, the royal inspector, and could no longer remain in hiding. How strange it is that we now meet again." Turning back to Nongok, he said, "Now tell me, who was that man in your bedroom?"

Nongok had been weeping throughout his story, and with her clothing soaked in tears, she said, "Does my husband not know my heart? If you had any doubts, why did you not come in that night to see for yourself? The person who was in our room is here at the court today. Would you like to see?"

---

9. A loyal minister of King Huai of Chu, who was rewarded with slander and banishment before drowning himself in the Miluo River. *Shiji* 84:2481–2491; Watson, *Records of the Grand Historian,* 1:499–508, esp. 507.

Nongok called for her maidservant Ongnan in the outer court. When she came, Nongok pointed to her and said, "This is the 'man' who wore your clothes that day."

Puzzled, Sŏnok asked, "Why would she have put on the cap and robes of a scholar?"

Nongok replied, "Do not ask me. Ask Ongnan."

Sŏnok turned to Ongnan: "What clothes were you wearing on that night six years ago?"

Ongnan was speechless for a long time. Finally she explained: "At that time I was just a child, and Lady Yi, who had been making a set of robes, wanted to be sure that all the measurements were correct. She told me to try them on so that she could see how they looked. Being young and foolish, I saw a cap that you had worn to the monastery and sent home; it was hanging on the wall, and I took it down and put it on. I was laughing when I said to her, 'Do I look like your husband?' Lady Yi laughed as well and then told me to take it off at once. So I did, and there has never been another time that I have worn a cap and robe."

Sŏnok realized how foolish he had been. Not trusting in his wife's fidelity, he had believed her to be so much less than what she really was. He wished he could die right then and there, as a sign of the love he felt for Nongok. He straightaway left the court and prostrated himself before his parents, crying out sorrowfully: "Your unworthy son doubted his wife's integrity. When I came of age, I left your protection and learned to esteem the grace that raised me.[10] You saw to it that we were cared for and always met us at the village entrance to ensure our safety. Then you could not know if your wretched son was dead or alive, which only caused you grave anxiety. I failed to use good judgment, and that imposter intent on destroying our family was the

---

10. *Shijing* 32: "Our mother toils and works."

result of my foolishness. Should I die ten thousand deaths, it would never suffice!"

Neither Sujŭng nor his wife knew what to make of what he was saying. "Who do you think you are, calling us your parents?"

Sŏnok grieved all the more and said, "How is it that my father and mother do not know their wretched son? Look closely and you will see that I am clearly Sŏnok."

Just then, the imposter Sŏnok also spoke as if grief stricken. "Alas, our family has been brought to ruin! When our morals have undergone such a shock, would that I could just depart this life to relieve you, my parents, of your anguish."

Sŏnok's parents looked closely at the false Sŏnok and saw that there was not a single difference between the two. They became all the more confused and stood there dumbfounded, as if drunk or mad.

The inspector brought Sujŭng and both Sŏnoks back into the court, bade them sit down, and then asked Sujŭng, "Do you not know who is who even now?"

Sujŭng responded to the question fearfully: "My eyesight has grown dim and I cannot distinguish between the two. But even if I had a good pair of eyes, it seems that the situation would be no different. In my muddle-headed old age, I have seen a scandal come to my family that is worse than any other in the past or present, and the blame rests all on me. Whom can I blame? I beg of you, and I forever prostrate myself before you, to resolve this confusion and tell me, who is my true son?"

The inspector chuckled and said, "Is it not written that a learned man cannot measure up to the ability of a father? If the father cannot recognize his own child, how could another possibly know?"

Opening the door to the next room, he summoned Yi Nongok. "It is known to you which of these is your husband. Please help your father-in-law to identify his son, thus relieving his anguish."

She spoke to Sŏnok's father. "Do you not recall that there is a blue spot on my husband's front tooth?"

Upon hearing this, Sujŭng suddenly remembered it as if awakening from a dream. He told both men to open their mouths and peered within. Of course, Hŭngnyong did not have a spot on his tooth while Sŏnok did. Only when he could see this for himself was the father's doubt resolved. He rejoiced at finding his true son and embraced him, weeping loudly. He was so overcome that his strength gave out, and he fainted. Sujŭng soon recovered, but his son Sŏnok still felt so confused that he didn't know what to do.

"Father, please do not grieve. In the olden days, was it not true that Confucius suffered peril at the hands of the people of Chen and Cai, who thought that he looked like the thief Yang Huo?[11] And did not the faithful servant Ji Xin[12] pose as the founder of the Han to fool the greatest hero under heaven, Xiang Yu, the king of Chu?[13] Since ancient times, it has been common for there to be confusion when people look alike. You, my parents, have suffered mental anguish since I left home, because he looks identical to me even down to the last hair. Oh, how you have suffered because of this breakdown of morals, greater than at any time throughout history! I am to blame for all of it. Please put your minds at ease."

Encouraging Sŏnok's father, the inspector asked, "Have you anything to say?"

Sujŭng stepped forward and said, "I am old and frail, and I was not able to distinguish my own son. This was the ruin of our family. And now, great inspector, you have extended your benevolence and have found my son, saving my family from destruction. This knowledge has penetrated my bones and shall never be forgotten. I beg you

---

11. The people of Kuang mistook Confucius for Yang, who had seized power in Lu (505 BCE). *Shiji* 47:1930 and *Lunyu* 9:5; Waley, *Analects,* 139, 244–245.

12. A general who saved the life of Liu Bang, founder of the Han, by a stratagem and was burnt alive by Xiang Yu. *Shiji* 8:373; Watson, *Records of the Grand Historian*, 1:64, 99, 303.

13. Xiang Yu (233–202 BCE), a warlord known for strength and valor, led a successful revolt against the Qin dynasty but lost the ensuing power struggle with Liu Bang.

to forgive my crime of not knowing which man was he—a crime that is unworthy of forgiveness even if I should die ten thousand deaths."

The inspector responded: "It was not because of my benevolence that you found your son. It was only because the king ordered me to look into this matter that it has all been resolved. As for your crime of not knowing your own son, it is not for me to do as I will. We must await orders from the king."

Sujŭng emerged from the court with his wife, saying, "That man is an imposter and this one is our son Sŏnok. I had forgotten that Sŏnok has a blue spot on his tooth and I was fooled by that scoundrel. Well, it is all over now, and there is no use regretting it." His wife suddenly realized that she too had forgotten, and she insisted on looking at Sŏnok's tooth to see that the blue spot was there just like before.

Then she took him by the hand and exclaimed, "Where did you go, my son, and why only now have you come back? I cannot begin to tell you how much trouble you have caused our family. But now merciful heaven has helped us and our family has been saved. How can we repay even a portion of what the inspector has done for us?"

Like shafts of sunlight after nine years of flood or clouds of rain falling after seven years of drought, they could not contain their joy and shouted together, "Long live the royal inspector!"

From that time forth, Sŏnok visited the parents of both houses frequently, and they talked without reserve. The joy felt by Nongok's parents was beyond measure, even while Hyŏngok stood rigid as if he were made of wood and stone.

Translated by Mark Peterson

Biographical Sketches—The Art of Chŏn

The biography (*chŏn*) of a historical person was written by a colleague, a friend, or a family member, usually in one of the following forms: "accounts of conduct" (*haengjang*); a "chronological life" (*yŏnbo*)—more like a curriculum vitae; a "tomb inscription" (*myoji*); an "epitaph" (*myop'yo, sindobi*); or a "sacrificial speech" (*chemun*), meaning a funeral oration. *Chŏn* were collected in official histories such as the *Historical Records of the Three Kingdoms* (1146), *History of Koryŏ* (1451), and *Veritable Records of the Chosŏn Kings* (*Chosŏn wangjo sillok,* covering the 472 years of reign of twenty-five kings in 1,893 chapters). The former two are compiled in an annal-biography format, and the latter, in an annalistic format. The *Historical Records* assigned ten chapters to group biography (*yŏlchŏn,* arrayed traditions or biographies), and *History of Koryŏ,* fifty chapters. In the *Veritable Records,* a person's death is noted under the month and year of his passing much more briefly than in the first two. These biographies were considered official.[1]

Essentially there were two kinds of biography being written: official and unofficial. The former may be further classified as either a biography that forms a part of an official history and is compiled by a court-appointed committee, or a biography that accompanies the collected works of a scholar-official. The subjects of both are identified by a personality type and role model, and each account is a series of anecdotes chosen according to the "praise and blame" principle of historiography. Anecdotes presented as examples of Confucian conduct possess added significance, since they aim to perpetuate Confucian ethical norms.

1. In Yi Saek's collected works, for example, his chronological life, accounts of conduct, epitaph, and sacrificial speech are placed at the head.

Unofficial biographies—we can call them prose portraits—were unofficial because they flout the official type. Prose portraits were usually preserved in literary miscellanies, with the intent of demonstrating what a man is like by examining what he says and does. The writer does not treat his subject in depth but peels back the surface of ordinary life by selecting details. He touches on the telltale aspects of a subject's personality such as his distinctive way of speaking, his personal views, or his idiosyncrasies.

The characteristics of these two kinds of biography may be summarized by saying that one emphasizes the public self; the other, the private. One attempts to describe the subject's career; the other, the moment. However, they share a number of features: relative indifference to the subject's external appearance; a lack of markedly contemporary detail; and a dearth of information about the subject's private life. Rhetorically, both types are epideictic in that an anecdote or episode is intended to imply praise or blame, even when there is no explicit moral comment.

Here are examples of how the writers of three Koryŏ literary miscellanies present the unofficial lives of historical persons:

Kim Puŭi (1079–1170) would sit decorously all day and read books. He did not like to compose poems; when he did, he would never fail to wash his brush in a bottle of ice water.—Yi Illo, *P'ahan chip*, 2:2

When Ch'oe U (d. 1249) presented the otherworldly monk Chisik with tea, incense, and a copy of the *Lengyen ching*,[2] the monk refused to write a letter of acknowledgment. "Have I not severed all ties with the world—how can I send a letter?" he replied.—Ch'oe Cha, *Pohan chip*, 3:33

Hong Ŏnbak (1309–1363) would take a bath every evening, put on his cap and gown, and worship the stars. He

---

2. *Śūraṅgama*(*-samādhi*) *sūtra* (Scripture of heroic-march concentration); *PDB*, 873.

never neglected this custom, even during his mission to
China or when supervising public works.—Yi Chehyŏn,
Nagong pisŏl, 1B:18

As these examples suggest, portraits in a miscellany often rely for
their effect on verbs expressing external action, certain observed be-
havioral traits, and, occasionally, quotations from direct speech.
The quotation attributed to Chisik above, by conveying his own
subjectivity, presents him more vividly to the reader. If a sparse narrative can re-create a memorable scene or a clever exchange, it can
also capture a special moment of feeling or thought—it can tell us
what a person is by what he says and does. More accomplished
pieces from the Chosŏn dynasty feature precise phrasing and deftly
wrought narrative, using verbs of external action augmented with
those of inward action as well. Conversely, by portraying the subjectivity inhabiting a third-person narrative, a writer can transform
that narrative from a statement about reality into a work of fiction.

From the fifteenth century, men of letters and affairs—in this
tradition, they were one—kept diaries in which they recorded
anecdotes, observations, and comments on various subjects. Their
interests were encyclopedic, and their habits of mind leisurely. Collections of these jottings, known as *chapki* (literary miscellany), include character sketches, poetry criticism, and miscellanea.

The *chapki* portrait galleries resemble the early seventeenth-
century English character books, but with some difference in procedure and aims. The writers who created Theophrastian characters in
England attempted to reveal a class through an individual's characteristic actions, each portrait delineating a type dominated by a single
vice or virtue. In contrast, our sketches usually deal not with personi-
fied abstractions ("He is the sort of man who . . .") but with historical
individuals. If a writer is to achieve brevity in depiction, he must present a telling detail in word, deed, or gesture. He is not recounting a
person's life, yet he should be able to reveal what sort of person his
subject is. The following examples from *The Storyteller's Miscellany*
(*P'aegwan chapki*), often considered a masterpiece in the form, show

a keen eye for the single action that reveals the qualities of a man's mind and character. They were written by Ŏ Sukkwŏn (fl. 1525–1554), an interpreter of Chinese who went to Ming China seven times.

Before taking the civil service examinations, Kim Suon (1409–1481) studied behind closed doors. One day he stepped out into the courtyard to urinate; only then did he notice the fallen leaves and realize that autumn had come. Our elders studied as diligently as he did. Later, when he was seriously ill and about to die, he told his juniors, "All of you should take heed not to study the *Doctrine of the Mean* and the *Great Learning*. I'm in agony, for I see only phrases from these two books!" (4:28)

Chŏn Im (d. 1509), magistrate of Seoul, received official preferment after passing a military service examination. He was rude and fierce of character. Once, seeing that the horse he rode had boils on its back, he cut into the back of his aged servant, saying, "You did not protect the horse from boils; now feel its pain." Later, when he was critically ill, he arose and became violent. He stared and bent his bow, yelling angrily, "What ghosts are you that dare kill me?" He then stomped with rage for a long while. (4:5)

The third minister without portfolio Cho Wŏngi (1457–1523) was frugal by nature. He once asked a furrier to make him a cape. Usually tailors use the thicker fur to make the outside and the thinner fur to line the interior.

On seeing this, Cho remarked, "What an unskilled worker you are. We wear capes to keep warm, but now you sew the thin fur on the inside and thick fur on the outside; this is no way to keep warm." He then told him to reverse the procedure.

He also could bear the cold; even in winter he wore only a coat and a lined jacket. Once he observed someone wearing socks in spring and asked, "Why do you wear those?"

The man replied, "Without them, the cold air might enter my stomach!"

Cho laughed and said, "The stomach is far from the feet. How could cold feet possibly harm the stomach?" (4:65)

By custom, three and seven days after a death the family of the deceased would take wine and cake to a shaman, who would speak of a new spirit descending and relate things of the past and future.

When my great-grandfather's (Hyoch'ŏm, 1405–1475) servants went to see a shaman after his death, he said to them through the medium, "All my life I shunned this sort of nonsense. You had better go home at once." (1:30)

In his portraits, Ŏ Sukkwŏn fastens on essential personality traits that can be illustrated with an anecdote. In this sense, Ŏ can be termed a biographer of the moment. His sketches owe much of their vitality to the vivid glimpses they give of an individual without a word of overt approval or disapproval. Each is an arresting, graphic piece that captures a man's mind and character. Ŏ is in perfect control of his materials, and his style never obscures his subject. The sketches whet the reader's curiosity to find out more about the lives of the interesting individuals they portray. Significantly, Ŏ cites eighteen works in the miscellany form and calls them *sosŏl* (small talk, or fiction); he knows that only fiction is capable of portraying the subjectivity of a third person *qua* third person—from the *P'ahan chip* to the *Somun swaerok* (Random records of trivia heard).

The twenty-five subjects of Yi Ok's (1760–1812) biographical sketches include men and women of various social classes and economic status. He is seldom a first-person narrator, typically adopting the third-person omniscient narrative form—he is not a participant in the events he recounts. Sometimes the narrator provides a physical description of the subject's appearance as seen from the outside but complements it by conveying the subject's perceptions, thoughts, and feelings—recognition of an interiority that is possible only in fiction. Through little details he reveals intimate knowledge of the subject, or instinctive sympathy, and he sometimes assigns a moral value to an act in order to eliminate ambiguities. On occasion, he provides passages of dialogue and quotes from letters. Often it is unclear whether the subject is his personal acquaintance or someone he knows from memory, whether it be from his own recollection or anecdotes picked up in passing.[3]

While covering the outward form of an official biography, by providing the subject's ancestry, birth, childhood, youth, and career, including the comments of contemporaries, Yi's narrator delights in the subject who does not conform to the norms of society, or who transgresses conventional class and gender expectations, revealing a rare independence of mind in a traditional hierarchical culture. Thus, when the subject's private thoughts break into written discourse, it is a momentous occasion. Acordingly, Yi's techniques of characterization are more akin to the methods of a creative writer than those of a moral historian or official biographer. His plot lines are episodic, and fictional elements predominate. In the absence of institutional documentation—he cannot prove that his story is historically true—his biographies illustrate a changing conception of the nature and purpose of biographical sketches together with a movement toward realism.

Six of Yi's biographical sketches, all translated by Youme Kim, follow.

3. Fictional narrative in traditional Korea often takes the form of an imaginary biography. A typical work carries in its title the graph *chŏn*, implying usually that it is a story of an invented character, and the name of the protagonist in the title: *X chŏn*—"The Tale of Hong Kiltong."

Yi Ok (1760–1812)

THE STORY OF A WOMAN OF THE SUCH'IK RANK

[SUCH'IK CHŎN]

Lady Yi, of the *such'ik* rank (6b), was attached to the palace of the crown prince and had enjoyed sexual relations with the prince. She must have felt considerable pain when the prince, who was mentally ill, died seven days after being imprisoned in a rice chest by his own father (July 13, 1762). Leaving the palace, she returned to her aunt's place, where she mortified her flesh and remained in complete isolation. Her story shows the complex way in which social and cultural patterns shape behavior—from her subjection in her assigned role to the masculine dominance perpetuated in social and palace codes, to the confinement of women generally in a patriarchal system. Any deeper motive in her suicidal self-loathing is left to the reader to fathom. Her aunt's setting free of the fish and shrimps is a parable about how they wished to be free of a confining social code. The formulaic "I say" is a parody of the historian's judgment usually rendered at the end of an individual biography.

The most right and ardent energy of heaven and earth is sometimes gathered in objects or persons. When *qi* is gathered in objects, it becomes the sun, moon, frost, murmuring streams, protruding rocks, pines and cypresses, the green of the bamboo, lotus flowers, peach blossoms, or chrysanthemums. When this same energy is gathered in a person, a man becomes a loyal official and a woman a faithful wife. The characteristics of strength, softness, and honesty are in such people. Nothing else shares the same characteristics or shape, but all things are the same in terms of gathering the right and ardent energy of heaven and earth.

I say: "Snow is always white, and its whiteness is not necessarily inferior to that of jade." People, however, highly value jade and disregard snow because they place a high value on jade's long-lasting whiteness. The *Book of Changes* says, "Lasting perseverance furthers."[1]

---

1. Wilhelm, *I Ching*, 1:15.

I say: "With regard to *qi,* strong *qi* becomes a man and soft *qi* becomes a woman. In dealing with great affairs and keeping great principles, a man may be necessarily superior to a woman. In old books, however, there were many women who never fell into evil throughout their lives, and few men kept their principles throughout their lives. Is this because a woman's disposition is extreme and hardly pacified once twisted? Alas! When a person faces a moral dilemma, death is easy and living is difficult. People who stabbed themselves with a short and sharp knife and drank a cup of poison seem to have known righteousness only and not appreciated their bodies. All creatures with blood coursing through their veins are eventually fated to die. With a mind that changes a thousand times even in a day, some consistently maintain themselves for several decades without fear or regret, like deeply rooted mountains and rocks. Their lives are actually not much different from death. How could the difficulty of living be compared to the difficulty of suicide? For this reason, it is said, "Living is difficult and death is easy." Indeed, maintaining one's life for a long period is more difficult.

A giant rock stood at Wŏram, west of the palace wall. The rock, very white and about one hundred *ch'ŏk*[2] tall, is located in the most wild and remote area outside the city wall. Near the rock was a small house where two women lived. One made a living through fortune-telling and needlework. She did not comb her hair and looked as if she carried a bird's nest on her head. Another always stayed in her room and did not look outside, so her neighbors would not know what she looked like. The two women always kept some ten fierce dogs to protect them and locked the door from inside day and night. If the one who made her living outside left the house, there was no cooking smoke from the chimney even if she was gone for five days.

Once, a neighbor set the house on fire by accident and flames spread throughout the building, but the woman in the room still did

2. *Ch'ŏk:* a measure of length, approximately one foot.

not emerge. The neighbor put out the fire just in time to save her from danger. An old woman in the village secretly peeped at her and saw only that she was covered by a single-layer quilt and lay in her bed facing the wall. This shows that the woman did not expose her face, even in her locked room. Although the other woman got along with people, she did not talk about her past. She sometimes bought small shrimps and fish in the market and released them in a lotus pond; she then looked at them and left, sighing as she departed.

A woman who had maintained a good relationship with her followed her, with much effort, and made her talk about her life. She only said, "Several years have passed since the lady in the room and I left the palace." She estimated that they left a year before 1763. Some took pity on them without knowing them well and others gossiped about them out of suspicion. Not even the women's closest neighbors knew the most basic details about them.

In the seventh month of 1791, during his morning assembly, the king summoned the magistrate of Seoul and the second minister of rites to issue a command: "About the policy of encouraging marriage issued from the five sections of Seoul, I received a report that a woman has lived alone to the west of the city for thirty years. Since the report, I have not been able to sleep for a long time because of my concern for her. Recently I sent a palace lady to examine her situation; I was told that she was forty-six years old and had entered the palace following her aunt. She won my father's favor, but no one looked after her, and she left the palace soon after her aunt did. It has been thirty years since then, and she has not seen the sun in the sky and has locked herself up in the room by herself. She has not gone outside, even when she needed to defecate or when her neighbor tested her with fire. Because I have come to know her situation well, I am considering erecting a memorial gate to celebrate her as an example. What are your opinions?"

All officials, including the chief state counselor, were astonished and admired the woman, and they granted her the rank of *such'ik* and set up the gate that day. The woman in the room is *such'ik,* and the other woman is her aunt. It was the villager's mistake that she was reported as an unmarried woman in the western district. After the royal order, people finally came to know her faithfulness in detail, and some lamented so much that they cried over her situation. It was reported that her surname was Yi.

I say: "While the lady Yi spent thirty years in her room, no one understood her behavior. I quietly fathom in my heart, not under pressure, that she did not see people, sky, or the sun because there was not a single day she did not shed tears. She probably did not expose her teeth even to smile. Much less comb her hair and bathe her body! Even her aunt did not do so; why should she? Her behavior was not from her consciousness of other's eyes but from deep within her heart. From the time she left the palace, when could she forget the royal favor and her suffering? Thirty years makes one generation, and she maintained her chastity the entire time. It is rare that during such a great ordeal a person could maintain her decision. It is natural that a fragrant smell comes from the valley when the orchids are in bloom and that a rainbow appears over the spring with a pearl in it. Her chastity came to be recognized by the world, although she did not want it. Near Wŏram, a white light of energy beamed and reached to the moon and stars every night for a long time. Sadly, however, no one recognized and visited her to pay respects. Alas! Alas!"

"Because Bo Yi[3] gathered bracken on the western hill and starved to death, he is a warning to evil and idle people in the world. The effect Lady Yi has had on society is not small, but I have some regrets. If she had been born as a man and faced national crisis, wouldn't she have revealed her loyalty by ripping her belly and disemboweling herself? Or wouldn't she have rammed her head into the stone step of the palace and smashed herself to death? Or wouldn't she have wailed out

3. Bo Yi and his brother Shu Qi refused to serve the Zhou dynasty and starved to death. Birch, *Anthology of Chinese Literature,* 103–105.

of deep grief and lamentation and died by shedding her blood? If she found herself in a situation that called for such loyal subjects and heroes as in the past, she would have performed what others could not and still more. Why did she only pull the quilt over her head, shut herself up in her room like a shadow, and keep back her tears for thirty years? Keeping one's chastity is difficult; doing so by dying is easy. Thus, I assume that heaven chose to gather the most extreme energy of chastity within her, not in any other, and gave her a trial through a great ordeal. Alas, alas! It is sad!"

The Story of a Humane Female Entertainer

[hyŏpch'ang kimun]

There was a female entertainer in Seoul whose beauty and artistic skills were the finest in her time. She had noble taste and did not show respect if guests were not rich or of high social status. Among the guests, moreover, she only served those who had a handsome look, fame, and an eye for the arts. Thus, she did not always have many guests. Among those she had served were civil officials from the Office of Special Counselors and Royal Secretariat and military officials from the office of a military commander. In addition, there were guests from rich households who wore splendid clothes and were known for their witty talk. The guests she rejected were eager to speak ill of her, but they did not know that she had high principles.

In the year ŭrhae (1755), many gentlemen were exiled for their involvement in a political event. One of the entertainer's favorite guests was charged, lost his position in the Office of Special Counselors and the Office of Royal Decrees, and was exiled to Cheju Island as a government slave. When she heard about him, she made the following announcement to others with whom she maintained close contact:

"Please prepare my bags for travel. I served him only for a day, as I do many others. Considering the past, altogether I have served guests for ten years, nearly one hundred people. They all enjoy fine meat and silk clothing and have not yet experienced any hardship. Yet he has been sentenced to starve on Cheju Island, and it would be to my dishonor if I should let my guest die in hunger. So I will follow him."

After crossing the sea with ample funds, she served him on Cheju Island lavishly and diligently.

She said to him: "It is certain that you cannot go back to Seoul. Living a short pleasurable life is better than a long miserable one. Why don't you pursue a pleasurable one?"

She provided wine every day and let him drink. When he was drunk she spent the nights with him, regardless of time. Before long he became sick and died. Then she arranged a funeral with a superb coffin and shroud. She even carried out the funeral preparations by herself. Giving ten letters and the leftover money to her neighbors, she said: "When I die, please wash and dress my body, and with this money transport my corpse to the southern hill in Kangjin. Also, please send these letters to Seoul."

Soon after, she drank heavily. She wailed and she died. The islanders took pity on her and carried out her request. They sent her letters to those she had served before in Seoul. The guests who received the letters were moved and thought her behavior laudable. They collected money and brought her body from the island, and obtained a good site to bury her. At that time, then, people finally recognized that she had a noble, righteous spirit and never depended on those with money and power.

Alas! It would be enough to say that a person like her kept her dignity. She is a heroic figure like Quanfu.[1] How can people compare her to other female entertainers who adorn their hair and pursue only money and profits? (Alas, how can I get her leftover incense and cosmetics so that those who seek only profits can learn by experience?) It is sad!

---

1. A brave and humane man of the Han (d. 131 BCE).

The Story of Literary Licentiate Sŏng

[Sŏng chinsa chŏn]

Human beings have existed for a long time. The degree of cunning worsens and deception flourishes every day. There was even such a case as this. A person forced the locked door of a house open while carrying the body of a person who had died of hunger on his back and fiercely called out to the master, angering him. When they finally came to blows, he shouted, "The master killed my friend. I will report him to the magistrate." Without knowing the circumstances, the magistrate could resolve the case only after the master had paid a heavy price. This was indeed a grave matter. However, with those who are extremely cautious in their behavior, the cunning dare not make a deal and swindlers dare not work their tricks. As the proverb goes, "It is better to be cautious about yourself than to make friends of three noble men." I regard the son of gentleman Sŏng as close to the highest example of one who is cautious in his behavior.

Sŏng Hŭiryong was from the Sangju area.[1] His home was rich. In a year of famine, many begged food from him. When a female servant carried a food table, another servant ran and reported to him, "A beggar carrying a bag snapped off the food table like a crow!"

Sŏng said, "He may be hungry. Give it away."

A little later, the servant came back and said, "The beggar is about to run away with dishes in his bag!"

"It's fine," responded Sŏng, who ordered the beggar to be brought to him. When he came, the beggar appeared ready to fight. Sŏng said, "Are you going to sell those dishes?"

"Yes."

"Sell them to me."

"I will not sell them for less than one thousand five hundred *yang*."

---

1. In North Kyŏngsang.

Sŏng ordered that one thousand five hundred *yang* be given. The beggar looked at Sŏng for a while, called his wife, who was waiting outside, to come see him, and said, "He is not a human being but a buddha."

The beggar untied his bundle, and there was the body of a dead baby. He said, "When I do something wrong to someone, he pushes me to drive me away. If he pushes me, I threaten him by saying that my baby was killed and then can get a large donation. Now I cannot use this trick, since you are discreet and cultivate yourself. I humbly decline your offer." Then he left the money and dishes and went away. In the end, Sŏng lost nothing.

I say: "If Sŏng had not behaved like that, a criminal case would have proceeded. If so, legal officials might have said, 'Sŏng's case is unclear,' and not given a decision for several years. Then how could Sŏng not have felt victimized? Alas! If an official with a sense of judgment like Ximen Bao (446–396 BCE)[2] were in charge of the case, a beggar would not dare commit such a crime."

The Story of a Wood Tender

[pumokhan chŏn]

In our language, a monk is called *chung,* an old monk *sujwa,* a novice monk *sangjwa,* a wood tender[1] *pumokhan,* and one who has returned to the laity *chungsokhan.* There was a Buddhist monastery on a mountain in the Chinch'ŏn area.[2] An old monk who was attended by a novice lived in the monastery. The old monk often called the novice and said, "Brew one *mal*[3] of rice wine."

---

2. A Chinese official in the state of Wei.
1. Or fire tender, a person who keeps wood in stock for the fires in temples.
2. In North Ch'ungch'ŏng.
3. A measure containing about 18 liters.

When the wine was ready, a wood tender suddenly visited the monastery from out of nowhere. The old monk had the novice bring a wine jar, and they found a remote and quiet place under a pine tree where they drank and talked to each other. Because they talked about the arcane principles of Buddhism, the novice could not understand them. When the wine ran out, the wood tender suddenly rose and went away. The novice made more wine after several months; the wood tender appeared without fail when the wine was aged, and when he came, he and the old monk would visit the same place. The novice, however, had not heard that they made a promise to meet again. A year passed while this went on.

One day, the wood tender was about to rise when the wine jar was empty and said in a pathetic voice: "Do you know what's going to happen on a certain day?"

"How can I not know?"

"What are you going to do?"

"I will just obey."

"Why don't you avoid it?"

"I came to this mountain because I had made up my mind."

"Then today is the last of your enjoyment in this world. Later, on that day, I will return to you."

"I see." Then they gazed at each other and parted.

When the day that the wood tender had mentioned approached, the old monk woke up at dawn, washed his body with scented water, put on his monk's robe, sat with his legs crossed, and invoked the name of Amitābha⁴ endlessly. In the evening, a disturbance arose because a tiger appeared on the mountain in front of the monastery. The old monk soon rose and came out. However, even before his robes were across the threshold, something rushed at him and clasped him in its mouth and ran away. Several monks followed, shouting, and when they reached the forest they found the old monk, whose body bore

4. "Infinite Light," the buddha who presides over the western paradise.

only the tiger's tooth marks and no other injury. They poured a liquid medicine in his mouth but failed to revive him. They washed and clothed the deceased and put him into a coffin made of willow. The day for cremation was settled, and it was the day that the wood tender had promised to visit. Before the cremation, he came and wailed sadly. He watched the cremation and went away when the fire was out.

The novice packed his bag and followed the wood tender stealthily. The wood tender admonished him, saying he should go back, but he did not listen. The wood tender entered a mountain valley passing curved paths and thorn bushes, and protruding rocks sharp as knives. The novice followed him determinedly. Whenever he fell, he rose and continued after him. Though his sandals were soaked with blood, he did not stop running. The whole day passed like this. In the evening, the wood tender finally said to him: "Come here. Why are you following me in spite of your suffering?"

"My deceased master was truly an extraordinary person, but I did not recognize it. That is already in the past. Who can I serve but you? I wish that you would accept me as your disciple."

"Ah, your effort is truly sincere, but what can I do with your life span?"

Then the novice asked his life span.

The wood tender responded, "You have only three more years to live. Your time will end before you master the path that can prolong your life. What you will have then is only extreme suffering that is pointless. It is better for you to return to the laity, enjoy meat and wine, and spend the rest of your life pursuing what pleases human nature. Why should I teach you?

The novice was stunned. He made a bow to the wood tender and returned to the monastery, pondering. The wood tender left without revealing his name and where he lived. After returning to secular life, the novice roamed through marketplaces as a celibate and told his story in detail, including the day of his death. Some did not believe his words, but sure enough he died on that day.

I say: "A proverb says, 'No outstanding singer in my village and no good writer among my classmates.' People in my country tend to slight themselves. Thus they believe the saying 'A Daoist transcendent lives in Yue'[5] or 'A buddha lives in Shu,'[6] but do not believe a transcendent or a buddha lives on some mountain in our own country. How can they possibly know that mountains in Yue and Shu are like those in our country? Also, if an unknown extraordinary being, hiding his talent, were to walk among us like the wood tender, people would hardly recognize him and would just pass him by. How can you be sure that a woman working in the field is not the Bodhisattva Who Observes the Sounds of the World in white clothes, or that a traveler passing by the lake is not Lü Tongbin (755–805)?[7] This story, which I heard from a monk at Chinch'ŏn, is an example of such an encounter. So it can be said that the story of Kim Ch'anghŭp's meeting with Namgung Tu[8] is entirely believable. Alas! How can I meet such an extraordinary person and know my fate?"

THE STORY OF STUDENT SIM

[SIMSAENG CHŎN]

Student Sim, a literatus in Seoul, was handsome and a model of elegance. On his way home one day, he saw a royal procession passing on Unjong Street. He also saw a sturdy female servant crossing the street while carrying someone on her back. From the size, Sim knew that the person being carried was not a child. That person was cov-

5. Yue: a state in modern Zhejiang.
6. Shu: an ancient state in modern Sichuan.
7. Chinese alchemist; see Needham, *Science and Civilization in China*, 2:159.
8. Samyŏn is the courtesy name of Kim Ch'anghŭp (1653–1722). Namgung Tu (1526–1620), a legendary Daoist hermit who is said to have met a transcendent, is the subject of Hŏ Kyun's "Namgung sŏnsaeng chŏn."

ered with a purple shawl. A young servant followed them holding a
pair of red silk shoes in her hands.

He followed them closely, not taking his eyes off the person under
the cover, and he sometimes came very near. When they reached the
Sogwangt'ong Bridge, a sudden gust lifted one side of the purple shawl.
It was indeed a lady. She had peach-colored cheeks and willow-shaped
eyebrows, wore a green upper blouse and a crimson skirt, and was
beautifully made up with rouge and powder. Just a glimpse was enough
for Sim to take in her extraordinary beauty. The lady herself had
taken notice of the handsome young man in blue clothes and a straw
hat who was following closely. She had been watching him through
the narrow opening in the cover. When the cover was blown open, four
willowlike eyes and starlike pupils met. Surprised and embarrassed,
she hid herself under the cover and was carried away. How could
Sim just let her go? He followed her again. When they arrived in front
of a red gate with a spiked top[1] on Sogongju-dong, the woman entered
the inner gate of her home.

Sim loitered there for a while as if he had lost something. Then he
encountered an old woman who lived next door and was willing to
answer his questions. The lady's father was a retired accountant in the
Ministry of Taxation who only had a fifteen- or sixteen-year-old
daughter who was not yet married. Sim asked where her room was in
the house. The old woman pointed with her finger: "If you turn at that
small intersection, you will see a plastered wall; the lady has a small
room on the other side of the wall." After hearing this, Sim could not
keep her out of his mind. Later that day, he made up a lie and told his
parents: "A friend of mine has asked me to come over, and I would
like to visit him this evening."

At the intersection, he waited until there were no passersby before
climbing over the wall and sneaking into the residence. A crescent
moon shed little light in the garden. Flowers were blooming outside

---

1. Erected before official buildings, palaces, or temples.

the window, and the window paper was bright with reflected lamp-light. Sim sat with his back pressed against the outer wall and waited, holding his breath.

The lady and two young servants were in the room. She was reading a work of popular fiction in a soft, quiet voice that rang sweet and clear like that of a baby oriole. At the third watch (11 p.m.–1 a.m.), the servants fell asleep and the lady put out the light and went to bed. However, something seemed to be on her mind and she did not fall asleep for a long time. Sim could not sleep either and dared not make even the faintest sound. He waited until the morning drum[2] was struck and then went back over the wall.

After that, Sim's visits became a nightly obsession. He went at dusk and returned home at dawn. He did this for twenty days in a row. The lady would read or do needlework in the early evening, and then put out the light at night and turn in, though sometimes she could not sleep. One night she said, "I feel unwell." She had taken to her bed in the early evening on the six or seven previous nights. Now she sighed deeply and beat on the wall a few times with her hands. Her plaintive moans could be heard outside the window, and they became worse day by day.

On the twentieth night, she suddenly emerged from the back veranda and came around the outer wall to where Sim sat. He rose with a sudden burst and clasped her in the dark. Without the slightest surprise, she said in a low voice, "Aren't you the gentleman I saw on the Sogwangt'ong Bridge? I've been aware of your visits for the past twenty days. Please do not hold me. If I should make a sound, you will never escape. But if you let me go, I will open the back door and let you in. Please release me."

Sim released her and decided to wait. She turned around and returned to her room. Then she called her servant and said, "Go to my

---

2. At about 4 a.m, the metal drum was struck thirty-three times to announce the end of curfew (*p'aru* or *parae*).

mother and ask her for a big padlock. It's very dark tonight, and I'm afraid of intruders." The servant went off and soon returned with a lock. The lady fastened the lock on the back door that she had promised to open, making loud noises on purpose. Then she put out the lamp and pretended to be asleep.

Sim was angry that she had deceived him. But he was elated to have had a chance to meet her even once. He remained all night outside the locked door and returned to his home at dawn. He went to her home the next day and again the day after. He felt no discouragement even though the back door remained closed. Even when it rained, he did not fail to visit, wearing a raincoat made of oiled paper. Ten more days passed. That night, the house was quiet and the people in it were asleep. After putting out the lamp, she too lay in silence for a long time. Then suddenly she roused herself and woke her servants. She told them to light a lamp and said, "Go and sleep upstairs tonight." The two servants did as she asked, and then she unlocked the door with a key that hung on the wall. Opening the door wide, she called: "Gentleman, please come in." Sim entered the room quickly, without hesitation. She locked the door again and told him: "Please have a seat for a while." She went to the upper rooms and soon came back with her parents. They were greatly surprised to see him.

"Please don't be startled and listen to my words," she said. "At the age of sixteen, I have never gone out. On the way home after the royal procession, my shawl was blown open by the wind, and I looked out and saw a young man in a straw hat on the Sogwangt'ong Bridge. Since then, he has come here in hiding and waited outside the door every night for the past thirty days and more. He has come in the rain, in the cold, and even after I made a point of locking the door and rejecting him. I have worried about it many times. I thought that if a story should get out that he was slipping in during the night and going away at dawn, who in the village would believe that he was actually standing outside by himself the entire time? That would make me the pheasant caught by a dog. Moreover, he is a gentleman from a noble family, one who does not know how to control himself, like a butterfly or a bee that only seeks flowers and doesn't care about any of the dangers. And who knows, he could fall ill soon, from being outside in bad weather. If he can't be saved, then it will be my fault even if I did not kill him. Although others may not know the real situation here, some good might still come out of it. Also, I am merely a girl from a middle-class family. I am hardly a beauty who conquers a city or makes fish hide in water or flowers feel shame. He, however, regarding a kite as a hawk, has devoted his true heart to me. If I do not follow him, heaven, displeased, will not bless me. I have already made up my mind. Dear parents, please don't worry. Ah! You are old and have no other children. I thought it would prove satisfactory if I could marry one day and have your son-in-law live with us and serve you while you were alive, and then perform the memorial services after you passed away. However, things have turned out differently. This seems to be the command of heaven, and there's little use in saying anything more."

The girl's parents were dumbfounded and had nothing to say. Nor could Sim say anything. He and the lady finally spent that night together. After his long yearning, how great was his pleasure! After that night, there was not a single day that he did not leave his home after dark and return at dawn. Because her family was rich, the lady made fine clothes for him. However, he could not wear them for fear of arousing his family's suspicion. With all of Sim's precautions, however, his family could not help growing suspicious about his habit of going out and staying away all night. As a result, he was ordered to remove himself to a Buddhist monastery on a mountainside and apply himself to his studies. While unhappy with the command, the combined pressure of family and friends gave him no choice but to take his books and move to the remote fortress on Mount Pukhan.

He had been at the monastery for about a month when he was handed a letter from the lady, written in the vernacular. Opening it, he found that it was a testament written to convey her imminent death. In fact, she had already died. The general contents of the letter were as follows:

> The spring weather is still chilly. How is your health in your studies at the monastery? Longing for you always, how can I possibly forget you? After you left me, I fell ill and it became severe enough to reach down to the marrow. Now all medicines are proving useless. After this, the only thing that awaits me is death. What is the good of extending such an unfortunate life as mine? But still, I have three lasting regrets that keep my eyes from closing.
>
> As an only child, I received all the love of my parents. So I wished to marry a suitable man on whom my parents could rely in their later years, one who could manage their affairs. However, as in the saying "Light is accompanied by shadow," my karma has become entangled. "The mistletoe and the love vine twine themselves on cypress and pine."[3] This is why I worried in vain, forgoing all pleasures, and have come to the point of death. Now my grizzled parents will have no one to rely on. That is my first regret.
>
> A woman, even a humble servant, has a husband and parents-in-law when she marries unless she is a female entertainer. There is no daughter-in-law whom her parents-in-law cannot recognize. (But I was deceived by another and was unable to see even a single old female servant of yours.) I have made shameful choices while living and will become a wandering ghost with nowhere to go after death. That is my second regret.
>
> Among the wife's duties to her husband, none is greater than preparing food to serve him and making clothes for him to wear. It has only been a short time since I met you. Nevertheless, I did make a few pieces of clothing for you. But I could not let you eat even a single bowl of rice in my home or wear a single suit I made for you, and I served you only in bed. That is my third regret.

3. *Shijing* 217:1; Waley, *Book of Songs,* 206.

I am heartbroken that I had to bid you farewell after a short meeting, only to fall ill and die without ever seeing you again. However, this is merely a woman's grief, with hardly any significance for a gentleman. As my thoughts reach this pass, my bowels seem ground to bits and my bones melted away with sorrow. The feeble grass bends before the wind. Although withered petals turn into mud, when can my grief possibly end?

Alas! Our secret meetings through the window are done. I hope you will not care about me and will devote yourself to your studies and soon achieve the dreams of your youth. I sincerely wish, many times over, that you maintain your health.

Sim burst into tears upon reading this letter. He cried sorrowfully, but what was the use? After that, he threw away his writing brush and turned to the military, becoming an official in the State Tribunal. He reached the rank of *kŭmorang*[4] and died young.

In appraisal I say: "I studied at a village school when I was ten years old and enjoyed hearing stories every day with my schoolmates. One day, my teacher told us Sim's story in detail and said, 'Student Sim was my schoolmate. I was there when he received the letter and burst into tears. I heard his story then and have never forgotten it.' He added, 'I do not suggest that you follow that gallant young gentleman. If a person can assert his will in an affair, to the point of moving even a lady in her boudoir, then how much more might you apply it to writing literary essays and passing your civil service examinations?' We thought the story was new at the time. I later read the *History of Love*[5] by Feng Menglong (1574–1646) and found similar stories in it. I add this as a supplement to the *History*."

4. Rank 6b.
5. *Qingshi* is a collection of love stories compiled by Feng Menglong after 1628.

THE STORY OF YI HONG

[YI HONG CHŎN]

People in the past may have been unsophisticated, but those in the present do value quick wits. Quick wits produces cunning, the type of craftiness that leads to slyness, and slyness creates deception. When deception is rampant, public morals are affected.

Inside the Great West Gate of Seoul was a large market, the lair of merchants selling fake goods. These merchants would assure customers that nickel was silver, goat's horn, a hawk's bill, and weasel fur a sable. They were actually fathers, sons, and brothers who set up their sales by pretending to make deals with each other and haggling over the price of their goods. Someone just in from the countryside would believe that the goods they haggled over were genuine and buy them at the asking price. In that market a seller could make a tenfold to a hundredfold profit. Moreover, there were pickpockets mingling with the crowd who would think nothing of using a sharp knife to rip open someone's bag or money belt if they thought something valuable was in it. When they were noticed and chased, they would run off to a side street, often the one where cold drinks made from fermented rice were sold. The street was winding and narrow. If the person in pursuit ever got close to the thief, a man carrying a load of bamboo baskets would suddenly block the way, saying, "Please buy one of my baskets!" and the chase would have to break off. For this reason people who went to the market were on guard to keep their goods and money safe, like warriors protecting their camp on a battlefield or a bride covering up her body. Still, however, they fell victim to deception. In the past, people of the Three Han era[1] were thought to be unsophisticated. But really, weren't there many like Paek Myŏnsŏn[2] among them? Did

---

1. Korea's confederated kingdoms period (c. 1st to 3rd cent.); the Samhan states were Mahan, Chinhan, and Pyŏnhan.
2. A notorious swindler in Seoul in the eighteenth century.

morality gradually decay and innocent people become crafty? Or did evil people exist in the remote past as well?

Yi Hong was from Seoul. He had good looks and could speak well, so that people seeing him for the first time never took him for a swindler. He wore good clothes and enjoyed good food and appeared to think little of wealth, but in fact he was poor. Yi could visit a noble household and emerge with ten thousand *yang*, which he had promised to invest in a profitable irrigation project, a line made plausible by the fact that he had once held a position in construction on the Ch'ŏngch'ŏn River.[3] Every day he was able to order beef and wine for his meal, and when he invited female entertainers to join him, none refused.

In the Anju area there was a female entertainer who was renowned as the greatest beauty in P'yŏngan province. Because she enjoyed the magistrate's favor, even the royal inspectors could not get to see her or invite her to their parties. Yi made a bet with his friends that he could go to Anju alone and succeed in meeting her within ten days. For the trip, he wore a silk military uniform and put his bags on a horse. Only a male servant wearing a hat accompanied him. Entering Anju, Yi mounted his horse and applied his whip. Everyone thought he was a wealthy Kaesŏng merchant.

He took quarters in the house of the entertainer. Her father was a retired soldier who had opened an inn. Yi made a deal with the father: "What I have with me are expensive goods. Please do not accept any other guests while I am here. I must wait for someone to come but cannot tell when he will arrive. I will pay your price in full on the day I leave. In addition, I care about food, so please prepare worthy meals. I do not care about the cost. You may set whatever prices you want for food and lodging."

The father believed that Yi was a merchant. He also noticed that Yi's bags were heavy, which suggested they were loaded with silver.

---

3. In North P'yŏngan. Beginning at Chŏgyu Pass, it eventually empties into the Yellow Sea.

"Oh, I have an excellent guest," he thought. He cleaned a room carefully and invited Yi to inspect it. Yi entered the room and looked around. He frowned and called for his servant: "Go and buy some oiled paper for the floor. How can I lie down in such a place even for a night?" He had the room repapered, put his bags by his bedside, and laid out wool bedding and a silk quilt. He then took out a thick account book, an abacus, and a small inkstone from his luggage. Shutting his door, he pretended to be engaged in accounting through the rest of the day.

The father bent his ear to the door crack and eavesdropped. Silk, spices, and medicinal stuffs were the goods that Yi and his servant were tallying. The father told his wife, a retired entertainer: "Our guest is a wealthy merchant. Once he sees our daughter, he will be entranced by her. If that happens, we will certainly be rich, far beyond what we're now getting from the magistrate."

The father quickly sent his daughter a message calling her back from the magistrate's office in P'yŏngyang.

When she entered his room, she said, "As the mistress of the house, I must make sure that everything is all right when a noble person such as yourself comes to stay in our humble lodging."

Yi replied, "Oh, don't bother. You needn't do anything." Yi kept working with his abacus as if he were busy, and did not appear to pay any attention to her. The father thought, "This gentleman is surely a great merchant. His cool behavior must be due to the fact that he has a great fortune and highly refined taste." That evening, the father said to him in private, "Wouldn't you like to meet my daughter? You were so indifferent to her that she feels mortified."

Yi did not show much interest and refused his offer several times, but finally seemed to agree, albeit reluctantly, to meet her. The entertainer prepared a lavish table of food and wine and did her best to please him, flirting through her singing and dancing. At length they passed the entire evening together. After that, she continued to attend to Yi over the course of the next three days.

But one day Yi seemed agitated and called the father over to ask him, with a worried look: "Have you heard about the western provinces being infested with thieves?"

"No."

"How long does it take to travel from Ŭiju to here?"

"A few days."

"Then the time has passed. Have there been any problems with horses?"

"Sir, is anything wrong?" the landlord asked.

Yi replied: "Goods from Peking were supposed to cross over the Yalu River on such and such a day and arrive here on such and such a day. However, they have not arrived yet, and I'm worried." He called his servant and said: "Go and take a look outside the West Gate." The servant returned in the evening and announced that he had heard nothing.

Yi seemed anxious from that day on, and after another three days, he called the landlord and said: "Because I have some expensive things in my possession, I haven't been able to go outside. But I'm feeling overcome with anxiety and cannot wait any longer. You are like a family member to me now, so I am going to leave my things in your care. Please watch over them. I must go and look into what is causing this delay." Yi locked his room and went off in a hurry. Once outside the inn, he immediately took a shortcut and proceeded back to the Ch'ŏngch'ŏn River. His journey had taken ten days in all.

The suspicions of the people in the house were aroused when Yi did not return. When they unpacked his bags, they found nothing in them but stones the size of a goose egg.

Another time, a local petty official went to Seoul to pay a tax to the military of a thousand strings of cash. While the official was considering where he would stay, Yi invited him to his home with a plan. "I have a good scheme," he said. "If you stick with me, you'll end up with money for travel and even have enough to enjoy a female entertainer as well."

The official willingly handed over all his cash, and Yi appeared to be working day and night on his plan. Ten days had passed when Yi suddenly began to praise the beautiful scenery of South Mountain. Together with the official, Yi bought a bottle of wine and climbed up to the remote area of P'aengnamkol.[4] He drank the wine by himself and began to wail.

"Tut, can't you hold a bottle of wine?" the official asked.

"Seoul is so beautiful," he replied. "Just look . . . but I can't linger here any longer, and it makes me weep."

Yi took out a rope from his sleeve and began to fasten a noose, intending to hang himself from a pine branch. Greatly startled, the official stopped him and asked his reason.

Yi responded: "It is because of you. I'm not the kind of man who can make off with another person's money, not even a penny. However, I've been taken advantage of, and all your money is gone. I want to repay you, but I'm poor and have no way. If I try to disappear, you will come after me with a vengeance and the situation will remain the same. So I might as well end it. Please don't stop me." Yi began to put his head through the noose and acted as if he would jump from the cliff immediately.

The official was extremely upset, and standing on his toes, he cried: "No, don't do it! You don't need to repay my money."

"How can you be serious? You only say those words because I'm about to die. Words are meaningless anyway. How can I make you keep this promise later? It's better for me to die now."

The official thought, "Whether he lives or dies, the end result will be the same: I will be out of the money. But if he dies, I will be in trouble." So the official took out brush and ink from his sleeve, wrote a note of forgiveness for the money, and tried to persuade Yi not to kill himself.

---

4. Corresponds to P'iltong Second Street.

"Well, now that you've done this, there's no reason for me to kill myself," Yi said. He shook the dust from his clothes and returned home. That night he drove the official out of his house and forbade him to come back.

An official from the Ministry of Penalties came to hear about the deception, however, and caused Yi to be seized. Then he sentenced him to one hundred strokes of the lash. Yi almost died from the beating but survived in the end.

Yi was known to practice archery, but his success in a military qualifying exam that year was not due to his skill. When the list of successful candidates was announced, he celebrated by having a parade bigger than all the others. The musicians all wore official uniforms made of blue ramie cloth and hat strings that smelled like sandalwood. In addition to their fee, Yi gave the musicians some cloth, a decorative towel, a folding screen painted with peony flowers, and an ornamental knife in a case made of rhinoceros horn. People said that Yi had cut the weeds on gravesites and sold *chewijŏn*[5] to raise money for the parade.

Yi's home was outside the West Gate. One day, while wearing a silk shirt embroidered with a floral pattern, he slowly entered the South Gate. He was pulling on his hat string and carrying a fan made of amber in his left hand. He saw a Buddhist monk, who struck a hand bell to ask him for an offering.

Yi called to the monk: "How long have you been standing here?"

"For three days."

"How much money have you gotten?"

"I've received some two hundred *p'un*."[6]

"My! You've been repeating "I trust in Buddha Amitābha" for three days and you only get two hundred *p'un*! You will be old and on the verge of death by the time you get enough money. I am rich and

---

5. Paddy fields set aside so that their produce will maintain annual ancestor-memorial services.

6. A unit of old copper coin, a penny. Ten *p'un* makes 1 *ton*.

have lots of children. It's been in my mind to do a good deed for the Buddha, so you are lucky. What shall I give as an offering?"

Yi thought for a moment and said: "I have some brassware. Would it be useful?"

The monk replied: "There is no better donation than having a buddha statue made in brass."

"Then follow me," said Yi. He led the monk through the South Gate. When they came to a tavern, he pointed to it and said, "Let's rest there." The barmaid warmed up some wine and brought some snacks. Yi drank ten cups of wine one after the other, fumbled with his silk pocket, and laughed loudly, saying: "I forgot to bring money for the wine today. Well, if I can borrow some from your sack, I will repay you right away." The monk paid the bill.

They went out and Yi asked the monk: "Are you coming with me?"

"Yes, of course."

"My brassware is quite old, and my family might try to stop you from taking it. You should carry it carefully."

"Offering the brassware is your decision, and how I carry it is up to me. How could I not take care of it?"

"As you say."

They went into another tavern and drank more wine, spending the monk's money. After three more rounds in taverns, the monk ran out of money.

As they were walking along, Yi said to the monk again: "People need to be perceptive in everything they do."

The monk replied: "That is how I have spent my life. I am aware of everything around me."

"You are right," said Yi. A few steps later, he turned and said: "The brassware is really big. Can you carry it?"

"Bigger is better," the monk answered. "Once you give it to me, even if it weighs a thousand *kŭn,*[7] I won't have any trouble carrying it."

"All right," Yi replied.

7. A traditional unit of weight, equal to 601 gm.

They had just crossed the Taegwangt'ong Bridge.[8] Yi turned into the street to the east and held his fan while pointing to the Injŏng Bell[9] in the massive bell pavilion. "There is the brassware. Be sure to carry it carefully."

Hearing this, the monk was stunned and stood there for a long time, looking over at South Mountain. Finally he turned and ran off. Yi slowly walked toward the Ch'ŏlchŏn Bridge.[10]

Yi's life was generally like that. These are only a few of the more noteworthy stories. He was notorious for deceiving people, and eventually he was punished and exiled to a remote place.

I say: "Only a big trick can take in all the world, including king and ministers and the common people alike. Yi's deception was of the lowest kind and hardly worth disputing. However, one who deceives the world can become a king, be honored, and finally make his house illustrious. Yi Hong was punished at the hands of the law because of his deceptions. It could be said that he actually deceived himself rather than others. This is sad."

Translated by Youme Kim

8. A bridge between Ch'ŏnggye Stream First and Second Streets.
9. A curfew bell at Chongno Second Street.
10. A bridge on Kwanch'ŏl Street.

ORAL LITERATURE

Introduction

Myths and legends are preserved in the memory of the race. This is the reason poets have traditionally pointed to Mnemosyne, the goddess of memory, as the source of their inspiration.

What myths and legends keep alive are the memories of heroes and heroines who are consequential to the welfare of society. This means that the hero is both an individual and a representative figure. It also means that the heroic is not a kind of person or action, but a way of looking at persons and actions.[1]

Premodern narratives, many written in verse, may be termed "higher narratives" in that they reflect different social orders than ours and are founded on different assumptions about the kinds of human experience that are suitable for literary development. The heroes in foundation myths, for example, are taken to be of greater stature than ourselves and rise above the horizon of literary realism. These heroes cover a great deal of space, time, and experience, and endure trials, ordeals, and suffering. They have a high purpose driving their quest or journey—the founding of a state—and they have access to elements, such as the supernatural, that are beyond the reach of ordinary humans. They possess superhuman strength, cleverness, and charisma, often augmented by magical powers. But their epic-like world is distinct from the divine, however much the two may impinge on each other.

In the West, "epic" is a term that was retrospectively devised well after the composition of the early epics by singers and bards. Like "romance," a medieval term for heroic narratives with antecedents in both classical antiquity and folklore, it may have been nostalgic at inception. The Western cultural presumption of the centrality of epic and romance has long influenced perception of works

1. Waith, *Ideas of Greatness*, 131.

with larger-than-life characters from other cultures, particularly when European literary practice is assumed to provide a norm against which other literatures may be evaluated. Although East Asia is rich with literary works that can be described as "epic-like" or "romance-like," each example will be found to embody some but not all features of the prescribed genre. Should they be found wanting when such deficiencies come to light? A more fruitful approach involves the adoption of a culturally neutral term like higher or elevated narrative to designate the genus to which individual species such as Western epic and romance and East Asian myths, legends, and *chuanqi* belong. From this vantage point, we can begin to examine foundation myths and other early narratives in Korea to see the common attributes of the exemplars. Gaining this perspective will then help us to consider in a more systematic and penetrating way the properties of higher narratives worldwide.

Foundation Myths

The Korean foundation myths, featuring personages such as Tangun, Chumong, Pak Hyŏkkŏse, and King Suro, first appear in ancient written records.[2] They divide geographically into those relating the founding of the northern kingdoms of Old Chosŏn and Koguryŏ and those that treat the southern kingdoms of Silla and Karak.

The Tangun myth and the Chumong myth deal with the founding of Old Chosŏn and Koguryŏ, respectively. They reveal similar structures of thought: both reflect a desire to imbue heaven and earth (or its waters) with sanctity. In these accounts, the male god, as the symbol of heaven, weds the goddess of the earth. Out of this holy union, which takes place in the secular world, the founder of a state is born. Northern myths describe the marriage between the gods of heaven and earth (or water), which leads to the birth of a state founder who then fulfills his destiny by establishing a state. Southern myths such as those of Pak Hyŏkkŏse and King Suro, by contrast,

2. *SY, KS,* and *Chewang ungi,* in the appendix to *SY,* Appendix, 50–53.

omit the explicit description of the marriage, which is represented symbolically, and begin with the birth of the founding father followed by the founding of the state.

The two types of myth show further differences in their portrayal of how the founder rises to power. In northern myths, the founding father is born into a state that is already established; he then becomes its ruler and goes on to establish another state. Southern myths bring the founder into a world without established states; he then creates a state and is made the first king. In this regard, southern myths contain a more primordial definition of state founding than their northern counterparts.

The Tangun myth relates the process by which the first kingdom that the Korean people inhabited, Chosŏn, came into existence. The main character is Tangun's father, Hwanung. But because Tangun is the one who establishes the kingdom of Old Chosŏn and is worshiped in ceremonies celebrating the state's founding, the myth is referred to as the Tangun myth. The first part deals with Hwanung's establishment of the sacred city; the second part relates the events leading to Tangun's birth. Historians interpret Hwanung as representing an outside group that worships the heavenly deity and Ungnyŏ (Bear Woman) as a symbol of an indigenous, bear-totem tribe. Their marriage and the subsequent founding of Chosŏn by their offspring, Tangun, are read as indicating the emergence of a new communal unit following the alliance between the two groups. Hwanung is read as a tribal chieftain who serves in the capacity of ceremonial officiator or high priest. The three talismans he receives from his father, Hwanin, refer to the sacred objects of mirror, bell, and sword in the Korean shamanist tradition. The three attendant ministers of wind, rain, and cloud may represent shamans who control the climate, indicating the chieftain of the agrarian tribe was viewed as having such authority. At the same time, this interpretation ascribes to the myth a firmly anthropocentric view of the world. Hwanung, though a heavenly deity, descends to the lower realm, and the bear and the tiger wish to overcome their animal nature and become human; the depiction of the divine and the beastly both yearning for the human world thus privileges the human realm. Moreover, the figure worshiped by later generations as the founding father is not the deity Hwanung but his son Tangun, seen as distinctly human. Such a humanistic approach is said to have provided the basic tenet of Taejong Kyo,[3] a native religion that worships Tangun.

The Chumong myth deals with the founding of Koguryŏ.[4] As the representative heroic myth in Korea, the Chumong myth combines the three generational myths of Haemosu, Chumong, and Yuri. Haemosu, a son of the heavenly emperor, marries Yuhwa, a daughter of the river earl, who then gives birth to Chumong; Chumong is raised in the palace of the king of Eastern Puyŏ, Kŭmwa, but flees to Cholbon, where he establishes the kingdom of Koguryŏ. He distinguishes himself and his state by forcing the surrender of the neighboring state of Songyang, which he then annexes to his kingdom. As a grandson of heaven and son of a union of heaven and earth (water), he has the power to invoke divine intervention, although such interference can be said to diminish the hero's valor and glory. He leads and serves his people, first as a warrior, then as a king. The myth stresses his strength, courage, and resourcefulness, but it does not describe his bow, arrow, armor, or horse (the paramount animal for the warrior in the heroic age). Many of the motifs common to heroic narratives are here: the miraculous birth, the exposed child, the contest/rivalry, the journey, divine intervention, early death, the marvelous, and the hero's ascent to heaven. At the same time, the sacred belief in heaven and water deities reveals that the Korean people honored such beliefs from antiquity.

The Pak Hyŏkkose myth is the foundation myth of Silla and survives in various written sources.[5] This myth consists only of tales related to the births of the dynastic founder and his wife. The details, however, make this royal couple descendants of gods of heaven and water respectively. The married couple ruled Silla and were worshiped

---

3. Established on the fifteenth of the first lunar month, 1909.

4. *SS* 13:129–131; *SY* 1:40–41; No et al., *Sinjŭng Tongguk yŏji sŭngnam*, 3:2a–8a; and *Chewang ungi*, 52.

5. *SY* 1:43–45.

as deities; reverence toward the deities of heaven and water as sacred entities was a central belief in Silla as well.

In the King Suro myth,[6] Suro is said to have emerged from an egg that was dug up from the earth at Mount Kuji, where a streak of violet connected sky and earth. After Suro was made king, he married Princess Hŏ Hwangok, who had sailed to his kingdom from the faraway Indian kingdom of Ayut'a (Ayodhya). The myth thus reveals a narrative structure that moves from the birth of the dynastic founder to his enthronement and ultimately to his marriage—characteristic of southern myths in general.

The Pak Hyŏkkose myth and the King Suro myth are the foundation myths of states, but they also detail the rise of two clans: the Pak of Kyŏngju and the Kim of Kimhae. Additional clan myths of Korea include the Three Clan myths of Cheju Island, as well as accounts describing the rise of the Ch'ae clan of P'yŏnggang and the Cho clan of Ch'angnyŏng. The Three Clan myths of Cheju Island appear in written sources and describe the rise of the Ko, Yang, and Pu clans.[7] Such myths portray the clan founders as originating from the soil and stress reverence toward the earth rather than a sacred belief in heaven. While the marriage process of the founders resembles that of King Suro, the depiction of the origins of agricultural and grazing practices indicates an attempt to trace the beginnings of an agricultural tribe.

The clan myths of the Ch'ae clan of P'yŏnggang and the Cho clan of Ch'angnyŏng belong to a folktale category that may be called "Intruder in the Night." These myths tell the story of various creatures such as otters, snakes, or turtles that are transformed; gain human aspect; visit maidens under the cover of night; and impregnate them. The child born from such a union becomes the founder of the clan. These myths differ from the foundation myths of states in that an earth female joins with a water male to give birth to the clan founder and the nature of paternity remains hidden. As such, the Intruder in

6. *SY* 2:108–120.
7. *KS* 57:53b–55a, and *Yŏngju chi*, with a postface dated 1450.

the Night myths might represent a variation of water god myths that emerged as the water god began to be superseded by the heavenly god in relative importance.

Foundation myths and classic archival records are known because they were preserved in literary Chinese. It is almost impossible to know how far the oral compositions were transformed into literary texts by the compilers, who worked within a literate culture. Unlike songs in vernacular poetic genres, their written versions reveal neither oral antecedents nor oral residue. It is possible, however, that the act or process of transcription led to tighter plots, with some embellishments in detail. Nevertheless, were it not for these texts, the Korean foundation myths and tales would not have been associated with known historical personages and places.

Legends

The legends and folktales in this volume were collected through oral dictation between 1967 and 1991. They are either recitations of memorized texts—not verbatim repetition—or genuine oral compositions. The presence in the original of dialects, incomplete sentences, pauses, and the recurrence of certain words and phrases indicates that the recorded versions were not polished by the collectors. For the sake of fluency, however, these telltale linguistic features have been kept to a minimum in translation. Most of the tradition bearers, as *Homo narrans* or storytelling human beings,[8] were in their sixties or even older when they were recorded: they were estimable figures commanding respect in their communities. Their mode of utterance, their highlighting of certain episodes or scenes, their gestures, and their intended humor, pathos, or irony are not easily transcribed in Korean, however, much less translated into English. Folklore, it is said, has several essential functions: apart from serving pedagogy and validating culture, it maintains conformity to accepted patterns of behavior while enabling human beings to escape in fantasy both

8. Niles, *Homo Narrans*, 18, 19.

from societal pressures and from their own biological and geographic limitations.[9]

Legends comprise a genre of oral literature in which the tales are believed to be true by those who tell them. They also have specific settings in both historical time and geographic location, and this specificity differentiates these narratives from folktales. A legend can thus be defined as "a traditional (mono) episodic, highly ecotypified, localized and historicized narrative of past events told as believable in a conversational tone. Psychologically, legend is a symbolic representation of folk belief and reflects the collective experience and values of the group to whose tradition it belongs."[10] Legends also stress the final downturn into tragedy: while the circumstances surrounding the birth of the hero are often omitted from the narrative, a detailed description of the death scene is a characteristic feature of the genre.

Legends are classified as national or regional according to how widely the sources are recognized. National legends deal with historical figures or events. Because the evidence for these stories can be found in the history of Korea, their truth is generally accepted by the Korean people. Such narratives may describe the founding of the Chosŏn dynasty, the establishment of the capital at Hanyang (now Seoul), or the life of Admiral Yi Sunsin (1545–1598), whose feats of valor during the Hideyoshi invasions are much famed. Regional legends, by contrast, have as their source the experiences of the inhabitants of the area and hence are limited by territorial considerations. Two examples of regional legends are "Brother and Sister Stūpas," associated with the physical structure located on Yŏnch'ŏn Peak of Mount Kyeryong in South Ch'ungch'ŏng, and "Dragon's Blood Hermitage," about T'ongdo monastery in Yangsan.

Another way to classify legends is to divide them into stories of people or of things according to the subject or the nature of the

---

9. Bascom, "Four Functions of Folklore"; John Niles lists six functions of oral narrative: "the *ludic*, the *sapiential*, the *normative*, the *constitutive*, the *socially cohesive*, and the *adaptive*" (*Homo Narrans*, 70, author's emphasis).

10. Tangherlini, *Danish Folktales, Legends, and Other Stories*, 180.

evidence. Most of the individuals who appear in legends are historical personages: the late Silla scholar and writer Ch'oe Ch'iwŏn (b.
857); a celebrated mid-Koryŏ general, Kang Kamch'an (948–1031),
who defeated the Khitan forces at Kwiju (1018); the great scholars
of Chosŏn, Sŏ Kyŏngdŏk (1489–1546), Yi Hwang (1501–1570), Yi
I (1536–1584), and Yi Chiham (1517–1578). These stories are
transmitted both orally and in literary Chinese. Oral legends about
people are not limited, however, to those who appear in historical
records. Famed geomancers like Tosŏn (827–898) and Pak Sangŭi
(d.u.), legendary physicians like Hŏ Chun (1546–1615) and Yu
It'ae (d.u.), and celebrated fortune-tellers like Hong Kyegwan (d.u.)
appear in oral legends as well. The story of Pak Munsu (1691–
1756), who served as a secret royal inspector, contains elements of
the mystical and supernatural. The legends of Ch'oe Ch'iwŏn, Kang
Kamch'an, Yi Chiham, and other notable Daoists—and many of the
celebrated Daoist narratives—find the heroes on the side of the common people. The benign protagonists of legend are often those possessed of exceptional wisdom and erudition who use these gifts to
help the people rather than serve the government.

Legends of things can further be divided into legends of natural
objects and man-made objects. Natural objects range from heavenly
bodies—the sun, moon, and stars—and topographic features like the
mountains and rivers to individual trees, lakes, and boulders.
The narratives show a variety of elements as well, ranging from the
mythical to the quasi-historical. Man-made objects include Buddhist
monasteries, stone stūpas, fortresses, bridges, works of calligraphy,
paintings, and sculptures. These narratives trace the events leading
to the completion of artworks or erected structures.

An example of a natural object legend is the story of Changja
Pond, which traces the origins of the pond. At the same time, the
legend belongs to a general category of folktale—the Sodom and Gomorrah type—that appears in many cultures. A father and son who
mistreat an old monk turn into a pond and die miserable deaths after
witnessing the decline of their household. The daughter-in-law, however, secretly gives the monk alms, and in return for her kindness the

monk informs her of a way to survive. But the daughter-in-law is unable to follow the instructions and is turned into stone in the end. This legend is associated with more than three hundred ponds across the country. In one reading, the heavenly entity represented by the old monk symbolizes the ideals toward which all human beings strive, while the miserly father and son are earthly beings who symbolize an obsession with mundane existence. The daughter-in-law who stands between the two is a middleman figure symbolizing the human dilemma poised between transcendent ideals and necessary reality.

Folktales

Folktales are recounted by tellers who do not consider the content of their narratives to be true or sacred. Because they value the tales as amusement, they make no attempt to present evidence that could establish their historical truth. Folktales are "fictional narratives that usually unfold in an unspecified time with unspecified characters; in many of these tales, magic is commonplace, and not unexpected. Folktales are traditionally circulated orally among members of a close, homogeneous social group."[11] This generality regarding time and space signifies that the world of folktales may be universal: the events of the narratives may take place anytime, anywhere, so long as people occupy that spatiotemporal plane. Similarly, the transmission of folktales is not limited by geographic considerations. If the tale can generate enough audience interest, it will secure transmission. For this reason, folktales show global tendencies. The particulars of the content, however, may differ according to the special cultural characteristics of the transmitting group.

Protagonists of folktales show much diversity in both social status and personal characteristics. Moreover, the process by which the main character gains an awareness of the conflict and resolves it is treated in a lighthearted manner. Typically he may get lucky, or else solve grave problems through naive and artless wisdom, or even by a simple trick. Particularly abundant in this category are humorous

---

11. Ibid., 171.

tales involving an idiot. For this reason, folktales are frequently regarded as funny; or, in more formal terms, as the fount of the aes-
thetics of humor.

A hundred different types of animal tales have been transmitted
through oral narratives—"The Dog and Cat Go Seeking a Jewel,"
for example, belongs in the Magic Ring category (Type 560).[12] Other
animal tales feature creatures such as crawfish, ants, frogs, spiders,
crabs, nightingales, pheasants, eagles, pigs, grasshoppers, mosquitoes, flies, fleas, bedbugs, lice, cows, terrapins, foxes, bears, and cocks.
Donkeys commonly appear instead of horses, and nonindigenous
animals like monkeys and lions are present as well. The animals
appearing most frequently in Korean folktales are tigers, foxes, dogs,
and toads.

"The Snaky Bridegroom" belongs to Type 425, the Search for
the Lost Husband category. The story of "Cupid and Psyche" belongs
to this category as well. The two stories are similar in outline: "Cupid and Psyche" is about the perseverance of Psyche, who ultimately
achieves reunion with Cupid and becomes a goddess despite the
punishments inflicted by Venus in her jealousy; "The Snaky Bridegroom" presents the story of a woman who loses her husband
through the jealous machinations of her elder sisters but ultimately
regains him through her perseverance.

Folk Songs

From ancient recorded history, Koreans have been known for their
love of singing and dancing. Folk songs, therefore, are still a living
phenomenon—exploring the power of the human voice, evoking
memories of the ethos of community, and reinforcing the people's
sense of identity. Singers have the power not only to move the audience but also to update the text by alluding to current fashions or
contemporary events. Common subjects include the farmer's work
and days, various phases of love relationships (especially parting and

---

12. See Aarne and Thompson, *Types of the Folktale*, for an extensive classification
system cataloging basic plots and tale types.

abandonment), modern life, and moral dilemmas in contemporary society. Some songs are known universally, such as "Arirang," while others are regional. The collection of Korean folk songs began in the twentieth century, especially from the 1960s on with the advent of the portable tape recorder. South Korea's educational broadcasting company has collected and classified them by province and issued CDs with accompanying lyrics. With the spread of industrial agriculture, however, work songs by farmers are increasingly hard to find.

Shamanist Narrative Songs

The shamanist oral tradition in Korea operated at the nexus of myth and ritual. From master to disciple, the verbatim transmission of accumulated knowledge, organized mnemonically, took prodigious memory and many years of hard work to accomplish. Before the advent of the portable tape recorder, written texts were the product of oral dictation to folklorists. The recital by the shaman Pae Kyŏngjae of Osan in Kyŏnggi province of the entire text of *The Abandoned Princess* in the 1930s is one example. Today songs are recorded at the site of the ritual. Important song texts exist in regional variations, and often there are differences between the dictated and transcribed versions. There is a lively interaction among the shamans, the supplicant who hosts the event, and the audience. Shamanist narrative songs are ritualized ideological discourse with an echo of voices from the past and should be appreciated with that context in mind.

In the past the typical shaman occupied the lowest social stratum and lived precariously, often viewed as a subversive figure by the lettered elite. Yet, while shamans endured suffering at the hands of local authorities, their faith and the rituals they performed brought solace to many, both the powerful and the powerless, the rich as well as the poor. Some of the written texts we possess are riddled with learned diction—Sino-Korean words and technical vocabulary from Buddhist, Daoist, and Confucian traditions—raising the intriguing question of how the unlettered shamans of the past managed to understand and commit those elements to memory, especially when they relied on oral rather than visual transmission. Whoever the redactors or interpolators were, they cultivated a hybrid textuality, an abstruse vocabulary intercut with a common vernacular.

P'ansori

P'ansori are oral narratives sung by a professional singer (*kwangdae*) accompanied by a single drummer. They emerged from shamanist narrative songs in Chŏlla province and were originally the property of a singer from a hereditary shaman household, usually the husband of a shaman. The singer sings, narrates, acts, and uses physical movement to create dramatic effects; the drummer beats the rhythm, supporting the action and chiming in. Except for a folding fan held by the singer (his/her badge) and a folding screen providing a backdrop, no stage props are used. *P'ansori* texts bear clear traces of an oral versemaking technique—use of story patterns, formulas, epithets, topoi, phonomimes, phenomimes, *sijo*, *kasa*, syntactic parallelism— and all these facilitated mnemonic composition. The mnemonic framework is provided by the plot—scenes, episodes, motifs, songs, and narratives—and the singer, capable of lengthy verbatim recall, managed diglossic situations with skill. Equipped with both narrative competence and performance skills, the singer's personality stamps his song, which is sung in a special register of the voice, the *p'ansori* register.

In 1753 Yu Chinhan (1711–1790), a scholar traveling through the southwest region, had the opportunity to hear a performance of the *Song of Ch'unhyang* and other *p'ansori* pieces. The following year, Yu wrote the "Song of Ch'unhyang," a heptasyllabic verse in two hundred couplets in literary Chinese. Woodblock editions of the *Song* began to be published in the nineteenth century, appearing mostly in Seoul and Chŏnju and generating their own textual communities. How did the song come to be written down? Did the singer learn the song from his teacher and memorize it, and did he then have enough literacy to write it down himself? Are we speaking here of a memorized text or a genuine oral composition? Sin Chaehyo (1812–1884), the first known redactor of *p'ansori* repertory who had dual competence in performance and in creating literary texts with copious allusions to Chinese works of verse and prose, can be said to have reshaped the tradition in order to preserve it. Most renowned singers presented the *Song of Ch'unhyang* in variant forms, exploring fully their power to suit performances to particular public spaces. Performance is thus an inextricable part of the meaning: the audience already knows the story but comes for the singer's ingenious interpretation—his art. The singing skill required for public performance was the product of years of apprenticeship and training, but recordings of variant performances suggest that exact verbal memorization of a text was neither encouraged nor practiced. The aspect of *p'ansori* performance that brought it to life was the fact that it was always affected by the place and occasion and reaction of the audience.

Mask Dance Plays

Mask dance plays originated as a popular part of village rituals and festivals, often serving to express the grievances felt by commoners against the social elites of the time. Among the staple themes of these plays were the foibles of apostate Buddhist monks, the hoodwinking of a decadent noble by his prankish servant, and the conflict between an ugly wife and a seductive concubine. The ritual significance of the plays emerged in scenes depicting the initiation of sexual union and childbirth, representing symbolic acts of invocation for bountiful harvests and other blessings for the coming year. As is common in ritual plays elsewhere, mask plays have all-male casts. The masks worn by the actors, with deep-set eyes, a prominent nose, and sometimes asymmetrical facial features, cover the entire face; a cloth covers the back of the head and secures the mask in place. Hahoe and Pongsan masks were made of black alderwood and lacquered; today most masks are made of paper, gourd, or wood. The colors of the masks symbolize the five directions of the compass: blue for east, white for west, red for south, black for north, and yellow for the center. The defeat of an old monk wearing a black mask by the young rake Ch'wibari in a red mask, for example, represents the victory of summer over winter. At the end of the play, the masks were usually burned in a symbolic sacrifice, to preserve their sacred purity; hence, few old masks remain today. Music for the play is provided by a double-reed oboe, a transverse flute, a two-stringed fiddle, an hourglass drum, a barrel drum, and a small gong. The plays are commonly performed at the New Year, the eighth day of the fourth lunar month, the fifth of the fifth lunar month, the fifteeenth of the eighth lunar month, and on other national holidays. The Yangju *pyŏlsandae* play excerpted in this volume has been designated by the Korean government as Intangible Cultural Asset No. 2.

Puppet Plays

Puppet plays originated in the Three Kingdoms period, and their contents were transmitted orally. The family name of the white-haired old man Pak Ch'ŏmji is homonymous with *pak* 'gourd.' Hong Tongji's family name is homonymous with *hong* 'red,' and his puppet is painted red from head to toe. Like the mask dance plays, the puppet plays retained elements of shamanist belief and dealt with themes such as the apostate monk, the triangular relationship of husband, wife, and concubine, and the oppression of the lower classes by the ruling elite. In this respect, both the puppet plays and mask dance plays expressed the antiauthoritarian and anticlerical features characteristic of folk literature in Korea.

Today one puppet play, *Kkoktu kaksi,* survives. Like *p'ansori,* its text reflects a history of oral composition in its exploitation of vernacular sound effects. The predilection for colorful vulgarisms, argot, obscenity, and scatology brings out the intended satire, humor, and pathos of the play. But while the language is open, unruly, heteroglossic, and polyphonic, it also interacts with literacy, as when Ch'wibari puns on letters of the Korean alphabet and on the tetrasyllabic lines from the *Thousand-Sinograph Primer*. Such a text is the product of a culture that was both oral and literate: when a schoolboy learned the Chinese classics in traditional Korea, he would recite a text aloud—by reading it out, he could hear his own voice amplifying his powers of retention and recall—and that recitation would be overheard by household members including servants and slaves (as Yi Toryŏng's male servant does in the *Song of Ch'unhyang*). Orality was close to—indeed, an intimate part of—the human lifeworld, and it was empathetic and participatory rather than objectively distanced, as it seems to be today.[13]

Foundation Myths

TANGUN

The *Wei shu* tells us that two thousand years ago, at the time of Emperor Yao, Tangun Wanggŏm chose Asadal as his capital and founded the state of Chosŏn. The *Old Record* notes that in olden times Hwanin's son, Hwanung, wished to descend from heaven and live in the world of human beings. Knowing his son's desire, Hwanin surveyed the three highest mountains and found Mount T'aebaek the most suitable place for his son to settle and help human beings. Therefore, he gave Hwanung three heavenly seals and dispatched him to rule over the people. Hwanung descended with three thousand followers to a spot under a tree by the holy altar atop Mount T'aebaek, and he called this place the City of God. He was the heavenly king Hwanung. Leading the earl of wind, the master of rain, and the master of clouds, he took charge of some three hundred sixty areas of responsibility, including agriculture, allotted life spans, illness, punishment, and good and evil, and brought culture to his people.

13. Ong, *Interfaces of the Word*, 276.

At that time a bear and a tiger living in the same cave prayed to holy Hwanung to transform them into human beings. The king gave them a bundle of sacred mugwort and twenty cloves of garlic and said, "If you eat these and shun sunlight for one hundred days, you will assume human form." Both animals ate the spices and avoided the sun. After twenty-one days the bear became a woman, but the tiger, unable to observe the taboo, remained a tiger. Unable to find a husband, the bear-woman prayed under the altar tree for a child. Hwanung transformed himself, lay with her, and begot a son called Tangun Wanggŏm.

In the fiftieth year of the reign of Emperor Yao, Tangun made the walled city of P'yŏngyang the capital and called his country Chosŏn. He then moved his capital to Asadal on Mount Paegak, also named Mount Kunghol, or Kŭmmidal, whence he ruled for 1,500 years. When, in the year *kimyo* (1122 BCE), King Wu of Zhou enfeoffed Jizi (Kija) to Chosŏn, Tangun moved to Changdanggyŏng, but later he returned and hid in Asadal as a mountain god at the age of 1,908.

CHUMONG

Tongmyŏng (Eastern Brilliance) appears to be a name for a god common to the Puyŏ peoples. After Chumong established Koguryŏ, it grew to be a mighty power in northeast Asia. The Tongmyŏng myth transmitted among the Puyŏ peoples was appropriated in Koguryŏ to embellish the legend of Chumong. It is preserved in artifacts such as the epitaph found on King Kwanggaet'o's stele, erected in 414, and in Chinese and Korean histories. The following is a prose version of the myth; originally in the *Old History of the Three Kingdoms*, it was quoted as a gloss to "The Lay of King Tongmyŏng," by Yi Kyubo (1168–1241), and preserved in the *Collected Works of Minister Yi of Korea (Tongguk Yi-sangguk chip)*.

In the third year of Shenque (59 BCE) of the Han dynasty, the Emperor of Heaven sent his son Haemosu to the old capital of Puyŏ (Ch. Fuyou). When Haemosu descended from heaven, he rode a five-dragon chariot while his retinue numbering in the hundreds all rode white swans floating on multihued clouds that gave forth music.[1] He dallied for more than ten days on Bear Heart Mountain before coming down; he wore a headdress made of crow feathers and carried a sword that shone like a dragon. He dealt with affairs of state in the morning and ascended back to heaven in the evening, so people called him the heavenly king.

On the Green River[2] north of the capital, the River Earl had three beautiful daughters. The eldest was called Willow Flower, the second Daylily Flower, and the youngest Reed Flower. One day the three girls set out from the Green River to play at Bear Heart Pond; their appearance was like that of the gods, soft and lustrous, and their jade ornaments jangled wildly so that they seemed just like Hangao.[3] Seeing them, King Haemosu told his courtiers: "If I marry one of them, I will surely have an heir." But when the girls saw the king, they immediately disappeared into the water.

The courtiers then said, "Why doesn't the king build a palace and wait for the girls to enter, after which he can close the door?" Whereupon Haemosu used his horsewhip to draw lines in the dirt—and suddenly a magnificent copper structure arose. In the middle of the room he set three places with goblets of wine. The three maidens came in, sat in the three places, and toasted one another with wine until they were quite inebriated. Having waited until they were drunk, the king then rushed out to close the doors. The girls were startled and tried to escape, but the eldest, Willow Flower, could not get away from the king.

---

1. This scene is read as symbolizing sunrise. The "Hae" of Haemosu's name means "sun" in Korea, and his appearance can be seen as the personification of the rising sun.

2. The present-day Yalu.

3. A female fairy in ancient China. According to the *Hanshi waijuan* (Han Ying's commentary on the *Book of Songs*), when Zeng Jiaofu of Zhou passed Hangao Terrace while on his way to Chu, he met two women whose jewels caught his eye, and he talked them into giving him the jewels.

An enraged River Earl sent a messenger demanding: "Who are you to detain my daughter?"

The king answered, "I am the son of the Emperor of Heaven, and I seek the hand of your daughter in marriage."

The River Earl sent his messenger again, saying, "If you, the son of the Emperor of Heaven, wish to seek my daughter's hand in marriage, you should send an intermediary. Is it not improper for you to have detained my daughter?"

The king, who now intended to call upon the River Earl, was unable to enter the room where the girl was captive, because of embarrassment, and decided to set Willow Flower free. But Willow Flower, who had come to love the king, would not leave. Instead she enjoined him, "We can go to the land of the River Earl in the five-dragon chariot."

The king called to heaven, whereupon the five-dragon chariot suddenly descended from the sky. As soon as Haemosu and the girl climbed into the chariot, wind and clouds arose and they found themselves at the palace of the River Earl. The River Earl greeted them with propriety, prepared a place for them, and said, "The way of marriage is the same everywhere under heaven. Why have you violated propriety and brought disgrace on my household? If you are truly the son of the Emperor of Heaven, you must have extraordinary powers."

The king responded, "That can only be seen through a test."

At that, the River Earl turned himself into a carp in the waters fronting his yard. The king turned himself into an otter and caught the carp. The River Earl then turned himself into a deer—whereupon the king turned himself into a wolf and chased the deer. Next the River Earl became a pheasant—but the king transformed himself into a falcon and attacked the pheasant. At last the River Earl realized that the king was indeed the son of the Emperor of Heaven and had the marriage conducted with full ritual. But fearing that the king might not take his daughter with him when he left, the River Earl put on a banquet and urged wine upon Haemosu, making him quite drunk. He then put the king and his daughter in a leather bag, placed them on the five-dragon chariot, and sent it off to heaven. But before the chariot could clear the water, the king awoke, grabbed the girl's golden hairpin, pierced the leather bag, emerged, and flew off to heaven alone.

Infuriated, the River Earl told his daughter, "You did not do as I said and have brought shame on my household."

He then had his courtiers stretch his daughter's lips to three feet and banished her to the Ubal River with only two slaves.[4]

The fisherman Kangnyŏk-puch'u reported to King Kŭmwa, "Lately there has been something in the weirs taking fish, but I do not know what kind of creature it is."

King Kŭmwa ordered the fisherman to catch the creature, but the net ripped open. So the fisherman made an iron net with which he brought in a woman sitting on a rock. Her lips were so long that she could not speak; only after they were trimmed three times was she able to talk. King Kŭmwa recognized that the woman was the consort of the son of the Emperor of Heaven and put her up in a detached palace. Impregnated by the sun shining on her, the woman gave birth to Chumong in the fourth month of the fourth year, *kyehae,* of Shenque (58 BCE). The newborn infant's crying was very loud, and his form was heroic and wonderful.

When Willow Flower bore Chumong, first she laid from her left armpit an egg the size of a peck. King Kŭmwa thought this strange and said, "It is inauspicious for a woman to lay a bird's egg."

He had his men throw the egg into a horse pasture, but the horses would not step on it. He then had it abandoned in deep mountains, but the wild beasts all protected it. There were always rays of the sun on the egg, even on cloudy days, so the king had the egg sent to its mother for her to tend.

---

4. Long lips—a reference to lips like a chicken's beak—are a motif of chicken and dragon myths. The case of Lady Aryŏng of Silla is an example.

Finally the egg opened and yielded a boy child who spoke before he was even one month old. He told his mother that flies were biting his eyes so he could not sleep and asked her to make him a bow and some arrows. His mother made him a bow and arrows of reeds, which he used to shoot flies resting on a spinning wheel; every arrow he loosed hit its mark. In the Puyŏ tongue, Chumong meant "skilled archer."[5]

As he grew older, he became more talented. King Kŭmwa had seven sons who always went hunting with Chumong. One day when the princes and their forty-odd attendants barely got one deer, Chumong shot many. Jealous, the princes grabbed Chumong, tied him to a tree, and took his deer. Chumong uprooted the tree and returned home. The crown prince Taeso told King Kŭmwa, "Chumong is courageous and has bold eyes. If we do not do something about him, there will surely be trouble later."

King Kŭmwa, seeking to test Chumong's intentions, had him tend horses. Nursing a sense of grievance, Chumong told his mother, "As the grandson of the Emperor of Heaven, I would rather die than feed horses for somebody else. I wish to go south and establish my own kingdom, but I do not dare do as I wish because my mother is here."

His mother replied, "This is what has troubled me day and night. I have heard that one needs a good horse for a long journey. I will choose one for you."

They went to where the horses were kept and drove them with a long whip. Terrified, the horses raced about, but one chestnut bay leaped over the fence, which was twice the height of a man. Chumong recognized that this was a superior horse and secretly pierced its

5. Chumong's archery skills suggest that the group that produced this myth was not agricultural but pastoral. This is borne out by the prominence of streams in the story as well, since water was an absolute necessity for people to be able to move their animals across broad lands in search of pasture. In the myth of Pak Hyŏkkŏse, reflecting an agricultural society, wells are prominent rather than streams.

tongue with a needle so that it could not eat or drink. Soon the horse began to waste away.

Upon touring the pastures, King Kŭmwa was delighted at the way all the other horses grew fat. The emaciated horse he gave to Chumong. Chumong then removed the needle and fed the horse well. With three men, Oi, Mari, and Hyŏppu, Chumong headed south to the Kaesa River, where they found no ferry. Afraid that the soldiers pursuing them might arrive at any moment, Chumong raised his whip to the sky and cried out, "I am the grandson of the Emperor of Heaven, the maternal grandson of the River Earl, and I have come here fleeing from danger. Gods of heaven and earth, take pity on me and quickly send a bridge."

He struck the river with his bow—whereupon fishes and turtles rose to form a bridge so that Chumong could cross. Soon the pursuing soldiers appeared. But when they reached the river, the fish and turtle bridge disappeared, and the soldiers already on it all drowned.

Earlier, when it had been time to depart, Chumong was unable to leave his mother. But she said, "Don't worry about your mother," and gave him bundles containing the seeds of the five grains. But Chumong, stricken at the thought of separating from her, forgot to take the barley seeds. As he was resting beneath a large tree, two doves flew up. Chumong said, "My divine mother must have sent the barley seeds," and shot the doves, knocking them both down with one arrow. He then opened their beaks, took out the barley seeds, and poured water on them. The doves then came back to life and flew away. Chumong sat himself down on a reed mat and established the ranks of king and ministers.

Songyang, the king of Piryu, was out hunting when he saw Chumong. Impressed by Chumong's extraordinary appearance, he called him over and prepared a place for him, saying: "Piryu is an isolated place by the sea, so I have never seen a superior man. It is very fortunate that I have met you today."

Chumong replied, "I am the grandson of the Emperor of Heaven and the king of the Western Country, so I dare to ask whom you succeeded as king."

Whereupon Songyang said, "I am descended of immortals and have been king for several generations. This area is too small to be divided between two kings. Since it has not been long since you set up your kingdom, is it not right that you should become my vassal?"

King Chumong responded, "I am the successor to the Emperor of Heaven while you, who are not the grandson of a god, insist on calling yourself king. If you do not submit to me, then surely heaven will kill you."

Songyang, who grew suspicious after hearing Chumong claim again and again to be the grandson of heaven, sought to test him, saying: "Let us shoot arrows together." He painted a deer, set it up within a distance of a hundred paces, and drew his bow. Even though his arrow did not strike the deer's navel, he managed to hit its body. King Chumong had a jade ring hung up over a hundred paces away and shot at the ring, smashing it like a roof tile. Songyang was taken aback.

King Chumong said, "My kingdom is new and still does not have the pomp and circumstance of drum and bugle. Thus when your Piryu envoy came, I was not able to greet him and send him away in proper royal fashion. That is why you took me so lightly."

Chumong's distinguished minister Pubunno stepped forth to say, "I will get the drums of Piryu for you, great king."

King Chumong asked, "How will you bring back something that another kingdom has hidden away?"

Pubunno responded: "This is what heaven has given. How can I not get it? Who knew that the king would rise to this level when he was in difficulty back in Puyŏ? The king has survived ten thousand dangers and is now known even west of the Liao River. This is due to the will of the Emperor of Heaven. There is nothing that the king cannot attain."

Pubunno and two others then went to the kingdom of Piryu and brought back the drums and bugles. The Piryu king sent a messenger to report the theft, but King Chumong, concerned that the messenger might see the drums and bugles, had them painted dark to look old. Songyang's messenger did not dare to dispute this and simply turned back. Because Songyang had sought to make King Chumong his vassal based on who set up his capital first, Chumong built a palace using rotten wood so that it looked to be a thousand years old. Songyang came, saw the palace, and did not dare to press the issue of whose capital was first.

King Chumong went hunting in the west, where he caught a white deer, hung it upside down at Crab Plain, made an incantation, and said, "I will not let you go unless heaven sends a great rain to wash away the royal capital of Piryu. If you want to escape this predicament, appeal to heaven."

The deer cried so piteously that the sound pierced the ears of heaven. Monsoon rains fell for seven days, and Songyang's capital was washed away. King Chumong, riding a duck-horse, stretched out ropes made of reeds to which all the people clung. Then King Chumong took his whip and drew a line in the water from which the flood subsided. In the sixth month, Songyang came and surrendered.

In the seventh month, a dark cloud covered Falcon Pass so that it could not be seen. But the voices of thousands of people and the sounds of cutting trees could be heard. King Chumong said, "Heaven is building a fortress for me." Then, for the first time in seven days, the mists cleared to reveal fortress walls and a palace terrace. King Chumong bowed to heaven and then took up residence there.

In the ninth month, King Chumong rose to heaven, never to return. At the time he was forty years of age. Crown Prince Yuri held a funeral on South Mountain using the jade whip Chumong had left behind.

Even as a child, Yuri had great integrity. When he was young, he busied himself shooting birds. One day he shot and broke a water pitcher carried by a woman on her head. Angrily, the woman berated him: "This fatherless child has shot and broken my pitcher."

Greatly embarrassed, Yuri fashioned a plug out of clay and fixed the pitcher like new. He then went home and asked his mother who his father was. His mother, teasing because he was so young, replied that he had no particular father.

In tears, Yuri said, "If I have no particular father, how can I face people from now on?" and he then tried to kill himself. Alarmed, his mother stopped him and said, "I was just teasing you. Your father is none other than the grandson of the Emperor of Heaven and the maternal grandson of the River Earl. He resented being the subject of Puyŏ, fled south, and set up a new kingdom. Will you not go and see it?"

Yuri answered, "My father is a king over his people while I, his son, am the subject of someone else. Even though I have no talent, I cannot but be ashamed."

His mother said, "This is what your father said when he left: 'I have hidden something in a pine tree on seven hills and seven valleys. Only he who finds it will be my son.'"

Yuri looked for it through all the hills and valleys. But he could not find it and returned home exhausted. He then heard a sad sound coming from one of the posts in the house. The post was a pine tree on a stone. The pine tree had seven corners. Figuring it out for himself, Yuri reasoned that seven hills and seven valleys were seven corners. He arose and went to the post, where he found a hole at the top. There he was delighted to discover a piece of a broken sword. In the fourth month of the fourth year of Hongjia of the Former Han dynasty (17 BCE), he escaped to Koguryŏ, where he presented the sword piece to the king. The king took out a piece of a broken sword and matched the two pieces together. They began to bleed and fused into one sword.

The king then said to Yuri: "If you are truly my son, then what kind of godlike powers do you have?" In response, Yuri shot himself up into the sky and rode a spear to the sun, thus demonstrating his extraordinary godlike powers. The king was delighted and made Yuri his crown prince.

Translated by John Duncan

PAK HYŎKKŎSE

In olden times Chinhan had six villages. The first was Yangsan village in Arch'ŏn, south of present-day Tamŏm monastery. Its chief was Arp'yŏng, who first descended on P'yoam Peak. He was the progenitor of the Yi clan of Kŭmnyang district. The second was Kohŏ village on Mount Tol. Its chief was Sobŏltori who first descended on Mount Hyŏng. He was the progenitor of the Chŏng clan in Saryang district, now called Namsan district, which includes villages in the south such as Kuryangbol, Madŭng, Odo, and Pukhoedŏk. The third was Taesu village on Mount Mu. Its chief was Kuryema, who first descended on Mount Yi. He was the progenitor of the Son clan in Chŏmnyang (Moryang) district. Now called Changbok district, it includes villages in the west such as Pakkok. The fourth was Chinji village on Mount Ch'wi. Its chief was Chibaek'o, who first descended on Mount Hwa. He is the progenitor of the Ch'oe clan in Ponp'i district, now called T'ongsŏn, which includes villages in the southwest such as Sip'a. Ch'oe Ch'iwŏn is from Ponp'i district. The old site is in front of Mit'an monastery, south of present-day Hwangnyong monastery—it is clearer to say that this is the site of the ancestral house belonging to the Ch'oe clan. The fifth was Kari village on Mount Kŭm. Its chief was Chit'a, who first descended on Mount Myŏnghwal. He was the progenitor of the Pae clan. Now called Kadŏk district, it includes villages in the southeast such as upper and lower Sŏjinaea. The sixth was Kaya village on Mount Myŏnghwal. Its chief was Hojin, who first descended on Mount Kŭmgang. He was the progenitor of the Sŏl clan of Sŭppi district, which includes villages in the east such as Muri, Inggumyŏ, and Kwŏlgok.

In view of this record, it appears that the progenitors of the six villages all came down from heaven. In the nineteenth year of King Yuri (32 CE), the names of the six districts were changed and six clan names were granted. According to current custom, however, Chunghŭng district is called Mother, Changhŭng district is Father, Imch'ŏn district is Son, and Kadŏk district is Daughter, but the reason is unknown.

On the first day of the third month of the first year, *imja,* of Dijie of the Former Han dynasty (69 BCE), the ancestors of the six villages, together with their children, gathered by the shore of the Al River. They said, "Because we have no ruler above to govern the people, the people are dissolute and do only what they wish. We should seek out a virtuous man to be our king, found a country, and lay out a capital."

When they climbed to a height and looked southward, they saw an eerie, lightning-like emanation by the Na Well under Mount Yang, while nearby a white horse seemed to kneel and bow. When they reached the spot, they found a red egg; the horse neighed and flew up to heaven when it saw men approaching.

When the people cracked the egg open, they found a beautiful infant boy with a radiant visage. Amazed by their discovery, they bathed the infant in the East Spring, and then he emitted light. Birds and beasts danced for joy, heaven and earth shook, and the sun and the moon became bright. They named the child King Hyŏkkŏse, or Bright, and titled him *kŏsŭrhan,* or king.

The people congratulated one another and said, "Now that the Son of Heaven has come down to be among us, we must seek a virtuous queen to be his mate." That day a hen dragon appeared near the Aryŏng well in Saryang district and produced from under her left rib an infant girl. Her features were unusually lovely, but her lips were like the beak of a chick. Only when the girl was given a bath in the North River in Wŏlsŏng did the beak fall off. The river was then called

Palch'ŏn. The people erected a palace at the western foot of Mount South and reared the two wondrous infants together. Since the boy had been born from an egg in the shape of a gourd, "*pak*" in Korean, they gave him the surname Pak; the girl was named after the well where she was born.

When the two reached the age of thirteen in the first year, *kapcha*, of Wufeng (57 BCE), the boy became king and the girl became queen.

They named the country Sŏrabŏl, Sŏbŏl, Sara, or Saro. And because of the circumstances of the queen's birth, the country was also called Kyerim, or Forest of the Cock, to commemorate the appearance of the hen dragon. According to another story, the country was so called because a cock crowed in the woods when Kim Alchi was found during the reign of King T'arhae. Later, Silla became the official name of the country.

After a sixty-one-year reign, Hyŏkkŏse ascended to heaven, and after seventy days his remains fell to earth. His queen is said to have followed him. The people wished to bury them in the same tomb, but a large snake appeared and stopped them. So the remains of each were divided into five parts (the head plus the right and left hands and feet) and buried. Called Five Tombs or Snake Tomb, the site is the present North Tomb at Tamŏm monastery. The heir apparent succeeded Hyŏkkŏse as King Namhae.

KIM SURO

Since the creation of heaven and earth there had been no name for the country of Karak or its ruler. The nine chiefs—Ado, Yŏdo, P'ido, Odo, Yusu, Yuch'ŏn, Sinch'ŏn, Och'ŏn, and Singwi—ruled over one hundred households with a population of seventy-five thousand, who lived on the hills and plains and plowed fields and dug wells.

In the eighteenth year, *imin*, of Jianwu in the reign of Emperor Guangwu of the Later Han (42 CE), on the day of the lustration festival, a strange voice called out from Mount Kuji in the north. Two or three hundred people gathered there. They heard the voice but could not see the speaker.

The voice asked, "Is anyone here?"

The chiefs replied, "Yes."

"Where is this place?'

"This is Kuji."

The voice continued: "Heaven commanded me to come here to found a new country and become your king, so I have descended. Dig the earth at the peak of the mountain, sing this song, and dance with joy to welcome your great king:

> O turtle, o turtle
> Show your head!
> If you do not,
> We'll roast and eat you.

Overjoyed, the nine chiefs sang and danced. Shortly afterward, they looked up and saw a purple rope descending from the sky to touch the earth; at the end of it hung a golden chest wrapped in red cloth. The chest contained six eggs round as the sun. Surprised and joyful, the people offered countless bows, wrapped the eggs again in cloth, and brought them to the house of Chief Ado, where they placed them on a table. Then they dispersed. When they returned at dawn, twelve days later, and opened the chest, the eggs had transformed into six infant boys with admirable appearances. The people had them sit on the table, bowed to them, and offered them utmost respect. The boys grew day by day. After more than ten days, they were nine feet (*ch'ŏk*) tall like King Tang of Yin and had the dragon face of the founder of the Han, eight-colored eyebrows like those of Emperor Yao, and double pupils like those of Emperor Shun. On the fifteenth day of the month they ascended the throne. The taboo name of the boy who first transformed was Suro, or Sunŭng, and the name of his country was Great Karak, or Kaya state. This was one of the six Kaya confederations. The other five boys became the rulers of the other five Kaya states. . . .

Suro had a temporary palace built that was roofed with uncut thatch in the interest of simplicity. The earthen steps of the palace were only three feet high.

Then, in springtime, in the first month of his second year, *kyemyo,* Suro declared: "I wish to establish a capital." He went to a newly re-claimed field (*sindapp'yŏng*) south of the temporary palace and viewed the mountain peaks in the four directions. Looking back at his sub-jects, he said, "This place is as small as a bean patch, but the hills and streams are beautiful and plentiful. It is fit to house the sixteen arhats[1] or the seven sages. Proper reclamation will make this a fine place." Before returning to his residence he marked out sites for the outer walls, some fifteen hundred steps round, and for palaces, halls, offices, ar-mories, and storehouses. Sturdy adults, workers, and artisans were conscripted, and construction went on from the twentieth day of the first month to the tenth day of the third month. The palaces and houses were built during the farmers' slack season, which lasted from the tenth month to the second month of the following year, *kapchin.* Suro chose an auspicious day and moved into his new palace, where he conducted the affairs of state diligently.

About this time the queen of King Hamdal in the country of Wanha conceived and gave birth to an egg. Out of the egg came a boy named T'arhae. He was three feet tall and his head one foot in dia-meter. T'arhae crossed the sea to Karak, entered the palace, and non-chalantly announced that he had come to take over the throne.

The king replied, "Heaven has commanded me to be king. I am to pacify the country and quiet the people. How can I go against the mandate of heaven and yield my throne, my country, and my people?"

---

1. "Worthy one," who has destroyed the afflictions and all cause for future rebirth and who thus will enter nirvāṇa at death (*PDB*, 62).

T'arhae proposed to settle the question with a contest in magic, and the king agreed. In the wink of an eye T'arhae became a hawk—whereupon the king became an eagle. T'arhae changed into a sparrow—whereupon the king changed into a falcon. Finally, both resumed their human forms.

T'arhae said, "I was a hawk before an eagle, a sparrow before a falcon. I escaped death because in your virtuous wisdom you do not wish to take life. I am not your equal."

Following the route taken by Chinese ships in a nearby ford outside of Ingyo, T'arhae departed. Fearing that T'arhae would foment rebellion, the king sent five hundred ships in pursuit. When T'arhae's ship fled toward Silla (Kyerim), the king's ships returned. . . .

On the twenty-seventh day of the seventh month of the twenty-fourth year, *musin,* of Jianwu (48 CE), the nine chiefs proposed to the king at the morning audience: "Since Your Majesty has descended to earth, you have not obtained a suitable mate. Please choose the most beautiful and virtuous of our daughters to enter the palace and become your wife."

The king replied, "My coming here was ordained by heaven, and heaven will choose my future queen as well. Please don't worry." He then ordered Chief Yuch'ŏn to sail to Mangsan Island with a light boat and a fast steed and wait there. He bade Singwi go to Sŭngjŏm.

Unexpectedly there appeared a ship with red sails and a red flag, sailing from the southwest to the north. When Chief Yuch'ŏn and others brandished torches, the passengers were eager to come ashore. Singwi galloped off to relay the news to the king. Upon hearing it,.the gladdened king sent the nine chiefs who held the mast and helm of the finest quality to welcome the ship and escort the passengers to the palace.

"He and I have never met," the princess said. "Am I to follow you so easily?"

When Chief Yuch'ŏn and the others returned to report what the princess had said, the king thought it proper. The king had a canopy built on a hill sixty feet southwest of the palace, on the lower slope of a mountain, and waited there with his officials. The princess had her boat moored at Pyŏlp'o Ford and walked up to the hilltop, where she removed her silk trousers and offered them as a gift to the mountain spirit. . . . As the princess approached the temporary quarters, the king went out to welcome her, and together they entered the canopy. The attending officials, in descending order of rank, greeted them from below the steps and then retired. . . .

When the king and his new queen were alone in the bedchamber, the queen calmly said to the king, "I am a princess from the Indian country of Ayodhya. My family name is Hŏ, my given name Hwangok (Yellow Jade). I am fifteen years old. In the fifth month of this year, when I was at home, my father and mother told me of a dream they had. In this dream the supreme deity of heaven appeared and said, 'The founding king of the state of Karak, Suro, has been sent by heaven. He is truly divine and holy. He has been busy governing his new country and has not yet chosen his wife, so you should send your daughter to be his queen.' Once those words were spoken, he ascended to heaven. His words to me still ring in my ears. 'Take leave of your parents and go there.' So I started on my voyage, with steamed dates and heavenly peaches to sustain me. Thus it is that I, with a lovely head and beautiful eyebrows,[2] stand before you now."

"Because of my divine nature," the king replied, "I knew that a princess would come from a distant land. I did not heed my officials' request that I marry a queen. Now that the wise and virtuous princess has come on her own, great is my fortune." The king passed two nights and one day with her. . . .

On the first day of the eighth month, the king and queen returned to the palace in a royal carriage, accompanied by courtiers in carriages and followed by a train of wagons loaded with exotic goods. . . .

2. *Shijing* 57:2; Waley, *Book of Songs*, 80.

One day the king told his officials: "The nine chiefs are heads of officialdom, but their names and titles are those of uncouth rustics, not of nobility. If they become known abroad, we would be ridiculed."Accordingly he changed Ado to Agung, Yŏdo to Yŏhae, P'ido to P'ijang, and Obang to Osang. Retaining the first graph but changing the second, he transformed Yusu and Yuch'ŏn to Yugong and Yudŏk, Sinch'ŏn to Sindo, and Och'ŏn to Onŭng. He replaced Singwi with homophones with a different meaning. He also adopted the Silla official system and established the ranks of Kakkan, Ajilgan, and Kŭpkan. For lower officials he followed the precedents of the Zhou and the system of the Han. This indeed was removing the old and adopting the new—a way of establishing government organization. Thereupon order prevailed in the country and family, and the king loved his subjects like his children. Though the king's teachings were not severe, they were majestic. Though his administration was not harsh, it was principled. . . . In that year (48 CE) his queen dreamed of a bear, conceived, and gave birth to a son, the heir apparent Kodŭng.

On the first day of the third month of the sixth year, *kisa,* of Zhongping in the reign of Emperor Ling of the Later Han dynasty (189 CE), the queen died at the age of 157. . . . The king spent many days mourning her death, and at last died ten years later, on the twenty-third day of the third month of the fourth year, *kimyo,* of Jianan of Emperor Xian. He was 158.

SŎK T'ARHAE

During the reign of King Namhae (4–24 CE), a boat came to anchor off the shores of Karak. King Suro of that country, together with his people, beat their drums and shouted in greeting. But the boat sailed away and reached Ajin Cove in the village of Hasŏji, east of the Forest of the Cock. Just then an old woman appeared on the shore of the inlet. Her name was Ajin Ŭisŏn, and she was the mother of a fisherman of King Hyŏkkŏse. Spying the boat from afar, she said, "There is no rock in the middle of the sea. Why does a flock of magpies circle above and cry?" She took a skiff and went to investigate. Magpies hovered over the boat, which bore a casket twenty feet long and thirteen feet wide. She towed the boat to shore and moored it at the foot of a grove of trees. She did not know whether it would be auspicious or not and informed heaven of what had happened. Then she opened the casket. In it were male and female slaves, seven treasures, and a handsome boy.

After seven days had passed, the boy said, "I am from the land of Yongsŏng, where has had twenty-eight dragon kings, all born from human wombs. They ascended the throne, one after another, at the age of five or six, and taught the people how to regulate their life. We have clans of eight ranks, but all ascended to the throne without elections. My father, King Hamdalp'a, married the daughter of the king of the land of Chŏngnyŏ, but she long remained barren and prayed for a son. After seven years, she gave birth to a huge egg. The great king had a casket made, put me into it, together with seven treasures and slaves, and loaded it on a boat. He had it launched and prayed that it would land in a destined place, found a kingdom, and establish a family. A red dragon came to guard the boat until it arrived here."

Then the boy, who was called T'arhae, climbed Mount T'oham with two slaves and other assistants trailing after him. They built a cairn where he stayed for seven days while looking for a suitable place within the city walls to settle. He saw a hill shaped like a three-day-old crescent moon—an ideal place for a long stay. When he went down from the mountain and approached the place, he found that it was Lord Ho's residence. The boy devised a ruse: he had a whetstone and charcoal buried around the house. The next day, he went to the door and declared that it was the house of his ancestors. Lord Ho denied this, and after quarreling without a resolution, they brought the case before the authorities. When the officials asked the boy for his proof, he replied, "We are a family of blacksmiths, but we were staying in a nearby village. During our absence some other person occupied our house. I beg you to dig up the ground and make a search." They found the whetstone and charcoal, so the house became his. Acknowledging the boy's shrewdness, King Namhae gave him his eldest daughter in marriage; she was Lady Ani.

Upon the death of King Yuri in the sixth month, *chŏngsa,* of the second year of Zhong-yuan of Emperor Guangwu (57 CE), T'arhae ascended the throne. Because he had taken over another's property under the pretext that it was his ancestors', his name became Sŏk (Old). Or perhaps it was because of the magpies that caused the casket to be opened: the *bird* radical was dropped from the graph *magpie,* leaving the one for Sŏk. His name T'arhae (Remove and Undo) alludes to the fact that he came out of an egg from a casket.

After a reign of twenty-three years, he died in the fourth year, *kimyo,* of Jianchu (79 CE) and was buried on the hill of Soch'ŏn. Later a god said, "Bury his bones with care." When dug up, his skeleton was three feet two inches in circumference, his body was nine feet seven inches tall, his teeth were closely set, appearing as one tooth, and his bones were closely joined—indeed, he was a peerless giant. His remains were broken up, remade into a statue, and enshrined in the palace. Then a god spoke again: "Bury his bones on East Peak." So he was enshrined there.

KIM ALCHI

On the fourth day of the eighth month of the third year, *kyŏngsin,* of Yongping in the reign of Emperor Ming of the Later Han (60 CE), Lord Ho was on his way to West Village in Wŏlsŏng when he saw a light emanating from the Sirim forest at night. Purple clouds stretched from the sky all the way down to the earth, a golden casket hung from the top of a tree, light was emanating from the casket, and a white cock was crowing under the tree. The lord informed the king of this event. When the king went to the forest and opened the casket, he found inside it an infant boy who was just getting up from a reclining position.

This recalled the auspicious event associated with Pak Hyŏkkŏse. The boy was named Alchi, meaning "small child" in our language. When the king returned with the boy in his arms, birds and beasts followed after him dancing in joy. The king chose an auspicious day and appointed him the crown prince, but later he yielded the position to Pasa and did not accede to the throne. Because he emerged from the golden casket, his family name was Kim (Gold).

Alchi gave birth to Yŏrhan. Yŏrhan gave birth to Ado, Ado to Suryu, Suryu to Ukpu, Ukpu to Kudo, Kudo to Mich'u, and Mich'u ascended the throne. The Kim clan of Silla began from Alchi.

THREE CLANS

According to the clans' oldest record, in remote antiquity when there were no human beings, three divine personages emerged from the ground through the hole named Mohŭng at the northern foot of Mount Chu.[1] The eldest of the three was Yang Ŭlla, the next was Ko Ŭlla, and the third, Pu Ŭlla.[2] All three wandered across the desolate plain and hunted, eating the meat and using the hide for clothes.

One day, reaching the eastern shore, they spied a wooden box with a seal. They opened the box. In it was a stone box, and an envoy clad in purple with a blue belt followed. They opened the box, which produced a colt, a calf, three maidens clad in blue, and seeds of the five grains. Only then did the envoy say, "I am an envoy from Japan. After siring three daughters, our king said, 'Three sons of a divinity have descended to the peak in the middle of the western sea to form a country, but they don't have spouses,' and he dispatched me with his three daughters, so I am here. Please marry them and succeed in your great undertaking." Then he went back to Japan, riding on the clouds.

---

1. According to *SS*, T'amna, now Cheju Island, began political contact with the Korean peninsula at the beginning of the fifth century.

2. The oldest among the three varies according to the source.

The three men married the three maidens[3] in the order of their age, found a place where the spring water was sweet and the soil fertile, and used arrow divinations to choose their own sites. Yang Ŭlla's settlement was called the first capital; Ko Ŭlla's, the second capital; and Pu Ŭlla's, the third capital. They planted the five grains for the first harvest, raised ponies and calves, and flourished day by day.

Legends

Mount Ch'iak and Sangwŏn Monastery

This tale incorporates the motif of an animal's gratitude and thus belongs to Type 554, the Grateful Animals category. It has appeared in many different versions over a long period of dissemination. The version here is an origin legend from Mount Ch'iak in Kangwŏn province. The story tells of a young man who happens upon two pheasants being attacked by a snake, and saves them. When later he is threatened with his own death, the pheasants sacrifice themselves to free him.

In a village to the east of Great Pass Ridge in Kangwŏn province, there was a young man famous for his ability to use a bow. He was set upon accomplishing something great, so one day he strapped his bow to his back and left his hometown, setting off on the road to Seoul. He walked for many days. He crossed mountains and he crossed water, and when night fell he slept under trees, at temples, or even by the roadside. One day, while on the road that goes through Mount Chŏgak in Wŏnju, he heard the sound of something moaning. He thought this strange, so he stood still and quietly tilted his ear and realized that the sound was coming from beneath the tree next to him. When he looked

---

3. The origin of the three maidens also varies.

closely by the edge of the road, he saw a large snake that had wrapped its entire body around two pitiful pheasants and was just at the point of putting them into its mouth. When he saw this, he quickly loaded his bow and shot at the snake. He hit the snake right in the middle of its body and killed it. The pheasants that the snake had wrapped itself around were so happy to escape death they didn't know what to do and, with a rustling of their wings, flew off to the west.

The young man then resumed his walk along the mountain path. As the day grew dark he began to look for shelter. With some difficulty he found a house and went in. There he found a beautiful woman holding a lamp, and he asked if he could spend the night. The woman readily agreed and brought him to the room opposite hers—he was to spend the night there. He looked around and saw that the house was a small cloister; in the front yard was a pillar with a bell. In his exhaustion, he lay down and immediately fell asleep. In his sleep he soon felt that he couldn't breathe, and he opened his eyes. A giant snake had wrapped itself around his body; its mouth was gaping open, ready to devour him. Now the woman in the house, who had transformed herself into the snake, said to the young man, "I am the wife of the snake you killed by the side of the road with your bow and arrow; tonight it is your turn to die." Just then the temple bell sounded with a clang. The snake was surprised to hear the sound of the bell and wondered who could have rung it. Quietly the snake began to unwind its body.

The bell clanged once more. Suddenly gripped with fear, the snake disappeared. The young man wondered how the bell could ring when the house was vacant with not a soul around, and he waited for the dawn. Then he went out to look at the bell. There he saw the two pheasants he had saved the day before. They were lying on the ground, their bones broken and beaks stained with blood. Both were dead. The young man took in what the pheasants had done for him out of gratitude, and he gave endless thanks. Nearby he found a good plot of land and buried them there.

His trip to Seoul was forgotten. Instead he improved the road to that place and built a monastery, which is now called Sangwŏn. And he became a monk. It is said that he consoled the spirits of the pheasants for as long as he kept watch over the temple. Later, they say, the name Mount Chŏgak was corrected to Mount Ch'iak (Pheasant Peak).

Translated by Timothy Tangherlini

Triple Star

This story from the legend tradition of Koreans living in the Yanbian region of China is similar to the classic tale about "four skilled brothers" (Type 653) who defeat a dragon and save a princess. In this version, three brothers live with their widowed mother, and each learns a different miraculous skill. When the sun is swallowed by a black dragon and disappears, the brothers unite to retrieve the sun and save the people from calamity. Even after they find the sun, the brothers continue to defend it, becoming the Triple Star (Samt'aesŏng). In recounting the origin of the Triple Star that protects the sun from the black dragon of the sea, this story can be considered a heroic legend of Korean sun worship.

If you look up into the night sky, you will see the unusually bright Three Brothers constellation flowing slowly across the sky from east to west. In our folk belief, this is known as the Triple Star. Since the olden days a beautiful story has been told about how it came to be.

A long time ago, in a place far away, there was a giant swamp named the Black Dragon Pool. At the edge of this swamp, in a sunny place at the foot of a hillock, there was a pleasant little village where triplets were born shortly after their father died. The triplets' newly widowed mother was a very strict and well-respected person. Because she wanted her sons to grow up to be useful and respectable people, when they were eight years old she pledged to send them away from home for ten years. So the triplets went out into the world, and there they immediately found their teachers.

For ten years, every day they honed their talents and learned new skills, and then they returned home. The oldest brother's skill was this: if he clapped his hands once while sitting on a cleverly made, beautiful cushion, he could travel ninety thousand tricents in the blink of an eye. The second brother's skill was this: if he closed one eye, he could see with the other eye ninety thousand tricents away, so clearly that it was as if he were reading the lines on his own palm. The third son was proficient in the eighteen common military arts; he could brandish the longsword like a bolt of lightning, and if he shot an arrow from his bow at the eye of a bird, he would get a hundred bull's-eyes in one hundred tries.

And so, having learned these skills, the triplets returned to their mother and worked in the fields. They set up an academy and taught skills to the young children of the village. That was not all they did. They applied themselves enthusiastically whenever there was difficult work to do, and so it was that in the village there was not one who did not praise them.

And then one year, during the summer, the day was clear and the sky was a deep blue. All of a sudden, a fierce gale began to rage from out of nowhere. A giant black raincloud hung heavy in the sky and heaven and earth were plunged into darkness. Lightning flashed and thunder boomed and the rain poured down in buckets. Suddenly the gale blew up violently again and it seemed that heaven and earth would be turned upside down. It became so pitch dark that you couldn't make out a single thing even if it was right in front of your eyes.

Nobody had ever experienced such bleakness before, and the people became flustered since they had no idea what to do. After a while, the violent gale and the torrential rains abated, and the day began to lighten. At last, people came out from behind their doors and saw that the clouds had disappeared and the sky had cleared up. But there was no trace of the sun and only stars studded the sky. The villagers believed that the sky hound had swallowed the sun. If they waited a while, they said, it would reappear. But regardless of how long they waited, the sun did not reappear. Soon the villagers were divided by arguments. If the sky hound had swallowed the sun, it would be unbearably hot and he'd immediately vomit it back up. But since the sun had not reappeared, some other misfortune must have occurred.

A day passed, two days passed, and the sun did not reappear. The people were wracked with anxiety and fear. Then they became sad and silenced by their melancholy. Even the birds stopped singing. Only the ferocious beasts still gathered, and one could hear their growls as they crept about the village.

On the third day, the mother sent for the triplets and said that since she had intended for them to be useful people, she had sent them off to learn their skills. Now the village was facing a truly serious problem, so she asked them sternly to put their skills to use: "You were born to be heroic men, and since this serious problem has arisen, do you think you can just sit quietly at your mother's knee? Don't come home until you have found the sun!"

The triplets hung their heads, and together they answered, "Yes," and stood up. Their mother tore her skirt into three strips and gave one to each of the boys as a headband. The triplets tied the strips firmly around their heads and made a firm oath that they would find the sun without fail and then return.

And so the triplets bade farewell to their mother and set out to find the sun. Using the oldest brother's skill, they got on a new cleverly made and beautiful cushion, and they looked all over the world, into every nook and cranny, but they didn't see the sun. Because of this, the oldest brother said that even if they searched blindly for the sun for nine years, it seemed they would not find it, so they should figure out a new method. In response, the second and third brothers said it would be good to find their three teachers and learn from them. So the triplets went and found their three teachers, and all six of them together considered all sorts of possibilities, but none of them could figure out where the sun had gone.

The oldest brother's teacher said to the two other teachers, "Our learning and skills cannot help us with this task, so it seems we must seek out even greater learning." Their teacher was now living at the foot of Perfume Mountain, and he suggested that it would be a good idea if they went there to get more learning. The other two teachers were pleased with his idea, and the idea of learning from their teachers' teacher pleased the triplets even more.

So the three teachers and the three brothers set off to find the old master at the foot of Perfume Mountain. The old master was a vigorous old man with silvery hair and a flowing beard, and the six—the three teachers and the triplets—found him in his straw house. He stroked his silvery gray beard and when he took their hands, it was if his youth flowed back into him and he spoke affectionately to them without end. The pupils told the old master their reason for seeking him out, so he taught them in great detail about the sun, the moon, and the stars, and about all things under heaven and earth. It was as if things became clearer and clearer in front of their eyes.

And then the old master told them why the sun had disappeared from the world. Here is what had happened. In the Black Dragon Pool there were two black dragons, a she-dragon and a he-dragon. Their bodies were ten tricents long and three hundred sixty fathoms wide, so they were gigantic, violent beasts. Whenever there were gusts of wind, it was because they were dashing mightily across the sky for ninety thousand tricents, racing each other. These two black dragons, once every several hundred or even several thousand years, fly into the night sky and wreak havoc. This time, from the night sky to the morning sky, they created the violent gale and rainstorm and wreaked terrible havoc. The she-dragon swallowed the sun and went to the top of the sky—and the he-dragon followed her. Now they were playing up above the sky. The old master heaved a great sigh and said, "So if in this world no superior and valiant warriors have been born, then the world will wallow in the darkness forever, and never be able to free itself."

The triplets were gathered, sitting on their knees in front of the old master, and they reaffirmed the stern oath they had made to their mother when they had received her order and tied the skirt strips around their heads and vowed not to return home until they had found the sun. The old master was overjoyed and his gloomy face became all smiles. He offered praise, saying that the mother was indeed the most admirable mother in the world for sending her sons without hesitation to search for the sun, and that the triplets were indeed the most remarkable youths in the world for offering their lives to find the sun.

And so the triplets and the three teachers who had received great knowledge from the old master returned to the village. The next day, at the edge of the Black Dragon Pool, the mother and the three teachers, along with the villagers, gathered to see the triplets off as they departed to do battle above the sky. Everyone shook their hands earnestly and asked them to win the battle with the black dragons, find the sun again, and then return. The triplets, one by one, said good-bye to the villagers; then they gathered and sat down in front of their mother and the three teachers.

"Now we are going to leave."

The three teachers each took hold of their pupil and lifted them to their feet. Over and over again, they implored them to fight bravely until the bitter end, wielding without fail their wisdom and their courage. Their mother adjusted her collar, brushed back her cascade of white hair, and spoke to the triplets:

"Children, people are born into the world and among the most righteous of works is to offer one's life for an honorable cause. You must rescue the sun! Nothing in the world can live without the sun. Now go!"

The triplets mounted the oldest brother's cushion and flew off to the top of the sky. As they soared into the boundless ninety-thousand-tricent sky, the second oldest brother patiently closed one eye, and shouted that he saw the two black dragons eighteen thousand tricents up above. The triplets then prepared to do battle and rose higher and higher. While the second brother pointed out the direction, the oldest brother drove the cushion and the third brother shouldered his bow and knapsack and stood holding the longsword at an angle across his body.

Those watching from the earth saw bolts of lightning high in the sky and heard the rumble of thunder. When the third brother brandished his sword, lightning flashed. And when the two dragons saw the triplets, they let out a frightful roar and attacked, fiercely creating thunder.

The battle was intense. Lightning shredded the sky from one side to the other and thunder rumbled across the heavens. After a while, the two black dragons were no longer able to repel the valiant triplets and they began to flee from one end of the sky to the other. The two dragons raced each other as they fled, neither one wishing to be last. The third brother put an arrow to his bowstring, pulled it back so that the bow looked like the full moon, and then let the arrow fly. It streaked across the sky like a shooting star, splitting the heavens in two, and stuck in the back of the she-dragon who had swallowed the sun.

The dragon was an incredibly fierce creature, and because the arrow struck it in the back and not in the head, the wound was not a mortal one. Nevertheless, the arrow was poisonous, and the she-dragon could not endure the pain of the wound. She bent her back and with a frightening noise that sounded like the sky was crumbling, she vomited the sun back out.

In an instant, the sun reappeared in the middle of the sky and the clear day of the bright heaven and earth returned. At the edge of the Black Dragon Pool, shouts of joy shook the earth and all of the people crowded around with joy. At the center of the swarm of people, the mother wiped her tears of joy with the hem of her new skirt, and smiles bloomed on the three teachers' faces over their pupils' victory.

And then the second brother's teacher closed one eye and looked up far into the sky and said, "The black dragon has vomited up the sun but still hasn't died. Now as the brothers are descending, they are fighting and . . . Oh dear! Oh dear! Even if we are growing old, we must help our pupils fight!"

Having said this, the three teachers made battle preparations and flew off into the sky. Then the triplets and the three teachers, supporting each other, joined in the attack. They fought with the two black dragons, and the dragons' bodies were covered with wounds, and from these wounds flowed fresh blood. Finally, the two dragons could not even think of attacking anymore, and they fled with all their might back toward the Black Dragon Pool.

One of the black dragons went straight down from high in the sky all the way to the pool with a clap of thunder that sounded as if the sky were being torn apart. An arrow had penetrated deep into the nape of the neck of that one, and the dragon sank into the pool with a frightening sound and disappeared. After a little while, the other dragon appeared high in the sky above the Black Dragon Pool. The triplets and the three teachers circled around that dragon and hacked and stabbed at it. And so, in a great hurry, it descended toward the pool with a sound like the splitting of the earth. Suddenly it fell at the edge. It crawled to the water, turned its head toward it, and then breathed its last. With a fierce glare in its eyes, it died.

The triplets had fought with great honor and triumphed. At the edge of the Black Dragon Pool, a shout of joy shook the earth, and the triplets and the three teachers embraced one another, and tears of happiness streamed down their faces. The triplets cried out, "Mother!" and, unable to conceal their joy, said they could now live once again with their mother and work in the fields, living happily.

Hiding her tears, so choked up by her happiness that she could say nothing, the mother embraced her three sons. She was happy, true, but suddenly a thought occurred to her. In an anxious voice, she asked, "Children, one of the dragons was killed. But the dragon that went down into the water, did it die or did it live?" While the triplets shook their heads, they explained that it was an incredibly fierce animal, and even though the arrow had struck true, the dragon had not died. The mother listened, surprised.

"And therefore, no one can know if it will swallow the sun again?" The triplets cast glances at their mother and were speechless, unable to offer an answer. The mother heaved a heavy sigh and said, "Children, don't worry about your mother. I'll be able to live as long as I can with the villagers. But from today on, you must go up into the sky and protect the sun forevermore." The triplets answered together, "Yes!" The three teachers and all the villagers without exception nodded in agreement when they saw this. They praised the mother as an honorable mother and the boys as the most magnificent sons in the world.

The sun set slowly over the western mountains, and the triplets, who intended to guard it forever and ever, prepared to fly up to the sky. The mother straightened her hair that had been mussed by the evening wind and, smiling, bade them farewell: "Oh, skillful and praiseworthy children! Night is falling! Please go up to the sky!"

The triplets took leave of their mother, their three teachers, and the villagers and once again flew up into the night sky. If you look from the earth up to the triplets, they look like three twinkling stars all in a row in the middle of the heavens. People say every night that these are the triplets who listened to their mother's words and protect the night sky, and they are called the Triple Star.

Translated by Timothy Tangherlini

The Dragon Pool and the Daughter-in-Law Stone

This legend, which traces the origin of a pool, belongs to the widely transmitted Wealthy Man and the Pool legend cycle found all over Korea wherever there are marshes. The story shares a similar plot with the story of Sodom and Gomorrah in the Bible, a worldwide motif. The present narrative illustrates the case of a rich miser who is destroyed by his abominable treatment of an eminent monk. It also relates the story of the miser's daughter-in-law, who escapes calamity through her charity to the same monk but is turned into stone for having broken the taboo against looking back. The story recorded here is related to the origin of the Dragon Pool located in Yongjŏng village, in Yongjŏn township, Changyŏn district, in Hwanghae province.

The Dragon Pool is located some twenty tricents from Changyŏn town, which is near Monggŭmp'o, famous for the popular ballad of the same name sung in the western region of Korea. The legend about it dates back to ancient times. It is said that in those days the present-day Dragon Pool was the site of the house of a wealthy old man. He was very rich—his rice crops exceeded several thousand sacks and he had built a splendid house. But he was a notorious miser, with his mind fixed on hoarding money and no interest in helping others, so people nicknamed him Pig. He gave nothing to those who came begging and refused Buddhist monks who came by for alms, too. Such was his ill repute.

About twenty tricents from the Dragon Pool village, there was a mountain called Mount Buddha, because of the large number of temples located on it. One summer an eminent monk, having heard about the ill-famed miser, visited his house—most likely on purpose— and begged for an offering while striking his wooden bell with a clapper. The old man said, "You wretch! You loathsome bonzes never till the soil or work. You just go around begging for food and live off of others. Go away! You won't get even a single grain of rice from my house."

Ignoring the miser's yelling, the monk kept on reciting the scripture and didn't budge. Infuriated, the miser picked up a shovel—in those days, it was called a spade—scooped up some cow dung out of the manure pile, and emptied it into the priest's satchel, saying, "We don't have any rice to give to you, so take this and be gone."

Undisturbed, the monk simply went on chanting "Homage to Amitābha." When he was about to step outside the house with the cow-dung sack slung over his shoulder, the miser's daughter-in-law, who had been watching the scene while washing rice at the well in the courtyard, said to the monk, 'My father-in-law was born ill-natured, so please don't take it too hard." Then she scooped up a bowlful of the rice she was washing and poured it into the priest's sack. The monk said to her, "In a short while, a great disaster will visit this household. Now quickly go inside your house and grab a couple of things you cherish most. And then run fast as you can to Mount Buddha."

The daughter-in-law hurried inside as she was told. She picked up her sleeping son and carried him on her back, put on top of her head the silk rolls she cut from the loom, and took along the family dog by calling it to follow. She started off toward Mount Buddha with her son on her back, the silk rolls on her head, and the dog tagging along. Suddenly the clear sky darkened, the thunder rumbled, and the lightning crashed. The daughter-in-law recalled the monk's warning: "Whatever you do, no matter what noises you hear, you should never turn around." But at the sudden roar of the thunder and the flashes of lightning, the woman did turn around. Instantly she turned into stone, as did her son, the rolls of silk, and the dog. Even now people say that a short distance downhill from Mount Buddha, there is a rock that looks like the fossilized daughter-in-law. It has a human shape and looks as if it is carrying something on top of its head. Below it there stands a doglike stone, too.

Going back to the story—when the lightning hit, the entire house of the miser disappeared, and in its place there appeared a huge pool hundreds of fathoms deep. As for the size of the pool, it is wider than a children's playground you might see today—about twice the size. The pool produces a lot of water, so much that it keeps making pounding noises, and if you go near you may feel the ground shaking. The amount of water is so great that it supplies the needs of hundreds of acres of rice paddy. Rain or drought, the water level of the pool never changes—no increase, no decrease. People often tried to measure the depths of the pool by dropping into it a silk thread with a stone tied on its end, but no matter how many threads were used, they could never reach the bottom—so deep was the pool.

Translated by Yung-Hee Kim

FOX HILL

This legend is in large part a biographical sketch of a master geomancer—a type of narrative transmitted in almost all regions of Korea. The story begins with a sick schoolboy who is stricken by a mysterious illness—a trick played by a fox. However, the boy becomes an extraordinary geomancer by successfully snatching a bead from the fox and swallowing it. The narrative transcribed here includes the etymology of the name of the hill where the fox died.

In the old days, what we know as Fox Hill had no name, and in the village nearby lived a boy of fourteen or fifteen. Do you know the district called Udu in the city of Ch'unch'ŏn? That's the place. In Udu-dong, there was a village school for Chinese classics—something similar to today's public schools—where the boy, a bright student with a good appetite and in good health, studied. After about three years, he grew very gaunt and pale. His mother wondered what had happened and asked him, "What's the matter with you? Do you feel sick?"

The boy answered, "No, I feel all right."

"Then why are you so pale?"

"I have no idea. Don't worry."

Eventually the boy became just like a stick, like a stone with paper pasted over it. No longer simply pale, he grew thinner and thinner. His mother, unable to bear the sight of her son, ran over to his teacher at school.

"I cannot send my son to this school anymore."

"What are you talking about?"

"As you may have noticed, my son looks sallow. But when I ask him why, he says nothing's the matter. All this has happened since he started studying here. So I will have him quit studying and stop coming to school."

"I see what you mean—I noticed the same. Let me talk to him alone after dismissing the other students. You may join me in listening to what he has to say."

After all the other students were sent outside, the teacher called to the boy, "You should stay here and play." And then he said, "Listen, something must have happened to you since you began studying here. You look pale, as if you are going to collapse and die soon. You have to tell your teacher without hiding anything. Your mother is here to listen, too, so tell us everything and be honest."

Thereupon the boy said, "Something funny has happened."

The teacher, with his curiosity alerted, said, "Really? What happened?"

"When I walk over the hill in the morning to come to school, there's nobody there. But when I return home in the evening, a beautiful girl appears without fail. And taking my hands and pulling me, she invites me to have a good time with her. As a male over fourteen, I cannot resist when she coaxes me by pulling my hands. When I go with her, all she does is hold my ears with her hands and kiss my lips. When she kisses me, I notice one side of her mouth is crimson, while the other side holds a white bead. She rolls the bead into my mouth, and when I spit it out, she puts it back in hers. She repeats this game for about two hours, and at the end, she puts the bead back in her mouth. Then she says that I should go home because we've had enough fun, and so I go home. That's about all the fun I've had, and I don't feel sick or anything."

The story made the teacher wonder, and something about it struck him as strange. He said, "Well, today or tomorrow, when the girl plays the same game with you, you should swallow the bead in one gulp instead of spitting it and putting it back in her mouth. Then fall on your back and look up at the sky. And then turn yourself over and look down at the ground."

Thus instructed, the boy started for home in the evening after school. As usual, the beautiful girl appeared and said, "Is that you? I've been waiting. Come, let's have fun before you go home." She held his ears and began to play with the bead, rolling it out of her mouth and putting it in his mouth, just as before. When the bead was placed in his mouth, the boy swallowed it in one gulp, just as his teacher had told him, whereupon the girl began tickling his sides to make him spit it out. She tickled him so hard that he fell on his face. He had no choice but to stare at the ground only, unable to look up at the sky. Because of the girl's tickling, he could not straighten himself up—all he could do was look down at the ground. He sprawled with his belly on the ground in order to keep the bead inside his stomach, out of her reach. The girl leaped up and then fell to the ground whimpering. When the boy looked at her more carefully, he discovered that she was not a girl but a big fox. She had turned back into a fox after losing the bead, and finally died. The boy said, "I see, you were not a girl but a beast!"

With the bead in his stomach, he went home and told his mother what had happened and repeated the same story to his teacher, too. The teacher said, "You stupid! I told you to look up at the sky no matter what happened or how ticklish you felt! How could you just stare at the ground?"

"I tried to, but her tickling was too much."

"Then you will only be able to see things thirty yards below the surface of the earth. Had you looked up at the sky first, you'd have become both an astrologer and a geomancer. But because you only looked down at the ground and didn't look up at the sky . . . ."

The boy grew up to be a superb geomancer, whose name I forget. The hill is still called Fox Hill, and it is so named because of what happened there long ago.

Translated by Yung-Hee Kim

THE CHILD GENERAL

This legend, told in every district of the country, is popularly referred to as the "Agi Changsu" legend. As evidence for the story, either a rock in the shape of a swift steed's footprint or the pond from which the steed sprang is mentioned. The child general exhibits remarkable talents, but his parents kill him out of fear that he might become a traitor, and he is thus unable to fulfill his potential—the tragedy of the story.

After the Chang clan settled, the Pak clan settled next. After they settled, our Pak family was the first to settle in this village. They called it Kumŏngdong. If you look at a map here, you can see Kumŏngdong. When the parents of the Pak family died, their offspring were unable to find them a proper burial place, so they were buried temporarily. One day a monk came and wanted to stay overnight. When he saw that the host looked as if he was in mourning, he asked, "Oh master, are you in mourning?"

"Yes, I'm in mourning."

"Did you find a burial place for your father?"

"I wasn't able to find a burial place, because we are poor. So I just buried him where I could."

Because he said that, the monk replied, "Well, I have seen a place in the mountains, so tomorrow let us go up there, you and the other mourners."

They woke up early and packed up their food and left. And if you ask where they went, that eastern village is now called Pŏngaet'ŏ. They called it "Tŏkpatche" back then. And so they went to the spot and the geomancer said, "Use this site right here." And when they looked there, right in front were three rocks, the three general rocks. And so the chief mourner said, "All right." That's what he said.

After the monk left, they buried the body there. And so they used the site. The next day the daughter-in-law of the Pak family started showing signs of pregnancy. One night, at midnight, according to the story, this child's mother looked at the child and saw that sweat was pouring off him, and that was strange. For three days, sweat poured off like this. Then this rosy-colored baby quietly got up and opened the door and went outside—the newborn baby. In front of him there was a large walnut tree, and he quickly climbed up and down, showing off his talents. He climbed down skillfully, and when he came down, he immediately went to his mother's bosom, and when she looked at him, the sweat poured from the child. So she told this to her father-in-law.

"We're in big trouble!" he responded.

"What is it?"

"What is to be done with a one–month-old child who wakes up and does all these tricks in the night? We must kill him," he said.

If the child didn't turn out well, he would become a traitor, but if he turned out well, he would be a loyal subject. This uncertainty wouldn't do. So they took a bag of red beans and pressed it down on the baby, and he squirmed, and they killed the boy.

Now, not three days later, the monk came by. He said, "There was a baby born at this house. Bring the child out."

And they said, "Oh no, it wasn't born, Oh, there's no baby."

"Quickly, bring the baby out!" That's what he said. "I'll take the baby with me. Bring him to me."

They said it hadn't happened, and the monk said the baby had absolutely been born and demanded that they bring it out.

'And so, finally, they bluntly told him the story. "He might not have turned out well, we didn't know if he'd become a traitor, and he seemed as if he'd kill our Pak family. So we pushed this down on him quite hard and killed him."

When the monk heard this, he pounded his chest, because he was exasperated.

"I was to take the baby and raise him myself—what am I to do now? You'll have another two soon; don't harm them and give them to me." This is what the monk said, and he left.

The next day, with a loud sound, a swift dragon steed arrived in the courtyard, bent all four of his knees, and sprang up. It quickly jumped across the courtyard, and then it lay down and died. A little later a pear tree grew there. So even today that place is called "Horse (or Dragon) Pear Tree Village." It was predicted that we'd have two more generals who would be born. To prevent that from happening, the Pak family dug up the graves of a young maiden and a young man, removed their corpses, and reburied them in front and in back of the pear tree. And so you can't budge it. Although it is our ancestor, we now eat the pears. And every year we talk about whether we should go and dig out the corpses. This tree has branched out. There aren't that many people here in our village, but even so we can't all agree on doing it.[1]

Translated by Timothy Tangherlini

BROTHER AND SISTER STŪPAS

This legend comes from Kyeryong village, Kongju county, South Ch'ungch'ŏng province. The story is of a monk who saves a tiger and, to repay this kindness, the tiger brings the monk a young girl from the outside world. Accepting their meeting as fate, the monk and the young girl agree to live as brother and sister, observing the path of Buddhism, and spend their life together like this. To commemorate this, people later built two pagodas and named them "Brother and Sister Stūpas." Even now in South Ch'ungch'ŏng province, halfway up the small peak of Mount Kyeryong, there are two stūpas standing side by side.

This legend has been passed down here, at the place called Kapsa; from here it is about ten tricents away. Mount Kyeryong there, that's

---

1. For a postmodern rewriting of the legend as a play, see Ch'oe Inhun's "Away, Away, Long Time Ago," in Peter H. Lee, *Modern Korean Literature*, 412–438.

where Kapsa is. If you go up the path behind Kapsa monastery, you'll find the brother and sister pagoda. They call them Brother and Sister Stūpas. There are two stūpas standing there at the boundary of uninhabited land. They've built a monastery there now.

There was a monk living alone there meditating, and he lived like that; he was a male monk. One day before dinner, a tiger came down and made a loud noise. It made a sound as if it were dying. This monk wasn't afraid of the tiger, since he was a monk who believed in the Buddha's teachings, and he wondered why the tiger was making this noise. So he went and looked outside, and this tiger was opening its mouth wide and writhing in pain, as though he were about to die. So the monk asked, "What's going on?"

The tiger's mouth was wide open and tears were streaming down its face. So the monk looked to see why the tiger's mouth was open like that, and he saw that something was caught in there. Now, a person whom the tiger had caught and eaten had injured him. The person's hairpin had got caught right there in the tiger's throat. So the monk removed it quickly. And when he removed it, the tiger shook himself, stood up, and nodded his head and just left.

So there in the hut the monk meditated again. Then one night he unexpectedly heard a sound, the sound of the tiger. He went outside and the tiger had come back again, the tiger from whose throat he had removed the hairpin. When the monk looked at him coming, he saw that the tiger was carrying a young girl on his back. The girl had fainted. So the monk could do nothing but bring the young girl into the hut. He carried her inside and massaged her whole body, and he gave her water and after a little while she recovered.

"How did it happen that a tiger carried you here on its back?" the monk asked.

The young girl said that she was at home at night, and when she got up to go to the toilet, she was suddenly lifted up and brought there. The monk asked where her home was, and she said that it was in Chŏlla province. In one day and one night she had been carried for several hundred tricents.

"Somewhere in Chŏlla province, somewhere," she said.

"But you must return to your home after you recover," the monk said. "I'll take you home."

"I'm not going," she replied. "Since the tiger brought me here like this, it must be fate. I too want to follow the path of Buddha and become a nun." And she wouldn't leave.

"You can't become a nun just like that. Men and women are different—how can we live together and meditate and become renunciates?" he said. "Young girl, you should return to the world, get married, and live a happy life." And even though he exhorted her frequently, she wouldn't go; she said she'd live there. The monk could do nothing else and didn't know how else to advise her, so they became like brother and sister for the sake of Buddhist practice. They didn't become husband and wife but lived there like brother and sister for the rest of their lives. They observed Buddhism and they meditated, and they only served the Buddha. Later the monks found out that there was a monastery on Mount Kyeryong and built two stūpas there. Brother and Sister Stūpas. They carved the names of the monk and nun into them. There, if you go down through a little entrance, you find the monastery called Tonghak in the middle. You have to go through Tonghak monastery to get to the stūpas.

Translated by Timothy Tangherlini

Folktales

The Dog and Cat Go Seeking a Jewel

This is the Korean version of a well-known Magic Ring story (Type 560). After eating a pheasant cock, an old couple has a son. At his wedding, a snake appears and threatens to eat him, because the pheasant the boy's parents ate was originally his. But the ingenious bride obtains a magic jewel in exchange for the groom's life and kills the snake with it. The couple happily marry and become rich. However, a neighbor covets the magic object and steals it, causing the couple to become poor again. Although this first part of the tale is absent in other versions, the part about the animals' search for the jewel is found in most variants.

Long ago there was a man who made his living by farming and chopping wood. One day, when he went to chop wood, the farmer saw a large pheasant. It was a huge male, and it was trapped, flapping wildly about.

"Hmm," thought the farmer. "There's something wrong with this fellow. I think I'll . . ." And he caught it. He caught the fellow, hung him on his load of wood, and brought him back home. When he put him down and had a look, he saw that it was a fine-looking pheasant, a fine red fellow. The farmer and his wife put the pheasant in a room and shut the door. And oh, they had a good time watching him run around in there.

"Why, enough of this," the farmer said finally. "Let's kill him and boil him up and eat our fill."

So the farmer and his wife butchered the pheasant and ate their fill. That night, with their bellies full, they slept together. Of course, they had slept together before, but hadn't produced any children. That night they remedied that, and after a certain amount of time passed, they had a beautiful boy.

In the old days, one would send a boy to school to learn the classics by the time he was six years old. And so their son was learning the classics there at the village school—he was tremendously smart. It was "Once told, knows tenfold"—that is to say, he could be taught one thing and he would know ten ways to apply it.

"Yeah, we had a fine son in our old age," said the farmer. Indeed, the lad grew as fast as a cucumber.

"*Aigu!*" said the farmer's wife. "I had my son so late. I wish I would at least have a daughter-in-law soon." She pronounced these wishful thoughts about her son's marriage all the time.

Well, after the son's marriage had been arranged, the day of the feast came around. Back then, you had to pick an auspicious day to hold a celebration like that. When they divined the day, it turned out that any day would be auspicious. But somehow the boy happened to be off studying. You see, there was this thing called "circling with the moon" to study with your teachers: this one on this month, that one on another month—alternating months like that. There was a mountain ridge about so big—you might say it was half a peak. The boy had crossed this ridge on his way to learn the classics. He'd gone to study that day, and he'd just gotten to the top of the ridge. He was almost on his way down when a huge snake appeared. Oh, this fellow opened his mouth wide, shooting his tongue out, and he blocked the path.

"Yeah! You're a respectable creature," said the boy. "What are you doing? Move aside."

But the snake didn't move aside. It was trouble.

The boy said, "Since you won't let me pass, is it your intention to eat me up?"

The creature nodded his head.

"Oh, no," the boy thought. "Now I'm dead." Yes, that's what's reliable sources say. So the boy pleaded with the snake. "My father had me late in life, and his wish was that he could see a daughter-in-law before his death. It will come true with the day of my wedding. It is on such and such a day. Let me go to fulfill my father's wish by getting married, and I'll come back to you straight away. Please, bide your time until then."

The serpent quietly slithered away.

Now the boy gave this some serious thought and he realized that he was, indeed, as good as dead. Knowing he was surely going to die, he lost his will to live.

The day of the feast was approaching fast. It was nearly upon them, and then it was time. They went to the bride's house and held the marriage ceremony. They prepared the bridal chamber, and the bride went inside. But they say the groom just refused and sat there.

The bride said, "Darling, you and I tied the hundred-year knot tonight. Why are you sitting there like some immovable object? What's the matter?"

"*Aigu!*" said the groom. "There's nothing I can say. Just remember that I must leave you like this."

"Oh, darling, what are you saying?" said the bride. "You're throwing your wife out on the wedding night? Is it because there's something wrong with me? What's going on?"

"I'm a man marked for death tonight, so there's no point in my laying a hand on your body. Before I'm gone, I want you to know that I went through with the marriage to fulfill my father's wish." And with that, he got up and ran off.

The new bride thought this over, and found it really quite unbelievable. She got up, still wearing her bridal headpiece, and followed her husband. She followed him to some isolated place, and as she went, the snake also approached, having agreed to meet again at that hour.

"Here I am," said the husband. "Come out and eat me if you wish." That damned snake came rushing forward with its jaws wide open. The bride was awestruck at the sight. Still wearing her headpiece, she rushed to her husband, who was still in his ceremonial clothes, and she hugged him tightly, wrapping him tightly in her skirt.

"Why is it that you're intending to eat this man?" the wife asked the snake.

In those days, snakes could speak. He answered, "This man's father ate food that was intended for me, and he was born thereafter. So there is nothing else I can do but eat him." The snake had hypnotized the pheasant in order to eat it. That's why it wasn't able to get away, and that's why the groom's father had been able to catch it—the very pheasant the snake had been toying with. And then he had cooked it and eaten it.

"Very well," said the bride. "But this is the man I've tied the hundred-year knot with. What am I to do if you eat him? I'm covering him up, and unless you tell me a way for him to save his life, I'm not letting him go."

The truth was, the snake couldn't possibly eat both of them at once. He slowly closed his eyes and just lay there a while, and then he jerked his head back and forth and spat out something the size of a garlic bundle: a jewel.

"What do you mean by spitting this up?" asked the bride.

"This has three facets," said the snake. "Take this facet and ask for rice, and rice will appear. Use the other facet to ask for money, and money will appear. As for the third facet, if you ask for your enemy to die, he will surely die."

"Then you die!" said the bride. She held the jewel up to the snake and commanded, "Die!"

The snake's eyes fluttered shut and he flopped over dead.

"Now we've got it made!" said the bride.

The husband, meanwhile, had already fainted. It was all over now, but this snake had had a lot of energy, so the wife felt very powerful. She lifted her husband and put him on her back and headed back to their house. She put him down, and then she was a frenzy of activity. She bought medicine good enough to restore the dead and fed it to him, and she tried all manner of things until he finally blossomed into a perfectly healthy man.

Now the bride went to the house of her in-laws and found that they lived in unimaginable poverty. Instead of the usual red-clay storage jars, they had small white jars, and they had covered them with green leaves. It was unbelievable. She went into the rooms, and they were tiny.

"I've found myself a good husband, but he lives in terrible poverty," she thought. "Well, as for me, it doesn't matter since I've got this treasure." She took the jewel and asked for rice, and rice came pouring out from somewhere into huge piles. They scooped it up, filled sacks, and stacked them up. Ah, now they could live. They had no money, so the bride asked for money and it appeared.

"Ah, that's enough for now," said the bride, because now they were well off.

Nearby there lived a man who had studied with the same teacher as the husband. He too was quite clever, but he was also dirt poor.

"Yeah," he said to the husband one day. "You were born and raised with me, and you're my friend, right? So how is it that you were so poor and suddenly you're showered in wealth?"

The husband told him the story. "We have a jewel in our house," he said finally. "That's how we live so well."

"Hey, then there are possibilities," said the friend. "You and I are so close, wouldn't it be nice if we both lived well? Let me borrow it."

"Oh, all right. Let's try it."

So he lent his friend the jewel, and the bastard took it and ran off.

In the husband's house he had a dog and a cat that had puppies and kittens. And when he lost the jewel and went back to living in poverty, he looked around one day and that damned pair of animals had disappeared somewhere together. "Yeah," he sighed, "life is so hard even the animals have run off. Damn it."

And where would they have gone? These two set off in search of the friend who had stolen the jewel. "We were eating well," they said. "Getting well fed, being well kept. And now life is hard because that bastard stole the jewel. Let's find him. Let's find that bastard, wherever he's gone."

They went boldly everywhere, and they came upon a great river. The cat couldn't swim very well, but the dog was a good swimmer. "Since you can't swim, get on my back," said the dog. "I'll take you across piggyback."

"All right, let's do it," said the cat.

The dog took the cat across on his back and let him off. They went on for a bit and found a great, wide field. Several thousand families were living there, and as the animals went right into the middle of the settlement, they found the largest house. The owners were probably quite wealthy.

"Hey, this house is pretty well off. So we have no choice but to go in there and steal something," they said. They went inside and found a large storage shed. And when they looked inside the shed, they saw there was nothing in the world it didn't contain. Food—all kinds of food. So they jumped right in, as hungry as could be. There were hind-quarters of beef, rice cakes—all kinds of food.

"Let's eat as much as our stomachs can hold," they declared. And they devoured as much meat as they could. Then they plopped right down in the middle of the room.

Well, as they sat there, a rat came in from somewhere. He had three-pronged whiskers, that rat, and he was the size of a large dog. He must have been quite old. The cat cried "Yeooooung!" and that rat collapsed with its tail in its crotch.

"There's nothing for you to be afraid of. I won't eat you up," said the cat. "Say, this house has a treasure, doesn't it? It's because he's got that treasure that the bastard who owns the place lives this well. Wouldn't be possible without it, right?"

It turned out that the owner of the house was the one who had stolen the jewel. He had made a stone box and sealed it in there. He slept with it right beside his head, so there was nothing much they could do.

As the cat thought about this one day, he realized he could not let it go on. He jammed his paw into the owner's bedroom door and opened it. He looked inside, and there that stone box was. He had sneaked around the front and back rooms, poked through the rice paper in the door of the owner's bedroom, and looked inside, and there it was. So the cat came back after seeing this, and when he returned, he said to the rat, "You. . . . There's a stone box right by the head of the old man who owns this house. There's going to be a certain jewel inside that stone box. You must get it for us. If you do, I'll spare you. Otherwise I'll exterminate you and your entire family."

Now the cat called the king of the rats and sat him down, and he said, "I'll spare you only if you get that jewel for me, however you do it. Otherwise I'll exterminate your entire species!"

When the rats heard this, there was quite an uproar. It looked like they were all going to die. "*Aigu!* I'll do it for you, sir!" said the king of the rats. He certainly didn't want to die. Whether or not he could do it, he had to answer yes. "Please, just give us one month's reprieve. It's not an easy thing to pull off."

"All right," said the cat. "I'll give you that month."

Now they just stayed in that storage shed filling their bellies. The cat, the dog, the rat—all three of them just stuffing themselves with all that food. Like an official decree that comes down from the county office these days, the rat circulated a decree near and far, ordering all the rodents to report on such and such a day at such and such an hour at such and such a place. He commanded it. And whether it was from Kyŏngsang or Hwanghae province, from every region, every province, every district, every village—all the rats came and assembled. And when they arrived, they were announced by their region: "Kangwŏn province is here!"

And the Kyŏngsang rats also streamed down there. They say the rats just came flooding in. They arrived. They gathered. And since there were millions and millions of them, they were bound to eat all the food stored in that shed. Now each rat that came also brought several others. These fellows dug underneath that bedroom and slowly sneaked in by gnawing tiny holes in the floor. They got in, but when they tried chewing through the stone box, they'd have two bites and their teeth would be ruined. It wasn't going to work that way. So they quickly took turns. One and then another fellow would gnaw away on the box, so eventually it was just not possible for there *not* to be a hole. They had a month's reprieve, and so they had to do it within that time. Well, they kept sneaking in there and gnawing away, and eventually there was a proper hole about so big in the box. But when the big rat wanted to go in, there wasn't room for him to fit through.

"This can't be done," he said. They sent in the tiniest fellow from some out-of-the-way place. "You! Go and fetch the jewel."

The smallest sort of backroom rat—it looked like *that* kind of rat might fit through the hole. They can get in and out of spaces like that. So the tiny fellow squeezed in and there was this jewel about the size of a garlic clump. He came out carrying it in his mouth and the big rat, who had been waiting, took it and ran off. Kneeling, he presented it to the cat. "Here, I've brought it," he said.

The cat saw that it was, indeed, the jewel. "Good," he said. "You've accomplished one of the great deeds of recent history. So you may eat every crumb of what's here and then part ways. That bastard's a thief, so you can clean out everything he's stolen. We'll be on our way now. Farewell. We're leaving."

The dog and the cat took the jewel and started for home. In their rush to return, they hadn't had anything to eat before they left that house. So after they had come a ways, they were so hungry they thought they might die. Then they had the misfortune of having to cross a river. It was night when they got to it. So again, the dog carried the cat, who carried the jewel in his mouth, on his back and swam across.

"Have you got a good grip with your teeth?" asked the dog.

"I've got a good grip," said the cat.

"You're holding tight?"

"I'm holding tight."

In order to answer the dog's questions, the cat had to open his mouth. Well, when they reached the middle of the river, he dropped the jewel. And what was he going to do now? What a damn shame it was. Like they say, it takes a decade of striving to become a buddha. They'd worked so hard to get the jewel, and now the cat had lost it. It breaks your heart to think about it. Well, they got across that river.

"What have you done with the jewel?" asked the dog. He wanted the cat to hand it over.

The cat told the dog that he could kill him—could do whatever he wanted to him. There was nothing he could do about the lost jewel now. The dog thought it over. "Well, our fate is already sealed," he said. "What good would it do to kill you now? And now I'm so hungry I could die. What should I do about that?"

They sneaked up and down the riverbank, and wouldn't you know it, someone was out there doing some night fishing. So they sat there quietly and waited while he went about his business. There was a plopping sound, and the fisherman unhooked a huge carp. The dog and cat kept an eye on it so they could steal it and eat it. The fisherman was so pleased about having caught that carp that he put it down and went back to the river. He sat there, holding his fishing rod, entirely preoccupied.

"Ya, let's steal that thing and eat it."

"We'll get caught if we eat it here. Let's make off with it."

So they grabbed the carp in their teeth and went a little ways before they stopped to devour it. "Let's eat it all up," said the dog. "I'm so hungry I could die."

They gobbled it up—eggs in the belly and all. They scooped out the intestines to eat. The dog bit into them and was trying to chew when he felt a sharp jolt of pain in his teeth. It was something hard. "Hey, what the hell is this?" he said, and he spat it out. It was the jewel. "I'll be damned," said the dog.

As you know, those big carp have large mouths. It was gulping and gulping away to drink the water, and just to make things turn out right in the end, the carp was gulping away when the jewel fell into the water. It went right down the fish's throat. Then, as luck would have it, the carp just happened to bite the line cast by that fisherman.

"Well, now we're all set," said the dog. "I guess God has come to our assistance." Since he had regained his strength from eating that whole carp, he took the jewel. "Let's hurry." They sped off faster than a car, and after a while they were back in their old home.

"Hey," said the dog, "I'm the one who eats and lives outside. You're the one who eats and sleeps indoors, so why don't you take the jewel and present it to our master?"

The master had thought the dog and cat were gone for good. But now they both appeared at once, so he was overjoyed to see them. "Where have you been?" he asked.

The cat walked right into the master's room and threw up. He spat up the jewel.

"*Aigu!*" said the master. "Where in the world did you find this?" He hugged and petted that cat and honored him more lavishly than his own great ancestor, all because he had found the jewel. Day and night, all he did was stroke the cat and buy meat to feed him.

Outside, the dog was brooding. He was getting good food, to be sure, but he wasn't getting treated as well as the cat. Well, when he gave the matter careful consideration, he was incredulous. "All right, you damned cat," he said. "You took all the credit for it, and now it's just you. Just wait, cat. There's some night when you're going to have to come outside. Then we'll see."

He bore a great grudge, obviously. So when the cat came out to relieve itself one night, the dog was lying in wait, and he bit him all the way through his narrow waist and flung him down. A little guy like the cat would die from that, wouldn't he? Well, he died. So it was at that time that the dog and cat became mortal enemies.

Translated by Heinz Insu Fenkl

THE STORY POUCH

This tale, known throughout Korea, belongs to the metafolklore category (stories about storytelling). A boy writes down all the old stories that the adults tell him, and he puts the slips of paper into a pouch he hangs on a pillar in his room. The boy grows to manhood, and on the night before he is to marry, a servant happens to hear the stories trapped inside the pouch plotting to kill him because he has kept them locked up and will not set them free. At the end, the boy, whose life is saved by the faithful servant that next day, finally releases the stories from the pouch. This tale instructs us on the basic nature of folktales and reminds us that stories are not just meant to be heard but must be passed on continually to freshen the oral tradition.

A long time ago, among the gentry, they'd hire a private teacher and sit their sons down to study with him. It was the same thing as a well-to-do family hiring a tutor these days. So this rich family had hired a private teacher to instruct their son, but the boy just wouldn't study.

When the sun went down, his father and the old neighbor would sit down and tell stories to each other, and the boy would write those stories down even while he was supposed to be studying. If he heard a tidbit one evening he'd write that down on a slip of paper, and fold it up. He set up a little pouch and stuffed the paper in there. After three years of doing this, he saw he had three full pouches. So he hung them up on the main pillar in his room. The boy had put in one story at a time for three years, so an incredible number of stories were stuffed in those pouches, all three of them jammed full.

In the fourth year, the boy was to be married. If he were living in a town like ours, he'd have been married off about as far as Hongch'ŏn. He'd have had to go over a mountain pass. But back then—why, they had to do it by palanquin, didn't they? He was going to leave the next day, and they had servants, so his father gave them their orders. "You take so-and-so's palanquin and receive such and such guests."

But one servant, the one who was going to lead the palanquin and take that young master over the pass—well, it was the middle of winter, and it suddenly snowed overnight, so he went to the young master's room to sweep the snow outside, and he was just outside the door. The young master wasn't there—the room was empty—but it was all abuzz with the sound of talking. It was the room that used to be the study. "Hmm," the servant thought. "The young master's not here, so what's all this talking coming from his room?" So he hid and he strained his ears to listen, and he heard a whole lot of voices chattering away.

"This bastard keeps us cooped up in a pouch and doesn't set us free," said a voice.

"Since they say this bastard's getting married over the hills tomorrow, we have to get him then," said another.

"We've just got to get him . . . ." Lots of sentiments like this were coming out in this discussion among the spirits.

"So how are we going to get him?" one of them asked.

"Listen to me," said another. "It's the middle of winter, so out of the blue we'll make a big wild pear appear at the top of the pass. The pear will dangle like this, with leaves spreading out like that, and when he sees it—ha—he'll bust a gut to eat it. We'll set it up just like that. And if this groom sticks it in his craw, he'll die. So let's do it."

Well, the servant who was supposed to lead the whole procession heard this, and he resolved that he must save his young master's life.

But the next morning, the father of the groom-to-be said, "Something important has come up. I know I told you to escort the young master today, but you'll have to tend to matters here at home instead."

"That won't do," said the servant. "I *have* to go."

"How dare you! Whose orders do you dare disobey?"

"I must go, even if it means having my head chopped off," said the servant.

The groom-to-be pondered this a while and realized it was rather strange. "What are you talking about?" he asked.

"I have no choice but to attend to you, young master," said the servant. Of course, that made the groom-to-be take a liking to him.

"Father, please. This time let's just let him go as you had originally planned."

"No, he must attend to the guests at home."

They weren't seeing eye to eye. Still, the servant said he had to go even if it meant his life. What could the father do when he said he'd go even if it meant he got his head chopped off? The son backed him up, so that's how the servant came to escort him.

Well, it was just like the spirits said. The procession was climbing this damned hill covered white with winter snow, and at the crest a wild pear tree appeared out of nowhere with wild pears dangling from it, and, ah, they were spectacularly ripe, and not many, either. Only two wild pears were dangling there.

"Hey, pick those for me," said the groom. "Now that we've reached the top, I'm thirsty."

Since the groom told him to pick the pears, the servant set down the palanquin. He went and pretended to pick them, and then he took them like they were stones and hurled them far away. It was as if his mind had snapped. "I misjudged," thought the groom. "If I had left him behind and brought someone else like Father said, then I'd have been able to eat those wild pears." Inside he had a twisted thought: "Sooner or later, he must be ready to die by my hand." And with that, he went to the wedding feast. Three days after they returned, he called the servant—the one who had thrown away the wild pears—and he came forward.

"You," said the groom. "What kind of grudge do you bear me that you'd throw away the wild pears I wanted so much to eat?"

"Young master, there's a reason for that. There is also a reason why I argued so stubbornly to accompany you."

"What is it?"

He spewed out the whole story. "When I went around to sweep the snow in front of the room where you study, the stories were plotting among themselves. They said that because you locked them up like that instead of setting them free, they were going to do away with you. And they said they were going to make the wild pears so you'd die if you ate them. And that's why I went to such lengths to show my devotion to you."

When the young master considered this, his story pouches came to mind. "Ah, you're right!" he said.

So the young master searched the room he used to study in. And the three story pouches he'd filled were hanging on the pillar, full to the brim with the stories he'd copied down, folded up, and crammed into them. So this fellow took the story pouches and ripped them open, letting all the stories out. Now, when he freed all those stories, all I managed to gather up was about half a pouch worth. And that's how the story ends.

THE TIGER AND THE CLOUDBURST

This story is a Korean variant of the Thief and Tiger tale (Type 177), which is found throughout the world. In this version a Chinese tiger comes to Korea and thinks that a "cloudburst" must be a frightful thing, after seeing people run into their homes to avoid one. When a cow thief mistakes the tiger for a cow and climbs on its back, however, the tiger thinks that this man must be the cloudburst and runs away. The tale is quite similar to the "The Tiger and the Persimmons," another widely known animal tale that features a dim-witted tiger.

This is a story about a thief who caught a tiger and got rich. You see, in the old days, Korea was the small country of Chosŏn, and a tiger from a small country was called a *horangi,* while a tiger from the great country of China was called a *pŏm.* So this tiger from China was quietly thinking to himself about how they said the country of Chosŏn was like a field of gold—that wonderful. He really wanted to go have a look at this Chosŏn, so he went "a thousand tricents without pause," as they say.

And so the Chinese tiger came creeping into this land of Chosŏn to a certain place, but the sun was setting. He finally sat down, intending to stay the night in that place, but it was that time of year—you know, summer—when they thresh the barley. He was looking straight down into a village from the mountain out front, and—ah—they were threshing barley. And they were all jumping up and down. They were having a cloudburst. It thundered, and they were all jumping up and down shouting, "It's a cloudburst!" And they jumped up and down for a while, saying a cloudburst was coming, and then everybody packed up and ran inside and locked their doors, and it all got quiet.

The tiger said: "*Ya!* In all of China I'm the most frightening creature—a fearsome tiger. But now that I'm here in Chosŏn, this fellow called the Cloudburst must be truly terrifying. It'd probably be the death of me, too, if that Cloudburst got me."

So he wanted to hide from the Cloudburst, and he went down to have a rest inside one of the houses where they were threshing barley. He went in—and it was the cowshed, of all places. And the cows, they were wide-eyed, probably thinking they were going to die—a tiger coming in and lying down with the cows like that. Well, they were all in an uproar since the tiger couldn't do a thing but lie there with them. While the Chinese tiger was just lying there, a cow thief happened to be passing by. He'd heard there were lots of cattle there, and he went in to feel them with his hands, intending to steal one. Well, he felt around, and in the far corner there was this one that was the largest, with a shaggy pelt and lots of meat on it. So he dragged this one out, but it didn't have a collar. He tied it up with whatever rope he could find and was dragging it out.

"*Aigu!* It's the Cloudburst! I'm in big trouble," thought the tiger. He couldn't put up a fight because he was being pulled by the scruff of his neck. The cow thief dragged him outside, tied the rope around his neck, and climbed onto his back and rode him off. The tiger couldn't resist him.

"You bastard Cloudburst, fall off!" thought the tiger. He was an agile wild mountain tiger, after all. He just took off into the mountains, faster than an airplane.

Now when this cow thief gave it a good think, he realized it wasn't a cow he was riding. He grabbed onto a clump of fur, because he knew he was going to die if he fell off. He was holding on to the fur for dear life, leaning forward, and there was no way he could get off because the tiger was going so damn fast. The cow thief finally looked down at what he was riding, and of course it wasn't a cow—it was a tiger. Now he knew that if he fell off the tiger was going to eat him, so he lay on his belly on the tiger's back, desperately clinging, since his life depended on it, and through the night they must have gone a myriad tricents. Along the way he saw some people transplanting rice seedlings, and they cursed at him: "Ah, some idiot is riding that tiger!"

He had to get off, but how? As they went along, they came to a certain place where there was a thick forest, and he jumped off. And as he jumped he saw this tree, an old tree, and he just leaped right into it.

"*Aigu!*" the tiger thought. "I've finally got rid of him. *Aigu!* It's a good thing he fell off."

In the old days, that was a time when even animals talked to each other, and as he continued on his way the tiger saw a bear up in a tree, snapping branches and eating the acorns.

"Hey," he said to the bear, "I'm so-and-so. I've just had a terrible time with the Cloudburst. What are you doing?"

"Ah, Mr. Tiger, where on earth have you been?" said the bear.

"*Aigu!* Don't even ask. I went to a place called Chosŏn and almost died at the hands of the Cloudburst. But how . . ."

"*Aigu!* Mr. Tiger, that's not a cloudburst, it's a man. You have to go catch him and eat him up," said the bear.

"Oh, how do I catch him?" asked the tiger. The bear's reply had made him hungry again. And since it was only a man after all, he decided he was going to eat him.

"Come on, come with me," said the bear. And the two of them made a plan. "I'll go over there, see. I'll lie at the top of the tree, and you, Mr. Tiger, dig a hole real quick. Then when he comes out, you, Mr. Tiger, eat him."

"All right."

So one went to lie up in the tree and the other started digging with his claws. As the tiger was digging, he kept looking around. "If that Cloudburst comes out again, we're in trouble," he said.

Meanwhile, up in the tree, the cow thief was thinking carefully. He was looking around and realized those big sacks he saw dangling down in front of him were the bear's testicles. It took him a while to figure this out. Now, the tiger was digging at the bottom and the bear was up top, sitting on his balls. The cow thief realized he was a dead man. No doubt about it. In those days they wore topknots, so he pulled out his hair tie, made a noose, and with a "To hell with it!" he suddenly pulled it tight around the bear's balls. The bear was ready to die from the pain.

When the tiger, digging away, looked over again, he saw the bear's expression was odd. "Hey, what's wrong with your face?" he asked.

"*Aigu!* I'm gonna die."

"See? I told you so. I am on top in China, but I went to Chosŏn and was beaten by the Cloudburst. See? I'll be on my way."

The thief yanked the noose really tight, and the bear fell over and died. When the man came down from the tree, he saw he'd caught a bear as big as a mountain, but there was nothing he could do with it. When he sauntered back down to the fields, the people were hustling and bustling about, transplanting rice.

"Hey, I'm the one that rode the tiger by here," he said. "I've caught a big bear, but I can't do anything with it by myself, so let's go and take care of it together."

So they all went together and claimed the bear, and that cow thief pulled out the bear's gallbladder and took the whole thing for himself. They say that what he got was far better than stealing a cow.

The Mud Snail Bride

Like "The Heavenly Maiden and the Woodcutter," "The Mud Snail Bride" is a tale widely known in Korea. Other versions have a tragic ending: the groom violates the interdiction not to look at the maiden taking a bath, and the two must separate.

Long ago there was a man who lived out in the wild in a place that was neither hill nor dale, and yet was close to the mountains and close to the fields. It was a wide grassy place like a public park. He'd lost his parents early and he was living alone, trying to find a way to get by all by himself.

"Oh, how will I manage?" he thought. After a while he bought himself a hoe and started to clear a patch of land. He tilled that field every day. He cooked for himself, he lived in a mud hut, and he tended to his field daily. After the tenth day he grew tired of it and he sat down. "Who will live with me when I've made myself into a farmer? Who will eat with me?"

From within the earth came the answer. "You'll eat with me, who else?" said a voice. It was decidedly strange. He didn't hear it again for a long time, but then, as he was resting again, he said, "Who will I live with after I till this land? Who will I eat with?" And a woman's voice answered, "You'll eat with me, who else?"

The young man took a liking to this voice, so every day he tilled the land, cultivated it, and turned it into a proper field. Then he would go back to his mud hut and at nightfall he would go to sleep. Every morning he would take his pot of rice and go out to till the field that would eventually feed him.

One day he wondered again, "Who will I eat and live with when I till this field?"

"You'll eat with me, who else?" came the voice.

"What on earth are you?" asked the young man.

"I won't tell you today," said the voice. "But I will tell you everything three days from now, so be patient and continue with your work."

The young man waited three days, working impatiently in his field, and after the third day he said, "Where is the person who said, 'You'll eat with me'?"

"Dig up a bowl of dirt and see," said the voice.

So the young man dug up a bowl of dirt and found a snail in it. It was a big owl snail. "What are you?" he asked, but it didn't say a word. It just bubbled and frothed, so he put it inside the water jug that was one of the items he had for keeping house. The next day he went and worked in the field again, and when he returned to cook for himself, he saw that the snail was still there.

Open the rice pot, cook the rice, sleep, and in the morning wake up and carry the food out to work in the field—that was his daily routine. But three days after he had put the snail inside the water jug, the young man went to cook himself some rice and found that it was already made in the pot. There were side dishes, too.

"This is strange," he said. When he tried the food, it tasted much better than his own cooking. So now he ate it and went to sleep. In the morning he ate the breakfast that had been prepared for him, and when he returned home after working into the night, once again someone had cooked the food.

"This is a strange thing," he said. Again he ate the food, but on the next day he thought, "Tomorrow evening, I'm going to have to come early and take a peek."

The next day after work, he returned to his house when it was about time to prepare dinner, and from under the rafters, he peeked into the kitchen. "What in the world is doing the cooking?" he thought. As he kept watch, it came time to prepare dinner, and from inside the water jug a beautiful maiden emerged. She neatly scrubbed the pot and cooked the rice. Now, she couldn't go to the market to shop; she just made the side dishes by chopping the kimch'i that was already there. Then with a splash, she plopped back inside the water jug.

"Aha! So you're the one," the young man said to himself. Now he knew. That night he ate, and the next day he went out to the field and returned early once again, before the sun went down. This time, when the beautiful maiden came out to scrub the pot and was stoking the fire to cook the rice, he grabbed her by the wrist.

"I'll get to the point," said the young man. "You are alone, and I am alone. Let's live together."

"It isn't time yet for us to live together," said the maiden.

"Then when shall it be?"

"In three days you and I will become husband and wife, even if you don't force me," said the maiden. "So let me go now and just concentrate on your work."

So he worked diligently as he was told to, and he waited anxiously for three days. Now when the third day came around the maiden didn't try to go back into the water jug. There was no need to grab her. She brought to the table the food she had prepared, but this time it was set for the two of them. When they had finished eating, they made a promise to each other: "Let's be husband and wife." And they lived together from that day.

Now this maiden was a beauty without equal, and the local folks spread the rumor far and wide that the man was living at a certain place with a beautiful woman.

The local magistrate must have become jealous. "Just how beautiful is she?" he said. One day he went to have a look and he saw that she was a beauty without equal. "Oh, she's more than a man of his standing deserves," he said. "I'll take her and make her one of my concubines."

The magistrate had an evil idea. He sent an official notice to the young man that said, "Give me your wife." It commanded the young man to appear before him.

When the young man came, the magistrate said, "Your wife is too good for a man of your station. Give her to me."

"Oh, how can that be?" said the young man.

"Well," said the magistrate, "then how did this rumor come about?"

The young man told the magistrate the whole story.

"Whatever your case may be, give me that wife of yours," said the magistrate.

"How could I do that?" said the young man. "Let me go home and ask."

"Very well. Go ask her and come back."

That night the young man went home and just lay there, not even eating.

"Why aren't you eating?" asked his wife.

"Oh, woman! I went to the magistrate today because he called me, and he told me to give you to him. How am I supposed to have an appetite?"

"Tell him you won't give me up. Tell him you won't, and he'll want you to play a game of chess with him."

"Oh, woman, I can't play chess. If I play him a game of chess over you, then I'll lose you, won't I?"

"Do as I say. When you play chess, he will naturally tell you to move first. When he does, tell him, 'Esteemed sir, you must move first.' When he makes his first move, a little blowfly will appear and sit on one of your pieces. Whichever way it flies, just put your piece where that fly lands."

"All right," said the husband. And he went to the magistrate as his wife had told him to do.

"So, what did she say?" asked the magistrate.

"She said, uh, she would not allow it."

"Then let's you and me play a game of chess over her," said the magistrate.

"How can you ask me to play a game of chess when I've never learned how?"

"Ah, it's because I intend to take your wife away from you."

"All right, let's play a round," said the young man. It wasn't as if he could refuse, since it was a command—and besides, he had been instructed to do so by his wife.

So the two of them sat facing each other and prepared to play. "You make the first move," said the magistrate.

"No, you're the magistrate. You play first."

The magistrate made the first move. The young man did exactly as his wife had told him, and a fly, so tiny you could hardly see it, lighted on the board. With a loud thump, the young man moved his piece there. Then the magistrate made his next move and the young man made his move, placing his piece where the fly landed. Every time the magistrate made a move, the fly would jump to another place on the board. They played through half the day.

"Chess is a man's game, but you play like a demon," said the magistrate. "I believed no one could beat me at the game of chess, but now it seems that chess will not do. I must devise another plan, so go get some sleep and come back tomorrow. But when you return tomorrow, it will be horses. I'll give you a horse and we'll go to the river. If you can't jump to the other bank, then let's agree that I get your wife."

So the young man returned home without even giving his consent. And again he sat there, sapped of strength, not able to eat. "It looks like I'll lose you after all," he said. "He told me he'll give me a horse tomorrow and that I'll have to jump across the river. If I can't, he'll take you away. But he's going to ride a good horse and give me a bad one, isn't he?"

"Of course. But do as I tell you."

"What shall I do?"

"Of course, the magistrate will probably ride a good horse. But if you look around the corner of the stable, you'll see a horse there that looks like a mangy old donkey. Ask the magistrate to give you that one. He'll laugh and he'll say to you, 'Why do you ask for the bad one and leave the good one for me?'

"Say to him, 'Oh, just give me that one. When would I ever have ridden a horse? I'm worried I might take a fall, so just give me that one.' He will reply, 'Then so be it.' Now, the magistrate's horse will take five steps back before he jumps, but you take ten steps back, and just when you are about to jump, say to the horse, 'Listen here, you nag, please let me keep the wife it took me so long to find.' Then jump."

Well, his wife's instructions got the young man all excited.

"You've returned?" the magistrate said the next day.

"Yes," answered the young man.

The magistrate mounted his thunderous horse and called out to his servant, "Drag out that mare there."

"Oh, I'm too afraid to ride that horse," said the young man. He bumbled about for a while until he found, off in one corner, the horse that looked like a donkey with mange. "Give me this one," he said, pulling it forward.

"Oh, surely not that one," said the magistrate.

"Please, I've never ridden a horse before and I'm scared. I'd like to ride this one."

"Well, what do you know," thought the magistrate. "I was going to give him a good horse since I'm stealing his wife, but that nag is probably going to stagger around and not even make it across the river."

"Very well," said the magistrate.

And that horse—it must have had some strength inside, but it just stood there without showing it, though it had the same strength as the good horse.

So the young man rode along on his old nag, and the villagers and the country folk came out to watch and have a laugh at him. "Ha, that crazy bastard," they said. "He shouldn't have made the bet in the first place. He should've just given it up. What kind of humiliation is he after, that he's riding that?" They jeered at him.

But the young man held his ground. "I've chosen this path, so I'm taking it," he said, and he rode on.

The magistrate jumped first. His horse took five steps back and jumped with a huff. But its hind legs got stuck in the river, and he had to struggle a long time before he got out again.

Now it was the young man's turn to jump. Just as his wife had told him, he took ten steps back and—*whack!*—he whipped the horse's flank. "Listen here, you nag," he whispered, "please let me keep the wife it took me so long to find." With a grunt, his horse leaped easily over the river.

The magistrate had no choice but to concede defeat. "Your wife is a gift given to you by heaven," he said. "What can I do but wish you a happy life as you are? But I cannot send you away empty-handed. I must at least reward you." And with that, they say the magistrate gave the young man nearly half of his wealth.

So they say this young man found his fortune when he dug in the dirt.

Translated by Heinz Insu Fenkl

The Father's Gifts

This tale, which is told in all parts of Korea, belongs to the "Three Lucky Brothers" category (Type 1650) common throughout the world. Before he dies, a poor man gives a millstone to the oldest son, a gourd and a bamboo cane to the second son, and a drum to the youngest son as their inheritance. The three sons become rich: the oldest son scares away bandits and takes their treasures, the second son marries the daughter of a wealthy family after saving her from a goblin, and the youngest son sells the king a tiger. Each, in his own parallel adventure, is able to make good use of his inheritance after all. This version was collected in Kongju county, South Ch'ungch'ŏng province, in 1960.

Out in the country, there once lived a poor father. He was so poor that all he had to leave his sons were a millstone, a gourd, a bamboo cane, and a drum.

From his deathbed, the poor father called his three sons together. "All I have to leave you are these paltry things," he told them. "When I die, live by your own good sense." With this, he gave the millstone to the oldest son, the gourd and the bamboo cane to the second son, and the drum to the youngest son, whereupon he drew his last breath and passed away.

The three sons held a funeral for their father and gathered to discuss how they were going to live from that day on. They decided to live separately and according to their own good sense, as their father had told them with his dying breath.

And so the three brothers left home, and they traveled together for a time until, finally, they came upon a three-forked road. There they made a pact to meet again, and then they split up.

The oldest son wandered aimlessly, carrying the millstone, until he found himself in the mountains at the end of the day. His legs were sore, he was hungry, and what's more, the weather was cold. He could not go any farther.

As he was looking all around for a place he might sleep, he found an old tree close by. He decided to spend the night there, so he went over and set down his millstone. But since he was so deep in the wilderness, he worried that some animal might come in the night, so he picked the millstone back up and climbed the tree. He set the millstone on a branch, and there he stayed the night, propped up against another branch.

Night fell quickly in the mountains. One moment the sun was setting behind the western peaks, and the next the mountains were buried in a thick darkness. Exhausted from wandering all day like a vagabond, the oldest son soon fell into a deep sleep. He hadn't slept long when he was awakened by a loud commotion. "Who could be making such a racket so deep in the woods?" he thought.

The oldest son quietly looked around and almost fainted at what he saw. Wouldn't you know it, the noise was coming from right under the very tree he was sleeping in! A gang of thieves in garish clothes were arguing among themselves as they divided up the money they had stolen.

"You have a thousand *yang* more than me."

"I have a thousand *yang* more?"

"You bastard, give it here. Why do you keep hiding it?"

"What was that you said?"

They went on like this until the Big Dipper tipped northward by more than a handspan—and still their bickering didn't end. Just then, the oldest son had an idea. He started to grind the millstone with all his might, and the millstone made a tremendous noise.

"*Ya!* It's big trouble! Thunder without a speck of cloud in the sky—it must be the wrath of heaven! Run for your lives!"

They had already been distracted by the money, but now they started to scatter in all directions without even pausing to think. Before the night was through, the oldest son escaped from that place with the money and the treasures that the thieves had left behind. He became a very rich man, thanks to the millstone.

The second son too wandered aimlessly like a vagabond. One day, at dusk, he rested his body on a stone offering table in front of a grave. It was pitch black that night, without a star in the sky. He was terribly lonely and even a bit scared. But he had no choice but to pass the night there.

In the middle of the night the second son heard the sound of footsteps approaching. He was already scared, but now he was so afraid his liver shrank to the size of a pea. He held his breath and listened to the footsteps. And wouldn't you know it, the footsteps stopped right at the edge of that very grave where he was! "Ah, now I'm dead," the second son was thinking. And then he heard:

"Hey there, Skeleton! Hurry and get up before the night's through. Tonight's the night we go to the rich man's house and steal the soul of his only daughter, ain't it?" It was a goblin.

When the second son saw this, he quickly collected himself. "I know!" he said nonchalantly. "That's why I was already up."

But the goblin seemed suspicious. "Why is there a human sound in your voice?" he said. "I don't believe you're a skeleton. What have you got to say?"

"Well now, you don't even trust me anymore. Have a feel to see if I'm lying or not."

"Then why don't you turn your head this way?"

Quickly the second son held out the gourd he had received from his father.

"Uh-huh, it's you without a doubt, since there's no hair on your head. But let's have a feel of your arm, just to be sure."

This time the second son held out the bamboo cane.

"Why is your forearm so thin? Since there's no moisture in the bone, you must have died a long time ago."

"You didn't know that till just now?"

"Never mind, let's hurry. We'll be late."

And so the second son and the goblin rushed down to the rich man's house. In the village, the rich man's family was quiet and oblivious in a deep sleep.

The goblin left the second son standing in front of the gate. "Look, you wait here," he said. "I'll go in and steal the daughter's spirit." And he went into the house.

The second son hardly had to wait—the goblin returned right away.

"What did you do with the daughter's spirit?" the second son asked.

"Here it is," said the goblin. "Right here—I'm holding it tight in my hands."

"Yeah? Well, instead of struggling with it in your hands like that, why don't you just put it into my pouch here?"

"Let's do that. But you have to tie the string really tight around the pouch," the goblin said as he put the spirit into the pouch the second son was wearing.

The two of them walked back toward the grave. They hadn't gotten very far—they had hardly left the village—when they heard a cock crow.

"Damn! What a nuisance," said the goblin. "I'll go ahead so you can take your time about it. I'll come find you tomorrow night." And with that he scurried off and disappeared somewhere.

That morning, the second son went back to the rich man's house, where everything was topsy-turvy and the clamorous sound of weeping filled the air.

He pretended not to know what was going on. "What has happened that you're all crying so mournfully?" he asked a servant.

"How on earth could something like this happen?" said the servant. "The master's daughter—she was perfectly healthy, and then just last night she passed away."

"Hmmm, is that so? Then I shall try to revive her."

As soon as he got the message that someone thought he could revive his daughter, the rich man came running out of the house. "Is it true? If so, I'll give you any amount of money—just bring my daughter back to life."

"Yes, I'll do my utmost," said the second son. He went into the room where the daughter's body lay and made sure no one was watching. He went up to the daughter's body, put his pouch right up to her nose, and untied the string. The daughter had been lying all stiff until then, but now she awakened and sat up with a big stretch.

Seeing his daughter come back to life, the rich man was so happy he didn't know what to do. He danced up and down with joy, and then he took the second son by the hand and said, "Thank you. How will I ever repay this debt? All of this must have been destined to happen. So if it pleases you, young man, I would like you to accept my daughter as your wife!"

As of that day, the second son married the rich man's daughter and inherited half his fortune, becoming a very rich man himself.

The youngest son walked on and on, carrying the drum his father had given him. Because he was the cheerful sort, he was wandering without even the slightest lonely or desolate thought. And so he found himself walking in a beautiful forest. His body felt a bit heavy, but as he was passing through such beautiful scenery, he dismissed his tiredness as nothing, and he sang as he walked. When he felt a particular surge of joy, he would even dance to the beat of his drum. And then a strange thing happened. Would you believe it? A huge tiger was doing a hobbly dance through a thicket of bodhi trees. The youngest son enjoyed this so much that he even forgot to be afraid, and he kept on beating his drum with a renewed fervor.

And the tiger came toward him, dancing with its front paws in the air.

The youngest son sang to the beat of his drum, and the tiger danced, and for a long time they went on like this, making their way down toward a village. The tiger was so preoccupied with his dancing that he came down to the village, too, without a thought.

"Goodness, I've never seen such a strange thing," the villagers said when they saw the tiger dancing to the beat of the drum, and they all tossed money at them. So the youngest son took the tiger from town to town, beating his drum and singing, and he made enough money to become as rich as his older brothers. The story spread quickly throughout the country, and soon it even reached the ears of the king.

"Well then, I would like to have a look, too," said the king, and he commanded his subjects to bring him the youngest son.

Beating his drum energetically, the youngest son brought the tiger into the palace. He sang with even more fervor to the beat of his drum, and the tiger, for his part, danced with many times his usual energy.

The king enjoyed himself so much that now he wanted to own the tiger. "I'll give you any amount of money, so sell it to me," he said.

"I am sorry," said the youngest son, "but this tiger is a treasure passed down from generation to generation in my family. How can I sell it so casually?" He refused repeatedly, but in the end the king bought the tiger for all of ten thousand *yang*. Now the youngest son was even richer.

The three brothers met again on the appointed day. When they learned that they had all become fabulously rich, the three embraced one another and danced with joy. And so, realizing that the seemingly worthless objects their father had given them had turned out to be precious gifts after all, they were once again grateful for their father's favor.

Translated by Heinz Insu Fenkl and Yoo-sup Chang

The Heavenly Maiden and the Woodcutter

A representative story known throughout Korea, this tale belongs to the Swan Maid family of folktales (Type 400). In this version the woodcutter becomes a rooster because he ignores his bride's advice. Another version presents a happy ending—the woodcutter does not come down to earth again.

A woodcutter was chopping wood by a stream when a deer, fleeing from a hunter, approached him. "Please hide me," said the deer. "The hunter is coming just over there."

The woodcutter shouldered the load of wood he had cut and hid the deer inside, covering him with the wood. But even so, he saw that the hunter was following him.

"Hey there! Hey, you!" called the hunter. "Didn't a deer just pass by here?"

"Yes, he was running that way," said the woodcutter. "He was running to the other side, over there."

After the hunter ran off in the direction the woodcutter had indicated, the deer came out of the woodpile. "Whew! Since I'm alive because of your help, I shall repay the favor."

"How will you repay me?" asked the woodcutter.

"There is a certain spot, at such and such a place, where you will find a well," said the deer. "Go there at night when the moon is full and you will see three heavenly maidens come down to bathe. When they have removed their clothes, you should hide one of the three sets of clothes. Not of the oldest or the second-oldest, but of the youngest maiden. Keep the clothes hidden, and give them back to her only when she has borne you three children."

So, on the fifteenth of the month, when the moon was full, the woodcutter went to that place as the deer had instructed. When he got there, just as the deer had said, there really were three maidens who had come down from heaven to bathe. Recalling what the deer had told him, the woodcutter quietly hid the youngest sister's clothes while she was bathing. Then he hid himself. When the three maidens had bathed, they came out and put on their clothes, but the youngest sister's clothes were missing. She was terribly anxious. "What happened? My clothes are gone!" she exclaimed.

The woodcutter waited in hiding until it came time and the two older heavenly maidens returned to the sky. But the youngest was unable to ascend because she could not find her clothes. It was only then that the woodcutter, having hidden the clothes in another place, came out from where he was hiding. And he said to the anxious maiden, "What's the matter? Why don't you come with me to my house?"

So now they went. The heavenly maiden followed the woodcutter and lived with him as his wife, and eventually they had one child, and then a second. But the heavenly maiden would sigh and lament every day, "Oh, I've lost my clothes and cannot find them. I'll never be able to return to heaven." The woodcutter felt so sorry for her that he returned her clothes to her the year she bore him their second child. When he gave her the clothes, she immediately put them on, and holding a child under each arm, she flew up into the sky. And that is how the woodcutter lost his wife.

So now he was brokenhearted and living as a bachelor, and one day the deer came to him again and asked, "Why did you give her the clothes after you had your second child, when I told you to give them to her after she bore you three?" Then the deer said, "Go back to that well at full moon. Since they no longer come down to bathe, having been tricked, they will draw the water up in a bucket. It will come down once, then twice, and when it comes down for the third time, throw out the water and climb inside."

So the woodcutter did exactly as the deer had instructed, and he was drawn up to heaven. When he arrived, his wife came with their two children. "How did you get here?" she asked.

"I came up because the deer told me how," said the woodcutter.

He intended to live there in heaven with her and the children, but his father-in-law—the father of the heavenly maiden—said, "If you want to live with my daughter, you must shoot an arrow down at a mortal."

So the woodcutter did as he was told, and he hit someone's only son right in the armpit. The boy who was struck by the arrow died. There was a funeral in the household, and it looked like it was the end of the world for that family. So now the woodcutter's wife told him, "Send someone down there and have them pull the arrow out." The woodcutter did just as his wife had instructed. The arrow was pulled from the boy's body, and he came back to life. It all worked out because he had followed the heavenly maiden's instructions.

The child lived, however, and so the father-in-law was still displeased. He commanded the woodcutter to do something else. But once again, in order that they could live together, his wife told him what to do, and when he did exactly as she had said, it all worked out. And so now they passed the father-in-law's tests and were able to live together in peace.

Now if the woodcutter had just kept quiet, things would have been fine. But one day, he said to his wife, "I've been here so long that I must go down to the mortal world and see my mother. I'll return after I pay her a visit."

When he said that, the heavenly maiden said, "Please, do not go down. No matter what. Don't go down. Because if you do, you will never be able to return."

"But one's parents are precious. And I haven't been able to fulfill my filial duties even for my one mother. It's been such a long time, I'll pay her a quick visit and come back up."

"Then if you really must go, go down to the mortal world but do not get off your horse. Visit your mother and return after talking to her from horseback." And then she added, "When you go down to the mortal world, do not eat pumpkin soup under any circumstances."

So the woodcutter went down to the mortal world. He rode a horse to his mother's house, and when he arrived he would not dismount because of what his wife had told him. Standing outside the door, he called to his mother, and she came running out.

"Oh! Where have you been all this time?" she said. She was overjoyed. "Hurry and come in," she said.

"Mother, I cannot come in," said the woodcutter. "I've come to see you and pay my respects, and then I must go."

"But I've prepared food for you every day you've been gone," she said. "And I've waited for you every day. So get down off that horse and come inside."

"Mother, if I go inside, I cannot leave," said the woodcutter. However, he had no choice but to obey his mother's wishes. He came down from the horse and ate the pumpkin soup she had made for him. And when he went outside again, the horse had already flown back to heaven. What was he to do now that the horse had gone? He had no way to return. So they say the woodcutter died. And when he died, he became a rooster. When a rooster crows, it sounds like "cock-a-doodle-doo!" and there's a tightness in its throat, as you know. Well, there's a reason for that. They say what the rooster is really saying is, "It's the pumpkin soup! The pumpkin soup! I can't return to heaven because I ate the pumpkin soup!"

THE SNAKY BRIDEGROOM

Known throughout Korea, this tale corresponds to the Search for the Lost Husband category (Type 425).

They say there was once an old woman who had a son who was born as a snake. In the old days they used to wear bamboo hats when they worked, and people used to keep them under the chimney. They say that after she had the baby, she covered him up with a bamboo hat. Well, that was the rumor, anyway.

There were three daughters. And when they heard that the old woman had had a baby, the oldest wanted to go have a look. She called on the old woman. "Grandma, Grandma," she said. "They say you had a baby, but wherever did you put it?"

"Go over to that corner and lift up the bamboo hat," said the old woman.

So she went and lifted the hat and there was a snake flicking, flicking, flicking its tongue. "Grandma, they say you had a baby," said the girl. "But what you've covered up here is a snake. How can you say you had a baby?" And she ran away.

Now the second daughter came to see the old woman's baby. "They say you had a baby, but where have you put him?"

The old woman told her to go over to that corner and lift up the bamboo hat. The girl lifted it and saw the snake and was frightened away just like her sister.

Finally, the youngest daughter came and said, "Grandma, Grandma, they say you had a baby, but where is it?"

"Go over to that corner and lift up the bamboo hat."

So she went and lifted up the bamboo hat, and the youngest daughter said, "Oh, Grandma, you've given birth to a fine snaky gentleman."

From that day on, the snake took a liking to the youngest daughter. They say when he was asked which of the three he preferred, he would reply that the youngest was the one he liked best. But when he was grown and ready to get married, his parents asked the oldest daughter, as was the custom.

She said, "Even if it means I never get married, I'm not going to marry a snake."

So they went and asked the second daughter, and she was frightened in just the same way. So they asked the youngest, and she said, "You'll have to get my mother's permission. I can't agree to it myself."

They got permission from her mother, and when they had it, the snake came out and said, "Mother, Mother, fetch me some water. Warm it up and add a cup of flour."

When she had heated the water, the snake took a bath, covered himself with the flour, and put on his clothes. He was transformed into a bridegroom, a pale and handsome young man. And so he got married.

During the wedding ceremony, he told the bride to put his cast-off snakeskin inside the collar of her wedding dress and wear it there. She was never to let anyone touch it. So the bride put it inside her collar and wore it, and he was a proper husband. They were married.

Now the other daughters became jealous of their sister. When her husband had to go away to Seoul for the civil service examination, they came visiting with something after he left. Seeing them, the youngest sister waited with the gate locked. But when she came out into the courtyard, they said, "Little sister, we brought you something tasty to eat."

They asked her to open the gate, but she would not. So the older sister said she was carrying a pot of black bean soup and her hands were getting burned.

"Hurry up and open the gate," she said, and the youngest daughter had no choice but to open it.

After she had let them in, her older sisters wanted to pick her head lice. Though she tried not to let them pick through her hair, they insisted so strongly that once again she had no choice. And then, before she knew it, they had taken the snakeskin from her collar and thrown it into the fire—and in an instant the sparks from the flame flew up and burned her husband's dining table.

And now it was time for the husband to return, but he did not come. Sensing that his wife had lost the snakeskin to her sisters, he did not return. So the wife went out in search of her husband.

Even wearing tattered clothes and with her face smudged black, the young wife was still very pretty. She traveled around making inquiries, and where they were planting crops she would stay and help with the planting. And as she was traveling, traveling far, if she saw people doing their laundry at the riverbank, she would stay and help them pound their clothes against the rocks, and if they were making preserves for the winter, she would help with the pickling. Slowly she made her way to Seoul.

Eventually she reached the city. She went to a straw-roofed house to beg for alms, and they gave her some money. Since she looked the way she did, they naturally thought she was a beggar and they gave her something, some millet. She tried to take it in a sack, but the sack had a hole in the bottom and the millet grains fell through. So she tried to pick them up with chopsticks, but that was a very hard task, and before long it was twilight. She was still picking up the millet grains when the sun went down.

"Please let me sleep here," she said.

"There's no place for you to sleep here."

"Please let me sleep here—even if it's under the floor in the crawl space," she pleaded.

"We could never get to sleep with a Blackie under our floor."

"I've failed everywhere else," she said. "Please, I'll sleep in the cattle trough and then be on my way."

So they told her to sleep in the cattle trough. Unbeknownst to the wife, she had come to the very house where her husband was living. As she was trying to sleep, the moon rose as bright as a full-bloom flower. The wife sang plaintively:

> Oh moon, oh moon, oh moon so bright
> My snaky dear is in your sight.
> But I, though I have two eyes here,
> I cannot see my snaky dear.

The husband was poring over his books when he heard the plaintive sound. "I've heard that voice somewhere before," he said. "My ears must be deceiving me." And he went back to his studying.

As he was again trying to concentrate on his reading, again he heard the song. With his anguish mounting, he was able to endure this two times. But on the third time he sent his personal attendant to find out what was making the sound. The servant went out into the courtyard and saw the creature singing plaintively:

> Oh moon, oh moon, oh moon so bright,
> My snaky dear is in your sight.
> But I, though I have two eyes here,
> I cannot see my snaky dear.

Once he had heard the song, the servant figured out what was going on. "Come here," he said to the husband. "It's like this," he explained. "She's a beggar. We gave her a handout during the day. She was picking up millet with chopsticks and couldn't get it all before the sun went down, so she asked for a place to sleep down there. She said she'd sleep in the cattle trough, and now she's singing that pathetic song."

At that the husband went outside. He pretended not to see her, and the wife sang the plaintive song once again.

"You, singing that song," said the husband. "Who are you? Show yourself. Please reveal yourself."

She couldn't exactly come out dressed like that, and looking the way she did. So she sang the song again:

Oh moon, oh moon, oh moon so bright,
My snaky dear is in your sight.
But I, though I have two eyes here,
I cannot see my snaky dear.

She sat there and sang the song again and again. She just kept singing and singing.

"You, old woman. Where are you from?" said the husband.

So finally, having recognized his voice, she told her story. "This and that happened, and you said not to show anyone my clothes. But my older sisters gave me such a hard time that I opened the gate for them. They said they wanted to pick my head lice, so I let them look for lice and they threw your snakeskin into the fire. And since you did not return, I traveled around to look for you, and I've finally found you here."

"So that's what happened," said the husband.

Finally they were together again. The husband dressed his wife in clean new clothes. They say he passed the civil service examination and they lived happily.

Translated by Heinz Insu Fenkl

Classical Archival Records

PRINCE HODONG

This story from the *Historical Records of the Three Kingdoms* (*Samguk sagi*) tells the tragic tale of Prince Hodong of Koguryŏ, who turned his wife against her father in order to gain military supremacy, only to meet his own subsequent demise through the machinations of a Koguryŏ queen.

In the fourth month of the fifteenth year of the reign of King Taemusin of Koguryŏ (32 CE), Prince Hodong was on an outing in Okchŏ in the northeast region. At the time, Cui Li, king of Luolang, who was on an excursion, saw Hodong and said, "I see from your visage that you are not an ordinary person. Are you not the son of King Taemusin of Koguryŏ?"

Together they returned to Luolang, and Cui Li gave his daughter to Hodong in marriage. Subsequently Hodong went back to Koguryŏ. He sent a secret messenger to Lady Cui: "If you go into the armory and destroy Luolang's drum and bugle, I will receive you with honor. If you don't, I will have nothing to do with you." Hodong had her do this because the drum and bugle in Luolang's armory would sound by themselves whenever enemy forces approached. Lady Cui took a sharp knife and stole into the armory, where she slashed the surface of the drum and cut the mouth of the bugle.

When Lady Cui reported this to Hodong, he prevailed on the Koguryŏ king to attack Luolang. Because the drum and bugle did not sound, Cui Li did not prepare for the attack. It was only when the attacking forces were under the fortress wall that Cui Li realized the drum and the bugle had been destroyed. He killed his daughter and came out of the fortress to surrender.[1]

In the eleventh month, Prince Hodong committed suicide. Hodong was the son of the king's second consort, the granddaughter of King Kalsa of Puyŏ. He was handsome and the king loved him dearly, which was why he gave him the name Hodong or "Good Child." The first consort was worried that the king might bypass her son and make Hodong the crown prince. She made a false charge about Hodong to the king, saying, "Hodong does not treat me with propriety, and I fear that he wants to make trouble." The king responded, "Do you despise him because he is someone else's son?" The first consort realized the king did not believe her. Fearing disaster, she sobbed, "I implore the king secretly to check the omens. If they are not as I say, then I will accept punishment." After that, the king came to suspect Hodong.

When someone asked Hodong why he did not explain himself, Hodong replied, "If I explain this affair, the first consort's misbehavior will come to light and it will cause the king to worry. Would you term that filial piety?" He then fell on his sword and killed himself.

KING SANSANG'S MARRIAGE TO A COUNTRY WOMAN

This story, also from the *Historical Records of the Three Kingdoms,* is interesting not only because of the way in which true love conquers social barriers but because of the role played by the pig, a sacred animal in the Korean shamanist tradition.

In the eleventh month of the twelfth year of King Sansang's reign (208 CE), a sacred pig to be used in sacrificial rites escaped. The official

---

1. Another version says that the Koguryŏ king, intent on destroying Luolang, sought Cui Li's daughter as his son's wife; after the marriage he sent her back to destroy Luolang's weapons.

responsible for the pig followed it all the way to Chut'ong village, where, although he chased it back and forth, he was unable to catch it. There was a beautiful and gentle smiling young woman of about twenty who captured the pig right in front of him. Thus the official was able to reclaim the pig.

Hearing of this, the king thought it wondrous and desired to see the young woman. He stole out at night, went to the woman's house, and sent one of his attendants in to talk to the inhabitants. Knowing that the king had come, they did not dare resist. The king went into a room and summoned the young woman, with the intention of bedding her. The woman said, "I dare not avoid the order of the king. If, by good fortune, I am to be with child, I hope you will not abandon me." The king agreed. It was late in the night when he arose and returned to his palace.

In the third month of the following year, the queen learned that the king had had relations with the woman of Chut'ong village. The jealous queen secretly sent soldiers to kill her. Hearing of this, the young woman dressed in men's clothing and ran away. Her pursuers captured her, however, and were preparing to kill her when the young woman said, "Have you come to kill me at the order of the king? Or is it at the order of the queen? I now have a child in my belly. In fact, it is the child of the king. If you kill me, you will also be killing the king's child."

The soldiers did not dare to harm her. They went back and reported what the woman had said. The queen was enraged because her desire to kill the young woman was unfulfilled. Hearing of this, the king went again to the young woman's house, where he said, "You are now pregnant. Whose child is it?" The young woman replied, "All my life, I have never even shared a seat with my own brothers. How, then, would I dare to approach a man of another family? The child in my belly now is indeed that which the king left there." The king comforted her and gave her generous presents. Then he returned to the palace and informed the queen, who no longer dared to harm the young woman.

In the ninth month, the Chut'ong village woman gave birth to a son. The king was delighted and said, "Heaven has given a son to succeed me." Because it all started with the affair of the sacrificial pig that allowed the king to meet the child's mother, he named the boy Kyoch'e (Sacred Pig) and made the mother his secondary queen. Earlier, when the Chut'ong village woman's mother had been pregnant with her, a shaman predicted that she would surely give birth to a queen. In happiness the mother named her daughter "Queenly Girl." In the tenth month, the king moved the capital to Hwando. In the first month of the king's seventeenth year on the throne (213 CE), the king made Kyoch'e the crown prince.

The Turtle and the Rabbit

This story, which is similar to turtle and rabbit stories elsewhere in the world, appears in the section of the *Historical Records of the Three Kingdoms* that relates Kim Ch'unch'u's diplomatic mission to Koguryŏ. After hearing this story, it is said, Kim realized the danger he was in and was able to escape back to Silla.

Long ago, the daughter of the Dragon King of the Eastern Sea had a heart disease. A physician told him that it could be treated if the king obtained a rabbit liver and mixed it with medicine. But there were no rabbits in the sea, so the king was powerless to help his daughter.

A turtle came to the Dragon King and said, "I can get a rabbit liver." The turtle then went ashore, where he spied a rabbit. He told it, "There is an island in the sea where the springs run clear, the rocks are clean, the forests are luxuriant, and the fruits are tasty. It is neither cold nor hot, and eagles do not transgress. If you go there, you can live in ease with no worries."

The turtle then put the rabbit on his back and swam out to sea. After going for two or three tricents, the turtle looked back at the rabbit and said, "The daughter of the Dragon King is ill. Because she needs a rabbit liver for her medicine, I am carrying you without concern for the effort it causes me."

The rabbit replied, "How sad! I am the offspring of the spirits of heaven and earth, so I can easily take out my organs, wash them, and put them back in. A little while ago, I was feeling down, so I took out my liver, washed it, and placed it temporarily beneath a rock. Taken with your sweet words, I came straight with you and left my liver behind. It will still be there. We should go back and get it. Then you will have what you came for. As for me, I can survive without a liver. It will work out well for both of us."

Believing the rabbit, the turtle turned back. When they reached the shore, the rabbit raced into the grass. He called back to the turtle, "What a fool you are. Who can live without a liver?" The chagrined turtle left without a word.

Translated by John Duncan

Pihyŏng and the Spirits

This account in the *Memorabilia of the Three Kingdoms* (*Samguk yusa*) relates how the song of Pihyŏng came into being because of King Chinji, who failed to tread the path of righteousness and was deposed. Pihyŏng expels demons in the human world and rules over the spirits—reflecting the Silla view of the relations between supernatural beings and the human world.

King Saryun, the twenty-fifth king of Silla, had the surname Kim and the posthumous title Chinji. His queen was Lady Chido, the daughter of Lord Kio. Chinji ascended the throne in the eighth year of the Chinese reign of Dajian (576), but after four years he was deposed for lasciviousness and misgovernment.

During his rule, there lived in Saryang district a woman of such beauty that she was called Peach Blossom Girl. The king heard of her and had her brought to the palace. When he made ready to approach her, she retorted: "It is not a woman's way to serve two husbands. To serve a husband of my own and to accept yet another—this even a king with all his majesty cannot force upon me."

"And if I were to have you killed?" the king asked.

The woman replied, "I would rather be beheaded in the marketplace."

The king teased: "But if your husband were no more, would it then sit well with you?"

"Yes, it might then be possible," the woman replied.

The king set the woman free, and in the same year he was deposed and died shortly thereafter. Three years later, the woman's husband died.

Ten nights after the husband's death, the king suddenly appeared to the woman and said, "You made me a promise long ago. Now that your husband is dead, will you be mine?"

The woman did not consent lightly and consulted her parents. They said, "How can you disobey a royal command?" and let her enter the bedchamber. After the seventh day the king vanished without a trace. The woman was pregnant, and when the time of delivery was at hand, heaven and earth shook and a baby boy was born. He was named Pihyŏng. Hearing of the strange incident, King Chinp'yŏng had the baby brought to the palace and reared there. When the boy reached age fourteen, he was given the post of clerk (*chipsa*).

When it was learned that the boy was going far afield every night in search of amusement, the king assigned fifty soldiers to keep watch over him. They reported that the boy would fly over Wŏlsŏng, heading west, and land on a hill above Hwangch'ŏn, where he would play with a band of spirits until the temple bell rang at dawn. When he heard this, the king summoned Pihyŏng and asked, "Is it true that you consort with spirits?"

"Yes," the boy replied.

The king continued: "Then have the spirits build a bridge across the stream north of Sinwŏn monastery."

With the royal decree Pihyŏng assembled the spirits, and by morning a stone bridge had been completed. It was called the Bridge of Spirits.

The king asked the boy again: "Is there a spirit who can return to life to assist me in governing?"

"One named Kiltal is worthy of the task," replied Pihyŏng. The following day the king had Kiltal brought to him and conferred upon him the title of clerk. He proved unequaled in honesty and loyalty.

At that time the prime minister Imjong had no son, and the king made him adopt Kiltal. Imjong asked Kiltal to build a gate tower south of Hŭngnyun monastery and sleep every night atop the gate. It was called Kiltal Gate.

One day Kiltal changed into a fox and ran away, but Pihyŏng had his spirits catch and kill him. After this, other spirits feared the name of Pihyŏng and stayed away, and the people composed a song:

Here is the house of Pihyŏng,
  The son of the king's spirit.
The flying and galloping spirits
  Will not stop and linger here.

It is the custom to paste the text of the song on our gates to drive away evil spirits.

THE BLACK ZITHER CASE

This story comes from the *Memorabilia of the Three Kingdoms*. The old man who emerges from the pond is a guardian spirit who punishes an evil monk for his misconduct. The story also explains the origin of the custom of eating glutinous rice on the fifteenth day of the first lunar month.

When Pich'ŏ (or Soji) traveled to Ch'ŏnch'ŏn Arbor in the tenth year, *mujin*, of his reign as the twenty-first king of Silla (488), a crow was heard to caw and a rat squeaked. What the rat said was: "Follow the crow wherever it flies"—whereupon the king ordered a horseman to follow the bird. The horseman traveled south toward P'ich'on, as far as the eastern foot of Mount South, where he stopped to observe a fight between two boars. Now, having lost sight of the crow, he began to wander about. Thereupon an old man emerged from a pond and presented him with a letter. On the outside was written: "If opened, two people will die—if not, only one man will die."

The horseman took the letter to the king, who said, "If two people are to perish by its being opened, then better not to open it—let only one die."

At this his astrologer remarked: "The two people are commoners, but the one must be the king himself." The king hearkened to this counsel and opened the letter. It read: "Shoot at the black zither case." The king returned to the palace at once and shot an arrow into the case. The case sprang open, revealing the queen enjoying the attentions of a monk whose job was to burn incense and cultivate the faith. Both were put to death.

Thereafter it has been our national custom to be discreet in speech and action and to remain idle on the first boar day, the first rat day, and the first horse day of the first month. On the fifteenth day of the month, called Crow Taboo Day, a day of sorrow and taboo, glutinous rice is offered to the bird even today. The king named the pond Sŏch'ul or Letter Issuing.

MILBON DRIVES AWAY GHOSTS

Found in the *Memorabilia of the Three Kingdoms,* this story is similar to the contest in magic between Haemosu and the river earl in the Koguryŏ foundation myth. When such a motif loses its proper function, it becomes only an interesting tale.

Queen Chindŏk (647–654), given name Tŏngman, was in critical condition. The master Pŏpch'ŏk was summoned, but his art had long been ineffective. There was a Dharma master Milbon, who was known for his virtuous deeds throughout the country, and the courtiers advised the queen to replace Pŏpch'ŏk with Milbon. When the queen received Milbon, he recited the *Healing Buddha Scripture* (*Yaksa kyŏng*)[1] beside her. When he finished, his six-ringed metal staff flew into the bedroom, struck an old fox together with Pŏpch'ŏk, and chased them into the lower courtyard. The queen's illness was cured. At that time, Milbon's brow emitted five mysterious lights, and those who witnessed this marveled.

When the chief minister Kim Yangdo was a child, his lips would stick together, his body would become stiff, and he could neither speak nor move. Each time this happened, he observed a large ghost followed by a horde of smaller ghosts entering the house and tasting all the food. When the shamans were called in to perform a ritual, the ghosts insulted them. Kim Yangdo wanted the ghosts to leave, but he could not speak. Kim's father called in a monk from Pŏmnyun monastery (his name has been lost) to recite a scripture. But the large ghost commanded a small ghost to strike the monk with an iron mallet, and the monk fell to the ground spitting blood and died. Several days later, a messenger was sent to bring Milbon from the palace. The messenger returned and said, "Dharma master Milbon says he accepts our request and will come."

Upon hearing this, all the ghosts paled. A small one spoke: "If he comes, we'll rue the day. It's best to avoid him."

"How can he hurt us?" the large ghost retorted arrogantly. But powerful gods from the four directions, bearing long halberds and wearing iron armor, suddenly appeared. They caught all the ghosts,

---

1. Also called Medicine King; *PDB*, 108–109.

bound them up, and took them away. Then countless heavenly gods came to take their places and they waited. Soon Milbon arrived. Even before he opened the scripture, Kim Yangdo's illness was cured. And now that he had regained his speech and could move his body, Kim Yangdo explained what had happened in detail. Because of this, Kim Yangdo became a devout Buddhist and remained so all his life. At Hŭngnyun monastery, he had the central image of the Buddha Amitābha cast, together with the bodhisattvas on its left and right sides, and he adorned the walls with golden murals.

Formerly Milbon had lived at Kŭmgok monastery. On one occasion, a close relative of Kim Yusin (595–673) required the care of an old householder (his identity is unknown). Kim Yusin's relative, Such'ŏn, had been seized with a malignant disease, and Kim Yusin asked the householder to look after him. Such'ŏn's friend Master Inhye from Middle Peak was visiting at the time, and he said insulting words to the householder: "From your attitude and posture, I can tell you are crafty and unreliable. How can you cure another's illness?"

"I received Lord Kim's order and came reluctantly," answered the householder.

"Observe my supernatural powers," boasted Inhye. He picked up an incense burner and chanted incantations. In a short while, five-hued clouds circled around his head and heavenly flowers rained down.

"Your power is truly wonderful. I too have power, though it is paltry, and wish to try it. Please stand before me."

Master Inhye did as he was asked. When the householder snapped his fingers, Inhye rose a fathom high, upside down, and in a moment came down with his head stuck in the ground like a driven stake. Those who were near pushed and pulled but to no avail. The householder departed, leaving Inhye standing upside down until the next dawn. The following day, Such'ŏn contacted Lord Kim, who dispatched the householder to release Inhye. Inhye never again showed off his trick.

The Storyteller Omurŭm

[CH'ŎNGGU YADAM]

This story from the *Unofficial Tales of Korea* relates how a talented storyteller was able to make an old man realize the error of his ways. Storytellers of this type were important entertainers in the late Chosŏn period.

There was a man with the surname O in the capital. He was well known for his storytelling ability and frequented the homes of high officials. He enjoyed eating cucumbers and seasoned greens, so people called him Omurŭm. That was because the pronunciation of his surname, O, was similar to the word for cucumber, and *murŭm* was the term for cooked greens.

One elderly member of the royal family had four sons. He had become wealthy by buying and selling things and was by nature quite stingy. Not only did he not give to others, he didn't even share his wealth with his four sons. If a close friend offered advice, he would simply reply, "I have my own ideas on that." He clung to his wealth over the years and never parceled it out to his sons. One day he called Omurŭm and had him tell a story. With a plan in mind, Omurŭm devised this tale.

"In the capital city there was a wealthy man called associate administrator Yi. He was wealthy and long-lived and had many sons, so people said he had been born under a lucky star. But this Yi, who was known as 'Old Moneybags,' had been poor in his youth and earned his riches through his own effort and hardship. Because of this, he was very tightfisted, to the point of giving a worn-out old fan to his sons or his brothers. As his death drew near, he thought back on his life and realized that all the affairs of this world are empty and that he had spent his life as a slave to the accumulation of wealth. No matter how he thought about it, as he lay there on his sickbed he realized there was nothing he could do to change it. So he summoned his children and gave them his final bequest: 'I have endured hardship throughout my life in order to accumulate wealth, so I am a rich man. But now, at the end of my life, I realize that I can take nothing with me. I regret having been so stingy in the past. When I face the funeral flag and see my name and position on it, I find the Pallbearers' Dirge inexpressibly sad, and I'm aware that in my lonely tomb where autumn leaves fall and the night rain drips I cannot spend even one penny. When you wrap my body and put it in the coffin, do not bind my hands. Instead I want you to drill holes on each side of the coffin and extend my hands out through them so that passersby can see that while I leave behind a mountain of wealth, I go to my grave empty handed.'

"After associate administrator Yi died, his children dared not go against his wishes and did as he had commanded. A short while ago, I encountered a funeral procession on the road. I thought it strange that the two hands of the deceased were outside the coffin. When I asked about it, I was told of Yi's deathbed injunction. The saying that one speaks well when one is about to meet death is indeed true."

Halfway through the story, it dawned on the old man that Omurŭm was indirectly talking about him. Although he felt that the story-teller was poking fun at him, he also realized the truth of his tale. He understood his folly and rewarded Omurŭm generously before sending him away. The next morning he divided his wealth among his sons, and gave generous gifts to other family members and friends as well. Afterward, he spent his days enjoying wine and zither music in a mountain pavilion and never once spoke of money.[1]

Generally it is not easy for a man suddenly to realize his folly after listening to just one story. Omurŭm belongs to the ranks of the great humorists. He is certainly as great as Chunyou Kun of Qi or Yu Meng of Chu, renowned wits of the Warring States period in ancient China.

1. *Lunyu* 8:4; Waley, *Analects*, 133.

RAIN SHOWER DESTINY

[CH'ŎNGGU YADAM]

Also from the *Unofficial Tales of Korea*, this story tells of a lonely old man whose life was changed because of two chance encounters in the rain nearly twenty years apart. The heavy traffic in the shops of the capital city seems to have encouraged the spread of various stories, of which this is only one example.

The medicine broker of Changdong, who had never married and had grown old alone, with neither child nor home, was in the habit of taking his food and lodging while traveling from medicine shop to medicine shop. One day in the fourth month, King Yŏngjo (1724–1776) was making a procession to Yuksang Palace when a sudden downpour caused the streams to overflow. Sightseers who had come out to watch the procession sought shelter from the rain in a medicine shop, so that the area under the eaves was crowded with people.

Sitting inside the medicine shop, the old medicine broker suddenly spoke up: "Today's rain reminds me of the rain I saw when crossing Bird Ridge in my youth."

The man sitting next to him responded: "What? Do you mean there is old rain and new rain?"

"Something sort of funny happened to me at that time, so I always remember it."

"Why don't you tell us the story?"

The old man began his tale. "It was summer, some years ago. At the time, the medicine shops in the capital had all run out of Japanese barberry root, so I was hurrying down to Tongnae to buy some. At midday, I was crossing Bird Ridge. Not long after passing the checkpoint, I was deep in the forest when I encountered a downpour like this one. I could barely see anything and was casting about for a place to get out of the rain when I saw a small hut at the foot of the mountain. I went into the hut, where I found a maiden who was past the age for marriage. I took off my clothes and was wringing the water out of them, but the maiden stayed right by my side and did not try to avoid me. Suddenly I became aroused and took her, but she didn't seem very disturbed. Soon the rain stopped, and I left the hut without even asking the maiden where she lived. Today's rain was so like the rain of that day that I am telling this story."

Suddenly a young man stepped out from under the eaves onto the wooden porch. "Who's the gent who was just talking of the rain on Bird Ridge?"

When the others in the room pointed to the old medicine broker, the young man bowed deeply before the old man and said, "Today, to my great good fortune, I have met my father."

All the onlookers were taken by surprise. The old man himself was at a loss and blurted out, "What is this all about?"

"My mother said that my father had a mark on his body. Please remove your clothes and show me."

The old medicine broker removed his clothing. The young man looked below the medicine broker's waist and said without hesitation, "You truly are my father."

The others on the porch pressed the young man for an explanation. "Tell us why you think he is your father."

"When my mother was still a maiden, she was watching the hut when she unexpectedly met a traveler in the rain. Soon after, she became pregnant and bore me. As I was growing up and learning to speak, I found that although all the other children had someone they called father, I didn't. I thought this strange and asked my mother. The story she told me was the same as the story this man just told. And while having relations with my father, she happened to notice that there was a dark mole on his left buttock. After hearing my mother's tale, at the age of twelve I set out on the road looking for my father. I have searched in all eight provinces and have been here to the capital no fewer than three times. After six years, I have finally found my father. Why should I not be happy?"

Then he turned to his father and said, "Father, is there any need for you to stay in the capital? I would like you to come to the country with me. I will farm diligently and take care of you. My mother has remained faithful to you, and her family is not poor, so you will not have to worry about your meals."

The onlookers thought this was indeed praiseworthy. The owner of the medicine shop, who had overheard the conversation from inside his room, came out and said, "So someone found his son. What a rare and wondrous thing this is. All your friends are overjoyed, and I can only imagine your feelings." The owner joined the son in urging the old man to go to the countryside.

The old medicine broker's joy knew no end, but he was a bit taken aback at the prospect of suddenly leaving the capital where he had spent so much of his life. Furthermore, he was worried about the travel expenses.

His son said, "Do not worry. I have a little money in my hands."

The others all urged the old man to go with his son and emptied their pockets to provide money for the trip, giving him five or six *yang*. Then the shop owner gave them ten or so more *yang*. When the rain stopped, the old man took leave of his friends and set out with his son. So the old medicine broker found a home, a wife, a son, and food to eat. They say that he spent the rest of his life in comfort and leisure.

Translated by John Duncan

Folk Songs

Folk songs sung in the thirteenth and fourteenth centuries were recorded in the Korean alphabet in compilations dating from the early sixteenth century. Songs from the Chosŏn period appear not to be very different from those that are sung today. After the 1930s, scholars of Korean literature began to collect folk songs in a concerted effort to preserve the indigenous culture. Although the lyrics of some had been recorded earlier, in Chinese, this effort led to the systematic collection of Korean folk songs. A project undertaken by the Academy of Korean Studies eventually resulted in the compilation of some six thousand songs (1984) from all over the country.

Various songs that deal with the trials of a woman living with in-laws describe the difficulties a young woman goes through after marriage. Transplanted to an unfamiliar and often hostile environment where she occupies the lowest place in the domestic hierarchy, the newly married woman must endure an endless cycle of physical work, undernourishment, and psychological abuse. In "Wretched Married Life," a folk song from Kŏch'ang, a young woman runs away from her husband's family after extreme mistreatment and becomes a Buddhist nun. The song reflects the abuses of a patriarchal Chosŏn society from the victim's perspective.

WRETCHED MARRIED LIFE

[SIJIPSARI NORAE]

On the third day of my marriage,
My in-laws asked me to weed a field
With a hoe made of wood.

When I reached the field,
It was hot as fire, and
The field was long as a ridgeline.
But I weeded three furrows.
When lunchtime came,
Everyone's lunch was brought
But no one brought mine for me.
When I entered my so-called home
And stood before the big gate,
My father-in-law asked,
"Daughter-in-law, daughter-in-law,
How many furrows have you weeded?"
"On a day hot as fire,
I've weeded three furrows
Of a long and stony field.
Everyone's lunch was brought
Except for mine."
"You wretched woman, get out!
You call that work
And ask for a meal?"
When I reached the middle of the courtyard
My husband's younger brother asked,
"Aunt, aunt, how many furrows did you weed?"
"On a day hot as fire,
I've weeded three furrows
Of an arid and stony field,
But no one brought me lunch."
"You wretched woman, you call that work
And ask for lunch when lunchtime comes?"
When I stepped up from the courtyard,
My sister-in-law asked,
"Sister-in-law, sister-in-law,
How many furrows have you weeded?"

"I've weeded three furrows
Of a long and stony field,
But no one brought me lunch."
"You wretched woman, go away,
You call that work and ask
For lunch when lunchtime comes?"
When I entered the kitchen,
My mother-in-law, holding a rice paddle, asked,
"Daughter-in-law, daughter-in-law,
How many furrows have you weeded?"
"On a day hot as fire,
I've weeded three furrows
Of a long and stony field.
Everyone else's lunch was brought
But no one brought mine."
"Wretched woman, you call that work
And ask for lunch when lunchtime comes?"
What they gave me to eat was
Year-old boiled barley
With a year-old soy sauce.
What they called a spoon was
A spade for scooping dung
At Scholar Chŏng's house.
Even that she did not just give
But threw it at me, and I ran to pick it up
And ate what they call a "meal."
An old woman in the neighborhood
Came to the kitchen and said,
"The world under heaven is earth,
So is earth in the underworld.
Have you really no place to live
Except for this household?"
I filled the crock with water

And told my mother-in-law:
"Mother, I am leaving,
I'm going to a temple."
"Hey, wretch! Go if you want.
My son can live without you."
I approached the male quarters
And told my father-in-law:
"I'm leaving, Father,
I'm going to a temple."
"Hey, wretch! Go if you want.
My son can live without you."
I went to my room and opened
The chest made of beech wood,
Cut a piece from my eight-strip skirt
To fashion a peaked nun's hat,
Used the rest for a pair of trousers and blouse.
Donning the peaked hat and
Carrying a knapsack on my back,
I went out into the courtyard:
"Listen, listen, father-in-law. Listen,
I'm going to a temple.
Listen, mother-in-law, too,
I'm going to a temple.
Sister-in-law, listen,
I'm going to a temple.
If your brother returns from Seoul,
Tell him I went to a temple."
So somehow I bade them farewell
And climbed to a temple with twelve gates.
I approached the first gate
And opened the door to the first room
Filled with young monks.
"Please shave my head, please."

"We can't do it for fear of gossip."
I opened the door to the second room
Filled with middle-aged monks.
"Please shave my head, please."
"We can't do it for fear of gossip."
I opened the door to the third room
Filled with old monks.
"Please shave my head, please."
"We can't do it for fear of gossip."
"When I am at this strait,
There will be no trouble,
So please shave my head."
I held a lamp in my hand, and
One monk shaved a side behind my ear.
My nun's robe was wet from tears.
I held a lamp in my hand, and
Another shaved both sides of my head.
I could not weep aloud:
"O listen, people in the world,
Is there no place for me to live
Under the sky without pillars,
That I've had my head shaved
With a young woman's face?"
After managing to pass three years
I the nun climbed a hill and saw
A gentleman approaching
Who looked like my own husband.
That gentleman said,
"Wouldn't there be a person like me
If you walked the four quarters?"
Looked at from the side it was he,
Looked at crossways it was he.
He was my man no matter how I looked,

It was clear that he was my husband.
I asked him to remove his hat—
Indeed, he was my husband!
Look how he behaved!
He dismounted from his horse in stocking feet,
Rushed toward me, grasped my hands,
Examined my face, and exclaimed,
"What's happened, what's happened?
What has happened to my wife?"
"I won't go back to your household.
Don't tell me nonsense, I won't return.
Now that I've had my head shaved,
I'll return after three more years of study.
If it were only between you and me,
I'd go with you this instant;
But I cannot stand, not at all,
My father-in-law's yelling,
Mother-in-law's bitching,
And sister-in-law's chattering.
So I won't go with you.
Return to your home alone and marry
A girl like a flower from a good family.
When you enjoy the company of gallant men,
Don't forget even in a dream my pitiful life,
Don't forget how I've suffered.
If you think of me in your dream,
Then even if I'm dead,
I'll tie grass to return your kindness."[1]

---

1. Wei Ke of Jin, whose kindness in marrying his father's favorite concubine to save her from being buried with her husband's corpse, was rewarded when her father tied grass knots to impede Wei's enemies in battle.

Parting from her like this,
The husband returned home.
His father came forward and said,
"Our daughter-in-law fled three years ago
Because you did not return."
The husband stopped taking food and water,
Entered the thatched hut in the rear garden,
And opened the door to her room.
Three feet of dust had settled.
A quilt, pillow, lovebird-embroidered bedding
Meant for two, a chamber pot,
A silver ring like a halter—
All scattered all over the room.
Where has the husband gone,
Not knowing how her innards burned?
If her father was a pharmacist,
Would he be able to cure her illness?
Where has his wife gone,
When could he return her kindness?
At last he died of heartache,
And that household became
A mugwort field abandoned.[2]

---

2. The ending is ambiguous. It can also refer to the wife, who died of illness. I have combined several incomplete versions of the song so that it makes sense in English. For another version, see *Hanguk kubi munhak taegye* 8, 5:454–463.

Shamanist Narrative Songs

THE ABANDONED PRINCESS

Also called *The Seventh Princess* (*Ch'il kongju*), the shamanist narrative song translated here as *The Abandoned Princess* is performed at a ritual (known as *chinogi or saenam kut*) to ensure the safe journey of the soul of the dead to the otherworld. The text exists in some forty versions with regional variations. The version transmitted around Seoul best preserves Princess Pari's mythic features: her heroic deeds, her attainment of sacred status, and the process of her deification as a goddess who governs all shamans and the underworld.

The story concerns the seventh daughter born to a royal family yearning for a son. Her birth is foretold in her mother's dream of the arrival of a heaven-sent child. A similar dream would portend the birth of a prince or a hero, but instead a princess is born—in this case an unwanted princess. When she is abandoned by her parents, "a sudden gale arises./Unexpectedly, crows and magpies descend/And cushion her with one wing, cover her with the other." The princess is put into a jade box, which is cast into the sea. Carried on the back of a golden turtle, the box is discovered by Śākyamuni Buddha, who asks an old man and old woman to rear the girl. When she reaches thirteen, her parents fall gravely ill. In a dream they are told they will die as retribution for casting out the child sent by heaven. But they locate the princess, and she returns to the palace. Among the seven daughters, it is only Princess Pari who consents to fetch the sacred water guarded by the Peerless Transcendent that will cure her parents. But in the underworld the Peerless Transcendent demands that she chop wood for three years, tend the fire for three years, and draw water for three years. He then demands that she marry him and bear seven sons—indeed, she offers herself as payment for the sacred water. After fulfilling all his demands, she returns to this world and revives her parents. But when her parents offer her half of their kingdom, she declines. She has traveled between the two worlds and cannot return permanently to the living. She forgives her parents and discharges her filial duty as a daughter. But by choosing to become a shaman goddess, she chooses the dark mysterious space, not the world of her parents. Her decision problematizes the inevitable separation between parents and daughters who, despite their filial love, must leave home. Thus she registers her anxiety and guilt about forsaking this world, including her own parents, especially her mother.

This narrative song, part of a ritual to assure the departed soul a safe journey, is termed "heroic" because of Princess Pari's arduous journey to the underworld, where she confronts the terror of darkness and silence and masters it. She is a model of forbearance, humility, courage, resourcefulness, and heroic energy. Moreover, the help rendered twice by Śākyamuni elevates her to the status of a hero with sacred powers. Oppressed by a patrilineal and patriarchal society because of her gender, she nevertheless discharges a great task and becomes a hero, indeed a deity, of the underworld—and thus is mythologized as a guardian of the souls of the dead. She appropriates divinity, which in traditional Korean culture is usually equated with maleness, and because she assists the departed souls, we will know her dark mysteries only after death. Princess Pari dramatizes the complexity of female filial emotion, including the institution of motherhood in patriarchy, and the female body as the privileged body. This narrative implicates a wider community of women in its production; her filiality is a collective expression that canonizes the social value of female virtue.

The version translated here is from Akamatsu Chijō and Akiba Takashi's *Chōsen fuzoku no kenkyū* (Studies in Korean shamanism), as narrated by a shaman named Pae Kyŏngjae in Osan, Kyŏnggi province, and annotated by Sŏ Taesŏk and Pak Kyŏngsin in *Sŏsa muga* (Shamanist narrative songs), 213–253.

This is a temple the state built with great effort,
And the temple's origin is in the southwest.[1]
Know the heavens!
Above, Indra's heavens;[2] below, the twenty-eight mansions;[3]
Great generals of the eight directions, Namong and Muong,[4] all
    have guarded it.
South of the Yangzi lies the Great Han; east of the sea lies
    Chosŏn.[5]

---

1. India.

2. Indra presides over the heavens of thirty-three divinities, constituting the second of the six heavenly realms in Buddhist cosmology; see *PDB*, 372.

3. Principal constellations in Chinese astronomy; see Needham, *Science and Civilization in China*, 3:239.

4. Two of the eight directional deities. Some identify Namong with the historical monk Naong (d. 1376) and Muong with Muhak (1327–1405).

5. Korea is so called because "it lies east of Parhae (Bohai)." See Peter H. Lee, *Songs of Flying Dragons*, 151.

The clan site of the founder of Chosŏn[6] is
Yŏnghŭng, near Tanch'ŏn, in Hamgyŏng province.
Above, on the hundredth memorial day, I lead the living to
    paradise.
Below, on the days of offering,[7] I lead the dead to paradise.
Red mountain wine made of red peonies, white mountain wine
    made of white peonies,
Quietly burning candles, incense fragrance, a cup of wine, and
    wailing;
Today is the day of hope for the spirits.
Kyŏnggi has thirty-seven counties, and Yangju is a large one,[8]
Ch'angdŏk palace, Ch'anghye palace, Kyŏngbok palace,
    Kyŏngdŏk palace,[9]
The lower palace and upper palace, tablets in the royal ancestral
    shrine,
Altars of soil and grain[10]—
Our king has succeeded to them all.
Their Majesties the king and queen have put on years,
The audience hall is silent, the queen's chamber empty.
The crown prince is fifteen years old.
"Where are the world's great diviners?
Go and ask our fortune," commands the king.
The ladies-in-waiting reply,
"We have our nameplates, please grant a list of gifts."
What are the gifts?
Five strings of silver coins and five of gold,

6. Refers to Yi Sŏnggye (1335–1408; r. 1392–1398).

7. On the six monthly fast days—the eighth, fourteenth, fifteenth, twenty-third, twenty-ninth, and thirtieth—nothing should be eaten after noon.

8. An old name for Seoul.

9. All were in Seoul except the last, built by Yi Sŏnggye, which was in Kaesŏng.

10. Altars symbolizing the state, at which national consecration ceremonies were conducted; Hucker, *Dictionary of Official Titles*, 5133.

Three *toe* and three *hop* of pearls,
One *ch'i* and five *p'un*[11] of cloth for the cassock,[12]
Three feet and three inches of silk he bestows.
They go bearing these royal gifts
To shaman Taji of Ch'ŏnha palace, shaman Moran of Chesŏk
  palace,
Shamaness Sosil of Chiha palace, and shaman Kangnim of
  Myŏngdo palace.
They cast pearls and grains of white rice on the white jade tray:
The first sign yields the shaman's fortunes,
The second tells of upper and lower gates,
The third tells the fortune of the two majesties.
"I fear to tell you but cannot deceive you.
If you hold a marriage ceremony in an unlucky year,
You'll have seven princesses.
If in a lucky year, three princes."
Thus they inform the king.
"One moment is as long as three autumns, one day as ten.
How can we await an auspicious year?"
The king calls all his officials
And orders the office of astrology to choose a day.
The third day of the third month is the first selection;
The fifth day of the fifth month, the second selection;
The seventh day of the seventh month,
When the Herd Boy and Weaver Maid[13] meet
On the bridge built by crows and magpies,
The chief of royal weddings makes the third selection.

11. One *toe* makes ten *hop*; *ch'i* is the Korean inch, equaling one tenth of a *cha*, and a
p'un is one-tenth of an inch.
12. *Kasawi* in the original; the meaning is unclear.
13. Constellations on opposite sides of the Milky Way, often invoked as a fit metaphor
for the separation of lovers. They are allowed to meet once a year when a bridge is built
across the vault of heaven.

Three thousand troops on the low road,
Five thousand on the high road,[14]
Cavalry in rows of five guard the royal carriage.
Courtiers in black belts prepare the bridal room in a separate
    palace.
The goose is presented on the jade table,[15] the nuptial cups
    exchanged.
All the officials cry, "Long live the king!"
His Majesty returns to T'ongmyŏng Hall,
And the queen[16] to the inner palace.
And the people cry, "Long live the king!"
Time flows like a river, heartless time flows like a stream.
In a gust of wind three summer months have passed,
And strange symptoms appear in the queen.[17]
The royal rice tastes raw,
The royal water tastes foul,
Golden glow tobacco tastes like grass,[18]
The royal soup tastes like soy sauce.
"Present the fruits of five hundred bearing trees
Brought through the four great gates to the inner palace."
Among lovebird-embroidered quilts and pillows,[19]
A breeze at the east window cannot reach the west window.[20]
When ladies-in-waiting inform His Majesty, he orders:
"Consult the shaman of Ch'ŏnha palace!"
Shaman Taji of Ch'ŏnha palace, shaman Moran of Chesŏk
    palace,

14. This may allude to the boundary between this world and the other world.
    15. At the marriage rite, the groom presents a wooden goose as a symbol of conjugal
fidelity.
    16. Her name is given as Ch'iltae; in another version it is Kiltae.
    17. The lines describe symptoms of pregnancy.
    18. The name of a tobacco produced in Kwangju.
    19. *Chatpyŏge*, a pillow made of chestnut wood, or simply an embroidered pillow.
    20. She finds her daily routine difficult and cannot move about.

They cast coral beads on the jade tray.
The first sign yields the shaman's fortune,
The second tells of upper and lower gates,
The third yields the royal fortune:
"When it comes to pass Your Majesty will know—
Had you married next year, a year of fortune,
A prince would have been born to rule with two brothers.
But you married in an unlucky year, so you will have the first
    princess."
Ladies-in-waiting report these words to both Their Majesties.
"What do they know?" they retort.
One, two months pass; in the third the fetus forms.
Small bones seem to melt, big bones are squeezed.[21]
Five and a half months pass;
"Midwives of the inner and outer chambers,
Royal messengers and servants,
All the officials and three thousand court ladies
Inquire at the inner palace morning, noon, and night."
After seven months, after nine months,
Black silk support before, blue silk support behind,[22]
"Present all cloths entering the four great gates to the inner
    palace!"
Prisoners are released in every town, the royal academy is
    closed,
Ten months have passed, the delivery room is ready.
After an easy labor and birth,
The queen turns around—a princess is born.
Ladies-in-waiting and three thousand court ladies
Announce to His Majesty the princess's birth.

---

21. The soreness of the pregnant woman is described.

22. A support (such as a bolster or pillow) to elevate her body or cushion her for
comfort.

His Majesty commands:

"Inquire of the queen about her dreams."

The queen replies, "I dreamed of this one day:

From one shoulder rose the moon,

And from the other rose the sun."

The king commands:

"To hold and carry, walk and nurse the baby,

The court lady for the royal son-in-law and supervision.

Blue silk support before, black silk support behind,

Among silk screens in the inner room,

Raise this baby with utmost care."

"May we humbly ask you to name this child?"

"Her name is Princess Pink Peach, another name Moon Girl."

O and alas! One soul among the dead,

Upon the first princess's birth

Released from three years' mourning,

Consoling the spirits in the underworld,

From ancestors' cause of grievance,

From the karma of earthly existence,

The dead man sheds his head cover, the dead woman her *yomo*
   cap,[23]

With prayers for rebirth in the land of happiness,

Becomes a man and journeys to Amitābha's Pure Land,

Upon this very day.

Time flows like a river, the princess is three years old.

Strange symptoms appear in the queen.

Among lovebird-embroidered quilts and pillows,

A breeze at the east window cannot reach the west window.

Small bones seem to melt, big bones are squeezed.

The royal rice tastes raw,

---

23. This might refer to the hollowed (indented) woman's cap.

The royal water tastes foul,
Golden glow tobacco tastes like grass,
The royal soup tastes like soy sauce.
"Present the fruits of five hundred bearing trees
Brought through the four great gates to the inner palace."
In three months, the fetus forms;
Five and a half months pass;
After seven months, after nine months,
The delivery room and six physicians are ready.
"Ladies-in-waiting and eunuchs
Attend the queen morning, noon, and night."
In the tenth month, pearl-sewn recliner cast aside,
Labor and birth over, the queen turns around to view the baby:
The second princess is born.
"I've given birth to girls. Surely I'll have a boy soon."
"To hold and carry, walk and nurse this baby,
The court lady for the royal son-in-law and supervision.
Black silk support before, blue silk support behind,
Among silk screens in the inner room,
Raise this baby with utmost care."
O and alas! One soul among the dead,
Upon the second princess's birth,
Pushes open the gates of Knife Mountain hell,
The gates of eighty-four thousand hells, and
Journeys to Amitābha's Pure Land, the land of happiness.

Time flows like a dream,
The second princess is three years old.
Strange symptoms appear again in the queen.
Among lovebird-embroidered quilts and pillows,
A breeze at the east window cannot reach the west window.
Small bones seem to melt, big bones are squeezed.
The royal rice tastes raw,

The royal water tastes foul,
Golden glow tobacco tastes like grass,
The royal soup tastes like soy sauce.
"Present the fruits of five hundred bearing trees
Brought through the four great gates to the inner palace."
In three months, the fetus forms;
Five and a half months pass;
After seven months, after nine months,
The delivery room and six physicians are ready.
"Ladies-in-waiting and eunuchs
Attend the queen morning, noon, and night."
In the tenth month, pearl-sewn recliner cast aside,
Labor and birth over, the queen turns around to view the baby:
The third princess is born.
"I've given birth to girls. Surely I'll have a boy soon."
"To hold and carry, walk and nurse the baby,
The court lady for the royal son-in-law and supervision.
Blue silk support before, black silk support behind,
Among silk screens in the inner room,
Raise this baby with utmost care."
O and alas! One soul among the dead,
Upon the third princess's birth,
Pushes open the gates of Knife Mountain hell,
The gates of eighty-four thousand hells, and
Journeys to Amitābha's Pure Land, the land of happiness.

Time flows like a dream,
The third princess is three years old.
Strange symptoms appear in the queen.
Among lovebird-embroidered quilts and pillows,
A breeze at the east window cannot reach the west window.
Small bones seem to melt, big bones are squeezed.
The royal rice tastes raw,

The royal water tastes foul,
Golden glow tobacco tastes like grass,
The royal soup tastes like soy sauce.
"Present the fruits of five hundred bearing trees
Brought through the four great gates to the inner palace."
The ladies-in-waiting inform His Majesty.
"Consult the diviner of Ch'ŏnha palace."
"Please, bestow the gifts," they ask.
He sends five strings of silver coins, five of gold,
Three *toe* and three *hop* of pearls,
One foot and one inch of cloth for the cassock,
Three feet and three inches of silk he bestows.
They go bearing these royal gifts
To shaman Taji of Ch'ŏnha palace, shamaness Sosil of Chiha
     palace,
Shaman Kangnim of Myŏngdo palace, and shaman Moran of
     Chesŏk palace.
They cast pearls and grains of white rice on the white jade tray:
The first yields the shaman's fortune,
The second tells of upper and lower gates,
The third tells the royal fortune.
"I fear to tell you but cannot deceive you.
You should have married in a year of auspice;
Since you married in an unlucky year,
The fourth princess will be born."
Ladies-in-waiting report these words to both Their Majesties.
"What do they know?" they retort.
One and two months pass, and in three months
The fetus forms;
Five and a half months pass;
"Midwives of the inner and outer chambers,
Royal messengers and servants,
All the officials and three thousand court ladies

Inquire at the inner palace morning, noon, and night."
After seven months, after nine full months,
Blue silk support before, black silk support behind,
"Present all cloths entering the four great gates to the inner
     palace!"
Ten months have passed, the delivery room is ready,
Labor and birth over, the queen turns around to view the baby:
The fourth princess is born.
"I've given birth to girls. Surely I'll have a boy soon."
"To hold and carry, walk and nurse the baby,
The court lady for the royal son-in-law and supervision.
Black silk support before, blue silk support behind,
Among silk screens in the inner room,
Raise this baby too with utmost care."
O and alas! One among the dead,
Upon this princess's birth
Released from three years' mourning,
Consoling the spirits in the underworld,
From ancestors' cause of grievance,
From the karma of earthly existence,
The dead man sheds his head cover, the dead woman her
     yomo cap,
With prayers for rebirth in the land of happiness,
Becomes a man and journeys to Amitābha's Pure Land,
Upon this very day.

Heartless time flows like a stream, like a dream,
The fourth princess is three years old.
Strange symptoms appear in the queen.
Among lovebird-embroidered quilts and pillows,
A breeze at the east window cannot reach the west window.
Small bones seem to melt, big bones are squeezed.
The royal rice tastes raw,

The royal water tastes foul,
Golden glow tobacco tastes like grass,
The royal soup tastes like soy sauce.
"Present the fruits of five hundred bearing trees
Brought through the four great gates to the inner palace."
In three months, the fetus forms;
Five and a half months pass.
After seven months, after nine months,
She rejects the pearl-sewn bolster.
Ten months pass, and after labor and birth,
The queen turns around to view the baby:
Another princess is born.
"I've given birth to girls. Surely I'll have a boy soon."
"To hold and carry, walk and nurse the baby,
The court lady for the royal son-in-law and supervision.
Blue silk support before, black silk support behind,
Among silk screens in the inner room,
Raise this baby with utmost care."
O and alas! One among the dead,
Upon the birth of the fifth princess,
Released from three years' mourning,
Consoling the spirits in the underworld,
From ancestors' cause of grievance,
From the karma of earthly existence,
The dead man sheds his head cover, the dead woman her
    yomo cap,
With prayers for rebirth in the land of happiness,
Becomes a man and journeys to Amitābha's Pure Land,
Upon this very day.

Time flows like a river, the princess is three years old.
Strange symptoms appear in the queen.
Among lovebird-embroidered quilts and pillows,

A breeze at the east window cannot reach the west window.
The ladies-in-waiting inform His Majesty.
"Consult the diviner of Ch'ŏnha palace!"
"Please, bestow the gifts," they ask.
Five strings of silver coins, five of gold,
Three *toe* and three *hop* of pearls,
Three feet and three inches of silk,
And one *ch'i* and one *p'un* of cloth for the cassock.
They go bearing these royal gifts
To shaman Taji of Ch'ŏnha palace, shamaness Sosil of Chiha
    palace,
Shaman Moran of Chesŏk palace, shaman Kangnim of
    Myŏngdo palace.
They cast pearls and grains of white rice on the white jade tray:
The first throw yields the shaman's fortune,
The second tells of upper and lower gates,
The third tells the royal fortune.
"Her Majesty is indeed with child;
But since you married in an unlucky year,
The sixth princess will be born."
"What do they know?" they retort.
One and two months pass, a fetus forms in the third,
Five and a half months pass;
"Midwives of the inner and outer chambers,
Royal messengers and servants,
All the officials and three thousand court ladies
Inquire at the inner palace morning, noon, and night."
After seven months, after nine full months,
Blue silk support before, black silk support behind,
"Present all cloths entering the four great gates to the inner
    palace!"
Ten months have passed, the delivery room is ready,
Labor and birth over, the queen turns around to view the baby:

Another princess is born.
"I've given birth to girls. Surely I'll have a boy soon."
"To hold and carry, walk and nurse the baby,
The court lady for the royal son-in-law and supervision.
Among silk screens in the inner room,
Raise this baby too with utmost care."
O and alas! One among the dead,
Upon the sixth princess's birth
Released from three years' mourning,
Consoling the spirits in the underworld,
From ancestors' cause of grievance,
From the karma of earthly existence,
The dead man sheds his head cover, the dead woman her
    yomo cap,
With prayers for rebirth in the land of happiness,
Becomes a man and journeys to Amitābha's Pure Land,
Upon this very day.

In the country of a thousand tricents of mountains and rivers,
Time flows by like a dream.
All six princesses are invested.
The queen again has strange symptoms.
Among lovebird-embroidered quilts and pillows,
A breeze at the east window cannot reach the west window.
Small bones seem to melt, big bones are squeezed.
The royal rice tastes raw,
The royal water tastes foul,
Golden glow tobacco tastes like grass,
The royal soup tastes like soy sauce.
"Present the fruits of five hundred bearing trees
Brought through the four great gates to the inner palace!"
Her face, once fair as a lotus,
Is now gaunt, pitiful to view.

With her delicate body, how can she endure?
His Majesty asks, "What are your dreams?"
"I saw perched on my right hand a purple falcon,
And on my left hand a white falcon.
I saw a golden turtle resting on my knees,
And the sun and moon rising from my shoulders.
On the main beam of Great Bright Hall,
I saw entwined blue and gold dragons."
This time the dream portends a prince.
"Ladies-in-waiting, consult the shaman of Ch'ŏnha palace."
"Please, bestow the gifts," they ask.
Five strings of silver coins, five of gold,
Three *toe* and three *hop* of pearls,
One *ch'i* and one *p'un* of cloth for the cassock,
Three feet and three inches of silk he bestows.
They go bearing these royal gifts
To shaman Taji of Ch'ŏnha palace, shamaness Sosil of Chiha
    palace,
Shaman Moran of Chesŏk palace, and shaman Kangnim of
    Myŏngdo palace.
They cast pearls and grains of white rice on the white jade tray:
The first throw yields the shaman's fortune;
The second tells of upper and lower gates;
The third tells the royal fortune.
"You will find out later,
It is clear that the queen is with child,
But since you married in an unlucky year,
She will give birth to a seventh princess."
So they report to His Majesty.
"However well they divine, what do they know?"
As her dreams foretold,
In the third month the fetus forms.
Five and a half months pass, seven months pass,

Inner and outer delivery rooms and six physicians stand ready.
"Royal messengers and servants
Inquire after the queen morning, noon, and night."
Proclaim in the five wards, notify eight provinces,
Post it on the four great gates; he approves
That the prison gates be open and prisoners set free.
After the eighth month, after the ninth month,
Now it's the tenth month, and she rejects the pearl-sewn bolster.
Labor and birth over, she turns around to view the baby:
It's the seventh princess.
Her Majesty the queen weeps royal tears.
His Majesty inquires: "Ladies-in-waiting,
In the deep, deep, deepest recess of the palace
Why is there the sound of a woman wailing?"
The ladies-in-waiting reply,
"We fear to tell you but cannot deceive you . . . ."
"Ladies-in-waiting, you too are brazen!
How can you face me?"
He strikes the desk with royal hand:
"What sins of my former lives were so great
Heaven has given me seven daughters?"
He scatters his incense box and stands.
"Who will worship at the altars of soil and grain?
Who will inherit the state and throne?
Who will inherit the country and people?"
His Majesty commands:
"Ladies-in-waiting, three thousand court ladies,
Take that baby and cast her in the rear garden!"
Her Majesty replies:
"They say the state law ignores blood ties
In the interests of the country,
But how can you cast her out?
One among courtiers and ladies-in-waiting,

Take her as a foster child."
"The state laws are not so,
There's nothing we can do."
Dressed in the seventh-day culottes and trousers,
A slip inscribed with the time of birth
Tied to her coat strings,
The baby is cast away in the rear garden.
Mountains are deep and waters still.
A sudden gale arises.
Unexpectedly, crows and magpies descend
And cushion her with one wing, cover her with the other.

It is a warm spring day.
With the royal guard and steward, His Majesty
Goes to view the blossoms and willows in the rear garden.
To the east he sees a wondrous light in the air
And hears crows and magpies crying loudly.
"A wondrous light in the air bodes well.
What's over there making the crows and magpies cry so
    noisily?"
Ladies-in-waiting reply:
"You told us to abandon the baby born this time.
We dared not defy your order,
So we cast her away in the rear garden.
One can still hear her cries faintly."
Her Majesty the queen commands:
"Retrieve the baby and bring her here."
Behold, black ants fill her ears,
Golden ants her mouth,
Small ants her eyes.
On Her Majesty's lotus face
Pearl-like tears flow two by two.
"They say the state law ignores blood ties

In the interests of the country.
But why cast her out so heartlessly?"
His Majesty commands: "Courtiers, I shall send her as an
    offering
To the dragon kings of the four seas to atone for my sins.
Let a box maker make a fine jade box."
The queen lays the baby within it,
At its mouth a jade bottle with milk from her breasts,
And ties to her coat strings a slip
Inscribed with the month and hour of her birth.
Her Majesty then pleads:
"How can you cast your own child into the sea?
Let some childless minister adopt her; or
If she must be abandoned, at least give her a name."
"Paridŏgi, the throwaway, Tŏjidŏgi, the castaway."
Loosely she closes the jade box with the golden turtle lock
And engraves in golden letters: "The Seventh Princess."
The minister of rites is called in.
He receives three cups of royal wine and takes the box on
    his back.
He leaves the palace gate but does not know where to go.
Then crows and magpies bow their heads to lead him,
And grasses and trees bend down.
One thousand tricents, two thousand tricents,
Three thousand tricents they go.
Kalch'i Mount and Kalchi'i Pass, Pulch'i Mount and Pulch'i
    Pass.[24]
Heave-ho heave-ho,[25] he goes calling the name of Amitābha.
He crosses the pass and then goes on,

24. Imaginary places.
25. *Ŏsadi taesadi*, "give a hard push or pull"; the difficulty of climbing seems to be implied.

Before them the River of Yellow Springs,
Behind, the River of Flowing Sands.
He casts her in the magpie shoals in the sea of blood.
First the foams rise; then pillars of waves surge high;
Third, the waters turn blood red.
Thunder and lightning quake.
Suddenly a golden turtle appears and, bearing the box upon its
    back,
Swims off somewhere into the Eastern Sea.
Crows and magpies gather to cushion her with one wing
And cover her with the other.
At night, clouds and fog lie thick,
During the day, clouds and fog lie thick.
World-Honored Śākyamuni is touring the four seas
With the honored Maudgalyāna[26] and Kāśyapa[27]
And has come to bestow babies on human beings.
"What is it over there
That makes the crows and magpies cry so long
And a wondrous light shine in the air?
If human, it is one favored by heaven,
If beast, it is one favored by heaven,
If spirit, it is one favored by heaven.
Go and see what it is."
"Lacking virtue, we can see nothing."
Then, holding the *Yellow Scripture*[28] in his hand,
Śākyamuni looks toward the west village of the great sea
As they row their stone boat speedily.
A jade box is left there!

---

26. An eminent arhat and a chief disciple of the Buddha; *PDB*, 498–499.
27. One of the seven Buddhas of antiquity preceding Śākyamuni, the current Buddha; *PDB*, 425.
28. Perhaps referring to the *Scripture of the Yellow Court* (*Huangting jing*), an early text on visualizations of human anatomy.

"If this were a boy I would make him my disciple;
But being a girl, she is of no use to me."
He hides the box in the hollow of a hazel tree.
Hemp skullcaps pulled down,
Purple packs upon their backs,
Singing the songs of hell,
An old man and woman who pray for merit[29] pass by.
World-Honored Śākyamuni asks:
"Are you human or are you ghosts?"
"We are not ghosts, or beasts.
We're an old man and woman praying for merit
And guarding this mountain."
World-Honored Śākyamuni speaks:
"Tell me, what is merit?
Building a bridge over deep waters to help the traveler,
Building a monastery to save mankind. Clothing the naked,
Feeding the hungry, giving water to the thirsty.
But to nourish the baby who has no mother's milk
Is the greatest merit of all.
How about taking this child and raising it?"
The old man and woman reply:
"In spring, summer, and fall we live in the fields,
In winter we stay in a cave."
"If you keep and raise this child,
You will have food to eat and clothes to wear,
And a small thatched cottage will appear."
In an instant, Śākyamuni is gone.
Clearly it is the Buddha's power.
They hear the baby's cries
Among green willows and yellow cuckoos,
Between the willows where yellow birds fly.

29. Or: old beggar man and old beggar woman.

They find a jade box whence the sounds come,
Examine it to find that the golden turtle lock is open.
Aejung Scripture for the parents,
Loyalty Scripture for the country,
Love Scripture for the wife and children,
And *Ch'ŏnji P'aryang Scripture*,[30]
They chant them all one by one,
And without a key the jade box opens.
They look inside: red ants fill her eyes,
Worms and snakes coil around her waist.
They wash her from bottom to top
In the current of Long-Flowing Stream,
Shed their long-sleeved cassocks and wash her twice more,
Taking off their long-sleeved fine garments.
And when they carry her and turn around,
A small cottage exquisitely stands there.

Eight, nine years go by.
Untaught, she is versed in the sciences of the heavens and the
    earth
As well as all the secret military arts.
One day she asks, "Grandma, Grandpa,
Even flying birds and crawling insects have their own parents.
Where is my own mother, where is my own father?
Find me my parents, please."
"Grandpa is your father and Grandma your mother."
"Grandma and Grandpa, please don't lie.
How can such old people have a child like me?"
Being childless and lonely, they had hoped to rely on her.
"Heaven is your father, and earth your mother."
"Heaven and earth give birth to myriad things,

30. All imaginary texts.

But how can they give birth to a human being?
Grandma and Grandpa, please tell me the truth."
"You cut a bamboo stalk in Chŏlla province,
Cut both ends to make a staff and hold it[31]
Through three years' mourning for a dead father.
Chŏlla bamboo is your father, and
Your mother is the paulownia on the back hill."
"The Chŏlla bamboo is far, far away,
I cannot inquire after it three times a day."
So the child daily sends regards
To the paulownia tree on the back hill.

Time flows like a river, and the girl is now fifteen.
One day they see in the child's washbasin
The sun and moon reflected there.
Thus time flows on like a river.
Their Majesties are gravely ill.
The king commands, "Go consult the shaman of Ch'ŏnha
    palace."
"Please, bestow the gifts."
He sends five strings of silver coins and five of gold,
One *ch'i* and one *p'un* of cloth for the cassock,
Three *toe* and three *hop* of pearls,
Three feet and three inches of silk.
They go bearing these royal gifts
To shaman Taji of Ch'ŏnha palace,
And shaman Moran of Chesŏk palace.
They cast pearls and grains of white rice on the white jade tray:
The first throw yields the shaman's fortune,
The second tells of upper and lower gates,

---

31. The chief mourner carries a bamboo staff in a man's funeral, and a paulownia
staff in a woman's.

The third the royal fortune.
"When it comes to pass Your Majesty will see
As surely as the sun sets in the Western Sea
And the moon rises from the Eastern Sea.
Your Majesties will die on the same day and hour.
Go find the seventh princess where you abandoned her."
Thus they report to the king and queen.
"If only we had left her on level ground,
Our ministers could find her.
But who can find her now?"
Both dream on the same day and time:
Six azure-clad boys descend from the beam of Great
    Bright Hall
And bow before them. Their Majesties ask,
"Are you human or are you ghosts?
Even flying birds cannot enter here;
How did you come in?"
"We are not human beings or ghosts.
We're the azure-clad boys of heaven,
Who came at the Jade Emperor's bidding
To take Your Majesty's life tablet
To store it in the city of the dead."
"But why is it so?
Did some ministers send a message of grievance?
Or the people complain about me?"
"Neither the people's complaint nor the ministers' grievance.
You sinned when you cast out the child sent by heaven,
So you will take ill and die
On the same day and at the same hour."
"But how can we be saved?"
"Seek the child and take her back.
When you seek the elixir of Three Blessed Mounts,
The sacred water of the Peerless Transcendent,

The magic pearl of the dragon king of the Eastern Sea,
The kayam plant of Mount Penglai,
And the suru plant of Ana Mountain,[32]
When you eat of these, you'll be saved."
Suddenly they awake; it was an empty dream.
At dawn the king summons his ministers:
"If one of you finds the abandoned child,
We'll reward him a thousand gold coins
And enfeoffment of myriad households.
Indeed, I shall grant him half the kingdom."
The ministers are silent.
"He who brings only the sacred water
Will be lord of myriad households."
"The Eastern Sea Dragon palace is a heavenly place,
The Western Sea Dragon palace is also a heavenly place.
Though we die, we cannot go there.
We would gladly look for her on flat land,
But who can find an abandoned child among the waters?"
Then the minister of rites speaks:
"For many generations my house has served the throne,
How can I sit idly now?
I shall find the princess, even if I perish on the way."
"What would you like to take with you?"
Bearing letters from the king, queen, and six princesses
And the small clothes of the seventh princess,
Escorted by palace ladies two by two,
They leave through the five garrison gates and palace gate,
But they do not know where to go.
Then crows and magpies bow their heads to guide them,
And grasses and trees bend down to lead them.
A country of a thousand tricents of mountains and rivers,

32. *Kayam*, "hazel tree" and *suruch'wi*, "herbs conferring immortality."

Mountains rise fold upon fold,
The cuckoo cries sadly.
Golden warblers flit among the willows,
Before the River of Yellow Springs,
Behind the River of Flowing Sands.
Kalch'i Mount and Kalch'i Pass,
Pulch'i Mount and Pulch'i Pass.
Invoking the name of Amitābha,
At last they come to Taesang Cloister.
An old man and woman praying for merit ask:
"Are you human or are you ghosts?
How have you come where
Flying birds and crawling insects cannot enter?"
"I've come to take you upon the king's orders."
"If I am indeed the daughter of a king,
Great were my sins to have been cast out the moment I was
    born."
"I bring the jacket you wore as a seven-day baby."
"How am I to recognize it?"
"I bring the record of the month and hour of your birth."
"How am I to remember it?"
"I bring letters from the king, queen, and six princesses."
"What do their letters mean to me? Bring me a sign!"
He has a golden vessel with drops of blood
From the thumbs of the king and queen.
He pricks the child's fourth finger:
The bloods blend and blossom like a cloud.
Now the girl agrees to go.
"Shall we await your command with the royal guards?
Shall we await your command with the princess's palanquin?"
"I who was cast out at birth,
What use have I for a palanquin?
Give me a horse, I shall ride alone."

She follows the minister of rites and presents herself at the
   palace gate.
The king and queen command: "Let the princess come in
   quickly."
They grasp one another's hands and shed royal tears.
"Did we abandon you in hatred? No, it was in anger.
We cast you out in anger. How did you bear the cold?
How did you bear the heat?
How did you bear the hunger?
How did you bear the longing for your parents?"
"I lived by the merit of an old man and woman."

A country of a thousand tricents of mountains and rivers,
Cruel time rushes past.
The illness of Their Majesties is grave.
"All the officials, ladies-in-waiting, and all people—
Will you fetch the Peerless Transcendent's sacred water to save
   the country?"
"That is not a medicine of this world.
How can we obtain it?"
They call the eldest princess: "Will you go to save your
   parents?"
"How can I go where three thousand court ladies cannot go?"
They call the second princess: "Will you go to save your
   parents?"
"How can I go where my elder sister cannot go?"
They call the third princess: "Will you go to save your parents?"
"How can I go where my two elder sisters cannot go?"
They call the fourth princess: "Will you go to save your
   parents?"
"How can I go where my three elder sisters cannot go?"
They call the fifth princess: "Will you go to save your parents?"
"How can I go where my four elder sisters cannot?"

They call the sixth princess: "Will you go to save your parents?"
"How can I go where my five elder sisters cannot?"
They call the seventh princess: "Will you go to save your
    parents?"
"I have no debt to this country.
But I'm grateful to my mother who bore me for ten months.
I shall go for my mother's sake."
"Would you have the royal guards or the princess's palanquin?"
"I shall ride alone," she says.
She wears a coarse top and bottom and outer coat,
Binds her hair in double knots,
Has a bamboo hat and an iron staff,
And a silver backpack with golden straps.
She receives the signatures of the king and queen and binds them
    to her belt,
She receives the signatures of the six princesses and binds them
    to her belt.
"Six elder sisters, three thousand court ladies,
Even if Their Majesties die on the same day and same hour,
Do not perform a funeral but await my return."
She bids farewell to the king, queen, and six princesses
And gallops out the palace gate but doesn't know where to go.
O and alas, one among the dead,
If it follows the seventh princess,
With prayer for rebirth in the Pure Land of the West,
Then it becomes a man and enters the land of happiness
Upon this very day.

She brandishes her staff once and goes a thousand tricents,
She brandishes it twice, and two thousand tricents,
She brandishes it thrice, and three thousand tricents.
What is the season now? It is the third month of spring, a
    pleasant time.

Plum and peach are in bloom,
Fragrant flowers and grasses wave gently.
Yellow warblers fly among the willows,
Parrots and peacocks preen, the cuckoo calls its mate.
The sun sets over the western mountain,
And the moon rises from the eastern peak.
She sits and scans a far-off golden rock
Covered with low pines with even branches.
There Śākyamuni explains the dharma
To Bodhisattva Kṣitigarbha[33] and Buddha Amitābha.
She draws near and bows thrice three times.
"Are you a human being or a ghost?
Here where flying birds and crawling insects cannot enter,
How did you come?"
"I am His Majesty's heir apparent on a mission of filial service.
Now I have lost my way.
Please, guide me by your grace."
World-Honored Śākyamuni replies:
"I have heard that the king has seven girls,
But this is the first I've heard of an heir apparent.
When they cast you out at the west village of the great sea,
I saved your wretched life.
But that was then.
You have traversed three thousand tricents on level earth,
But how can you go three thousand tricents on a steep path?"
"Though I die on the way, I will go."
"Take this gift of an udumbara flower.[34]
When you come to a great sea, wave this flower
And the sea will become hard ground."

---

33. "Earth Store," a bodhisattva with the power to rescue beings born in the hells; *PDB*, 448.

34. In the original, *nahwa*, "gauze flower," referring to the udumbara or *ficus glomerata*. It is said to bloom only once every one thousand or three thousand years; *PDB*, 934.

Before her she sees walls of thorns and iron reaching to the sky.
She remembers the Buddha's words and waves the flower:
Armless demons, legless demons, eyeless demons,
A hundred million demons jump and croak like frogs,
Open the gates of Knife Mountain hell
And Fire Mountain hell,
The eighty-four thousand hells.
Souls headed for the ten kings of hell are sent there,
Souls destined for hell are sent there.
O and alas! One soul among the dead,
With rotten ears and rotten mouth,
If he hears prayers and repeats them to all the bodhisattvas,
He follows Princess Pari and enters
The Pure Land of the West, the land of happiness,
On this very day.

She views a place afar—
To the east a gate of blue glass,
To the west a gate of white glass,
To the south a gate of red glass,
To the north a gate of black glass,
And in the center the gate of chastity,
And there stands the Peerless Transcendent.
His height seems to reach the sky,
Face like a rice cake, eyes like an oil cup for a lamp,
Nose like a clay bottle, hands large as kettle lids,
Feet three feet and three inches long,
So dreadful and frightful he is.
She backs away and bows three times.
The Peerless Transcendent asks:
"Are you a human being or a ghost, that you enter here
Where flying birds and crawling insects cannot?
How did you enter and where do you come from?"

"I am an heir apparent on a mission of filial service."
"If you came to fetch the water, what payment do you bring?
And for the herbs, what payment do you bring?"
"In my haste I forgot to bring anything."
"Then draw the water for three years,
Tend the fire for three years,
Gather the herbs for three years."
After thrice three years of life there,
The Peerless Transcendent speaks to her:
"You seem a prince behind, but a woman before.
Why not tie a marriage bond,
Bear me seven sons and then return? How about that?"
"If it's for my parents' sake, I'll do it."
Heaven and earth for a canopy, creepers for a pillow,
Grass for a bed, a cloud bank for shade,
The morning star for a lamp.
In the first watch she gives her consent,
In the second watch she stays,
And throughout the night they tie the marriage knot.

She bears seven sons, and one day she speaks:
"However great our love may be,
I have delayed my mission for my parents.
I dreamed in the first watch a silver bowl was shattered
And in the second a silver spoon broken.
Surely the king and queen must have died at the same time.
I must hurry now to save them."
"Take it in your golden crock,
The water you drew is healing water.
Take the herbs you gathered,
For they bring flesh and bone to life.
But first, won't you view the sea with me?"
"I don't care to view the sea."

"Then come view the back hill's flowers."

"I don't care to see the flowers."

"I lived alone as a bachelor,

But now, how can eight bachelors live?

Please, take the seven boys with you."

"I'll do that for my parents' sake."

Big children walk and small ones are carried on backs.

Then the Peerless Transcendent asks her,

"What if I were to follow you?"

"It is said that wife should follow husband;

But for my parents' sake, let it be so.

I came alone; now nine bodies return."

Before the River of Yellow Springs,

Behind the River of Flowing Sands.

Princess Pari asks, "What are those boats row on row

Over the magpie shoals in the sea of blood?"

"Those carry souls that in the former life

Were filial to parents, loyal to the state,

Loved their brothers, and kept harmony in their homes."

O and alas! One among the dead goes forth,

At the first shrine receives the ritual coins,

At the second the preliminary purification ritual,

At the third food for three messengers of the underworld,

The iron gate, the bamboo gate, the lotus hall,

The forty-ninth-day ritual for the soul of the dead.

He receives gold and silver coins,

Invokes the name of the Buddha, and

Rides the boat to the Pure Land of the West, the land of
     happiness.

She asks, "Those bottomless boats on the sea of blood,

Crying like summer frogs as they go,

What boats are they?"

"Those carry souls who in the former life were unfilial,
Betrayed the state, didn't love their brothers,
Gave with small measure and took with large measure,
Gave bad rice for alms and harmed others.
Now those boats carry their souls, crying,
To the hundred million four thousand hells."
"And what are those boats without rowers?"
"Those are the boats of souls
Who in the former life had no offspring,
And now drift on the sea."
"Herdboys on Mount Ch'o,
In the capital's broad square over there,
Why are the people gathered?"
"We'll tell you if you pay a toll."
"And what's the toll?"
She gives them seven feet and seven inches of the silk
That strapped the baby to her back.
Then the herdboy speaks:
"Unborn babies may not know it,
But those who came forth from the womb know
That the king and queen died on the same day
And today is the state funeral.
Are you a human being or a ghost?
The seventh princess has gone three thousand tricents to seek the
    sacred water,
But there is no news whether she is alive or dead."
Startled, the seventh princess hastens.
Hiding seven sons in a thicket
And the Peerless Transcendent in the forest,
She stares at the funeral flags—indeed, they're the king's,
She sees the dragon robe and dirge—they're the king's.
Loosening their hair, the ministers announce death.
"Ladies-in-waiting, attend within the curtains,

People and ministers, guard outside the curtains,
Lower the small bier, lower the large bier."
She raises the coffin lids and drives the people back,
Loosens the seven knots that bind each corpse,
Infuses breath into their flesh,
Infuses breath into their bones,
Inserts magic pearls into their eyes,
Pours sacred water into their mouths,
And they revive at the same time.
The king arises: "I've slept deeply.
Have we come out to view the sea
Or to view the flowers on the back hill?"
"Not to view the sea, or the flowers;
Your Majesties died, and we're in the funeral procession.
The seventh princess went three thousand tricents
To the Weakwater to obtain the sacred water,[35]
And you have revived on this day and hour."
His Majesty cancels the funeral, declares it an outing,
And returns to T'ongmyŏng Hall,
And the queen to the inner palace.
All the officials and three thousand court ladies all shout,
"Long live the king!"
Myriad people cry in unison, "Long live the king!"
His Majesty summons the seventh princess:
"All my officials and ministers have inquired of us,
'Why has the seventh princess not come?'
'She has sinned, she married the Peerless Transcendent
And bore him seven sons.'
The sin is not yours but mine.
Should I give you half my kingdom?

---

35. The name of a transcendent stream on which not even a feather can float. Needham, *Science and Civilization in China* 3:608–611.

Or all the clothes brought through the four great gates?"
"Had I once held the kingdom, I'd now desire it.
Had I once had the clothes, I'd want them again.
But I never knew fine food and clothes at my parents' knee,
So I will become the progenitor of shamans."

Above, on the hundredth day, she leads the living to paradise,
Below, on the six fast days, she leads the dead to paradise.
Above, an embroidered jacket made from Chinese silk,
Below, a long skirt, embroidered shoes, and a staff,
A bell at her hand, broad red sash at her waist,
A fifty-ribbed fan in one hand,[36]
She governs all shamans.[37]

"Present the Peerless Transcendent, my son-in-law," the king
    commands.
"His gauze cap will catch upon the south gate."
"Dig out the earth beneath the gate and enter."
"His waist will hit the sides of the north gate."
"Pull down the sides and have him enter."
The Transcendent stands in the broad court before T'ongmyŏng
    Hall.
His height is great.
"Messengers, measure the height of the princess and our
    son-in-law."
"His height is thirty-three heavens and thirty-three feet.
The princess's is twenty-eight lunar mansions and twenty-eight
    feet."
"Then you are indeed a heaven-joined pair.
For the prince who measures to the thirty-three heavens,

36. This action describes the appearance of the princess as the prototypical shaman.
37. Literally, "body governing spirit."

Ring the cymbals;
For the princess who measures to the twenty-eight lunar
    mansions,
Ring the large gong."
The king grants them food and garments.
The son-in-law will have offerings on the road
With many dishes on the large table.
World-Honored Śākyamuni shall receive
The first-, second-, forty-ninth-, and one hundredth-day rites.
Herdboy Kangnim on a hill with peaches and plums
Shall receive the seven-feet-and-seven-inch silk towel,
Grandma praying for merit shall have hemp cloths
At the gate of thorns and of iron.
Grandpa praying for merit shall have
Offerings of *pŏlch'o namhyang*.[38]
And seven sons, two *ton* and one *p'un* of money offerings.

In the first court, Great King Guang of Qin,[39]
Hear the prayers of my myriad subjects,
Preach the dharma to ferry all living beings across.
Homage to Buddha Amitābha and Bodhisattva Kṣitigarbha.
In the second court, Great King of the First River,
Hear the prayers of my myriad subjects,
Preach the dharma to ferry all living beings across.
Homage to Buddha Amitābha and Bodhisattva Kṣitigarbha.
In the third court, Great King Di of Song,
Hear the prayers of my myriad subjects,
Preach the dharma to ferry all living beings across.
Homage to Buddha Amitābha and Bodhisattva Kṣitigarbha.
In the fourth court, Great King of the Five Offices,

38. Unknown.
39. The ten kings of hell are invoked here.

Hear the prayers of my myriad subjects,
Preach the dharma to ferry all living beings across.
Homage to Buddha Amitābha and Bodhisattva Kṣitigarbha.
In the fifth court, Great King Yama,
Hear the prayers of my myriad subjects,
Preach the dharma to ferry all living beings across.
Homage to Buddha Amitābha and Bodhisattva Kṣitigarbha.
In the sixth court, Great King of Transformation,
Hear the prayers of my myriad subjects,
Preach the dharma to ferry all living beings across.
Homage to Buddha Amitābha and Bodhisattva Kṣitigarbha.
In the seventh court, Great King of Mount Tai,
Hear the prayers of my myriad subjects,
Preach the dharma to ferry all living beings across.
Homage to Buddha Amitābha and Bodhisattva Kṣitigarbha.
In the eighth court, Great Impartial King,
Hear the prayers of my myriad subjects,
Preach the dharma to ferry all living beings across.
Homage to Buddha Amitābha and Bodhisattva Kṣitigarbha.
In the ninth court, Great King of the Capital,
Hear the prayers of my myriad subjects,
Preach the dharma to ferry all living beings across.
Homage to Buddha Amitābha and Bodhisattva Kṣitigarbha.
In the tenth court, Great King Who Turns the Wheel of Rebirth,
Hear the prayers of my myriad subjects,
Preach the dharma to ferry all living beings across.
Homage to Buddha Amitābha and Bodhisattva Kṣitigarbha.
Hear the prayers of my myriad subjects,
Preach the dharma to ferry all living beings across.
Homage to Buddha Amitābha and Bodhisattva Kṣitigarbha.

Released from three years' mourning,
Consoling the spirits in the underworld,

Released from the ancestors' cause of grievance,

From the karma of earthly existence,

The dead man shed his head cover, the dead woman her
yomo cap,

With prayers for rebirth in the land of happiness.

When you go to the Pure Land,

Open the gate of Knife Mountain hell and the gate of Fire
Mountain hell,

Open the gate of Poisonous Snakes hell and the gate of Ice
Cold hell,

When you go to the land of happiness.

The wide dark road leads to hell,

The bright narrow road, to the land of happiness,

The bright large road, to the heavenly palace in the Milky Way.

Leave aside the wide dark road, take the bright large;

When the road spirit detains you,

Offer the straw sandals from your feet;

When the lady of the grave detains you,

Offer seven outer knots and seven inner knots,

Untie the fourteen knots and present them to her.

When an evil spirit detains you,

Offer your undershirt.

When the mountain spirit detains you,

Offer your funeral banners and wooden fan.

When you meet the earth spirit,

Give him the upper and lower shrouds;[40]

When you come to the great rocks[41] and sharp rocks,

Offer a bag of your toenails, fingernails, and hair.

When you reach the twelve gates,

---

40. Spread on the lower and upper parts of the dead in the coffin.

41. *Chigye*, perhaps a rock that stands on the boundary between earth and the underworld.

Offer three thousand monks' caps.
When you reach the Great King's hall,
Transmit the meditation practice of Chŏngt'o monastery
And the cultivator's mystic syllables.
With wet rotten mouth and wet rotten ears,
Invoke the Buddha's name as you go in.
Don't follow the immortal officials robed in blue,
But follow the ones robed in red.
Take the road of the red-robed officials.
Though flourishing rhododendron, azalea, cockscomb, balsam,
Pine, juniper, and cedar thickly line the way,
Don't pluck the flowering twigs,
Don't look behind you,
Go to the high supreme Lotus Terrace,[42]
Seek an immortal lady to become an immortal, and enter the
    Jasper Lake.
Homage to Buddha Amitābha and Bodhisattva Kṣitigarbha.
Word by word, line by line, with rotten ears and mouth,
Recite the prayers as you go:
Homage to Buddha Amitābha and Bodhisattva Kṣitigarbha.
First, I cleanse the east, purifying it to a place of worship,[43]
Second, I cleanse the south and obtain coolness,
Third, I cleanse the west and complete the Pure Land,
Fourth, I cleanse the north and become eternally healthy.
As this place of enlightenment is purified, without flaw or
    maculation,
I now keep and recite these sublime mystic syllables,
Vowing to bestow love and compassion and secretly watch over
    everyone.
Bodhisattva Who Observes the Sounds of the World

42. Where the Buddha and bodhisattvas sit.
43. See *Sŏngmun ŭibŏm*, 97, translated in Buswell, *Zen Monastic Experience*, 239.

With a Thousand Hands and Eyes!
Homage to Buddha Amitābha,
Homage to Buddha Amitābha,
Homage to Buddha Amitābha.
I lead the former dead, latter dead, all the dead ancestors,
Generation after generation, son after son,
This is the day they go to the land of happiness.

P'ansori

P'ansori is an oral narrative performed on stage by a professional singer (*kwangdae*) who uses mimetic and conventional body movements and gestures, as well as songs, to project his characters. Accompanied by a single drummer, the singer dons no special costumes, wears no mask, and uses no props except for a fan (and sometimes an onstage screen). As with other vernacular poetic genres, performance traditions helped to preserve and maintain the art of *p'ansori*.

This art form emerged from shamanist narrative songs in Chŏlla province, in the southwestern part of Korea. The singer was usually from a hereditary shaman household; in fact, he was often the husband of a shaman, "who had served as an accompanist or assistant to his wife, eventually emerging as a professional actor and singer on his own."[1] The traditional shaman was a spiritually empowered woman who acted as a medium for spirits and gods and consequently had the ability to heal the sick, summon the dead, and drive out demons. Yet, while the shaman was a professional mnemonist, a ritual specialist, and a repository of tales and songs, proverbs and riddles, she was also a socially abject figure in the community. How

---

1. Pihl, *Korean Singer of Tales*, 20.

were these singers/redactors able to take full advantage of the representative power in language? Textual analysis of *p'ansori* shows heteroglossia at its most exuberant, the diglossic and dialogic imagination working to embody the experiential richness of the world. Moreover, the process of composition, starting from the original text or ur-form and progressing through different versions with the accretion of additional episodes and interpolated songs, reveals a collaborative re-creation that epitomizes the fluidity of the oral tradition. Here Paul Zumthor's notion of *"mouvance,"*[2] an aesthetic principle of transmission leading to changes that were intended and perceived as improvements to the received text, is useful. Successive singers and redactors shaped each oral performance by revising the text for a new audience—a simultaneous dialogue between performer and tradition and performer and audience. In this art, the ur-form becomes irrelevant because each surviving redaction is ultimately authorized by its singer. *P'ansori* is an anonymous collective oral work that lives through its variants in a state of perpetual re-creation.[3]

Song of the Faithful Wife Ch'unhyang

There are some 120 different editions of the *Song of Ch'unhyang*—in varying lengths, in literary Chinese and in the vernacular, and in narrative fiction as well as in *p'ansori*. The earliest extant version, written down by Yu Chinhan (1712–1791), is in literary Chinese and consists of two hundred heptasyllabic couplets. The *Song* he heard, however, was already part of the popular culture, and the broad outline of the plot was known in advance. We may speculate that the earliest version of the *Song* was composed orally in performance. Thereafter the text was almost exclusively transmitted in performances, some of which have survived in written versions. Among multiple retellings of the *Song,* the one I have chosen is the Wanp'an woodblock edition (d.u.), meant to be sung, titled *Song of the Faithful Wife Ch'unhyang (Yŏllyŏ Ch'unhyang sujŏl ka)*. This version focuses on Ch'unhyang; it is the richest in sound and sense, form and style, and probably the most literary as well as the most readable. Written from a pluralistic narrative perspective, with different voices and their corresponding value systems, it is

---

2. *Essai de poétique médiéval*, translated as *Towards a Medieval Poetics*, 42–45.
3. Doane and Pasternack, *Vox Intexta*, 227; Zumthor, *Oral Poetry*, 183.

polyphonic and heteroglossic, recognizing and exploiting to the fullest the intralingual and interlingual features of the language.

The story of Ch'unhyang, known to all Koreans, revolves around the daughter of a wealthy retired female entertainer (Wŏlmae) and Second Minister Sŏng, who meets and marries Student Yi. When his father, the magistrate of Namwŏn, is transferred to a position at court, Yi follows him to Seoul to prepare for the civil service examinations. Meanwhile, a new magistrate, Pyŏn Hakto, arrives and demands that Ch'unhyang become his mistress. When she refuses, because she is married, she is tortured and put in prison. Yi returns to Namwŏn as a secret royal inspector, however, in time to save his beloved.

The *Song* is set in the Korean city of Namwŏn, in the southeastern part of Chŏlla province, famed for its many historic and religious sites. Above all, Namwŏn is known as the birthplace of Ch'unhyang. The administrative complex lies in the center of the walled town; a shrine to loyal officials is to the northwest, a jail to the northeast. The district school is north of the wall almost at the midpoint. Sŏnwŏn monastery is to the northeast, the shrine to Guan Yu (d. 219) to the southwest. Southwest of the walled town are the precincts of a walled and gated park named Great Cold Tower Park (Kwanghallu Wŏn), considered an exceptionally pleasant place. At the north corner there is a shrine to Ch'unhyang, with her fulllength portrait in the midst of a bamboo grove, the bamboo representing fidelity and constancy. Some steps south are Great Cold Tower, where Ch'unhyang and Student Yi meet for the first time; the Palace on the Moon; and the Milky Way watercourse, constructed by drawing water from Smartweed River nearby, with Magpie Bridge (Ojakkyo) over it. The bridge figures prominently in the story of the Herd Boy and Weaver Maid—constellations (Altair and Vega) fated to be separated on the east and west sides of the Milky Way throughout the year except once, on the seventh night of the seventh month, when magpies build a bridge for them to cross over the vault of heaven. On the lake are representations of three sacred seamounts in Chinese mythology—Yŏngju (Yingzhou, or Mount Halla), Pongnae (Penglai, or the Diamond Mountains), and Pangjang (Fangjang, or Mount Chiri).

Ch'unhyang is born in answer to her mother's prayers, and the association of the birth of the heroine with the divine indicates that Ch'unhyang is the personification of Consort Fu, daughter of the Chinese culture hero Fu Xi, who drowned in the Luo River and became a river goddess. She is Fu incarnate—and nature sends harbingers, as in the case of heroes and saints. Even as a child, Ch'unhyang distinguishes herself with talent, learning, and virtue—qualities that define a class.

The nine songs presented in this excerpt constitute the core of the *Song of Ch'unhyang*, and most versions contain all or nearly all of them.

Accompanied by her maid Hyangdan, Ch'unhyang comes out to play on a swing:

CH'UNHYANG ON THE SWING

Unable to resist the spring feeling
At the singing of birds,
A fair girl plucks a spray of azaleas
And puts them in her hair;
She picks a white peony
And puts it in her mouth;
Lifting the unlined gauze in her garment,
She bends to rinse her hands
And takes a mouthful of water to cleanse her mouth
In the clear water of a flowing stream;
She picks up a pebble and
Throws it at the orioles in the willow.
Was this not "Striking the oriole to wake it up?"[1]
She strips the leaves off the willow
And scatters them on the water.
Snow-white butterflies and bees,
Holding the stamens,
Dance in pairs, swaying;
Golden orioles
Flit among the trees.
Great Cold Tower is beautiful,
But Magpie Bridge is better—
Truly the loveliest in all Chŏlla province.
If this is indeed Magpie Bridge,
Where are Herd Boy and Weaver Maid?
In such a beautiful place,
How can there be no poetry?

1. Refers to Jin Changxu's poem "Chunyuan," in *Quan Tangshi* 768:8813.

Student Yi is feeling lonely; he imagines all sorts of things, and cannot help but mumble to himself. He wishes to identify this female transcendent on the swing, and sings:

WHO IS SHE?

Xi Shi followed Fan Li[2]
On a skiff to the Five Lakes,
So she shouldn't be here.
Lady Yu sang a sad song before she turned
To Xiang Yu in the moonlight at Kaixia,[3]
So she couldn't be here.
Lady Wang Jiaojun left Tanfeng Palace
And went to the desert
Where now she lies in her Green Tomb,[4]
So she couldn't be here.
Ban Jieyou shut herself in Changxin Palace[5]
Where she sang her sad song,
So she couldn't be here;
Zhao Feiyan left Shaoyang Palace
After attendance in the morning,[6]
So she couldn't be here.
Is this a transcendent of the Luo River,
A transcendent on Mount Shaman?
His soul flew away to heaven
Bearing his body weary—
Truly he was still single.

---

2. Xi Shi, a famous beauty from Yue, followed Fan Li (c. 5th cent. BCE) on a skiff to the Five Lakes.

3. Lady Yu parted from Xiang Yu, hegemon of Chu, with a sad song on a moonlit night at Kaixia; see Watson, *Records of the Grand Historian*, 1:70.

4. Wang became a bride of the khan of the Xiongnu in 33 BCE. Her tomb is so called because it is supposed to stay green throughout the year.

5. "Favored Beauty" (c. 48–46 BCE) served the Han emperor Cheng but had to retire to Lasting Trust Palace. *Hanshu* 97B:3983–3988.

6. "Flying Swallow" (d. 6 BCE), who replaced Favored Beauty in Cheng's affections.

Unable to collect his thoughts, Yi goes to his room and spends hours in anguish while waiting until dusk. As soon as the yamen is closed and dusk has ushered in the night, Yi and his servant boy steal out, heading for Ch'unhyang's house. Yi wants to marry her right then and there and obtains Wŏlmae's consent. Both are sixteen years old (fifteen by Western count)—a nubile age since boys age fifteen and girls age fourteen were allowed to marry. So an informal wedding takes place in Ch'unhyang's mother's house without an exchange of gifts, a nuptial procession, or the bridegroom's visit to the bride's home to present a wooden goose, symbol of conjugal fidelity. After a feast, Wŏlmae asks Hyangdan to prepare the bedroom. At this point Yi learns from Wŏlmae that after Magistrate Sŏng passed away in Seoul, Ch'unhyang was raised by a single mother and never knew her biological father. After a second night, their joy is renewed and they jointly compose an impromptu love song:

SONG OF LOVE

Love, love, my love,
Love high as Mount Shaman under the moon
Shining upon the seven hundred tricents of Grotto Court Lake.
Love deep as water at the horizon's end,
Deep as heaven and the emerald sea,
Love high as the top of Mount Jade under the bright moon,
Enjoying itself on myriad peaks of the autumn mountains—
Love like spending years in the study of dance
And asking for one who plays the pipe[7]—
Love that shines like the evening sun and moon
Upon the peach and plum blossoms seen through the screen—
Love that abounds in winsome smiles and graces

---

7. Lu Jiaolin (635–684), in "Changan gui," *Quan Tangshi* 41:522–523. The text reverses lines 17 and 18 and gives only four graphs to fit the *p'ansori* meter: "Tell me of her who plays the pipes off into purple mist—/she has spent her years of beauty in the study of dance" (Owen, *Poetry of Early T'ang*, 106).

With a new moon powdered white,
Love that brings us together through three lives,
Bound by the old man under the moon[8]—
Love between husband and wife without reproach—
Love like a well-rounded peony on the eastern hill
Amid the rain of blossoms—
Love entwined and bound
Like a net in the sea off Yŏnp'yŏng[9]—
Love joined on end like a brocade woven by
Weaver Maid in the Silver River—
Love sewn tightly
Like seams in the quilt of a singing girl,
Love drooping
Like fronds of weeping willow by the river—
Love piled up like grains
In the southern and northern granaries—
Love deeply etched in every corner
Like silver and jade inlays in the chest—
Love enjoyed by golden bees and white butterflies
As they hold pink flowers
And dance in spring breezes—
Love that floats like a pair of mandarin ducks
Bobbing on the clear green stream—
Love of Herd Boy and Weaver Maid
On the night of Double Seven—
Love of Xingzhen, pupil of Master Liuguan,[10]
Frolicking with the eight fairies—
Love of Xiang Yu, whose strength can pluck up the hills,
Meeting with beautiful Lady Yu—
Love of the brilliant emperor of Tang

---

8. Traditionally, the matchmaker who uses red strings to tie the marital knots between husband and wife.

9. Two islands off the southern shore of Hwanghae province, known as a fishing spot.

10. The protagonist in *A Dream of Nine Clouds*.

For his precious consort Yang[11]—
Love swaying gracefully
Like the sea roses along Bright Sand Beach[12]—
You're indeed my love, all of you is love—
Ŏhwa tungdung, my love,
O my lovely one,
My love!

Yi wishes to commemorate love and his beloved in monuments more lasting than bronze. The body is the source of language, yet language outlasts the body.

LIFE AFTER DEATH

When you die, I'll tell you what you'll be:
You will be a sinograph—
Graphs for earth, for female,
For wife, and the radical for woman.
When I die, I'll become graphs
For heaven, husband, male,
The body of the son attached to the woman radical
Making the graph for good.
Love, love, my love!

When you die, I'll tell you what you'll be:
You'll become water—
Water in Silver River,
Water of waterfalls,
Of myriad acres of emerald seas,
Of clear valley brooks, of jade valley brooks,
Ending in a long river for the whole region.
Even during a seven-year drought,

11. Xuanzong's undying love for Yang Guifei is the subject of Bo Juyi's "Song of Everlasting Sorrow."

12. Well-known beach in Wŏnsan, South Hamgyŏng.

You'll become the water of yin and yang
Overflowing always and sinking to the bottom.

When I die, I'll become a bird,
Not a cuckoo,
Or a blue bird at Jasper Lake,
Or a blue crane, white crane, or roc,
But a mandarin duck
That never leaves its mate,
Bobbing on the green waters—
Love, love,
Ŏhwa tungdung, that's me.
Love, love, my fascinating love!

"No, I don't want to be any such thing."
All right, then. I'll tell you what you'll be after death.
When you die, you won't be the great bell at Kyŏngju,
Or that in Chŏnju, or Songdo,
But the one in Chongno in the capital.
When I die, I'll become the clapper of the bell,
In accordance with the thirty-three heavens and twenty-eight mansions.
After the beacon on Mount An[13] flares three times,
After the beacon on Mount South flares twice,
The first sound of the Chongno bell—
Every time it rings,
People will think,
Only the bell:
But inside ourselves we'll know
It's Ch'unhyang's clang, my clang.
Let the two of us conjoin,
Love, love, my fascinating love!

"No, I don't like that either."
Then, when you die, what will you be?

13. In Imje county, Kangwŏn province.

You will become a mortar,
I'll become a pestle when I die,
The mortar made by Jiang Taigong[14]
At the hour, day, month, year of the White Monkey . . .
And when I pound, clang clang,
You'll know it's me.
Love, love, my love,
My charming love!

"I don't like it, I don't want to be that either."
Why do you say that?

"Why must I be
At the bottom
In this life and the next?"
"Then, when you die, I'll put you on top.
You'll be the upper plate of a millstone,
And I the lower plate.
When slender hands of young handsome faces
Hold the millstone and turn,
Like round heaven and square earth together,
Then you'll know it's me."
"Still I don't like it and won't be that either.
When I was born, this top part was given only to me.
For what sort of grudge
Was I given an extra orifice?
I don't want anything."

"Then when you die, I'll tell you what you'll be;
Be a sea rose on long Bright Sand Beach;
When I die, I'll be a butterfly
And nibble with antenna
While you brush it with pollen.
When spring winds blow,

14. A counselor to King Wen of Zhou, who found him fishing in the Wei River.

We'll dance swaying—
Love, love, my love
My charming love!
If I look here, you're my love;
If I look there, you're my love.
If all this is my love,
How can I live caught up in love?
Ohǒ tungdung, my love!
My beloved, my love!
When you smile sweetly,
The peony, king of flowers,
Seems half open
After a night's drizzle.
Wherever I look, I see my love!
My charming love!

SONG OF THE GRAPH SŬNG

Let's play at riding—
Like the Yellow Lord who drilled his men, making clouds and fog,
And caught Chiyou in the Zhuolu wilderness[15]
While beating the victory drums
In the leading chariot—
Like Great Yu of Xia in his land-rumbling chariot
When he tamed the nine-year flood,
Like Master Red Pine riding on a cloud,[16]
Or Lü Tongbin on his egret,[17]
Like Li Bo, a banished transcendent, on a whale,
Or Meng Haojan on a donkey,[18]

15. Chiyou is the god of war. *Shiji* 1:3–4; Birrell, *Chinese Mythology,* 132–134.
16. Rain master under Shennong.
17. Eighth-century alchemist; see Needham, *Science and Civilization in China,* 2:159.
18. A Tang poet (689–740).

The divine Great Unique[19] on a crane,
A Chinese emperor on an elephant,
Our king in a carriage,
Three state counselors in sedan chairs,
Six ministers in carriages,
A military general in his war carriage,
Magistrates on their palanquins,
The magistrate of Namwŏn in a special carriage,
Even old fishermen on a leafy boat at sunset—
Yet I have nothing to ride on.
This night at the third watch,
I'll ride on Ch'unhyang's belly,
Hoisting the quilt for a sail,
My member as an oar,
And enter into her sunken spring—
As without effort I cross
The waters of yin and yang,
If I take you as my horse to ride,
Your pace may vary—
I will be the groom
Gently holding your reins.
You may trot and canter,
Go rough and hard,
Gallop like a piebald horse.[20]

Meanwhile, Yi's father, the current magistrate of Namwŏn, has been appointed a sixth royal secretary in Seoul and orders his son to depart the following day ahead of him. Yi tells his mother about Ch'unhyang, only to be scolded, and he goes to her house with his news.

---

19. In Chinese mythology, the supreme sky god who resides in a palace at the center of heaven, marked by the pole star. Needham, *Science and Civilization in China*, 3:260.

20. In this song Yi offers lessons to his new wife, hitherto innocent of amorous experience, to initiate her into the various moves and caresses of erotic love. Just as there is a homology between hunting and sexuality in early Greek poetry, there is a homology between combat and sexual intercourse in Chinese and Korean fiction.

At first Ch'unhyang suggests that he should go to the capital first and she will follow. But Yi tells her they must part, because he will not be accepted at court if their love becomes known. At this, Ch'unhyang loses her composure and sobs in protest. In desperation, Yi thinks he can smuggle her into the palanquin with the ancestral tablets, but resigning herself to the inevitable, she offers her beloved a cup of wine before he mounts his horse. She sings the "Song of Parting," each word ending in one of the homonyms *chŏl* (break off, cut off) and *chŏl* (chastity, moral integrity).

After some months, a new magistrate, Pyŏn Hakto, is appointed. The narrator enumerates his faults: he makes errors of judgment, forgets his moral training, and behaves irresponsibly. At the first meeting with his officials, Pyŏn inquires about Ch'unhyang. His curiosity has been kindled by rumors about her beauty. The first item on his official agenda is to inspect all the female entertainers registered in his town. After a survey of eighteen girls, Pyŏn notices that Ch'unhyang's name is not on the list and asks her whereabouts. The head of slaves and the chief clerk in the personnel section tell him that Ch'unhyang is not a female entertainer and is known to be the faithful and cloistered wife of Yi Mongnyong. Pyŏn orders his men to fetch her at once. While the soldiers are on their way to Ch'unhyang's house, she sings:

SONG OF MUTUAL LOVE

> I want to go, I want to go,
> I want to follow my love.
> I'll go a thousand tricents,
> Ten thousand tricents,
> I'll brave storms and rain,
> Scale the high peaks,
> Where even wild falcons, tamed falcons,
> Peregrine falcons, trained falcons rest
> Beyond Tongsŏn Pass.

If he will come and look for me,
I will take off my shoes,
Carry them in my hands,
Race to him without pause.
My husband in Seoul,
Does he think of me?
Has he forgotten me utterly?
Has he taken another love?

Brought before Pyŏn who asks her to be his mistress, Ch'unhyang answers that she is married and would rather die than serve him. She says, "If I betray my husband to become your concubine, it would be treason just as if a minister were to forget his own country and betray his king. If the rape of a married woman is not a crime, what is?"

The soldiers drag Ch'unhyang to the courtyard and throw her to the ground. Pyŏn orders them to "bind her to the chair, break her shinbones, and submit a report of her execution." The jailor begins to flog her with a club. At each stroke, she shouts out her response, punning on each count—*one* sincere and firm heart; a chaste wife does not serve *two* husbands; *three* bonds; *four* classes/limbs; *five* relations/elements; and the like:

SONG OF TEN STROKES

One sincere and firm heart
Is to follow *one* husband.
One punishment
Before *one* year's over,
But not for a moment will I change.

A chaste wife does not serve *two* husbands—
Hence there can't be *two* husbands.
Though beaten and left for dead,
I'll never forget Master Yi.

"*Three* dependencies"[21] is a heavy law;
I know *three* bonds and five relations.
Though I am punished and exiled *three* times,
I'll never forget my husband—
Master Yi of Samch'ŏng Street.

A magistrate, a king's official,
Disregards the affairs of *four* classes;
He rules exercising his power,
And doesn't know the people
In the forty-eight wards of Namwŏn resent him.
Even if you sever my *four* limbs,
I'll live and die with my husband,
Whom I cannot forget in life or death.

The *five* relations remain unbroken;
Husband and wife have separate duties.
Our tie, sealed by the *five* elements,
Cannot be torn apart.
Sleeping or waking,
I cannot forget my husband.
The autumn moon on the phoenix tree
Is watching over my love.
Will a letter come today?
Will news come tomorrow?
My innocent body
Does not deserve death.
Don't convict me unjustly—
Aego, aego, my lot!

Six times *six* is thirty-*six*—
Kill me *six*ty thousand times;

---

21. That she follows the wishes of her father, husband, and eldest son. See Ch'ü, *Law and Society in Traditional China*, 102–103.

Six thousand joints in my body
Are all tied by love—
My heart cannot be changed.

Have I committed the *seven* wifely faults?[22]
Why should I receive *seven* punishments?
With a *seven*-foot sword,
Cut me up
And kill me quickly.
Bureau of Punishment,
Don't hesitate when you strike,
I, all *seven* jewels of my face, die!

This fortunate Ch'unhyang's body
Met a renowned official
Among the magistrates of *eight* provinces.
Governors and magistrates of *eight* provinces—
You're sent to rule the people,
Not to inflict cruel punishments.

In the *nine* bends of my bowels and innards,
My tears will make a *nine*-year flood.
With tall pines on the *nine* hills[23]
I'll build a boat for a clear river,
Go quickly to Seoul,
Lay my case before the king
In the *nine*fold palace;
I'll then step down *nine* steps,
Go to Samch'ŏng Street,
Meet my love joyfully
And vent my grudge
Tied in knots.

22. Failure to produce a son; adultery; extreme disobedience; extreme talkativeness; theft; jealousy; and grave illness. Ibid., 118–123.
23. *Shijing* 184:1; Waley, *Book of Songs*, 158.

Though I live *ten* times,
After escaping death nine times,
My mind is made up for eighty years—
A hundred thousand deaths
Won't change it.
Will never change it.
Young Ch'unhyang, just sixteen,
How sad the wronged wretch beaten to death!
The full moon
Is hidden in the clouds,
My husband in Seoul
Has withdrawn to Samch'ŏng Street—
Moon, moon, do you see him?
Why can I not see where he is?

Playing the zither of *twenty-five* strings[24] in the moonlight,
I cannot restrain my sorrow.
Wild goose, where are you going?
On your way to Seoul,
Take a message to my beloved
Who lives in Samch'ŏng Street.
Note every detail of how I look now,
Do not, by any means, forget.

Pyŏn orders the soldiers to put Ch'unhyang in a cangue and take her to prison. Ch'unhyang prizes her chastity so highly that she is willing to die for it. Not to marry twice, or not to serve two husbands, was a general norm of Confucian morality—indeed, Confucian

---

24. Holsinger, in *Music, Body, and Desire in Medieval Culture*, comments on "pain's fundamental audibility . . . that produce(s) sounds that can be heard and felt (192–194)," "a commonplace association between torture and song" (198), and "devotional writers (who) imagined . . . the unique propensity of musical sonority to embody and channel extreme somatic experience, particularly pain" (208). Here one can say that the unremittent percussive beatings felt by Ch'unhyang's body in pain produce her song.

discourse emphasized it for several centuries. Ch'unhyang wishes to preserve the dignity of a married woman. Even a lowborn has the freedom to maintain human dignity.

In prison Ch'unhyang sings:

WHAT WAS MY CRIME?

What was my crime?
I've not stolen government grain.
Why was I beaten so savagely?
I've not killed anyone.
Why was I put in a yoke and fettered?
I've not plotted rebellion,
Why was I bound hand and foot?
I've not committed adultery,
What is this punishment for?
The waters of three rivers for ink,
The blue sky for paper,
I'll protest my sorrow
And petition the Jade Emperor.
My heart burns with longing for my husband.
My sigh becomes a wind
That blows those flames;
I shall die in vain.
The single chrysanthemum,
Its constancy is great!
The green pine in the snow
Has kept faith for myriad years.
The green pine is like me,
The yellow chrysanthemum like my husband.
My sad thoughts—
What I shed are tears,
What soak me are sighs.
My sighs as a wind,

My tears as a drizzle,
The wind will drive the muzzling rain,
Blowing and splashing
To wake my beloved.
Herd Boy and Weaver Maid,
Meeting on the seventh night,
Never broke a promise
Even when the Silver River blocked them.
What water then divides me
From where my husband is?
I never hear news from him.
Rather than live in longing,
It's better to die and forget him—
Better to die
And become a cuckoo in the empty hills,
At the third watch when
The pear blossoms are white beneath the moon,
To sing sadly in my husband's ears;
Or become a mandarin duck on the clear river,
Calling in search of its mate,
And show him
My love and tender feelings;
Or become a butterfly in spring
With two scented wings,
Glorying in the spring sun,
And settle on his clothes;
Or become a bright moon in the sky,
Rising when night comes
And shedding my bright light
On my beloved's face.
With stagnant blood from my innards
I'd draw his likeness,
Hang it as a scroll on my door
To see when I go in and out.
A peerless beauty, chaste and faithful,

Has been treated cruelly.
Like white jade of Mount Jing[25]
Buried in dirt,
Like a fragrant herb of Mount Shang[26]
Buried in weeds,
Like a phoenix that played in the beech tree
Making its nest in the thorn patch . . .
From olden days sages and worthies
Died innocent—
Benevolent rulers like Yao, Shun, Yu, Tang
Were imprisoned
By evil Jie and Zhou
But were set free and became holy lords.
King Wen of Zhou
Who ruled the people with bright virtue,
Was imprisoned in Yuli by Zhou of Shang.
Confucius, greatest of all the sages,
Because he looked like Yang Huo,
Was imprisoned in Kongye,[27]
But he became a great sage—
When I think of these things,
Will my innocent body
Live to see the world again?
Stifling sorrow!
Who will come to rescue me?
Would my husband in Seoul
Come here as an official
And save me
Close to death?
Summer clouds on strange peaks—

25. *Han Feizi* 4:13–14; Watson, *Han Fei Tzu*, 80–83.
26. Four white beards retired to Mount Shang at the end of the Qin; *Shiji* 55:2044–2045.
27. Yang seized power in Lu (505 BCE) and the people of Kuang mistook Confucius for Yang. *Lunyu* 9:5; Waley, *Analects*, 139, 244–245.

Do the high hills block his way?
Will he come only when the highest peaks
Of the Diamond Mountains are flat?
Will he come only when at the fourth watch
A yellow crane painted on the screen
Stretches its wings
And caws at dawn?
Aego, aego, my wretched fate!

Her only hope is her husband, who must come as an official, for only such a person has the power to chastise the evil magistrate Pyŏn. Her song ends on a note of impossibility: the Diamond Mountains becoming flat, and a painted yellow crane, another symbol of the nobility of mind, crowing at dawn.

While dozing in prison, Ch'unhyang has a dream. When a blind man passes by the prison, Ch'unhyang asks him to divine her fortune.

CH'UNHYANG'S DREAM

Your dream is a good one.
When the flower falls, the fruit can form;
When the mirror breaks, the sound is loud,
Only when it bears fruit
Will the flower fall.
If the mirror breaks,
Should there not be a sound?
A scarecrow over the door
Makes everyone look up;
When the sea runs dry,
You can see the dragon's face.
When the mountain crumbles, the earth becomes flat.
Good! It's a dream that foretells
You'll ride on a sedan chair drawn by two horses.
(Ch'unhyang sees a crow cawing twice overhead;
She raises her hands to shoo it away.)

Just a moment! Doesn't the crow caw *kaok kaok?*
That's good.
Ka is a graph for good;
Ok for a house.
A beautiful joyful event will come;
Your lifelong sorrow will end.
Don't worry at all.
Even if you were to pay me a thousand *yang,*
I wouldn't take it.
Wait and see.
When you gain riches and honor,
Don't pass me over.
Now I'll take my leave.

Meanwhile, Yi in Seoul studies day and night and passes his civil service examinations with distinction. The king compliments him and appoints him a secret royal inspector of Chŏlla province, the post he has wanted. Then he directs his agents and soldiers to meet in Namwŏn on such and such a day. Accompanied by one or two lower-ranking officials, his routine is to walk around in disguise, wearing tattered clothes and a crushed cap.[28] As a secret inspector, he is not expected to inconvenience the village chief, and he often carries his own dried cooked rice and camps outside the village. When necessary he displays the horse warrant[29] to disclose his identity. If he finds a corrupt magistrate, he confiscates the magistrate's official seal and dismisses him from office.

Half-dreaming and half-awake, Ch'unhyang thinks her husband has come, with a gilded cap on his head and a black-rimmed red court

28. Yi's disguise has a narrative function in the *Song.* It conceals his social persona (comprising his status, education, and speech), and since he can preserve the secret of his identity from all save his own wife, her maid, and his mother-in-law, the narrative's disguise episodes generate comic, ironic, or dramatic effect depending on whom he encounters.

29. Usually with the image of two horses engraved on one side that confirm his authority to mobilize soldiers and servants and use horses kept at the stations.

robe. They embrace each other and begin to talk of myriad dear memories. When she hears him calling, she asks: "Is that voice real or in a dream? It's a strange voice."

To Wŏlmae: "What are you talking about? You say my husband has come. Can I see him in reality? (She grasps his hand between the bars and immerses herself in memories and grief.)

To her husband: "*Aego, aego!* Is it really you? I must be dreaming. Now I can easily see the one I have longed for. I have no regrets even if I should die. Why were you so heartless? Mother and I are wretched. Since you left, I have passed days and nights thinking of you; for days and months my heart has been burning. I have been beaten till I was almost dead. Have you come to save me? I don't care whether I live or die, but what has happened to you?"

To her mother: "I longed for my husband in Seoul as people long for rain after seven years of drought. Did he long for me? A tree planted gets rotten, the stūpa built with labor collapses. Alas, there is no help for my lot. Mother, please let me feel no regret after I'm gone. The silk coat I used to wear is in the inlaid wardrobe. Please take it out and exchange it for the best ramie cloth from Hansan and make him a decent coat. Sell my white skirt and buy him a horsehair hat, headband, and shoes. My silver hairpin shaped like a rice cake with imprinted flower patterns, my encased ceremonial knife with amber handle, my jade ring in the box—sell them too and make him an unlined inner jacket and short pants. Sell the contents in the drawers of the wardrobes with dragon and phoenix designs for what you can get and use the money to buy him some dainty side dishes. After I am dead, look after him as though I were still alive."

To her husband: "Listen, my beloved husband. Tomorrow is the magistrate's birthday. If he gets drunk, he will probably summon me, and with unkempt hair tied up on my head, I will stagger to the yamen and be beaten to death. You must pick up my body like a hired man and take it to Lotus Hall, where we spent our first nights. Then lay me out with your own hands in a quiet place, dress me for burial, and comfort my soul. Please don't remove my clothes but bury me as I am in a sunny place. Then, after you have achieved high office, come back and rebury me in a fine linen shroud. Have me borne in a simple but elegant bier, not to the front or back of Mount South, but straight to Seoul, and bury me near your ancestral plot. On my epitaph carve eight graphs: "Grave of Ch'unhyang, Chaste Wife, Unjustly Killed." It will serve as a legend for a constant wife who awaited her husband, perished, and finally turned to stone. The sun that sets behind the western hills will rise again tomorrow; but poor Ch'unhyang, once gone, will never return. Requite my wrongs. *Aego, aego!* My wretched lot! My poor mother will lose me, and destitute, will become a beggar, asking for food from house to house and dozing off here and there beneath the hill. When her strength fails, the jackdaws from Mount Chiri, flapping their wings and cawing, will peck out her eyes since no one will be standing by to scare them away. *Aego, aego!*"

At Pyŏn's birthday party, Yi is given a seat and proposes that everyone compose a verse on a given rhyme. His heptasyllabic quatrain goes:

> Fine wine in a golden cup is a thousand people's blood,
>> Viands on jade dishes are a thousand people's flesh.
> When the grease of the candle drips, the people's tears are falling;
>> When the noise of music is loud, the people's grudges grow louder.

Pyŏn and his officials fail to fathom the intent of the verse. Yi summons his troops, who shout, "The royal inspector comes!" Yi removes Pyŏn from office and suspends his corrupt officials. Ch'unhyang, together with others wrongly jailed, is brought in. Yi then puts his wife to the test ("Will you refuse to be my mistress?"), and she makes the last public declaration of her fidelity: "All you officials who come here are indeed notorious. Please listen to me, inspector in embroidered robes! Can the wind break the layered rocks of a cliff? Can the snow change the verdure of the pine and bamboo? Do not ask such a thing. Have me killed quickly." Only then does the inspector say: "Raise your eyes and look at me!" When she sees that the new inspector on the dais is none other than her own husband, she laughs and cries at the same time. There is no limit to her joy.

Mask Dance Plays

With their origin in village rituals and festivals, the Pukch'ŏng mask dance and Hahoe *pyŏlsin* mask play still retain the features of ceremony. The Pongsan mask dance play in Hwanghae, the Yangju *pyŏlsandae* around Seoul, and the T'ongyŏng *Ogwangdae* in South Kyŏngsang, by contrast, show evidence of development in the direction of drama. They are performed by masked actors and involve both dance and dialogue. Each play consists of several acts that are independent of one another. A modicum of conflict smacking of folk humor and farce can be found in the roles of the old monk, the gentleman, and the old woman. In the Yangju *pyŏlsandae* play, when the old monk and young shaman are about to be joined, Ch'wibari (the young rake) enters, takes the shaman away, and impregnates her. In the Pongsan mask dance play, the old woman and the young girl fight for the favor of a man. The victory of the young man and woman is interpreted as originating from the ceremony for the god of fertility. In the gentleman (*saennim*) scene of the Yangju *pyŏlsandae* play, the servant Malttugi ridicules three brothers who are portrayed as foolish hypocrites trying to hide their incapacity, while the servant is portrayed as a figure of spirit and wit who exposes their hypocrisy.

YANGJU *PYŎLSANDAE* PLAY

Performed on the eighth day of the fourth month, the fifth of the fifth month, and the fifteenth of the eighth month in Yangju, Kyŏnggi, the Yangju *pyŏlsandae* is thought to have followed the pattern of the *Pon sandae* play of the Seoul area, which is now lost. The character and sequence of eight scenes resemble those of the Pongsan mask dance play. In the following scene, the *saennim* (a member of the literati; translated as "gentleman") is ridiculed and humiliated.

Scene 7: Gentleman

Malttugi, servant of the gentleman and son of the old man
Soettugi, servant of the gentleman
Saennim, prudish gentleman-scholar
Sŏbangnim, young master
Toryŏnnim, young bachelor of the literati family

MALTTUGI (*enters with Saennim, Sŏbangnim, and Toryŏnnim and stands facing the musicians. Soettugi and his wife are already present in front of the musicians*): Servant at a temporary lodging!

SOETTUGI: What motherfucker comes to me—who's on inside duty at a government office—and shouts "Servant at a temporary lodging"?

MALTTUGI: You motherfucker! You say you do an indoor job when people are crowding the hills and fields?

SOETTUGI: "Motherfucker"! What kind of talk is that? Even when people are bustling about all over the hills and fields, when a husband and wife sit together, that is an "indoor job."

MALTTUGI: I see. You two are sitting, and you call it an "indoor job."

SOETTUGI: Right!

MALTTUGI: You motherfucker. I'm glad to hear your voice.

SOETTUGI: (*abruptly stands up and bows*): Hey there!

MALTTUGI: Hey! I haven't seen you for a long time—like straws in the gruel for the cattle. Do you have pain in your cock?[1]

---

1. *Chok* (foot, or penis).

SOETTUGI: Oh, my cock!

MALTTUGI: Hey, by the way, I'm hard up.

SOETTUGI: What's the matter?

MALTTUGI: My young master and a young bachelor were on their
way to take the civil service examination, but they got so
obsessed with sightseeing that they lost count of how many
days had passed. Now they're asking me to find temporary
lodging for them. But I don't have any close friends or relatives
here. In the midst of all the bustling, night fell and I didn't know
what to do. But I've met you at just the right time. Please, find
us some temporary lodging.

SOETTUGI: Hey! Those fuckers are crazy about sightseeing and asked
you to find lodging? All right. You must be in a fix. I'll try to
find something. (*circles around the playground several times,
saying he's looking for lodging, and stops in front of Malttugi*)
I've found a place.

MALTTUGI: I drove a few stakes in the ground, enclosed them with
belts, and made a door facing the sky.

SOETTUGI: Fuck! That thing must look like a Western-style house.

MALTTUGI: Right! Well then. When those bastards try to enter, they'll
have to stand on their heads.

SOETTUGI: Right!

MALTTUGI: Hey there! That gentleman is outside, so I've got to bring
him in.

SOETTUGI: Why should I invite those motherfuckers in?

MALTTUGI: Whatever you say, there's no other way. Considering our
good friendship, you're the one to bring them in.

SOETTUGI: I see. Considering our good friendship and your situation,
that's right.

MALTTUGI: Are you sure?

SOETTUGI: Yes. (*Soettugi stands in front of the group while Malttugi
stands in the back holding a whip. In between stand the*

gentleman-scholar, young master, and young bachelor. He
wields his whip and, saying "oink oink oink," walks them into
a pigpen in the middle of the playground.)

GENTLEMAN: Hey, Malttugi!

MALTTUGI: Yes, sir!

GENTLEMAN: Who found this temporary lodging?

MALTTUGI: I didn't find it, sir, because I've got no relatives here. And
not knowing where to go during the rush hour, I asked a fellow
I know named Soettugi to help, and he found it.

GENTLEMAN: I see. It's very tidy and clean—I like it.

MALTTUGI: We decided to find a two-story place because, being sons
of the gentleman, you might prefer two parts so that you can
smoke without disturbing others.

GENTLEMAN: I see.

SOETTUGI: (*to Malttugi*): What's your position in the house?

MALTTUGI: I'm a steward.

SOETTUGI: You rascal! Let's see. Why does a steward wear a split-
bamboo hat worn by lowly fellows?

MALTTUGI: No, that isn't so. I'm a secondary son of that family.

SOETTUGI: I see. You're a secondary son.

MALTTUGI: Well, then. Go inside and greet the gentleman-scholar.

SOETTUGI: Why should I greet that motherfucker?

MALTTUGI: Because when that gentleman holds a position, he'll
advance by climbing the ladder of success. Then you'll find
some sort of job.

SOETTUGI: Well, maybe so. His voice tells me he'll be an important
person. He looks like dried inner bark of arrowroot.

MALTTUGI: He'll be sure to hold an official position. Go see him.

SOETTUGI: (*circles around the gentlemen to the tune of* t'aryŏng *and*
upon seeing them, says): I thought you were a son of the
gentleman, but you're nothing more than a mongrel. With a
cloth beancurd wrapper on your cap, a flower in your hand, full

dress attire, and a knapsack on your back, you must be the son of a male shaman. (*to the young master*) You've a cap, all right, full dress, a flower fan, and a knapsack on your back. You're the son of a male shaman, too. Bad fellows? (*to the young bachelor*) You wear a villain's cap and a military uniform, a knapsack on your back, and a fan in your hand. This fellow can't possibly be a son of the gentleman. (*coming to Malttugi*) Hey! I looked at them and found that they're sons of male shamans, not from the ruling class.

MALTTUGI: You may be right. But their family is so poor, they had to rent their clothing from a store. That's why the colors don't match.

SOETTUGI: Right! In any case, they're not sons of the literati.

GENTLEMAN: Malttuk!

MALTTUGI: Yes, sir.

GENTLEMAN: Damn fellow! Where have you been?

MALTTUGI: I've been looking for you.

GENTLEMAN: Where?

MALTTUGI: After I brushed the pony, fitted him with a tigerskin saddle, and rode to Mount South in front and Mount South outside, Ssanggye-dong, Pyŏkkye-dong, passed Ch'ilp'ae, P'alp'ae, Tolmoru, quietly crossed Tongjak-tong, then entered through South Gate, passed by One Gan Jang, Two Mok Ward, Three Ch'ŏng-dong, Four Jik Hill, Five Palace Sites, Six Ministries, Seven Kwanan, Octagonal Pass, Nine Rigae, Ten Cha Pavilion, and Tabang-kol, alias Child's Head, Kamt'ujŏn-kol, alias Adult's Head, then crossed Harelip's Bridge, Blind-man's Bridge, then to Paeugae, and Annnegŏri,[2] and then I searched up and down and looked around but could not even find a puppy or children of yours. So I asked an old friend, who

2. A list of street names in old Seoul, cleverly arranged based on puns.

told me you went to the playground. So here I came and looked for you all over. And then I found you, my great-grandson's only son.

SOETTUGI: (*upon hearing what Malttugi has said*): Hey, hey, hey! I didn't want to let him into the house. But when I thought about the favor I might ask from him later, I decided I had no choice but to greet him.

MALTTUGI: Do it then!

SOETTUGI: Sir, another man's servant inquires after your health. If you receive me improperly, you'll be beheaded and posthumously punished and your bones will be broken to smithereens. (*enters to pay his respects. Pressing his hands together in front while thrusting his right foot forward, he enters frivolously.*) Ah, gentleman, I . . . (*The scholar is silent. After bowing to him, Soettugi returns to Malttugi.*) Hey, he might be a real noble; he is dignified.

MALTTUGI: No question about it. He's a reserved person.

SOETTUGI: Well, what kind of family does he come from?

MALTTUGI: His family is like this. On Moving Day, they open the door of the household shrine, twine a straw rope a span long, and pull one end of it. Then they come out in a row and put one of their legs in the dog dish while keeping the other leg out and making "slurp slurp" sounds. That kind of family.

SOETTUGI: They're pigs, then.

MALTTUGI: Right! Go greet the young master.

SOETTUGI: (*going to him*): Ah, young master . . . (*looking at him*) I . . . (*comes to Malttugi*) He is a real gentleman.

MALTTUGI: When you bow to the gentleman-scholar, he looks like a dog's bottom. When you bow to the young master, he looks like a dog's butt. The last person over there is the young bachelor from the main family. Go and greet him sincerely. If not, you'll be beheaded and posthumously punished till not a bone remains. Go!

SOETTUGI: I think it likely. I've got no choice but to go.

MALTTUGI: To discuss the gentleman's family is our fault.

SOETTUGI: (*going to the young bachelor*): Ah, young bachelor! Young bachelor!

TORYŎNNIM: Are you well?

SOETTUGI: (*coming to Malttugi*): He was a true-blue gentleman. If we greet the likes of him, some would ask, "Are your mom and dad fucking well?" But instead he asked whether I was well. He is a dignified gentleman.

MALTTUGI: Of course!

SOETTUGI: Hey, hey! I've got no choice but to greet him again.

MALTTUGI: What do you plan to do?

SOETTUGI: If I couldn't have a cup of wine, I'd sweep the upper and lower courtyards clean. After one cup, two cups, or three cups, my face would get ruddy, I'd go visit the upper and lower houses, shuck all available clams,[3] old and new, and say I'm a disciple of Soettugi who loves to eat Yonghae Yongdong mackerel, shad, yellowtail, conch.

MALTTUGI: What a fucking long greeting that is. That's all right. Look here, gentleman-scholar. Someone's servant Soettugi asked me to convey his greetings to you. If you receive them improperly, you'll be beheaded and posthumously punished, and not one piece of your bones will remain. He's one who would sweep the upper and lower houses when he couldn't have a single cup of wine. And after one cup, two cups, or three cups, his face would turn ruddy and he'd travel between the upper and lower houses, shucking all the available clams, old and new, and eating Yonghae Yongdong mackerel, shad, yellowtail, and conch such as young fellows come to shuck and eat.

GENTLEMAN: (*abruptly opening his fan*): Look, you!

MALTTUGI: Yes, sir.

---

3. Clams (vagina).

GENTLEMAN: By saying such absurd things, you've behaved excessively badly to the gentleman who's been traveling on the
streets. Where on earth can you find such motherfuckers? (*sits,
dignified*) Malttuk!

MALTTUGI: Yes, sir.

GENTLEMAN: Arrest the servant Soettugi and bring him here.

MALTTUGI: (*carries the struggling Soettugi upside down*): I've arrested and brought him, sir!

GENTLEMAN: What happened to that fellow's face? Did he fight in
the Chŏngju campaign?

MALTTUGI: No, sir. I'm bringing him upside down so your mother
won't swoon and die when she sees him.

GENTLEMAN: Then pull out his head and turn him around so I can
see his face.

MALTTUGI: Yes, I've done it. (*turns Soettugi quickly*)

GENTLEMAN: What's that wriggling behind?[4]

MALTTUGI: That's what your mother plays with at night.

GENTLEMAN: Damn you!

SOETTUGI: Motherfucker, I've definitely got a name. But why do you
call me "damn you"?

GENTLEMAN: Look, damn you! If you have a name, what is it?

SOETTUGI: Yes, I've got a name fit for you to call. The letters *a* in
adang and *pon* in *pongae*.

GENTLEMAN: *A* in *adang, pongae pon?*

SOETTUGI: No, not that way. As a gentleman you studied the *Thou-
sand Sinograph Primer*, which begins "*hanŭl ch'ŏn tta chi*" . . .
Don't you read it straight down as "*ch'ŏn chi hyŏn hwang*"?
You should read my name straight down as well.

GENTLEMAN: *Pŏna* . . .

SOETTUGI: Why do you read in the opposite way?

---

4. Refers to the penis.

GENTLEMAN: That motherfucker's name is quite uncanny and coarse. *Aaa!*

SOETTUGI: You behave rampageously. Quick, combine the two letters together. Otherwise it's futile to call them out for ten years and three months.

GENTLEMAN: (*finally*): *Abon.*[5]

MALTTUGI: Yes.

GENTLEMAN: (*insulted by his own servant, he is indignant*): Pardon servant Soettugi, but arrest my servant Malttugi.

SOETTUGI: Yes. That's a smart command. (*Snatches Malttugi's hat and puts it on and snatches his whip and holds it in his hand.*) Since you frequent the gentleman's household, you've wielded power. But you, damn fellow, you lost your power ten years ago. What once rose must fall. I'll make you suffer.

MALTTUGI: Ah, you're drunk.

SOETTUGI: Wine? What wine? Let's go! Let's go. (*Leads Malttugi and goes in.*) According to your order, sir, I've arrested him and brought him here.

GENTLEMAN: Lay him down and flog him. Give him a single stroke, then a pretend stroke, then strike him severely.

SOETTUGI: Yes, sir! That's a smart order. (*to himself*) Your eyes tell me you're a fellow who would take money from a child. What crime has he committed to deserve flogging? (*When he is ready to strike, Malttugi says he'll pay money if he strikes lightly. Soettugi nods.*)

GENTLEMAN: Look, damn you.

SOETTUGI: Yes, sir!

GENTLEMAN: You two schemed to fuck your mothers?

SOETTUGI: No, sir. He thinks if I flog him he'll die in your presence and asked me to give him a pretend stroke.

GENTLEMAN: No!

5. Father.

SOETTUGI: Then what is it? I'm in a tight situation.

GENTLEMAN: No!

SOETTUGI: He'll give you ten *yang* without fail.

GENTLEMAN: No!

SOETTUGI: What shall I do? I'll add five *yang* more and make it fifteen *yang*. Fifteen!

GENTLEMAN: Fifteen *yang?*

SOETTUGI: Does that sound attractive to you?

GENTLEMAN: Damn fellow!

SOETTUGI: Yes, sir!

GENTLEMAN: The person sitting in the last seat is the young bachelor from the main family. It's been nineteen years since he received the wedding gifts from his future family. Send fourteen *yang,* nine *ton,* and nine *p'un,* five *ri* to his family.[6] And with the remainder buy yourself a cup of wine, mix it with cold water, and drink. Then you'll get diarrhea like the runs you get after eating a lot of turnips in December, and then drop dead.

SOETTUGI: Yes, gentleman-scholar. It is a smart order. (*The gentleman's group exits through the musicians' section.*)

MALTTUGI (*standing*):

> In the deep green waters and blue hills,
> Green-yellow dragons wiggle . . .

(*Malttugi and Soettugi dance facing each other and exit.*)

6. All are traditional monetary units: one *ton* (0.1325 ounces) is equivalent to ten *p'un;* which is equivalent to ten *ri.*

Puppet Play

The puppet play is performed by a group of roving actors who tour the country. The stage is a desk, covered with white cloth, big enough for three men to crouch behind. The puppeteer hides behind the stage, manipulates the puppets, and engages in dialogue. Like the mask dance play, the puppet play consists of a number of scenes, some featuring a gentleman and an old woman. But it also includes scenes absent from mask dance plays such as Hong Tongji's subduing of a large snake in Yonggang, the building and demolishing of a temple, and the falconry scene excerpted below.

Also known as the Pak Ch'ŏmji or Hong Tongji play, *Kkoktu kaksi* is the only puppet play preserved in Korea. It has been designated Korea's Intangible Cultural Asset No. 3. The falconry scene exposes the oppressive behavior of the power-wielding official, and in it the naked Hong shatters the governor's authority. Pak Ch'ŏmji acts as actor, narrator, and commentator. The family names of these characters reflect their identities: Pak, the white-haired old man, is homonymous with *pak* "gourd," and Hong is homonymous with *hong* "red." The puppet for Hong Tongji is painted red from head to toe.

KKOKTU KAKSI

The Falconry Scene

PAK: Hey! We're in trouble.
MUSICIAN: What's the trouble now?
PAK: The governor of P'yŏngan is arriving.
(*Pak exits, the governor enters.*)
MUSICIAN: Well, that's a problem.

GOVERNOR: Are you Pak or Mang?

PAK: Hey, who's looking for me?

MUSICIAN: The governor is looking for you.

PAK: (*goes near*): Yes, I'm at your service.

GOVERNOR: Are you Pak?

PAK: Yes, I'm Pak or Mang.

GOVERNOR: If you're Pak, listen. Who has improved the road? Arrest him and bring him in.

PAK: Yes, sir. Hey! We're in trouble.

MUSICIAN: Why do you say that?

PAK: I've been ordered to arrest the one who did the road repairs and bring him in.

MUSICIAN: Of course, we should arrest him. Leave it to me.

PAK: Let's do it your way.

MUSICIAN: Hey, Chindung!

HONG: (*from inside*): I'm having a meal.

MUSICIAN: Whether you have food or whatever, you have a windfall coming. Come quickly.

HONG: (*the back of his head appearing first*): Why, what's up?

MUSICIAN: You rascal! You came out the wrong way.

HONG: (*turning around*): No wonder it was dark in front. Why did you call me?

MUSICIAN: The governor says you did a good job on road improvements and wishes to reward you. Hurry to him.

HONG: Yes, I've got to go. (*approaches the governor*) Yes? I wait for your order, sir.

GOVERNOR: Are you the rascal who improved the road?

HONG: Yes, sir.

GOVERNOR: Commander!

COMMANDER: Yes, sir.

GOVERNOR: Turn him facedown and flog his buttocks. What kind of road repairs leave my horse's legs all broken? (*The director approaches Hong to flog him.*)

HONG: Yes, yes! I'm sorry. I'll do as you command.

GOVERNOR: I'll forgive you this time only. Withdraw at once! (*Hong exits, farting. The governor is about to exit, but enters again.*)

PAK: Look here. The governor was about to go on an outing. But seeing a high fortress, he thinks there must be a lot of pheasants and is ready to go out for a pheasant hunt.

MUSICIAN: Tell him to come out.

PUPPET MASTER: (*from inside*): P'yŏngan governor's pheasant hunt!

MUSICIAN 1: P'yŏngan governor's pheasant hunt!

MUSICIAN 2: Governor, governor, pheasant hunt!

PUPPET MASTER: (*from inside*): Governor, governor's hawking.

GOVERNOR: Hey, Pak or Mang!

PAK: Who's calling me?

MUSICIAN: The governor is.

PAK: (*goes near him*): Yes, sir!

GOVERNOR: Are you Pak? If so, listen. I found the high fortress good, and pheasants must be there. So I'm out for a pheasant hunt. Go quickly and engage an advance guard.

MUSICIAN: You, old man! Go over there and keep watch. I'll engage an advance guard. Hey, Chingdung over the hill!

HONG: (*from inside*): I'm relieving myself.

MUSICIAN: Come out quickly.

HONG: What do you say?

MUSICIAN: Instead of eating three or four times a day and idling, try working for wages for the governor. He wants a chaser.

HONG: How much will he pay?

MUSICIAN: Ten thousand *yang*.

HONG: I'll go then. (*He approaches the governor.*) Yes, sir!

GOVERNOR: Are you naked?

HONG: No, sir! I've put on my aunt's blouse and pants.

GOVERNOR: That rascal is using a vulgar allusion. Damn rascal! The bush clover field is infested with crawling insects. Get rid of them to the best of your ability. (*Hong butts Pak in the brow with his head and pretends to chase the pheasants. Everyone present mimics hunting pheasants.*) Hey, Pak!

PAK: Who's calling me?

MUSICIAN: The governor wishes to reward you for engaging a good chaser.

PAK: Yes, Pak or Mang is coming!

GOVERNOR: If you are Pak, listen. Thanks to the advance guard you engaged, we had a good hunt. But I've got no travel money for the return trip, so go and sell one pheasant quickly.

PAK: I've already prepared a hundred and fifty *yang,* so please cross the hill with my younger brother as a guide.

GOVERNOR: Good. Good-bye.

PAK: He is gentle. Obscenely gentle. (*Pak follows the governor and exits.*)

The Bier Scene

PAK: Hush! I'm in trouble.

MUSICIAN: What's up?

PAK: On his way home with the pheasants, the governor took a nap at Tongsŏl Ridge in Hwangju and was bitten in the balls by ants. He died instantly.

MUSICIAN: Then a bier will show up.

PAK: Right. (*The sound of a pallbearers' procession.* Oho ohae iya . . . *The bier enters, followed by Pak.*) Oh my, oh my, oh my.

MUSICIAN: Hello, old man.

PAK: Yeah.

MUSICIAN: Whose bier is that where they weep so sadly?

PAK: Isn't it ours?

MUSICIAN: You wretched fellow. That's the governor's.

PAK: I thought it was ours. That's why no tears came no matter how much I wept. Somehow I thought it was pointless.

MUSICIAN: What a fool you are!

PAK: Shucks. Look, let's watch the procession. Oh, how well it's fixed up! P'yŏngan is a big province, so we get Confucian students with double biers carrying seven-*p'un* coins. Oh, what a foul smell! He died without farting. Hey look! Is there a funeral tablet?

MUSICIAN: Of course.

PAK: Where?

MUSICIAN: There in front.

PAK: Ah, there it is. *Hoi hoi.* (*mimics reading*) Ha ha ha.

MUSICIAN: Why do you laugh?

PAK: It reads: "Nameless Person's Coffin."

MUSICIAN: Does it mean a bier without a chief mourner? You can see the chief mourner there, so you'll pay dearly if you say such nonsense.

PAK: What? What? There's a chief mourner?

CHIEF MOURNER: What did you say, damn rascal?

PAK: Yes, yes! I said it was a splendid procession.

CHIEF MOURNER: Well then. All right.

PAK: Let's express our condolences.

CHIEF MOURNER: Good idea.

PAK: *Oi oi oi.*

CHIEF MOURNER: *Kkolgo naego . . .*[1]

PAK: Hey, you! What kind of chief mourner is that who doesn't say "*aigo*" when I say "*oi*," but says "*kkolgo naego*"?

MUSICIAN: Ah, because he lacks sense.

PAK: Even if he lacks sense, let me try again. *Oi oi.* (*pretends to keen*)

CHIEF MOURNER: *Kkolgo naego . . .* A beggar from last year survived and returned. Yŏngdŏk Hall is newly built, and a record that dates from when the beam was put up follows the rules.

---

1. The keening of the mourner is humorously imitated.

PAK: What an eccentric chief mourner he is! A chief mourner sings the beggar's song. Hell, I'm leaving.

CHIEF MOURNER: Hey, Pak!

PAK: Are you looking for a certain Pak who looked for wooden shoes with clogs on a rainy day?

MUSICIAN: The chief mourner wishes to reward you for your good repair work on the road. Go quickly to him.

PAK: Yes.

CHIEF MOURNER: Are you Pak?

PAK: Darn! How disgusting! He's still wet behind the ears but calls me Pak or Mang. Even if he is a chief grave keeper, it's "Hey Pak, hey Mang." Yes, whether I am a Pak or a Mang . . .

CHIEF MOURNER: If you're Pak, listen. Several days have passed since we heard a rumor that the procession was coming. How have you improved the road if the pallbearers have all sprained an ankle? You'd better engage one new bearer.

PAK: Ho ho! Is this a reward? Pallbearers sprained an ankle, so engage a new one.

MUSICIAN: I'll get one, so you go back home. Hey hey, Chindung across the hill!

HONG: (*from inside*): After a bit of rice, now I'm relieving myself.

MUSICIAN: It is rotting! Come out quickly!

HONG: All right.

MUSICIAN: Damn fellow! You came out from the side.

HONG: I thought it was funny.

MUSICIAN: Damn you! You're going to be rich. For the governor of P'yŏngan's funeral party is looking for a day laborer.

HONG: Whose funeral?

MUSICIAN: P'yŏngan governor's.

HONG: Oh, it is a rich man's then. Are there rice cakes?

MUSICIAN: Of course.

HONG: Wine too?

MUSICIAN: Wine too.

HONG: Dried persimmons and dates too?

MUSICIAN: Of course!

HONG: Lentil pancakes too?

MUSICIAN: Yes.

HONG: Dog meat soup as well?

MUSICIAN: Damn you! What dog meat soup?

HONG: Then what's there?

MUSICIAN: Everything is there except what isn't there.

HONG: Everything?

MUSICIAN: Yes.

HONG: Then I wish to offer my condolences to the chief mourner.

MUSICIAN: Of course.

HONG: (*goes near*): I bring kind regards.

CHIEF MOURNER: Within the gate or outside, who's that naked rascal? The naked should not come near.

HONG: Hoho! I came here to carry the bier.

CHIEF MOURNER: That naked fellow can't come near the bier.

HONG: Everything goes wrong! Everything goes wrong! He says the naked can't come near the governor's bier.

MUSICIAN: Yeah, yeah. There is a good plan.

HONG: What?

MUSICIAN: Do what I tell you. Ask whether the mourners and pallbearers have removed their crotches and buried them in the warm part of the room.

HONG: Yeah, yeah. I'd pay dearly for such a remark.

MUSICIAN: It's all right.

HONG: No, I'm afraid.

MUSICIAN: Aren't you the strong man in seven villages?

HONG: Yes, that's right. I'm the strong man of seven villages. If I can't do it with force, then I'll kick with my foot and strike with my fist. If I can't live in this world, then I'll live in the other world . . . (*about to pounce*) Hey, I can't.

MUSICIAN: Damn you! Go on!

HONG: Right! I should try. (*hesitates*) Chief mourner, sir!

CHIEF MOURNER: Why are you calling me?

HONG: Did you and the pallbearers remove your crotch and bury it in the warm part of the room?

CHIEF MOURNER: Oh boy! This naked fellow speaks well. Then carry the bier to the very best of your ability.

HONG: Oh boy! It's done. I trembled with fear for nothing. I'm going to view the funeral procession. There should be bits of rice cakes around here. Yes, I found an apple here.

MUSICIAN: Hey, damn you! That's not an apple. It's the top of the bier.

HONG: I mistook it for an apple. What an awful smell! He must have died without relieving himself.

MUSICIAN: You'll have a hell of a time from the chief mourner.

(*The sound of the procession.* Ohŏ ŏhŏyŏ ŏhŏ ŏhŏyŏ. *They carry the bier, and Hong pushes it with his lower belly.*)

Biographical Notes

An Minyŏng (fl. 1870–1880). A secondary son and professional singer; co-compiler of *Sourcebook of Songs* (*Kagok wŏllyu*, 1876). He was a poet of flowers, noted for addressing ten songs to plum blossoms.

Cho Chonsŏng (1553–1627). A disciple of Sŏng Hon (1535–1598) and Pak Chihwa (1513–1592); passed the higher examination in 1590. During the Japanese invasion he traveled to Ming China seeking military reinforcement; during the Manchu invasion of 1627 he served the crown prince. His four *sijo* are preserved in *Songs of Korea* (*Haedong kayo*, 1763).

Cho Hwi (fl. 1568–1608). Little is known about his career.

Cho Myŏngni (1697–1756). Passed the 1731 examination; served as mayor of Seoul.

Cho Sik (1501–1572). Lived an idyllic life on Mount Turyu (Chiri), never taking office. The *sijo* presented here expresses his sorrow over the death of King Myŏngjong (1545–1567).

Cho Sŏnggi (1638–1689). Scholar and writer; dedicated to learning. Author of "Showing Goodness and Stirred by Rightness" (*Ch'angsŏn kamŭi rok*).

Cho Wihan (1558–1649). Passed the 1601 and 1609 examinations and fought against the Manchu in 1627. Author of "The Story of Ch'oe Ch'ŏk" (*Ch'oe Ch'ŏk chŏn*).

Ch'oe Cha (1188–1260). Passed the 1212 examination and served as a Hallim academician under King Kojong. His works are collected in *Pohan* *chip* (Supplementary jottings in idleness) and *Ch'oe Munch'ŏng kajip* (Works of Ch'oe Cha).

Ch'oe Ch'iwŏn (b. 857). Journeyed to Tang China in 868, where he won the "presented scholar" degree after six years of study. That same year (874), he was appointed secretary to the military commander Gao Bien when the Huang Chao rebellion broke out. He returned to Korea in 885 and is said to have spent his last years at Haein monastery. He was posthumously awarded the title of marquis (1023), and his collected works are published in China. The *Selections of Refined Literature in Korea* (*Tong munsŏn,* 1478) preserves 146 of his poems.

Ch'ŏn Kŭm (d.u.). Little is known about her except for a single *sijo* preserved in the *Hwawŏn akpo,* an anonymous anthology of 650 *sijo* compiled at the end of the nineteenth century.

Chŏng Chisang (d. 1135). Passed the 1114 examination and held a series of court posts, including that of censor (1129). In 1135 he was implicated in a rebellion and executed.

Chŏng Ch'ŏl (1537–1594). Chŏng's political career was turbulent owing to factional strife at court. He was subtle in his use of language, often relying on a cunning juxtaposition that presented a familiar word in a new light. The Sŏngju edition of 1747, the most complete edition of his *Pine River Anthology,* contains five *kasa* and seventy-nine *sijo*. See Peter H. Lee, *Pine River and Lone Peak*, 43–86.

Chŏng Kŭgin (1401–1481). Passed the higher examination in 1453 but retired to a country village when Sejo usurped the throne from Tanjong, his young cousin. He was awarded the posthumous title of minister of rites.

Chŏng Yagyong (1762–1836). Strongly influenced by Catholicism, taking John as his baptismal name; a champion of practical learning. For his ideas on a variety of topics, including land, tools and techniques, the wickedness of petty officials, music, and philosophy, see the selections in *Sourcebook*, vol. 2.

Chŏnggwan, Great Master (1533–1609). Became a monk at age thirteen; a disciple of Great Master Sŏsan (1520–1604).

Ch'ŏyong (fl. 875–886). Author of "Song of Ch'ŏyong" (c. 879), probably the most famous of all Silla songs. Traditionally he was thought to have been a shaman, since he expelled the demon not by confrontation but by means of a song, shaming the demon into submission. His identity remains a topic of speculation.

Chu Ŭisik (1675–1720). Passed the military examination during the reign of Sukchong (1674–1720); a professional singer who left fourteen *sijo*.

Ch'ungdam, Master (fl. c. 742–765). Author of "Statesmanship" and "Ode to Knight Kip'a," a eulogy for a member of the *hwarang*.

Hŏ Kyun (1569–1618). Passed the higher examination in 1594; served as third royal secretary and minister of punishments. Hŏ was executed in 1618 after being accused of participating in a group of secondary sons' plans for a coup. His story "The Tale of Hong Kiltong" (*Hong Kiltong chŏn*) is acknowledged as Korea's first work of fiction in the vernacular.

Hŏ Nansŏrhŏn (1563–1589). Elder sister of Hŏ Kyun. Studied poetry with Yi Tal; her poems in Chinese were well thought of in Ming China and Japan. For translations, see Chang and Saussy, *Women Writers of Traditional China*, 209–215 and 698–700.

Hongnang (fl. 1576–1600). A famous female entertainer from Hongwŏn, South Hamgyŏng. She entertained the poet Ch'oe Kyŏngch'ang on his tour of duty in the north country in 1573; when he was about to return to the capital, she sent him the song presented here.

Hŭimyŏng (fl. 742–765). Author of "Hymn to the Thousand-Eyed Sound Observer."

Hwang Chini (c. 1506–1544). The most famous and most accomplished of all Korean women poets. Hwang lived in Kaesŏng and had a host of admirers; her virtuosity appears most effectively in her love songs.

Hwang Hŭi (1363–1452). Passed the 1389 examination; served King Sejong as chief state counselor for eighteen years. Hwang was known as an incorruptible and beneficent minister.

Hyegyŏng, Princess (1735–1815). Wife of Crown Prince Sado and mother of Chŏngjo; author of *A Record of Sorrowful Days* (*Hanjung nok*).

Im Che (1549–1587). Passed the 1577 examination; a disciple of Sŏng Hon. Scorning the factional strife at court, Im led a retired life. His poetry is known for its bold extravagance. Tradition has it that the song presented here was composed when he visited the tomb of Hwang Chini to pay tribute to her memory.

Inp'yŏng, Prince (1622–1658). Third son of King Injo; taken as a hostage by the Manchu in 1640. Known for his calligraphy and painting, Inp'yŏng became the Korean envoy to Peking in 1650.

Iryŏn (1206–1289). A master of the Meditation school of Korean Buddhism. During the Mongol invasions, Iryŏn compiled the *Memorabilia of the Three Kingdoms* (*Samguk yusa*, 1285), a collection of folktales and other accounts of the early history of the Korean kingdoms, including fourteen Silla songs (*hyangga*) in *hyangch'al* orthography and the first description of Korea's mythical founder, Tangun.

Kakhun (d.u.). Little is known of this scholar monk, except that he was a friend of famous writers such as Yi Illo (1152–1220), Yi Kyubo (1168–1241), and Ch'oe Cha (1188–1260). Yi Illo comments that Kakhun's poetry resembled that of Jia Dao (779–843), a Tang monk who returned to laity and was the author of a collection of verse, *Changjiang ji.*

Kil Chae (1353–1419). After the fall of Koryŏ, Kil refused the honors bestowed upon him by the new dynasty, lived concealed in the countryside, and devoted himself to nurturing disciples. Moved by the pathos of life, he composed the *sijo* presented here.

Kim Ch'anghyŏp (1651–1708). Passed the 1682 examination but consistently declined offers from the court, especially after his own father, Kim Suhang, was ordered to commit suicide in 1689. Kim's reputation as a man of letters and thinker has never been disputed.

Kim Ch'ŏnt'aek (c. 1725–1776). A professional singer and poet; compiled the first anthology of *sijo*, *Songs of Green Hills* (*Ch'ŏnggu yŏngŏn*, 1728). *Songs of Korea* (*Haedong kayo*) contains fifty-seven *sijo* of his.

Kim Ingyŏm (b. 1707). Composed the "Grand Trip to Japan" (*Iltong changyu ka*, 1763) while serving as a secretary on a Korean diplomatic mission to Japan.

Kim Ku (1488–1534). Composed the song presented here to wish King Chungjong a long life during the king's surprise visit to the Office of Special Advisers.

Kim Kwanguk (1580–1656). Passed the 1606 examination; served King Injo during the Manchu invasions. Sent to Peking as an envoy in 1654. Kim is the author of a cycle of fourteen *sijo*, "Songs of Chestnut Village" (*Yulli yugok*), in praise of a simple life.

Kim Manjung (1637–1692). Ranked first in the 1665 higher examination; held a number of official positions, rising to the level of minister. Exiled first to Sŏnch'ŏn, North P'yŏngan, in 1687–1688, for defending the harsh punishment meted out to a high minister, and again to Namhae, South

Kyŏngsang, in 1689. *A Dream of Nine Clouds* was written to console his mother, probably during his first exile. Kim consistently championed the use of the vernacular despite its marginal use and status among the literati of the day.

Kim Sangyong (1561–1637). Passed the 1582 examination; a disciple of Sŏng Hon. When the fortress on Kanghwa Island fell into the hands of the invading Manchu, Kim climbed atop the south gate and blew himself to pieces with gunpowder. He left behind some twenty *sijo*.

Kim Sisŭp (1435–1493). As an infant prodigy, Kim was examined by King Sejong and awarded a royal gift. At the news of Sejo's usurpation of the throne in 1455, he shaved his head and became a tireless traveler. Versed in the meditation schools of Buddhism and Daoism, Kim is the author of *New Stories from Gold Turtle Mountain* (*Kŭmo sinhwa*), a collection of five tales of wonder in literary Chinese. His works are collected in the *Maewŏltang chip* (Works of Kim Sisŭp, 1602).

Kim Sŏnggi (c. 1725–1776). First an archer, then a master of the black zither and other musical instruments; known in his day for his singing voice.

Kim Sujang (1690–1769). Clerk during the reign of Sukchong and a professional singer; compiled *Songs of Korea* (*Haedong kayo*, 1763), in which he is represented by 117 *sijo*.

Kim Yŏng (fl. 1776–1800). Passed the military examination and rose to reach the rank of minister of punishments. He left seven *sijo* songs.

Kim Yuk (1580–1658). Imported European books on algebra and the Western calendar in 1644; as chief state counselor, encouraged land reform and the use of copper cash in 1651. For Kim's contribution to development of a market economy, see *Sourcebook*, 2:73–74 and 110–112.

Kwŏn Homun (1532–1587). Passed the 1561 examination but did not take office and lived below Mount Ch'ŏngsong all his life. A disciple of

Yi Hwang, Kwŏn is the author of a cycle of eighteen *sijo, Hangŏ sipp'al kok*.

Kwŏn P'il (1569–1612). Gifted poet who failed the higher examination by miswriting one sinograph; a disciple of Chŏng Ch'ŏl. Kwŏn had little interest in a worldly career, devoting himself to wine and poetry instead. Eventually caught up in political intrigue, he was exiled at the age of forty-two and took his life on the way there.

Kyerang (Yi Hyanggŭm, 1513–1550). Famous entertainer from Puan, North Chŏlla; adept at poetry, the black zither, and dance. Using the pen name "Plum Window," she left some seventy pieces in Korean and Chinese, but her collected works are no longer extant.

Kyunyŏ, Great Master (923–973). Buddhist exegete and poet; his songs were translated into Chinese by Ch'oe Haenggwi in 967, and his biography was written by Hyŏngnyŏn Chŏng in 1075.

Maeng Sasŏng (1360–1438). Renowned minister in the early fifteenth century; known as a man with a pure heart and clean hands.

Myŏngok (late 16th cent.). Little is known about her, except that she was an entertainer from Suwŏn with the professional name "Bright Jade."

Nam, Lady, of Ŭiryŏng (1727–1823). Educated lady who wrote travel records and diaries in the vernacular; author of "Viewing the Sunrise."

Nŭngun (d.u.). Little seems to be known about her.

O Cham (fl. 1274–1308). A sycophant of King Ch'ungnyŏl; putative author of "The Turkish Bakery."

Ŏ Sukkwŏn (fl. 1525–1554). Passed the documentary style examination, becoming an instructor of documentary style (1515). He then served in the Office of Diplomatic Correspondence and went to Ming China seven times.

He is remembered for two books: *Kosa ch'waryo* (Selected essentials on verified facts, 1554) and *P'aegwan chapki* (The storyteller's miscellany). See Peter H. Lee, *Story of Traditional Korean Literature*.

Pak Chiwŏn (1737–1805). Champion of practical learning and author of satirical stories exposing the literati to scorn and ridicule. For the diary he kept on a journey to Peking in 1780, see "A Conversation in Peking" in *Sourcebook*, 2:120–125.

Pak Hyogwan (fl. c. 1850–1880). Professional singer and a favorite of Taewŏngun, King Kojong's father. Compiled, with An Minyŏng, the *Sourcebook of Songs* (*Kagok wŏllyu*, 1876). He left thirteen *sijo*.

Pak Illo (1561–1643). Author of sixty-eight *sijo* and seven *kasa*. Pak joined the army in 1592 to fight the Japanese invaders. In 1599 he passed the military examination and became the commander of Chorap'o, a garrison on Kŏje Island. In 1605 he was named a shipmaster in Pusan but ended his military career in the same year. See Peter H. Lee, *Pine River and Lone Peak*, 87–140.

Pak P'aengnyŏn (1417–1456). Passed the 1438 and 1447 examinations; one of the six ministers who plotted the restoration of Tanjong when the usurper Sejo forced the abdication of his fourteen-year-old cousin in 1445. The six were apprehended and tortured to death by Sejo.

Pongnim, Prince (1619–1659). Second son of King Injo; ascended the throne as Hyojong (r. 1649–1659). Having spent eight years of his youth as a hostage in Qing China, he wanted to erase the shame of Manchu subjugation but died before he could realize his ambition.

Pyŏn Wŏngyu (fl. 1881–1884). Interpreter of Chinese who accompanied the Korean ambassador Kim Yunsik to China for talks with Li Hongzhang, the diplomat and general who directed Chinese policy in Korea. Pyŏn was known for his poetry and calligraphy.

Sigyŏngam, Monk (fl. 1270–1350). Learned monk whose essays reflect the perspective of the Korean Meditation school of Buddhism.

Sinch'ung (fl. 737–757). Author of the Silla song "Regret"; became prime minister in 757 and later retired to a cloister.

Sin Hŭm (1566–1628). Passed the 1586 examination, eventually reaching the rank of chief state counselor. Served both Sin Ip and Chŏng Ch'ŏl during the Japanese invasion. He was known as an accomplished scholar of Neo-Confucianism as well as a skilled writer in Chinese.

Sin Sukchu (1417–1475). Passed the 1438 examination; went to Japan as a secretary in the Korean diplomatic mission of 1443. Sin helped King Sejong in his research on East Asian languages and rose to become chief state counselor (1462). His works are collected in the *Pohanjae chip.*

Sŏ Kyŏngdŏk (1489–1546). Passed the examination but preferred a life of retirement at Hwadam, outside the east gate of Kaesŏng. A tireless thinker who devoted his life to the study of Neo-Confucian metaphysics, Sŏ is said to have withstood the charm of Hwang Chini; one source says she was his pupil. For his philosophical position, see *Sourcebook,* 1:607–610.

Sŏng Hon (1535–1598). A man of wide learning who refused to enter public life. During the Japanese invasion, however, he was summoned by the crown prince and served the government. His philosophical position is encapsulated in his correspondence with Yi I; see *Sourcebook,* 1:633–641.

Sŏng Sammun (1418–1456). One of the six martyred ministers who plotted the restoration of Tanjong when the usurper Sejo forced the abdication of his fourteen-year-old cousin in 1445. Sŏng was tortured and quartered, expressing at a crucial moment his undying loyalty to his lord. His works are collected in the *Sŏng Kŭnbo chip* and *Sŏng Kŭnbo sŏnsaeng chip* (or *Maechukhŏn chip*).

Song Sun (1493–1583). Journeyed to Ming China as an envoy in 1547; then retired to Tamyang, South Chŏlla, and led a quiet life.

Sŏngjong, King (1470–1494). Ninth king of Chosŏn. The song presented here was addressed to Yu Hoin, his favorite courtier.

Sŏsan, Great Master (Hyujŏng, 1520–1604). Passed the clerical examination in 1549; took command of the monkish army, by royal command, in 1592. Because of his successful military campaigns, he became a folk hero. See *Sourcebook,* 1:658–665

T'aego, National Preceptor (1301–1382). Became a monk at age thirteen; passed the clerical examination in 1325. In 1346 he went to Yuan China and became a master of the Linji school of meditation. On returning to Korea in 1348, he became royal preceptor of King Kongmin and then national preceptor.

Tŭgo or Tŭgogok (fl. 692–702). Member of the *hwarang* headed by Knight Chungman. The ode presented here was composed to lament his comrade Knight Chukchi's death.

U T'ak (1262–1342). Studied Neo-Confucianism and was versed in the *Book of Changes.* Two songs are attributed to him.

Wŏlmyŏng, Master (fl. c. 742–765). Monk, poet, and author of two Silla songs, "Song of Tuṣita Heaven" and "Requiem for a Dead Sister."

Wŏn Ch'ŏnsŏk (fl. c. 1401–1410). Tutor of Yi Pangwŏn, future king of Chosŏn. The song presented here is one of two attributed to him.

Yi Chehyŏn (1287–1367). Passed the 1301 examination at the age of fifteen; journeyed to Yuan China at least six times to accompany the Korean kings in residence at the Mongol court. Translated into Chinese nine folk songs current in his day, under the title *A Small Collection of Folk Songs*

(*So akpu*). His collected works, first published in 1363, were reprinted in the fifteenth, seventeenth, and nineteenth centuries.

Yi Chŏngbo (1693–1766). Passed the 1732 examination; excelled in calligraphy and poetry in both literary Chinese and the vernacular. He left seventy-eight *sijo*.

Yi Chono (1341–1371). Passed the 1360 examination. The clouds in the *sijo* presented here symbolize villainous courtiers who pursue fame and wealth rather than serve the country and its people.

Yi Chonyŏn (1269–1343). Passed the 1284 examination; served as director of the Office of Royal Decrees. When his advice to King Ch'unghye to amend a wanton lifestyle was not heeded, Yi resigned.

Yi Hyanggŭm. *See* Kyerang.

Yi Illo (1152–1220). Ranked first in the 1180 examination; served fourteen years in the academy of letters and office of historiography, then as head of the royal archives. A poet, historian, and scholar, Yi excelled in both verse and prose. His *Jottings to Break Up Idleness* (*P'ahan chip*), the first literary miscellany in Korea, was published in 1260, but two other collections by Yi are no longer extant. Anthologies preserve 129 of his poems. See Peter H. Lee, *Story of Traditional Korean Literature,* 89–154.

Yi Kae (1417–1456). Passed the 1447 examination; one of the six martyred ministers who tried to restore the rightful ruler Tanjong and were tortured to death by the usurper Sejo.

Yi Kyubo (1168–1241). Passed the 1190 examination; accompanied the court to Kanghwa Island during the Mongol invasion and rose to be first privy counselor. His collected works (published in 1241 and 1251) contain some two thousand poems and provide invaluable information on the history of the Three Kingdoms, including the text of the "Lay of King Tongmyŏng," the foundation myth of Koguryŏ.

Yi Myŏnghan (1595–1645). Passed the 1616 examination; opposed the peace treaty with the Manchu and was transported to Shenyang (Mukden). Known for his devotion to Neo-Confucian metaphysics.

Yi Ok (1760–1812). A politically marginalized outsider, Yi avoided political issues in the twenty-five biographical sketches *(chŏn),* poems, essays, and one play he wrote, focusing instead on the sharply observed life of city dwellers in the late eighteenth and early nineteenth centuries.

Yi Saek (1328–1396). Passed the local examination at field headquarters to qualify for the metropolitan and palace examinations at the Mongol capital (1353–1354); then served in the Hanlin Academy and office of historiography.

Yi Sŏkhyŏng (1415–1477). Passed the 1441 examination; a member of the Hall of Worthies under King Sejong.

Yi Sunsin (1545–1598). The Korean admiral who with his "turtle ship" defeated the Japanese navy during the invasions of 1592–1598. See the *Record of the Black Dragon Year.*

Yi T'aek (1651–1719). Passed the 1676 military examination; served as navy commander. Two *sijo* are attributed to him.

Yi Tal (fl. 1568–1608). Known as one of the Three Tang-Style Masters who emulated the poetry of the High Tang.

Yŏngjae, Monk (fl. c. 785–798). A Silla monk who believed in the power of poetry to touch the heart. In "Meeting Bandits" he transcends the moment to find a truth that he and the bandits can share.

Yu, Lady (n.d.). Author of "Lament for a Needle."

Yu Mongin (1559–1623). Passed the 1589 examination. Yu's political career was checkered at best; after being implicated in a rebellion, he and his son were executed in 1623. He is the author of a collection of unofficial historical narratives.

Yu Ŭngbu (d. 1456). A military official and one of the six ministers who plotted the restoration of Tanjong, the deposed boy king. Yu was tortured to death by the usurper Sejo for his role in the plot.

Yun Sŏndo (1587–1671). Generally regarded as the most accomplished poet in the *sijo* form, Yun left seventy-five songs. His political career was turbulent, and he spent fourteen years in exile. He is best known for "Songs of Five Friends" (1642), a cycle of six songs, and "The Angler's Calendar" (1651), a cycle of forty songs.

Yungch'ŏn, Master (fl. c. 579–632). Little is known about Yungch'ŏn apart from the miracle-working "Song of the Comet," which seems to have removed the dreadful apparition from the sky.

Bibliography

EAST ASIAN SOURCES

Abe Yoshio. *Nihon Shushigaku to Chōsen*. Tokyo: Tokyo daigaku shup-pankai, 1965.

Akamatsu Chijō and Akiba Takashi. *Chōsen fuzoku no kenkyū*. Tokyo: Ōsakayagō shoten, 1937–1938.

Anon. *Akchang kasa*. Taejegak, 1973.

———. *Ch'unhyang chŏn (Yŏllyŏ Ch'unhyang sujŏl ka)*. Edited by Ku Chagyun. Hanguk minjok munhak taegye 10. Minjung sŏgwan, 1976.

———. *Imjin nok*. Edited by So Chaeyŏng and Chang Kyŏngnam. Hanguk kojŏn munhak chŏnjip 4. Koryŏ taehakkyo Minjok munhwa yŏnguso, 1993.

———. *Siyong hyangak po*. In *Wŏnbon Hanguk kojŏn ch'ongsŏ*. Taejegak, 1972.

An Taehoe. *Chosŏn hugi sop'ummun ŭi silch'e*. T'aehaksa, 2003.

Cao Yin et al. *Quan Tangshi*. Beijing: Zhonghua, 1960.

Chang Hyohyŏn. *Hanguk kojŏn sosŏlsa yŏngu*. Koryŏ taehakkyo ch'ulp'anbu, 2004.

Chang Tŏksun, ed. *Im Kyŏngŏp chŏn, Pakssi chŏn, Ch'oe Koun chŏn*. Hŭimang ch'ulp'ansa, 1978.

Chang Tŏksun and Ch'oe Chinwŏn, eds. *Hong Kiltong chŏn, Imjin nok, Sinmi nok, Pakssi puin chŏn, Im Kyŏngŏp chŏn*. Hanguk kojŏn munhak chŏnjip 1. Posŏng munhwasa, 1978.

Ch'oe Cha. *Pohan chip*. In *Koryŏ myŏnghyŏn chip*, vol. 2. Sŏnggyungwan taehakkyo Taedong munhwa yŏnguwŏn, 1973.

Ch'oe Hang et al. *Yongbi och'on ka*. 2 vols. Keijō: Keijō teikoku daigaku, 1937–1938. Reprint of the 1612 woodblock edition.

Ch'oe Kwan. *Bunroku Keichō no eki.* Tokyo: Kodansha, 1994.

Chŏng Ch'ŏl. *Songgang chŏnjip.* Taedong munhwa yŏnguwŏn, 1964.

Chŏng Hŭidŭk. *Wŏlbong haesang nok. Haehaeng ch'ongjae* 8. Kojŏn kugyŏk ch'ongsŏ 85, 1982.

Chŏng Inji et al., eds. *Koryŏ sa.* 3 vols. Yŏnse taehakkyo Tongbanghak yŏnguso, 1955–1961.

Chŏng Pyŏnguk. "Akki ŭi kuŭm ŭrobon pyŏlgok ŭi yŏŭmgu." *Kwanak ŏmun yŏngu* 2 (1977): 1–26.

———. *Chŭngbop'an Hanguk kojŏn siga non.* Singu munhwasa, 1999.

Chŏng Pyŏnguk and Yi Sŭnguk, eds. *Kuun mong.* Hanguk kojŏn munhak taegye 9. Minjung sŏgwan, 1992.

Chŏng Yagyong. *Chŏng Tasan chŏnsŏ.* Edited and published by Munhŏn p'yŏnch'an wiwŏnhae, 1961–1962.

———. *Yŏyudang chŏnsŏ.* 6 vols. Kyŏngin munhwasa, 1982.

Chōsenshi henshūkai, ed. *Chōsen shi.* 42 vols. Keijō: Chōsen sōtokufu, 1932–1940. Reprint, Kyŏngin munhwasa, 1982.

Haehaeng ch'ongjae. In Kojŏn kugyŏk ch'ongsŏ. Minjok munhwa ch'ujinhoe, 1975–.

Hanguk chŏngsin munhwa yŏnguwŏn, ed. *Hanguk kubi munhak taegye.* 82 vols. Hanguk chŏngsin munhwa yŏnguwŏn, 1980–1988.

———, ed. *Hanguk minjok munhwa taebaekkwa sajŏn.* 27 vols. Hanguk chŏngsin munhwa yŏnguwŏn, 1991.

Hanguk kososŏl yŏnguhoe, ed. *Hanguk kososŏl ron.* Asea munhwasa, 1991.

Han Ugŭn et al., trans. *Yŏkchu Kyŏngguk taejŏn.* 2 vols. Hanguk chŏngsin munhwa yŏnguwŏn, 1992.

Hŏ Kyun. *Hong Kiltong chŏn.* Edited by Yi Ihwa. Asea munhwasa, 1983.

Hwang Sin. *Ilbon wanghwan ki. Haehaeng ch'ongjae* 8. Kojon kugyŏk ch'ongsŏ 85, 1982.

Im Kijung, ed. *Hanguk kasa munhak chuhae yŏngu.* 21 vols. Asea munhwasa, 2005–.

———. *Kohwaltchabon yŏktae kasa chŏnjip.* 50 vols. Tongsŏ muhwawŏn, 1987–1998.

Iryŏn. *Samguk yusa.* Edited by Ch'oe Namsŏn. Minjung sŏgwan, 1954.

Kang Hang. *Kanyang nok. Haehaeng ch'ongjae* 2, Kojŏn kugyŏk ch'ongsŏ 79, 1982.

Kang Hanyŏng, ed. *Sin Chaehyo P'ansori sasŏl chip.* Hanguk kojŏn munhak taegye 12. Minjung sŏgwan, 1974.

———, ed. *Ŭiyudang ilgi, Hwasŏng ilgi.* Singu munhwasa, 1974.

Ki Chahŏn and Yu Kŭn. *Tongguk sinsok Samgang haengsilto.* Reprint, Taejegak, 1974.

Kim Chinse. "Kososŏl ŭi chakka wa tokcha." In *Hanguk kososŏl ron,* 53–71. Asea munhwasa, 1991.

Kim Chunhyŏng. *Hanguk p'aesŏl munhak yŏngu.* Pogosa, 2004.

Kim Ilgŭn, ed. *Ch'inp'il ŏngan ch'ongnam.* Kyŏngin munhwasa, 1974.

Kim Kidong, ed. *Kojŏn sosŏl chŏnjip.* 30 vols. Asea munhwasa, 1980.

———, ed. *P'ilsabon kojŏn sosŏl chŏnjip.* 10 vols. Asea munhwasa, 1980.

Kim Kyŏngjin. *Ch'ŏnggu yadam.* Kyomunsa, 1996.

Kim Myŏngjun. Akchang kasa *yŏngu.* Taeunsaem, 2004.

Kim Pusik. *Samguk sagi.* Edited by Yi Pyŏngdo. 2 vols. Ŭryu, 1977.

Kim Pyŏngguk, ed. *Hyŏndaeyŏk Kuun mong.* 2 vols. Sŏul taehakkyo ch'ulp'anbu, 2007.

Kim Sisŭp. *Kŭmo sinhwa.* Translated by Sim Kyŏngho. Hongik ch'ulp'ansa, 2000.

Kim Sŏnghwan, ed. *Hanguk yŏktae munjip ch'ongsŏ mongnok.* 3 vols. Kyŏngin munhwasa, 2000.

Kitajima Manju. *Chōsen nichinichi ki, Kōrai nikki.* Tokyo: Soshiete, 1982.

Kojŏn sosŏl yŏnguhoe, ed. *Hanguk kososŏl ron.* Asea munhwasa, 1991.

Kongzi jiayu. Sibu beiyao. Shanghai: Zhonghua shuju (between 1927 and 1936).

Kwŏn Tuhwan, ed. *Kojŏn siga.* Hanguk munhak ch'ongsŏ 1. Haenaem, 1997.

Li Fang, ed. *Taiping guangji.* 10 vols. Beijing: Zhonghua, 1961.

Naba Toshisada. "Geppō kaijōroku kōshaku." *Chōsen gakuhō* 21–22 (1961): 1–65.

Naitō Shunpo. *Bunroku Keichō eki ni okeru hirojin no kenkyū.* Tokyo: Tokyo daigaku shuppankai, 1976.

No Sasin et al., eds. *Sinjŭng Tongguk yŏji sŭngnam.* Kojŏn kanhaenghoe, 1958.

Nuki Masayuki. *Hideyoshi ga katenakatta Chōsen bushō.* Tokyo: Dōjidaisha, 1991.

Ŏ Sukkwŏn. *P'aegwan chapki.* In *Taedong yasung.* Chōsen kosho kankōkai, 1909–1911.

Pak Chiwŏn. *Yŏnam chip.* Kyŏngin munhwasa, 1982.

Pak Hŭibyŏng, ed. *Hanguk hanmun sosŏl kyohap kuhae.* Somyŏng, 2005.

Pak Illo. *Nogye sŏnsaeng chip. Yijo myŏnghyŏn chip* 3. Taedong munhwa yŏnguwŏn, 1973.

Pak Wansik. *Hanguk hansi ŏbusa yŏngu.* Ihoe ch'ulp'ansa, 2000.

Qian Qianyi, ed. *Qianzhu Dushi.* 2 vols. Hong Kong: Zhonghua, 1973.

Qu You. *Jiandeng xinhua.* In *Shida jinshu,* vol. 7. Beijing: Zhongguo wenshi chubanshe, 2002.

Shangshu. Sibu congkan. Shanghai: Shangwu yinshuguan (1936).

Shiba Ryōtarō. "Kokyō wasurejigataku sōrō." In *Shiba Ryōtarō zenshū* 29: 373–404. Tokyo: Bungei shunjū, 1981.

Sim Chaewan. *Kyobon yŏktae sijo chŏnsŏ.* Sejong munhwasa, 1972.

Sin Yonggae et al., eds. *Sok Tong munsŏn.* Kyŏnghŭi ch'ulp'ansa, 1966–1967.

Sŏ Kŏjŏng et al., eds. *Tong munsŏn.* 3 vols. Kyŏnghŭi ch'ulp'ansa, 1966–1967.

Sŏng Hyŏn, ed. *Akhak kwebŏm.* Yŏnse taehakkyo Inmun kwahak yŏnguso, 1968.

Sŏ Taesŏk, ed. *Kubi munhak.* Hanguk munhak ch'ongsŏ 3. Haenaem, 1997.

Sŏ Taesŏk and Pak Kyŏngsin, eds. *Sŏsa muga.* Koryŏ taehakkyo Minjok munhwa yŏnguso, 1996.

Sunzi. Sibu beiyao. Shanghai: Zhonghua shuju (between 1927 and 1936).

Takakusu Junjirō and Watanabe Kaigyoku, eds. *Taishō shinshū daizōkyō.* 100 vols. Tokyo: Taishō issaikyō kankōkai, 1924–1934.

Wu Rusong. *Li Weigong wendui jiaozhu.* Beijing: Zhonghua, 1983.

Yi Chehyŏn. *Ikchae chip.* In *Koryŏ myŏnghyŏn chip,* vol. 2. Sŏnggyungwan taehakkyo Taedong munhwa yŏnguwŏn, 1973

Yi Chiyŏng, ed. *Ch'angsŏn kamŭi rok.* Hanguk kojŏn munhak chŏnjip 10. Munhak tongne, 2010.

Yi Chongch'an. *Chosŏn kosŭng hansi sŏn.* Tongguk taehakkyo Pulchŏn kanhaeng wiwŏnhoe, 1978.

Yi Hyegu. *Sinyŏk Akhak kwebŏm.* Kungnip kugagwŏn, 2000.

Yi Hyŏnbo. *Nongam chip.* In *Yijo myŏnghyŏn chip,* vol. 3. Taedong munhwa yŏnguwŏn, 1973.

Yi Illo. *P'ahan chip.* In *Koryŏ myŏnghyŏn chip,* vol. 2. Sŏnggyungwan taehakkyo Taedong munhwa yŏnguwŏn, 1973.

Yi Kangok. *Chosŏn sidae irhwa yŏngu.* T'aehaksa, 1998.

Yi Kyubo. *Tongguk Yi-sangguk chip.* Tongguk munhwasa, 1958.

Yi Minhŭi. *16–19 segi sŏjŏk chunggaesang kwa sosŏl sŏjŏk yut'ong kwangye yŏngu.* Yŏngnak, 2007.

Yi Ok. *Yi Ok chŏnjip.* Translated by Silsi haksa kojŏn munhak yŏnguhoe. 3 vols. Somyŏng, 2001.

Yi Saek. *Mogŭn mungo.* In *Yŏgye myŏnghyŏn chip.* Taedong munhwa yŏnguwŏn, 1959.

Yi Sangbo, ed. *Inhyŏn wanghu chŏn.* Ŭryu, 1974.

Yi Sangt'aek, ed. *Kojŏn sosŏl.* Hanguk munhak ch'ongsŏ 2. Haenaem, 1997.

Yi Wŏnsŏp. *Koryŏ kosŭng hansi sŏn.* Tongguk taehakkyo Pulchŏn kanhaeng wiwŏnhoe, 1978.

Yu Hŭich'un. *Miam ilgi ch'o.* 5 vols. Chōsen sōtokufu, 1936–1938.

Yun Sŏndo. *Kosan yugo.* In *Yijo myŏnghyŏn chip,* vol. 3. Taedong munhwa yŏnguwŏn, 1973.

WESTERN SOURCES

Aarne, Antti. *Verzeichnis der Märchentypen* (Index of Folktale Types). Folklore Communications 3. Helsinki, 1910.

Aarne, Antti, and Stith Thompson. *The Types of the Folktale: A Classification and Bibliography.* 2nd revised ed. Folklore Fellows Communications 184. Helsinki: Suomalainen Tiedeakademie, 1964.

Bakhtin, M. M. *The Dialogic Imagination.* Edited by Michel Holquist. Austin: University of Texas Press, 1981.

Bantly, Francisca Cho. *Embracing Illusion: Truth and Fiction in the* Dream of the Nine Clouds. Albany: State University of New York Press, 1996.

Bascom, William. "Four Functions of Folklore." *Journal of American Folklore* 67 (1954): 333–349. Quoted in Robert A. Georges and

Michael Owen Jones, *Folkloristics: An Introduction* (Bloomington: Indiana University Press, 1995), 189.

Beecher, Donald A., and Massimo Ciavolella, trans. *Jacques Ferran: A Treatise on Lovesickness.* Syracuse, NY: Syracuse University Press, 1990.

Birch, Cyril, ed. *Anthology of Chinese Literature: From Early Times to the Fourteenth Century.* New York: Grove Press, 1965.

Birrell, Anne. *Chinese Mythology: An Introduction.* Baltimore: Johns Hopkins University Press, 1993.

Buswell, Robert E. *The Zen Monastic Experience.* Princeton, NJ: Princeton University Press, 1992.

Buswell, Robert E., Jr., and Donald S. Lopez Jr., eds. *The Princeton Dictionary of Buddhism.* Princeton, NJ: Princeton University Press, 2014.

Carson, Anne. *Eros the Bittersweet: An Essay.* Princeton, NJ: Princeton University Press, 1986.

Caruth, Cathy, ed. *Trauma: Explorations in Memory.* Baltimore: Johns Hopkins University Press, 1995.

———. *Unclaimed Experience: Trauma, Narrative, and History.* Baltimore: Johns Hopkins University Press, 1985.

Chan, Wing-tsit. *A Source Book in Chinese Philosophy.* Princeton, NJ: Princeton University Press, 1963.

Chang, Kang-i Sun, and Haun Saussy, eds. *Women Writers of Traditional China: An Anthology of Poetry and Criticism.* Stanford, CA: Stanford University Press, 1999.

Ch'oe Yŏngho, Peter H. Lee, and Wm Theodore de Bary, eds. *Sources of Korean Tradition: From the Sixteenth to the Twentieth Centuries.* New York: Columbia University Press, 2001.

Ch'ü T'ung-tsu. *Law and Society in Traditional China.* Paris: Mouton, 1961.

Cohn, Dorrit. *The Distinction of Fiction.* Baltimore: Johns Hopkins University Press, 1999.

Conze, Edward. *Buddhist Wisdom Books, Containing the Diamond Sutra and the Heart Sutra.* London: Allen and Unwin, 1958.

Damrosch, David. *What Is World Literature?* Princeton, NJ: Princeton University Press, 2003.

Deuchler, Martina. *The Confucian Transformation of Korea: A Study of Society and Ideology.* Cambridge, MA: Harvard University Press, 1992.

Doane, A. N., and Carol Braun Pasternack, eds. *Vox Intexta.* Madison: University of Wisconsin Press, 1991.

Earnshaw, Doris. *The Female Voice in Medieval Romance Lyric.* New York: Peter Lang, 1988.

Eckert, Carter J., et al. *Korea Old and New: A History.* Ilchokak, 1990.

Felman, Shoshana, and Dori Laub, M.D. *Testimony: Crises of Witnessing in Literature, Psychoanalysis, and History.* New York: Routledge, 1992.

Finnegan, Ruth. *Oral Poetry: Its Nature, Significance and Social Context.* Cambridge: Cambridge University Press, 1977.

Foley, J. M. *How to Read an Oral Poem.* Urbana: University of Illinois Press, 2002.

———. *Immanent Art: From Structure to Meaning in Traditional Oral Epic.* Bloomington: Indiana University Press, 1991.

Frankel, Hans H. "The Plum Tree in Chinese Poetry." *Asiatische Studien* 6 (1952): 88–115.

Frye, Northrop. *Anatomy of Criticism: Four Essays.* New York: Atheneum, 1968.

Fusek, Lois. *Among the Flowers: The Hua-chien chi.* New York: Columbia University Press, 1982.

———. "The 'Kao-T'ang Fu.'" *Monumenta Serica* 30 (1972–1973): 329–425.

Galassi, Jonathan. "The Great Montale in English." *New York Review of Books* 59, no. 17 (November 8, 2012): 65–67.

Goodrich, L. Carrington, and Fang Chao-ying, eds. *Dictionary of Ming Biography, 1368–1644.* 2 vols. New York: Columbia University Press, 1976.

Graham, A. C. *The Book of Lieh-tzu.* London: John Murray, 1960.

Griffith, Samuel B. *Sun Tzu: The Art of War.* Oxford: Clarendon Press, 1963.

Haboush, Jahyun Kim, trans. *The Memoires of Lady Hyegyong; The Autobiographical Writings of a Crown Princess of Eighteenth-Century Korea.* Berkeley: University of California Press, 1996.

Hamburger, Käte. *The Logic of Literature.* Translated by Marilyn J. Rose. Bloomington: Indiana University Press, 1973.

Hawkes, David. *Ch'u Tz'u: Songs of the South.* Oxford: Clarendon Press, 1959.

———. *A Little Primer of Tu Fu.* Oxford: Clarendon Press, 1967.

Hightower, James Robert. *The Poetry of T'ao Ch'ien.* Oxford: Clarendon Press, 1970.

Holsinger, Bruce W. *Music, Body, and Desire in Medieval Culture: Hildegard of Bingen to Chaucer.* Stanford, CA: Stanford University Press, 2001.

Hucker, Charles O. *A Dictionary of Official Titles in Imperial China.* Stanford, CA: Stanford University Press, 1985.

Hummel, Arthur W., ed. *Eminent Chinese of the Ch'ing Period.* 2 vols. Washington, DC: US Government Printing Office, 1943–1944.

Jauss, H. R. "Literary History as a Challenge to Literary Theory." In *Toward an Aesthetic of Reception,* 3–45. Minneapolis: University of Minnesota Press, 1982.

Karlgren, Bernhard. *The Book of Odes.* Stockholm: Museum of Far Eastern Antiquities, 1950.

Kato, Eileen. *The Heart Remembers Home.* Tokyo: Japan Echo Inc., 1979.

Kelleher, M. Theresa. "Back to Basics: Chu Hsi's *Elementary Learning* (*Hsiao-hsüeh*)." In *Neo-Confucian Education: The Formative Stage,* ed. Wm Theodore de Bary and John W. Chaffee, 219–251. Berkeley: University of California Press, 1987.

Kim, Youme. "The Life and Works of Yi Ok (1760–1812)." PhD diss., University of California at Los Angeles, 2014.

Lau, D. C., trans. *Mencius.* Harmondsworth: Penguin, 1970.

———, trans. *Tao Te Ching.* Harmondsworth: Penguin, 1972.

Lee, Janet Y. "Reinterpreting 'Lovesickness' in Late Chosŏn Literature." PhD diss., University of California at Los Angeles, 2014.

Lee, Peter H., ed. *Anthology of Korean Literature: From Early Times to the Nineteenth Century.* Honolulu: University of Hawai'i Press, 1981, 1990 (with revisions).

———. *Celebration of Continuity: Themes in Classic East Asian Poetry.* Cambridge, MA: Harvard University Press, 1979.

———, ed. *The Columbia Anthology of Traditional Korean Poetry.* New York: Columbia University Press, 2002.

———, ed. *A History of Korean Literature.* Cambridge: Cambridge University Press, 2003.

———. *Lives of Eminent Korean Monks: Haedong kosŭng chŏn.* Cambridge, MA: Harvard University Press, 1969.

———, ed. *Modern Korean Literature: An Anthology.* Honolulu: University of Hawai'i Press, 1990.

———, ed. *Myths of Korea.* Jimoondang, 2000.

———, ed. *Oral Literature of Korea.* Jimoondang, 2005.

———. *Pine River and Lone Peak: An Anthology of Three Chosŏn Dynasty Poets.* Honolulu: University of Hawai'i Press, 1991.

———. *The Record of the Black Dragon Year.* Seoul: Institute of Korean Culture, Korea University; Honolulu: Center for Korean Studies, University of Hawai'i, 2000.

———. *Songs of Flying Dragons: A Critical Reading.* Cambridge, MA: Harvard University Press, 1975.

———, ed. *Sourcebook of Korean Civilization.* 2 vols. New York: Columbia University Press, 1993–1996.

———. *The Story of Traditional Korean Literature.* Amherst, NY: Cambria Press, 2013.

Lee, Peter H., and Wm Theodore de Bary, eds. *Sources of Korean Tradition.* Vol. 1. New York: Columbia University Press, 1997.

Legge, James. *The Chinese Classics.* 5 vols. Hong Kong: Hong Kong University Press, 1960.

Linley, David. *Lyric.* London: Methuen, 1985.

Liu, James J. Y. *Chinese Theories of Literature.* Chicago: University of Chicago Press, 1975.

Liu, Wu-chi, and Irving Yucheng Lo, eds. *Sunflower Splendor: Three Thousand Years of Chinese Poetry.* Garden City, NY: Doubleday, 1975.

Luo Guanzhong. *Three Kingdoms: A Historical Novel.* Translated by Moss Roberts. Berkeley: University of California Press, 1998.

Ma, Y. W., and Joseph S. M. Lau, eds. *Traditional Chinese Stories.* New York: Columbia University Press, 1978.

Mair, Victor H., ed. *The Columbia Anthology of Traditional Chinese Literature.* New York: Columbia University Press, 1994.

———, ed. *The Columbia History of Chinese Literature.* New York: Columbia University Press, 2001.

Mather, Richard B., trans. *A New Account of Tales of the World.* Minneapolis: University of Minnesota Press, 1976.

McCann, David. *Early Korean Literature: Selections and Introductions.* New York: Columbia University Press, 2000.

Needham, Joseph. *Science and Civilization in China.* Vol. 2, *History of Scientific Thought*; Vol. 3, *Mathematics and the Sciences of the Heavens and the Earth.* Cambridge: Cambridge University Press, 1956, 1987.

Nienhauser, William H., Jr., ed. *The Indiana Companion to Traditional Chinese Literature.* Bloomington: Indiana University Press, 1986.

Niles, John D. *Homo Narrans: The Poetics and Anthropology of Oral Literature.* Philadelphia: University of Pennsylvania Press, 1999.

Ong, Walter J. *Interfaces of the Word: Studies in the Evolution of Consciousness and Culture.* Ithaca, NY: Cornell University Press, 1977.

Owen, Stephen. *The Great Age of Chinese Poetry.* New Haven, CT: Yale University Press, 1981.

———. *The Poetry of Early T'ang.* New Haven, CT: Yale University Press, 1977.

Palumbo-Liu, David. *The Poetics of Appropriation: The Literary Theory and Practice of Huang Tingjian.* Stanford, CA: Stanford University Press, 1993.

Pihl, Marshall. *The Korean Singer of Tales.* Cambridge, MA: Harvard University Press, 1994.

Preminger, Alex, and T. V. F. Brogan, eds. *The New Princeton Encyclopedia of Poetry and Poetics.* Princeton, NJ: Princeton University Press, 1993.

Renoir, Alain. *A Key to Old Poems: The Oral-Formulaic Approach to the Interpretation of West-Germanic Verse.* University Park: Pennsylvania State University Press, 1988.

Robinson, David M. *Empire's Twilight.* Cambridge, MA: Harvard University Asia Center, 2009.

Rutt, Richard, trans. *The Book of Changes (Zhouyi): A Bronze Age Document.* Durham East-Asia Series, no. 1. Curzon: 1996.

Rutt, Richard, and Kim Chong-un, trans. *Virtuous Women*. Seoul: Korean National Commission for Unesco, 1974.

Sadie, Stanley, ed. *The New Grove Dictionary of Music and Musicians*. 2nd ed. 29 vols. London: Macmillan, 2001.

Scarry, Elaine. *The Body in Pain: The Making and Unmaking of the World*. New York: Oxford University Press, 1985.

Schafer, Edward H. "The Idea of Created Nature in T'ang Literature." *Philosophy East and West* 15 (1965): 153–160.

Sorensen, Clark W. "The Mystery of Princess Pari and the Self-Image of Korean Women." *Anthropos* 83 (1988): 403–419.

Tangherlini, Timothy. *Danish Folktales, Legends, and Other Stories*. Seattle: University of Washington Press, 2014.

Teiser, Stephen F. *The Scripture on the Ten Kings*. Studies in East Asian Buddhism 9. Honolulu: University of Hawai'i Press, 1994.

Thompson, Stith. *Motif Index of Folk Literature: A Classification of Narrative Elements in Folktales, Ballads, Myths, Fables, Medieval Romances, Exempla, Fabliaux, Jestbooks, and Local Legends*. 6 vols. Bloomington: Indiana University Press, 1989.

Vos, Frits. "Tales of the Extraordinary: An Inquiry into the Contents, Nature, and Authorship of the *Sui chŏn*." *Korean Studies* 5 (1981): 1–25.

Wack, Mary Frances. *Lovesickness in the Middle Ages: The* Viaticum *and Its Commentaries*. Philadelphia: University of Pennsylvania Press, 1990.

Waith, Eugene. *Ideas of Greatness: Heroic Drama in England*. London: Routledge and Kegan Paul, 1971.

Waley, Arthur. *The Analects*. London: Allen & Unwin, 1949.

———. *The Book of Songs*. London: Allen & Unwin, 1954.

Watson, Burton, trans. and ed. *The Columbia Book of Chinese Poetry*. New York: Columbia University Press, 1984.

———, trans. *The Complete Works of Chuang Tzu*. New York: Columbia University Press, 1968.

———, trans. *Han Fei Tzu: Basic Writings*. New York: Columbia University Press, 1964.

———, trans. *Records of the Grand Historian of China*. 2 vols. New York: Columbia University Press, 1961.

————, trans. *Su Tung-p'o.* New York: Columbia University Press, 1965.

Wilhelm, Richard. *The I Ching or Book of Changes.* Translated by Cary F. Baynes. 2 vols. New York: Pantheon, 1950.

Ziolkowski, Jan M. *Fairy Tales from before Fairy Tales: The Medieval Latin Past of Wonderful Lies.* Ann Arbor: University of Michigan Press, 2007.

Zumthor, Paul. *Essai de poétique mediéval.* Paris: Seuil, 1972. Translated by Philip Bennett as *Towards a Medieval Poetics.* Minneapolis: University of Minnesota Press, 1992.

————. *Oral Poetry: An Introduction.* Translated by Kathryn Murphy-Judy. Minneapolis: University of Minnesota Press, 1990.

Index

About the Editor

With some twenty books to his credit, Peter H. Lee, professor emeritus of Korean and comparative literature at the University of California, Los Angeles, is widely credited as having pioneered the study of Korean literature in the West. Lee made important contributions to the field of Korean studies by spearheading the development of a series of basic reference tools and comprehensive anthologies that have been crucial to training a generation of students. His massive two-volume *Sourcebook of Korean Civilization* (1993–1996) represents the first comprehensive anthology of Korean culture to appear in any language other than Korean. Lee has also compiled and edited anthologies of Korean literature, both traditional and modern.

Lee has received many honors for his scholarship, including fellowships from the American Council of Learned Societies, the Bollingen Foundation, the Guggenheim Foundation, and the National Endowment for the Humanities. He is the recipient of Korea's most prestigious national awards, including the Presidential Award.

Lee received his graduate degrees from Yale University and Ludwig-Maximillian University in Munich. He also studied at the University of Fribourg in Switzerland, the University of Florence, and the University of Oxford. He has taught at Columbia University, the University of Hawai'i, and served as a Distinguished Scholar at Peking University under the auspices of the National Academy of Sciences.